The Mammoth Book of

MEN O'WAR

Also available

The Mammoth Book of
MEN O'WAR

Edited by
Mike Ashley

Merry Christmas

Robbie

Loads of love

from

Dad & Mom

Robinson
LONDON

Dec /2000

Robinson Publishing Ltd
7 Kensington Church Court
London W8 4SP

First published in the UK by Robinson Publishing 1999

A copy of the British Library Cataloguing in Publication data is
available from the British Library

ISBN 1–84119–060–8

Printed and bound in the EC

10 9 8 7 6 5 4 3 2 1

CONTENTS

COPYRIGHT AND ACKNOWLEDGMENTS

I would like to thank Alexander Kent for his foreword. I would also like to thank Judith Higgins and Stephen Holland for their help in providing valuable research material. All of the stories are copyright in the name of the individual authors as follows. Every effort has been made to trace the holders of copyright. In the event of any inadvertent transgression of copyright the editor would like to hear from the author or their representatives via the publisher.

INTRODUCTION

Mike Ashley

Way back in 1740 James Thomson penned the words which we still sing joyously today, especially at the Last Night of the Proms: "Rule Britannia, Britannia rule the waves." Well, Britain may no longer "rule the waves", but our naval heritage is still a strong part of our national identity, from the time of the great voyages of Sir Frances Drake and Sir Walter Raleigh through to the time of Horatio Nelson and Trafalgar.

This anthology looks at just some of that wonderful heritage. The bulk of the book concentrates on the wars between Britain and France, particularly the Napoleonic period, but it broadens the canvas slightly. The first story is set in 1788, just before the French Revolution, when Britain was still recovering from the loss of the American colonies, and it ends in 1862 with a mighty river battle during the American Civil War. The penultimate story looks in detail at the last ever battle between sailing ships.

In total there are eighteen stories of naval warfare and intrigue, stretching around the globe, from as close to home as the Cornish coast and Boulogne, to as far afield as the West Indies and Tasmania, touching, en route, the whaling fleets of the North Atlantic and the China Fleet in the East Indies. The stories are by such notable authors as Patrick O'Brian, Richard Woodman, C.S. Forester, Walter Jon Williams, Showell Styles, Harriet Hudson and others, with some classic material from Frederick Marryat, Herman Melville and Cutcliffe Hyne. You will encounter many famous characters from history as well as a few surprises.

For those who want to explore this world further, I have appended a bibliography of key Napoleonic naval fiction.

So with no more ado I shall hand over to Mr Alexander Kent to set us on our way.

FOREWORD

Alexander Kent

The great and lasting interest in this country's maritime past is hardly surprising, and all too often taken for granted. We are an island race; we have the sea in our blood; you can be born nowhere which is more than eighty miles from it. Almost a dismissal of a thousand years of colourful and often violent history.

For centuries, vessels of every kind have left these shores to explore, to discover new lands and peoples, eventually to foster trade, and to protect it by whatever means were necessary. The man-of-war was as vital in the days of sail as, in more recent memory, those lines of rusty ships in convoy which through two world wars were the margin between victory and slavery.

And yet in spite of all modern advances in the technology of war, with weapons so sophisticated and overwhelming that they have all but outstripped the minds and capacities of those who might be called upon to commit them to conflict, that splendid, brutal image of a fighting ship under full sail can still seize and hold a listener's or a reader's attention.

I speak of listeners, because who, after all, were the first real storytellers? The true sailorman was the only one who ever travelled vast distances to the other ends of the earth. He could embellish, even lie a little, for who would dispute him? And there were plenty ready to listen, to be entertained or to be lured to that life, tempted to become like him. The blue jacket and the tarred hat, the parrot and the eye patch were not so far removed from the truth, and the sailor's greatest legacy, perhaps, his language of the sea, remains with us in everyday usage. *Taken aback, first-rate, between the devil and the deep, by and large* and many, many more were all naval expressions. Although they are now often used in different context, they are still very much alive.

But, for me, to write about the ships and men of those far-off days was something else. I had been a well-established author for ten years or so when my American publisher at the time suggested I should think about putting into words what had always been deep inside me. I had served in the Royal Navy, and my experiences had led me to write of my own war. On the face of it, everything should have gone against me. I came from a long line of soldiers, the red coats and the green, and it was almost taken for granted that I would follow the drum. I had lived beside the Thames and had always loved boats, but of all the unlikely vessels which made me look askance at the army, it was a troopship that was to change everything, far more than I could have imagined. A troopship out of Southampton was a weekly occurrence in those days of Empire, and we sailed all the way to Singapore: Gibraltar, round the Cape and across the Indian Ocean. To the soldiers, it was undoubtedly boring, uncomfortable and restrictive. But to a seven year old boy, from the first throb of engines and the slow movement away from the pier, it was a magic voyage.

When we eventually returned home to England, I could not wait to be taken to Portsmouth, and to see Nelson's *Victory*. And looking back, in spite of some of the things I saw and shared in the Atlantic and other theatres of war, I never lost that memory. That sudden feeling of awareness.

But to write about it. . . .

The first thing I discovered was that it was not enough to think of the period in question: I had to be in it. In research, for instance, when going through old newspapers and log books, personal letters and diaries, I had to ask myself, not *what were they doing then*?, but *what are they doing now?* It was a far cry from the swift torpedo and the mindless violence of the dive-bomber.

Research is always enjoyable, or should be, and in this country there is material everywhere. But as I was already an experienced writer when my American publisher made me the offer I could not refuse, I knew full well that research is another way of putting off the main event. Most of the writers I meet have entirely different methods of working, but all admit to the unalterable fact. *Page One, Chapter One*: The empty horizon.

People ask me, "What is it like? How does it feel?" Perhaps like an open film set, the characters off stage and waiting to assemble. Or like being there yourself, sharing the changes of light, feeling the wind, like being a part of it. And sometimes none of these things.

One of the main differences between writing about more modern ships and the days of sail was soon apparent. In the eighteenth and nineteenth centuries, almost every one important was visible at any given time. You have to know where each seaman stands for every duty he performs, what he can see and hear when orders are passed to make or shorten sail, or to engage an enemy.

In some ways you learn *with* them, especially the new men, probably never aboard a ship before, dragged from their homes or villages by the hated and feared press gangs. There were no training depots or establishments as there were when I entered the navy, somewhere to give you time to "test the water". You were on board a King's ship. The rest was survival. Only the marines were trained ashore. For the others, from midshipman to post-captain, landman to experienced sailor and warrant rank, it was a question of learning by example, and by leadership.

And gradually you come to know and understand your characters, so that you triumph or suffer with them.

It is difficult when I am asked, "Why did you let so-and-so die? I liked him!" How can you expect someone to believe that

you have so little control over what you have started? If start it
you did. Richard Bolitho would describe it as Fate, Thomas
Herrick, less confident perhaps, as Lady Luck. But eventually
the work, as publishers term it, is finished. Your part, anyway.

When the first Richard Bolitho story was published I was
soon to discover still more differences from my other writing
self. I had always received many letters from readers, often from
those who had experienced something similar to the events in a
particular book, or from friends or relatives of those who had. It
had always been there, this affinity with the sea, often amongst
people who had scarcely seen it, except maybe from the port of a
high-flying jet, or on a weekend's holiday. It is a closeness,
something still hard to accept, harder to understand. The
ordinary foot soldier slogging through France after the Ger-
mans' first breakthrough was worn out, retreating, but felt no
sense of defeat when so many others would have given in, with
the sea blocking any hope of escape. All it said on his scrap of
paper was the word "Dunkirk". Most of them had never heard
of it. All of them clung to the old trust: *just get me to the sea, and
I'll get home.*

But after the first of the Bolitho books was published I
realised that over half of the letters I received were from
women, asking searching questions about the lives and times
of those characters, the world they knew, and exchanged for the
uncertain security of the ocean.

It took a lot of thought and the second book in the series
before I understood. With the passing of sail there were many
improvements in the lot of the sailor, and the sea officer's
greatest enemies, time and distance, were largely overcome.
But we had lost something nevertheless. That sense of true
independence and self-reliance the moment a ship was sailing
alone, out of sight of land, was gone forever, and with it the code
of honour and gallantry, even at the cannon's mouth.

And there is the character of ships to consider.

How can something built of wood or steel possess character,
other than that bestowed by her masters? Even in my navy I was
soon to learn. I first went to sea in an elderly destroyer, one left
over from the Great War, a true veteran in every sense of the

word. But to us she was not only our protection, and our means of hitting at the invisible enemy; she was our home. *Personal.* Over the years she had acquired a slight list which was always with us. And yet, if some outsider from our chummy ships dared to mention it, we would take it as a criticism, something not to be tolerated. I can clearly recall being sent below after dodging a bomb during an air attack on a convoy we were escorting. A near miss, but I can see it now: there was a hole in the side of the lower messdeck, with the sea curling past just a couple of feet below. Sea-boot stockings hanging up to dry, an unfinished letter left on a messdeck table at the first clamour of the alarm for action stations. I felt a sense of outrage.

As one of Richard Bolitho's first captains said, "Your duty is to me, to this ship, and the King. In that order!" Things had not changed all that much.

But a ship's character is there. Ignore it at your peril. And in the days of sail, and long, long passages without news of world events, or even if you were still at war with the foe you had been ordered to seek out, the hull which contained those same men shared every mile logged, every shot fired. They fought for one another, and for their ship. The cause was left at the gates of Admiralty.

And what of today's navy, and the men and women who are steering it into a new century? I often visit ships and naval establishments for research purposes, and to keep up to date, as well as for other, less formal reasons, and it is always a pleasure for me, as I enjoy the sense of belonging. The faces and voices I meet may have changed, adjusted to the high-tech world about them, but look more closely, and you can imagine the same ones at the Nile or Trafalgar.

A fellow writer recently proclaimed that the men and the deeds of Nelson's navy were only a memory. *We shall never see their like again,* he said.

In this collection of sea stories he is proved wrong.

In fact, they have never left us.

THE STEEPLE ROCK

Richard Woodman

We begin in 1788, the year before the French Revolution. Britain was still smarting from the loss of the Thirteen Colonies in America, much to the delight of Europe. Most of continental Europe had sided with the Colonies against Britain, and they regarded Britain as a third-rate power. The one thing that Europe did appreciate about Britain was its navy – the largest and most efficient fleet in the world. Even in times of peace the British navy patrolled the seas, guarding the island and her possessions. It was the fleet and Britain's island status that made Britain comparatively safe from invasion.

This first story focuses on the activities of Trinity House in protecting both the Royal Navy and the merchant fleet from harm around Britain's coast, with its relay of lighthouses, buoys and beacons. It introduces us to Nathaniel Drinkwater, the hero of fourteen novels by Richard Woodman (b. 1944). The events described fall chronologically between the first two books in the series, **An Eye of the Fleet** *and* **A King's Cutter***.*

1. The Surveying Party – April 1788

"Well, Mr Drinkwater, behold the Cornish shore with all its rocky marvels. It looks benign enough today, and I hope it will suit our purposes and remain so for a further sennight . . ."

Captain Judd's voice tailed off as he turned his head and stared to the westward. The line of the horizon had a peculiar sharpness to it, as though acknowledging its business as the threshold to the vast Atlantic Ocean that lay beyond its rim. Above, the sky was a pale grey, a single tone of overcast that lay like a sheet obscuring any discernible signs or portents of the weather to come. The sight seemed to rob Judd of any further speech and Drinkwater suppressed a smile. Captain Judd, a man of fifty-odd years of age, did not like his present task. He was an east-coast man, happiest when dodging among the shoals that lay in profusion between the South Foreland and the Dudgeon, sniffing and examining the lead's arming and pronouncing, with a confidence that was absolute, that they were off the Haisbro' Tail, or the Outer Gabbard. Drinkwater had learned to admire the consummate skill of the man, not only in the matter of cabotage, but in his ability to handle his big cutter. The *Argus* was a Trinity House buoy-yacht, a heavy, if somewhat ornate vessel, intended to maintain the increasing number of buoys, beacons and offshore lighthouses that came under the management of the Court of Elder Brethren of the Trinity House in London. She was a maid-of-all-work, with comfortable quarters aft for the Brethren (when they chose to go to sea on one of their tours of inspection), a pair of heavy working boats stowed on chocks amidships, and a foredeck upon which a heavy, pawled windlass spoke of her more robust function, overhauling the moorings of seamarks. Additional evidence of this appeared on her topsides, where sheets of copper protected her spirketting and a hefty baulk of oak extended outboard in the form of a davit; and aloft, where her stout mast supported an equally stout derrick with its outfit of topping lift, guys and fall.

The usual station of the buoy-yacht *Argus* was the River Thames. From her moorings at Deptford, she worked to seaward, down stream to the wide expanse of the dangerous

Estuary, where she laboured amid the buoys and beacons of the Swin, the King's and the Knob Channels as they threaded through the maze of banks and shoals. She was commonly seen in Harwich, and ventured farther north to assist her sister buoy-tender based at Great Yarmouth, or rounded the North Foreland to anchor in the Downs and tend the buoys placed off the Goodwin Sands. But she rarely ventured far to the westward, for there was only the Eddystone lighthouse off Plymouth, and that was tended by its own small yacht, and the isolated lights on the Caskets, which were serviced from Alderney. Apart from the lighthouses at St Agnes, in the Isles of Scilly, and a few isolated stations on the Welsh coast, much of the west coast of England still lay in primitive darkness – dangerous to seamen as they sought the entrance to the Bristol and St George's Channels after long passages across the Atlantic when overcast weather had made the determination of their latitude uncertain.

Captain Judd, a master of coastal arcana, was instinctively uneasy about his vessel's situation, the more so since a new buoy-yacht was about to be launched from the yard of Randall and Brent at Rotherhithe, and Judd nursed the ambition to command her. He did not want anything to go wrong, to foul up his chances; and the loss of Mr Drinkwater, his competent young mate, even if only for a week, meant he had to linger on this accursed and treacherous coast. It was true that he had a full cargo of coals for St Agnes, but he knew that the road off St Mary's was not the best holding ground for a ship's anchor, and the anxiety gnawed at his entrails. He was used to the glutinous ooze of the Thames, in which an anchor's palms embedded themselves with satisfying security. He turned his attention to the shore, now only a league away. Well, even St Mary's Road would be preferable to the narrow estuary off which they now lay. He turned to his second mate who stood expectantly by the tiller.

"Very well, Mr Carslake, don't start the heads'l sheets but lay her on the other tack and heave her to." Then he turned to the man beside him: "You have everything ready?"

Drinkwater suppressed a smile. Judd was a fretful fellow, possessed of a demon of anxiety. Drinkwater had had the starboard boat loaded and ready since mid-forenoon. "I do, sir . . ."

"You do have two compasses?"

"I have two boat compasses, sir, and they agree. I worked six azimuths yesterday . . ."

"And sufficient paper . . ."

"I have sufficient paper and pencils, pen and ink, and a sextant." Drinkwater adjusted his footing as *Argus* changed her trim, rolling as she came up into the light, southerly breeze which blew across the almost westerly swell. "There is one thing, though, Captain Judd."

"What? What is that?"

"I shall need some money, sir, for our . . ."

"Yes, yes, of course, for your subsistence. I have it ready in the cabin. Come below . . . Mr Carslake, you have the deck; as soon as she is steady, swing the starboard gig out."

"Aye, aye, sir."

Judd moved towards the companionway and disappeared below. Waiting for him to descend, Drinkwater caught Carslake's eye, which winked. Drinkwater smiled. Both of the yacht's officers liked Judd, but privately they referred to him as "Fuss-pot".

Drinkwater stepped from the gloom of the tiny space at the base of the companionway into the cabin. It was lit through a row of stern-lights which would not have disgraced a frigate. He removed his tricorne, stooping his shoulders as he ducked after Judd. The yacht's master took a key from his pocket, opened a small locker secured to the bulkhead and took out a purse and a scrap of paper, motioning Drinkwater to sit at his desk. Drinkwater unclipped the inkwell, dipped the shortened goosequill and scribbled his signature on the receipt.

"I have provided you with seven guineas, Mr Drinkwater. I think it superior to your needs, but you must have sufficient funds to carry out your task. However, I shall require that you account for every penny, *every* penny, mark you, that you disburse upon this duty."

"I understand, sir."

"And you are conversant with the task?"

"Perfectly, sir," Drinkwater replied, adding with what he hoped was a perfect suppression of exasperation at "Fuss-

pot's" endless concern, "we have gone over the problem sufficiently."

"That is as well, it remains that you discover the matter."

"Indeed, sir. Let us hope that, as you say, the weather holds.
If it does not . . ."

"Then you shall travel overland to Falmouth and rejoin me
there."

"But what about the gig?"

"Leave it in the charge of some responsible person, the parish
priest will do. I can return for the boat, but I don't want you and
your men absent for longer than is absolutely necessary." Judd
held out his hand. "Good luck."

The two men shook hands. "You may think me anxious, Mr
Drinkwater, but in due course, I hope, you will understand the
concerns that beset a commander. You are yourself embarking
on detached service, in command of a boat. I am aware of your
previous service in His Majesty's Navy and value that highly,
but do you guard against *all* the dangers hereabouts. They
might not all be quite as obvious as you think. You will have to
be quartered in a tavern, but beware the dangers of drink, not
for yourself, but the men. Mead and Foster have a liking for the
stuff, but they are also good men in a boat . . ."

"Captain Judd," Drinkwater broke in, smiling the lopsided grin
that charmed through its absence of insolence, wrinkling the pale
line of the sabre cut on his cheek, "I am aware of all the dangers of
the land, believe me. I shall see you in a week, here or in Falmouth,
and with my commission executed to the best of my ability."

"Very well, Mr Drinkwater, very well." It was Judd's turn to
smile. A spare man of middle-height, he ran his hand over the
thinning hair that was drawn into a tight queue at his nape. It
was a gesture of dismissal, and Drinkwater was relieved to see it.
He turned and, pocketing the purse, picked up his hat. Briefly
ducking into his own tiny cabin to pick up his gear, he noticed
its absence. He smiled briefly at the small watercolour on the
bulkhead, a painting done years ago by Elizabeth, long before
she became his wife. It showed the former American schooner
Algonquin, lying in Falmouth, a prize to the frigate *Cyclops*. He
kissed his finger tips and touched it for good luck.

A moment later Drinkwater emerged on deck and turned forward. Amidships, in the starboard waist and hanging onto the heavy double-burton of the running backstay, Carslake made him a mock bow. "Your chariot hawaits, Mister Mate". Drinkwater stared down into the boat lying alongside. "For Gawd's sake don't *you* start fussing, Nat. I've 'ad hall your dunnage put in the boat." Carslake held up his hand. "No, no, I ain't forgotten nuffink; yer bleedin' tin tubes, yer watercolours, the whole festerin' lot's in the boat. There's nuffink else to do but be off wiv you. 'Ere you are."

"Thank you, Mr Carslake," Drinkwater responded with mock formality, taking the proffered boat-cloak and throwing it about his shoulder as he grinned into Carslake's broad, red face. A raw cockney raised in the stews of Wapping, between, as he himself boasted, low tide and Trinity High Water, Carslake had first shipped forward. Sheer ability and intelligence had, by the time he was thirty, gained him a place amid the yacht's small afterguard and he rather enjoyed such vulgar banter with a former naval midshipman, who had briefly held an acting commission as lieutenant.

Drinkwater clambered over the rail, waited his moment, and jumped down into the gig. Settling himself in the stern with the boat-cloak about him, he tucked the tiller under his arm and looked along the boat. Six men had been detailed to attend him and, each with his small, round bag of kit, now sat expectantly.

"Toss oars," he ordered. "Let go forward." The painter was cast off onboard *Argus* and coiled down in the gig's bow. The bowman shoved the boat clear of the big cutter's side and Drinkwater gave a wave.

"Heads'l sheets there! Midships the hellum!" Judd's voice shouted, and Drinkwater saw the backed staysail and jib suddenly released. For a moment they flogged before the lee sheets tamed them. *Argus* drew swiftly ahead as the gap between the buoy-yacht and her boat widened. Then, as he drew past, Judd's face looked down on them. "In a week then, Mr Drinkwater."

"Aye, aye, sir," Drinkwater replied and then called," down oars . . . Standby . . . Give way together!" Putting the tiller over, he turned the gig for the shore and when he looked back, the big cutter, the huge red Trinity ensign flapping languidly above the end of her boom, was already diminishing with distance. "Very well, lads, a nice easy stroke. We've about five miles to pull."

The estuary of the River Carrow debouched into the Atlantic between two granite headlands. The northernmost fell almost sheer to the sea before a great buttress of rock seemed to lean upon it, so that it extended in a series of low steps down to the tideline and beyond. The short spur thus formed was hidden by the surface of the water, though betrayed by the swirling disruption it caused to both flood and ebb tide visible on a calm day. On the southern side the headland was grander, splendid enough to be named Pen Carrow. A great grey cliff, seamed with cracks and fissures, some so large that the locals called them "zawns", and criss-crossed with tiny ledges upon which nested thousands of seabirds; white kittiwakes, black guillemots, dark brown razorbills and the charming little sea-parrots called puffins. The screams of these birds grew louder as the gig approached, the extent of their habitations exposed as the boat drew past a series of isolated rocks, remnants of the ancient extension of the southern headland, long since destroyed by the sea's attrition. Drinkwater regarded them with interest, for he thought they might hold the key to his task. They would have names, he thought, given them by the local fishermen, though they were shown as mere dots upon the imperfect chart he had brought with him.

He felt the boat lift beneath him and looked astern. They had pulled in almost between the two headlands and, as he stared over his shoulder, he saw the low swell humping up so that it obscured the horizon. Foster, the man pulling stroke oar, nodded at the approaching swell. "It be the bar," he said flatly, as he tugged on his oar.

Drinkwater nodded. Here the Atlantic drove the sand of the seabed into the river mouth, while the river, contrariwise, tried to push its way out to sea. The depth would be much less here, a submarine ledge, hence the steepening of the swell. It would break violently in an onshore wind, even at high water, and must have caused agonies to Captain Poynton when his ship was caught on this lee shore. Drinkwater looked about him. Poynton must have been driven across this very bar on a wild, winter forenoon last January. Had it not been for Poynton's experience and his influence with the Court of Trinity House, Drinkwater thought it unlikely that he and his boat's crew would have been dumped here for a week.

"What's all this for then, Mr Drinkwater?" asked Foster. Grunts of curiosity came from the other oarsmen as the gig passed under the shadow of Pen Carrow. Drinkwater recalled they had been told only that they were to gather dunnage for a week's absence from the *Argus* for a surveying party. Such temporary detachment was not unusual, but it was time he told them what the specific purpose of their absence was.

"Well, lads, last January the slaver *Montrose*, bound from the West Indies to her home port of Liverpool, made her landfall hereabouts. Half a gale was blowing from the west and the weather was thick. The master, Captain Edward Poynton, let both anchors go when he found the land under his lee. As the weather cleared, he discovered he had fetched up to seaward of the bar we have just crossed. His anchors were holding and the lead showed him he was in about twelve fathoms with a fine sandy bottom. All seemed well and, despite the proximity of the land, they thought they could ride the gale out, but, if the worst came to the worst, they might make a run through here." Drinkwater gestured about him, at the towering slopes that formed the entrance to the river.

"Bit narrow," said Foster, staring up at the beetling cliffs as he threw his weight back on his oar-loom. "You'd need a deal of nerve to drive a ship through here with a following gale."

"That," Drinkwater went on, silently agreeing with Foster, "was what Poynton deposed. Anyway, the wind shifted three or four points and the weather cleared as the gale increased. The wind-rode ship swung to the change of wind and then, quite suddenly, both anchor cables parted and the ship drove over the bar and fetched up under the Head there. Poynton and four others escaped with their lives. Of the rest, and the *Montrose*

herself, there was not a trace the following day. Poynton had his
fortune sunk in the ship; moreover, he swore that the cables
were in good condition and that something other than the
violence of the wind caused them to part. He made representa-
tions to the Trinity House to discover if any wreck was known
to exist in the area, upon which his cables might have fouled,
but none was known of, nor rumoured. But this Captain
Poynton is a determined man, and petitioned the Brethren.
Now we are come to try and discover the cause of his loss."

"She was underwritten at some value then, sir?" queried
Ross over Foster's shoulder. A slim, wiry man, Ross's ability to
read and write assured his presence in any surveying party.

"Indeed, Ross, at some considerable value, I understand."

The men seemed content with the explanation. Judd had
confided in Drinkwater that he had heard that Poynton had
promised a substantial bequest to the Trinity House, if an effort
was made to determine the cause of the loss of the *Montrose* and
the realisation of her insured value. "Wheels within wheels,"
Judd had concluded obliquely.

The headlands fell astern and the gig emerged into the broad
estuary of the River Carrow beyond. The transition was remarkable, the sea retreated astern, a narrow, grey sleeve
glimpsed between the retreating capes, while on either side
grass and woodland spread out, the small town of Porthcarrow
nestling on the southern bank, in the lee of Pen Carrow, behind
a small stone breakwater. Drinkwater tugged on the tiller and
headed the gig for the cluster of stone cottages which scrambled
up the hillside about the square, grey tower of a church. It
looked an idyllic spot to quarter oneself for a week.

2. Porthcarrow

"I don't have a room and you'll not find one, Mister, not here,
nor in The Plough in Upper Town."

"There would be the finding of two meals a day, and I have
six men to feed and accommodate . . ."

"The answer would be the same: no."

Drinkwater frowned. He had not expected such open hostility

from the landlord of The Anchor and Hope. It was an ironically-named tavern, given his situation. He stared about him. There were three or four elderly men in the low-ceilinged taproom and they stared at him from their benches, clay-pipes poised as though his presence had suspended their conversation.

"We are not the press."

"We know that, Mister. You'm from Lunnon . . . The Trinity House, no doubt. We had Cap'n Poynton down here a month or two back, askin' about rocks and wrecks and suchlike, and swearing black murder about wreckin'. That were false witness, Mister, and we don't like such things, when the Cap'n knew full well that his cables parted . . . Maybe," the landlord added, "the mermaids cut them."

The company roared with laughter at this witticism.

"That's as maybe," Drinkwater broke in, "but has nothing to do with me. I have a simple task to carry out and I'd be obliged if –" he turned and stared back at the circle of old men, "if any of you would care to put up myself and six seamen for a few days. I shall pay well," he added, certain that the inducement would arouse someone's cupidity. For an instant he thought he detected a flicker of interest in the eyes of the old fishermen, but then they turned away and, murmuring amongst themselves, resumed their interrupted game of cribbage.

Drinkwater swung back to the landlord, then took his departure. As he lifted the latch on the door, the landlord called after him. "You can sleep on the strand, Mister, near your boat," and the advice was accompanied by another rumble of laughter from the cribbage players.

Outside the seamen were sitting on benches, their backs to the tavern wall, their faces uplifted to the late afternoon sunshine. They had gathered about them a knot of curious children and the glances of the townsfolk as they went about their business. Drinkwater was nonplussed. For a moment he stood uncertainly as his men looked up at him, expecting some instructions. Then an idea struck him and, just as Foster opened his mouth and asked "Well, sir . . . ?" Drinkwater said, "stay here, I shall be about half an hour."

He found the rectory without difficulty, a fine house set back from the lane which rose up the back of Pen Carrow, and knocked upon the door, recalling his encounter with Elizabeth in similar circumstances. A plain, severely-dressed woman appeared in the doorway and Drinkwater removed his hat.

"I wish to see the incumbent, Ma'am. Upon a matter of some urgency and importance," he added as the woman hesitated. It was clear she was a servant, not, as he had briefly thought, the mistress of the house.

"What name?" she asked curtly.

"Nathaniel Drinkwater. I am an officer of the Trinity House."

"*The Trinity*?" she asked with some astonishment.

Suppressing his amusement, Drinkwater seized the advantage. "The Trinity," he confirmed. He noticed the atmosphere of the house was stale, redolent of cooking and unemptied chamber pots, and did not resent being left upon the doorstep. The rector might be, as Judd put it, a person of some importance, but he was clearly not a man insistent upon the thing most next to Godliness.

The woman reappeared, a man accompanying her. He was unwigged, dressed in waistcoat and breeches, both of which were stained with snuff and his neck-linen was none too clean. He brought with him the sweet smell of old sweat and had the appearance of a man aroused from sleep.

"Well, sir, who are you?"

Drinkwater smelt brandy upon the rector's breath as he repeated his name. "I seek accommodation for myself and six men, and I am refused at the Anchor and Hope. I am on official duty on behalf of the Trinity House, London . . ."

"He ain't from the bishop, Mary," the rector said sharply, and the woman melted away, rebuked. "Damned fool," the rector muttered, then he addressed Drinkwater. "What is your business here?"

Drinkwater explained, but was cut short. "So, you act on behalf of that troublesome fellow Poynton . . ."

"He lost his ship, sir, he has, er, a natural anxiety to determine the cause . . ."

"The cause, I hear, Mister Drink . . ."

"Drinkwater."

"Quite so, the cause was well known to be the failure of his anchor cables."

"He does not believe so . . ."

"And what do you believe?"

"I have an open mind, sir. I am not his creature. I am on official duty and, at the moment, I seek lodgings."

"And there is no room at the inn, eh?" The rector smiled, a peculiarly unpleasant grimace, revealing a row of stained teeth.

"I was hoping," Drinkwater said, though the prospect of sleeping under the rector's roof was most displeasing, "that you would be able to help me . . ."

"Help you? You mean accommodate yourself and your sailors here?" The idea of Christian charity seemed entirely foreign to the rector.

"I should pay, sir," Drinkwater said sharply.

"I should insist upon it, sir, but the matter's quite impossible." The rector put a finger in his ear, waggled it and removed it, examining the adhesion to its extremity. Then he looked at Drinkwater and shrugged.

"Very well, I am sorry to have troubled you." Drinkwater turned away, exasperated. The rector's attitude, added to that of the landlord of the Anchor and Hope, boded ill. It was clear that this was not just a lack of local hospitality; this was hostility. Drinkwater could not imagine what Captain Poynton had done to upset the inhabitants of Porthcarrow, but whatever it was, it was going to prevent him finding lodgings for his men, and already the shadows were lengthening.

"Where are you going?" the rector called boorishly after him. Drinkwater turned his head without arresting his retreat. "To rig a sail and sleep under my boat on the beach, damn it."

"Wait!"

Drinkwater stopped and turned. The rector came out under the porch and, cupping his hands, bellowed "Billie!" A moment later a small, ragged boy appeared, and the rector bent to chuck his cheek and give him some instruction after which the boy ran off. Straightening up, the rector announced, "Mr Goodhart has the farm at the end of the lane. I've told him to take you and your men in at half a sovereign a night . . ."

"Have you, sir. That is most kind of you," Drinkwater responded ironically, but the rector had turned away and Drinkwater finished his sentence addressing the rectory's slammed door.

The barn was at least plentifully supplied with straw and the farmer's wife gave them a hearty breakfast. Drinkwater had been unable to negotiate a lesser charge than the exorbitant rate arranged by the rector, and Mr Goodhart had belied his name. Nevertheless, the morning promised well, with no trace of either the previous day's overcast, or its wind. As they pulled out through the heads, an ebb tide sweeping them seawards, Drinkwater, putting the unpleasantness of Porthcarrow behind him, considered the day's work. Mead, Foster and two others, named Thorn and Kerr, manned the oars, while in the bow Wynn, having got out the boat anchor, made the lead ready, a large pot of tallow on the bottom-boards beside him. In the stern sheets with Drinkwater, the literate Ross prepared pencils and note-tablet, while Drinkwater readied his compasses, pegged a large sheet of paper on his drawing board and tucked his precious sextant under the after thwart.

"We've a good position from Poynton which was where the *Montrose* lay after the shift of wind. We know the direction of the gale and the scope of cable she had veered, so," Drinkwater explained to the gig's crew, "that will be our datum point."

"Have you any idea what we are looking for, Mr Drinkwater?" Ross asked, looking up.

"Yes," Drinkwater said with a confident grin. "I think I have. It's called a steeple rock."

3. The Steeple Rock

The phenomenon of the steeple rock was one well known to the officers of the Trinity House. The most famous of them lay off the Land's End. Known as the Wolf Rock, it had defied all attempts to mark it with a beacon, for only its peak broke the surface of the sea, and was constantly swept by the monstrous swells of the Atlantic Ocean. This made it the most dangerous of the known hazards off the coast of Southern Britain, for the only notice of its presence was a swirl of white foam at low tide, and an occasional ominous howl as air compressed in its fissures vented, and gave the rock its name. Close to the rock there was deep water, so the danger manifested itself as a needle of hard granite, somewhat like the steeple of a church, upthrust from the bed of the sea.

More complex reefs, composed of several rocks, like the Eddystone, could often be seen by vigilant lookouts even at night, or in stormy weather. The very name "eddy-stone" indicated the means by which the reef made its presence known. Moreover, such reefs could support a lighthouse, as had been established at both the Eddystone and the Caskets, but steeple rocks presented an insuperable danger. Furthermore, a steeple rock could lurk unknown below the surface of the sea, ready to catch the bottom of a vessel passing overhead at low tide and in the trough of a great wave perhaps, or simply to rend a straining anchor cable snagged about its jagged flanks. That, at least on the basis of Poynton's account, was what Judd and Drinkwater had concluded had occurred to the unfortunate *Montrose*.

Drinkwater had no reason to disbelieve Poynton's account, for it had been sworn before a notary. The references to the *Montrose*'s master he had encountered in Porthcarrow, however, began to shake this simple viewpoint, and the loss of certainty increased as the day dragged by and they found nothing. The second day was no more successful, and the grins of the fishermen of Porthcarrow as they passed the Trinity House gig, engaged on their own business, were infuriating. On the evening of the third fruitless day, Drinkwater brought the gig into Porthcarrow in their company. The local fishing boats consisted of line and pot boats, and larger luggers which, although they had seen much of these boats, they had had no contact with, for it was clear the fishermen deliberately ignored the interlopers.

"Sent us to bleedin' Coventry, the whores'ns," Foster succinctly put it.

As they pulled the gig inside the breakwater and made its

painter fast to a ring in the wall, Drinkwater caught the eye of a young man in an adjacent line-boat.

"I wish to hire your boat, tomorrow," he said. "I will pay you five shillings."

He saw the gleam in the fisherman's eye; five shillings was a huge sum of hard money, well worth a day off his grounds. Drinkwater's generosity provoked a sharp interest among his own crew, but the young man turned away without a word, busying himself with the coiling down of a line.

"I addressed you, sir, in a perfectly respectful tone." Drinkwater made a second attempt. "I am offering you five shillings for the hire of your boat . . ."

The young fisherman looked up. "No! My boat's not for hire, bugger you," and scrambling forward, the fisherman grabbed his painter, hauled his boat alongside the wall and climbed a rope hanging down the wall. Drinkwater sighed and Ross caught his eye.

"He were upset, Mr Drinkwater. It hurt him to turn down five shillings . . ."

"It'd hurt me," put in Foster, to a chorus of agreement.

"Follow him, Ross, find out where he lives. He'll have a wife or a mother who might be more pliant. Go with him, Foster, make it look casual. Just find out where he lives."

"We might need a drink, sir, if he goes in a tavern . . ."

Drinkwater fished a coin out of his pocket. "Here's thruppence, now get on with it."

"Aye, aye, sir," Foster grinned and winked at his disconsolate fellows.

"They're a bloody rum lot hereabouts," said Mead as they began to take the gear out of the boat. "Suspicious as Frenchmen . . ."

"What d'you want his boat for, sir?" asked Kerr.

"I want to make a sweep. To stretch a weighted line between two boats and drag it along the bottom. It's going to be the only way to locate this damned rock. I thought it would be quite large, now I'm not so sure."

"There's somefink Ross said, Mister Drinkwa'er," put in Mead.

"What's that?"

"Well, sir, if this rock cut fru the *Mon'rose*'s cables, couldn't them bleedin' cables have broke the rock . . ." Drinkwater stared incredulously at Mead. It was certainly possible . . . "Ross found an old carrot in that barn, d'you see, sir, an' 'e hexplained it to me, like. The carrot broke . . ."

"Yes, of course, that's quite possible. D'you know that never occurred to me." It was obvious when he thought of it. The weight of a ship under the impulse of a strong wind, even with her topmasts sent down and her lower yards a-portlast, was considerable. Add the additional strain conferred by the surge of the breaking seas, and the thing was not only possible, it was quite likely. Drinkwater felt certainty oozing back into him, along with the realisation that he had been foolish in making too many assumptions.

"That don't explain the unfriendliness of these poxy fisherfolk," said Thorn, adding, as he indicated the sextant and compasses, "I suppose we've got to hump this lot back up to the barn, Mr Drinkwater?"

"I'm afraid you have, Thorn. Shall we get on with it and see what Mrs Goodhart has got for us to eat this evening."

After two days, Mrs Goodhart seemed not to share the hostility of the rest of the inhabitants of Porthcarrow, perhaps because she was a farmer's wife and not one of the bigotted fisherfolk, perhaps because half a sovereign a day put several shillings into her own purse. She and her husband, Drinkwater had gleaned, worked land owned if not by the rector, then by the squire in whose gift the rector's parish lay.

They had eaten Mrs Goodhart's stew before Foster and Ross appeared in the farmhouse's kitchen. They were amiably drunk, and pitched into their portions of stew before Ross edged up to Drinkwater, whose position as officer in charge gave him the privilege of the only spare upright chair in the room. It had been another long day, and Drinkwater was soporific with food and the warmth of the kitchen. He leaned back and drowsily asked, "Well, Ross? What news?"

"Found his home, sir. Lives with a handsome young bint and a babe near the quay."

"Very well." Drinkwater roused himself. "You can show me when you've eaten."

An hour later the two men descended to the town. It was almost dark under the shadow of Pen Carrow, which rose dark and sharp against the twilight. Lights were appearing here and there and the narrow streets were almost deserted, though an old woman shuffled past them muttering to herself, a young man and a girl drew back into an alleyway, and a dog urinated against a doorpost. The town smelt of rotting fish, for piles of nets lay outside the doorways, awaiting repair by the women.

Ross led Drinkwater quickly to a tarred, black door outside which stood a pair of boots, a pair of oars and a coil of light line, left in readiness for the morning.

"This is the place, sir."

Drinkwater knocked on the door, lifted the latch and gently eased it open. The hinges had dropped and it scraped on the flagstones. The young fisherman lay slumped at a table, asleep on his arms. At the opposite end, a young woman looked up from the basin of water in which she was scouring her pots. The astonishment in her eyes turned quickly to alarm and she called "John!" so that the young man stirred.

"Don't be alarmed, Ma'am. You clearly know who I am, but you may not know that your husband refused to hire me his boat . . ."

"John!" she called again, and this time a wail came from a crib beside the fire.

"Did you know I offered him five shillings?" Drinkwater persisted, gesturing to the baby. "It would have bought some comforts for you and your child."

Drinkwater saw the fact strike her, but she was too frightened to say more than, "John, wake up!" The alarm woke the baby, whose squalling filled the room and the fisherman lifted his head from the table. The intruders swam into focus and the legs of his chair squealed against the flagstones as he rose, unsteady with drink, food and fatigue.

"What the hell do you want?"

"I only want to know why you won't let me hire your boat tomorrow."

"Get out of my house!"

"Name your price, man. You owe it to your wife and child."

"What'ave you said to 'im?" he said to his wife.

She had scooped up the child and swayed from side to side, patting its head as the wailing subsided. "Nothing, John, they just bursted in . . ."

"Five shillings . . ."

"I don't want your five shillings, damn you . . ."

"John, think . . ."

"Hold your tongue woman. As for you," the fisherman pushed himself clear of the table and confronted Drinkwater, "we don't want you round here! Not you no more than Poynton. Take my advice and get out while you can. I don't know what the bloody rector be doing encouraging you to stay, damn his drunken soul. Just get out of my house."

"I don't think we are doing . . ." Ross began, but Drinkwater had already come to the same conclusion.

"I am sorry to have troubled you," he said to the woman and backed out into the street.

"There's something not right," remarked Ross as they walked down the dark street and turned uphill towards the church.

Drinkwater woke early. The sun had yet to rise, and although the air was filled with birdsong, it failed to raise his spirits, for he was greatly troubled by the apparent impossibility of his task, the unpleasantness of the previous evening and the knowledge that he was running out of time. The conviction that Ross might be right, and the *Montrose*'s cables had demolished the steeple rock even as the cables were cut through, was less strong as he lay in the straw, listening to the snoring of the seamen about him. It was just too much of a coincidence, however attractive it might seem after a long, unsuccessful day. If the rock remained in existence he simply *had* to find it, and the thought prevented him from falling asleep again. He lay thinking, assuming the rock was there, and then it occurred to him there was something he could do, something simple. Brushing the straw from his person he pulled on his shoes, picked up his coat and stumbled out into the yard. Dishevelled and sticky from sleep, he set off up the damp flank of Pen Carrow.

An hour later he arrived at the summit, his legs aching. Like most seamen, although capable of keeping his balance in difficult circumstances, he found walking arduous and the rising sun, though low, was already warm on his back. As soon as he had gained the vantage point he sought, he settled himself on an outcrop of rock high above the river mouth. From this vantage point he could see the swirl of the river as it ran into the sea, its stream adding to the ebbing tide. Delicate filigrees of foam formed necklaces about the rocks below him, off Pen Carrow, and the continuing windless conditions ensured there was no sea, the surface of which was not even ruffled in the prevailing calm. A low swell, perhaps left over from some long dead gale, perhaps presaging a blow far out in the Atlantic to the westward, seemed to make the ocean breathe in a slow, languid undulation. Drinkwater realised he could expect no more perfect conditions for his observations.

Carefully, he scrutinised the scene below. Almost at once he detected something interesting. About the rocks were set the tiny spar buoys of the fishermen. These small stakes, each with a weft of torn cloth to distinguish it, was anchored to a crab or lobster pot on the seabed. They were mostly tucked close in to the rocks, the habitat favoured by the lobsters. But, while there was a sprinkling across the estuary, marking lesser outcrops, three or four were clustered about a single spot. Could that be the location of the steeple rock? Drinkwater felt his heart-beat quicken. Wondering why he had not thought of this before, he pulled his notebook from his pocket. Of course, he thought, quickly thumbing through the leaves, everything looked quite different at sealevel, but the position was very different from the one Poynton had given, and about which they had been so unsuccessfully searching.

He found Poynton's bearings and regarded the scene before him. The bearing to the north east was incontrovertible and, moreover, ran right through the cluster of dan buoys. Drinkwater broke out in a sweat of anticipation. The second bearing ran to "a sharp rock", and Drinkwater realised that Poynton had not laid his compass upon the slab of granite he himself knew as The Mewstone, but at a lesser, more pointed rock which at sea level lay

directly in line with The Mewstone, when erroneously viewed
from the assumed position. Interpretation of the bearing was
therefore anomalous and, Drinkwater thought chiding himself,
he had made a false assumption. On the morning that Drinkwater
had first located the supposed position, these two rocks had been
in the eye of the sun, and he had assumed The Mewstone to be the
"sharp rock" to which Poynton, in the extremity of his situation,
had referred. Both revised bearings crossed over the cluster
of pots, but, if he had it aright, the third remained stubbornly
obdurate. Poynton had written simply "S° Headland SE1/4E",
and there seemed no way that a bearing of South East a Quarter
East could be made to pass through anything other than the rock
outcrop on the summit of Pen Carrow upon which Drinkwater
now sat. He tried visually transferring the bearing through the
dan buoys and then he smote his head for a silly fool. Just behind
him, hidden by a fold in the cropped grass from an observer in a
small boat, rose another. From the quarter-deck of a ship, it
would, he thought, appear as the summit of the south headland.
Drinkwater had fallen into a simple but effective trap, making
assumptions that, had he acted with less impetuous certainty,
would have saved him much time and labour.

"God's bones," he swore, thrusting himself to his feet.
"What a callow fool I've been!" He began to run back to the
farm, not noticing the line of cloud gathering on the western
horizon, or the gently increasing undulation in the breathing
Atlantic. As he ran gasping into the yard he met Ross. Anxiety
was plain on the seaman's face.

"Where've you been, sir? We've been looking everywhere for
you."

"Why, what's the matter?"

"We went down to the boat, sir, thinking you were down
there, and the buggers have stove it!"

4. The Matter of a Boat

The gig had been removed from its mooring off the breakwater
and dragged up the beach a quarter of a mile upstream. Here an
axe had been taken to its bottom and a dozen ribs had been

chopped through, the garboard on both sides of the hog were split and, for good measure, several adjacent planks on either side had been beaten in. Drinkwater's blood ran cold at the sight. Outrage at the act combined with a furious frustration that he was so close to his objective and was now deprived of the means to achieve it. His only consolation was that their instruments remained safe. For a moment he strode up and down in a lather of conflicting emotion, and then he decided what he should do. Appealing to the justices, one of which was almost certainly the rector, was likely to avail him nothing. He must get a boat and finish his task in defiance of local opposition. Then perhaps he could contemplate what action he should take against these fisherfolk who nursed so intense a hatred of strangers that they would commit such an act as deliberate wrecking. Making up his mind, he turned to his men, who stood awaiting his decision.

"Well, they've done their best to dissuade us, but I've been out this morning and I wish to make another attempt to locate this rock." He looked at the men and tried to gauge their mood; it was clear they were waiting for him to finish. "Foster and Mead, you've both served in the navy, haven't you?"

"Aye, sir." The two men shifted their feet in the sand and a buzz of flies rose from the dried bladder-wrack they disturbed.

"So have I, sir," said Wynn.

"Good," Drinkwater replied. "I intend to commandeer one of the inshore boats. I would rather none of these people was hurt because if they are we'll not get back ashore alive, but if we employ a little subterfuge, I think we may be lucky. Now, Ross, Thorn and Kerr, are you game for this?"

"Aye, sir, of course."

"That's as well. Now, this is what we are going to do."

The men responsible for wrecking the *Argus's* gig had broken its oars into several pieces. The looms of these had been recovered by Drinkwater's men and hidden up their sleeves as they shuffled disconsolately back through the little town.

"Not a word," Drinkwater had ordered. "Not a scowl at a single soul. You may kick a dog out of your way, but you must appear defeated. We are going to retire from this place . . ."

It was clear from the men lounging in their doorways, that many of them had deferred putting to sea that morning, in order to be available if a show of force was put up by the Trinity House party. From their penury it was clear that few could afford a day off in such fine weather. Drinkwater was therefore gambling on their going to sea as soon as they were certain that he and his men had gone. In this Drinkwater obliged them before the church clock struck nine, amused that two boys were sent to trail them as the Trinity House party set out inland, along the single track which climbed uphill towards Bodmin.

Long before noon the boys grew bored and turned back. Determined to maintain his deception, Drinkwater trudged on so that, to anyone watching with a glass, he and his men would be seen crossing the moor and vanishing over the horizon. As they marched, the men speculated on the reason behind the hostility of the fisherfolk of Porthcarrow. Their opinions varied; most regarded the natives as retarded primitives, suspicious of any outsiders. Ross, on the other hand, claimed that there was another more sinister reason.

"They're wreckers," he said firmly. "The place is stuffed with the booty from wrecked ships, *that's* why they didn't want Poynton sniffing round and that's why they don't want us snooping about."

Drinkwater paid little attention to the easy discourse of the men. They seemed able to shrug off the events of the morning with ease. Ross, Drinkwater considered, might well be correct, but then Ross and his cronies were not responsible for the gig, or the discovery of that damned steeple rock.

They had bought a loaf and a flagon of cider from Mrs Goodhart before their departure and ate it once over the brow of the hill. After a short rest, they began to work their way back towards Porthcarrow, off the beaten track, finding a small spinney to hole up in until late afternoon. As the sun began to wester amid a riot of cloud which presaged a change in the weather, Drinkwater gave his final instructions.

It was almost dark when they set off again. Drinkwater was

not anxious to return to Porthcarrow until the fishing boats had come in and the menfolk were dozing about their hearths, so the church clock was again chiming nine as they reached the first cottage on what they knew was called Church Street. But if they had thought to find the tiny harbour deserted, they were mistaken, for a group of men were manning a large lugger, and Drinkwater was compelled to retire to the churchyard, hide among the tombstones and revise his plans.

He left the men crouching amid the graves and set off to watch thc harbour, only to find that in the interim the lugger had sailed and the quay was now deserted. Staring out across the river, he saw the jagged outline of the lugger's sails as she moved out into the tide, heading for sea. Drinkwater went back to the churchyard and waved his men on. The moon had yet to rise, and they moved swiftly onto the stone quay. After the tension of the day, the ease with which they stole the young fisherman's boat was a relief. Before casting off, Drinkwater opened the lay of the standing boatrope fastened to the iron ring on the quay wall, and through the splayed strands he inserted a folded leaf of his pocketbook. It was a promise to pay five shillings for the hire of the boat on his return.

Drinkwater kept the boat inshore as they edged out between the headlands. He could still see the lugger, but thought it most unlikely that anything of the following boat, creeping under the massive shadow of Pen Carrow, was visible from seaward. What concerned him more was the steepening swell and the fresh breeze that met them as they emerged from the shelter of the land.

He had intended that they should lay off The Mewstone to await daylight, then to locate the rock before hue and cry caught up with them. He had left the promissory note to distract the boat's owner, so confident was he now of finding the steeple rock. But the deterioration in the weather, which could only worsen, meant they must start at once. Fortunately, there was sufficient light to see the dark masses of the two headlands and the rocks, and it would not take them long to work their way onto the position. Fortunately too, the boat contained a tub of light line, well furnished with hooks, but terminating at one end in a small boat-anchor, or killick. This would considerably simplify matters and, armed with his new knowledge of the dan buoys, Drinkwater headed the boat further to the south than hitherto.

Despite the wind, which was from the south west, they were also lucky in that this threw the assumed position of the rock in the lee of The Mewstone. They must take advantage of the shelter and, as the boat's crew bent to the oars, Drinkwater explained his reasons for making this last effort and was gratified to hear grunts of approval.

"It's make all our trials and tribulations worthwhile," said Ross as he shipped his oar and prepared to assist Drinkwater.

"We might even 'ave this boat back on its moorin's afore any of those daft buggers wake up!" put in Mead, and his fellow oarsmen laughed agreeably.

In the end the discovery of the steeple rock was simple, though it took five attempts. The first three were disrupted by heavy swells which rolled down upon the wallowing boat at an inappropriate moment, and the fourth was abandoned when they ran foul of one of the dan buoys that revealed the presence of submarine rocks. This and its crab-pot had to be lifted, but thanks to the long line left in its tub by the boat's owner, Drinkwater was able to perfect his technique and at the fifth sweep, the line came up all standing.

"I think we have the thing," he said as the boat's head jerked round. "Now just pull easily and take the weight of the boat off the line. Kerr you heave in and tell me when the line's up-and-down."

Drinkwater had dropped the killick clear on the landward side of the estimated position of the steeple rock. He had then taken the boat in a wide sweep round the assumed location, with Ross carefully paying out the line over the boat's transom. From time to time Ross had sworn as the hooks caught him, and the four false starts tested all their patience, but the fifth went smoothly, despite the slop of the waves and the spatter of spray that made them curse the chill. But by encircling the rock with the line, they were able to pass a bight of the fishing line about it, girding it and thus effectively capturing it. The critical moment came as the loop was completed and tugged the boat's head round so that she was moored to the killick with the line about the rock, almost replicating the situation Poynton's *Montrose* had been in the previous January.

By gently pulling the boat forward until the line led vertically down into the sea, they would bring her over the very spot. As they did so, Kerr in the bow dipped his lead repeatedly as Drinkwater, his sextant held horizontally and lining up two of the three objects he had selected for the best triangulation, prepared to fix the position of the steeple rock for posterity.

Kerr seemed to be dibbing over the bow for an eternity, and Drinkwater was almost praying as he shook with the effort of trying to retain the images in both sextant mirrors. But at last, just as it seemed he could retain the posture no longer, Kerr shouted with triumph.

"Rock, sir, no doubt! Hard as flint and two, no two-and-a-half fathoms off the soft sand about it!"

"Well done," Drinkwater called, "now maintain station boys, don't lose the bugger . . ." Frantically he took his first set of angles, then, bent double, he ducked into the bottom of the boat where Ross had the boat's lamp alight. Carefully Drinkwater read the angle off the silvered arc, his eyes streaming with the effort. He dictated them to Ross who wrote them down, then he stood again. "Still holding, Kerr?"

"Bouncing right a-top the bugger, sir."

"Hold it another moment, then . . ." Drinkwater struggled with the second angle. The two angles bisected adjacent chords of two circles, the left extreme of the right-hand angle resting on the vertical cliff where Pen Carrow fell into the estuary, which in turn became the right extreme of the left-hand angle. The Euclidean solution to this plane triangulation, that the angle subtending a chord at the circumference of a circle was half that subtended at the centre, was simple on paper, but resolving it in practice, in a wildly dancing boat, in the dark, was beset by practical difficulties. Strained though Drinkwater's skill and patience were, he sat down with a grunt of triumph, having captured the second angle, and read it off to Ross by the lamplight. The two angles gave the intersection of the two circles, and beneath that geometric certainty, lay the elusive steeple rock.

For a further half an hour they pulled about the site, roughly establishing the extent of the rock and finding it was indeed a steeple, no more than two or three feet across, yet rising from the seabed some fifteen feet. It was a sheer needle of granite and one, it seemed, quite capable of severing a pair of heavy rope cables if they were sawed across its striated surface for a while. Concentrating thus upon their task, it was only when they began to consider that it was complete, that Mead remarked that "it was blowing a bit now."

Drinkwater looked up. The lee of The Mewstone in which they had been working had been perfect, but beyond it, the wind had already kicked up a vicious sea. Astern of them the bar was now covered with heavy breaking waves, grey-white in the growing light of dawn. They were another quarter-of-an-hour recovering the fisherman's line and killick, by which time the wind was not only freshening, but was veering, blowing ever more directly into the estuary of the Carrow. When the killick had been lifted, Drinkwater set the boat's head towards the bar.

"Give way, my lads."

There were only four oars in the boat, so the unoccupied men sat shivering, ready to relieve their companions as they pulled for the wild barrier of breaking waves that bestrode the hidden obstruction of the submerged sand-bar. The noise of the break-ers mingled horribly with the howl of the rising gale. Drink-water fought the kick of the tiller as the boat tried to swing round under the impetus of the following seas. The eyes of the crew were astern, where the crests of each succeeding wave rose higher and higher above them. The surface of the sea steepened as they ran into shallower water until, with a savage roar, one broke above them and, lifting the boat and flinging it forward, roared past on either side in a welter of white water.

As the crest passed under them, the boat dragged on the reverse slope of the onrushing wave. Drinkwater roared, "You idlers! Prepare to bale! We may not be so lucky next time." Then they were in the wind-shadow of the next crest, felt the indifferent mass of it raising them as the boat was accelerated again, felt the slam of it against the broad transom, and then the dip of the bow and the surging rise of the cartwheeling stern. "Hold on!" bellowed Drinkwater, as the sudden chilling shock of cold seawater seemed to fill the whole world.

5. A Warm Welcome

The wave passed swiftly beneath them before they pitchpoled and the boat fell back on an even keel. It was filled to the thwarts with water, but they were through the worst, and although the wind blew strongly onshore, they had passed the bar into calmer water.

The "idlers" needed no second bidding and baled frantically, Kerr with his bonnet, Ross with his cupped hands until Drinkwater, securing the sextant and boat compass in their wooden boxes, threw Ross his own hat. And once they were between the headlands the oarsmen ran their oar-looms across the boat and joined their baling mates. Swamping a boat was, while not a common occurrence, a not unfamiliar predicament to the seamen of Trinity House. The most dangerous aspect of their situation was the long, hook-infested line of the boat's rightful owner. No-one escaped its vicious barbs as they mastered their plight, but in due course – cold, wet and hungry – they plied their oars again and headed for the grey breakwater.

"Looks like they've discovered the missing boat, sir," Kerr called from forward.

It was already daylight and Drinkwater could see the figures gathering on the quay.

"Have any of you still got your broken oar-looms," Drinkwater asked, "or were they all washed away?"

"I've got mine," responded Foster, "jammed it under bottom boards."

"And I've mine . . ."

"And me . . ."

"Looks as though you might need them," Drinkwater said, standing up in the stern, retrieving his sodden hat from Ross and clapping it on his head. "Now a nice clip of a stroke there, Foster. Let's show these cod ends we know what's what, eh?"

*   *   *

Drinkwater put on a bold front as the boat was pulled smartly round the end of the breakwater into the pool within its compass.

"Oars!" he commanded. "Hold water larboard!" The boat spun round, its stern heading for the ringbolt and its standing boatrope. Kerr was ready in the bows. "Hold water all!" The boat came to a stop and Kerr picked up the rope. As he did so, Drinkwater, still standing in the stern sheets, looked up at he men lining the quay and staring down at them. The young fisherman he knew simply as "John" was there and in his hand a slip of white paper fluttered in the wind. So, he was aware of the five shillings owing for the hire of his boat. Drinkwater swept the wet hat from his head and made a small bow from the waist.

"Good morning, gentlemen," he said, then turning to the young fisherman, added, "I'm obliged to you for the use of your boat, John, and see, it is returned to you early enough for you to go fishing, if you'll risk your neck out there in this weather . . ."

"Why, you damned trickster . . ." an older man began, but Drinkwater was in no mood for repartee and continued addressing John.

"Your fellow fishermen wantonly destroyed the *Argus*'s gig and I had, perforce, to avail myself of your kind offer to hire me your own boat for five shillings."

"Oi made no such offer," protested John as a stare of mistrust passed among his mates on the quay.

"Did you not? Well your wife seemed to indicate something of the sort when we visited you the other evening."

"That's a damn lie!"

Having precipitated an immediate altercation between the unfortunate John and his colleagues, and thus diverted attention from themselves, Drinkwater gathered up his sextant box. "Disembark nice and quietly, lads, no pushing or shoving."

"You'd better go first, Mr Drinkwater," Mead offered.

"Well, if you insist . . ." Drinkwater stepped the length of the boat over the thwarts and, clambering up the rope, found a pair of leather boots confronting him as he raised his eyes over the edge. He looked up. "If you are thinking of kicking me in the teeth, sir, I should think again. If I choose to take proceed-

ings against you, rather than claim my boat was damaged on
rocks and I lost it, I shall have at least one of you hanged. As it is
I've completed my business and can truly go to Falmouth
without further delay . . . Now, let me up, if you please . . ."

The crowd fell back with a buzz of comment at the news.
Rising to his feet, Drinkwater bent, recovered the sextant box
from Kerr and waited for his crew to muster on the quay.
Turning to the crowd about him, he remarked pleasantly, "You
have a fine steeple rock in the approaches to Porthcarrow,
gentlemen, but I guess you already knew that, and could have
saved me a deal of labour and anxiety, had you chosen to."

"We mean you no harm, Mister," said the man whose boots
Drinkwater had confronted. "But the sooner you're out of here
the better for all of us." The announcement was greeted with a
chorus of assent.

"Well then," Drinkwater said, "you had better arrange for
that ruffian at the Anchor and Hope to serve us a breakfast, and
allow us to dry our clothes there . . ."

"You've half an hour to get out of town . . ."

"Breakfast, sir, before I do another damned thing . . ."

But this argument was scotched before it proceeded further.
Attention was demanded by a cry from the bottom of Church
Street. Drinkwater could not make out what was said, but
suddenly the crowd was moving away, shouting at the man
standing in the narrow gap between the houses which marked
Church Street's junction with the quayside. Then they were
almost alone; only the young fisherman John lingered uncertainly, looking anxiously after his fellows but clearly reluctant
to relinquish his contact with five shillings.

"Here, fellow," Drinkwater said, beckoning him back and
reaching into his pocket. "The five shillings is yours if you'll
just put a word in for us in the Anchor and Hope."

"Why you're a bad, wicked man, sir, and that's the truth."
The man came hesitantly back towards them, holding his hand
out.

"The Anchor and Hope, John," Drinkwater insisted. "Then
the five bob's yours." He turned to his men. "Come lads,
breakfast."

They had to beat upon the tavern door, but when the landlord appeared, Drinkwater stood quietly and let the fisherman explain their needs in a low voice. He caught the words, "hurry up" and "the alarm's been raised", which turned the landlord from anger at being roused, to an obvious compliance. The fisherman turned to Drinkwater. "'Tis fixed," he said shortly and held out his hand.

"Come, Landlord, some rum punch for my lads, and then a hearty breakfast of whatever your wife has to hand. We've been up all night and have a King's appetite, eh lads?"

"My money," demanded the fisherman.

Drinkwater began counting it out into the man's grubby, split hand. "What's all the hurry, John? Come, stay and have a drink . . ." Drinkwater saw the man hesitate. "Join us in a bite. I don't imagine," he added drily, "that it will be long in coming."

"Oi, er, oi'd, er . . ."

"You know there's no hurry, John. You know as well as I do that you'll not get a ship over that bar until high water, and that's four hours away. By then," Drinkwater continued, taking the proffered rum from Kerr and offering it to the fisherman, "the weather'll make it impossible. You were expecting her yesterday, that's why you wanted us out of town, isn't it, eh?"

"How the devil . . . ?" John stopped himself, but he had already given the game away and it fell silent in the taproom. Drinkwater motioned the young man to take the rum punch. Having served them, the landlord had disappeared to raise his wife and cook up the demanded breakfast. John found himself surrounded by the Trinity seamen.

"You bastards are wrecking," Ross said accusingly.

"No, no, we ain't wrecking," John protested vehemently.

"No, no, they're not wrecking," Drinkwater said, "but they are expecting contraband. They're smuggling, and a full cargo, if I'm not mistaken."

"How d'you know . . . ?" John began, alarm written across his pleasant, guileless face, but at that instant the door crashed open and three men with clubs came in, seized the wretched fisherman and dragged him out into the street, where they began belabouring him.

"I think we need those oar-looms, lads," said Drinkwater, fisting his pewter tankard and slamming it down on the head of one of John's assailants. The fight was short-lived. With one of their number knocked bleeding and unconscious to the ground, the other two men ran off. With an odd solicitude, Kerr and Wynn helped John to his feet. Blood poured down his face from a gash to his head and his face was ashen.

"Ross," Drinkwater said sharply, "do you run to his cottage and get his wife. Those bastards have concussed the poor devil."

"Aye, the bloody landlord had a hand in it," Foster said.

"Seen our bloody breakfast off, then, the bugger!"

"Ow d'you know about this 'ere smugglin' then, sir?"

"I guessed," replied Drinkwater. "Ross gave me the lead, but these men aren't deliberate wreckers. Oh, certainly they'd plunder a wreck if they had the chance. I think they'd have had a go at Poynton's *Montrose* if there was any of it left, and maybe they've been dragging the site in the hope of some plate, but smuggling's a different matter. The rector's in it up to his breeches, and probably the squire, but we haven't had the pleasure of *his* acquaintance."

"So what do we do now, sir?"

"Have our breakfast and then . . . Well, I can't see Captain Judd working the *Argus* round the Land's End for a week, so we had better make our rendezvous in Falmouth."

"That's a fair march from here, sir," Foster said, regarding his empty pot ruefully. "And we was up all last night after marching all day yesterday."

"An' our clothes is intol'rably wet, sir."

Drinkwater looked round the circle of faces and grinned. "We could stay here until tomorrow if one or two of you could persuade the landlord of the fact. I don't suppose there are too many to argue the point just at the moment." Foster agreed, as did Mead and Wynn. "This fellow still looks grim," Drinkwater added, regarding the fisherman stretched upon the adjacent bench.

At this point the door opened again and Ross led the man's wife into the taproom. 'Help the lady home with her husband," Drinkwater said wearily.

*   *   *

After the fisherman's wife had been calmed, told what had happened and seen home, they settled to a belated and resentfully-served breakfast. Following this, Drinkwater and his men dozed as their outer garments dried before the fire. It was late morning before any of the Trinity men stirred, but a gust of wind blew the taproom door open and a swirl of rain blew in. Drinkwater woke with a start, stretching and feeling the agony of returning circulation to his cramped and numbed limbs. Slowly he recalled his circumstances, and then, thinking of the injured fisherman and the hours of idleness before he could lead his men out of this benighted place, he decided to see how the wretched fellow was.

Stepping out into the narrow street, Drinkwater was almost swept off his feet by a gust of wind. Having struggled to the fisherman's house he knocked and went in. The young man was conscious, his head bandaged with a clean rag, and his wife was peeling potatoes. The fisherman stirred, his face puffing with anger at the intrusion, but Drinkwater held up his hand.

"I'm sorry about your injury, John," he said, "but it was your own people who hit you. At least you are not concussed."

John subsided and shook his head. "There's trouble, Mister, an' there'll be more afore this is all ower. Reckon you owes me more than five shilling."

Drinkwater ignored the last remark. "I know there's trouble, but what is it?"

"It's nowt to do with you, sir, and I'd keep out of it."

Drinkwater nodded. In his pocket he found a shilling and, leaning forward, he placed it on the blanket covering the sleeping child in his crib. "Fine baby," he said, smiling at the woman.

"John, like his father," she said smiling back at him. "You married, sir?" He nodded. "But no children?"

"But no children. Tell me, is Big John involved with this smuggling . . . ?"

She looked across at her husband. "Be silent, woman," he said. "There's trouble enough already."

"What *is* this trouble?" Drinkwater persisted.

"There's a damned ship due. She's late like you said an' now they've got her anchored off the bar . . ."

"Just like the *Montrose*, eh?"

"Aye, jus' like the bloody *Montrose*! An' just like the *Montrose* she'll go all to pieces and we'll lose her an' the cargo, an' then that poor little bastard," John nodded at the child, "will have to drag himself to sea like his father an' his gran'father . . ."

"Don't talk like that . . ." his wife cut in, but Drinkwater was already leaving them to their domestic misery, glad at least that the poor, young fellow was alive. Returning to the Anchor and Hope, Drinkwater made an announcement.

"You're welcome to remain here, but I'm going up on Pen Carrow head. I think we might have a wreck on our hands by darkness." The door slammed behind Drinkwater.

"On *our* bloody hands," Foster protested, "what's a wreck got to do with us?"

"He's like a bloody bulldog," Ross remarked, half admiringly.

6. Rescue

The scene from Pen Carrow was stupefying. The fishermen of Porthcarrow were scattered about the slope of the headland, huddled in impotent little groups, oddly like flotsam, Drinkwater thought, washed hither and thither, from the quay to this lonely, wind-scoured spot, by the circumstances from which they wrested their existence. He felt sorry for them, standing there, watching the small brig as she snubbed at her cable. Whatever the brig's cargo, the attempt to evade duty was a determined, well-planned operation, only spoiled by the weather. Drinkwater could not imagine why they had let her get so close inshore, but concluded those responsible must have decided to cross the bar before the weather precluded it altogether. One thing was certain, the brig could not linger offshore. Every day's delay increased the chances of word of her presence reaching Bodmin or Launceston and the Excisemen arriving. Now they stood watching any chance of landing their precious cargo ebb away.

"*You* could get her in, sir." Drinkwater turned to find Ross beside him. "We could get aboard and you could get her in . . ."

"What the hell are you suggesting, Ross?" Drinkwater frowned at the able seaman. "You know what Foster said, the entrance is too narrow."

"*Foster* said it was too narrow . . ." Ross left the sentence hanging for a moment. "Look sir," he went on, "none of these fishermen is used to handling a brig of that tonnage. They're cod-heads, good at their trade, but ignorant. On the other hand, the crew of the brig probably don't fancy lying this close inshore on an unfamiliar coast. She ain't registered in Porthcarrow, is she? And I don't suppose anything much larger than a lugger is, but we . . . you, me, Wynn, Mead, even Foster and the others, we're used to working inshore. You'd not lose your nerve, sir."

"Wouldn't I? How the deuce d'you know that?"

"Cause I've seen you."

"You don't want to leave the brig to her fate, do you Ross?"

"Doesn't seem right, somehow, sir." Ross paused.

"Well, that's true . . ." The mad idea gathered momentum in Drinkwater's active mind. "Very well. We'd better ask these villains for the loan of one of their boats again." And with that, Drinkwater, having located the fisherman whose boots he had become acquainted with earlier that day, walked down the hill towards him.

"We've put a pilot aboard," said the villainous man, whom Drinkwater now knew as Jacob. "He's a fisherman like ourselves, but he was a prisoner in France during the American War and he speaks the lingo."

"She's a French vessel then?"

Jacob turned and looked at him. "Aye, as you'll find out if you gets aboard her." They sat in the stern sheets of the lugger as eight oarsmen pulled her out to sea against the wind and the swell that now, near the top of the tide, swept in between the headlands.

"Your pilot went out in the lugger this morning then," Drinkwater said.

"Aye. This lugger." Jacob smacked the rail beside him. "She came back in while you were at the inn."

They sat in silence. It was increasingly difficult to talk as the

wind howled about them, the big lugger bucked into the sea and
sheets of spray shot aft, stinging their faces and inducing the
painful wind-ache that followed. After a few minutes, Jacob
turned to Drinkwater. "Why are you doing this, Mister? So's
you can turn us all over to the Riding Officers?"

Drinkwater grinned. "No Jacob. I know nothing beyond the
fact that there's a vessel in distress off Pen Carrow. It is our
duty to assist, if it is humanly possible. But let's get her inside
the heads and lying to an anchor in the stream first. It brings ill
luck to count your chickens before they're hatched."

The seas on the bar were less violent now the tide had risen, but
the state of the sea beyond was wild in the extreme. So strong
had the wind become, that the crests had ceased to break, but
were torn off and shredded, their disintegrating atoms streaming to leeward with the force of buckshot. Pulling directly to
windward, they could do little beyond inch the big lugger
forward with tedious, back-breaking slowness. The oarsmen
had fallen into a numbing rhythm, and Drinkwater admired
their stout fortitude as they swayed, back and forth in faultless
unison. Ahead of the lugger's stem, Drinkwater could now see
the brig, her bow rising high out of the water as she breasted the
incoming seas, her single cable stretched tightly and leading
steeply down into the water. Their own progress was barely
discernible, but over a period of half an hour, the brig was
noticeably closer.

"The tide's turned," Drinkwater now had to shout, to make
Jacob hear, "we're being carried to seaward by the ebb."

While this afforded them some assistance in getting out to the
brig, it increased the danger of bringing the vessel in, since not
only would the strength of the tide grow inexorably against
them – something which the power of the wind would easily
overcome – but with the wind and tide in opposition, even
steeper seas would run in the estuary and, worse still, across the
bar itself. Whilst it may have been possible to pass the bar at a
lower state of the tide in good weather, to do so in these
conditions could result in the brig striking the bottom. If that
were to happen she might break up. It was not a prospect

Drinkwater wished to dwell upon. Besides, they were running out of time.

Then they began to get a little shelter from the plunging hull and, shielded from the worst of the wind, they made better progress, watched by half a dozen heads peering over the brig's rail.

"Keep going, lads, not far now." Drinkwater turned to Jacob. "I want all my men aboard. You may have to make several approaches, but do your damnedest."

"Aye, aye, sir."

Something about the way Jacob responded led Drinkwater to ask, "Have you ever served in the navy?"

Jacob nodded and spat to leeward.

"So have I, Jacob."

"You, Mister?"

"Aye, Jacob. As Acting Lieutenant."

"*Acting* Lieutenant? Then you were a midshipmite."

Drinkwater nodded and, despite his precarious situation, grinned. "We all suffer bad luck, Jacob, but *especially* if you're a midshipmite in His Britannic Majesty's Navy."

"*Were* a midshipmite, Mister," Jacob growled. "You're bugger all now."

A moment later the brig, yawing and sawing at her cable, loomed above the lugger as it surged up and down her dun-coloured starboard side. A short pilot's ladder had been flung over the side and, as the boat rose, Drinkwater made a leap for it. The instant both his feet felt the rungs, he scrambled upwards, for fear the lugger rose again and caught his ankles against the brig's side. Clambering over the rail he jumped down on the deck and cast about him.

Drinkwater recognised the fisherman-cum-pilot, and the worried-looking master. He bowed. "*M'sieur*." He struck his breast and said "Drinkwater *à votre service. Attendez-vous votre*, er," he gestured aloft, "*hunier*" he said, recalling the French for topsail and gesturing to that on the foremast.

"*Pourquoi*?"

Drinkwater turned and gestured that the brig would proceed through the heads. The master violently shook his head, countering with equal insistence that they remained at anchor.

Drinkwater held out his right arm and sawed it across his left fist, and then pointed downwards before flattening his hands and waving them laterally in a universal gesture of failure. The master turned to the fisherman who tried to address the master's concerns.

"Tell him there's a steeple rock in this area, that the *Montrose* was lost here with two cables down, that he doesn't have a hope in hell unless he gets under way without more delay. Tell him the tide's on the ebb and I haven't come out here to argue with him. Tell him to have his men ready to loose his foretopsail, cut his cable and be ready to give her a stern board and cast her head to starboard."

Drinkwater turned to his own men, the last of which was Foster. "I want you on the forebraces. Except you, Foster. You get forward with that knife of yours and start cutting the cable." Drinkwater turned to the master again. "Captain, get that festering *hunier* ready, stand-by the bloody clewlines!"

The unfortunate Frenchman stood uncertainly for a moment, then a tremor ran through the whole fabric of the brig. From forward a cry of alarm was raised as the cable began to part, and the French master bawled his orders.

"Get forrard, you men!" Drinkwater shouted. "Let fly the starboard and heave aft the larboard forebraces!" Drinkwater bellowed at his men and turning aft to the heavy tiller by which the brig was steered, he threw his weight on it, forcing it over to starboard. Even before the brig's crew had let go the fore topsail's clew and buntlines, with a second tremor, helped by Foster's knife, the cable parted. The brig gathered sternway and, with the rudder hard a-port, her head fell off to starboard. With a slam aloft, the half-sheeted topsail slammed aback against the foremast.

Drinkwater stared intently astern, watching Poynton's "sharp rock" draw closer, aware that the French master was beside him, muttering anxiously. "*M'sieur, m'sieur, regardez –*"

But Drinkwater needed no bidding. The fore topsail was now all a-tremble as the wind caught the weather luff. "Let go and haul!" he shouted, adding to the French master, "*Capitaine, m'aider!*"

Both men threw themselves on the tiller and, in defiance of the brig's momentum astern, forced the tiller right across the deck so that, as the gale caught the after side of the topsail, the stern board was arrested, the brig's bow continued its starboard swing and she gathered headway. A moment later, the vessel was spinning round, her bowsprit raking the northern headland, as Drinkwater and the French captain steadied her for the centre of the channel and the tumbling mass of breakers thundering across the bar.

From their standing start, they seemed now to have gained the speed of an arrow as they raced towards the fearful sight. The topsail had been sheeted home and, as the brig steadied on the entrance to the Carrow, the foreyards were squared. They were committed, committed to the narrow vent through which the river funnelled to the sea. Drinkwater felt his knees knock with sudden, terrifying panic. This was sheer madness! He could not believe the self-conceit that had led him to harken to Ross's flattery. He felt certain that, in a few minutes, as they passed into that hideous welter of green, grey and white water, he would feel the fatal impact of the keel on hard sand, see the masts whip and hear the shrouds part with the twang of fiddle strings.

"*Mon Dieu!*" Beside him, the Frenchman blasphemed as the bowsprit stabbed upwards at the sky above Pen Carrow. Drinkwater felt the stern fall into the trough of the following sea, heard again the sudden hush as a wave reared over their stern, and then felt the stern lift, lift with such sudden violence that he could feel the compression acting on his legs and spine. The bowsprit drove downwards and even the topsail seemed to shiver in the lee of the breaker.

Now, now would be the instant the brig drove her forefoot into the sand bar and the masts would go by the board as they cartwheeled, broached and became a helpless wreck . . .

But there was no impact; instead the bow seemed to lift with an astonishingly graceful majesty. Riding up, the brig was borne forward in triumph on the crest of the wave as it broke beneath them and foamed on beyond the quivering hull. There was a second, less terrifying pitch and scend, exhilarating after the first, and then they were through, the headlands rising on either side. It seemed for a moment that the lower yardarms would scrape the cliffs, but they sped past, sailing in across the placid waters of the estuary. Behind the brig, the lugger, under a scrap of sail, followed in their wake.

Fifteen minutes later, the brig, the *Rozelle* of Quimper, lay at her second bower anchor off Porthcarrow, and Drinkwater was shaking the hand of the French master who insisted on planting a kiss of each of his cheeks.

As Drinkwater gathered his men and gear together on the quayside, he was aware that a crowd was assembling at the foot of Church Street.

"Looks like trouble, Mr Drinkwater," Foster said.

As the Trinity House men approached, the fishermen spread out, barring their exit from the breakwater. Jacob stood truculently at their head and Drinkwater walked straight up to him.

"Come now, Jacob, stand aside. There has been enough bother."

"Why did you help us, Mister?" The question was accompanied by a rumble of agreement. "Aye, why . . . ?" "Why . . . ?" "Tell us!"

"Why?" Drinkwater set down his bundle and faced Jacob. "Because I must explain the loss of a fine gig, damn you, Jacob. As you and your fine friends hereabouts all know well, she was lost as I boarded the brig *Rozelle* to render assistance." He turned to the men standing in a semicircle behind him. "Wasn't she, lads?" he asked them with a wink.

Ross caught on quicker than the others. "Aye, sir, lost she was, rendering assistance to the brig *Rozelle*."

It clearly took a moment longer for Drinkwater's subterfuge to sink in among the fishermen. The subtlety seemed to occur to someone in the crowd after a moment, and the word was whispered to Jacob who, his eyes fixed on Drinkwater, remained suspicious.

"And what of the brig *Rozelle*, Mister?"

"I shall report her arrival here when I reach the Custom House at Falmouth, Jacob."

Jacob squinted at the young officer, convinced he was being

outwitted. "That'll be tomorrow then?" a man next to Jacob asked, his intelligent eyes picking up Drinkwater's intention.

"Perhaps the day after if we can find decent lodgings in Porthcarrow," Drinkwater responded quickly. "We have been up all night," he added, gesturing at the men about him, "and I'm deuced tired."

"We could find you a decent berth, Mister," said the man with intelligent eyes.

"Not at Mrs Goodhart's," chipped in Foster. "She don't serve no ale."

"No, not at Mrs Goodhart's, Jacob," Drinkwater added grinning, "the Anchor and Hope will do very well, if you please."

The man with the intelligent eyes whispered into Jacob's ear and the fishermen's leader nodded reluctantly, still half-bemused at his good fortune.

"I'll slit your gizzard if you've tricked me, Mister."

"Stand aside man. I've a steeple rock to mark on a chart, a report to write and some sleep to catch up with. I'm too tired to trick a monkey."

At Jacob's order the fishermen fell back and, slinging their dunnage over their shoulders, the Trinity House men headed for the tavern. "I told you you could do it, Mister Drinkwater," Ross said, falling in step beside the mate of the *Argus*. "But did you really do it to explain the loss of the gig?"

"Don't ask me, Ross. As I said, I'm tired . . ."

Drinkwater wondered if the explanation would really satisfy old "Fuss-Pot" Judd. Perhaps, he reflected, he should have paid more attention to Judd's advice to avoid *all* the dangers hereabouts. Well, it was too late now; but it was true, that young fisherman's wife was a damned handsome young woman.

SIEGE OF TOULON

Showell Styles

The French Revolutionary Wars began on 20 April 1792 when the French Assembly declared war on Austria. The Hapsburg Emperor, Leopold II, was the brother of French queen Marie Antoinette, and he continued to support the French monarchy. Leopold entered into an alliance with Prussia against France, but he died before hostilities began. The French took advantage of his death to invade Austria. The start of the war was a scrappy affair with neither side well prepared. The first real victory was at Valmy, east of Paris, on 20 September 1792, where the French defeated the Prussian army. The patriotic fervour arising from the battle gave the French government the opportunity to declare a republic. The fates of the French king and queen were sealed. Louis XVI was executed on 21 January 1793 and Marie Antoinette nine months later.

    Until 1793, Britain had remained neutral, even when the French invaded Belgium, but Britain had an alliance with Holland, which was an obvious French target. France could not invade Holland without also becoming the enemy

*of Britain. On 1 February 1793 France declared war on
Britain and Holland. On 9 March France also declared
war on Spain. Hostilities were now in earnest. The involvement of Britain, however, had extended the war from
land to sea.*

*There was not total support within France for the republic
and during 1793 a series of internal rebellions broke out. One
of these was at Toulon, which turned to Britain for help.
Toulon was also the first important engagement for a young
French captain, Napoleon Bonaparte.*

*The following story is by Showell Styles (b. 1908) who
has written many books set during the Napoleonic period.
It is taken from* Path to Glory *(1952), which traces the
exploits of Captain (later Admiral) Sir Sidney Smith
(1764–1840).*

Sir Sidney Smith was jogging adventurously down a dusty
mountain-track in the Balkans with his servant Titus Wright,
blissfully ignorant that his country was at war.

He had left an England at peace and convinced that she would
remain so in spite of Burke's fulminations in the House. The
notion of travelling clean across Europe to Constantinople had
fascinated him; it presented a prospect of new scenes and
adventures such as his restless spirit craved. He took Wright
with him as servant and companion, and travelled slowly, with
many a divergence, through the Low Countries and Hanover,
across Saxony and Bohemia, into Hungary.

Here he was nearly poisoned by drinking foul water and was
only restored to health after weeks of careful nursing by Wright.
On his farther journey southward into the marches of the Turkish
Empire no news of war reached him. At Adrianople, in October, a
merchant repeated a rumour that there had been fighting on the
shores of the far-off northern sea. But not until early November,
when he and his servant, burnt almost black by the weather,
arrived in Constantinople, did Sir Sidney hear the truth – that
England had been at war with France for nearly ten months.

Within three days Captain Smith was aboard a Turkish brig sailing for Smyrna, where he hoped to pick up a passage to Gibraltar, or at least to Sicily. But at Smyrna there were terrible tales of rape and murder and cutting-off of heads in all the ports of France. No master would take his ship beyond Cape Matapan.

Captain Smith was very far from despairing. For one thing he had reliable news that Hood was at Toulon; this would shorten his passage from 2000 to 1,500 sea miles – he might join the English fleet as much as a week earlier. For another, Wright, in his foraging sallies from the evil-smelling wine-shop on the Smyrna quays where they had found lodging, had come upon two English seamen prowling about the alleys. They had, so they said, been abandoned there by their ship, a merchantman; and they added that there were others in like plight, all of them eager to get clear of Smyrna and strike a blow at the Frogs. As soon as he heard this Captain Smith dispatched his henchman to bring these seamen to the wine-shop.

Behold, then, Captain Sir Sidney Smith seated in the gloomiest corner of Hussin's gloomy wine-shop on a November evening. Hussin had few customers, and they squatted, huddled in their robes, at the low tables sipping syrupy wine and taking no notice of the Englishman. There was, indeed, little to indicate the Frankish race of this stranger. Over a Greek tailor's conception of British naval uniform he wore a vast sheepskin cloak acquired in Nish, on his head was a cap of warm fur such as the Kurds affected; and the beak-nosed features tanned very dark by a year's wanderings might have hailed from anywhere south of the Black Sea.

But for all his twenty-nine years it was still a boyish face, and the eager tilt of the chin as Titus Wright entered the shop held all the old confident expectation of adventure.

Wright, his gigantic form swathed in a gaudy robe, looked like some eastern *djinn* until he doffed his fur cap and showed his square English face a-grin.

"Seven I've got, sir," he muttered, bending down to speak to the captain. "In poor shape, but seamen every man."

"Bring them in," said the captain.

As Wright turned to obey he called to the proprietor of the place, a huddled heap dozing in a far corner.

"Hussin! Nine glasses of wine – and bring rugs."

The wizened little Turk hastened to do his bidding. While he was spreading dirty rugs on the dirtier floor about the table at which Sir Sidney was sitting, the door opened again, letting in a swirling gust from the quays and Wright with seven ragged men.

Wright led his companions forward, stood to attention and knuckled his forehead.

"Crew reportin' for orders, sir," said he.

The seven ragamuffins shuffled and stared at the man in the chair. Sir Sidney had flung back the sheepskin cloak to reveal a blue frock-coat and somewhat soiled white breeches. He scanned in turn the faces displayed to him by the wavering lamplight. An unshaven, bleary-eyed gang they were.

"Very good," he said tersely. "Sit down, men. You'll take wine with me, I beg."

Grinning sheepishly, they squatted in a half-circle on the rugs. Wright handed the wine which Hussin had brought. The captain raised his glass.

"Success to our arms and confusion to the Frogs," he said.

"Amen," said a sharp-featured little man as he tossed off his drink and smacked his lips. The others drank in silence, appreciatively, staring the while at their host. The captain leaned forward, running his eye over the row of dark expectant faces.

"I'm sailing to join Lord Hood at Toulon," he said incisively. "Any man who sails with me will do the same. Is that clear?"

The sharp-featured man leered up at him, contorting his face into an expression of extraordinary cunning.

"An' no questions asked, cully?" he demanded.

"My name," said the captain without rancour, "is Sir Sidney Smith, captain in His Majesty's Navy. You will say 'sir' when you speak to me."

"Aye aye, sir," he muttered. "But I'm wishful to know . . ."

"No questions will be asked, except for your name and qualifications as a seaman."

"I'm game, then," said the little man defiantly. "James Boxer, that's me – gunlayer, sir."

Captain Smith gave no indication that he now knew the man for a deserter from a King's ship. Wright recorded the name in his book, and one by one the others signified their agreement: Coulson, Beecroft, Carroll, Morris, Humpherson and Lee – all, according to their own statement, able seamen.

"Very good," said the captain, when Wright had finished. "We sail for Toulon with the first light tomorrow."

They stared at him open-mouthed.

"No ship'll put to sea, sir," said one. "Me and Tom Carroll's been trying . . ."

"We shall be obliged," interrupted the captain calmly, "to help ourselves to a ship."

Boxer, the gunlayer, slapped his thigh and chuckled.

"Steal one, eh? By hookey, sir, that's the game!"

Sir Sidney frowned down his nose at him.

"I am not in the habit of thieving from those who are not our enemies, Boxer," he said. "I shall leave what money I have with me in payment. Unhappily it is considerably short of the amount required to purchase the ship I have in mind, but I cannot allow that to stand in the way of my duty."

He glanced over his shoulder at the chattering Turks and beckoned his hearers to draw closer. They did so eagerly.

"The ship I have in mind," said the captain, in a low voice, "is the two-masted felucca lying alongside the north quay. I have ascertained that she is victualled for a voyage to Tunis. That should provide for us. Her sails and rigging appear in good order. Two men are in the habit of sleeping on board. I shall command. Mr Wright" – the big man jumped at the unaccustomed title – "will act as lieutenant, Boxer will act as quartermaster."

"My heye!" chuckled the gunlayer. " 'Ere's promotion for Jimmy Boxer . . ."

He ended with a suppressed yelp and a glare at Wright, who had kicked him on the ankle.

"Attend to me, now," rapped the captain. "I want every man on the north quay before dawn tomorrow, but you'll keep out of sight until you hear me whistle. On that signal you, Boxer, with Carroll and Beecroft, will board her and truss up the two men on board. They are to be bound and gagged but not otherwise hurt – mind that. Coulson, you'll cut her for'ard mooring. Morris, you'll deal with the after mooring. You've knives?"

"Yes, sir."

"Mr Wright, with Lee and Humpherson, will get sail on her as quickly as possible," Sir Sidney went on. "I trust I've made myself clear. If any man is in doubt, let him speak up now."

The men muttered to each other, but their faces showed excitement and determination.

"Very good." Sir Sidney stood up. "Mr Wright, allocate positions for the morning to your men, in three parties. I don't want them to wait in a bunch. The *kalif* has a patrol walking the port at night. Carry on."

The men scrambled to their feet, knuckling their foreheads in awkward salute.

"Lord 'elp us!" gasped Boxer to Wright, as they emerged from the wine-shop into the fury of the night wind. "We'll drown tomorrow!"

"You'll drown if the captain says so," growled Wright. "Not otherwise, d'ye see?"

Which sufficiently indicates the convictions of the newly promoted lieutenant as to his master's capabilities.

In fact, the boundless self-confidence which to many appeared as arrogance and rashness was Sir Sidney Smith's weakness as well as his strength. Not infrequently this led to a narrow escape from the failure of his schemes; but sometimes his airy taking-for-granted of men's integrity and capabilities put them on their mettle, and so it was with the seven ragamuffins of Smyrna. Weeks of debauchery had softened their moral fibre, bad and meagre rations had weakened their bodies. But something about this cool, hawk-faced gentleman challenged their manhood, and they responded. An hour before dawn every man of the seven was on the north quay, crouching behind the piled bales of merchandise.

Captain Smith, pacing slowly along the quay with his sheep-skin cloak drawn tightly round him, did not even consider the possibility of his crew failing him. He had succeeded in obtaining a crude chart of the Cyclades, and he would need it if he were to get safely through that densely clustered archipelago to the open sea beyond Cape Matapan. He would not need to call in for water until he reached Messina. In his pocket were two gold coins, all he possessed. The rest of his money was left in trust with Hussin, to be delivered, on pain of reprisal, to one Enver Ali, the owner of the felucca he proposed to command.

He was approaching the dark shape of the felucca when a figure, gigantic in the gloom, materialized from behind a pile of casks.

"All's taut, sir," whispered Wright. "Two Dagoes snorin' in the after cabin. I've took the liberty of casting-off the extra mooring they'd rigged for'ard, sir."

"Very good."

Captain Smith threw a glance at the long huddle of flat-roofed houses that loomed along the quay. Not a light showed; the quay was deserted as far as the darkness permitted him to see. The rain, chill and invisible, drove at him, stinging his cheeks. The *kalif*'s patrol would be sheltering in some corner – if indeed it was going its rounds in this weather.

"Stand by, Mr Wright," he said, and putting two fingers to his teeth whistled shrilly.

At once dark figures came running out of the gloom. Wright stepped forward.

"After cabin, Boxer!" he muttered. "Coulson and Morris, stand by for the word."

With the exception of the two at the mooring ropes the party dropped on to the slippery deck of the felucca. Captain Smith groped his way aft to the tiller, his mind busy with calculations of wind and sail. From somewhere below his feet came muffled noises – thumps, oaths, startled appeals to Allah instantly stilled. Wright was growling instructions as he and his two men struggled with the unfamiliar brailings of the lateen sails. Simultaneously two white bundles were dumped unceremoniously over the side on to the wet stones of the quay.

"Cast off!" rapped the captain.

The big sails stiffened and filled. The felucca heeled and went plunging away into the dark. The whole operation had taken no more than five or six minutes.

Sunrise found them plunging ahead with a quartering wind, the drab hills of Asia Minor opening farther on either hand as the gulf widened towards the Ægean. Captain Smith relinquished the tiller to Lee, who claimed experience as a helmsman, and made a rapid inspection of his craft. She was a 40-foot keel, decked forward and aft to form foc'sle and after cabin.

Wright, a roll of cloth in his hand, ducked out of the foc'sle as the captain descended to the waist.

"Best I can do, sir," he said. "There's a halyard ready rigged."

"Bend it on, Mr Wright, and pipe all hands, if you please."

He clambered to the tiny after deck. The half-dozen men, mustered by Wright, came stumbling aft.

"Men," said Captain Smith, raising his voice against the tumult of wind and wave, "this craft is henceforth one of His Majesty's Ships, and subject to naval discipline. I name her the *Swallow*, fleet tender. God save the King!"

He doffed his fur cap, and Wright ran up his improvised flag to the peak. An ensign had been impracticable with his crude materials, but he had made a very passable St George's Cross, red on a white ground; an admiral's flag, but that could not be helped. The men raised a cheer. None of them, least of all the captain of the *Swallow* – he whose hope it was shortly to command a ship of the line – saw anything at all ridiculous about this ceremony. A sudden glint of sunshine illuminated the tiny flag like an omen.

"Mr Wright," barked Captain Smith, "hands to breakfast."

On the morning of 3 December, nearly three weeks after the *Swallow* tender sailed from the port of Smyrna, Lord Hood's squadron lying at anchor in the outer bay of Toulon was surprised by a sudden popping of small artillery. This was the *Swallow*'s brass carronade saluting the Admiral's flag.

The Admiral himself was on his quarterdeck when the tiny

craft came racing between the great wooden hulls of the line-of-battle ships with the green water creaming under her forefoot. He watched her approach, scowling. The state of things in the port, the dissension between French and Spanish and Neapolitans, above all the notoriously bile-stirring *mistral*, combined to put him into the worst of tempers. His flag-captain, Lambert, was surprised into incautious speech by sight of the *Swallow*'s ensign.

"There's an Admiral of the Fleet aboard that felucca, sir, if her flag's anything to go by!" he chuckled.

"Thank you, captain, I've eyes of my own," snapped Admiral Hood.

A midshipman came running up to *Victory*'s quarterdeck. "Felucca hails us, sir," he panted. "Says she's the *Swallow* tender, Captain Sir Sidney Smith."

Lord Hood's leathery face wrinkled itself in a malevolent grin.

"Tell him he may come alongside," he said.

"Aye aye, sir. Pipe the side, sir?"

"No, damn it!" exploded the Admiral. "Pipe the side of my flagship for a half-pay captain a year late reporting for duty?" he fulminated. "I'll see him damned first, Swedish knight or not! Look at the mountebank – not even in uniform!"

Sir Sidney was wearing his sheepskin mantle and fur cap. Before he leapt for the ladder leading to the entry port, however, he threw off these unofficial garments. He arrived on the flagship's quarterdeck in salt-stained blue coat and worn white breeches much spotted with tar, and walked briskly up to the Admiral, who received his salute with a grim nod.

"Captain Sir Sidney Smith, sir, reporting for duty with eight seamen, from Smyrna. I have the *Swallow* tender –"

"You'll please to render a full report to my flag-captain, *Sir* Sidney," said the Admiral harshly. "In particular, you will give your reasons for wearing that flag at your peak – which I order you instantly to haul down."

"Aye aye, sir." The captain of the *Swallow* gave no sign of discomposure at this unpromising reception. "And my men, sir?"

"Damn your men, sir!" rasped the Admiral ill-temperedly.
"Do what you like with 'em – don't badger me!"

Captain Smith stood his ground.

"If I've your permission to victual and refit, sir –"

"Yes, yes, yes!"

The Admiral stumped away.

This interview was the only contact with his superior Captain
Smith obtained for a fortnight after his arrival in Toulon.

Captain Smith was in any case quite capable of looking after
himself. On the strength of the Admiral's few words he
wheedled out of Lambert a comprehensive authority to draw
on naval stores for his requirements. Aided by Wright, he set
his men to work re-rigging the felucca until he had her as smart
as a man-of-war's tender. The long voyage through Mediterranean winter storms had toughened the ragamuffins of Smyrna
and taught them to rely on each other and on their captain, and
they worked with a will. After long persistence and many
applications, the captain got them entered for pay on the books
of the *Diomede*, with whose commander he had some acquaintance. And in the intervals between these activities, since no one
attempted to give him any orders, he made excursions with
Wright into the port of Toulon, with the purpose of picking up
information and acquiring a knowledge of the inner harbours.

Each time he visited the port he found the townspeople, those
enthusiasts who had so boldly proclaimed their allegiance to
Louis XVII some months ago, more apprehensive than before.

The town was in a state of siege. On the great amphitheatre of
hills that rises steeply behind the double bay stood a strong
enceinte of forts and batteries, planned to cover the harbours
from attack by sea, from the south. On the north side of this wall
Carnot, the military genius of the new Republic, was massing
infantry and artillery day by day. Reliable reports said that he
had already 30,000 men there and innumerable batteries of siege
guns. To defend this 15-mile line of fortifications there were
some 18,000 troops, of which 2,000 were English regulars from
Gibraltar, and 1,500 seamen and marines from the fleet; the
remainder were a hotchpotch of French Royalists, Neapolitans,
Spaniards and Piedmontese.

Captain Smith, hiring a mule, rode up to the fortifications himself on a grey day in the middle of December and found little to encourage him. The marine officer who welcomed him had no doubt of his own ability to hold the portion of the line allotted to him, but had every doubt of his neighbours, a Spanish regiment. The camp could be seen at no great distance across the arid hills; a city of tents stretching as far as the eye could see on either hand, with single ant-like figures or coloured masses of men moving to and fro.

"These confounded forts aren't built for landward defence," complained the marine officer, "and if we have to retreat, sir, they command our whole line – and the harbours as well."

Captain Smith pointed to a grey bastion at the western end of the long semicircle of forts and tenailles and batteries. It crowned the summit of a steep hill directly overlooking the Grande Rade, where rode the English fleet like models in a basin.

"With that one fort in their hands," he observed, "the Frogs hold a master-key. They can rake your defences from the rear and at the same time fire on the town, the quays, and the shipping. Damme, major, if I were a French artilleryman I'd concentrate all my fire on that fort!"

The marine looked at him with respect.

"You're quite right, sir. That's Fort Aiguillette, and Lord Mulgrave knows it's the key-point. He's put the two battalions of ours from Gib there. All the same, God help us if there's any Jean Crapaud that tumbles to your conclusion."

Sir Sidney rode away down the steep tracks to the port in a thoughtful frame of mind. He would have been more thoughtful still had he known that a sullen little ferret of an artilleryman from Corsica was at that very moment urging Citizen-General Carnot to concentrate on taking Fort Aiguillette. As it was, he reached the conclusion that the defences of Toulon were bound to fall within a day or two of Carnot's first mass attack. And in the inner harbour lay thirty-one French warships.

Captain Smith considered those warships as the cockboat took him past them on his way back to the *Swallow*. Half of them had their Republican crews on board, prisoners under hatches. Since the port must eventually be abandoned, therefore, those ships should be destroyed. As soon as he reached his tiny craft the captain wrote a letter to the Admiral submitting that this should be done, adding that the arsenal and the powder-storage ships ought also to be destroyed at the same time. Receiving no reply to this, he occupied himself in the preparation of a plan and in fitting the felucca to be rowed by sweeps in case his plan ever materialized. Two more days passed before the Republican army made their assault.

The felucca was jerking uneasily at her anchor and the night wind thrummed in her rigging; a storm from the north drove ragged clouds across the moon. On the ridge of hills above the straggling lights of Toulon another kind of storm was raging. From all along the 15 miles of undulating crest came the bright orange flashes of the guns and their ceaseless boom and rumble. Carnot had begun his bombardment.

All that stormy day it continued. At noon a rabble of Spanish soldiery, packed into barges, came out to be embarked in the ships of the Spanish squadron.

Balls began to fall among the outlying houses of the port during the afternoon. Hard on the heels of the news that Fort Balaquier had fallen came boatload after boatload of Neapolitans, many of them wounded; and with them came the first pitiful refugees from the town. Still the British colours fluttered from Fort Aiguillette. They would not stay there another twenty-four hours if the relentless bombardment continued. And there in the inner harbour, ten of them moored in a close tier absolutely inviting the use of a fire-ship, lay those thirty-one great fighting ships waiting to fall into the hands of the enemy again.

Captain Smith had himself rowed to the flagship, taking his plan with him in his pocket. Captain Lambert received him, informed him that the Admiral had been in Council of War with the French, Spanish, Neapolitan, Piedmontese and British leaders since noon, and politely hurried him over the side again.

Night brought no slackening of the bombardment. From the town came sounds of tumult and a glare ruddier than that of the gunfire. It was said that the Republican elements in Toulon had set fire to the gaol, liberating the imprisoned criminals.

Morning found the waters of the Grande Rade crowded with small craft of every sort conveying Royalist refugees to the safety of the English ships. There were French Royalist soldiers, too – and Neapolitans, and Spanish, fleeing from the imminent wrath of the Republic. Of O'Hara's Gibraltar battalions, of Lord Hood's marines, there was no sign. And over Fort Aiguillette a shred of colour still told of resistance, as did the rumble of gunfire farther east along the fortifications. Captain Smith set his crew to work preparing his little ship for action.

Although he was convinced that the British commander would be neglecting his plain duty if he failed to destroy those thirty-one ships before the inevitable evacuation of Toulon, he felt no animosity against the Admiral who refused to consider it. He was well aware that Admirals had other factors to take into their calculations besides those that were obvious to their subordinates; and he was himself a disciplinarian. But Sir Sidney's logical mind, focussed always upon the golden pathway of duty that led to glory, regarded obedience to orders only as a means – though the surest means – of keeping his feet on that pathway. To obey an order that would prevent him following the path was, to him, no part of his duty. Thus, without the slightest doubt as to the rightness of his decision, Captain Smith had decided to make an independent attempt to destroy at least some of the ships as soon as the evacuation began.

Fortunately for the *Swallow* and her crew this desperate intention was forestalled. About noon the bombardment on the distant hills intensified. An hour later, through a gap in the great wreaths of dun-coloured smoke that coiled lazily under the pale blue sky, the flat grey shape of Fort Aiguillette appeared. Above its walls floated the Tricolour of the Republic. Captain Bonaparte had won his objective.

Along the line of fortifications the guns still boomed, but it could only be a matter of a few hours before the defenders were overwhelmed – and in a matter of minutes the Republican shot would be falling on Toulon and the inner harbour. Captain

Smith pictured the final abandonment of the defences: the battered troops pouring down to the harbour to embark, the victorious French hard on their heels, the Toulon Republicans harassing the embarkation. There should be gunboats to cover that embarkation. He got into his cock-boat and was rowed to the *Victory*.

Captain Lambert met him as he stepped on board.

"I was about to send a boat for you, Sir Sidney," he said hurriedly. "Lord Hood requires your presence – Council of War in his cabin now. They've decided to order a withdrawal."

The gorgeous uniforms were crowded round a table with Admiral Hood presiding. The Spanish Admiral Langara was there, Sir Hyde Parker, Sir Gilbert Elliott, General Dundas, and four foreign officers unknown to Captain Smith.

Lord Hood, his wrinkled face drawn with worry, scowled at the newcomer and turned abruptly to the council.

"Captain Sir Sidney Smith, gentlemen, is an officer eminently suitable for this command." There was perhaps a touch of irony in his tone; the command involved a three-to-one chance of death.

"Captain Smith," he continued rapidly, swinging round to face his officer, "our troops will begin to withdraw an hour after sunset. Six gunboats, three of ours and three Spanish, will cover the embarkation. You will command these and such small craft as can be spared, and you'll remain until the last man is embarked."

"Aye aye, sir."

"You'll make contact with the governor of Toulon beforehand and you'll give such aid to him and the Royalist civilians as you can. You understand your orders hey?"

"Yes, sir. And the French warships, sir?"

"What about them, pray?" growled the Admiral irritably.

"I submit that I should attempt to destroy them, sir."

"Nonsense, sir! You'll obey orders!" roared Hood, banging the table. "Carry on!"

"Aye aye, sir."

Captain Smith turned away. Before the cabin door closed behind him he heard Admiral Langara begin a protest.

"But consider, my lord, if it were possible to destroy these ships . . ."

He heard no more; but so much was encouraging. He flung himself into the business in hand without pause. The six lieutenants, three English and three Spanish, who were to command the gunboats came on board the *Swallow* and received concise orders before he dashed into the inner harbour and up to the governor's house. The streets of Toulon were an inferno. The guns were already firing on the town from Fort Aiguillette, and the intermittent crash and rumble of falling masonry added to the terror of the hurrying crowds of refugees making for the harbour.

Captain Smith wasted no time in imparting his orders to the governor. At a little after three he boarded his felucca, to find a lieutenant of the Admiral's staff awaiting him.

"I'm instructed to deliver this to you in person, sir," the lieutenant explained, handing over a sealed note. "The *Vulcan* fireship, Lieutenant Hare, is added to your flotilla and a supply of combustibles will arrive on board within half an hour."

Captain Smith's eyes were bright as he broke the seal and read the Admiral's wavering scrawl.

"Victory," 18 December, 3 p.m.

My dear Sir Sidney,
You must burn every French ship you possibly can, and consult the Governor the proper hour of doing it, on account of the bringing off the troops.

Very faithfully yours,
Hood.

The new-fallen night was hideous with sound and lurid with red and orange light. From Fort Aiguillette, where *chef de bataillon* Bonaparte raged among his gunners, from the heights of Malbousquet from the captured batteries on the eastward hills, the flash and roar of the Republican artillery made continuous eruption. In Toulon itself three fires, caused either by the gunfire or by the rioters in the streets, doubled their red glare in the waters of the harbour so that the *Swallow* tender seemed to float upon a sea of blood.

Captain Smith, erect and eager on the tiny after deck of the felucca, glanced astern to where the six gunboats, in two lines of three, crawled like many-legged beetles in his wake. Farther astern still the *Vulcan* fireship was being towed, a decrepit little brig loaded with powder and combustibles.

The felucca, rowed by thirty men, was passing through the narrows between the Grande Rade and the Petite Rade or inner harbour, and the dark waters ahead were crowded with a jumble of craft bearing the last of the refugees from the town. "Mr Wright," commanded Captain Smith, "make the signal."

Wright had his slow-match burning. A rocket hissed and rose from the felucca's deck. The three Spanish gunboats altered course and headed away to larboard.

Hood's tardy order, putting upon the captain the double responsibility of covering the embarkation of the retreating troops and destroying thirty-one French ships, had called for every ounce of Sir Sidney's energy and organizing power. Apart from the fireship, he had received no extra forces for his work. Since the embarkation must be covered at all costs, he had reserved the three British gunboats for this task, though that meant leaving the Spaniards to sink the powder-ships and burn the twenty-one warships which Hare's fire-ship would leave untouched. The *Swallow*'s part was to be the destruction of the arsenal.

Sir Sidney glanced astern. The British gunboats were spreading out now, to take their stations. Their guns would cover the quays where already barges and naval small-craft waited to take off the rearguard of the troops. Beyond the gunboat on the extreme left he could see the frigate *Iris*; she was laden with a thousand barrels of powder, and the Spaniards should by now be preparing to knock a hole in her bottom. *Vulcan* was taking her position.

"Here they come, sir!" said Wright suddenly.

The *Swallow* was leaving the quays on her larboard beam, heading for the arsenal at the head of the basin, but he could see the swirl and tumult in the crowd as the red uniforms came bursting through to the boats. Then the loom of waterside buildings hid them from view. But it was something to know that the withdrawal was beginning according to plan.

"Smartly alongside, now!" snapped the captain.

As the felucca slid alongside a broad flight of landing-stairs, Wright popped his head up from below the after deck.

"Mr Middleton, sir – musket ball broke his arm above the elbow."

"I'll manage somehow, sir," came Middleton's strained voice as he tried to rise.

Captain Smith leapt down into the waist and picked up the canvas bag from the lieutenant's side.

"Come on, Mr Tupper!" he snapped. "Five minutes in that mast-house and five in the stores is all you'll get."

He ran up the stairs, Tupper hard at his heels. Thirty paces away across the dark stones of the quay was the black square of the arsenal's main door. Tupper went racing off to the building on the right. Captain Smith, stepping over a dead galley-slave, slipped and almost fell in the spreading pool of the man's blood. Then he was at the door. Across it lay the body of a man in uniform – the guard placed there by the governor. Breathing a prayer that the mob had not thought to search the body for keys, the captain bent over him. Here they were – in his side pocket. Captain Smith's hand was steady as he turned the key in the big lock and pushed open the heavy door. A black cavern fronted him, and he stepped inside. Two strides, and his hand touched ranked powder-barrels.

There was no fumbling as he made his preparations: the bundle of combustible wedged between two powder-casks with the end of the slow-match securely attached; the long coil led away towards the door. He knelt in the darkness with the other end of the match held between his knees, took up the flint and steel and struck.

The third time set the slow-match sputtering. Then he was running for the main door. The fiery glow of the open quay was like day after the blackness of the arsenal. The whistle of musket balls was about him as he reached the stairs.

"Tupper?" he gasped.

"Here, sir – mast – house and store well alight."

"Push off, then – and give way quickly, men!"

The gap between them and the quay widened swiftly. 50 yards, 100, 150 – a great sheet of yellow flame leapt upwards from the quay, the blast of the following thunder-clap whipping the captain's coat like a hurricane of a split second's duration. The Republicans would never get that powder, at least.

"Begging pardon, sir" – Wright was at Captain Smith's elbow – "you heard the first explosion, belike? Those lubberly Dons set the *Iris* afire, 'stead o'sinking her, and she blew up. I'll swear to it they've sunk the *Union* gunboat into the bargain, sir!"

The captain had no doubt that Wright spoke the truth. It was just the sort of imbecile thing the Spaniards would do, to save themselves the trouble of sinking the powder-ship properly. And that gunboat had been close to the *Iris* . . .

"See what speed you can get out of her," he jerked at Wright.

Back towards the wider waters of the basin flew the *Swallow*. Sir Sidney was conscious of a curious sense of relief, such as a man experiences when he comes suddenly into shelter out of a roaring gale. It was a second or two before he realized that the cannonade from the forts had ceased. That must mean that the Republicans were swarming down from the heights to enter the town.

The whole harbour was brightly lit now. The great torch of the flaming arsenal astern and the row of burning ships ahead threw a yellow glare over all and turned the water to liquid gold. All manner of craft were pulling frantically out from the port, heading for the narrows leading to the English ships. Fort Aiguillette was firing out to sea, aiming at the waiting ships. The time was getting short. The Republican troops would be entering the streets of Toulon by now. There was no sign of the flames which should mark the ships fired by the Spaniards . . .

"Boat ahoy! What craft's that?"

The high-pitched hail came from a barge packed with Piedmontese troops and rowed by English sailors.

"Easy!" ordered Sir Sidney, and his crew rested gratefully on their oars. "*Swallow* tender, Captain Sir Sidney Smith!" he replied. "Report to me progress of withdrawal, if you please."

A diminutive midshipman in the stern screeched reply.

"All away, sir – this is the last barge."

"Where are the gunboats?"

The boy's voice came faintly across the widening gap.

"Back to fleet . . . heard Captain Herries order . . . withdraw, in absence . . . senior . . ."

The words were drowned in a chorus of cries and oaths.

"Give way, all!" The captain turned to Lee. "Make for the *Iris*."

The jagged black shell of the powder-frigate still smouldered low on the water. A flight of musket-balls hummed through the rigging, and Sir Sidney glanced at the quay whence that volley had come. White breeches and cross-belts could be seen in the flickering glare; those were the van of Carnot's victorious army. He realized that unless the Spanish gunboats were still endeavouring to destroy the remaining French ships the *Swallow* was alone under the guns of an enemy port.

"Men in the water – larboard bow!" came Boxer's hail.

It was half an hour since the *Union* had been sunk by the Spaniard's carelessness. It was just possible that these were survivors.

Two men were hauled on board, where one of them – a seaman – instantly collapsed. The other was Lieutenant Hare. He dragged himself up to the quarterdeck, a dripping, blackened scarecrow well-nigh exhausted but sustained by a fire of anger.

"Thank heaven you came, sir," he stuttered, as great shivers shook his frame. "We were almost done. Ball from the fort sank my boat – only two of us left. The fire-ship did her job, sir."

Sir Sidney nodded. "Have you seen anything of the *Union*'s crew?"

"I s-saw those bastard Dons sink her with their tomfool explosion, sir – no survivors, I fear." Hare raised shaking fists. "And – you know that was all they did, sir? Blew up the powder-ship and cleared?"

The captain stiffened. "You mean, Mr Hare, that they made no attempt to sink the ships of the line?"

"I mean just that, sir, the crab-gutted, lubberly –" Blasphemies . . . forced themselves between Lieutenant Hare's trembling lips.

Something passed close overhead with a whooping sound. Up out of the water 100 yards away rose a tall column of red-glittering spray. Wright bobbed up at the captain's elbow.

"Begging pardon, sir, but I reckon that's Fort What's-its-name – turned a gun on us. Shall I get under way for the fleet?"

Captain Smith pointed beyond the smouldering hulk of the *Iris* to where, to the left of the still-burning tier of warships, the dark shapes of the rest of the Toulon Fleet lay at anchor.

"I wish to go alongside the first of those ships," he said.

As he spoke another shot from the fort splashed close to the felucca's starboard quarter. Wright glanced at the white upheaval of water and then at the captain. His dark face split into a grin.

"Aye aye, sir," he growled, and turned to yell at the oarsmen.

"Mr Hare," said Captain Smith, "you have done your duty and I shall see that the Admiral hears of it. For the present, you will take that man of yours into the after-cabin. I intend to do what I can to remedy the errors of the Dons."

"But – you mean to burn those ships, sir?" Hare stammered. "The fort will sink you, sure as . . ."

"Thank you, Mr Hare. I command here."

The captain's eye took in the rags of clothing which the shivering man was endeavouring to hold round him. He whipped off his own coat and flung it over the lieutenant's shoulders.

"And tell Mr Tupper to prepare what combustibles remain," he added.

It is recorded of *chef de bataillon* Bonaparte that his initiative brought those light field-pieces of which he was so fond thundering down the hillsides into Toulon on the heels of the Republican vanguard. Some few Royalists still maintained a desperate resistance in the main square, not far from the quays of the inner basin. The square was swept as by an instantaneous plague, leaving a heaving prostrate mass. No one remained standing; but not all those who lay were dead or dying.

It was immediately after this episode that an officer came running up from the quays and gained Bonaparte's ear.

"The English!" he panted. "They're still burning ships in the harbour! Those fools in Fort Aiguillette . . ."

The little Corsican ordered his weary gunners and their pieces to the Quai de Vauban. They had six field-pieces in position on the Quai de Vauban in twenty minutes. Across a quarter of a mile of black water flecked with red loomed the ships in the inner basin, and one of them – the *Héros*, seventy-four – was already a mass of flames. By the light of that vast torch the flank of the warship next in line was illuminated, and against it in black silhouette the *Swallow* tender made an admirable mark as she lay waiting for her captain.

Captain Smith and Lieutenant Tupper, having successfully dealt with the *Héros*, were having more trouble with the *Thémistocle*. This was one of the ships that had French prisoners on board. Sir Sidney called for Boxer and a party of six armed with cutlasses to board the ship, and knocked away the bars from the hatches. 200 Frenchmen, pale and terrified, tumbled up from below. They were ordered over the side to swim ashore, some who were unable to swim being taken into the felucca. It was while Tupper and the captain were below lighting their bundles of inflammable stuff that the cannon on the Quai de Vauban opened fire.

Sir Sidney felt the thud and the shudder of the big vessel as the balls splintered her side. He shouted to Wright to get the felucca round to the other side of the *Thémistocle* and darted below again to make certain that his fire was catching.

Shielded by the great bulk of the *Thémistocle* they were safe from shore gunfire. But already she was well ablaze – the roaring of the flames could be heard plainly. To linger there was impossible. The captain gave the order to make for the harbour entrance.

Weary as he was, and bitter at the thought of those eighteen unharmed ships left for the enemy to use, Captain Smith yet felt the intoxicating thrill of excitement as the *Swallow* began to move out of her shelter. Those gunners ashore would be ready and waiting, and the felucca would have to run the gauntlet of their fire for at least five minutes before she could slip round the corner out of the basin and through to the Grande Rade . . .

The *Swallow* leapt beneath him. A spar came smashing down – the felucca's main yard – and struck him a blow on the right arm, numbing it completely. The *Swallow* was swinging round – what was Lee about? But Lee was no longer at the helm, and a great piece of the after bulwarks had gone. Captain Smith seized the tiller with his left hand and headed the felucca for the dark opening between flame-lit buildings that was the entrance.

Wright was shouting at him from amidships.

"Three oars gone, sir, larboard side. Four killed – and I reckon she's took a ball aft below waterline, sir."

"Damme, that's not so bad," said the captain cheerfully. "Take three starboard oars in – and keep rowing, men."

They were gliding behind the flaming hulk of the *Héros* now. If he could keep it between himself and the cannon the gunners would be helpless. "Look to that shot-hole, Wright," he added.

Wright dashed into the cabin and then emerged to rip up the felucca's bottom-boards.

"We'll need to bale her, sir!" he shouted. They were nearly at the entrance now, and out of danger from the cannon on the quay. Sir Sidney remembered suddenly the Grosse Tour that commanded the eastern side of the entrance. Would the French have reached it yet? It was a long way from the main port . . .

A sheet of water rose with a swishing noise from overside and fell across the felucca, drenching him from head to foot. Fort Aiguillette was trying its marksmanship on the *Swallow* now – and she was becoming momently more sluggish.

"Shall I send a man to the helm, sir?" Wright asked.

"No, damme! Put every spare hand to baling, those Frogs as well. We've a long way to go yet."

The captain's heart warmed to Wright as the big man worked; he had Lieutenants Tupper and Hare slaving to plug the shot-holes in an instant, had found balers – two buckets, a saucepan, even the French soldiers' round caps – without hesitation.

They were passing through the narrows now, and the dark bastions of the Grosse Tour were silent. Splashes on either beam simultaneously told that the forts were firing at him, but now the glare of the fires was falling astern and the felucca was slipping into the friendly darkness of the outer harbour.

Captain Smith measured with his eye the space of black water between the *Swallow* and the nearest English ship – they were near enough for him to recognize her as the *Victory*. A bare mile to go; but the water was over the bottom-boards now. The guns were still firing from the forts, but there was no sign of the fall of shot.

Very slowly now the *Swallow* moved forward under the impulse of the two dozen oars. She seemed weary – at the end of every stroke it was as if she halted and sighed. The rest that lay in the deeps beneath her called to her battered timbers . . .

"Boat fine on the larboard bow, sir !" called Wright suddenly, and bellowed without waiting for his captain's reply. "Guard-boat ahoy! *Swallow* tender! We're sinking – take us on board!"

The answering hail was drowned by a string of shrill objurgations from Boxer. The six French prisoners, stopping work with the balers, had rushed to the side to peer at the dim shape of the guard-boat. Beneath the slight alteration of trim the *Swallow* rolled, very gently, but with a kind of inevitability, and the black water rushed into her and over her. The *Victory*'s guard-boat, coming up within three minutes, found and picked up twenty-nine men.

For the rest of the *Swallow's* crew there were hot drinks and blankets as soon as they were got up the flagship's side; but for her captain there was yet a duty to be fulfilled. The Admiral required his report at once, said Captain Lambert.

In the big stern-cabin Lord Hood sat at his table under a swinging lantern. Captain Smith came in and stood stiffly in front of him, dripping sea-water. His breeches were torn and soiled, blood from a splinter-cut on his cheek mingled with the water that ran down his face. He made his report with his customary assurance.

Lord Hood heard him in scowling silence.

"Thirteen ships destroyed?" he repeated when the captain

had ended. "That means eighteen left, hey? Why didn't you destroy those, sir – hey?"

"I did my utmost, sir," said Captain Smith, lifting his head a little higher.

The Admiral nodded. He knew all about the defection of the Spanish gunboats. Much as he disliked this mountebank of a Swedish knight he could not but admit that he had done his utmost. When he spoke again his tone had softened to a growl.

"And your ship, captain? The – hum – *Swallow* tender?"

Captain Smith seemed to have difficulty in replying. The Admiral looked up sharply, peering at the lean, stained face under the smoky light of the lantern. There were tears in the mountebank fellow's eyes.

BILLY BUDD

Herman Melville

Our setting moves away from Britain and France to the newly formed United States, and to the work of Herman Melville. Melville (1819–91) is best remembered today for his novel about the great white whale, Moby Dick, which we shall return to later in this anthology. Melville had joined the navy as a cabin boy in 1839, an experience he relived in Redburn *(1849). He spent eighteen months on a whaler in the South Pacific and had other adventures in the South Seas before enlisting as an ordinary seaman on the frigate* United States *in 1843. His year at sea on this man-of-war formed the basis for* White-Jacket *(1850), another brooding novel. Thereafter Melville settled down to writing, rapidly establishing a reputation with his first few novels. His popularity flagged after* Moby Dick *(1851), although he continued to write until his death in 1891. He was not rediscovered until 1920, and it was not until 1924 that his last novel,* Billy Budd, *unpublished at the time of his death, was brought into print. Some people may be more familiar with* Billy Budd *through the*

*film directed in 1962 by Peter Ustinov or the opera based
on it by Benjamin Britten, first performed in 1951. It is a
stark study of good versus evil set against the unremitting
background of the sea.*

1

In the time before steamships, or then more frequently than
now, a stroller along the docks of any considerable seaport
would occasionally have his attention arrested by a group of
bronzed mariners, man-of-war's men or merchant-sailors in
holiday attire ashore on liberty. In certain instances they would
flank, or, like a bodyguard, quite surround, some superior
figure of their own class, moving along with them like Alde-
baran among the lesser lights of his constellation. That signal
object was the "Handsome Sailor" of the less prosaic time alike
of the military and merchant navies. With no perceptible trace
of the vain-glorious about him, rather with the offhand un-
affectedness of natural regality, he seemed to accept the spontaneous homage of his shipmates. A somewhat remarkable
instance recurs to me. In Liverpool, now half a century ago,
I saw under the shadow of the great dingy street-wall of Prince's
Dock (an obstruction long since removed) a common sailor, so
intensely black that he must needs have been a native African of
the unadulterate blood of Ham. A symmetric figure much above
the average height. The two ends of a gay silk handkerchief
thrown loose about the neck danced upon the displayed ebony
of his chest; in his ears were big hoops of gold, and a Scotch
Highland bonnet with a tartan band set off his shapely head.

It was a hot noon in July, and his face, lustrous with
perspiration, beamed with barbaric good humor. In jovial
sallies right and left, his white teeth flashing into view, he
rollicked along, the center of a company of his shipmates. These
were made up of such an assortment of tribes and complexions
as would have well fitted them to be marched up by Anacharsis
Cloots before the bar of the first French Assembly as Repre-

sentatives of the Human Race. At each spontaneous tribute rendered by the wayfarers to this black pagoda of a fellow – the tribute of a pause and stare, and less frequent an exclamation – the motley retinue showed that they took that sort of pride in the evoker of it which the Assyrian priests doubtless showed for their grand sculptured Bull when the faithful prostrated themselves.

To return.

If in some cases a bit of a nautical Murat in setting forth his person ashore, the handsome sailor of the period in question evinced nothing of the dandified Billy-be-Damn, an amusing character all but extinct now, but occasionally to be encountered, and in a form yet more amusing than the original, at the tiller of the boats on the tempestuous Erie Canal, or, more likely, vaporing in the groggeries along the towpath. Invariably a proficient in his perilous calling, he was also more or less of a mighty boxer or wrestler. It was strength and beauty. Tales of his prowess were recited. Ashore he was the champion, afloat the spokesman; on every suitable occasion always foremost. Close-reefing topsails in a gale, there he was, astride the weather yard-arm-end, foot in the Flemish horse as "stirrup", both hands tugging at the "earing" as at a bridle, in very much the attitude of young Alexander curbing the fiery Bucephalus. A superb figure, tossed up as by the horns of Taurus against the thunderous sky, cheerily hallooing to the strenuous file along the spar.

The moral nature was seldom out of keeping with the physical make. Indeed, except as toned by the former, the comeliness and power, always attractive in masculine conjunction, hardly could have drawn the sort of honest homage the Handsome Sailor in some examples received from his less gifted associates.

Such a cynosure, at least in aspect, and something such too in nature, though with important variations made apparent as the story proceeds, was welkin-eyed Billy Budd, or Baby Budd as more familiarly under circumstances hereafter to be given he at last came to be called, aged twenty-one, a foretopman of the British fleet toward the close of the last decade of the eighteenth

century. It was not very long prior to the time of the narration
that follows that he had entered the King's Service, having been
impressed on the Narrow Seas from a homeward-bound English merchantman into a seventy-four outward-bound, H.M.S.
Indomitable; which ship, as was not unusual in those hurried
days having been obliged to put to sea short of her proper
complement of men. Plump upon Billy at first sight in the
gangway the boarding officer Lieutenant Ratcliffe pounced,
even before the merchantman's crew was formally mustered on
the quarter-deck for his deliberate inspection. And him only he
elected. For whether it was because the other men when ranged
before him showed to ill advantage after Billy, or whether he
had some scruples in view of the merchantman being rather
short-handed, however it might be, the officer contented himself with his first spontaneous choice. To the surprise of the
ship's company, though much to the lieutenant's satisfaction,
Billy made no demur. But, indeed, any demur would have been
as idle as the protest of a goldfinch popped into a cage.

Noting this uncomplaining acquiescence, all but cheerful one
might say, the shipmates turned a surprise glance of silent
reproach at the sailor. The shipmaster was one of those worthy
mortals found in every vocation, even the humbler ones – the
sort of person whom everybody agrees in calling "a respectable
man." And – nor so strange to report as it may appear to be –
though a plowman of the troubled waters, lifelong contending
with the intractable elements, there was nothing this honest
soul at heart loved better than simple peace and quiet. For the
rest, he was fifty or thereabouts, a little inclined to corpulence, a
prepossessing face, unwhiskered, and of an agreeable color – a
rather full face, humanely intelligent in expression. On a fair
day with a fair wind and all going well, a certain musical chime
in his voice seemed to be the veritable unobstructed outcome of
the innermost man. He had much prudence, much conscien-
tiousness, and there were occasions when these virtues were the
cause of overmuch disquietude in him. On a passage, so long as
his craft was in any proximity to land, no sleep for Captain
Graveling. He took to heart those serious responsibilities not so
heavily borne by some shipmasters.

Now while Billy Budd was down in the forecastle getting his kit together, the *Indomitable*'s lieutenant, burly and bluff, no-wise disconcerted by Captain Graveling's omitting to proffer the customary hospitalities on an occasion so unwelcome to him, an omission simply caused by preoccupation of thought, unceremoniously invited himself into the cabin, and also to a flask from the spirit-locker, a receptacle which his experienced eye instantly discovered. In fact he was one of those sea dogs in whom all the hardship and peril of naval life in the great prolonged wars of his time never impaired the natural instinct for sensuous enjoyment. His duty he always faithfully did; but duty is sometimes a dry obligation, and he was for irrigating its aridity, whensoever possible, with a fertilizing decoction of strong waters. For the cabin's proprietor there was nothing left but to play the part of the enforced host with whatever grace and alacrity were practicable. As necessary adjuncts to the flask, he silently placed tumbler and water-jug before the irrepressible guest. But excusing himself from partaking just then, he dismally watched the unembarrassed officer deliberately diluting his grog a little, then tossing it off in three swallows, pushing the empty tumbler away, yet not so far as to be beyond easy reach, at the same time settling himself in his seat and smacking his lips with high satisfaction, looking straight at the host.

These proceedings over, the master broke the silence, and there lurked a rueful reproach in the tone of his voice: "Lieutenant, you are going to take my best man from me, the jewel of 'em."

"Yes, I know," rejoined the other, immediately drawing back the tumbler preliminary to a replenishing. "Yes, I know. Sorry."

"Beg pardon, but you don't understand, Lieutenant. See here now. Before I shipped that young fellow, my forecastle was a rat-pit of quarrels. It was black times, I tell you aboard the *Rights* here. I was worried to that degree my pipe had no comfort for me. But Billy came, and it was like a Catholic priest striking peace in an Irish shindy. Not that he preached to them or said or did anything in particular, but a virtue went out of him, sugaring the sour ones. They took to him like hornets to treacle; all but the buffer of the gang, the big shaggy chap with the fire-red whiskers. He indeed, out of envy, perhaps, of the newcomer, and thinking such a 'sweet and pleasant fellow', as he mockingly designated him to the others, could hardly have the spirit of a gamecock, must needs bestir himself in trying to get up an ugly row with him. Billy forebore with him and reasoned with him in a pleasant way – he is something like myself, Lieutenant, to whom aught like a quarrel is hateful – but nothing served. So, in the second dog watch one day the Red Whiskers, in presence of the others, under pretense of showing Billy just whence a sirloin steak was cut – for the fellow had once been a butcher – insultingly gave him a dig under the ribs. Quick as lightning Billy let fly his arm. I dare say he never meant to do quite as much as he did, but anyhow he gave the burly fool a terrible drubbing. It took about half a minute, I should think. And, Lord bless you, the lubber was astonished at the celerity. And will you believe it, Lieutenant, the Red Whiskers now really loves Billy – loves him, or is the biggest hypocrite that ever I heard of. But they all love him. Some of 'em do his washing, darn his old trousers for him; the carpenter is at odd times making a pretty little chest of drawers for him. Anybody will do anything for Billy Budd; and it's the happy family here. But now, Lieutenant, if that young fellow goes – I know how it will be aboard the *Rights*. Not again very soon shall I, coming up from dinner, lean over the capstan smoking a quiet pipe – no, not very soon again, I think. Aye, Lieutenant, you are going to take away the jewel of 'em; you are going to take away my peacemaker!" And with that the good soul had really some ado in checking a rising sob.

"Well," said the officer, who had listened with amused interest to all this, and now waxing merry with his tipple, "well, blessed are the peacemakers, especially the fighting peacemakers! And such are the seventy-four beauties some of which you see poking their noses out of the portholes of yonder warship lying to for me," pointing through the cabin window at the *Indomitable*. "But courage! don't you look so downhearted, man. Why, I pledge you in advance the royal approbation. Rest assured that His Majesty will be delighted to know that in a time when his hardtack is not sought for by sailors with such avidity as should be, a time also when some shipmasters privily resent the borrowing from them a tar or two for the services, His Majesty, I say, will be delighted to learn that *one* shipmaster at least cheerfully surrenders to the King the flower of his flock, a sailor who with equal loyalty makes no dissent. – But where's my beauty? Ah," looking through the cabin's open door, "here he comes; and, by Jove – lugging along his chest – Apollo with his portmanteau! – My man," stepping out to him, "you can't take that big box aboard a warship. The boxes there are mostly shot-boxes. Put your duds in a bag, lad. Boot and saddle for the cavalrymen, bag and hammock for the man-of-war's man."

The transfer from chest to bag was made. And, after seeing his man into the cutter and then following him down, the lieutenant pushed off from the *Rights-of-Man*. That was the merchant ship's name, though by her master and crew abbreviated in sailor fashion into *The Rights*. The hard-headed Dundee owner was a staunch admirer of Thomas Paine, whose book in rejoinder to Burke's arraignment of the French Revolution had then been published for some time and had gone everywhere. In christening his vessel after the title of Paine's volume the man of Dundee was something like his contemporary shipowner, Stephen Girard of Philadelphia, whose sympathies, alike with his native land and its liberal philosophers, he evinced by naming his ships after Voltaire, Diderot, and so forth.

But now, when the boat swept under the merchantman's stern, and officer and oarsmen were noting – some bitterly and others with a grin – the name emblazoned there, just then it was that the new recruit jumped up from the bow where the coxswain had directed him to sit, and waving his hat to his silent shipmates sorrowfully looking over at him from the taffrail, bade the lads a genial good-bye. Then, making a salutation as to the ship herself, "And good-bye to you too, old *Rights of Man*."

"Down, sir!" roared the lieutenant, instantly assuming all the rigor of his rank, though with difficulty repressing a smile.

To be sure, Billy's action was a terrible breach of naval decorum. But in that decorum he had never been instructed, in consideration of which the lieutenant would hardly have been so energetic in reproof but for the concluding farewell to the ship. This he rather took as meant to convey a covert sally on the new recruit's part, a sly slur at impressment in general, and that of himself in especial. And yet, more likely, if satire it was in effect, it was hardly so by intention, for Billy, though happily endowed with the gaiety of high health, youth, and a free heart, was yet by no means of a satirical turn. The will to it and the sinister dexterity were alike wanting. To deal in double meanings and insinuations of any sort was quite foreign to his nature.

As to his enforced enlistment, that he seemed to take pretty much as he was wont to take any vicissitude of weather. Like the animals, though no philosopher, he was, without knowing it, practically a fatalist. And it may be that he rather liked this adventurous turn in his affairs, which promised an opening into novel scenes and martial excitements.

Aboard the *Indomitable* our merchant-sailor was forthwith rated as an able seaman and assigned to the starboard watch of the foretop. He was soon at home in the service, not at all disliked for his unpretentious good looks and a sort of genial happy-go-lucky air. No merrier man in his mess, in marked contrast to certain other individuals included like himself among the impressed portion of the ship's company; for these when not actively employed were sometimes, and more particularly in the last dog watch when the drawing near of twilight induced reverie, apt to fall into a saddish mood which in some partook of sullenness. But they were not so young as our foretopman, and no few of them must have known a hearth of some sort; others may have had wives and children left, too probably, in uncertain circumstances, and hardly any but must have had acknowledged kith and kin, while for Billy, as will shortly be seen, his entire family was practically invested in himself.

2

Though our new-made foretopman was well received in the top and on the gun decks, hardly here was he that cynosure he had previously been among those minor ship's companies of the merchant marine, with which companies only had he hitherto consorted.

He was young, and, despite his all but fully developed frame, in aspect looked even younger than he really was, owing to a lingering adolescent expression in the as yet smooth face all but feminine in purity of natural complexion but where, thanks to his seagoing, the lily was quite suppressed and the rose had some ado visibly to flush through the tan.

To one essentially such a novice in the complexities of factitious life, the abrupt transition from his former and simpler sphere to the ampler and more knowing world of a great warship – this might well have abashed him had there been any conceit or vanity in his composition. Among her miscellaneous multitude, the *Indomitable* mustered several individuals who, however inferior in grade, were of no common natural stamp, sailors more signally susceptive of that air which continuous martial discipline and repeated presence in battle can in some degree impart even to the average man. As the *handsome sailor* Billy Budd's position aboard the seventy-four was something analogous to that of a rustic beauty transplanted from the provinces and brought into competition with the highborn dames of the court. But this change of circumstances he scarce noted. As little did he observe that something about him provoked an ambiguous smile in one or two harder faces among the bluejackets. Nor less unaware was he of the peculiar favorable effect his person and demeanor had upon the more intelligent gentlemen of the quarter-deck. Nor could this well have been otherwise. Cast in a mould peculiar to the finest physical examples of those Englishmen in whom the Saxon strain would seem not at all to partake of any Norman or other admixture, he showed in face that humane look of reposeful good nature which the Greek sculptor in some instances gave to his heroic strong man, Hercules. But this again was subtly modified by another and pervasive quality. The ear, small and shapely, the arch of the foot, the curve in mouth and nostril, even the indurated hand dyed to the orange-tawny of the toucan's bill, a hand telling alike of the halyards and tar bucket;

but, above all, something in the mobile expression, and every chance attitude and movement, something suggestive of a mother eminently favored by Love and the Graces; all this strangely indicated a lineage in direct contradiction to his lot. The mysteriousness here became less mysterious through a matter of fact elicited when Billy at the capstan was being formally mustered into the service. Asked by the officer, a small brisk little gentleman, as it chanced among other questions, his place of birth, he replied, "Please, sir, I don't know."

"Don't know where you were born? Who was your father?"

"God knows, sir."

Struck by the straightforward simplicity of these replies, the officer next asked, "Do you know anything about your beginning?"

"No, sir. But I have heard that I was found in a pretty silk-lined basket hanging one morning from the knocker of a good man's door in Bristol."

"*Found* say you? Well," throwing back his head and looking up and down the new recruit; "well, it turns out to have been a pretty good find. Hope they'll find some more like you, my man; the fleet sadly needs them."

Yes, Billy Budd was a foundling, a presumable by-blow, and, evidently, no ignoble one. Noble descent was as evident in him as in a blood horse.

For the rest, with little or no sharpness of faculty or any trace of the wisdom of the serpent, nor yet quite a dove, he possessed that kind and degree of intelligence going along with the unconventional rectitude of a sound human creature, one to whom not yet has been proffered the questionable apple of knowledge. He was illiterate; he could not read, but he could sing, and like the illiterate nightingale was sometimes the composer of his own song.

Of self-consciousness he seemed to have little or none, or about as much as we may reasonably impute to a dog of Saint Bernard's breed.

Habitually living with the elements and knowing little more of the land than as a beach, or, rather, that portion of the terraqueous globe providentially set apart for dance-houses, doxies, and tapsters, in short what sailors call a "fiddlers' green," his simple nature remained unsophisticated by those moral obliquities which are not in every case incompatible with that manufacturable thing known as respectability. But are sailors, frequenters of fiddlers' greens, without vices? No; but less often than with landsmen do their vices, so called, partake of crookedness of heart, seeming less to proceed from viciousness than exuberance of vitality after long constraint; frank manifestations in accordance with natural law. By his original constitution aided by the co-operating influences of his lot, Billy in many respects was little more than a sort of upright barbarian, much such perhaps as Adam presumably might have been ere the urbane Serpent wriggled himself into his company.

And here be it submitted that, apparently going to corroborate the doctrine of man's fall, a doctrine now popularly ignored, it is observable that where certain virtues pristine and unadulterate peculiarly characterize anybody in the external uniform of civilization, they will upon scrutiny seem not to be derived from custom or convention, but rather to be out of keeping with these, as if indeed exceptionally transmitted from a period prior to Cain's city and citified man. The character marked by such qualities has to an unvitiated taste an untampered-with flavor like that of berries, while the man thoroughly civilized even in a fair specimen of the breed has to the same moral palate a questionable smack as of a compounded wine. To any stray inheritor of these primitive qualities found, like Kaspar Hauser, wandering dazed in any Christian capital of our time, the good-natured poet's famous invocation, near 2000 years ago, of the good rustic out of his latitude in the Rome of the Caesars, still appropriately holds:

> Honest and poor, faithful in word and thought,
> What has thee, Fabian, to the city brought.

Though our Handsome Sailor had as much of masculine beauty as one can expect anywhere to see, nevertheless, like the beautiful woman in one of Hawthorne's minor tales, there was just one thing amiss in him. No visible blemish indeed, as with the lady; no, but an occasional liability to a vocal defect. Though in the hour of elemental uproar or peril he was everything that a sailor should be, yet under sudden provocation of strong heart-feeling his voice, otherwise singularly musical, as if expressive of the harmony within, was apt to develop an organic hesitancy, in fact more or less of a stutter or even worse. In this particular Billy was a striking instance that the arch interferer, the envious marplot of Eden, still has more or less to do with every human consignment to this planet of earth. In every case, one way or another he is sure to slip in his little card, as much as to remind us – I too have a hand here.

The avowal of such an imperfection in the Handsome Sailor should be evidence not alone that he is not presented as a conventional hero, but also that the story in which he is the main figure is no romance.

3

At the time of Billy Budd's arbitrary enlistment into the *Indomitable* that ship was on her way to join the Mediterranean fleet. No long time elapsed before the junction was effected. As one of that fleet the seventy-four participated in its movements, though at times, on account of her superior sailing qualities, in the absence of frigates, despatched on separate duty as a scout and at times on less temporary service. But with all this the story has little concernment, restricted as it is to the inner life of one particular ship and the career of an individual sailor.

It was the summer of 1797. In the April of that year had occurred the commotion at Spithead, followed in May by a second and yet more serious outbreak in the fleet at the Nore. The latter is known, and without exaggeration in the epithet, as the Great Mutiny. It was indeed a demonstration more menacing to England than the contemporary manifestoes and conquering and proselyting armies of the French Directory.

To the British Empire the Nore mutiny was what a strike in the fire brigade would be to London threatened by general arson. In a crisis when the kingdom might well have anticipated the famous signal that some years later published along the naval line of battle what it was that upon occasion England expected of Englishmen, *that* was the time when at the mast-heads of the three-deckers and seventy-fours moored in her own roadstead – a fleet, the right arm of a Power then all but the sole free conservative one of the Old World – the bluejackets, to be numbered by thousands, ran up with huzzahs the British colors with the union and cross wiped out; by that cancellation transmuting the flag of founded law and freedom defined into the enemy's red meteor of unbridled and unbounded revolt. Reasonable discontent growing out of practical grievances in the fleet had been ignited into irrational combustion as by live cinders blown across the Channel from France in flames.

The event converted into irony for a time those spirited strains of Dibdin – as a song-writer no mean auxiliary to the English Government at the European conjuncture – strains celebrating, among other things, the patriotic devotion of the British tar:

And as for my life, 'tis the King's!

Such an episode in the Island's grand naval story her naval historians naturally abridge, one of them (G. P. R. James) candidly acknowledging that fain would he pass it over did not "impartiality forbid fastidiousness." And yet his mention is less a narration than a reference, having to do hardly at all with details. Nor are these readily to be found in the libraries. Like some other events in every age befalling states everywhere including America, the Great Mutiny was of such character that national pride along with views of policy would fain shade it off into the historical background. Such events cannot be ignored, but there is a considerate way of historically treating them. If a well-constituted individual refrains from blazoning aught amiss or calamitous in his family, a nation in the like circumstance may without reproach be equally discreet.

Though after parleyings between Government and the ring-leaders, and concessions by the former as to some glaring abuses, the first uprising – that at Spithead – with difficulty was put down, or matters for the time pacified; yet at the Nore the unforeseen renewal of insurrection on a yet larger scale, and emphasized in the conferences that ensued by demands deemed by the authorities not only inadmissible but aggressively insolent, indicated – if the Red Flag did not sufficiently do so – what was the spirit animating the men. Final suppression, however, there was, but only made possible perhaps by the unswerving loyalty of the marine corps and voluntary resumption of loyalty among influential sections of the crews.

To some extent the Nore Mutiny may be regarded as analogous to the distempering irruption of contagious fever in a frame constitutionally sound, and which anon throws it off.

At all events, of these thousands of mutineers were some of the tars who not so very long afterwards – whether wholly prompted thereto by patriotism, or pugnacious instinct, or by both – helped to win a coronet for Nelson at the Nile, and the naval crown of crowns for him at Trafalgar. To the mutineers those battles and especially Trafalgar were a plenary absolution and a grand one: for all that goes to make up scenic naval display, heroic magnificence in arms, those battles, especially Trafalgar, stand unmatched in human annals.

4

Concerning "The greatest sailor since our world began." – TENNYSON

In this matter of writing, resolve as one may to keep to the main road, some bypaths have an enticement not readily to be withstood. I am going to err into such a bypath. If the reader will keep me company I shall be glad. At the least we can promise ourselves that pleasure which is wickedly said to be in sinning, for a literary sin the divergence will be.

Very likely it is no new remark that the inventions of our time have at last brought about a change in sea warfare in degree corresponding to the revolution in all warfare effected by the original introduction from China into Europe of gunpowder. The first European firearm, a clumsy contrivance, was, as is well known, scouted by no few of the knights as a base implement, good enough peradventure for weavers too craven to stand up crossing steel with steel in frank fight. But as ashore knightly valor, though shorn of its blazonry, did not cease with the knights, neither on the seas, though nowadays in encounters there a certain kind of displayed gallantry be fallen out of date as hardly applicable under changed circumstances, did the nobler qualities of such naval magnates as Don John of Austria, Doria, Van Tromp, Jean Bart, the long line of British Admirals and the American Decaturs of 1812, become obsolete with their wooden walls.

Nevertheless, to anybody who can hold the present at its worth without being inappreciative of the past, it may be forgiven, if to such an one the solitary old hulk at Portsmouth, Nelson's *Victory*, seems to float there, not alone as the decaying monument of a fame incorruptible, but also as a poetic reproach, softened by its picturesqueness, to the *Monitors* and yet mightier hulls of the European ironclads. And this not altogether because such craft are unsightly, unavoidably lacking the symmetry and grand lines of the old battleships, but equally for other reasons.

There are some, perhaps, who, while not altogether inaccessible to that poetic reproach just alluded to, may yet on behalf of the new order be disposed to parry it; and this to the extent of iconoclasm, if need be. For example, prompted by the sight of the star inserted in the *Victory*'s quarter-deck designating the spot where the Great Sailor fell, these martial utilitarians may suggest considerations implying that Nelson's ornate publication of his person in battle was not only unnecessary, but not military, nay, savored of foolhardiness and vanity. They may add, too, that at Trafalgar it was in effect nothing less than a challenge to death, and death came; and that but for his bravado the victorious admiral might possibly have survived the battle, and so, instead of having his sagacious dying injunctions overruled by his immediate successor in command, he himself when the contest was decided might have brought his shattered fleet to anchor, a proceeding which might have averted the deplorable loss of life by shipwreck in the elemental tempest that followed the martial one.

Well, should we set aside the more disputable point whether for various reasons it was possible to anchor the fleet, then plausibly enough the Benthamites of war may urge the above.

But the *might-have-been* is but boggy ground to build on. And, certainly, in foresight as to the larger issue of an encounter, and anxious preparations for it – buoying the deadly way and mapping it out, as at Copenhagen – few commanders have been so painstakingly circumspect as this same reckless declarer of his person in fight.

Personal prudence, even when dictated by quite other than selfish considerations, surely is no special virtue in a military man; while an excessive love of glory, impassioning a less burning impulse, the honest sense of duty, is the first. If the name *Wellington* is not so much of a trumpet to the blood as the simpler name *Nelson*, the reason for this may perhaps be inferred from the above. Alfred in his funeral ode on the victor of Waterloo ventures not to call him the greatest soldier of all time, though in the same ode he invokes Nelson as "the greatest sailor since our world began."

At Trafalgar, Nelson on the brink of opening the fight sat down and wrote his last brief will and testament. If under the presentiment of the most magnificent of all victories to be crowned by his own glorious death, a sort of priestly motive led him to dress his person in the jeweled vouchers of his own shining deeds; if thus to have adorned himself for the altar and the sacrifice were indeed vainglory, then affectation and fustian is each more heroic line in the great epics and dramas, since in such lines the poet but embodies in verse those exaltations of sentiment that a nature like Nelson, the opportunity being given, vitalizes into acts.

5

Yes, the outbreak at the Nore was put down. But not every grievance was redressed. If the contractors, for example, were no longer permitted to ply some practices peculiar to their tribe everywhere, such as providing shoddy cloth, rations not sound or false in the measure, not the less impressment, for one thing, went on. By custom sanctioned for centuries, and judicially maintained by a Lord Chancellor as late as Mansfield, that mode of manning the fleet, a mode now fallen into a sort of abeyance but never formally renounced, it was not practicable to give up in those years. Its abrogation would have crippled the indispensable fleet, one wholly under canvas, no steam power, its innumerable sails and thousands of cannon, everything in short, worked by muscle alone; a fleet the more insatiate in demand for men, because then multiplying its ships of all grades against contingencies present and to come of the convulsed Continent.

Discontent foreran the two mutinies, and more or less it lurkingly survived them. Hence it was not unreasonable to apprehend some return of trouble sporadic or general. One instance of such apprehensions: in the same year with this story, Nelson, then Vice Admiral Sir Horatio, being with the fleet off the Spanish coast, was directed by the admiral in command to shift his pennant from the *Captain* to the *Theseus*, and for this reason: that the latter ship, having newly arrived on the station from home, where it had taken part in the Great Mutiny, danger was apprehended from the temper of the men, and it was thought that an officer like Nelson was the one, not indeed to terrorize the crew into base subjection, but to win them, by force of his mere presence, back to an allegiance, if not as enthusiastic as his own, yet as true. So it was that for a time on more than one quarter-deck anxiety did exist. At sea, precautionary vigilance was strained against relapse. At short notice an engagement might come on. When it did, the lieutenants assigned to batteries felt it incumbent on them, in some instances, to stand with drawn swords behind the men working the guns.

6

But on board the seventy-four in which Billy now swung his hammock, very little in the manner of the men and nothing obvious in the demeanor of the officers would have suggested to an ordinary observer that the Great Mutiny was a recent event.

In their general bearing and conduct the commissioned officers of a warship naturally take their tone from the commander, that is if he have that ascendancy of character that ought to be his.

Captain the Honorable Edward Fairfax Vere, to give his full title, was a bachelor of forty or thereabouts, a sailor of distinction even in a time prolific of renowned seamen. Though allied to the higher nobility his advancement had not been altogether owing to influences connected with that circumstance. He had seen much service, been in various engagements, always acquitting himself as an officer mindful of the welfare of his men, but never tolerating an infraction of discipline; thoroughly versed in the science of his profession, and intrepid to the verge of temerity, though never injudiciously so. For his gallantry in the West Indian waters as flag-lieutenant under Rodney in that admiral's crowning victory over De Grasse, he was made a post-captain.

Ashore in the garb of a civilian scarce anyone would have taken him for a sailor, more especially that he never garnished unprofessional talk with nautical terms, and, grave in his bearing, evinced little appreciation of mere humor. It was not out of keeping with these traits that on a passage when nothing demanded his paramount action, he was the most undemonstrative of men. Any landsman observing this gentleman not conspicuous by his stature and wearing no pronounced insignia, emerging from his cabin to the open deck, and noting the silent deference of the officers retiring to leeward, might have taken him for the King's guest, a civilian aboard the King's ship, some highly honorable discreet envoy on his way to an important post. But in fact this unobtrusiveness of demeanor may have proceeded from a certain unaffected modesty of manhood sometimes accompanying a resolute nature, a modesty evinced at all times not calling for pronounced action, and which, shown in any rank of life, suggests a virtue aristocratic in kind.

As with some other engaged in various departments of the world's more heroic activities, Captain Vere, though practical enough upon occasion, would at times betray a certain dreaminess of mood. Standing alone on the weather side of the quarter-deck, one hand holding by the rigging, he would absently gaze off at the blank sea. At the presentation to him then of some minor matter interrupting the current of his thoughts he would show more or less irascibility, but instantly he would control it.

In the navy he was popularly known by the appellation "Starry Vere." How such a designation happened to fall upon one who, whatever his sterling qualities, was without any brilliant ones, was in this wise: a favorite kinsman, Lord Denton, a free-hearted fellow, had been the first to meet and congratulate him upon his return to England from his West Indian cruise; and but the day previous turning over a copy of Andrew Marvell's poems had lighted, not for the first time however, upon the lines entitled "Appleton House," the name of one of the seats of their common ancestor, a hero in the German wars of the seventeenth century, in which poem occur the lines,

> This 'tis to have been from the first
> In a domestic heaven nursed,
> Under the discipline severe
> Of Fairfax and the starry Vere.

And so, upon embracing his cousin fresh from Rodney's great victory wherein he had played so gallant a part, brimming over with just family pride in the sailor of their house, he exuberantly exclaimed, "Give ye joy, Ed; give ye joy, my starry Vere!" This got currency, and the novel prefix serving in familiar parlance readily to distinguish the *Indomitable*'s captain from another Vere his senior, a distant relative an officer of like rank in the navy, it remained permanently attached to the surname.

7

In view of the part that the commander of the *Indomitable* plays in scenes shortly to follow, it may be well to fill out that sketch of him outlined in the previous chapter.

Aside from his qualities as a sea officer Captain Vere was an exceptional character. Unlike no few of England's renowned sailors, long and arduous service, with signal devotion to it, had not resulted in absorbing and *salting* the entire man. He had a marked leaning toward everything intellectual. He loved books, never going to sea without a newly replenished library, compact but of the best. The isolated leisure, in some cases so wearisome, falling at intervals to commanders even during a war cruise, never was tedious to Captain Vere. With nothing of that literary taste which less heeds the thing conveyed than the vehicle, his bias was toward those books to which every serious mind of superior order occupying any active post of authority in the world naturally inclines: books treating of actual men and events no matter of what era – history, biography, and unconventional writers, who, free from cant and convention, like Montaigne, honestly and in the spirit of common sense philosophize upon realities.

In this love of reading he found confirmation of his own more reasoned thoughts – confirmation which he had vainly sought in social converse – so that, as touching most fundamental topics, there had got to be established in him some positive convictions, which he forefelt would abide in him essentially unmodified so long as his intelligent part remained unimpaired. In view of the troubled period in which his lot was cast this was well for him. His settled convictions were as a dike against those invading waters of novel opinion, social, political, and otherwise, which carried away as in a torrent no few minds in those days, minds by nature not inferior to his own. While other members of that aristocracy to which by birth he belonged were incensed at the innovators mainly because their theories were inimical to the privileged classes, not alone Captain Vere disinterestedly opposed them because they seemed to him incapable of embodiment in lasting institutions, but at war with the peace of the world and the true welfare of mankind.

With minds less stored than his and less earnest, some officers of his rank, with whom at times he would necessarily consort, found him lacking in the companionable quality, a dry and bookish gentleman as they deemed. Upon any chance withdrawal from their company one would be apt to say to another, something like this: "Vere is a noble fellow, Starry Vere. Spite the gazettes, Sir Horatio" meaning him with the Lord title "is at bottom scarce a better seaman or fighter. But between you and me now don't you think there is a queer streak of the pedantic running through him? Yes, like the King's yarn in a coil of navy-rope?"

Some apparent ground there was for this sort of confidential criticism, since not only did the captain's discourse never fall into the jocosely familiar, but in illustrating of any point touching the stirring personages and events of the time he would be as apt to cite some historic character or incident of antiquity as that he would cite from the moderns. He seemed unmindful of the circumstance that to his bluff company such remote allusions, however pertinent they might really be, were altogether alien to men whose reading was mainly confined to the journals. But considerateness in such matters is not easy to natures constituted like Captain Vere's. Their honesty prescribes to them directness, sometimes far-reaching like that of a migratory fowl that in its flight never heeds when it crosses a frontier.

8

The lieutenants and other commissioned gentlemen forming Captain Vere's staff it is not necessary here to particularize, nor needs it to make any mention of any of the warrant officers. But among the petty officers was one who, having much to do with the story, may as well be forthwith introduced. His portrait I essay, but shall never hit it. This was John Claggart, the master-at-arms. But that sea title may to landsmen seem somewhat equivocal. Originally, doubtless, that petty officer's function was the instruction of the men in the use of arms, sword or cutlass. But very long ago, owing to the advance in gunnery making hand-to-hand encounters less frequent and giving to niter and sulphur the pre-eminence over steel, that function ceased; the master-at-arms of a great warship becoming a sort of chief of police charged among other matters with the duty of preserving order on the populous lower gun decks.

Claggart was a man about five-and-thirty, somewhat spare and tall, yet of no ill figure upon the whole. His hand was too small and shapely to have been accustomed to hard toil. The face was a notable one, the features all except the chin cleanly cut as those on a Greek medallion; yet the chin, beardless as Tecumseh's, had something of strange protuberant heaviness in its make that recalled the prints of the Rev. Dr Titus Oates, the historic deponent with the clerical drawl in the time of Charles II and the fraud of the alleged Popish Plot. It served Claggart in his office that his eye could cast a tutoring glance. His brow was of the sort phrenologically associated with more than average intellect; silken jet curls partly clustering over it, making a foil to the pallor below, a pallor tinged with a faint shade of amber akin to the hue of time-tinted marbles of old. This complexion, singularly contrasting with the red or deeply bronzed visages of the sailors, and in part the result of his official seclusion from the sunlight, though it was not exactly displeasing, nevertheless seemed to hint of something defective or abnormal in the constitution and blood. But his general aspect and manner were so suggestive of an education and career incongruous with his naval function that when not actively engaged in it he looked like a man of high quality, social and moral, who for reasons of his own was keeping incog. Nothing was known of his former life. It might be that he was an Englishman, and yet there lurked a bit of accent in his speech suggesting that possibly he was not such by birth, but through naturalization in early childhood. Among certain grizzled sea gossips of the gun decks and fore-castle went a rumor perdue that the master-at-arms was a *chevalier* who had volunteered into the King's navy by way of compounding for some mysterious swindle whereof he had been arraigned at the King's Bench. The fact that nobody could substantiate this report was, of course, nothing against its secret currency. Such a rumor once started on the gun decks in reference to almost anyone below the rank of a commissioned officer would, during the period assigned to this narrative, have seemed not altogether wanting in credibility to the tarry old wiseacres of a man-of-war crew. And indeed a man of Claggart's accomplishments, without prior nautical experience entering the navy at mature life, as he did, and necessarily allotted at the start to the lowest grade in it; a man too who never made allusion to his previous life ashore, these were circumstances which in the dearth of exact knowledge as to his true antecedents opened to the invidious a vague field for unfavorable surmise.

But the sailors' dog-watch gossip concerning him derived a vague plausibility from the fact that now for some period the British navy could so little afford to be squeamish in the matter of keeping up the muster rolls, that not only were press gangs notoriously abroad both afloat and ashore, but there was little or no secret about another matter, namely that the London police were at liberty to capture any questionable fellow at large, and summarily ship him to the dockyard or fleet. Furthermore, even among voluntary enlistments there were instances where the motive thereto partook neither of patriotic impulse nor yet of a random desire to experience a bit of sea life and martial adventure. Insolvent debtors of minor grade, together with the promiscuous lame ducks of morality, found in the navy a convenient and secure refuge. Secure, because once enlisted aboard a King's ship, they were as much in sanctuary as the transgressor of the Middle Ages harboring himself under the shadow of the altar. Such sanctioned irregularities, which for obvious reasons the government would hardly think to parade at the time and which consequently, and as affecting the least influential class of mankind, have all but dropped into oblivion, lend color to something for the truth whereof I do not vouch, and hence have some scruple in stating; something I remember having seen in print, though the book I cannot recall; but the same thing was personally communicated to me now more than forty years ago by an old pensioner in a cocked hat with whom I had a most interesting talk on the terrace at Greenwich, a Baltimore Negro, a Trafalgar man. It was to this effect: in the case of a warship short of hands whose speedy sailing was imperative, the deficient quota in lack of any other way of making it good, would be eked out by drafts culled direct from the jails. For reasons previously suggested it would not perhaps be easy at the present day directly to prove or disprove the allegation. But allowed as a verity, how significant would it be of England's straits at the time, confronted by those wars which like a flight of harpies rose shrieking from the din and dust of the fallen Bastille. That era appears measurably clear to us who look back at it, and but read of it. But to the grandfather of us gray beards, the more thoughtful of them, the genius of it presented an aspect like that of Camöen's Spirit of the Cape, an eclipsing menace mysterious and prodigious. Not America was exempt from apprehension. At the height of Napoleon's unexampled conquests, there were Americans who had fought at Bunker Hill who looked forward to the possibility that the Atlantic might prove no barrier against the ultimate schemes of this French upstart from the revolutionary chaos who seemed in act of fulfilling judgment prefigured in the Apocalypse.

But the less credence was to be given to the gun-deck talk touching Claggart, seeing that no man holding his office in a man-of-war can ever hope to be popular with the crew. Besides, in derogatory comments upon anyone against whom they have a grudge, or for any reason or no reason mislike, sailors are much like landsmen – they are apt to exaggerate or romance it.

About as much was really known to the *Indomitable*'s tars of the master-at-arms' career before entering the service as an astronomer knows about a comet's travels prior to its first observable appearance in the sky. The verdict of the sea quidnuncs has been cited only by way of showing what sort of moral impression the man made upon rude uncultivated natures whose conceptions of human wickedness were necessarily of the narrowest, limited to ideas of vulgar rascality – a thief among the swinging hammocks during a night watch, or the man-brokers and landsharks of the sea ports.

It was no gossip, however, but fact, that though, as before hinted, Claggart upon his entrance into the navy was, as a novice, assigned to the least honorable section of a man-of-war's crew, embracing the drudgery, he did not long remain there.

The superior capacity he immediately evinced, his constitutional sobriety, ingratiating deference to superiors, together with a peculiar ferreting genius manifested on a singular occasion, all this capped by a certain austere patriotism abruptly advanced him to the position of master-at-arms.

Of this maritime chief of police the ship's corporals, so called, were the immediate subordinates, and compliant ones, and this, as is to be noted in some business departments ashore, almost to a degree inconsistent with entire moral volition. His place put various converging wires of underground influence under the chief's control, capable when astutely worked through his understrappers, of operating to the mysterious discomfort, if nothing worse, of any of the sea commonalty.

9

Life in the foretop well agreed with Billy Budd. There, when not actually engaged on the yards yet higher aloft, the topmen, who as such had been picked out for youth and activity, constituted an aerial club lounging at ease against the smaller stunsails rolled up into cushions, spinning yarns like the lazy gods, and frequently amused with what was going on in the busy world of the decks below. No wonder then that a young fellow of Billy's disposition was well content in such society. Giving no cause of offense to anybody, he was always alert at a call. So in the merchant service it had been with him. But now such a punctiliousness in duty was shown that his topmates would sometimes good-naturedly laugh at him for it. This heightened alacrity had its cause, namely, the impression made upon him by the first formal gangway punishment he had ever witnessed, which befell the day following his impressment. It had been incurred by a little fellow, young, a novice, an after-guardsman absent from his assigned post when the ship was being put about – a dereliction resulting in a rather serious hitch to that maneuver, one demanding instantaneous promptitude in letting go and making fast. When Billy saw the culprit's naked back under the scourge gridironed with red welts, and worse; when he marked the dire expression on the liberated man's face as with his woolen shirt flung over him by the executioner he rushed forward from the spot to bury himself in the crowd, Billy was horrified. He resolved that never through remissness would he make himself liable to such a visitation or do or omit aught that might merit even verbal reproof. What then was his surprise and concern when ultimately he found himself getting into petty trouble occasionally about such matters as the stowage of his bag or something amiss in his hammock, matters under the police oversight of the ship's corporals of the lower decks, and which brought down on him a vague threat from one of them.

So heedful in all things as he was, how could this be? He could not understand it, and it more than vexed him. When he spoke to his young topmates about it they were either lightly incredulous or found something comical in his unconcealed anxiety. "Is it your bag, Billy?" said one; "well, sew yourself up in it, bully boy, and then you'll be sure to know if anybody meddles with it."

Now there was a veteran aboard who because his years began to disqualify him for more active work had been recently assigned duty as mainmastman in his watch, looking to the gear belayed at the rail roundabout that great spar near the deck. At off times the foretopman had picked up some acquaintance with him, and now in his trouble it occurred to him that he might be the sort of person to go to for wise counsel. He was an old Dansker long anglicized in the service, of few words, many wrinkles, and some honorable scars. His wizened face, time tinted and weather-stained to the complexion of an antique parchment, was here and there peppered blue by the chance explosion of a gun cartridge in action. He was an *Agamemnon* man; some two years prior to the time of this story having served under Nelson when but Sir Horatio in that ship immortal in naval memory, and which, dismantled and in part broken up to her bare ribs, is seen a grand skeleton in Haydon's etching. As one of a boarding party from the *Agamemnon* he had received a cut slantwise along one temple and cheek, leaving a long pale scar like a streak of dawn's light falling athwart the dark visage. It was on account of that scar and the affair in which it was known that he had received it, as well as from his blue-peppered complexion, that the Dansker went among the *Indomitable*'s crew by the name of "Board-her-in-the-smoke."

Now the first time that his small weazel eyes happened to light on Billy Budd, a certain grim internal merriment set all his ancient wrinkles into antic play. Was it that his eccentric unsentimental old sapience, primitive in its kind, saw or thought it saw something which in contrast with the warship's environment looked oddly incongruous in the Handsome Sailor? But after slyly studying him at intervals, the old Merlin's equivocal merriment was modified; for now when the twain would meet it would start in his face a quizzing sort of look, but it would be but momentary and sometimes replaced by an expression of speculative query as to what might eventually befall a nature like that, dropped into a world not without some man traps and against whose subtleties simple courage lacking experience and address and without any touch of defensive ugliness is of little avail; and where such innocence as man is capable of does yet in a moral emergency not always sharpen the faculties or enlighten the will.

However it was, the Dansker in his ascetic way rather took to Billy. Nor was this only because of a certain philosophic interest in such a character. There was another cause. While the old man's eccentricities, sometimes bordering on the ursine, repelled the juniors, Billy, undeterred thereby, revering him as a salt hero would make advances, never passing the old *Agamemnon*-man without a salutation marked by that respect which is seldom lost on the aged, however crabbed at times or whatever their station in life.

There was a vein of dry humor, or what not, in the mastman; and, whether in freak of patriarchal irony touching Billy's youth and athletic frame or for some other and more recondite reason, from the first in addressing him he always substituted "Baby" for "Billy," the Dansker in fact being the originator of the name by which the foretopman eventually became known aboard ship.

Well then, in his mysterious little difficulty going in quest of the wrinkled one, Billy found him off duty in a dog watch ruminating by himself seated on a shot-box of the upper gun deck now and then surveying with a somewhat cynical regard certain of the more swaggering promenaders there. Billy recounted his trouble, again wondering how it all happened. The salt seer attentively listened, accompanying the foretopman's recital with queer twitchings of his wrinkles and problematical little sparkles of his small ferret eyes. Making an end of his story, the foretopman asked "And now, Dansker, do tell me what you think of it."

The old man, shoving up the front of his tarpaulin and deliberately rubbing the long slant scar at the point where it entered the thin hair, laconically said, "Baby Budd, *Jimmy Legs*", meaning the master-at-arms, "is down on you."

"*Jimmy Legs!*" ejaculated Billy, his welkin eyes expanding; "what for? Why he calls me *the sweet and pleasant young fellow*, they tell me."

"Does he so?" grinned the grizzled one; then said "Ay, Baby Lad, a sweet voice has *Jimmy Legs*."

"No, not always. But to me he has. I seldom pass him but there comes a pleasant word."

"And that's because he's down upon you, Baby Budd."

Such reiteration along with the manner of it, incomprehensible to a novice, disturbed Billy almost as much as the mystery for which he had sought explanation. Something less unpleasingly oracular he tried to extract; but the old sea-Chiron, thinking perhaps that for the nonce he had sufficiently instructed his young Achilles, pursed his lips, gathered all his wrinkles together, and would commit himself to nothing further.

Years, and those experiences which befell certain shrewder men subordinated lifelong to the will of superiors, all this had developed in the Dansker the pithy guarded cynicism that was his leading characteristic.

10

The next day an incident served to confirm Billy Budd in his incredulity as to the Dansker's strange summing up of the case submitted. The ship at noon going large before the wind was rolling on her course, and he below at dinner and engaged in some sportful talk with the members of his mess chanced in a sudden lurch to spill the entire contents of his soup pan upon the new scrubbed deck. Claggart, the master-at-arms, official rattan in hand, happened to be passing along the battery in a bay of which the mess was lodged, and the greasy liquid streamed just across his path. Stepping over it, he was proceeding on his way without comment, since the matter was nothing to take notice of under the circumstances, when he happened to observe who it was that had done the spilling. His countenance changed. Pausing, he was about to ejaculate something hasty at the sailor, but checked himself, and, pointing down to the streaming soup, playfully tapped him from behind with his rattan, saying in a low musical voice peculiar to him at times: "Handsomely done, my lad! And handsome is as handsome did it too!" And with that passed on. Not noted by Billy, as not coming within his view, was the involuntary smile, or rather grimace, that accompanied Claggart's equivocal words. Aridly it drew down the thin corners of his shapely mouth. But everybody taking his remark as meant for humorous, and at which therefore as coming from a superior they were bound to laugh, "with counterfeited glee" acted accordingly; and Billy, tickled, it may be, by the allusion to his being the Handsome Sailor, merrily joined in; then addressing his messmates exclaimed: "There now, who says that Jimmy Legs is down on me!" "And who said he was, Beauty?" demanded one Donald with some surprise. Whereat the foretopman looked a little foolish recalling that it was only one person, Board-her-in-the-smoke, who had suggested what to him was the smoky idea that this master-at-arms was in any peculiar way hostile to him. Meantime that functionary, resuming his path, must have momentarily worn some expression less guarded than that of the bitter smile, and usurping the face from the heart, some distorting expression perhaps, for a drummer-boy, heedlessly frolicking along from the opposite direction and chancing to come into light collision with his person, was strangely disconcerted by his aspect. Nor was the impression lessened when the official, impulsively giving him a sharp cut with the rattan, vehemently exclaimed: "Look where you go!"

11

What was the matter with the master-at-arms? And, be the matter what it might, how could it have direct relation to Billy Budd, with whom, prior to the affair of the spilled soup, he had never come into any special contact official or otherwise? What indeed could the trouble have to do with one so little inclined to give offense as the merchant ship's *peacemaker*, even him who in Claggart's own phrase was "the sweet and pleasant young fellow"? Yes, why should *Jimmy Legs*, to borrow the Dansker's expression, be *down* on the Handsome Sailor? But, at heart and not for nothing, as the late chance encounter may indicate to the discerning, down on him, secretly down on him, he assuredly was.

Now to invent something touching the more private career of Claggart, something involving Billy Budd, of which something the latter should be wholly ignorant, some romantic incident implying that Claggart's knowledge of the young bluejacket began at some period anterior to catching sight of him on board the seventy-four – all this, not so difficult to do, might avail in a way more or less interesting to account for whatever of enigma may appear to lurk in the case. But in fact there was nothing of the sort. And yet the cause, necessarily to be assumed as the sole one assignable, is in its very realism as much charged with that prime element of Radcliffian romance, *the mysterious*, as any that the ingenuity of the author of the *Mysteries of Udolpho* could devise. For what can more partake of the mysterious than an antipathy spontaneous and profound, such as is evoked in certain exceptional mortals by the mere aspect of some other mortal however harmless he may be, if not called forth by this very harmlessness itself?

Now there can exist no irritating juxtaposition of dissimilar personalities comparable to that which is possible aboard a great warship fully manned and at sea. There, every day among all ranks, almost every man comes into more or less of contact with almost every other man. Wholly there to avoid even the sight of an aggravating object one must needs give it Jonah's toss or jump overboard himself. Imagine how all this might eventually operate on some peculiar human creature the direct reverse of a saint.

But for the adequate comprehending of Claggart by a normal nature these hints are insufficient. To pass from a normal nature to him one must cross "the deadly space between". And this is best done by indirection.

Long ago an honest scholar my senior said to me in reference to one who like himself is now no more, a man so unimpeachably respectable that against him nothing was ever openly said though among the few something was whispered, "Yes, X is a nut not to be cracked by the tap of a lady's fan. You are aware that I am the adherent of no organized religion, much less of any philosophy built into a system. Well, for all that, I think that to try and get into X, enter his labyrinth and get out again, without a clue derived from some source other than what is known as *knowledge of the world* – that were hardly possible, at least for me."

"Why," said I, "X, however singular a study to some, is yet human, and knowledge of the world assuredly implies the knowledge of human nature, and in most of its varieties."

"Yes, but a superficial knowledge of it, serving ordinary purposes. But for anything deeper, I am not certain whether to know the world and to know human nature be not two distinct branches of knowledge, which, while they may coexist in the same heart, yet either may exist with little or nothing of the other. Nay, in an average man of the world, his constant rubbing with it blunts that fine spiritual insight indispensable to the understanding of the essential in certain exceptional characters, whether evil ones or good. In a matter of some importance I have seen a girl wind an old lawyer about her little finger. Nor was it the dotage of senile love. Nothing of the sort. But he knew law better than he knew the girl's heart. Coke and Blackstone hardly shed so much light into obscure spiritual places as the Hebrew prophets. And who were they? Mostly recluses."

At the time my inexperience was such that I did not quite see the drift of all this. It may be that I see it now. And, indeed, if that lexicon which is based on holy writ were any longer popular, one might with less difficulty define and denominate certain phenomenal men. As it is, one must turn to some authority not liable to the charge of being tinctured with the Biblical element.

In a list of definitions included in the authentic translation of Plato, a list attributed to him, occurs this: "Natural Depravity: a depravity according to nature." A definition which, though savoring of Calvinism, by no means involves Calvin's dogmas as to total mankind. Evidently its intent makes it applicable but to individuals. Not many are the examples of this depravity, which the gallows and jail supply. At any rate, for notable instances, since these have no vulgar alloy of the brute in them but invariably are dominated by intellectuality, one must go elsewhere. Civilization, especially if of the austerer sort, is auspicious to it. It folds itself in the mantle of respectability. It has its certain negative virtues serving as silent auxiliaries. It never allows wine to get within its guard. It is not going too far to say that it is without vices or small sins. There is a phenomenal pride in it that excludes them from anything mercenary or avaricious. In short the depravity here meant partakes nothing of the sordid or sensual. It is serious, but free from acerbity. Though no flatterer of mankind it never speaks ill of it.

But the thing which in eminent instances signalizes so exceptional a nature is this: though the man's even temper and discreet bearing would seem to intimate a mind peculiarly subject to the law of reason, not the less in his heart he would seem to riot in complete exemption from that law, having apparently little to do with reason further than to employ it as an ambidexter implement for effecting the irrational. That is to say: toward the accomplishment of an aim which in wantonness of malignity would seem to partake of the insane, he will direct a cool judgment sagacious and sound.

These men are true madmen, and of the most dangerous sort, for their lunacy is not continuous but occasional, evoked by some special object; it is probably secretive, which is as much to say it is self-contained, so that when, moreover, most active, it is to the average mind not distinguishable from sanity, and for the reason above suggested, that, whatever its aims may be – and the aim is never declared – the method and the outward proceeding are always perfectly rational.

Now something such an one was Claggart, in whom was the mania of an evil nature, not engendered by vicious training or corrupting books or licentious living but born with him and innate, in short "a depravity according to nature."

12. Lawyers, Experts, Clergy: An Episode

By the way, can it be the phenomenon, disowned or at least concealed, that in some criminal cases puzzles the courts? For this cause have our juries at times not only to endure the prolonged contentions of lawyers with their fees, but also the yet more perplexing strife of the medical experts with theirs? But why leave it to them? Why not subpoena as well the clerical proficients? Their vocation brings them into peculiar contact with so many human beings, and sometimes in their least guarded hour, in interviews very much more confidential than those of physician and patient; this would seem to qualify them to know something about those intricacies involved in the question of moral responsibility; whether in a given case, say, the crime proceeded from mania in the brain or rabies of the heart. As to any differences among themselves these clerical proficients might develop on the stand, these could hardly be greater than the direct contradictions exchanged between the remunerated medical experts.

Dark sayings are these, some will say. But why? Is it because they somewhat savor of Holy Writ in its phrase "mysteries of iniquity"? If they do, such savor was far from being intended, for little will it commend these pages to many a reader of today.

The point of the present story turning on the hidden nature of the master-at-arms has necessitated this chapter. With an added hint or two in connection with the incident at the mess, the resumed narrative must be left to vindicate, as it may, its own credibility.

13. Pale ire, envy and despair

That Claggart's figure was not amiss, and his face, save the
chin, well molded, has already been said. Of these favorable
points he seemed not insensible, for he was not only neat but
careful in his dress. But the form of Billy Budd was heroic; and
if his face was without the intellectual look of the pallid
Claggart's, not the less was it lit, like his, from within, though
from a different source. The bonfire in his heart made luminous
the rose-tan in his cheek.

In view of the marked contrast between the persons of the
twain, it is more than probable that when the master-at-arms in
the scene last given applied to the sailor the proverb *Handsome
is as handsome does* he there let escape an ironic inkling, not
caught by the young sailors who heard it, as to what it was that
had first moved him against Billy, namely, his significant
personal beauty.

Now envy and antipathy, passions irreconcilable in reason,
nevertheless in fact may spring conjoined like Chang and Eng in
one birth. Is Envy then such a monster? Well, though many an
arraigned mortal has in hopes of mitigated penalty pleaded
guilty to horrible actions, did ever anybody seriously confess to
envy? Something there is in it universally felt to be more
shameful than even felonious crime. And not only does everybody disown it but the better sort are inclined to incredulity
when it is in earnest imputed to an intelligent man. But since its
lodgment is in the heart, not the brain, no degree of intellect
supplies a guarantee against it. But Claggart's was no vulgar
form of the passion. Nor, as directed toward Billy Budd, did it
partake of that streak of apprehensive jealousy that marred
Saul's visage perturbedly brooding on the comely young David.
Claggart's envy struck deeper. If askance he eyed the good
looks, cheery health, and frank enjoyment of young life in Billy
Budd, it was because these went along with a nature that, as
Claggart magnetically felt, had in its simplicity never willed
malice or experienced the reactionary bite of that serpent. To
him, the spirit lodged within Billy and looking out from his
welkin eyes as from windows, that ineffability it was which

made the dimple in his dyed cheek, suppled his joints, and, dancing in his yellow curls, made him preeminently the Handsome Sailor. One person excepted, the master-at-arms was perhaps the only man in the ship intellectually capable of adequately appreciating the moral phenomenon presented in Billy Budd. And the insight but intensified his passion, which, assuming various secret forms within him, at times assumed that of cynic disdain – disdain of innocence – To be nothing more than innocent! Yet in an esthetic way he saw the charm of it, the courageous free-and-easy temper of it, and fain would have shared it, but he despaired of it.

With no power to annul the elemental evil in him, though readily enough he could hide it; apprehending the good, but powerless to be it; a nature like Claggart's surcharged with energy as such natures almost invariably are, what recourse is left to it but to recoil upon itself, and, like the scorpion for which the Creator alone is responsible, act out to the end the part allotted it.

14

Passion, and passion in its profoundest, is not a thing demanding a palatial stage whereon to play its part. Down among the groundlings, among the beggars and rakers of the garbage, profound passion is enacted. And the circumstances that provoke it, however trivial or mean, are no measure of its power. In the present instance the stage is a scrubbed gun deck, and one of the external provocations a man-of-war's-man's spilled soup.

Now when the master-at-arms noticed whence came that greasy fluid streaming before his feet, he must have taken it – to some extent willfully, perhaps – not for the mere accident it assuredly was, but for the sly escape of a spontaneous feeling on Billy's part more or less answering to the antipathy on his own. In effect a foolish demonstration he must have thought, and very harmless, like the futile kick of a heifer, which yet, were the heifer a shod stallion, would not be so harmless. Even so was it that into the gall of Claggart's envy he infused the vitriol of his contempt. But the incident confirmed to him certain telltale reports purveyed to his ear by "Squeak", one of his more cunning corporals, a grizzled little man, so nicknamed by the sailors on account of his squeaky voice and sharp visage ferreting about the dark corners of the lower decks after interlopers, satirically suggesting to them the idea of a rat in a cellar.

From his Chief's employing him as an implicit tool in laying little traps for the worriment of the foretopman – for it was from the master-at-arms that the petty persecutions heretofore adverted to had proceeded – the corporal, having naturally enough concluded that his master could have no love for the sailor, made it his business, faithful understrapper that he was, to foment the ill blood by perverting to his chief certain innocent frolics of the good-natured foretopman, besides inventing for his mouth sundry contumelious epithets he claimed to have overheard him let fall. The master-at-arms never suspected the veracity of these reports, more especially as to the epithets, for he well knew how secretly unpopular may become a master-at-arms, at least a master-at-arms of those days zealous in his function, and how the bluejackets shoot at him in private their raillery and wit; the nickname by which he goes among them, *Jimmy Legs*, implying under the form of merriment their cherished disrespect and dislike.

But in view of the greediness of hate for patrolmen, it hardly needed a purveyor to feed Claggart's passion. An uncommon prudence is habitual with the subtler depravity, for it has everything to hide. And in case of an injury but suspected, its secretiveness voluntarily cuts it off from enlightenment or disillusion; and, not unreluctantly, action is taken upon surmise as upon certainty. And the retaliation is apt to be in monstrous disproportion to the supposed offense; for when in anybody was revenge in its exactions aught else but an inordinate usurer? But how with Claggart's conscience? For though consciences are unlike as foreheads, every intelligence, not excluding the Scriptural devils who "believe and tremble", has one. But Claggart's conscience, being but the lawyer to his will, made ogres of trifles, probably arguing that the motive imputed to Billy in spilling the soup just when he did, together with the epithets alleged, these, if nothing more, made a strong case against him;

nay, justified animosity into a sort of retributive righteousness.
The Pharisee is the Guy Fawkes prowling in the hid chambers
underlying the Claggarts. And they can really form no conception of an unreciprocated malice. Probably, the master-at-arms'
clandestine persecution of Billy was started to try the temper of
the man; but it had not developed any quality in him that
enmity could make official use of or even pervert into plausible
self-justification; so that the occurrence at the mess, petty if it
were, was a welcome one to that peculiar conscience assigned to
be the private mentor of Claggart. And, for the rest, not
improbably it put him upon new experiments.

15

Not many days after the last incident narrated something befell
Billy Budd that more graveled him than aught that had previously occurred.

It was a warm night for the latitude, and the foretopman,
whose watch at the time was properly below, was dozing on the
uppermost deck, whither he had ascended from his hot hammock, one of hundreds suspended so closely wedged together
over a lower gun deck that there was little or no swing to them.
He lay as in the shadow of a hillside, stretched under the lee of
the booms, a piled ridge of spare spars amidships between
foremast and mainmast and among which the ship's largest
boat, the launch, was stowed. Alongside of three other slum-
berers from below, he lay near that end of the booms which
approaches the foremast, his station aloft on duty as a foretopman being just over the deck station of the forecastlemen,
entitling him according to usage to make himself more or less
at home in that neighborhood.

Presently he was stirred into semiconsciousness by somebody, who must have previously sounded the sleep of the
others, touching his shoulder, and then, as the foretopman
raised his head, breathing into his ear in a quick whisper, "Slip
into the lee forechains, Billy; there is something in the wind.
Don't speak. Quick, I will meet you there," and disappeared.

Now Billy, like sundry other essentially good-natured ones,

had some of the weaknesses inseparable from essential good nature, and among these was a reluctance, almost an incapacity, of plumply saying *no* to an abrupt proposition not obviously absurd on the face of it, nor obviously unfriendly, nor iniquitous. And being of warm blood he had not the phlegm tacitly to negative any proposition by unresponsive inaction. Like his sense of fear, his apprehension as to aught outside of the honest and natural was seldom very quick. Besides, upon the present occasion, the drowse from his sleep still hung upon him.

However it was, he mechanically rose, and, sleepily wondering what could be in the wind, betook himself to the designated place, a narrow platform, one of six, outside of the high bulwarks and screened by the great deadeyes and multiple columned lanyards of the shrouds and backstays, and, in a great warship of that time, of dimensions commensurate to the hull's magnitude, a tarry balcony in short overhanging the sea, and so secluded that one mariner of the *Indomitable*, a nonconformist old tar of a serious turn, made it even in daytime his private oratory.

In this retired nook the stranger soon joined Billy Budd. There was no moon as yet; a haze obscured the starlight. He could not distinctly see the stranger's face. Yet from something in the outline and carriage, Billy took him to be, and correctly, one of the after-guard.

"Hist! Billy," said the man in the same quick cautionary whisper as before; "you were impressed, weren't you? Well, so was I," and he paused, as to mark the effect. But Billy, not knowing exactly what to make of this, said nothing. Then the other: "We are not the only impressed ones, Billy. There's a gang of us. Couldn't you – help – at a pinch?"

"What do you mean?" demanded Billy, here thoroughly shaking off his drowse.

"Hist, hist!" the hurried whisper now growing husky, "see here", and the man held up two small objects faintly twinkling in the nightlight, "see, they are yours, Billy, if you'll only –"

But Billy broke in, and in his resentful eagerness to deliver himself his vocal infirmity somewhat intruded: "D-D-Damme, I don't know what you are d-driving at, or what you mean, but you had better g-g-go where you belong!" For the moment the fellow, as confounded, did not stir; and Billy, springing to his feet, said, "If you d-don't start I'll t-t-toss you back over the r-rail!" There was no mistaking this, and the mysterious emissary decamped, disappearing in the direction of the mainmast in the shadow of the booms.

"Hallo, what's the matter?" here came growling from a forecastleman awakened from his deck doze by Billy's raised voice. And as the foretopman reappeared and was recognized by him: "Ah, Beauty, is it you? Well, something must have been the matter for you st-st-stuttered."

"Oh," rejoined Billy, now mastering the impediment, "I found an after-guardsman in our part of the ship here and I bid him be off where he belongs."

"And is that all you did about it, foretopman?" gruffly demanded another, an irascible old fellow of brick-colored visage and hair, and who was known to his associate forecastlemen as "Red Pepper." "Such sneaks I should like to marry to the gunner's daughter!" by that expression meaning that he would like to subject them to disciplinary castigation over a gun.

However, Billy's rendering of the matter satisfactorily accounted to these inquirers for the brief commotion, since of all the sections of a ship's company the forecastlemen, veterans for the most part and bigoted in their sea prejudices, are the most jealous in resenting territorial encroachments, especially on the part of any of the afterguard, of whom they have but a sorry opinion, chiefly landsmen, never going aloft except to reef or furl the mainsail, and in no wise competent to handle a marlinspike or turn in a deadeye, say.

16

This incident sorely puzzled Billy Budd. It was an entirely new experience, the first time in his life that he had ever been personally approached in underhand intriguing fashion. Prior to this encounter he had known nothing of the after-guardsman, the two men being stationed wide apart, one forward and aloft during his watch, the other on deck and aft.

What could it mean? And could they really be guineas, those two glittering objects the interloper had held up to his eyes? Where could the fellow get guineas? Why even spare buttons are not so plentiful at sea. The more he turned the matter over, the more he was nonplussed, and made uneasy and discomfited. In his disgustful recoil from an overture which though he but ill comprehended he instinctively knew must involve evil of some sort, Billy Budd was like a young horse fresh from the pasture suddenly inhaling a vile whiff from some chemical factory and by repeated snortings tries to get it out of his nostrils and lungs. This frame of mind barred all desire of holding further parley with the fellow, even were it but for the purpose of gaining some enlightenment as to his design in approaching him. And yet he was not without natural curiosity to see how such a visitor in the dark would look in broad day.

He espied him the following afternoon in his first dog watch below, one of the smokers on that forward part of the upper gun deck allotted to the pipe. He recognized him by his general cut and build, more than by his round freckled face and glassy eyes of pale blue, veiled with lashes all but white. And yet Billy was a bit uncertain whether indeed it were he – yonder chap about his own age chatting and laughing in free-hearted way, leaning against a gun, a genial young fellow enough to look at, and something of a rattlebrain, to all appearance. Rather chubby too for a sailor, even an after-guardsman. In short the last man in the world, one would think, to be overburthened with thoughts, especially those perilous thoughts that must needs belong to a conspirator in any serious project, or even to the underling of such a conspirator.

Although Billy was not aware of it, the fellow, with a sidelong watchful glance, had perceived Billy first, and then noting that Billy was looking at him thereupon nodded a familiar sort of friendly recognition as to an old acquaintance, without interrupting the talk he was engaged in with the group of smokers. A day or two afterwards, chancing in the evening promenade on a gun deck to pass Billy, he offered a flying word of good fellowship, as it were, which, by its unexpectedness and equivocalness under the circumstances, so embarrassed Billy that he knew not how to respond to it, and let it go unnoticed.

Billy was now left more at a loss than before. The ineffectual speculations into which he was led were so disturbingly alien to him that he did his best to smother them. It never entered his mind that here was a matter which, from its extreme questionableness, it was his duty as a loyal bluejacket to report in the proper quarter. And, probably, had such a step been suggested to him, he would have been deterred from taking it by the thought, one of novice magnanimity, that it would savor overmuch of the dirty work of a telltale. He kept the thing to himself. Yet upon one occasion he could not forbear a little disburthening himself to the old Dansker, tempted thereto perhaps by the influence of a balmy night when the ship lay becalmed; the twain, silent for the most part, sitting together on deck, their heads propped against the bulwarks. But it was only a partial and anonymous account that Billy gave, the unfounded scruples above referred to preventing full disclosure to anybody. Upon hearing Billy's version, the sage Dansker seemed to divine more than he was told, and, after a little meditation during which his wrinkles were pursed as into a point, quite effacing for the time that quizzing expression his face sometimes wore: "Didn't I say so, Baby Budd?"

"Say what?" demanded Billy.

"Why, *Jimmy Legs* is *down* on you."

"And what," rejoined Billy in amazement, "has *Jimmy Legs* to do with that cracked after-guardsman?"

"Ho, it was an after-guardsman then. A cat's-paw, a cat's-paw!" And with that exclamation, which, whether it had reference to a light puff of air just then coming over the calm sea, or subtler relation to the after-guardsman, there is no telling, the old Merlin gave a twisting wrench with his black teeth at his plug of tobacco, vouchsafing no reply to Billy's impetuous question, though now repeated, for it was his wont to relapse into grim silence when interrogated in skeptical sort as to any of his sententious oracles, not always very clear ones, rather partaking of that obscurity which invests most Delphic deliverances from any quarter.

Long experience had very likely brought this old man to that bitter prudence which never interferes in aught and never gives advice.

17

Yes, despite the Dansker's pithy insistence as to the master-at-arms being at the bottom of these strange experiences of Billy on board the *Indomitable*, the young sailor was ready to ascribe them to almost anybody but the man who, to use Billy's own expression, "always had a pleasant word for him." This is to be wondered at. Yet not so much to be wondered at. In certain matters, some sailors even in mature life remain unsophisticated enough. But a young seafarer of the disposition of our athletic foretopman is much of a child-man. And yet a child's utter innocence is but its blank ignorance, and the innocence more or less wanes as intelligence waxes. But in Billy Budd intelligence, such as it was, had advanced, while yet his simple-mindedness remained for the most part unaffected. Experience is a teacher indeed, yet did Billy's years make his experience small. Besides, he had none of that intuitive knowledge of the bad which in natures not good or incompletely so foreruns experience, and therefore may pertain, as in some instances it too clearly does pertain, even to youth.

And what could Billy know of man except of man as a mere sailor? And the old-fashioned sailor, the veritable man-before-the-mast, the sailor from boyhood up, he, though indeed of the same species as a landsman, is in some respects singularly distinct from him. The sailor is frankness, the landsman is finesse. Life is not a game with the sailor, demanding the long head; no intricate game of chess where few moves are made in straightforwardness, and ends are attained by indirection; an oblique, tedious, barren game hardly worth that poor candle burnt out in playing it.

Yes, as a class, sailors are in character a juvenile race. Even their deviations are marked by juvenility. And this more especially holding true with the sailors of Billy's time. Then, too, certain things which apply to all sailors do more pointedly operate here and there upon the junior one. Every sailor, too, is accustomed to obey orders without debating them; his life afloat is externally ruled for him; he is not brought into that promiscuous commerce with mankind where unobstructed free

agency on equal terms – equal superficially, at least – soon
teaches one that unless upon occasion he exercise a distrust keen
in proportion to the fairness of the appearance, some foul turn
may be served him. A ruled undemonstrative distrustfulness is
so habitual, not with businessmen so much, as with men who
know their kind in less shallow relations than business, namely,
certain men-of-the-world, that they come at last to employ it all
but unconsciously, and some of them would very likely feel real
surprise at being charged with it as one of their general char-
acteristics.

18

But after the little matter at the mess Billy Budd no more found
himself in strange trouble at times about his hammock or his
clothes bag or what not. While, as to that smile that occasionally
sunned him, and the pleasant passing word, these were, if not
more frequent, yet if anything more pronounced than before.

But, for all that, there were certain other demonstrations
now. When Claggart's unobserved glance happened to light on
belted Billy rolling along the upper gun deck in the leisure of the
second dog watch, exchanging passing broadsides of fun with
other young promenaders in the crowd, that glance would
follow the cheerful sea-Hyperion with a settled meditative
and melancholy expression, his eyes strangely suffused with
incipient feverish tears. Then would Claggart look like the man
of sorrows. Yes, and sometimes the melancholy expression
would have in it a touch of soft yearning, as if Claggart could
even have loved Billy but for fate and ban. But this was an
evanescence, and quickly repented of, as it were, by an im-
mitigable look, pinching and shriveling the visage into the
momentary semblance of a wrinkled walnut. But sometimes
catching sight in advance of the foretopman coming in his
direction, he would, upon their nearing, step aside a little to
let him pass, dwelling upon Billy for the moment with the
glittering dental satire of a Guise. But upon any abrupt unforeseen encounter a red light would flash forth from his eye like a
spark from an anvil in a dusk smithy. That quick fierce light was

a strange one, darted from orbs which in repose were of a color nearest approaching a deeper violet, the softest of shades.

Though some of these caprices of the pit could not but be observed by their object, yet were they beyond the construing of such a nature. And the thews of Billy were hardly compatible with that sort of sensitive spiritual organization which in some cases instinctively conveys to ignorant innocence an admonition of the proximity of the malign. He thought the master-at-arms acted in a manner rather queer at times. That was all. But the occasional frank air and pleasant word went for what they purported to be, the young sailor never having heard as yet of the "too fair-spoken man."

Had the foretopman been conscious of having done or said anything to provoke the ill will of the official, it would have been different with him, and his sight might have been purged if not sharpened. As it was, innocence was his blinder.

So was it with him in yet another matter. Two minor officers – the armorer and captain of the hold, with whom he had never exchanged a word, his position in the ship not bringing him into contact with them – these men now for the first began to cast upon Billy when they chanced to encounter him that peculiar glance which evidences that the man from whom it comes has been some way tampered with and to the prejudice of him upon whom the glance lights. Never did it occur to Billy as a thing to be noted or a thing suspicious, though he well knew the fact, that the armorer and captain of the hold, with the ship's yeoman, apothecary, and others of that grade, were, by naval usage, messmates of the master-at-arms, men with ears convenient to his confidential tongue.

But the general popularity that our Handsome Sailor's manly forwardness upon occasion, and his irresistible good nature, indicating no mental superiority tending to excite an invidious feeling – this good will on the part of most of his shipmates made him the less to concern himself about such mute aspects toward him as those whereto allusion has just been made.

As to the after-guardsman, though Billy for reasons already given necessarily saw little of him, yet when the two did happen to meet, invariably came the fellow's off-hand cheerful recognition, sometimes accompanied by a passing pleasant word or two. Whatever that equivocal young person's original design may really have been, or the design of which he might have been the deputy, certain it was from his manner upon these occasions that he had wholly dropped it.

It was as if his precocity of crookedness (and every vulgar villain is precocious) had for once deceived him, and the man he had sought to entrap as a simpleton had, through his very simplicity, ignominiously baffled him.

But shrewd ones may opine that it was hardly possible for Billy to refrain from going up to the after-guardsman and bluntly demanding to know his purpose in the initial interview, so abruptly closed in the forechains. Shrewd ones may also think it but natural in Billy to set about sounding some of the other impressed men of the ship in order to discover what basis, if any, there was for the emissary's obscure suggestions as to plotting disaffection aboard. Yes, the shrewd may so think. But something more, or, rather, something else, than mere shrewdness is perhaps needful for the due understanding of such a character as Billy Budd's.

As to Claggart, the monomania in the man – if that indeed it were, as involuntarily disclosed by starts in the manifestations detailed, yet in general covered over by his self-contained and rational demeanor – this, like a subterranean fire was eating its way deeper and deeper in him. Something decisive must come of it.

19

After the mysterious interview in the forechains, the one so abruptly ended there by Billy, nothing especially germane to the story occurred until the events now about to be narrated.

Elsewhere it has been said that in the lack of frigates (of course better sailers than line-of-battle ships) in the English squadron up the Straits at the period, the *Indomitable* was occasionally employed not only as an available substitute for a scout, but at times on detached service of more important kind. This was not alone because of her sailing qualities, not common in a ship of her rate, but quite as much, probably, that the character of her commander, it was thought, specially adapted him for any duty where under unforeseen difficulties a prompt initiative might have to be taken in some matter demanding knowledge and ability in addition to those qualities implied in good seamanship. It was on an expedition of the latter sort, a somewhat distant one, and when the *Indomitable* was almost at her furthest remove from the fleet, that in the latter part of an afternoon watch she unexpectedly came in sight of a ship of the enemy. It proved to be a frigate. The latter perceiving through the glass that the weight of men and metal would be heavily against her, invoking her light heels crowded sail to get away. After a chase urged almost against hope and lasting until about the middle of the first dog watch, she signally succeeded in effecting her escape.

Not long after the pursuit had been given up, and ere the excitement incident thereto had altogether waned away, the master-at-arms ascending from his cavernous sphere made his appearance cap in hand by the mainmast respectfully waiting the notice of Captain Vere, then solitary walking the weather side of the quarter-deck, doubtless somewhat chafed at the failure of the pursuit. The spot where Claggart stood was the place allotted to men of lesser grades seeking some more particular interview either with the officer of the deck or the captain himself. But from the latter it was not often that a sailor or petty officer of those days would seek a hearing; only some exceptional cause would, according to established custom, have warranted that.

Presently, just as the commander absorbed in his reflections was on the point of turning aft in his promenade, he became sensible of Claggart's presence, and saw the doffed cap held in deferential expectancy. Here be it said that Captain Vere's personal knowledge of this petty officer had only begun at the time of the ship's last sailing from home, Claggart then for the first, in transfer from a ship detained for repairs, supplying on board the *Indomitable* the place of a previous master-at-arms disabled and ashore.

No sooner did the commander observe who it was that now deferentially stood awaiting his notice, than a peculiar expression came over him. It was not unlike that which uncontrollably will flit across the countenance of one at unawares encountering a person who though known to him indeed has hardly been long enough known for thorough knowledge, but something in whose aspect nevertheless now for the first provokes a vaguely repellent distaste. But coming to a stand, and resuming much of his wonted official manner, save that a sort of impatience lurked in the intonation of the opening word, he said: "Well, what is it, Master-at-Arms?"

With the air of a subordinate grieved at the necessity of being a messenger of ill tidings, and while conscientiously determined to be frank, yet equally resolved upon shunning overstatement, Claggart, at this invitation or rather summons to disburthen, spoke up. What he said, conveyed in the language of no uneducated man, was to the effect following if not altogether in these words, namely, that during the chase and preparations for the possible encounter he had seen enough to convince him that at least one sailor aboard was a dangerous character in a ship mustering some who not only had taken a guilty part in the late serious troubles, but others also who, like the man in question, had entered His Majesty's service under another form than enlistment.

At this point Captain Vere with some impatience interrupted him: "Be direct, man; say impressed men."

Claggart made a gesture of subservience and proceeded.

Quite lately he (Claggart) had begun to suspect that on the gun decks some sort of movement prompted by the sailor in question was covertly going on, but he had not thought himself warranted in reporting the suspicion so long as it remained indistinct. But, from what he had that afternoon observed in the man referred to, the suspicion of something clandestine going on had advanced to a point less removed from certainty. He deeply felt, he added, the serious responsibility assumed in making a report involving such possible consequences to the individual mainly concerned, besides tending to augment those natural anxieties which every naval commander must feel in view of extraordinary outbreaks so recent as those which, he sorrowfully said it, it needed not to name.

Now at the first broaching of the matter Captain Vere, taken by surprise, could not wholly dissemble his disquietude. But as Claggart went on, the former's aspect changed into restiveness under something in the witness's manner in giving his testimony. However, he refrained from interrupting him. And Claggart, continuing, concluded with this:

"God forbid, your honor, that the *Indomitable*'s should be the experience of the –"

"Never mind that!" here peremptorily broke in the superior, his face altering with anger, instinctively divining the ship that the other was about to name, one in which the Nore Mutiny had assumed a singularly tragical character that for a time jeopardized the life of its commander. Under the circumstances he was indignant at the purposed allusion. When the commissioned officers themselves were on all occasions very heedful how they referred to the recent events, for a petty officer unnecessarily to allude to them in the presence of his captain, this struck him as a most immodest presumption. Besides, to his quick sense of self-respect, it even looked under the circumstances something like an attempt to alarm him. Nor at first was he without some surprise that one who so far as he had hitherto come under his notice had shown considerable tact in his function should in this particular evince such lack of it.

But these thoughts and kindred dubious ones flitting across his mind were suddenly replaced by an intuitional surmise which though as yet obscure in form served practically to affect his reception of the ill tidings. Certain it is that, long versed in everything pertaining to the complicated gun-deck life, which like every other form of life has its secret mines and dubious side, the side popularly disclaimed, Captain Vere did not permit himself to be unduly disturbed by the general tenor of his subordinate's report. Furthermore, if in view of recent events prompt action should be taken at the first palpable sign of recurring insubordination, for all that, not judicious would it be, he thought, to keep the idea of lingering disaffection alive by undue forwardness in crediting an informer even if his own

subordinate and charged among other things with police surveillance of the crew. This feeling would not perhaps have so
prevailed with him were it not that upon a prior occasion the
patriotic zeal officially evinced by Claggart had somewhat
irritated him as appearing rather supersensible and strained.
Furthermore, something even in the official's self-possessed
and somewhat ostentatious manner in making his specifications
strangely reminded him of a bandsman, a perjurious witness in
a capital case before a court-martial ashore of which when a
lieutenant he, Captain Vere, had been a member.

Now the peremptory check given to Claggart in the matter of
the arrested allusion was quickly followed up by this: "You say
that there is at least one dangerous man aboard. Name him."

"William Budd. A foretopman, your honor –"

"William Budd," repeated Captain Vere with unfeigned
astonishment; "and mean you the man that Lieutenant Ratcliffe
took from the merchantman not very long ago – the young
fellow who seems to be so popular with the men – Billy, the
Handsome Sailor, as they call him?"

"The same, your honor; but, for all his youth and good looks,
a deep one. Not for nothing does he insinuate himself into the
good will of his shipmates, since at the least all hands will at a
pinch say a good word for him at all hazards. Did Lieutenant
Ratcliffe happen to tell your honor of that adroit fling of
Budd's, jumping up in the cutter's bow under the merchantman's stern when he was being taken off? It is even masked by
that sort of good-humored air that at heart he resents his
impressment. You have but noted his fair cheek. A man trap
may be under his ruddy-tipped daisies."

Now the Handsome Sailor, as a signal figure among the crew,
had naturally enough attracted the captain's attention from the
first. Though in general not very demonstrative to his officers,
he had congratulated Lieutenant Ratcliffe upon his good fortune in lighting on such a fine specimen of the *genus homo*, who
in the nude might have posed for a statue of young Adam before
the Fall. As to Billy's adieu to the ship *Rights-of-Man*, which
the boarding lieutenant had indeed reported to him but in a
deferential way more as a good story than aught else, Captain

Vere, though mistakenly understanding it as a satiric sally, had but thought so much the better of the impressed man for it, as a military sailor, admiring the spirit that could take an arbitrary enlistment so merrily and sensibly. The foretopman's conduct, too, so far as it had fallen under the captain's notice, had confirmed the first happy augury, while the new recruit's qualities as a *sailorman* seemed to be such that he had thought of recommending him to the executive officer for promotion to a place that would more frequently bring him under his own observation, namely, the captaincy of the mizzentop, replacing there in the starboard watch a man not so young whom partly for that reason he deemed less fitted for the post. Be it parenthesized here that since the mizzentopmen, having not to handle such breadths of heavy canvas as the lower sails on the mainmast and foremast, a young man if of the right stuff not only seems best adapted to duty there, but in fact is generally selected for the captaincy of that top, and the company under him are light hands and often but striplings. In sum, Captain Vere had from the beginning deemed Billy Budd to be what in the naval parlance of the time was called a "*king's bargain*," that is to say, for His Britannic Majesty's Navy a capital investment at small outlay or none at all.

After a brief pause during which the reminiscences above mentioned passed vividly through his mind and he weighed the import of Claggart's last suggestion conveyed in the phrase "pitfall under the daisies," and the more he weighed it the less reliance he felt in the informer's good faith, suddenly he turned upon him and in a low voice: "Do you come to me, Master-at-Arms, with so foggy a tale? As to Budd, cite me an act or spoken word of his confirmatory of what you in general charge against him. Stay," drawing nearer to him, "heed what you speak. Just now, and in a case like this, there is a yardarm-end for the false witness."

"Ah, your honor!" sighed Claggart, mildly shaking his shapely head as in sad deprecation of such unmerited severity of tone. Then, bridling – erecting himself as in virtuous self-assertion, he circumstantially alleged certain words and acts, which collectively, if credited, led to presumptions mortally inculpating Budd. And for some of these averments, he added, substantiating proof was not far.

With gray eyes impatient and distrustful essaying to fathom to the bottom Claggart's calm violet ones, Captain Vere again heard him out, then for the moment stood ruminating. The mood he evinced, Claggart, himself for the time liberated from the other's scrutiny, steadily regarded with a look difficult to render – a look curious of the operation of his tactics, a look such as might have been that of the spokesman of the envious children of Jacob deceptively imposing upon the troubled patriarch the blood-dyed coat of young Joseph.

Though something exceptional in the moral quality of Captain Vere made him, in earnest encounter with a fellow man, a veritable touchstone of that man's essential nature, yet now as to Claggart and what was really going on in him his feeling partook less of intuitional conviction than of strong suspicion clogged by strange dubieties. The perplexity he evinced proceeded less from aught touching the man informed against – as Claggart doubtless opined – than from considerations how best to act in regard to the informer. At first indeed he was naturally for summoning that substantiation of his allegations which Claggart said was at hand. But such a proceeding would result in the matter at once getting abroad, which in the present stage of it, he thought, might undesirably affect the ship's company. If Claggart was a false witness – that closed the affair. And therefore before trying the accusation he would first practically test the accuser, and he thought this could be done in a quiet undemonstrative way.

The measure he determined upon involved a shifting of the scene, a transfer to a place less exposed to observation than the broad quarter-deck. For although the few gun-room officers there at the time had, in due observance of naval etiquette, withdrawn to leeward the moment Captain Vere had begun his promenade on the deck's weather side; and though during the colloquy with Claggart they of course ventured not to diminish the distance, and though throughout the interview Captain Vere's voice was far from high and Claggart's silvery and low, and the wind in the cordage and the wash of the sea helped

the more to put them beyond earshot; nevertheless, the interview's continuance already had attracted observation from some
topmen aloft and other sailors in the waist or further forward.

Having determined upon his measures, Captain Vere forthwith took action. Abruptly turning to Claggart he asked,
"Master-at-Arms, is it now Budd's watch aloft?"

"No, your honor." Whereupon, "Mr Wilkes!" summoning
the nearest midshipman, "tell Albert to come to me." Albert
was the captain's hammock-boy, a sort of sea-valet in whose
discretion and fidelity his master had much confidence. The lad
appeared. "You know Budd the foretopman?"

"I do, sir."

"Go find him. It is his watch off. Manage to tell him out of
earshot that he is wanted aft. Contrive it that he speaks to
nobody. Keep him in talk yourself. And not till you get well aft
here, not till then let him know that the place where he is wanted
is my cabin. You understand. Go. Master-at-Arms, show
yourself on the decks below, and when you think it time for
Albert to be coming with his man, stand by quietly to follow the
sailor in."

20

Now when the foretopman found himself closeted there, as it
were, in the cabin with the captain and Claggart, he was
surprised enough. But it was a surprise unaccompanied by
apprehension or distrust. To an immature nature essentially
honest and humane, forewarning intimations of subtler danger
from one's kind come tardily if at all. The only thing that took
shape in the young sailor's mind was this: yes, the captain, I
have always thought, looks kindly upon me. Wonder if he's
going to make me his coxswain. I should like that. And maybe
now he is going to ask the master-at-arms about me.

"Shut the door there, sentry," said the commander; "stand
without, and let nobody come in. Now, Master-at-Arms, tell
this man to his face what you told of him to me," and stood
prepared to scrutinize the mutually confronting visages.

With the measured step and calm collected air of an asylum

physician approaching in the public hall some patient beginning to show indications of a coming paroxysm, Claggart deliberately advanced within short range of Billy, and, mesmerically looking him in the eye, briefly recapitulated the accusation.

Not at first did Billy take it in. When he did, the rose-tan of his cheek looked struck as by white leprosy. He stood like one impaled and gagged. Meanwhile the accuser's eyes removing not as yet from the blue dilated ones, underwent a phenomenal change, their wonted rich violet color blurring into a muddy purple, those lights of human intelligence losing human expression, gelidly protruding like the alien eyes of certain uncatalogued creatures of the deep. The first mesmeric glance was one of serpent fascination; the last was as the hungry lurch of the torpedo-fish.

"Speak, man!" said Captain Vere to the transfixed one, struck by his aspect even more than by Claggart's. "Speak! defend yourself." Which appeal caused but a strange dumb gesturing and gurgling in Billy, amazement at such an accusation so suddenly sprung on inexperienced nonage; this, and, it may be, horror of the accuser, serving to bring out his lurking defect and in this instance for the time intensifying it into a convulsed tongue-tie; while the intent head and entire form straining forward in an agony of ineffectual eagerness to obey the injunction to speak and defend himself, gave an expression to the face like that of a condemned Vestal priestess in the moment of being buried alive, and in the first struggle against suffocation.

Though at the time Captain Vere was quite ignorant of Billy's liability to vocal impediment, he now immediately divined it, since vividly Billy's aspect recalled to him that of a bright young schoolmate of his whom he had once seen struck by much the same startling impotence in the act of eagerly rising in the class to be foremost in response to a testing question put to it by the master. Going close up to the young sailor, and laying a soothing hand on his shoulder, he said: "There is no hurry, my boy. Take your time, take your time." Contrary to the effect intended, these words so fatherly in tone doubtless touching Billy's heart to the quick, prompted yet more violent efforts at

utterance – efforts soon ending for the time in confirming the
paralysis, and bringing to his face an expression which was as a
crucifixion to behold. The next instant, quick as the flame from
a discharged cannon at night, his right arm shot out, and
Claggart dropped to the deck. Whether intentionally or but
owing to the young athlete's superior height, the blow had taken
effect full upon the forehead, so shapely and intellectual-look-
ing a feature in the master-at-arms, so that the body fell over
lengthwise, like a heavy plank tilted from erectness. A gasp or
two, and he lay motionless.

"Fated boy," breathed Captain Vere in tone so low as to be
almost a whisper, "what have you done! But here, help me."

The twain raised the felled one from the loins up into a sitting
position. The spare form flexibly acquiesced, but inertly. It was
like handling a dead snake. They lowered it back. Regaining
erectness Captain Vere with one hand covering his face stood to
all appearance as impassive as the object at his feet. Was he
absorbed in taking in all the bearings of the event and what was
best, not only now at once to be done, but also in the sequel?
Slowly he uncovered his face, and the effect was as if the moon
emerging from eclipse should reappear with quite another
aspect than that which had gone into hiding. The father in
him, manifested toward Billy thus far in the scene, was replaced
by the military disciplinarian. In his official tone he bade the
foretopman retire to a stateroom aft (pointing it out) and there
remain till thence summoned. This order Billy in silence
mechanically obeyed. Then, going to the cabin door where it
opened on the quarter-deck, Captain Vere said to the sentry
without, "Tell somebody to send Albert here." When the lad
appeared his master so contrived it that he should not catch
sight of the prone one. "Albert," he said to him, "tell the
surgeon I wish to see him. You need not come back till called."
When the surgeon entered – a self-poised character of that grave
sense and experience that hardly anything could take him aback
– Captain Vere advanced to meet him, thus unconsciously
intercepting his view of Claggart, and, interrupting the other's
wonted ceremonious salutation, said, "Nay, tell me how it is
with yonder man," directing his attention to the prostrate one.

The surgeon looked, and for all his self-command, somewhat started at the abrupt revelation. On Claggart's always pallid complexion, thick black blood was now oozing from nostril and ear. To the gazer's professional eye it was unmistakably no living man that he saw.

"Is it so then?" said Captain Vere, intently watching him. "I thought it. But verify it." Whereupon the customary tests confirmed the surgeon's first glance, who now, looking up in unfeigned concern, cast a look of intense inquisitiveness upon his superior. But Captain Vere, with one hand to his brow, was standing motionless. Suddenly, catching the surgeon's arm convulsively, he exclaimed, pointing down to the body, "It is the divine judgment on Ananias! Look!"

Disturbed by the excited manner he had never before observed in the *Indomitable*'s captain, and as yet wholly ignorant of the affair, the prudent surgeon nevertheless held his peace, only again looking an earnest interrogation as to what it was that had resulted in such a tragedy.

But Captain Vere was now again motionless, standing absorbed in thought. But again starting, he vehemently exclaimed: "Struck dead by an angel of God! Yet the angel must hang!"

At these passionate interjections, mere incoherences to the listener as yet unapprised of the antecedents, the surgeon was profoundly discomposed. But now, as recollecting himself, Captain Vere in less passionate tone briefly related the circumstances leading up to the event.

"But come, we must dispatch," he added. "Help me to remove him (meaning the body) to yonder compartment," designating one opposite that where the foretopman remained immured. Anew disturbed by a request that, as implying a desire for secrecy, seemed unaccountably strange to him, there was nothing for the subordinate to do but comply.

"Go now," said Captain Vere with something of his wonted manner, "go now. I shall presently call a drum-head court. Tell the lieutenants what happened, and tell Mr Mordant," meaning the captain of marines, "and charge them to keep the matter to themselves."

21

Full of disquietude and misgiving, the surgeon left the cabin.
Was Captain Vere suddenly affected in his mind, or was it but a
transient excitement, brought about by so strange and extraordinary a happening? As to the drumhead court, it struck the
surgeon as impolitic, if nothing more. The thing to do, he
thought, was to place Billy Budd in confinement and in a way
dictated by usage, and postpone further action in so extraordinary a case to such time as they should rejoin the squadron,
and then refer it to the admiral. He recalled the unwonted
agitation of Captain Vere and his excited exclamations so at
variance with his normal manner. Was he unhinged? But
assuming that he is, it is not so susceptible of proof. What
then can he do? No more trying situation is conceivable than
that of an officer subordinate under a captain whom he aspects
to be, not mad indeed, but yet not quite unaffected in his
intellect. To argue his order to him would be insolence. To
resist him would be mutiny.

In obedience to Captain Vere he communicated what had
happened to the lieutenants and captain of marines, saying
nothing as to the captain's state. They fully shared his own
surprise and concern. Like him too they seemed to think that
such a matter should be referred to the admiral.

22

Who in the rainbow can show the line where the violet tint ends
and the orange tint begins? Distinctly we see the difference of
the colors, but when exactly does the one first blendingly enter
into the other? So with sanity and insanity. In pronounced
cases, there is no question about them. But in some supposed
cases, in various degrees supposedly less pronounced, to draw
the exact line of demarcation few will undertake – though for a
fee some professional experts will. There is nothing namable
but that some men will undertake to do it for pay.

Whether Captain Vere, as the surgeon professionally and
privately surmised, was really the sudden victim of any degree

of aberration, one must determine for himself by such light as this narrative may afford.

That the unhappy event which has been narrated could not have happened at a worse juncture was but too true. For it was close on the heel of the suppressed insurrections, an aftertime very critical to naval authority, demanding from every English sea commander two qualities not readily interfusible: prudence and rigor. Moreover, there was something crucial in the case.

In the jugglery of circumstances preceding and attending the event on board the *Indomitable*, and in the light of that martial code whereby it was formally to be judged, innocence and guilt personified in Claggart and Budd in effect changed places. In a legal view the apparent victim of the tragedy was he who had sought to victimize a man blameless; and the indisputable deed of the latter, navally regarded, constituted the most heinous of military crimes. Yet more. The essential right and wrong involved in the matter, the clearer that might be, so much the worse for the responsibility of a loyal sea commander inasmuch as he was not authorized to determine the matter on that primitive basis.

Small wonder then that the *Indomitable*'s captain, though in general a man of rapid decision, felt that circumspectness not less than promptitude was necessary. Until he could decide upon his course, and in each detail, and not only so, but until the concluding measure was upon the point of being enacted, he deemed it advisable, in view of all the circumstances, to guard as much as possible against publicity. Here he may or may not have erred. Certain it is, however, that subsequently in the confidential talk of more than one or two gun rooms and cabins he was not a little criticized by some officers, a fact imputed by his friends and vehemently by his cousin Jack Denton to professional jealousy of "Starry Vere". Some imaginative ground for invidious comment there was. The maintenance of secrecy in the matter, the confining all knowledge of it for a time to the place where the homicide occurred, the quarter-deck cabin; in these particulars lurked some resemblance to the policy adopted in those tragedies of the palace which have occurred more than once in the capital founded by Peter the Barbarian.

The case indeed was such that fain would the *Indomitable*'s captain have deferred taking any action whatever respecting it further than to keep the foretopman a close prisoner till the ship rejoined the squadron and then submitting the matter to the judgment of his admiral.

But a true military officer is in one particular like a true monk. Not with more of self-abnegation will the latter keep his vows of monastic obedience than the former his vows of allegiance to martial duty.

Feeling that unless quick action was taken on it, the deed of the foretopman, so soon as it should be known on the gun decks, would tend to awaken any slumbering embers of the Nore among the crew, a sense of the urgency of the case overruled in Captain Vere every other consideration. But though a conscientious disciplinarian he was no lover of authority for mere authority's sake. Very far was he from embracing opportunities for monopolizing to himself the perils of moral responsibility, none at least that could properly be referred to an official superior or shared with him by his official equals or even subordinates. So thinking, he was glad it would not be at variance with usage to turn the matter over to a summary court of his own officers, reserving to himself as the one on whom the ultimate accountability would rest, the right of maintaining a supervision of it, or formally or informally interposing at need. Accordingly a drumhead court was summarily convened, he electing the individuals composing it, the first lieutenant, the captain of marines, and the sailing master.

In associating an officer of marines with the sea lieutenants in a case having to do with a sailor, the commander perhaps deviated from general custom. He was prompted thereto by the circumstance that he took that soldier to be a judicious person, thoughtful, and not altogether incapable of grappling with a difficult case unprecedented in his prior experience. Yet even as to him he was not without some latent misgiving, for withal he was an extremely good-natured man, an enjoyer of his dinner, a sound sleeper, and inclined to obesity. A man who though he would always maintain his manhood in battle might not prove altogether reliable in a moral dilemma involving aught of the tragic. As to the first lieutenant and the sailing master, Captain Vere could not but be aware that, though honest natures, of approved gallantry upon occasion, their intelligence was mostly confined to the matter of active seamanship and the fighting demands of their profession. The court was held in the same cabin where the unfortunate affair had taken place. This cabin, the commander's, embraced the entire area under the poop deck. Aft, and on either side, was a small stateroom, the one room temporarily a jail and the other a deadhouse, and a yet smaller compartment leaving a space between, expanding forward into a goodly oblong of length coinciding with the ship's beam. A skylight of moderate dimension was overhead, and at each end of the oblong space were two sashed porthole windows easily convertible back into embrasures for short carronades.

All being quickly in readiness, Billy Budd was arraigned, Captain Vere necessarily appearing as the sole witness in the case, and as such temporarily sinking his rank, though singularly maintaining it in a matter apparently trivial, namely, that he testified from the ship's weather side, with that object having caused the court to sit on the lee side. Concisely he narrated all that had led up to the catastrophe, omitting nothing in Claggart's accusation and deposing as to the manner in which the prisoner had received it. At this testimony the three officers glanced with no little surprise at Billy Budd, the last man they would have suspected either of the mutinous design alleged by Claggart or the undeniable deed he himself had done.

The first lieutenant, taking judicial primacy and turning toward the prisoner, said, "Captain Vere has spoken. Is it or is it not as Captain Vere says?" In response came syllables not so much impeded in the utterance as might have been anticipated. They were these: "Captain Vere tells the truth. It is just as Captain Vere says, but it is not as the master-at-arms said. I have eaten the King's bread and I am true to the King."

"I believe you, my man," said the witness, his voice indicating a suppressed emotion not otherwise betrayed.

"God will bless you for that, your honor!" not without stammering said Billy, and all but broke down. But immediately was recalled to self-control by another question, to which with the same emotional difficulty of utterance he said, "No, there was no malice between us. I never bore malice against the master-at-arms. I am sorry that he is dead. I did not mean to kill him. Could I have used my tongue I would not have struck him. But he foully lied to my face and in presence of my captain, and I had to say something, and I could only say it with a blow, God help me!"

In the impulsive aboveboard manner of the frank one the court saw confirmed all that was implied in words that just previously had perplexed them, coming as they did from the testifier to the tragedy and promptly following Billy's impassioned disclaimer of mutinous intent – Captain Vere's words, "I believe you, my man."

Next it was asked of him whether he knew of or suspected aught savoring of incipient trouble (meaning mutiny, though the explicit term was avoided) going on in any section of the ship's company.

The reply lingered. This was naturally imputed by the court to the same vocal embarrassment which had retarded or obstructed previous answers. But in main it was otherwise here, the question immediately recalling to Billy's mind the interview with the after-guardsman in the forechains. But an innate repugnance to playing a part at all approaching that of an informer against one's own shipmates – the same erring sense of uninstructed honor which had stood in the way of his reporting the matter at the time though as a loyal man-of-war-man it was incumbent on him, and failure so to do if charged against him and proven, would have subjected him to the heaviest of penalties – this, with the blind feeling now his, that nothing really was being hatched, prevailed with him. When the answer came it was a negative.

"One question more," said the officer of marines, now first speaking and with a troubled earnestness. "You tell us that what the master-at-arms said against you was a lie. Now why should he have so lied, so maliciously lied, since you declare there was no malice between you?"

At that question unintentionally touching on a spiritual

sphere wholly obscure to Billy's thoughts, he was nonplussed, evincing a confusion indeed that some observers, such as can readily be imagined, would have construed into involuntary evidence of hidden guilt. Nevertheless he strove some way to answer, but all at once relinquished the vain endeavor, at the same time turning an appealing glance toward Captain Vere, as deeming him his best helper and friend. Captain Vere, who had been seated for a time, rose to his feet, addressing the interrogator. "The question you put to him comes naturally enough. But how can he rightly answer it, or anybody else, unless indeed it be he who lies within there?" designating the compartment where lay the corpse. "But the prone one there will not rise to our summons. In effect, though, as it seems to me, the point you make is hardly material. Quite aside from any conceivable motive actuating the master-at-arms, and irrespective of the provocation to the blow, a martial court must needs in the present case confine its attention to the blow's consequence, which consequence justly is to be deemed not otherwise than as the striker's deed."

This utterance, the full significance of which it was not at all likely that Billy took in, nevertheless caused him to turn a wistful interrogative look toward the speaker, a look in its dumb expressiveness not unlike that which a dog of generous breed might turn upon his master, seeking in his face some elucidation of a previous gesture ambiguous to the canine intelligence. Nor was the same utterance without marked effect upon the three officers, more especially the soldier. Couched in it seemed to them a meaning unanticipated, involving a prejudgment on the speaker's part. It served to augment a mental disturbance previously evident enough.

The soldier once more spoke, in a tone of suggestive dubiety addressing at once his associates and Captain Vere: "Nobody is present – none of the ship's company, I mean who might shed lateral light, if any is to be had, upon what remains mysterious in this matter."

"That is thoughtfully put," said Captain Vere; "I see your drift. Aye, there is a mystery; but, to use a Scriptural phrase, it is 'a mystery of iniquity,' a matter for psychologic theologians to discuss. But what has a military court to do with it? Not to add that for us any possible investigation of it is cut off by the lasting tongue-tie of – him in yonder," again designating the mortuary stateroom. "The prisoner's deed – with that alone we have to do."

To this, and particularly the closing reiteration, the marine soldier, knowing not how aptly to reply, sadly abstained from saying aught. The first lieutenant, who at the outset had not unnaturally assumed primacy in the court, now overrulingly instructed by a glance from Captain Vere, a glance more effective than words, resumed that primacy. Turning to the prisoner, "Budd," he said, and scarce in equable tones, "Budd, if you have aught further to say for yourself, say it now."

Upon this the young sailor turned another quick glance toward Captain Vere; then, as taking a hint from that aspect, a hint confirming his own instinct that silence was now best, replied to the lieutenant, "I have said all, sir."

The marine – the same who had been the sentinel without the cabin door at the time that the foretopman, followed by the master-at-arms, entered it – he, standing by the sailor throughout these judicial proceedings, was now directed to take him back to the after compartment originally assigned to the prisoner and his custodian. As the twain disappeared from view, the three officers, as partially liberated from some inward constraint associated with Billy's mere presence, simultaneously stirred in their seats. They exchanged looks of troubled indecision, yet feeling that decide they must and without long delay. As for Captain Vere, he for the time stood unconsciously with his back toward them, apparently in one of his absent fits, gazing out from a sashed porthole to windward upon the monotonous blank of the twilight sea. But the court's silence continuing, broken only at moments by brief consultations in low earnest tones, this seemed to arm him and energize him. Turning, he to-and-fro paced the cabin athwart, in the returning ascent to windward climbing the slant deck in the ship's lee roll, without knowing it symbolizing thus in his action a mind resolute to surmount difficulties even if against primitive instincts strong as the wind and the sea. Presently he came to a

stand before the three. After scanning their faces he stood less as
mustering his thoughts for expression than as one only deliberating how best to put them to well-meaning men not intellectually mature, men with whom it was necessary to demonstrate
certain principles that were axioms to himself. Similar impatience as to talking is perhaps one reason that deters some minds
from addressing any popular assemblies.

When speak he did, something both in the substance of what
he said and his manner of saying it, showed the influence of
unshared studies modifying and tempering the practical training of an active career. This, along with his phraseology now
and then, was suggestive of the grounds whereon rested that
imputation of a certain pedantry socially alleged against him by
certain naval men of wholly practical cast, captains who nevertheless would frankly concede that His Majesty's Navy mustered no more efficient officer of their grade than "Starry
Vere."

What he said was to this effect: "Hitherto I have been but the
witness, little more; and I should hardly think now to take
another tone, that of your coadjutor, for the time, did I not
perceive in you – at the crisis too – a troubled hesitancy,
proceeding, I doubt not, from the clash of military duty with
moral scruple – scruple vitalized by compassion. For the compassion, how can I otherwise than share it? But, mindful of
paramount obligation, I strive against scruples that may tend to
enervate decision. Not, gentlemen, that I hide from myself that
the case is an exceptional one. Speculatively regarded, it well
might be referred to a jury of casuists. But for us here acting not
as casuists or moralists, it is a case practical, and under martial
law practically to be dealt with.

"But your scruples: do they move as in a dusk? Challenge
them. Make them advance and declare themselves. Come now,
do they import something like this: if, mindless of palliating
circumstances, we are bound to regard the death of the master-
at-arms as the prisoner's deed, then does that deed constitute a
capital crime whereof the penalty is a mortal one? But in natural
justice is nothing but the prisoner's overt act to be considered?
How can we adjudge to summary and shameful death a fellow

creature innocent before God, and whom we feel to be so? Does that state it aright? You sign sad assent. Well, I too feel that, the full force of that. It is Nature. But do these buttons that we wear attest that our allegiance is to Nature? No, to the King. Though the ocean, which is inviolate Nature primeval, though this be the element where we move and have our being as sailors, yet as the King's officers lies our duty in a sphere correspondingly natural? So little is that true that, in receiving our commissions, we in the most important regards ceased to be natural free agents. When war is declared are we, the commissioned fighters, previously consulted? We fight at command. If our judgments approve the war, that is but coincidence. So in other particulars. So now. For suppose condemnation to follow these present proceedings. Would it be so much we ourselves that would condemn as it would be martial law operating through us? For that law and the rigor of it, we are not responsible. Our vowed responsibility is in this: that however pitilessly that law may operate, we nevertheless adhere to it and administer it.

"But the exceptional in the matter moves the hearts within you. Even so too is mine moved. But let not warm hearts betray heads that should be cool. Ashore in a criminal case will an upright judge allow himself off the bench to be waylaid by some tender kinswoman of the accused seeking to touch him with her tearful plea? Well the heart here denotes the feminine in man, is as that piteous woman and, hard though it be, she must here be ruled out."

He paused, earnestly studying them for a moment, then resumed.

"But something in your aspect seems to urge that it is not solely the heart that moves in you, but also the conscience, the private conscience. But tell me whether or not, occupying the position we do, private conscience should not yield to that imperial one formulated in the code under which alone we officially proceed?"

Here the three men moved in their seats, less convinced than agitated by the course of an argument troubling but the more the spontaneous conflict within.

Perceiving which, the speaker paused for a moment, then, abruptly changing his tone, went on.

"To steady us a bit, let us recur to the facts. In wartime at sea a man-of-war's-man strikes his superior in grade, and the blow kills. Apart from its effect, the blow itself is, according to the Articles of War, a capital crime. Furthermore –"

"Aye, sir," emotionally broke in the officer of marines, "in one sense it was. But surely Budd purposed neither mutiny nor homicide."

"Surely not, my good man. And before a court less arbitrary and more merciful than a martial one that plea would largely extenuate. At the Last Assizes it shall acquit. But how here? We proceed under the law of the Mutiny Act. In feature no child can resemble his father more than that Act resembles in spirit the thing from which it derives – War. In His Majesty's service – in this ship indeed – there are Englishmen forced to fight for the King against their will. Against their conscience, for aught we know. Though as their fellow creatures some of us may appreciate their position, yet as navy officers, what reck we of it? Still less recks the enemy. Our impressed men he would fain cut down in the same swath with our volunteers. As regards the enemy's naval conscripts, some of whom may even share our own abhorrence of the regicidal French Directory, it is the same on our side. War looks but to the frontage, the appearance. And the Mutiny Act, war's child, takes after the father. Budd's intent or nonintent is nothing to the purpose.

"But while, put to it by those anxieties in you which I cannot but respect, I only repeat myself – while thus strangely we prolong proceedings that should be summary – the enemy may be sighted and an engagement result. We must do; and one of two things must we do: condemn or let go."

"Can we not convict and yet mitigate the penalty?" asked the junior lieutenant here speaking, and falteringly, for the first.

"Lieutenant, were that clearly lawful for us under the circumstances, consider the consequences of such clemency. The people," meaning the ship's company, "have native sense; most of them are familiar with our naval usage and tradition, and how would they take it? Even could you explain to them – which our official position forbids – they, long molded by arbitrary discipline, have not that kind of intelligent responsiveness that might qualify them to comprehend and discriminate. No, to the people the foretopman's deed, however it be worded in the announcement, will be plain homicide committed in a flagrant act of mutiny. What penalty for that should follow, they know. But it does not follow. *Why*? they will ruminate. You know what sailors are. Will they not revert to the recent outbreak at the Nore? Aye. They know the well-founded alarm – the panic it struck throughout England. Your clement sentence they would account pusillanimous. They would think that we flinch, that we are afraid of them – afraid of practicing a lawful rigor singularly demanded at this juncture lest it should provoke new troubles. What shame to us such a conjecture on their part, and how deadly to discipline. You see then, whither, prompted by duty and the law, I steadfastly drive. But I beseech you, my friends, do not take me amiss. I feel as you do for this unfortunate boy. But did he know our hearts, I take him to be of that generous nature that he would feel even for us on whom in this military necessity so heavy a compulsion is laid."

With that, crossing the deck he resumed his place by the sashed porthole, tacitly leaving the three to come to a decision. On the cabin's opposite side the troubled court sat silent. Loyal lieges, plain and practical, though at bottom they dissented from some points Captain Vere had put to them, they were without the faculty, hardly had the inclination, to gainsay one whom they felt to be an earnest man, one, too, not less their superior in mind than in naval rank. But it is not improbable that even such of his words as were not without influence over them, less came home to them than his closing appeal to their instinct as sea officers in the forethought he threw out as to the practical consequences to discipline, considering the unconfirmed tone of the fleet at the time, should a man-of-war's-man's violent killing at sea of a superior in grade be allowed to pass for aught else than a capital crime demanding prompt infliction of the penalty.

Not unlikely they were brought to something more or less akin to that harassed frame of mind which in the year 1842 actuated the commander of the US brig-of-war *Somers* to resolve, under the so-called Articles of War, Articles modeled

upon the English Mutiny Act, to resolve upon the execution at
sea of a midshipman and two petty officers as mutineers
designing the seizure of the brig. Which resolution was carried
out though in a time of peace and within not many days sail of
home – an act vindicated by a naval court of inquiry subsequently convened ashore. History, and here cited without
comment. True, the circumstances on board the *Somers* were
different from those on board the *Indomitable*. But the urgency
felt, well-warranted or otherwise, was much the same.

Says a writer whom few know, "Forty years after a battle it is
easy for a noncombatant to reason about how it ought to have
been fought. It is another thing personally and under fire to
direct the fighting while involved in the obscuring smoke of it.
Much so with respect to other emergencies involving considerations both practical and moral, and when it is imperative
promptly to act. The greater the fog the more it imperils the
steamer, and speed is put on though at the hazard of running
somebody down. Little ween the snug card-players in the cabin
of the responsibilities of the sleepless man on the bridge."

In brief, Billy Budd was formally convicted and sentenced to
be hung at the yardarm in the early morning watch, it being now
night. Otherwise, as is customary in such cases, the sentence
would forthwith have been carried out. In wartime, on the field
or in the fleet, a mortal punishment decreed by a drumhead
court – on the field sometimes decreed by but a nod from the
general – follows without delay on the heel of conviction,
without appeal.

23

It was Captain Vere himself who of his own motion communicated the finding of the court to the prisoner, for that purpose
going to the compartment where he was in custody and bidding
the marine there to withdraw for the time.

Beyond the communication of the sentence, what took place
at this interview was never known. But in view of the character
of the twain briefly closeted in that state-room, each radically
sharing in the rarer qualities of our nature – so rare indeed as to

be all but incredible to average minds however much cultivated
– some conjectures may be ventured.

It would have been in consonance with the spirit of Captain
Vere should he on this occasion have concealed nothing from
the condemned one – should he indeed have frankly disclosed
to him the part he himself had played in bringing about the
decision, at the same time revealing his actuating motives. On
Billy's side it is not improbable that such a confession would
have been received in much the same spirit that prompted it.
Not without a sort of joy indeed he might have appreciated
the brave opinion of him implied in his captain making such a
confidant of him. Nor as to the sentence itself could he have
been insensible that it was imparted to him as to one not
afraid to die. Even more may have been. Captain Vere in the
end may have developed the passion sometimes latent under
an exterior stoical or indifferent. He was old enough to have
been Billy's father. The austere devotee of military duty
letting himself melt back into what remains primeval in
our formalized humanity may in the end have caught Billy
to his heart even as Abraham may have caught young Isaac on
the brink of resolutely offering him up in obedience to the
exacting behest. But there is no telling the sacrament, seldom
if in any case revealed to the gadding world, wherever under
circumstances at all akin to those here attempted to be set
forth two of great Nature's nobler order embrace. There is
privacy at the time, inviolable to the survivor, and holy
oblivion, the sequel to each diviner magnanimity, providentially covers all at last.

The first to encounter Captain Vere in act of leaving the
compartment was the senior lieutenant. The face he beheld, for
the moment one expressive of the agony of the strong, was to
that officer, though a man of fifty, a startling revelation. That
the condemned one suffered less than he who mainly had
effected the condemnation was apparently indicated by the
former's exclamation in the scene soon perforce to be touched
upon.

24

Of a series of incidents within a brief term rapidly following each other, the adequate narration may take up a term less brief, especially if explanation or comment here and there seem requisite to the better understanding of such incidents. Between the entrance into the cabin of him who never left it alive, and him who when he did leave it left it as one condemned to die, between this and the closeted interview just given, less than an hour and a half had elapsed. It was an interval long enough, however, to awaken speculations among no few of the ship's company as to what it was that could be detaining in the cabin the master-at-arms and the sailor; for a rumor that both of them had been seen to enter it and neither of them had been seen to emerge, this rumor had got abroad upon the gun decks and in the tops; the people of a great warship being in one respect like villagers taking microscopic note of every outward movement or nonmovement going on. When, therefore, in weather not at all tempestuous all hands were called in the second dog watch, a summons under such circumstances not usual in those hours, the crew were not wholly unprepared for some announcement extraordinary, one having connection too with the continued absence of the two men from their wonted haunts.

There was a moderate sea at the time, and the moon, newly risen and near to being at its full, silvered the white spar-deck wherever not blotted by the clear-cut shadows horizontally thrown of fixtures and moving men. On either side the quarter-deck the marine guard under arms was drawn up; and Captain Vere, standing in his place surrounded by all the wardroom officers, addressed his men. In so doing his manner showed neither more nor less than that property pertaining to his supreme position aboard his own ship. In clear terms and concise he told them what had taken place in the cabin: that the master-at-arms was dead; that he who had killed him had been already tried by a summary court and condemned to death; and that the execution would take place in the early morning watch. The word *mutiny* was not named in what he said. He refrained too from making the occasion an opportunity for any preachment as to the maintenance of discipline, thinking perhaps that under existing circumstances in the navy the consequence of violating discipline should be made to speak for itself.

Their captain's announcement was listened to by the throng of standing sailors in a dumbness like that of a seated congregation of believers in hell listening to the clergyman's announcement of his Calvinistic text.

At the close, however, a confused murmur went up. It began to wax. All but instantly, then, at a sign, it was pierced and suppressed by shrill whistles of the boatswain and his mates piping down one watch.

To be prepared for burial Claggart's body was delivered to certain petty officers of his mess. And here, not to clog the sequel with lateral matters, it may be added that, at a suitable hour, the master-at-arms was committed to the sea with every funeral honor properly belonging to his naval grade.

In this proceeding, as in every public one growing out of the tragedy, strict adherence to usage was observed. Nor in any point could it have been at all deviated from, either with respect to Claggart or Billy Budd, without begetting undesirable speculations in the ship's company, sailors, and more particularly men-of-war's men, being of all men the greatest sticklers for usage.

For similar cause, all communication between Captain Vere and the condemned one ended with the closeted interview already given, the latter being now surrendered to the ordinary routine preliminary to the end. This transfer under guard from the captain's quarters was effected without unusual precautions – at least no visible ones.

If possible not to let the men so much as surmise that their officers anticipate aught amiss from them is the tacit rule in a military ship. And the more that some sort of trouble should really be apprehended, the more do the officers keep that apprehension to themselves, though not the less unostentatious vigilance may be augmented.

In the present instance the sentry placed over the prisoner had strict orders to let no one have communication with him but the chaplain. And certain unobtrusive measures were taken absolutely to insure this point.

25

In a seventy-four of the old order the deck known as the upper
gun deck was the one covered over by the spar-deck, which last,
though not without its armament, was for the most part exposed
to the weather. In general it was at all hours free from hammocks; those of the crew swinging on the lower gun deck and
berth deck, the latter being not only a dormitory but also the
place for the stowing of the sailors' bags, and on both sides lined
with the large chests or movable pantries of the many messes of
the men.

On the starboard side of the *Indomitable*'s upper gun deck,
behold Billy Budd under sentry lying prone in irons in one of
the bays formed by the regular spacing of the guns comprising
the batteries on either side. All these pieces were of the heavier
caliber of that period. Mounted on lumbering wooden carriages, they were hampered with cumbersome harness of
breeching and strong side tackles for running them out. Guns
and carriages, together with the long rammers and shorter
lintstocks lodged in loops overhead – all these, as customary,
were painted black; and the heavy hempen breechings, tarred
to the same tint, wore the like livery of the undertakers. In
contrast with the funereal hue of these surroundings the prone
sailor's exterior apparel, white jumper and white duck trousers, each more or less soiled, dimly glimmered in the obscure
light of the bay like a patch of discolored snow in early April
lingering at some upland cave's black mouth. In effect he is
already in his shroud or the garments that shall serve him in
lieu of one. Over him but scarce illuminating him, two battle
lanterns swing from two massive beams of the deck above. Fed
with the oil supplied by the war contractors (whose gains,
honest or otherwise, are in every land an anticipated portion of
the harvest of death) with flickering splashes of dirty yellow
light, they pollute the pale moonshine, all but ineffectually
struggling in obstructed flecks through the open ports from
which the tompioned cannon protrude. Other lanterns at
intervals serve but to bring out somewhat the obscurer bays,
which, like small confessionals or side-chapels in a cathedral,

branch from the long dim-vistaed broad aisle between the two batteries of that covered tier.

Such was the deck where now lay the Handsome Sailor. Through the rose-tan of his complexion no pallor could have shown. It would have taken days of sequestration from the winds and the sun to have brought about the effacement of that. But the skeleton in the cheekbone at the point of its angle was just beginning delicately to be defined under the warm-tinted skin. In fervid hearts self-contained some brief experiences devour our human tissue as secret fire in a ship's hold consumes cotton in the bale.

But now lying between the two guns, as nipped in the vice of fate, Billy's agony, mainly proceeding from a generous young heart's virgin experience of the diabolical incarnate and effective in some men – the tension of that agony was over now. It survived not the something healing in the closeted interview with Captain Vere. Without movement, he lay as in a trance. That adolescent expression previously noted as his, taking on something akin to the look of a slumbering child in the cradle when the warm hearth-glow of the still chamber at night plays on the dimples that at whiles mysteriously form in the cheek, silently coming and going there. For now and then in the gyved one's trance a serene happy light born of some wandering reminiscence or dream would diffuse itself over his face, and then wane away only anew to return.

The Chaplain coming to see him and finding him thus, and perceiving no sign that he was conscious of his presence, attentively regarded him for a space, then, slipping aside, withdrew for the time, peradventure feeling that even he, the minister of Christ, though receiving his stipend from Mars had no consolation to proffer which could result in a peace transcending that which he beheld. But in the small hours he came again. And the prisoner now awake to his surroundings noticed his approach and civilly, all but cheerfully, welcomed him. But it was to little purpose that in the interview following the good man sought to bring Billy Budd to some godly understanding that he must die, and at dawn. True, Billy himself freely referred to his death as a thing close at hand; but it was something in the way that children will refer to death in general, who yet among their other sports will play a funeral with hearse and mourners.

Not that like children Billy was incapable of conceiving what death really is. No; but he was wholly without irrational fear of it, a fear more prevalent in highly civilized communities than those so-called barbarous ones which in all respects stand nearer to unadulterate Nature. And, as elsewhere said, a barbarian Billy radically was; as much so, for all the costume, as his countrymen the British captives, living trophies, made to march in the Roman triumph of Germanicus. Quite as much so as those later barbarians, young men probably, and picked specimens among the earlier British converts to Christianity, at least nominally such and taken to Rome (as today converts from lesser isles of the sea may be taken to London), of whom the pope of that time, admiring the strangeness of their personal beauty so unlike the Italian stamp, their clear ruddy complexion and curled flaxen locks, exclaimed, "Angles" (meaning *English*, the modern derivative), "Angles do you call them? And is it because they look so like angels?" Had it been later in time one would think that the Pope had in mind Fra Angelico's seraphs, some of whom, plucking apples in gardens of the Hesperides, have the faint rose-bud complexion of the more beautiful English girls.

If in vain the good Chaplain sought to impress the young barbarian with ideas of death akin to those conveyed in the skull, dial, and crossbones on old tombstones, equally futile to all appearance were his efforts to bring home to him the thought of salvation and a saviour. Billy listened, but less out of awe or reverence perhaps than from a certain natural politeness, doubtless at bottom regarding all that in much the same way that most mariners of his class take any discourse abstract or out of the common tone of the workaday world. And this sailor-way of taking clerical discourse is not wholly unlike the way in which the pioneer of Christianity, full of transcendent miracles, was received long ago on tropic isles by any superior *savage* so called – a Tahitian, say, of Captain Cook's time or shortly after that time. Out of natural courtesy he received, but did not appropriate. It was like a gift placed in the palm of an outreached hand upon which the fingers do not close.

But the *Indomitable*'s chaplain was a discreet man, possessing the good sense of a good heart. So he insisted not in his vocation here. At the instance of Captain Vere, a lieutenant had apprised him of pretty much everything as to Billy; and since he felt that innocence was even a better thing than religion wherewith to go to judgment, he reluctantly withdrew, but in his emotion not without first performing an act strange enough in an Englishman, and under the circumstances yet more so in any regular priest. Stooping over, he kissed on the fair cheek his fellow man, a felon in martial law, one who, though on the confines of death, he felt he could never convert to a dogma; nor for all that did he fear for his future.

Marvel not that having been made acquainted with the young sailor's essential innocence (an irruption of heretic thought hard to suppress) the worthy man lifted not a finger to avert the doom of such a martyr to martial discipline. So to do would not only have been as idle as invoking the desert, but would also have been an audacious transgression of the bounds of his function, one as exactly prescribed to him by military law as that of the boatswain or any other naval officer. Bluntly put, a chaplain is the minister of the Prince of Peace serving in the host of the God of War – Mars. As such, he is as incongruous as that musket of Blücher, etc., at Christmas. Why then is he there? Because he indirectly subserves the purpose attested by the cannon; because too he lends the sanction of the religion of the meek to that which practically is the abrogation of everything but brute force.

26

The night so luminous on the spar-deck but otherwise on the cavernous ones below, levels so like the tiered galleries in a coal mine – the luminous night passed away. But, like the prophet in the chariot disappearing in heaven and dropping his mantle to Elisha, the withdrawing night transferred its pale robe to the breaking day. A meek shy light appeared in the East, where stretched a diaphanous fleece of white furrowed vapor. That light slowly waxed. Suddenly *eight bells* was struck aft, responded to by one louder metallic stroke from forward. It was four o'clock in the morning. Instantly the silver whistles were heard summoning all hands to witness punishment. Up through the great hatchways rimmed with racks of heavy shot, the watch below came pouring, overspreading with the watch already on deck the space between the mainmast and foremast, including that occupied by the capacious launch and the black booms tiered on either side of it, boat and booms making a summit of observation for the powder-boys and younger tars. A different group comprising one watch of topmen leaned over the rail of that sea-balcony, no small one in a seventy-four, looking down on the crowd below. Man or boy none spake but in whisper, and few spake at all. Captain Vere – as before, the central figure among the assembled commissioned officers – stood nigh the break of the poop deck facing forward. Just below him on the quarter-deck the marines in full equipment were drawn up much as at the scene of the promulgated sentence.

At sea in the old time, the execution by halter of a military sailor was generally from the foreyard. In the present instance, for special reasons the mainyard was assigned. Under an arm of that lee yard the prisoner was presently brought up, the Chaplain attending him. It was noted at the time, and remarked upon afterwards, that in this final scene the good man evinced little or nothing of the perfunctory. Brief speech indeed he had with the condemned one, but the genuine Gospel was less on his tongue than in his aspect and manner toward him. The final preparations personal to the latter being speedily brought to an end by two boatswain's mates, the consummation impended. Billy stood facing aft. At the penultimate moment, his words, his only ones, words wholly unobstructed in the utterance, were these: "God bless Captain Vere!" Syllables so unanticipated coming from one with the ignominious hemp about his neck – a conventional felon's benediction directed aft toward the quarters of honor; syllables, too, delivered in the clear melody of a singing bird on the point of launching from the twig, had a phenomenal effect, not unenhanced by the rare personal beauty of the young sailor spiritualized now through late experiences so poignantly profound.

Without volition as it were, as if indeed the ship's populace were but the vehicles of some vocal current electric, with one voice from allow and aloft came a resonant sympathetic echo: "God bless Captain Vere!" And yet at that instant Billy alone must have been in their hearts, even as he was in their eyes.

At the pronounced words and the spontaneous echo that voluminously rebounded them, Captain Vere, either through stoic self-control or a sort of momentary paralysis induced by emotional shock, stood erectly rigid as a musket in the ship-armorer's rack.

The hull deliberately recovering from the periodic roll to leeward was just regaining an even keel, when the last signal, a preconcerted dumb one, was given. At the same moment it chanced that the vapory fleece hanging low in the East was shot through with a soft glory as of the fleece of the Lamb of God seen in mystical vision, and simultaneously therewith, watched by the wedged mass of upturned faces, Billy ascended, and, ascending, took the full rose of the dawn.

In the pinioned figure arrived at the yard-end, to the wonder of all no motion was apparent, none save that created by the ship's motion, in moderate weather so majestic in a great ship ponderously cannoned.

27. A digression

When, some days afterward, in reference to the singularity just mentioned, the purser, a rather ruddy rotund person more accurate as an accountant than profound as a philosopher, said at mess to the surgeon, "What testimony to the force lodged in will power," the latter – saturnine, spare and tall, one in whom a discreet causticity went along with a manner less genial than polite – replied, "Your pardon, Mr Purser. In a hanging scientifically conducted – and under special orders I myself directed how Budd's was to be effected – any movement following the completed suspension and originating in the body suspended, such movement indicates mechanical spasm in the muscular system. Hence the absence of that is no more attributable to will power as you call it than to horsepower – begging your pardon."

"But this muscular spasm you speak of, is not that in a degree more or less invariable in these cases?"

"Assuredly so, Mr Purser."

"How then, my good sir, do you account for its absence in this instance?"

"Mr Purser, it is clear that your sense of the singularity in this matter equals not mine. You account for it by what you call will power, a term not yet included in the lexicon of science. For me, I do not, with my present knowledge, pretend to account for it at all. Even should we assume the hypothesis that at the first touch of the halyards the action of Budd's heart, intensified by extraordinary emotion at its climax, abruptly stopped – much like a watch when in carelessly winding it up you strain at the finish, thus snapping the chain – even under that hypothesis how account for the phenomenon that followed?"

"You admit, then, that the absence of spasmodic movement was phenomenal."

"It was phenomenal, Mr Purser, in the sense that it was an appearance the cause of which is not immediately to be assigned."

"But tell me, my dear sir," pertinaciously continued the other, "was the man's death effected by the halter, or was it a species of euthanasia?"

" 'Euthanasia,' Mr Purser, is something like your 'will power': I doubt its authenticity as a scientific term – begging your pardon again. It is at once imaginative and metaphysical – in short, Greek. But," abruptly changing his tone, "there is a case in the sick bay that I do not care to leave to my assistants. Beg your pardon, but excuse me." And rising from the mess he formally withdrew.

28

The silence at the moment of execution and for a moment or two continuing thereafter, a silence but emphasized by the regular wash of the sea against the hull or the flutter of a sail caused by the helmsman's eyes being tempted astray, this emphasized silence was gradually disturbed by a sound not easily to be verbally rendered. Whoever has heard the freshet-wave of a torrent suddenly swelled by pouring showers in tropical mountains, showers not shared by the plain; whoever has heard the first muffled murmur of its sloping advance through precipitous woods, may form some conception of the sound now heard. The seeming remoteness of its source was because of its murmurous indistinctness since it came from close by, even from the men massed on the ship's open deck. Being inarticulate, it was dubious in significance further than it seemed to indicate some capricious revulsion of thought or feeling such as mobs ashore are liable to, in the present instance possibly implying a sullen revocation on the men's part of their involuntary echoing of Billy's benediction. But ere the murmur had time to wax into clamor it was met by a strategic command, the more telling that it came with abrupt unexpectedness.

"Pipe down the starboard watch, Boatswain, and see that they go."

Shrill as the shriek of the sea hawk the whistles of the boatswain and his mates pierced that ominous low sound, dissipating it; and yielding to the mechanism of discipline the throng was thinned by one half. For the remainder, most of them were set to temporary employments connected with trimming the yards and so forth, business readily to be got up to serve occasion by any officer-of-the-deck.

Now each proceeding that follows a mortal sentence pronounced at sea by a drumhead court is characterized by promptitude not perceptibly merging into hurry, though bordering that. The hammock, the one which had been Billy's bed when alive, having already been ballasted with shot and otherwise prepared to serve for his canvas coffin, the last offices of the sea-undertakers, the sailmaker's mates, were now speedily completed. When everything was in readiness a second call for all hands, made necessary by the strategic movement before mentioned, was sounded, and now to witness burial.

The details of this closing formality it needs not to give. But

when the tilted plank let slide its freight into the sea, a second
strange human murmur was heard, blended now with another
inarticulate sound proceeding from certain larger seafowl,
whose attention having been attracted by the peculiar commotion in the water resulting from the heavy sloped dive of the
shotted hammock into the sea, flew screaming to the spot. So
near the hull did they come that the stridor or bony creak of
their gaunt double-jointed pinions was audible. As the ship
under light airs passed on, leaving the burial spot astern, they
still kept circling it low down with the moving shadow of their
outstretched wings and the croaked requiem of their cries.

Upon sailors as superstitious as those of the age preceding
ours, men-of-war's men, too, who had just beheld the prodigy
of repose in the form suspended in air and now foundering in
the deeps; to such mariners the action of the seafowl, though
dictated by mere animal greed for prey, was big with no prosaic
significance. An uncertain movement began among them, in
which some encroachment was made. It was tolerated but for a
moment. For suddenly the drum beat to quarters, which
familiar sound, happening at least twice every day, had upon
the present occasion a signal peremptoriness in it. True martial
discipline long continued superinduces in average man a sort of
impulse of docility, whose operation at the official sound of
command much resembles in its promptitude the effect of an
instinct.

The drumbeat dissolved the multitude, distributing most of
them along the batteries of the two covered gun decks. There, as
wont, the guns' crews stood by their respective cannon erect
and silent. In due course the first officer, sword under arm and
standing in his place on the quarter-deck, formally received the
successive reports of the sworded lieutenants commanding the
sections of batteries below, the last of which reports being
made, the summed report he delivered with the customary
salute to the commander. All this occupied time, which in
the present case was the object of beating to quarters at an
hour prior to the customary one. That such variance from usage
was authorized by an officer like Captain Vere, a martinet as
some deemed him, was evidence of the necessity for unusual

action implied in what he deemed to be temporarily the mood of his men. "With mankind," he would say, "forms, measured forms, are everything; and that is the import couched in the story of Orpheus with his lyre spellbinding the wild denizens of the wood." And this he once applied to the disruption of forms going on across the Channel and the consequences thereof.

At this unwonted muster at quarters, all proceeded as at the regular hour. The band on the quarter-deck played a sacred air, after which the chaplain went through the customary morning service. That done, the drum beat the retreat, and, toned by music and religious rites subserving the discipline and purpose of war, the men in their wonted orderly manner dispersed to the places allotted them when not at the guns.

And now it was full day. The fleece of low-hanging vapor had vanished, licked up by the sun that late had so glorified it. And the circumambient air in the clearness of its serenity was like smooth white marble in the polished block not yet removed from the marble dealer's yard.

29

The symmetry of form attainable in pure fiction cannot so readily be achieved in a narration essentially having less to do with fable than with fact. Truth uncompromisingly told will always have its ragged edges; hence the conclusion of such a narration is apt to be less finished than an architectural finial.

How it fared with the Handsome Sailor during the year of the Great Mutiny has been faithfully given. But though properly the story ends with his life, something in way of sequel will not be amiss. Three brief chapters will suffice.

In the general rechristening under the Directory of the craft originally forming the navy of the French monarchy, the *St Louis* line-of-battle ship was named the *Athéiste*. Such a name, like some other substituted ones in the Revolutionary fleet, while proclaiming the infidel audacity of the ruling power was yet, though not so intended to be, the aptest name, if one consider it, ever given to a warship, far more so indeed than the *Devastation*, the *Erebus* (the *Hell*) and similar names bestowed upon fighting ships.

On the return passage to the English fleet from the detached cruise during which occurred the events already recorded, the *Indomitable* fell in with the *Athéiste*. An engagement ensued, during which Captain Vere, in the act of putting his ship alongside the enemy with a view of throwing his boarders across her bulwarks, was hit by a musket ball from a porthole of the enemy's main cabin. More than disabled he dropped to the deck and was carried below to the same cockpit where some of his men already lay. The senior lieutenant took command. Under him the enemy was finally captured and though much crippled was by rare good fortune successfully taken into Gibraltar, an English port not very distant from the scene of the fight. There Captain Vere with the rest of the wounded was put ashore. He lingered for some days, but the end came. Unhappily he was cut off too early for the Nile and Trafalgar. The spirit that spite its philosophic austerity may yet have indulged in the most secret of all passions, ambition, never attained to the fullness of fame.

Not long before death, while lying under the influence of that magical drug which, soothing the physical frame, mysteriously operates on the subtler element in man, he was heard to murmur words inexplicable to his attendant: "Billy Budd, Billy Budd." That these were not the accents of remorse would seem clear from what the attendant said to the *Indomitable*'s senior officer of marines, who, as the most reluctant to condemn of the members of the drumhead court, too well knew, though here he kept the knowledge to himself, who Billy Budd was.

30

Some few weeks after the execution, among other matters under the head of *News from the Mediterranean*, there appeared in a naval chronicle of the time, an authorized weekly publication, an account of the affair. It was doubtless for the most part written in good faith, though the medium, partly rumor, through which the facts must have reached the writer, served to deflect and in part falsify them. The account was as follows:

"On the tenth of the last month a deplorable occurrence took place on board H.M.S. *Indomitable*. John Claggart, the ship's master-at-arms, discovering that some sort of plot was incipient among an inferior section of the ship's company, and that the ringleader was one William Budd, he, Claggart, in the act of arraigning the man before the captain was vindictively stabbed to the heart by the suddenly drawn sheath knife of Budd.

"The deed and the implement employed sufficiently suggest that, though mustered into the service under an English name, the assassin was no Englishman, but one of those aliens adopting English cognomens whom the present extraordinary necessities of the service have caused to be admitted into it in considerable numbers.

"The enormity of the crime and the extreme depravity of the criminal appear the greater in view of the character of the victim, a middle-aged man respectable and discreet, belonging to that minor official grade, the petty officers, upon whom, as none know better than the commissioned gentlemen, the efficiency of His Majesty's Navy so largely depends. His function was a responsible one, at once onerous and thankless, and his fidelity in it the greater because of his strong patriotic impulse. In this instance, as in so many other instances in these days, the character of this unfortunate man signally refutes, if refutation were needed, that peevish saying attributed to the late Dr. Johnson, that patriotism is the last refuge of a scoundrel.

"The criminal paid the penalty of his crime. The promptitude of the punishment has proved salutary. Nothing amiss is now apprehended aboard H.M.S. *Indomitable*."

The above, appearing in a publication now long ago superannuated and forgotten, is all that hitherto has stood in human record to attest what manner of men respectively were John Claggart and Billy Budd.

THE RESCUE

Kenneth Bulmer

In Europe, the Treaty of Campo Formio in 1797 had brought an end to the war between France and Austria (known as the War of the First Coalition). France's main enemy now was Britain. Bonaparte was rising in prominence in France, and would achieve even greater status after his campaigns in Egypt and the Levant.

The following story is set in 1799. It is an early episode from the hapless career of George Abercrombie Fox, whose adventures were told by Kenneth Bulmer in a long series of books written under the alias of Adam Hardy. This episode, which stands on its own, comes from the third book in the series, Siege *(1973) – the title referring to the Siege of Acre.*

The sea was the enemy. George Abercrombie Fox, lieutenant temporarily in command of His Britannic Majesty's fourteen-gun brig *Raccoon*, chafed to clear Palermo harbour and stand away for Acre. But the elements dictated otherwise and here he was, stormbound, and summoned to an evening of cards with the Kintleshams whilst his vessel lay penned within the harbour by a dead foul wind running a gale, that whipped the sea into a foam-flecked nightmare of confused violence.

Fox cursed as sea water sluiced up from a wave breaking full on the sea wall and pelted all across his shabby finery. He blinked his eyes fiercely and peered across that white-running devil's cauldron of a sea. The waves contused into knots of blackness which the wind scythed into gobbets of hurtling whiteness.

The vessel out there was doomed. She had run aground on rocks that would have torn her bottom out as a butcher guts a rabbit. The lucky ones out there would be already dead. The unlucky ones would be clinging on with torn fingernails and bleeding hands, shuddering as each wave smashed down on them, unable to hear anything save the shriek of the wind and the pound of the seas. At Fox's back the good people of Palermo, including the Neapolitan court, were sheltering within doors and only groups of seafaring folk and fishermen clustered near Fox, talking and shouting, gesticulating in the wind.

"They're all done for, sir!" shouted Midshipman Grey. He added in the formula: "Poor devils!"

Fox didn't bother to reply. The people on the wrecked vessel were doomed; it had been their misfortune to have shipped aboard a vessel whose captain hadn't the sense to give the coast a wide berth and sheer off to gain maximum searoom before the blow came. It was just possible a boat might live in that sea; Fox had no doubts that no boats that would swim were left aboard the wreck. Cascades of broken water burst above the black mass. The day was dying early as the gale drove furiously over Sicily. He turned away. Waiting for him tonight there were dinner, cards, lamplight and gleaming female shoulders.

Of that not inconsiderable catalogue the dinner, most of all, tempted Fox. Then the cards – and he had made up his mind that he would only play all square and above board if no one got across his hawse. Then the luxury of real wax candles, which, to a marshboy from the Thames, embodied the realisation that times had changed, albeit too slowly and not enough. And, lastly – and how mocking and forlorn a pleasure! – the gleaming female shoulders. Poor Sophie. Poor fat good-natured simple Sophie. Her fat shaking shoulders would gleam in that soft expensive candlelight well enough; but they would gleam with sweat. She would sigh and ogle him and flutter her fan and utter little crooning noises over him. He was paying, was George Abercrombie Fox, the London scum who had come up through the hawsehole, he was paying deeply for his pretensions and his clawing assault on the citadel of Interest.

It would take a deal of resolution tonight not to drink so much that he would become stupid and unconcerned.

He dashed spray from his face and cursed again. Thought of Interest that so corrupted the Royal Navy made him fret with a keener pang over this damnable gale. Since Commander Mortlock had died – Fox could still conjure to his mind's eye that glistening veined eyeball naked in the man's injured face – the temporary command of *Raccoon* had been his through the kind influence of Lord Kintlesham, fat Sophie's father, with Sir William Hamilton, and through the Ambassador's wife with the admiral. But this sloop was a plum. There were very few quarterdeck brigs afloat and for the command of one of them to fall to a rapscallion like George Abercrombie Fox was more than a mere miracle, it was by all standards that Fox had known in his life an impossibility.

But, in command he was, a lieutenant without epaulette, and unless he could get to sea and actually be at sea, any day might bring down a greater force of Interest to take his command away. He was only a lieutenant. He had not been appointed to command *Raccoon* as a commander – they would have called him master and commander up to four years ago, but then the admiralty had at last struck the anachronistic "master" from the title.

These dark thoughts broke as Mr Midshipman Grey shouted into the wind, his eager face streaming with spray, all his classic profile wonderfully displayed. "My God, sir! There's a woman aboard!"

Fox picked her out in an instant. The wreck had shifted, exposing more of the deck to his gaze. Unmistakably the form of a woman clung to the stump of the mizzen mast, her long white skirts trailing with each resurgence of the water which broke in torrential sheets across the taffrail – or what was left of it. Cordage writhed in that wind like Medusa's hair. Staring straight into the wind Fox saw the specks of people and the white loose mass that was a woman clinging to that spray-drenched, wave-battered, doomed mass of timbers.

"These fools will take women to sea." Fox blinked his eyes again as spray lashed. Both his eyes were functioning perfectly well. He had no desire to wait here and watch a ship being devoured by that sea he loved and loathed. The fang-teeth of the rocks were biting into the hull, a frenzied chomping that would reduce the hull to mere random timbers. Her masts had gone by the board in the first shock; but, still attached by a single line, one spar kicked and thrust like a toothpick in the fist of a demented sea-giant.

He had to lean over against the wind. God help a poor sailorman on a night like this. Although – no one was going to help those poor devils on the wreck now. He thought of the wax candles and the dinner that beckoned. Why couldn't those pitiful survivors be decently washed overboard when she struck? Why did they have to cling on like limpets in a rip, drenched, battered, lost and waiting for death? Again Fox stared over the white-running sea. He studied that maelstrom with those eyes that were working very well and with a brain that figured and calculated without, as it were, a by-your-leave from his will.

Waves poured in long confused masses towards the rocks and broke and split and reared lofting high. The roar was a continuous beating sound. The wreck was being pushed over the rocks as the bottom fell out plank by plank. Only the lame and simple of mind went to sea, and if they were halfway sane when they signed on they'd be as mad as the next in no time. As mad as George Abercrombie Fox.

Beyond the angle of the sea wall a swathe of calmer water showed where the locals beached their boats. Well, they would know the vagaries of the weather and the currents hereabouts and they would know, too, that only a madman would venture to take a boat out into that sea . . .

Fox gripped Grey's arm and swung him about.

His left hand held his hat clapped onto his head, as Grey also held his, and Fox had to release the midshipman to point.

Grey's face showed puzzlement, then shock, then a strange kind of fierceness completely lost on Fox.

Grey's lips formed words half dashed-away by the gale.

"It could be done, sir. My oath – but it'd be a thing to do!"

Just why he had made up his mind to do what he now fully intended Fox could never be sure. Perhaps it was just connected with that scrap of white soaked dress out there where the waves spouted and the wind howled and the spume cut like daggers and the splintered timbers of the wreck lurched agonisedly towards total disintegration. He put his mouth alongside Grey's ear.

"Rouse out these volunteers, Mr Grey." He rattled off the men he wanted, good men all. He did not stop to think what their reactions would be; they were members of his crew and he, although a lowly lieutenant, was their captain and therefore their Lord God Almighty aboard *Raccoon*. That they would volunteer, all of them to a man, if he gave them the chance in competition with the rest of the crew, that, also, he knew.

He began to stride briskly down to the beached Sicilian boats. By the time the men joined him, sweating and yet quiet, most of them with massive duffles of waterproof clothing, he had selected the most likely boat. He had picked her from the some fifteen or so specimens available, double-ended craft, high forward and aft with gaily-painted planks and strakes. He chose this one with an eye to her breadth and apparent seaworthiness. The bung was found and rammed in. His men stared at him, their faces shining in the wind-driven spray, their eyes hard and calculating, and he saw more than one of the men rub a horny hand down across his mouth.

He did not speak but gave his commands in curt stabbing gestures. They ran the boat out. People up on the wall would be looking over and speculating and no doubt considering them as good as lost and if the owner of the boat put in an appearance now Fox had no time for argument.

Leaving the rudder and tiller alone he shipped a long steering oar in the notch cut in the stern. The men scrambled aboard. Grey was in the bows. The men grasped the looms of the oars and waited, staring at him.

For just a betraying instant he wished that Affleck was rowing stroke oar – that same cheerful stubborn stupid Affleck whom he had not seen since leaving *Tiger*. But Josephs was rowing stroke, a massive man, a good man at the loom with the big burly body and bunched muscles that made him cock of the boat's crew – and more besides. His own coxswain, Phillips, crouched in the sternsheets and would, without doubt, have to assist with the steering oar.

Not a man of the boat's crew had murmured or refused to be ordered to volunteer. That, Fox expected; he had no time now to consider how very strange it was, given the kind of man he was and knew himself to be. He had no time to worry about anything else at all as he gave a savage nod, the men took their first challenging stroke that put the boat under his control and they shot forward from the relatively calm water out into the full violence of the gale.

As soon as he felt the power of the sea upon the boat and realised the efforts he must put out with the steering oar to keep her head into the waves and wind as he crabbed along, he knew just what kind of a bloody idiot he was.

The men bent and heaved and he could plainly feel the power of each surge forward, for with the feathering and lift of the oars the boat seemed to stop as though it had run into a brick wall. The blades thrashed through the water. Each yard forward was bought at the cost of prodigious effort. The wreck was half invisible beneath flying sheets of spray. The wind howled in maniacal fury. The sound drove him to a kind of half-crouching stoop at each stroke of the oars. The wreck was approaching; but slowly, slowly.

The boat leaped and heaved, pitched and rolled. It kept trying to fall away and Fox had to make huge sweeping thrusts with the steering oar. His clothes were wet through and com-

pletely ruined. Water ran down over him as though he stood
beneath the ship's pump of a three-decker manned by iron-
thewed colossi. He blinked water away from his eyes. Still they
were performing well. The contused knots of waves flung
themselves at the boat. She struggled and reared and the oars
drew back and went down and were dragged through the water.
Slowly, painfully slowly, the boat edged through that wild-
erness of water.

Grey was shouting something but of course the words were
whipped away instantly. Fox cast a single quick glance inboard.
Water sloshed. Someone would have to bale; he would think
about that when they had reached the wreck. The sun was dying
in a crimson violence in the sky that matched the grey and black
and silver violence of the sea.

They were close enough now for him to see a man wave an
arm from the wreck. The next instant everything there was
obscured as a wave burst; when the deck was clear the arm
waved again. The woman in the white dress still clung to the
mizzen; probably she was lashed there.

Now they could match their movements as they rose and fell.
The boat was going up and down an enormous distance and Fox
had to judge his moment. Just to leeward of the wreck and the
fanged rocks a swathe of calmer water stretched like a pocket-
handkerchief, rippling and roiling. Once inside it the motion of
the boat eased. Fox tried to shout his orders and gave up at once.
He would have to rely on hand signals and the native wit of his
crew.

Now came the part of the job where experience would
count. The slightest mistake would take the boat crushing
into the wreck; a misjudgment of the wave pattern as the
rollers surged in to break across the rocks, the swirling
undertow as they poured around the wreck or the thrust
of the wind would take him and his boat's crew to perdition
in a twinkling.

Spray licked and flung across the wreck and the wind drove it
straight into his face. He blinked angrily and stared ahead,
judging his distance, heaving with all his squat strength on the
steering oar. He brought the boat's head around to meet a

jagged wave, saw the patterns coalesce in his mind, and thrust
his head on and up, his chin jutting – he couldn't spare a hand
from the steering oar at this juncture. The men hauled at the
looms with frantic effort. The boat shot ahead, lunging, and as
Fox laid her as near alongside as he dared on the upswing of a
wave the first of the survivors came sliding and sprawling down
the canted wet decks and into the boat. Grey was hauling them
in as he might throw carcasses into a stores lighter. The woman
was being helped down by two men. They more fell onto the
maindeck than used the ladders, which were smashed, in any
case. This vessel had been of that species where quarterdeck
and poop are in one, a merchantman styling, and on the second
swooping run of the boat as it rose on a wave they managed to
contrive the woman into the foresheets. A lad leaped boldly
from the splintered deck as the boat rose. He landed solidly but
lightly, like a cat, and at once scrambled towards the woman.

Here came Grey, clawing his way over the thwarts, putting
his mouth next to Fox's ear, bawling.

"That's all of them, sir. Ten and the woman."

Ten! So few – and yet these were those whom Fox had
consigned to the deep as the unlucky ones. He nodded and
Phillips who was putting his weight onto the steering oar hauled
hard over. Fox wanted to turn within the slightly sheltered
space in lee of the wreck. Only by the most prodigious effort was
he able to succeed. The boat was going up and down like the
pendulum of a runaway clock, leaping from the crests of the
running waves, battered at by the wind, cavorting and surging
and rolling – but they were round and the men were finding the
oars easier to pull so that Fox could concentrate on using them
as balancing mechanisms. The wind and the waves were driving
them forward now in smothers of foam and spray. They must
present a remarkable spectacle to the observers on shore. Most
of the time they must be hidden from view. Then they would
shoot out like a cork, a dark fish-shape hurtling through the
water rather than over it.

If he missed that scrap of relatively calmer beach he'd pile up
on the sea wall. They'd have a period of damned hard pulling
then. He bent over, temporarily releasing the steering oar to

Phillips, got his face alongside Joseph's bristly cheek and
bawled in his ear.

" 'vast pulling . . . Pull on my orders . . ."

Josephs understood the fragmentary half-wind-blown words.
Now Phillips and their captain at the steering oar could do the
work and when Fox felt the boat swinging and moving to
broach to he could nod the oars into giving a few savage strokes
to bring their head back on line again. He wanted to conserve
what strength the men had left. Grey already had the survivors
baling. The woman had someone's coat thrown over her – then
Fox saw it was Grey's boat cloak, for the boy stood with his best
uniform as sodden and ruined as Fox's own.

The memory of that chase when the French frigate had so
relentlessly pursued *Raccoon*, heavily-laden with Lord Kintlesham's marbles of ancient Rome, and Grey had fallen overboard, popped up oddly into Fox's mind. He had risked a very
great deal in backing his foretopsail and lowering the jolly boat
to pick up Grey. The middy had bounded on deck, dripping,
his face shining, and Fox had had to remind himself with some
force that he was a loner, a man apart, a mere Thames
marshboy masquerading as an officer in the Royal Navy, he
who had been a ship's boy, and that between him and these
scions of the upper classes could be no friendship, no affection.
But Grey persisted in regarding Fox with some kind of
possessive pride, as though proud of serving under this short,
unlovely, shabby lieutenant.

The boat surged and heaved sickeningly. The steering oar
thrashed through the water. Spume flew. The bows reared up
and fell away and the bend of the sea wall sped past like a
racehorse. They roared through white water. The balers were
working under the intemperate orders of young Grey. Water
bellowed everywhere. Fox's left eye hinted at a little ring of that
confounded purple and black and he blinked and cursed and the
constriction of sight vanished.

"Now!" he yelled at Phillips, the words quite inaudible in the
uproar.

The steering oar ploughed through the water, the starboard
side oars all gave way with manic tugs, the larboard held in the

water so that they bent beneath the strain and the water built up shining blowing mounds before them.

For an instant as the boat spun Fox thought they were all overset. The boat reeled. Then they shot into the lee of the wall and the wind shrieked past over their heads and left them in a kind of numbed glass sphere of bellowing silence and the bowman was standing up and hauling the boathook out and the bows were touching and, incredibly, it was all over.

Now Fox realised how soaked he was. He shivered. These fancy clothes, shabby already, but his best, were completely ruined. He stomped up onto the stern thwart and, angry and contemptuous of his own feelings, leaped ashore.

"Mr Grey, would you be good enough to have these poor creatures seen to?"

Already people were hurrying down to them. He didn't want, still, to meet the owner of the boat. His men were running her along ready to return her to her place among her fellows. The survivors were crowding up, miserable and numb. The lad was kneeling over the woman in the white dress, who lay on the stones, water trickling away from her. Her face was as white as the dress. The boy was holding her hands. Fox could not see his face; but he recognised with an instant intuitive leap of sympathy, just what it was he was witnessing.

There were many things that must be done; but he hesitated and then went across.

The boy looked up and his face, lean and hungry and with black-smudged pits for eyes, showed like a shining mask of wax in the thickness of the water upon it.

"She's dead," he said. He shook his head, not believing. "Dead – my mother – dead . . ."

George Abercrombie Fox put his hand on the rough wet cloth over the boy's shoulder. He could not find anything to say.

A MIDSHIPMAN
AT COPENHAGEN

John Finlayson

*The following story is something of a novelty as it comes
from an otherwise unpublished set of memoirs by Commander John Finlayson (1786–1845). Finlayson was
enlisted into the Royal Navy in 1798, when he was
only eleven, on HMS St George, a 98-gun second rate
three-decker, which had been built at Portsmouth in
1785 and would ultimately be wrecked off Jutland in
1811. The St George took part in most of the major
Napoleonic naval campaigns and the following is a first-
hand account of the Battle of Copenhagen in 1801. It
was at Copenhagen that Nelson placed his telescope
against his blind eye so as to disobey orders with the
famous remark, "I see no signals."*

In the month of September 1798 we were ordered round to Plymouth to join the Channel Fleet, then under the command of Earl St Vincent.

We sailed from Plymouth in the latter end of the same month, with several other line-of-battle ships to join the Admiral off Ushant, where we remained cruising, watching to prevent the French Fleet escaping. During this time, till the month of December, we had very frequent heavy gales, but our Admiral could never think of bearing up for a port in the channel, and his remark was that none but lubbers would ever do so. However, about the middle of the month, a heavy gale from the south west put us all on the alert, and so hard did it blow, and with so heavy a sea, that all hands were employed nearly the whole of the night in housing the middle-deck guns. The night, I remember, was a very bad one, and our good Captain, who at that time had a severe touch of the gout, was standing with both feet in tubs to keep them dry the greatest part of the night, watching very intensely the movements of the flagship. At daylight the Admiral's ship appeared without her main topmast, and the gale so far mastered him that, on the day becoming clear, he made the signal to bear up for Torbay. Such was the force of the gale that we passed a sloop of war supposed to be the *Vultigem*, and a cutter bottom up.

The fleet anchored in Torbay late in the evening, and the next morning all hands were employed watering, etc., and preparing again for sea. At this time the French Fleet was expected to put to sea every day, and Ireland was reported to be the place of their destination.

On 27 January 1799 our old and highly respected Captain gave me the rating of "Midshipman", which in those days was considered great promotion, the Captains having it in their power to promote those youngsters whom they considered the most deserving. About 10 March, to our regret, he was superseded by Captain Sampson Edwards, an excellent good man, and at the latter end of the same month, the fleet having recruited their water, provisions, etc., put to sea under the command of Lord Bridport, and proceeded to our old cruising ground, off Ushant, where we watched the motions of the French Fleet, expecting they would make a start. But in April, to our great regret, we found that they had actually made their escape from Brest.

Small vessels were despatched in all directions to give information to any and all of His Majesty's Ships they might fall in with, and off we started. God knows it was a good start for us all, after being so long a time cruising off Brest. The only consolation we had had was to take a peep occasionally at our French friends, snugly lying in harbour; yet after all our watching they gave us the slip. We bent our course towards the coast of Ireland, supposing they had made for that country, which was at that time in a very disturbed state. On our way we fell in with a lugger which gave the Admiral information that the French Fleet was bound for Cape Clear. But it appeared that they, instead of making for Ireland, had proceeded towards the westward. Our fleet was augmented to twenty-six sail of the line, many frigates and smaller vessels, but after cruising about for some days the Admiral made up his mind to despatch twelve sail of the line, under the command of Rear-Admiral Sir Charles Cotton, to join Lord Keith off Cadiz, supposing the enemy's fleet had made for that Port.

It was on a Sunday morning all in the beautiful month of May 1799, the signal was made for a Midshipman. It fell to my lot to answer our signal by going on board, and I had orders that all women were to leave the ships immediately, the sailors and officers at this time being allowed to have their wives at sea with them. When I returned on board, the Captain, and others who had their wives on board, were dismayed to learn that they had to leave immediately, and that the *Dolly*, hired cutter, was to take them into the Cove of Cork and land them. By four o'clock in the afternoon all the females were on board this said *Dolly*, and it may be supposed that in twelve sail of the line there were a great many females altogether. Having had the unpleasant job of escorting the Captain's Lady and servant on board, I found that the dear little *Dolly* was as full as any cutter of her size should be, particularly as it was blowing hard for a summer's day, and a very ugly sea running at the time. At six p.m. the *Dolly*, with her valuable cargo on board, parted company for the Cove of Cork and the squadron made sail to the south and west.

The whole of the Midshipmen was thrown into a very great dilemma. The fact was that the sailors' wives were our washerwomen; particularly unfortunate for all, for you must know that Midshipmen had never more rigging than they knew what to do with.

I now began to study the signals and was appointed Signal Midshipman, which I found no sinecure. From daylight until dark were my hours, but one thing which made it easier was my having excellent good glasses.

The *St George* reached the Mediterranean in time to take part in Lord Keith's pursuit of the combined French and Spanish Fleets back through the straits and into the Atlantic. Cadiz was empty. The pursuit continued until, on 13 August, the enemy slipped into Brest, less than twenty-four hours ahead of the unfortunate Keith.

In October we were ordered to Plymouth to refit, for we were so overrun with rats that the beef and pork cask was actually eaten through, and the meat eaten from the bones. The ship, now lying in Cawsand Bay, was cleared as much as possible to give the men a chance to catch the rats, and some dozens were caught in cages purposely made for them.

Our old First Lieutenant was a very strict but good officer, and kept all hands in their proper places. As regards the comfort of the Mids., we were as well off as our pockets would admit, which were not at all times overflowing with cash, although we received our six months' wages regularly when in the channel. Still, we found quite enough to do to make the two ends meet when the pay day came. As for prize money, it was quite out of the question, and as we were at times hard run to obtain a fresh meal when we came into harbour, except the ship's allowance, it was generally salt beef one day, salt pork the other.

From the month of December 1799 until March 1800 we were cruising with the Channel Fleet, occasionally putting into Torbay from disturbance of the weather. About 24 April, Earl St Vincent again took command of the fleet from Lord Bridport. Later, Lord Allen Gardner, with six or seven sail of the line, my old ship being one, was ordered into Plymouth to refit. We considered it was time, and as our Commander-in-Chief was well noted for keeping his ships at sea, we were, as may be supposed, glad to get a little respite from our toils and fagging in the channel. About 15 March we once more joined our comrades off our well-known cruising ground, Ushant, occasionally looking and taking a peep at our old friends the French Fleet. Our cruise was expected to be a very long one, and not a very pleasant one during the winter. We began (we Mids.) to wonder how our wardrobes would stand affliction. On Friday evening after the last dog-watch, plans were laid and we began to take stock, determined that two out of each mess should commence the operation of washing a shirt for each in the pump-well, but a difficulty arose about water; for being so long out of it after a certain time, it was being served so much to each Mess. But what with plundering, and purchasing with grog from one Mess or the other, and a little with peas water, we could manage to rub out pretty decently six or eight shirts, sometimes a dickey or two. White stockings, if not too black or dirty, we could chalk or pipe-clay.

Our mess utensils generally comprised a black bottle for a candlestick, two or three broken pieces of plates, or biscuits as substitutes, one rusty knife, one fork with three prongs, two of which were broken, amongst twelve or fourteen Mids. One of the worst things we were generally put to for was a cloth to boil a plum pudding in. However, finding we could not find a decent cloth, we made shift with a night-cap, taking care it was clean before filled. This was our last resource on the Christmas Day of 1800, when all hands, or nearly so, dined on that day together in the gun-room. About six were lucky in being asked to dine in the Wardroom and with the Captain. It was blowing very hard, and although placed so low as the gun-room is of a three-decker, we found great difficulty in keeping what crockery we could muster on the table.

We youngsters were now obliged to attend very strictly to our schoolmaster, who also held the appointment of chaplain. Our Captain being a great disciplinarian, kept us very closely to our studies, and particularly our navigation, and keeping the ship's way or reckoning, which was on the cabin table every day when at sea by 1.30 p.m.

The schoolmaster was inclined to lift his hand too often to his mouth, and at times could scarcely speak plainly. This soon came to the knowledge of our Captain, and very shortly after he was removed to sick quarters.

About the beginning of February 1801, the ship being re-fitted, we were ordered round to Torbay to join the fleet. We left Cawsand Bay with a fine fresh wind from the north north-west, smooth water and wind offshore, with double-reefed topsails, courses, jib and spanker. About noon, with no warn-ing, we were laid on our beam-ends with a heavy squall. Fortunately the jib-boom, fore-yard, main topmast and cross-jack yard, in one moment went over the side, in the slings, and the ship righted. It was fortunate because there were at the time several of the lee lower deck ports open, so for the short time the ship lay on her side things looked serious. The wreck was very shortly cleared, and we made the best of our way to Torbay, the wind proving more favourable. We anchored, and from the state of our masts and yards, we expected to have been ordered back to Cawsand Bay, but no, our old Earl St Vincent had orders for us that he could not by any possible means allow the ship to be ordered back. The carpenters of the fleet were set to work. A cross-jack and fore-yard were soon replaced, and the news soon flew through the ship that we were to hoist blue at the fore, the flag of Lord Nelson, and that we were to be sent on some secret expedition.

About the 12th, everyone on board was in motion, the flag was hoisted (it having been on board the *San Josef*), and His Lordship joined. Captain Sir Thomas Hardy was appointed and took command of the ship, our old Captain having ex-changed ships.

By a deal of interest, I was allowed to remain on board with several other youngsters. At this time Signal Midshipmen were in great demand, and I was made Signal Mate over four or five youngsters who had joined the ship with His Lordship, about eighteen to twenty youngsters then being our complement. I recollect it was blowing so hard on the day the flag was shifted from the *San Josef* that His Lordship could not leave the ship. Every eye was looking out to see the man whom England had made so much of, and we expected that our expedition, let it be where it may, would still add to England's glory and our Admiral's renown.

About the 20th we sailed from Torbay for Portsmouth. We arrived on the 22nd, and remained until 2 March making preparations for our expedition, when we left for Yarmouth, and arrived at that anchorage on the 6th. My knowledge of the squalls, and His Lordship being very particular in regard to the answering and repeating of signals, brought me more and more every day into the notice of His Lordship. We found, lying in Yarmouth Roads, Admiral Sir Hyde Parker with fifteen sail of the line (small ships about fifty sail). I was now apprenticed Midshipman of the Admiral's Barge, as well as Signal Mate.

His Lordship on the 10th went on shore, where he met with his brother, the Rev. Mr Nelson, who accompanied His Lordship on board and remained on board until the next day when I landed him in the Admiral's Barge.

On the 12th the fleet left Yarmouth Roads for the North Sea. As may be supposed, my attention and exertion was called into practice as regarding the signals. Having two or three very steady, expert men, we managed to receive the approbation of His Lordship, and many times he has patted me on the head, when observing the expedition that was used to give satisfaction. From this time, every day, when the weather would permit, all hands were employed exercising great guns and small arms, hoping the time would not be long before we should have occasion to put our improvements in that respect into practice.

However, we had some heavy weather until, on the 18th, we made the Naze of Norway, when the weather became more favourable, and the whole of the fleet, ships of the line, frigates and gun brigs, innumerable again, were nearly collected. We may have passed through the sound, but for what reason no one could tell, but the disappointment was very perceptible in His Lordship's movement and gesture.

On the 21st it blew hard, and the whole of the fleet anchored for twenty-four hours and did not arrive off Elsinore until the 24th. Our ambassador, the Hon. Mr Vansittart, had proceeded to Elsinore and returned to the fleet on the day we anchored. The terms they had offered, not being accepted, they parted for England on the 25th. By this time, everyone was on tiptoe, preparation making, etc.

The wind now was strong and favourable, and it was expected that the Admiral would have taken advantage and have passed through. While these delays were going on, His Lordship was very anxious, and a council of war having been held on board the *London*, it was determined that the fleet should proceed through the belt.

On the 26th the whole fleet weighed, with the intention of proceeding through the belt, and had not gone far along the coast of Zealand, before some of the small craft got on the rocks. On this His Lordship proceeded on board the *London*. After some time consulting Admiral Sir Hyde Parker in the forenoon, the plan was changed, and the whole of the fleet returned to its former anchorage. The greatest number of the gun brigs were commanded by some of the oldest lieutenants in the service.

On the 27th a flag of truce was sent on shore at Elsinore to the Governor, but on its return it was said that terms could not be arranged. The *Elephant* (Captain Foley), which had joined the fleet on the 26th, brought us the melancholy intelligence of the loss of His Majesty's Ship *Invincible*, Rear Admiral Totty, on a sand-bank off Yarmouth.

On the 29th His Lordship shifted his flag from the *St George* to the *Elephant*. On his Lordship leaving the ship, he called me from the poop, and turning to Captain Hardy, asked how long I had served. I replied two years and upwards. His Lordship patted me on the head and said, "We must leave you for a future day. However, Hardy," said His Lordship, "as Mr Gill, who has only joined the ship a few days, was strongly recommended, let him go instead of the youngster," (meaning myself), "but the boats of the reserve squadron will be assisting in the battle. Let him go in any of the boats he may wish himself."

At this time, as may be supposed, everyone was on the alert, and expecting every hour we should be engaged with the

Danish or Swedish batteries. The whole fleet at this time was perfectly clear for battle, and as may be supposed, knowing the request of His Lordship to Captain Hardy, I was all alive as to what boat I should like best.

On the 30th, a breeze from the north west sprang up, which would carry us through the sound. The fleet was soon under way, and formed into the order of battle previously arranged. It was a beautiful sight to see the old ship in such state, and everyone ready to do their duty to their king and country in upholding the dignity of both.

Although we had not His Lordship's flag flying, still my anxiety, as regarded the answering and repeating of signals, was as much as ever. I was told that his ship, meaning the *St George*, would still bear the credit of repeating signals.

The morning of the 30th was a beautiful one. The *Edgar*, with the fleet of bomb and gun-vessels, had taken up her position the day before off Cronenburgh Castle, ready to give the Danes a dose, should the batteries molest us in passing.

The moment the Danes saw our fleet was determined to pass the sound and had formed the line and made sail, they, about 10 a.m., opened their fire on our leading ships. At the same time the *Edgar*, and her fleet of bombs, etc., opened their fire on the batteries. Our ship was stationed nearly in the centre of the line, astern of the Commander-in-Chief, and certainly it was one of the most beautiful sights possible to see such a noble fleet, in spite of the Danish batteries, passing with that ease, as if nothing was going on. The Swedish batteries remaining silent, gave the fleet an opportunity of keeping more on the Swedish shore. By that means, the headmost kept more over towards it, out of reach of the Danes, which kept up heavy fire of shot and shell, our ships occasionally giving them a shot in return, but finding neither did any harm, nor indeed did the Danish shot, although falling in showers a cable length from the fleet. It was certainly a laughable thing to hear the remarks of our tars when the shot or shell fell short.

About midday the whole of the fleet came to an anchor between the Island of Huen and Copenhagen. So soon as the fleet had anchored, the Commander-in-Chief, with His Lord-

ship and several Captains, left in the barge to reconnoitre the
Danish Harbour. We found they were prepared for us by the
number of floating batteries, etc., which appeared to be moored
for the protection of the city and arsenal.

The night also of the 30th was employed by some of our most
intelligent masters and pilots, several of whom we had brought
from England with us, in sounding and laying down fresh
buoys, the Danes having removed the old ones or misplaced
them to mislead our fleet.

On 1 April we were in hopes we should have made an April
Fool of the Danes, but the fore part of the day was employed as
the day previous in asserting the exact position of the shoals as
well as the number of ships we should have to contend with.

In the afternoon a council of war was held on board the
London, the Commander-in-Chief's ship. The intelligence we
had from the *London* was that Nelson was or had been much
vexed by some difficulty having been made as to the mode of
attack. His Lordship, having made up his mind, offered his
services, and without any more hesitation the Commander-in-
Chief gave him two more line of battle ships than he requested,
with the frigates, bombs, and gun-brigs.

We had increased our number of youngsters to about twenty-
two, and His Lordship having shifted on board the *Elephant*,
most of them found that they came short of a good breakfast, so
when His Lordship was on board, never less than four, with the
Signal Midshipman, sat down to breakfast. The whole number
generally that sat down to breakfast was from twelve to fourteen.

On the afternoon of the 1st, His Lordship with his squadron
weighed and took up his position near the shoal which lay
between him and the Danish Flotilla. The Commander-in-
Chief with his squadron also the next morning (2 April)
weighed and attempted to take the position that His Lordship
had left the night before, but the wind during the night had
changed.

About 7 a.m. the signal was made for all boats to be in
readiness for service. I, of course, was on the alert, and had
some days previously provided myself with the arms and

ammunition that was usually required. About 8 o'clock the
Commander-in-Chief made the signal to anchor the ships, not
being able to make way against a strong current and a head
wind. I was sent for by Capt. Hardy. He said, "Well, youngster,
are you prepared for your expedition? Recollect His Lordship
promised you should have your choice to go in any boat you
pleased." I had made up my mind before, and informed the
Capt. that if he had no objection I should prefer the Admiral's
barge. We had three boats which were to go and assist on board
any ship that might require them. Nelson's division at this time
getting under way, the signal was made by the Commander-in-
Chief for all boats appointed for particular service to assemble
alongside the *London* to receive their orders. Those of us who
had, as we called it, the good luck to be ordered or allowed to go
in the boats, went round and took our leave by shaking hands
with our messmates, and I with one who was very dear to me,
with a very strong injunction to do my duty, and obey most
strongly any orders I might receive from my superior officers.
At 9 a.m. the boats had assembled alongside the Commander-
in-Chief's ship the *London*. We were ordered to proceed on
board the *Elephant*, provided we could pull up against the tide
and wind, but at a time like this our brave tars, twenty in
number, at the oars, gave their whole might and strength to
their work. Our crew consisted of the twenty seamen at the oars,
one coxswain, one sergeant and six marines, one lieutenant and
myself.

We had got about half-way to the fighting squadron when the
action began, and that, if possible, increased the exertions of our
boats' crews to get on board the *Elephant* for instructions. As we
approached the battle I felt rather curious in my inside, but the
closer we got, the more confident I felt. We at last got within
range of the Danish shot, which began to pass over us and fall in
all directions around us. I was sitting on the larboard side of the
Lieutenant, who sat in the centre of the stern-sheets, and the
Sergeant of Marines on my left. We were cheering our lads up,
when in a moment a spent shot, a twelve-pounder, struck the
Sergeant in the back and knocked the breath out of him. He fell
in the bottom of the boat and never either spoke or moved. This

was a great shock to me. I scarcely knew what I said or did. The Lieut in a jocular way said, "Well, youngster, what think you of this?" I said I should think much better of it if he would allow me to exchange places, as I thought the next shot might take me as quickly as it had the Sergeant out of the world. However, the Lieut would not exchange places with me, and I thought his ideas may have been something like my own as regards the next shot.

"Now, youngster," says he, "feel the Sergeant's pulse; see if he is dead or not." However, I tried the wrist, and pronounced him dead, quite dead. As this was no time to think about burying the dead as we should have wished, we threw the Sergeant overboard, wishing him a safe passage to the "other world".

We arrived alongside the *Elephant* in the middle of the battle. We were all except two boat-keepers ordered on the quarter deck, and I observed His Lordship walking up and down giving directions, when the Signals Officer told His Lordship that the Commander-in-Chief had No. 39 flying, and after a few moments I heard His Lordship ask if No. 16 was hoisted. Knowing the signals and considering myself still His Lordship's Signal Midshipman, although not taken aboard with him, for reasons already named, I was anxious to see and hear all I could, and was asked by His Lordship if the signals, said to be flying on board the *London* were correct. I said "Yes," and just at this moment who should be carried along but poor Gill, who had taken my place as Signal Midshipman. However, he was not so seriously hurt, and after some time returned again to his duty. This was a dreadful sight to me, who had never seen a shot fired in anger before, and what with the poor fellows falling and the shot from the Danes, I thought I should never return again to my old friends or shipmates. We were then ordered to take a message to the *Glatton*, and in so doing it was wonderful how we escaped the shot that flew in all directions. The whole of the time I thought of nothing but the quick death of the Sergeant.

On our return on board the *Elephant*, about noon (the Danes at this time were slackening their fire and many were drawing out, burning and disabled), we, with other ships' boats, were ordered to assist the prizes, and to pick up as many as possible of the poor Danes, who were jumping overboard from the blazing hulks. We saved a great many, some without arms or legs, and others in some way or other dreadfully wounded, and put them on board for the moment on the first ship we could get near.

Observing one of the Danish line-of-battle ships drifting from the scene of action towards the anchorage, we were, with the *London*'s barge, ordered to take possession of her. On our receiving this order, it came to a good race between the two barges which should have the honour of first boarding her. However, the race was even, and both boats threw their oars up at the same time. Our boat being next the ship, the trial was then between myself and the youngster of the *London*'s boat, each being forward with the boat-hook, ready to hook on to the ship, so as to have the first chance of getting up the side. The youngster either by accident or purpose contrived to strike me in the mouth with his boat-hook, which broke one of my teeth and cut my lip very much. However, I succeeded in reaching the quarter deck before him. My Lieut having taken possession and finding no anchor on board, our time was employed in preparing to bring the ship up with two of her maindeck guns and hawsers. When this had been effected we had time to look around us. It is impossible to describe the state of her cockpit and 'tweendecks with the dead, dying and wounded, it appearing that the doctors had left their stations in the heat of the battle. However, my friends began to laugh at the idea of my being wounded in the mouth, a circumstance I had forgotten in the bustle. On seeing my friend, the youngster, I put the question as to his depriving me of one of my teeth. His reply being anything but what I considered it should be, I told him I should not put up with such conduct, and being backed by my own shipmates I thought I could do no less than shew him I had a spirit above slavery and challenged him to try who was the best man. Off jackets and to it we went. This was on the main deck, and after a few rounds I found I had the best of it by his giving in, but not before both having had a few rolls among the dead and wounded, and as may be supposed, our clothes shewed good proof that we had been attempting to swab the decks with them. After a short time we were brought together and shook hands, then turned to and assisted each other in cleaning our clothes as well as we could. We left the ship in charge of those sent on purpose, and in the evening joined our old ship again.

The next morning His Lordship again hoisted his flag: in the meantime he had paid his respects to the Crown Prince, in conjunction with several of his Captains.

While waiting for the settling of the armistice we were preparing to lighten the ship by discharging the greatest part of our guns and provisions. However, the youngsters, not having much to do, we on Thursday, it being a very fine day, asked permission of our First Lieut to man the barge and take a pull to stretch our arms. About 1 p.m., off we started. Being in my fifteenth year and the oldest out of eighteen, I took command of the helm, and away we started towards the crown battery, which was distant about three miles, and we pulled slowly round the battery between it and two fine 74s, Danish, moored inside. We had passed outside some distance, when we to our surprise heard a whiz pass over our heads, and looked astern whence we supposed the ball had come, when whiz came another, which we observed had been fired from a small boat pulling in great haste after us. Thinking we had now got ourselves into a scrape, we lay on our oars until the said boat approached, apparently a man-of-war's boat, Danish, with a pendant in the bow. After a short time we heard someone hail us, "Boat ahoy, you must come with us to the Commodore." Keeping some distance away, we talked it over among ourselves, when I, having to give the casting vote, very politely asked our Danish friend that if he would come alongside we would take him in style on board his Commodore. But, shrugging his shoulders, he begged to be excused. Finding we had the heels of them, we took him in tow, and by his directions proceeded as fast as we could towards the Commodore, who had his flag on board a very fine and, to outward appearance, handsome ship. It was not long before we were tossing our oars alongside, and from the laughter we heard from the Officers and ship's company, they appeared to like the joke of sixteen youngsters towing a small boat with only four men and one officer alongside of their own ship, for before we came near the Officer begged we would cast off the tow, but no, alongside we went. An Officer in uniform on the gangway spoke to us in very good English, saying he would send two seamen down to take care of the boat, which was done, and as I was the coxswain, it was agreed that I should mount the side and show my boat's crew the way. Up we went and were received on the quarter deck by several officers in their uniform. One, who appeared to be the Commodore, and in full dress, approached us and shook hands and welcomed us on board. "But," said he, "young gentlemen, I am very sorry that I shall be under the necessity of detaining you all as my prisoners until I hear or have orders from my sovereign to set you at liberty." From those words, some of my boat's crew began to pipe their eye. I said, "Perhaps, sir, you are not aware that we are Lord Nelson's youngsters, and only on a cruise for part time." He said, "I am very sorry, but I must do my duty, and while I send on shore for instruction my First Lieut will show you all round my ship." I thought this was all very well and I began to think the next pleasant thing we should have imposed on us would be to put us under the care of a Marine.

However, we followed the Officer, after thanking the Commodore for his politeness. After going round her 'tween-decks and seeing everything that could be seen, which was not a very great novelty to us, on the quarter deck we mounted, when we were again received by the Commodore, and by him very politely taken into the cabin, where lo and behold, to our very great surprise, we found a table laid out with a profusion of all kinds of fruit and wine. Addressing himself to us, "Now," said he, "young gentlemen, allow me the pleasure of taking a glass of wine with you all; sit down and take some fruit." We said we were very much obliged but if he had no objection we would drink his health and take our departure, for it was now growing late. "Yes," said he, "you appear to be a fine set of young lads, ready for anything, and as you no doubt were not aware of the articles of the armistice I shall allow you to depart," and shaking us all by the hands he bade us, "good afternoon."

As you may suppose, we were not very long resuming our seats, and once more started for our old ship. On going on board, we were all summoned before the Captain, who after hearing our story gave us a severe reprimand, with strict orders not to be allowed a boat for pulling again for some time.

On going down to our berth in the cockpit, and telling our story to the oldsters, we had a regular three cheers for the old Commodore, and promised that if ever he should come our way we would treat him in the same way he had Nelson's youngsters. Perhaps if not in wine and fruit, it would be some good old rum and salt pork, if nothing better happened to be in the lockers.

Our fleet was at this time refitting and preparing for further service, and it was not many days before the whole squadron was reported ready. The fleet, under the command of Sir Hyde Parker, Commander-in-Chief, took the opportunity of a fair wind and crossed the shoals. The *St George* drawing so much water, it was found necessary that we should be lightened, and word was sent for an American ship lying at the mole dismantled and waiting for a cargo. The Captain, not wishing to give his ship for the service we required him for, we sent the boats of the ship and brought her out. At the same time as the rest of the boats' crews were getting topmast on end and preparing the ship for sea, some of the boats towed the American ship alongside. By this time the rest of the fleet had passed over the grounds. We here can show what British sailors can do. With the American ship we had five brigs, bomb tenders, also alongside, and everything being prepared, the hands were turned up, commenced discharging the lower and upper deck guns, shot, water and provisions, and by noon the vessel and tenders were all under way. With a fair wind we crossed the shoals, anchored again at 4 p.m. and commenced discharging the tenders.

At 10 p.m. news came that the Swedish Fleet was out. His Lordship immediately ordered his gig, with six men, his Cox-swain and Mr Bradley, the Master of the *Edgar*, and left for Bornholm, which place the squadron was cruising off. On His Lordship leaving the ship, many were the good wishes for his safe arrival on board the *Elephant*, his old ship, on board of which he had won so many laurels. The *St George*, in the meantime, anchored in Kirge Bay with the squadron, weighed under the Commander-in-Chief's orders and was making the best of its way towards Revel. On the *St George* joining the squadron again under Nelson he again hoisted his flag. The Swedes, having returned into port, after hearing of the death of the Russian Emperor, the whole of our fleet sailed for Kirge Bay, when a few days after Sir Hyde Parker received orders to return to England.

As you may suppose, it was to the delight of the whole fleet when the news became known that His Lordship was to take command.

Sir Hyde Parker in a day or two left the fleet and made sail for England, so, as soon as he was out of sight, the signal was made to prepare for sailing and to hoist in all launches. By this time our mosquito fleet of gun brigs, etc., had disappeared; consequently my duty became less arduous regarding them, and as Commander-in-Chief's ship we had then only to make instead of repeating signals.

On 7 May the fleet weighed and made sail for the island of Bornholm, where they anchored. It was blowing very hard. Leaving part of the fleet here, His Lordship proceeded with ten sail of the line, two brigs and one schooner, for the port of Revel.

On the 12th we anchored in the outer roads, and found that only three days before our arrival the Russian Fleet had left for Cronstadt. Our Admiral sent on shore to know if they would return a salute, if given, which was answered in the affirmative; but after the salute had been given, for some time none was returned. However, this delay or neglect was not to be passed over by His Lordship, who sent an officer on shore to know the cause. The reply was that the officer of the fort had neglected to do so, and was put under arrest. However, the salute was returned, but at a late hour, and by the request of His Lordship the officer was released.

On the 13th His Lordship went on shore and dined with the Governor. In the meantime, all hands were employed watering and receiving supplies of fresh meat and vegetables, and as you may suppose, the soft tommy stood no chance with the "Mid".

On the 14th all bustle to receive the Governor, he promising to return the visit. He was accompanied by a very young officer commanding a regiment of hussars. Every attention was paid to him and other military officers in showing them the inside of a British man-of-war.

It appeared from what we could learn that His Lordship had sent a letter to St Petersburgh, for on the 16th an answer was received. I recollect well being at His Lordship's table when the letter arrived; he appeared very much agitated, and in the middle of dinner he retired to his after cabin, and in the space of a quarter of an hour returned again. The signal was made to prepare for sea. The fleet weighed in the evening without waiting for the supply of fresh provisions which had been contracted for. This quick movement of His Lordship's struck everyone that things were not or had not been going on in a satisfactory manner. However, the fleet stood off for the night; there being only two or three hours dark a brig was left at Revel to bring the provisions after the fleet. In the morning the fleet proceeded down the Baltic, and when off Bornholm we were joined by a squadron under Captain Murray. His Lordship then sent a detachment for Kirge Bay, to procure provisions and water. Another detachment was sent to Rostock for the same purpose, and His Lordship with the remainder of the fleet proceeded to Rostock.

The great attention paid by His Lordship to the comforts of the ships' crews was very remarkable, he frequently causing a small quantity of almost every article of provision when fresh supplied to be put on his own table.

His general hour for rising was from four to five o'clock, when he expected everything on the upper decks to be in order, particularly the poop, the front of which was his quarter deck until breakfast, which took place at six a.m. This meal I was invariably invited to, and the company generally amounted to from ten to twelve, His Lordship frequently passing his jokes, keeping all hands laughing, so that I frequently wished he would leave his jokes for some other time, but while on deck he would keep the bunting in motion. His dinner-table was well kept, and the whole of the ship was expected to be in order by eight o'clock, thus giving the whole of the day for exercise or anything else that might be required.

On our return to Bornholm, the Russian frigate *Venus*, with an Admiral's flag, met us with despatches for His Lordship. The *Latona* also, with Lord St Helens, met us on his way to St Petersburgh.

At Rostock no time was lost in procuring a supply of provisions and water. The moment it was known that Nelson was in the roads, many of the inland towns sent deputations with their record books to have His Lordship's name written by himself, and with many invitations for him to land, but he never landed while in the Baltic. Boats were continually roaming round our ship the *St George* with persons of respectability in them to catch a momentary sight of him.

The day after our arrival, 26 May, a Russian lugger joined with despatches from the Emperor, as we understood, a reply from those His Lordship had forwarded from Revel. I always found plenty of employment at the signals, and if the barge was sent away I had the honour of being in her. On the lugger leaving the fleet with an answer to the despatches he had brought, he fired a salute. I recollect His Lordship asking Mr Davon if he heard that little fellow salute, meaning the lugger. "Well," says he, "there is now peace with Russia, depend on it." By this time we had got clear of nearly all our mosquito fleet, the gun brigs, the greatest plague I had, for in making the signal for one of their Lieutenants there was generally two or three who would answer the signal, and when they came on board and were told they were not wanted, His Lordship would laugh most heartily and say it would do those old gentlemen, meaning the Lieutenants, good to have a pull before breakfast, and would frequently invite some to stay and breakfast with him.

After being at anchor some days off Rostock we were getting under way for Kirge Bay when we received the intelligence that the Duke of Mecklenburgh-Strelitz, the Queen's brother, was on his journey to visit His Lordship, and shortly after His Royal Highness was received on board with all the attention the sudden visit could give time for, and His Lordship accompanied him throughout the ship.

On the 5 or 6 June we returned to Kirge Bay, but remained there only a few days to complete our water, which could not be done in Rostock Bay. From what we could learn, His Lordship intended very shortly to return home, much to the regret of the whole fleet. We made our last cruise with His Lordship's flag on board between 9 and 13 June off Bornholm, on which day the orders were received from His Majesty to invest Rear Admiral Graves with the Order of the Bath, and the sanction of the Admiral for His Lordship to return to England.

On 14 June every preparation was made to carry His Majesty's instructions into effect, and Admiral Graves, being in a very ill state of health, he was assisted up the side, and immediately invested by His Lordship laying the sword on the Rear Admiral's shoulder in the name of the King. He accompanied this with a very dignified and animated speech. This was the last good action His Lordship performed in the Baltic Sea.

Sir Charles Maurice Pole arrived a few days afterwards in a frigate, and received the chief command. Lord Nelson's resignation was attended with infinite regret to the whole fleet, and there appeared a deep depression of spirits upon the occasion, and not more so than with myself, although on his leaving the ship he told me he hoped I should continue to hold that good name I had gained from my strict attention to my duty, that Captain Hardy was going to remain, and would not lose sight of me while on board. Sir Charles was accompanied by Captain Nichol as Captain of the Fleet, Captain Hardy as Captain of the Ship. The orders of thanks and of praise to the fleet on his leaving will never be forgotten by those who had the honour of sailing under his orders, and I saw many tears starting from the eye of many a good sailor and officer on the flag being struck and hoisted on board the *Kite* brig on 19 June, showing that he had the good of the country at heart, not wishing to deprive the service of a fine frigate.

THE BATTLE
OF ELEPHANT BAY

Richard Butler

The tendrils of the Napoleonic Wars stretched far afield. There was a brief lull in Anglo-French hostilities following the Treaty of Amiens on 25 March 1802, but it was an uncertain peace. In the far colonies, where news took far to travel, no one could be sure just what games the French were playing. So it was with considerable distrust that the English in Australia viewed the appearance of the French Le Géographe, *purportedly on a scientific expedition to chart the coast. It led to a little-known incident which is amusingly recounted here.*

Richard Butler was born and educated in England and emigrated to Australia in 1963. He taught in Tasmania and Victoria until the publication of his fourth novel, The Buffalo Hook *(1974), when he embarked on a dual career as a writer and professional actor. He has published nineteen books including the historical novels* The Men That God Forgot *(1975),* A Blood-Red Sun at Noon *(1980) and* The Devil's Coachman *(1981).*

As dawn flushed the eastern sky with pink, the vessel materialized like a ghost ship, wallowing drunkenly on the Pacific swell under a flapping, ragged foretopsail and jib. Long ribbons of weed trailed astern and, as the winter sun came up, the lookout on South Head, the entrance to Port Jackson, could see that the flush deck was deserted apart from the skeletal figure in rags that clung to the helm. "Christ Almighty!" He stared down in superstitious awe. It was like a hulk out of Hell, doomed to sail the seas until the end of time. "What d'yer make o'that, Mr Long?"

The Petty Officer stared through his glass and whistled through his teeth. "Never seen no barky come 'ere in that state, I ain't. No colours but she ain't one of ourn."

"What, then?"

"Frenchie – they build thirty-gun corvettes like that. And one thing's for sure – she ain't a-goin' to get through the Heads on that tack, not nohow." He snapped the telescope shut. "Signal the settlement, Jem."

In the study of Government House 4 miles down the harbour, the round-faced, balding Captain Philip Gidley King, R.N., was engaged in the discouraging task of composing dispatches for London that would be out of date when they arrived. As indeed were those he received, so that news had only recently reached him concerning the Peace of Amiens that had ended the war with France in March 1802, three months earlier. He was interrupted by a loud crash as his door burst open, followed by the somewhat unconventional entry of a naval officer on his hands and knees.

The portly Governor sighed and laid down his pen. Not for the first time, he wondered why he hadn't put the fellow on a ship for England years ago. Trubshaw, tall and gangling with protuberant blue eyes, was still a midshipman at the age of thirty-six, being as clumsy as an ox and almost as witless. But at the same time he was so likable and desperately eager to please that it was difficult to chastise him. King said, with the rounded vowels of his native Cornwall, "I beg you will not carry ceremony to excess, Mr Trubshaw. Remember that I am but the Governor of New South Wales, not the Cham of

Tartary, so prostration is unnecessary. A simple bow will suffice."

"My apologies, sir." Scarlet-faced, the tall Acting Lieutenant Percival Trubshaw scrambled to his feet. He had come out to New Holland in '88 with King who, when made Governor, had awarded him his unofficial rank and taken him on as his aide, knowing that sometimes loyalty, honesty and industry can be of far more value than brains. "I tripped, sir –"

"Just so. And?"

"And fell against the door which flew open, thus –"

"Dammit, sir, what is the purpose of your visit?"

"The purpose, sir? To be sure. Purpose. Ah, yes. Sir, Lieutenant Curtis sends his duty and desires to report a French corvette in difficulty off the Heads. He requests permission for me to take a boat out and bring her in."

"You?" After twenty-four years in the navy. Trubshaw could handle a boat as well as the next but he hated the French as a dog hates cats. "Very well. But I trust you will remember that, although French, they are nonetheless distressed mariners?"

"Depend upon it, sir, I shall treat the crapauds just as if they were ordinary human beings."

"She's almost certainly one of Nicolas Baudin's corvettes, *Le Géographe* or *Le Naturaliste*. They are on a scientific expedition. You recall that Lieutenant Flinders met Captain Baudin at Encounter Bay last April?"

"Indeed, sir. How fitting he should meet them in a bay of that name!"

King sighed again. "It was because of that encounter that Flinders named the bay. Off you go, then. And take Scoggin as your coxswain." It might be wise to have the fatherly Scoggin on hand just in case . . .

"Aye, aye, sir." Trubshaw gave a jerky bow, hesitated as if unsure what to do next and then exited awkwardly through the door.

King raised his eyes heavenward and then returned to his paperwork.

*   *   *

The Frenchman was perilously close to the foot of South Head when Trubshaw took his launch out into the Pacific swell. "Silly buggers! Caught on a lee shore," he said. "Pull hard, now, lads! We should just do it!"

But it was a close-run thing. The white surf seemed a proverbial biscuit-toss away as the dozen seamen swarmed up the corvette's side and ran to the braces. But, as the flapping sails tautened, the sea began to chuckle along the salt-stained hull and the Frenchman heeled, her bow swinging obediently towards the harbour entrance. Trubshaw went below. then came back hurriedly, his handkerchief to his nose.

Scoggin had relieved the semi-conscious helmsman. "Lucky we got the wind dead astern, sir."

"You're right! A Chinese river scow ain't in it!"

Governor King was waiting on the jetty when Trubshaw went ashore followed by two French officers and a civilian. "Sir, may I name Lieutenant Henry Guss . . . Gusset."

One of them coughed diffidently. "I am Lieutenant Jean-Paul Marais." He was young, good-looking and spoke excellent English. "This is Lieutenant Henri Guisset and this Monsieur Aristide Legaillon."

"Of the corvette *Lee Geography*," Trubshaw said. "Gentlemen, this is Captain King, Governor of His Majesty's Colony of New South Wales." As they made their bow Trubshaw added, "Lieutenant Gusset is their First Officer. Monsewer Leg-Iron is a naturalist. They say they are the only fit men left on board."

If they are fit, God save the rest, King thought. He turned to rap out an order to a passing overseer. All three were unshaven and filthy, their clothes white with salt. The First Officer was sagging with exhaustion. Marais was deathly pale. Legaillon's face, bony and black-bearded, showed the sores of the early stages of scurvy. "You must report to the infirmary directly, gentlemen. What of Captain Baudin?"

"Sir, he sends his regrets that illness prevents him from waiting upon you," Marais said. "He suffers from the dysentery."

Legaillon, tall and stooped, said haltingly, "There was much sickness when your Lieutenant Flinders came aboard in April but *Capitaine* Baudin wished to conceal it. Then, when we the scientists persuade 'im we mus' make for Port Jackson, 'e sail round Van Diemen's Land. The weather, it was very bad. Many men dead –" He broke off to watch the overseer bring up a gang of convicts, who began to carry the sick men ashore on stretchers.

"You went south of Van Diemen's Land?" King said, astonished. "Did he not know of the passage through the Bass Strait that would have saved him weeks?"

"First Officer Guisset, 'e protest but the Captain does not listen. The sickness also was caused by neglect of the Captain –"

King cut in. "Indeed?" It was contrary to naval etiquette for him to listen to such criticism, much less take part in it. "Lieutenant Trubshaw will escort you to the hospital, gentlemen." To Trubshaw: "Then I should be obliged if you would attend me at Government House."

On the way to Dawes Point, Marais made polite conversation. The other two tramped along in silence. At the clean, airy hospital, the Scottish Chief Surgeon Balmain examined them, then ordered them to bed. "I canna for the life of me understand why ye havena been taking lime juice," he said. "Ye'll be astonished how quickly scurvy yields to anti-scorbutic treatment."

Marais protested that he was not ill, but was given a nightshirt like the others. He was scarcely in bed when an uncommonly good-looking girl in a high-necked grey gown came in with a mug. She offered it without a word, without a smile.

"What is it?"

"Ha! So ye speak English." She was tall for a girl and slim, her skin clear and slightly tanned. She had hair like polished copper and the greenest eyes he'd ever seen.

He said, "My mother was English. What is it?"

"It's only the juice of limes, for Heaven's sake! D'ye think we'd poison ye?"

He took the mug and drank, wrinkling his face at the sourness. "Thank you, pretty one." She was certainly pretty – even beautiful – and should be readily available, since nurses, like actresses, were only one step removed from harlots. "I am not ill, you understand? Perhaps tonight, when your duty is finished and you are free, we might meet –"

"I'm never free."

"Never? But you do not work always?"

"Not always. The regulations allow me time to sleep and eat." She smiled bleakly. "This is a prison colony, remember."

"*Que diable!* Then you are . . . that is to say – ?"

She shrugged. "That is to say, I'm a convicted felon." And went out, her skirt swaying gracefully.

Trubshaw found the Governor drinking sherry with Major Francis Grose, Commandant of the New South Wales Corps. "Pray help yourself to a glass, Mr Trubshaw," King said. "You've had a hard forenoon watch. I fear. What does the Chief Surgeon have to say about our French guests?"

"That, if they take lime juice, they'll be well in no time. If you ask me, I think they're gammoning us. Coming it the sick-bay moocher."

The Governor frowned. "Come now, Lieutenant, they're not malingering, they're really sick. I am unable to comprehend how any Captain could allow scurvy to gain such a grip."

Grose, resplendent in his scarlet and yellow, said, "Lieutenant Flinders told me that Baudin lost fifty deserters at Mauritius. No authority, eh? Just bear-leader for a band of crackbrained scientists. Seems harmless enough."

"Never trust Johnny Crapaud, Major!" Trubshaw's slightly protuberant blue eyes were filled with patriotic fervour. He waved a hand, spraying himself with sherry. "Mark my words, this scientific expedition's all my eye! They're here to spy out the land!"

"Indeed?" King sipped his sherry calmly. "To what end?"

"The seizure of the Colony, sir! They're the spearhead of an invasion fleet!"

Grose stared. "That's coming it a bit high, don't you think? We are at peace, after all."

"Peace? Ha! You may think me somewhat septic, Major –"

"Septic?" The Governor raised an eyebrow. "I hope not."

"Sceptic, then. Doubting, like that Thomas cove. But all the world knows that this so-called peace is merely a truce. Arranged, in my opinion, by that cunning First Consul Bonaparte so that he may rebuild the fleet that our heroic Nelson savaged at the Nile and Copenhagen."

"Possibly so, Lieutenant," King said. "But a truce suits our book as well, d'ye see, since My Lord Sidmouth and the Tories desire a breathing space in which to repair our shattered finances."

"That's as may be, sir. But why does Boney need a fleet if he fights on land, eh? Why, it is because he wishes to build an empire and to do that you must command the seas. The Frogs failed in India and Canada fifty years ago. Bonaparte failed in Egypt in '98. Now the wretch has his eye on New Holland." He swigged what was left of his sherry.

King said. "Hardly likely, Lieutenant." He saw the Major grin disbelievingly behind Trubshaw's back. "But now it is turned two o'clock. So, gentlemen, perhaps you would do me the honour of dining with Mrs King and me?"

Lieutenant Marais, suffering only from debilitation, was discharged after two days. In that time, he had made no attempt to further his acquaintance with the red-haired nurse. *A convict! Who knows what crimes she has committed?* But, as he was leaving, she came in to change his bed. "So ye're off then?" she said.

"Yes." He inclined his head politely. "I must thank you for taking care of me."

A shrug. " 'Tis nought. Ye'll be going home?"

"*Oui.* It will be good to see France again."

"In spite of the state it's in?"

"What do you mean?" He stared at her.

"I mean ye aimed at Liberty, Equality and Fraternity and what have ye got? Your King and Queen murdered, a reign of terror and your leaders squabbling while your people starve. It was your precious revolution that sent me to this place."

"How so?"

"Me father and I belonged to the United Irishmen Movement. We believed all the lies you French told us. We supported Wolfe Tone's rebellion of '98 after we'd been promised French aid." Her lovely face flushed at the recollection. "There was no aid. We were tried for treason and told we were lucky to be transported instead of hanged."

"*Alors*, your father is here?"

She said brutally, "Aye, in the cemetery."

"I am very sorry."

"He's better off where he is." She looked at the door. "Ye'd best be going."

"You never told me your name."

"Ye never asked. It's Sheilagh O'Rourke."

"I am Jean-Paul Marais."

"I know. It's on the register." She held out a hand. "Goodbye, Lieutenant." Her grip felt strong and firm.

"*Au 'voir*. Until I see you again."

"It's hardly likely." Boots were heard in the passage. "Go now."

Outside, he bowed to Governor King, Lieutenant Trubshaw and the Chief Surgeon, on their way to pay a call on Captain Baudin.

They found him staring morosely at the ceiling. As he began to sit up: "*Non, non!*" King said. "*Ne vous* – that is to say, do not disturb yourself – *déranger* . . . Damnation! How's your French, Balmain?"

"Not as good as yours, sir."

"I speak a little the English." Baudin propped himself up, a small, narrow-shouldered man with a long nose and black eyes like boot buttons. King thought he looked somewhat like a field-mouse.

"Excellent!" King said. Introductions were performed. The Surgeon excused himself and left.

Baudin said, "I thank you for your 'ospitality of the most generous, *Monsieur le Gouverneur*. Also I offer my excuses for no salute with guns when we enter the 'arbour".

"Why, sir, pray do not mention it, I beg."

"Be seated, if you please." King sat on the only chair,

Trubshaw behind him, eyeing Baudin suspiciously. "We 'ave 'ad an unfortunate voyage. Many men lost. But I 'ave a good crew, good officers. Guisset, Marais – good men."

"That is certainly a compensation. May I inquire if you have completed your scientific researches?"

"*Oui*. We 'ave collected the plants, noted the animals –"

"And drawn charts, sir, no doubt?" Trubshaw asked meaningly.

"*Bien sûr*."

"And what are your plans, sir?" King asked.

"Why, to return to France, *naturellement*, as soon as possible."

As Surgeon Balmain had said, recovery from scurvy was usually swift. Apart from one death, all the French were discharged from hospital within the week, although many had lost teeth or hair. The weather was cold but fine, so Aristide Legaillon suggested that he and the tough First Officer Guisset should take a stroll. Clear of the settlement, he said, "Report your progress with the officers."

"Most will join the mutiny. There is a general contempt for Baudin. To those who hesitated, I spoke, as you suggested, of Citizen Fouché and his method of dealing with those disloyal to the Republic." He paused. Even mentioning the name of the dreaded Police Minister made him feel uneasy. During the Terror, Joseph Fouché's excesses had horrified even his blood-soaked fellow-revolutionaries. Legaillon was one of his agents. "The men, of course, will follow their officers. I have not approached Lieutenant Marais. He is too close to the English."

Legallon's death's-head face twisted in a smile. "Quite right, Lieutenant. If he is *too* friendly with them he will have to go the same way as Baudin."

"Is that really necessary, Citizen? Captain Baudin is an incompetent fool but nonetheless –"

The spy sneered. "He is an anachronism. What they used to call a man of honour. He knows nothing of our plan and regards the English as his hosts. He would never act against them. He must die."

"And your men of science?"

"Will obey orders." Legaillon stared across the vast harbour. "This delay is unfortunate. But at least it gives us an opportunity to observe the defences here."

"Then we take Van Diemen's Land."

"Yes. After all, we have a right to it. Du Fresne was there in '72, long before the English. We will establish a base from which to attack the mainland when the First Consul sends more ships and troops."

During the next few weeks the French settled in, living on board their ship, well-behaved and well-liked for the most part. Then, to Legaillon's annoyance, *Le Naturaliste* arrived at the beginning of July – in a very different condition from her sistership, being well-found, her men in excellent health. Guisset, half relieved, said, "This puts an end to your plan, eh, Citizen?" Her captain, Emmanuel Hamelin, was a bluff, forthright mariner who could not be expected to look kindly on mutiny and murder aboard *Le Géographe*.

"*Point du tout!*" snapped Legaillon. "A way will be found."

July passed, then August. The scientists studied the flora and fauna of Port Jackson, Legaillon being particularly busy with his notebook. The French ships were provisioned and *Le Géographe* fitted out with a new suit of sails, but Baudin seemed in no hurry to leave. Instead, he begged to remain and observe the transit of Mercury in October. Meanwhile he dined at Government House and met the notables of the Colony, all of whom agreed he was far too civilized to be a Frenchman.

He was not the only one in no hurry to leave. Sailors vanished into the forest. Young Aumont, a red-haired eighteen-year-old *aspirant de Marine* was brought before Baudin on a charge of desertion.

"You plead guilty?"

"Yes, my Captain. Things are happening on this ship. There are plots –"

"Silence! You know the sentence? Death by hanging."

The midshipman paled but his back stiffened. "I accept your punishment, my Captain."

Baudin nodded. "In view of your age I am altering the charge to absence without leave. You are confined to the ship until further notice."

Like Legaillon, Trubshaw was not pleased by the arrival of *Le Naturaliste*. He complained to the Governor. "Mark my words, sir, before you can say Boney, Port Jackson will be full of French ships, with Frogs strutting about topping it like the Great Panjandrum and eating their heads off. Then, when Boney gives the word, we'll be told to sling our hooks."

"Mr Trubshaw," King said sharply, "your prejudice is becoming tiresome and I must ask you not to raise the matter again. I find Captain Baudin a perfect gentleman and your suspicions are quite unfounded."

"If you say so, sir. But please to remember that these ships are thirty-gun corvettes. We've nothing to match them this side of India."

Lieutenant Marais had taken to walking to Dawes Point every day. And eventually he encountered the pretty red-haired nurse. "Mademoiselle O'Rourke, good day!" he said. "I am enchanted to see you again!"

She looked pleased. "Ye're quite recovered, then?"

"Perfectly. Thanks to my nurse, I am as fit as a – what? A louse, *n'est-ce pas?*"

She smiled. "A flea."

"Ah, thank you! You are taking a stroll?"

"Ah, to be sure," she said tartly. "I might even take tea with the Governor's wife."

"I am sorry." He looked embarrassed. "I forgot –"

"Ach, it's of no consequence. I'm on an errand for the Chief Surgeon. Good day to ye, Lieutenant."

"Wait! You will permit me to walk with you?"

"I will not! An officer in the company of a convict?"

"This officer is honoured and charmed to be in such company. *Allons, mam'selle!*" He offered his arm.

"Are ye mad?" She looked about anxiously. "Very well. Ye may walk with me but I cannot take yer arm."

They set off down the west side of Sydney Cove and into the town. On the way he discovered that she was from Cork and had attended a convent school. In turn, he told her he came from Le Havre, where his father was a notary. He had joined the navy at the age of twelve, full of ambition. But thirteen years had brought disillusionment as he had seen the fleet of well-designed, well-built ships ruined by incompetent Admirals and a corrupt ministry. "My father wished me to carry on his profession," he said bitterly. "I often wish I had."

He discovered that she was often sent on errands, and he hung about the hospital whenever he was off watch. He enjoyed being with her – enjoyed her slim grace, her quick wit, her intelligence and her warm, compassionate nature. From her smile when they met, he thought she, too, enjoyed his company. But time was slipping away. And on a spring morning in October, with the harbour sparkling blue under a cloudless sky, she said, "There's talk ye'll be leaving soon."

"It is true." It was as if a cloud had passed over the sun. "I shall miss you."

She said softly, "And I you, Jean-Paul."

He took her hand. "Sheilagh, I want to tell you how much I –"

"Don't say it!" She snatched her hand away. "There can be nothing between us! Nothing! You will go and I must stay."

He saw the tears shining in her emerald eyes. He said slowly, "What if I could take you with me?"

"On your ship? Don't be foolish! How could ye?"

"I think I know a way. Would you trust me and take it?"

"And escape from this place? Can a duck swim!" A quick look round. She reached up and kissed him on the lips.

He hurried back on board *Le Géographe*. He had to see Midshipman Aumont urgently . . .

The Governor gave a dinner for the French on the day before they sailed. Captain Hamelin was clearly anxious to put to sea, Baudin less so. He made a graceful speech of thanks for the hospitality he had received.

"A decent enough fellow, eh, Lieutenant?" the Governor said to Trubshaw afterwards.

"Oh, they can all do the civil, sir." He lowered his voice. "But they're a decadent lot. I saw one of their lieutenants – the English speaking one – kissing a midshipman earlier this evening."

"Indeed?" King raised an eyebrow. "But, of course, the French do it as a greeting –"

"This was no greeting, sir. Very – passionate it was. Ugh! Disgusting!"

"Ah well, they've gone and that's an end to it."

But they had not all gone. Next morning Governor King was informed by a pop-eyed, breathless Trubshaw that the proprietor of the Anchor Inn had found a French officer in bed with one of his chambermaids.

"Is that a good reason for interrupting my breakfast?" King asked coldly.

"Sir, there's more. This cove – Aumont, a midshipman – has told the wench he could not stay in Port Jackson because it would soon be in French hands." Trubshaw added smugly, "As I foretold, sir, did I not?"

"To the point of boredom, Mr Trubshaw." King rang for more toast. "Oh well, I suppose I must speak to the fellow."

The red-haired midshipman looked very young and very frightened and the Governor had no difficulty in getting him to talk. Understanding him was another matter since his English was on a par with the Governor's French, but King managed to elicit the information that a French settlement was to be established in Van Diemen's Land, and that a French invasion fleet would arrive at an appropriate moment to use it as a base for an assault on Port Jackson.

When he had been dismissed, King sat drumming his fingers on his desk. "Damnation! I would never have believed Baudin capable of such duplicity."

"I would, sir. He was always something of an enema to me."

"Enigma," King said absently. "But what is to be done? Flinders has taken *Investigator* to explore the north coast. That leaves only the schooner, *Cumberland*, to defend the Colony."

"*Cumberland*'s sound enough, sir, if rather small," Trubshaw said eagerly. "I could take her south and keep an eye on the

Frogs. With the southerly we've got, they can't have gone far."
The 29-ton schooner was certainly small but she was also very
fast, having been primarily intended for chasing boats seized by
absconding convicts.

"Aye." Keeping an eye would do no harm. "But no rashness,
you understand, Lieutenant?"

"Certainly not, sir."

"I will give you a letter for Captain Baudin, expressing my
astonishment at his actions. In French, so there may be no
misunderstanding. If necessary you may hoist the flag to
emphasize that Van Diemen's Land is ours – take half a dozen
Marines for the ceremony. But no insult to the French Navy or
their Government, mind." The thought of being responsible
for a renewal of the war made him break out in a cold sweat.
"Take Scoggin."

"Aye, aye, sir. I will sail with the next tide." Trubshaw
almost danced away. O bliss! His own command at last!

Cumberland sailed next day under a leaden sky and into an
equally grey Pacific blown into whitecaps. But the wind had
backed easterly so, with her deck tilted like a roof, she went
racing south. '14 knots, Scoggin!" Trubshaw shouted to his
coxswain. "We'll be there in no time!" *But where?* He stared
into the grey murk and rain squalls, unwilling to admit that the
entire French Navy could be hidden in them.

He was fortunate, however. Two days later, halfway across
Bass Strait, they came upon a sealer bound for Port Jackson.
She reported two vessels under French colours anchored in
Elephant Bay on the eastern coast of King Island. Trubshaw
turned west and ran before the wind.

During the night, the weather eased and the sky cleared. As
the dawn came up out of the Pacific behind him, Trubshaw saw
the grey hump of an island ahead. He stood on as the island
turned green, touched with sunlight. Then a wide, shallow bay,
with the colony of sea elephants that had given it its name. At
the northern end, a ship at anchor, flying the tricolour. White
tents on shore.

Tents? Good God, a settlement!

*　　*　　*

On shore, Legaillon cursed as he watched the English schooner approach. On the previous day he had prevailed upon Baudin to send *Le Naturaliste* back to France with the scientific specimens. Today Captain Baudin was to be the victim of a shooting accident in the woods. Now this! *Merde!*

"Enemy in sight! Hands to battle stations!" bawled Trubshaw. *God, it's the Battle of the Nile all over again!*

Yells and total confusion, the hands having no idea where to go.

"Close her and put a shot across her bow!"

"But, sir, she's at anchor!" Scoggin said. "T'ain't no use tellin' 'er to 'eave to!"

"Out tompions!" Trubshaw yelled, ignoring him. "Aim your guns!"

"Sir! We got two 6 pounders again their thirty cannon! They can blow us into firewood if they turns nasty."

"Both together!" shrieked Trubshaw. "Fire!" Scoggin put his hands over his eyes to shut out the vision of balls ripping into the French ship.

So he did not see the weak puffs of smoke or the little balls soaring 10 feet in the air, to splash into the sea. "Damnation seize it! The blasted powder's damp!" Trubshaw cursed bitterly. "Reload!"

On shore, the sentry woke the Captain. "Sir, it appears that the English wish to salute us."

Baudin felt unwell. He wished he had not sent Hamelin back to France: he should have gone himself. His head ached as he struggled out into the blinding sunlight in time to see a second pair of projectiles plopping into the sea close to the schooner's bow. He squinted into the sun. "The English, they always salute with ball?" he asked as Guisset came up.

"Ah, the English, they are mad to be tied, so who can make sense of what they do? Perhaps they have come for the Irish convict?"

In view of her Irish nationality and Marais' obvious affection, Baudin, a great romantic, had agreed to take her to France. "It

is possible, although it seems a great deal of fuss just for one girl.
But, if that is the case, they have only to ask and I must,
naturally, hand her over without delay."

Trubshaw glared at the French camp. *Damn their impudence!
Settling down snug as pigs in pease-straw!* "Corporal! You know
the drill for flag-hoisting?"

The Corporal of Marines was still struggling into his uniform
coat. "Well, sir, to tell the truth, I ain't never done it –"

"Oh, you'll soon get the hang of it. Look sharp now! Hop into
the boat! Who has the flag?"

"Flag, sir? We ain't got but the one on the jack, sir."

"Then fetch it, you oaf! How can we have a flag-hoisting
ceremony without a flag?"

Sheilagh, looking delightful in Aumont's shirt and breeches,
stood at the rail of *Le Géographe* with Lieutenant Marais. "I
know that officer. He is the Governor's aide, Lieutenant Trubshaw." She pointed. "Look! One of the Marines has gone back
on board. He's lowering the flag. But now he's jumping into the
sea with it!"

"You stupid lubber!" yelled Trubshaw. "What the hell are you
doing in the water?"

"He fell in, sir," said the Corporal reproachfully. He extended an oar to the floundering Marine. "Can 'appen to
anybody –"

"Don't answer back!" Trubshaw snatched the dripping flag
and began to wring it out. "Row for the shore! Look for a tall
tree!"

"Ain't no tall ones, sir. Little bushes, like, mostly."

"We can't hoist the flag on a bush, you fool! We'll use an
oar."

The glare of the sun had driven Baudin back to his tent.
Legaillon joined the First Officer. "They dig a hole with a
bayonet! Why?"

Guisset shook his head. "Is it possible that they wish to plant an oar? Ah, now it falls down. The Officer dances about. Clearly we are dealing with lunatics."

Legaillon glowered at them. "Whatever folly they are engaged in, I wish they would finish and go away. We cannot deal with Baudin while they are here."

"Why do we not just order them to leave? We outgun them."

"My orders are to avoid any confrontation that might lead to war. The First Consul is not ready."

"Corporal, I 'opes as I won't 'ave to pay for me broken bayonet?" whined the Marine.

"Belay that row!" Trubshaw wondered if Nelson had had such idiots under his command. The oar now stood upright but nobody had thought to fasten the flag to it. "Take down the oar and secure the flag!"

"What wiv, sir?" The bo'sun asked. "We ain't got no nails nor nuffin'—"

"Then tie it on, dammit!"

Marais stared at the wet flag, dangling from the oar that leaned drunkenly. "They have hoisted it upside down! A sign of distress!"

Sheilagh said, "Now the redcoats are lining up. The Officer is making a speech. What in the name of God are they about?"

". . . In the name of His Britannic Majesty, King George the Third!" bawled Trubshaw. He put away the paper by which he had laid claim to Van Diemen's Land. "Now, Corporal, let's have a smart volley over the Frog tents!"

"Sir, some of the lads ain't what you might call marksmen, like—"

"For Christ's sake, Corporal, all they've got to do is fire in the bloody air! Get on with it and see if you lobsters can't do something right for a change!"

"Yes sir! Squad, hun! Righ-eet dress!"

The six Marines shuffled into a wavering line.

"Eye-ees front! Preeee-sent ahhm!"

Muskets twitched uncertainly.

"Load!"

They ripped the cartridges open, rammed in the ball and wadding.

"Preee-sent! Fire!"

A crash. A blast of smoke. Shrieks and French oaths from the tents.

"Jesus!" said the Corporal.

Legaillon was flat on the ground, cursing horribly. "They are not only mad but homicidal!"

Guisset, who had scorned to duck, looked at the holes in the tents from which half-naked sailors were pouring. "Surely now we may fire back?"

"How many times must I tell you? We must not precipitate a conflict. It will all go into my report to Citizen Fouché." He stared along the beach. Trubshaw was marching towards them at the head of his Marines. "Now what?"

Trubshaw came up. "You Frenchies there! Take me to Captain Baudin directly."

Guisset snarled an insult that, luckily, Trubshaw could not understand. Legaillon said, "You 'ave damage our tents!"

"You've no right to have bloody tents here, Leg-Iron! Take me to your *Capitaine* and be *vite* about it!"

Legaillon turned, fuming, and led the way.

Baudin was standing outside his tent, looking stunned. He returned Trubshaw's somewhat perfunctory bow. "You 'ave fired on us, *m'sieu!*"

"Nothing of the kind! *Nous raisons le* flag, that is *tout.* Where's your other *bateau?*"

Legaillon glared at him. "*Le Naturaliste* 'as return to France."

Baudin said, "I wish an explanation of your conduct."

"Ha! You do, eh?" Trubshaw produced King's letter. "Then read this, *monsewer.*"

Baudin read it. Raised his eyebrows. "I do not comprehend. Your Governor accuses me of ingratitude. Of seizing land. It is not so! You must take my reply, denying his charge!"

"You've set up *le* camp *ici!*"

Legaillon snapped, "Only while we conduct the observations scientific!"

"*Combien de* days will that take?"

Baudin said, "Two. Three, per'aps."

"Then I'll wait until you sling your hook." When they looked blank: "Until you *poussez* off!"

Legaillon choked back his rage. "We only make notes of the plants, the animals. It will waste your time, *m'sieu*."

"You are trespassing! It's my duty to see you off the premises!"

Legaillon's bearded face flushed with rage. "This insult I report to my Government!"

"Pray do, Leg-Iron. Meanwhile we'll stay *ici* and do *le* fishing. *Bong jaw!*"

On the following day, Lieutenant Guisset took *Le Géographe* out into the Bass Strait. "Homeward bound, eh?" he said to the officer of the watch. "But I do not think the Captain will see France. He is very ill."

Marais nodded. "It has not been a happy voyage. I observe that Monsieur Legaillon also keeps to his cabin. Is he unwell?"

"He thinks of a certain interview that awaits him in Paris. One at which he must keep calm and not lose his head." Guisset chuckled unsympathetically. "And you? You will marry your Midshipman, eh?"

"*Bien sûr*. And I will leave the service. I have a mind to settle in Le Havre and become a notary."

"You are wise. Soon there will be war again." Guisset stared at the grey storm clouds driving up from Antarctica. "We will reef topsails, if you please, Lieutenant."

"The beginning of a settlement, eh? At Elephant Bay! By George, you were right all along, Lieutenant! And you scared them off – two thirty-gun corvettes!"

"Only one, sir," Trubshaw said modestly.

"Well done, Mr Trubshaw! Well done indeed! I think you'll find that their Lordships will approve your being made full Lieutenant without the usual examination." The Governor waved the French Captain's letter. "But I must say, I'm damned disappointed in Baudin. Swears he had no aggressive intent, while all along –"

"He was gammoning, sir, just as I said. It puts me in mind of that old Johnny who told us not to trust Greeks bearing gifts."

"But, Lieutenant," the Governor said, bemused, "the French were not bearing gifts!"

"That, sir," Trubshaw said, "makes it even worse. Damned miserly set of coves!"

THE CHINA FLEET

Patrick O'Brian

Tempers soon began to fray over the enactment of the Treaty of Amiens. France had its own interpretation of the terms in relation to Piedmont, which seemed to flout the Treaty, and in the face of that Britain became reluctant to complete its obligations with regard to evacuating Malta. No one was prepared to change their views, and in May 1803 Britain declared war on France. Hostilities would endure for the next seven years.

Today when you think of sea stories of the Napoleonic period one name stands proud, that of Patrick O'Brian, the consummate author of the Jack Aubrey and Stephen Maturin novels. O'Brian based Aubrey on the successful but rather unorthodox Thomas Cochrane (1775–1860), later Lord Dundonald. Cochrane undertook some remarkable exploits during the Napoleonic Wars, though did not always receive the credit he deserved, partly because his peers and rivals were envious of the amount of prize-money he accumulated. In just two months in 1805 he amassed £75,000.

Sadly Mr O'Brian has written no short stories featuring Jack Aubrey, so I have selected a self-contained episode from HMS Surprise *(1973) which contains some of his best writing of naval action. Events have moved to the Indian Ocean. Aubrey, in command of the* Surprise, *has encountered the China Fleet, which is taking goods to the value of six million pounds to India. Also in the Indian Ocean, however, is a French squadron under the command of Rear Admiral Linois. Aubrey realizes it is down to him to ensure that the China Fleet does not fall into French hands.*

It was in longitude eighty-nine east that the frigate caught them. A string of lights had been seen towards the end of the middle watch, and as the sun came up most of the *Surprise*'s people were on deck to contemplate the cloud of sails that stretched along the horizon: thirty-nine ships and a brig in two separate bodies.

They had scattered somewhat in the night, and now they were closing up in response to their Commodore's signals, the laggards crowding sail on the moderate north-east breeze. The leeward division, if such a wandering heap could be called a division, was made up of country ships bound for Calcutta, Madras or Bombay, and some foreigners who had joined them for safety from pirates and to profit by their exact navigation; it straggled for 3 miles along the distant sea. But those to windward, all sixteen of them the larger kind of Indiamen that made the uninterrupted voyage from Canton to London, were already in a formation that would not have done much discredit to the navy.

"And are you indeed fully persuaded that they are not men-of-war?" asked Mr White. "They look wonderfully like, with their rows of guns; wonderfully like, to a lands-man's eye."

"They do, do they not?" said Stephen. "It is their study so to appear; but I believe that if you look closer you will see water-butts placed, *stowed*, between the guns, and a variety of bales on deck, which would never be countenanced in the service. And the various flags and streams that fly in the appropriate places are quite different. I am not prepared to say just in what the difference lies, but to the seaman it is instantly apparent – they are not the *royal* insignia. Then again, you will have noticed that the Captain has given orders to close them; which I conceive he would scarcely have done, had they been an enemy fleet of such magnitude."

"He said, 'Keep your luff,' and followed it with an oath," said the chaplain, narrowing his eyes.

"It is all one," said Stephen. "They speak in tropes, at sea."

From his perch in the main crosstrees Pullings summoned William Church aloft, a very small midshipman in his first voyage, who seemed rather to have shrunk than to have grown in the course of it. "Now, younker," he said, "you are always nattering about the wealth of the Orient and the way you never seen none of it in Bombay nor parts east, but only mud and flies and a mortal lot of sea: well, now, just take a look through this spyglass at the ship wearing the pendant. She's the *Lushington*: I made two voyages in her. Then next astern there's the *Warley*: a very sweet sailer – works herself, almost – and fast, for an Indiaman: trim lines – you could take her for a heavy frigate, if you had not been aboard. You see they carry forestaysails, just as we do: they are the only merchantmen you will ever see with a forestaysail. Some call it impertinence. And then the one with her topsail atrip, that they are making such a cock of trimming – Judas Priest, what a Hornchurch fair! They have forgot to pass the staysail sheet – you see the mate in a passion, a-running along the gangway? I can hear him from here. It is always the same with these Lascars: they are tolerable good seamen, sometimes, but they forget their ABC, and they can't be got to do their duty brisk, no, not if it is ever so. Then on her quarter, with the patched inner jib, that's the *Hope*: or maybe she's the *Ocean* – they're much of a muchness, out of the same yard and off of the same draught. But any gait, all of 'em you see in this weather line, is what we call 1,200-tonners; though to be sure some gauges 13 and even 1,500 ton, Thames measurement. *Wexford*, there, with her brass fo'c'sle 8-pounder winking in the sun, she does: but we call her 1,200-ton ship."

"Sir, might it not be simpler to call her a 1,500-ton ship?"

"Simpler, maybe: but it would never do. You don't want to be upsetting the old ways. Oh dear me, no. God's my life, if the Captain was to hear you carrying on in that reckless Jacobin, democratical line, why, I dare say he would turn you adrift on a 3-inch plank, with both your ears nailed down to it, to learn you bashfulness, the way he served three young gentlemen in the Med. No, no: you don't want to go arsing around with the old ways: the French did so, and look at the scrape it has gotten them into. But what I called you up here for, was to show you this here wealth of the Orient. Just you look ahead of the Commodore to the leading ship, *Ganges*, if I don't mistake, and now cast your eye to old slowbelly in the rear, setting his topgallants and sagging to leeward something cruel. Look hard, now, because you will not likely see such a sight again; for there you have a clear six millions of money, not counting the officer's private ventures. Six million of money: God love us, what a prize!"

The officers who were wafting this enormous treasure across the ocean in their leisurely East-India fashion were well rewarded for doing so; this pleased them, because, among other things, it allowed them to be magnificently hospitable; and they were the most hospitable souls afloat. No sooner had Captain Muffit, the Commodore, made out the frigate's tall mainmast in the light of dawn, than he sent for his chief steward, his head Chinese and his head Indian cook; and signals broke out aboard the *Lushington*: the one to the *Surprise: Request honour of Captain's and officers' company to dinner*, the other to the convoy, *All ships: pretty young female passengers required dine frigate's officers. Repeat young. Repeat pretty.*

The *Surprise* ran within a cable's length of the *Lushington*. Boats plied to and fro along the fleet, bringing young women in silk dresses and eager officers in blue and gold. The Indiaman's splendid stateroom was filled with people, filled with cheerful noise – news of Europe, of India and the farther East; news of the war, of common acquaintances, gossip; inane but cheerful conversation; riddles! toasts to the Royal Navy, to the Honourable East-India Company, to trade's increase – and the frigate's officers filled themselves with splendid food, with charming wine.

*   *   *

Two days later the *Surprise*, alone on a misty heaving sea, was trying it. The carpenter and his crew had wrought all morning, and now, dinner having been cut short, the long mast was swaying up through the intricate tracery of the rigging. This was a delicate task in a heavy swell, and Jack had not only heaved to but he had stopped the midday grog: he wanted no fuddled enthusiasm heaving on the top-rope, and he knew very well that the delay would stimulate zeal – that no one would put up with a moment's dawdling – that no man would presume to pause to gasp in the oppressive, thundery heat for fear of what his mates would do.

Up and up it went, and peering with half-closed eyes into the glare of the covered sun, he guided it inch by inch, co-ordinating the successive heaves with the pitching of the ship. The last half foot, and the whole ship's company held its breath, eyes fixed on the heel of the mast. It crept a little higher, the new top-rope creaking in the block and sending down a cloud of shakings: then with a jerk and a shudder along its whole length the heel lifted over the top-cap.

"Handsomely, handsomely!" cried Jack. A trifle more: at the masthead the bosun flung up his hand. "Lower away." The top-rope slackened; the heel of the mast settled down inside the step; and it was done.

The Surprises let out a universal sigh. The maintopsail and forecourse dropped like the curtain at the end of a harrowing drama; they were sheeted home, and the bosun piped belay. The frigate answered at once, and as he felt the way on her, Jack gazed up at the new royal-mast, rigidly parallel with the topgallant and rising high above with a splendid promise of elastic strength: he felt a dart of pure joy, not merely because of the mast, nor because of the sweet motion of the ship – his own dear ship – nor yet because he was afloat and in command. It was a plenitude of being –

"On deck, there," called the Lookout in a hesitant, deprecating howl. "Sail on the larboard bow. Two maybe." Hesitant, because reporting the China Fleet for a third time was absurd; deprecating because he should have done so long ago, instead of staring at the perilous drama of the mast.

His hail excited little interest, or none: grog was to be served out the moment the mast was secured and the yard across. Willing hands, well ahead of orders, were busy with the two pair of shrouds, the stoppings on the yard; impatient men were waiting in the crosstrees ready to clap on the braces. However, Jack and his First Lieutenant looked attentively at the hazy ships, looming unnaturally large some 4 miles ahead and growing rapidly clearer as the frigate sailed towards them – she was making 5 knots already on the steady north-east wind.

"Who is that old-fashioned fellow who carries his mizen-topmast staysail *under* the maintop?" said Stourton. "I believe I can make out two more behind them. I am astonished they should have come up with us so soon; after all . . ."

"Stourton, Stourton," cried Jack, "it is Linois. Haul your wind! Hard a-port, hard over. Let fall the maincourse, there. Strike the pendant. Forestaysail: maintopgallant. Marines, Marines, there: clap on to the mainbrace. Bear a hand, bear a hand. Mr Etherege, stir up your men."

Babbington came running aft to report the foreroyalyard across, and the frigate's sudden turn, coinciding with a heavy roll, threw him off his balance: he fell sprawling at his Captain's feet. "Butcher!" cried Jack, "Mr Babbington, this is carrying a proper deference too far."

"Yard across, sir, if you please," said Babbington: and seeing the wild glee on Jack's face, the mad brilliance of his eye, he presumed on their old acquaintance to say, "Sir, what's afoot?"

"Linois is afoot," said Jack, with a grin. "Mr Stourton, backstays to that mast at once, and preventers. Do not let them set up the shrouds too taut; we must not have it wrung. All stuns'ls and kites into the tops. Give her what sail she can carry. And then I believe you may prepare to clear for action."

Slinging his glass, he ran up the masthead like a boy. The *Surprise* had spun round on her heel; she was now steadying on her course, close-hauled and heading north, leaning far over to larboard as the sail increased upon her and her bow-wave began to fling the water wide. The Frenchmen were fading a little in the haze, but he could see the nearest signalling. Both had been sailing on a course designed to intercept the *Surprise* – they had seen him first – and now they were following his turn in chase. They would never fetch his wake unless they tacked, however; they had been too far ahead for that. Beyond them he could make out a larger ship: another farther to the south-west, and something indistinct on the blurred horizon – perhaps a brig. These three were still sailing large, and clearly the whole squadron had been in line abreast, strung out to sweep 20 miles of sea; and they were standing directly for the path the slow China Fleet would traverse next day.

Thunder had been grumbling and crashing since the morning, and now in the midst of a distant peal there was the sound of a gun. The Admiral, no doubt, calling in his leeward ships.

"Mr Stourton," he called, "Dutch ensign and two or three hoists of the first signal-flags that come to hand, with a gun to windward – two guns."

The French frigates were cracking on: topgallant staysails appeared, outer jib, jib of jibs. They were throwing up a fine bow-wave, and the first was making perhaps 8 knots, the second 9; but the distance was drawing out, and that would never do – his very first concern was to find out what he had to deal with.

Below him the deck was like an ant-hill disturbed; and he could hear the crash of the carpenters' mallets below as the cabin bulkheads came down. It would be some minutes before the apparent confusion resolved itself into a trim, severe pattern, a clean sweep fore and aft, the guns cast loose, their crews standing by them, every man at his station, sentries at the hatchways, damp fearnought screens rigged over the magazines, wet sand strewn over the decks. The men had been through these motions hundreds of times, but never in earnest: how would they behave in action? Pretty well, no doubt: most men did, in this kind of action, if they were properly led: and the Surprises were a decent set of men; a little over-eager with their shot at first, perhaps, but that could be dealt with . . . how much powder was there filled? Twenty rounds apiece was yesterday's report, and plenty of wads: Hales was a good conscientious gunner. He would be as busy as a bee at this moment, down there in the powder-room.

This drawing away would never do. He would give them another two minutes and then take his measures. The second frigate had passed the first. She was almost certainly the thirty-six gun *Sémillante*, with 12-pounders on her maindeck: the

Surprise could take her on. He moved out on to the yardarm for a better view, for they lay on his quarter and it was difficult to count the gun-ports. Yes, she was the *Sémillante*; and the heavy frigate behind her was the *Belle Poule*, 40, with 18-pounders – a very tough nut to crack, if she was well handled. He watched them dispassionately. Yes, they were well-handled: both somewhat crank, probably from want of stores; and both slow, of course; they must be trailing a great curtain of weed, after so many months in this milk-warm water, and they were making heavy weather of it. Beautiful ships, however, and their people obviously knew their duty – *Sémillante* sheeted home her foretopmast staysail in a flash. In his opinion *Belle Poule* would do better with less canvas abroad; her foretopgallant seemed to be pressing her down; but no doubt her captain knew her trim best.

Braithwaite appeared, snorting. "Mr Stourton's duty, sir, and the ship is cleared for action. Do you choose he should beat to quarters, sir?"

"No, Mr Braithwaite," said Jack, considering: there was no question of action yet awhile, and it would be a pity to keep the men standing about. "No. But pray tell him I should like sail to be discreetly reduced. Come up the bowlines a trifle and give the sheets half a fathom or so – nothing obvious, you understand me. And the old number three foretopsail is to be bent to a hawser and veered out of the lee sternport."

"Aye, aye, sir," said Braithwaite, and vanished. A few moments later the frigate's speed began to slacken; and as the strain came on to the drag-sail, opening like a parachute beneath the surface, it dropped further still.

Stephen and the chaplain stood at the taffrail, staring over the larboard quarter. "I am afraid they are coming closer," said Mr White. "I can distinctly see the men on the front of the nearer one: and even on the ship behind. See, they fire a gun! And a flag appears! Your glass, if you please. Why, it is the English flag! I congratulate you, Dr Maturin; I congratulate you on our deliverance: I confess I had apprehended a very real danger, a most unpleasant situation. Ha, ha, ha! They are our friends!"

"*Haud crede colori*," said Stephen. "Cast your eyes aloft, my dear sir."

Mr White looked up at the mizen-peak, where a tricolour streamed out bravely. "It is the French flag," he cried. "No. The Dutch. We are sailing under false colours! Can such things be?"

"So are they," said Stephen. "They seek to amuse us; we seek to amuse them. The iniquity is evenly divided. It is an accepted convention, I find, like bidding the servant –" A shot from the *Sémillante*'s bow-chaser threw up a plume of water a little way from the frigate's stern, and the parson started back. "– say you are not at home, when in fact you are eating muffin by your fire and do not choose to be disturbed."

"I often did so," said Mr White, whose face had grown strangely mottled. "God forgive me. And now here I am in the midst of battle. I never thought such a thing could happen – I am a man of peace. However, I must not give a bad example."

A ball, striking the top of a wave, ricocheted on to the quarterdeck by way of the neatly piled hammocks. It fell with a harmless dump and two midshipmen darted for it, struggled briefly until the stronger wrested it away and wrapped it lovingly in his jacket. "Good heavens," cried Mr White. "To fire great iron balls at people you have never even spoken to – barbarity is come again."

"Will you take a turn, sir?" asked Stephen.

"Willingly, sir, if you do not think I should stand here, to show I do not care for those ruffians. But I bow to your superior knowledge of warfare. Will the Captain stay up there on the mast, in that exposed position?"

"I dare say he will," said Stephen. "I dare say he is turning over the situation in his mind."

Certainly he was. It was clear that his first duty, having reconnoitred the enemy, was to reach the China Fleet and do everything possible to preserve it: nor had he the least doubt that he could outsail the Frenchmen, with their foul bottoms – indeed, even if they had been clean he could no doubt have given them a good deal of canvas, fine ships though they were: for it was they who had built the *Surprise* and he who was sailing her – it stood to reason that an Englishman could handle a ship better than a Frenchman. Yet Linois was not to be underestimated, the fox. He had chased Jack in the Mediterranean through a long summer's day, and he had caught him.

The two-decker, now so near that her identity was certain – the *Marengo*, 74, wearing a rear-admiral's flag – had worn, and now she was close-hauled on the larboard tack, followed by the fourth ship and the distant brig. The fourth ship must be the *Berceau*, a twenty-two gun corvette: the brig he knew nothing about. Linois had *worn*: he had not tacked. That meant he was favouring his ship. Those three, the *Marengo*, *Berceau* and the brig, standing on the opposite tack, meant to cut him off, if the frigates managed to head him: that was obvious – greyhounds either side of a hare, turning her.

The last shot came a little too close – excellent practice, at this extreme range. It would be a pity to have any ropes cut away. "Mr Stourton," he called, "shake out a reef in the foretopsail, and haul the bowlines."

The *Surprise* leapt forward, in spite of her drag-sail. The *Sémillante* was leaving the *Belle Poule* far behind, and to leeward; he knew that he could draw her on and on, then bear up suddenly and bring her to close action – hammer her hard with his 32-pounder carronades and perhaps sink or take her before her friends could come up. The temptation made his breath come short. Glory, and the only prize in the Indian Ocean . . . the pleasing image of billowing smoke, the flash of guns, masts falling, faded almost at once, and his heart returned to its dutiful calculating pace. He must not endanger a single spar; his frigate must join the China Fleet at all costs, and intact.

His present course was taking Linois straight towards the Indiamen, half a day's sail away to the east, strung out over miles of sea, quite unsuspecting. Clearly he must lead the Frenchmen away by some lame-duck ruse, even if it meant losing his comfortable weather-gauge – lead them away until nightfall and then beat up, trusting to the darkness and the *Surprise*'s superior sailing to shake them off and reach the convoy in time.

He could go about and head south-east until about ten o'clock: by then he should have fore-reached upon Linois so far that he could bear up cross ahead of him in the darkness and so double back. Yet if he did so, or offered to do so, Linois, that deep old file, might order the pursuing frigates to hold on to their northerly course, stretching to windward of the *Surprise* and gaining the weather-gauge. That would be awkward in the morning; for fast though she was, she could not outrun *Sémillante* and *Belle Poule* if they were sailing large and she was beating up, as she would have to beat up, tack after tack, to warn the China Fleet.

But then again, if Linois did that, if he ordered his frigates northwards, a gap would appear in his dispositions after a quarter of an hour's sailing, a gap through which the *Surprise* could dart, bearing up suddenly and running before the wind with all the sail she could spread, and passing between the *Belle Poule* and the *Marengo*, out of range of either; for Linois's dispositions were based upon the chase moving at 9 or 10 knots – no European ship in these waters could do better, and hitherto *Surprise* had not done as well. *Berceau*, the corvette, farther to leeward, might close the gap; but although she might knock away some of his spars, it was unlikely that she could hold him long enough for the *Marengo* to come up. If she had a commander so determined that he would let his ship be riddled, perhaps sunk – a man who would run him aboard – why then, that would be a different matter.

He looked hard over the sea at the distant corvette: she vanished in a drift of rain, and he shifted his gaze to the two-decker. What was in Linois's mind? He was running east-south-east under easy sail: topsails, forecourse clewed up. One thing Jack was certain of was, that Linois was infinitely more concerned with catching the China Fleet than with destroying a frigate.

The moves, the answers to those moves on either side, the varying degrees of danger, and above all Linois's appreciation of the position . . . He came down on deck, and Stephen, looking attentively at him, saw that he had what might be called his battle-face: it was not the glowing blaze of immediate action, of boarding or cutting out, but a remoter expression altogether – cheerful, confident, but withdrawn – filled with natural author-ity. He did not speak, apart from giving an order to hitch the runners to the mastheads and to double the preventer-back-stays, but paced the quarterdeck with his hands behind his back, his eyes running from the frigates to the line-of-battle

ship. Stephen saw the First Lieutenant approach, hesitate, and
step back. "On these occasions," he reflected, "my valuable
friend appears to swell, actually to increase in his physical as
well as his spiritual dimensions: is it an optical illusion? How I
should like to measure him. The penetrating intelligence in the
eye, however, is not capable of measurement. He becomes a
stranger: I, too, should hesitate to address him."

"Mr Stourton," said Jack. "We will go about."

"Yes, sir. Shall I cast off the drag-sail, sir?"

"No: and we will not go about too fast, neither: space out the
orders, if you please."

As the pipes screeched "All hands about ship" he stood on
the hammocks, fixing the *Marengo* with his glass, pivoting as
the frigate turned up into the wind. Just after the cry of
"Mainsail haul" and the sharp cutting pipe of belay, he saw
a signal run up aboard the flagship and the puff of a gun on her
poop. The *Sémillante* and the *Belle Poule* had begun their turn
in pursuit, but now the *Sémillante* paid off again and stood on.
The *Belle Poule* was already past the eye of the wind when a
second gun emphasised the order, the order to stand on northwards and gain the weather-gauge, and she had to wear right
round to come up on to her former tack. "Damn that," murmured Jack: the blunder would narrow his precious gap by
quarter of a mile. He glanced at the sun and at his watch. "Mr
Church," he said, "be so good as to fetch me a mango."

The minutes passed: the juice ran down his chin. The French
frigates stood on to the north-north-west, growing smaller.
First the *Sémillante* and then the *Belle Poule* crossed the wake
of the *Surprise*, gaining the weather-gauge: there was no changing his mind now. The *Marengo*, her two tiers of guns clearly
to be seen, lay on the starboard beam, sailing a parallel course.
There was no sound but the high, steady note of the wind in the
rigging and the beat of the sea on the frigate's larboard bow.
The far-spaced ships scarcely seemed to move in relation to one
another from one minute to the next – there seemed to be all the
peaceful room in the world.

The *Marengo* dropped her foresail: the angle widened half a
degree. Jack checked all the positions yet again, looked at his

watch, looked at the dog-vane, and said, "Mr Stourton, the stuns'ls are in the tops, I believe?"

"Yes, sir."

"Very well. In ten minutes we must cast off the drag-sail, bear up, set royals, stuns'ls aloft and alow if she will bear them, and bring the wind two points on the quarter. We must make sail as quick as ever sail was made, brailing up the driver and hauling down the staysails at the same time, of course. Send Clerk and Bonden to the wheel. Lower the starboard port-lids. Make all ready, and stand by to let go the drag-sail when I give the signal."

Still the minutes dropped by; the critical point was coming, but slowly, slowly. Jack, motionless upon that busy deck, began to whistle softly as he watched the far-off Linois: but then he checked himself – he wanted no more than a brisk topgallant breeze. Anything more, or anything like a hollow sea, would favour the two-decker, the tall, far heavier ship; and he knew, to his cost, how fast these big French 74s could move.

A last glance to windward: the forces were exactly balanced: the moment had come. He drew a deep breath, tossed the hairy mango stone over the side, and shouted, "Let go there." An instant splash. "Hard a-port." The *Surprise* turned on her heel, her yards coming round to admiration, sails flashing out as others vanished, and there close on her starboard quarter was her foaming wake, showing a sweet tight curve. She leapt forward with a tremendous new impulse, her masts groaning, and settled on her new course, not deviating by a quarter of a point. She was heading exactly where he had wanted her to head, straight for the potential gap, and she was moving even faster than he had hoped. The higher spars were bending like coach-whips, just this side of carrying away. "Mr Stourton, that was prettily executed: I am very pleased."

The *Surprise* was tearing through the water, moving faster and faster until she reached a steady 11 knots and the masts ceased their complaint. The backstays grew a shade less rigid, and leaning on one, gauging its tension as he stared at the *Marengo*, he said, "Main and fore royal-stuns'ls."

The *Marengo* was brisk in her motions – well-manned – but the move had caught her unawares. She did not begin her turn until the *Surprise* had set her royal studdingsails and her masts were complaining again as they drove her 500 tons even faster through the sea: her deck leaning sharply, her lee headrails buried in the foam, the sea roaring along her side, and the hands standing mute – never a sound fore and aft.

Yet when the *Marengo* did turn she bore up hard to bring the wind on her starboard quarter, settling on a course that would give her beautiful deep-cut sails all possible thrust to intercept the *Surprise* at some point in the south-west – to cut her off, that is to say, if she could not find another knot or so. At the same time, the flagship sent up hoist after hoist of signals, some directed, no doubt, at the still invisible corvette to leeward, and others to bring the *Sémillante* and the *Belle Poule* pelting down after the *Surprise*.

"They will never do it, my friend," said Jack. "They did not send up double preventer-stays half an hour ago. They cannot carry royals in this breeze." But he touched a belaying pin as he said this: royals or no, the situation was tolerably delicate. The *Marengo* was moving faster than he had expected, and the *Belle Poule*, whose earlier mistake had set her well to leeward, was nearer than he could wish. The two-decker and the heavy frigate were the danger; he had no chance at all against the *Marengo*, very little against the *Belle Poule*, and both these ships were fast converging upon his course. Each came on surrounded by an invisible ring 2 miles and more in diameter – the range of their powerful guns. The *Surprise* had to keep well out of these rings, above all out of the area where they would soon overlap; and the lane was closing fast.

He considered her trim with the most intense concentration: it was possible that he was pressing her down a trifle aft – that there was a little too much canvas abroad, driving her by force rather than by love. "Haul up the weather-skirt of the main-course," he said. Just so: that was distinctly sweeter; a more airy motion altogether. The dear *Surprise* had always loved her headsails, "Mr Babbington, jump forward and tell me whether the spritsail will stand."

"I doubt it, sir," said Babbington, coming aft. "She throws such an almighty bow-wave."

Jack nodded: he had thought as much. "Spritsail-topsail, then," he said, and thanked God for his new strong royal-mast, that would take the strain. How beautifully she answered! You could ask anything of her. Yet still the lane was narrow enough, in all conscience: the *Marengo* was crowding sail, and now the *Surprise* was racing into the zone of high danger. "Mr Callow," he said to the Signal-Midshipman, "strike the Dutch colours. Hoist our own ensign and the pendant." The ensign broke out at the mizen-peak; a moment later the pendant, the mark of a man-of-war and no other, streamed from the main. The *Surprise* was particular about her pendant – had renewed it four times this commission, adding a yard or two each time – and now its slim tapering flame stretched out 60 feet, curving away beyond her starboard bow. At the sight, there was a general hum of satisfaction along the deck, where the men stood tense, strongly moved by the tearing speed.

Now he was almost within random-shot of the *Marengo*'s bow guns. If he edged away the *Belle Poule* and the *Sémillante* would gain on him. Could he afford to hold on to this present course? "Mr Braithwaite," he said to the Master's Mate, "be so good as to heave the log."

Braithwaite stepped forward, paused for a moment at the sloping lee-quarter to see where he could toss it into a calm patch outside the mill-race rushing along her side, flung the log wide through the flying spray, and shouted "Turn!" The boy posted on the hammock-netting with the reel held it high; the line tore off, and a moment later there was a shriek. The Quartermaster had the boy by one foot, dragging him inboard; and the reel, torn from his hand, raced away astern.

"Fetch another log, Mr Braithwaite," said Jack with intense satisfaction, "and use a fourteen-second glass." He had seen the whole line run off the reel only once in his life, when he was a midshipman homeward-bound in the packet from Nova Scotia: and the *Flying Childers* boasted of having done it too – the *Childers* also claimed to have lost their boy. But this was no time to be regretting the preservation of young puddinghead, Bent Larsen – for although it was clear that at this speed they would do it, that they would cross the *Marengo* and start to increase the distance within a few minutes, yet nevertheless they were running towards the nearest point of convergence, and it was always possible to mistake by a few hundred yards. And some French long brass 8s threw a ball very far and true.

Would Linois fire? Yes: there was the flash and the puff of smoke. The ball fell short. The line was exact, but having skipped five times, the ball sank 300 yards away. So did the next two; and the fourth was even farther off. They were through, and now every minute sailed carried them farther out of range.

"Yet I must not discourage him," said Jack, altering course to bring the *Surprise* a little closer. "Mr Stourton, ease off the foresail sheet and hand the spritsail-topsail. Mr Callow, signal, *enemy in sight: ship of the line, corvette and brig bearing east, two frigates bearing north-north-west. Request orders*, with a gun to windward. Keep it flying and repeat the gun every thirty seconds."

"Yes, sir. Sir, may I say the corvette is bearing south-east now?"

She was indeed. The lifting rainstorm showed her on the *Surprise*'s larboard bow, well ahead of the *Marengo*, and to leeward. The turning wind in the squall had set her half a mile to the west. Grave: grave.

It was in the corvette's power to bring him to action, unless he edged away into the extreme range of the frigates – the *Sémillante* had overhauled the *Belle Poule* once again. But to bring him to close action the corvette would have to stand his raking fire, and it would need a most determined commander to take his ship right in against such odds. He would probably bear up at long gunshot and exchange a distant broadside or two. Jack had no sort of objection to that – on the contrary: ever since he had set the *Surprise* for the gap, showing what she could really do in the way of speed, giving away her qualities, he had been trying to think of some means of leading Linois on in a hopeful chase that would take him far to the southward before nightfall. The signal was well enough in its way, but its effect would not last. The drag-sail would scarcely take again – they must have smoked it; but a yard coming down with a run as though it had been shot away, why, that would answer. And he could give any of them the mizen or even the maintopsail.

"Mr Babbington, the corvette will engage us presently. When I give the word, let the maintopsail come down with a run, as though her fire had had effect. But neither the yard nor the sail must be hurt. Some puddening on the cap – but I leave it to you. It must look like Bedlam, all ahoo, and yet still be ready to set.''

It was just the kind of caper Babbington would delight in; Jack had no doubt of his producing an elegant chaos. But he would have to go briskly to work. The *Berceau* was coming down under a cloud of canvas, as fast as ever she could run; and as Jack watched he saw her set her fore-royal flying. She was steering to cross ahead of the *Surprise* – she lay on her beam at this moment – and although she was now within range she held her fire.

''Mr Babbington,'' cried Jack, without taking his eyes from the *Berceau*, ''should you like your hammock sent up?''

Babbington slid down a backstay, scarlet with toil and haste. ''I am sorry to have been so slow, sir,'' he said. ''All is stretched along now, and I have left Harris and Old Reliable in the top, with orders to keep out of sight and let go handsomely when hailed.''

''Very good, Mr Babbington. Mr Stourton, let us beat to quarters.''

At the thunder of the drum Stephen took the startled chaplain by the arm and led him below. ''This is your place in action, my dear sir,'' he said in the dimness. ''These are the chests upon which Mr M'Allister and I operate; and these'' – waving the lantern towards them – ''are the pledgets and tow and bandages with which you and Choles will second our endeavours. Does the sight of blood disturb you?''

''I have never seen it shed, in any quantity.''

''Then here is a bucket, in case of need.''

Jack, Stourton and Etherege were on the quarterdeck; Harrowby stood a little behind them, conning the ship; the other officers were at the guns, each to his own division. Every man silently watched the *Berceau* as she ran down, a beautiful, trim little ship, with scarlet topsides. She was head-on now, coming straight for the frigate's broadside; and Jack, watching closely through his glass, could see no sign of her meaning to bear up. The half-minute signal-gun beside him spoke out again and again and again, and yet still the *Berceau* came on into the certainty of a murderous raking fire. This was more determination than ever he had reckoned on. He had done the same himself, in the Mediterranean: but that was against a Spanish frigate.

Another 200 yards and his heavy carronades would reach the *Berceau* point-blank. The signal-gun again; and again. "Belay there," he said; and much louder, "Mr Pullings, Mr Pullings – a steady, deliberate fire, now. Let the smoke clear between each shot. Point low on her foremast."

A pause, and on the upward roll the purser's gun crashed out, the smoke sweeping ahead. A hole appeared in the corvette's spritsail and a cheer went up, drowned by the second gun. "Steady, steady," roared Jack, and Pullings ran down the line to point the third. The ball splashed close to the corvette's bow, and as it splashed she answered with a shot from her chaser that struck the mainmast a glancing blow. The firing came down the line, a rippling broadside: two shots went home in the corvette's bows, another hit her chains, and there were holes in her foresail. Now it began forward again, and as the range narrowed so they hit her hard with almost every shot or swept her deck from stem to stern – there were two guns dismounted aboard her, and several men lying on the deck. Broadside after deliberate broadside, the whole ship quivering in the thunder – the jets of flame, the thick powder-smoke racing ahead. Still the *Berceau* held on, though her way was checked, and now her bow-guns answered with chain-shot that shrieked high through the rigging, cutting ropes and sails as it went. "A little more of this, and I shall not need my caper," thought Jack. "Can he mean to lay me aboard? Mr Pullings, Mr Babbington, briskly now, and grape the next round. Mr Etherege, the Marines may –" His words were cut off by a furious cheer. The *Berceau*'s foretopmast was going: it gave a great forward lurch, the stays and shrouds parted and it fell in a ruin of canvas, masking the corvette's forward guns. "Hold hard," he cried. "Maintop, there. Let go."

The *Surprise*'s topsail billowed out, came down, collapsed; and across the water they hear a thin answering cheer from the shattered corvette.

A forward gun sent a hail of grape along the *Berceau*'s deck, knocking down a dozen men and cutting away her colours.

"Cease fire there, God rot you all in hell," cried Jack. "Secure those guns. Mr Stourton, hands to knot and splice."

"She struck," said a voice in the waist, as the *Surprise* swept on. The *Berceau*, hulled again and again, low in the water and by the head, swung heavily round, and they saw a figure running up the mizen-shrouds with fresh colours. Jack took his hat off to her Captain, standing there on his bloody quarter-deck 70 yards away; the Frenchman returned the salute, but still, as his remaining larboard guns came to bear he fired a ragged broadside after the frigate, and then, as she reached the limit of his range, another, in a last attempt at preventing her escape. A vain attempt: not a shot came home, and the *Surprise* was still far ahead of the *Marengo* on her larboard quarter and the two frigates away to starboard.

Jack glanced at the sun: no more than an hour to go, alas. He could not hope to lead them very far this moonless night, if indeed he could lead them at all for what was left of the day. "Mr Babbington, take your party into the top and give the appearance of trying to get things shipshape – you may cockbill the yard. Mr Callow – where is that Midshipman?"

"He was carried below, sir," said Stourton. "Hit on the head."

"Mr Lee, then. Signal, *partial engagement, heavy damage; request assistance. Enemy bearing north-north-east and north-north-west*, and carry on with the half-minute gun. Mr Stourton, a fire in the waist would do no harm: plenty of smoke. One of the coppers filled with slush and tow might answer. Let there be some turmoil."

He walked to the taffrail and surveyed the broad sea astern. The brig had gone to the assistance of the *Berceau*: the *Marengo* maintained her position on the larboard quarter, coming along at a fine pace and perhaps gaining a little. As he expected, she was signalling to the *Sémillante* and the *Belle Poule* – a talkative nation, though gallant – and she was no doubt telling them to make more sail, for the *Belle Poule* set her main-royal, which instantly carried away. For the moment everything was well in hand.

He went below. "Dr Maturin," he said, "what is your casualty-list?"

"Three splinter-wounds, sir, none serious, I am happy to report, and one moderate concussion."

"How is Mr Callow?"

"There he is, on the floor – on the *deck* – just behind you. A block fell upon his head."

"Shall you open his skull?" asked Jack, with a vivid recollection of Stephen trepanning the gunner on the quarterdeck of the *Sophie*, exposing his brains, to the admiration of all.

"No. Oh, no. I am afraid his condition would not justify the step. He will do very well as he is. Now Jenkins here had a truly narrow escape, with his splinter. When M'Alister and I cut it out –"

"Which it came off of the hounds of the mainmast, sir," said Jenkins, holding up a wickedly sharp piece of wood, 2 feet long.

"– We found his innominate artery pulsing against its tip. The twentieth part of an inch more, or a trifling want of attention, and William Jenkins would have become an involuntary hero."

"Well done, Jenkins," said Jack. "Well done indeed," and he went on to inquire after the other two – a forearm laid open, and an ugly scalp-wound. "Is this Mr White?" catching sight of another body.

"Yes. He was a little overcome when we raised John Saddler's scalp and desired him to hold it while we sewed it on: yet there was virtually no blood. A passing syncope: he will be quite recovered by a little fresh air. May he go on deck, presently?"

"Oh, this minute, if he chooses. We had a slight brush with the corvette – such a gallant fellow: he came on most amazingly until Mr Bowes brought his foremast by the board – but now we are running before the wind, far out of range. Let him come on deck by all means."

On deck the black smoke was belching from the frigate's waist, streaming away ahead of her, the ship's boys were hurrying about with swabs, buckets and the fire engine, Babbington was roaring cursing in the top, waving his arms, all hands looked pleased with themselves and sly; and the pursuers had gained a quarter of a mile.

Far on the starboard beam the sun was sinking behind a

blood-red haze; sinking, sinking, and it was gone. Already the night was sweeping up from the east, a starless night with no moon, and pale phosphorescent fire had begun to gleam in the frigate's wake.

After sunset, when the French sails were no more than the faintest hint of whiteness far astern, to be fixed only by the recurrent flash of the admiral's top-lantern, the *Surprise* sent up a number of blue lights, set her undamaged main-topsail, and ran fast and faster south-westwards.

At eight bells in the first watch she hauled to the wind in the pitchy darkness; and having given his orders for the night, Jack said to Stephen, "We must turn in and get what sleep we can: I expect a busy day tomorrow."

"Do you feel that M. de Linois is not wholly deceived?"

"I hope he is, I am sure: he ought to be, and he has certainly come after us as if he were. But he is a deep old file, a through-going seaman, and I shall be glad to see nothing to the east of us, when we join the China Fleet in the morning."

"I've brought you a mug of coffee, Doctor," said Pullings, looming at his side. "And when you have drunk it up, I am going to call the skipper. He will be most uncommon pleased." He still spoke in his quiet night-watch voice, although the idlers had been called already, and the ship was filling with activity.

"What will please him so, Thomas Pullings? You are a good creature, to be sure, to bring me this roborative, stimulating drink: I am obliged to you. What will please him so?"

"Why, the Indiamen's toplights have been in sight this last glass and more, and when dawn comes up I dare say we shall see them a-shaking out the reef in their topsails just exactly where he reckoned to find 'em: such artful navigation you would scarcely credit. He has come it the Tom Cox's traverse over Linois."

Jack appeared, and the spreading light showed forty sail of merchantmen stretched wide along the western sea; he smiled, and opened his mouth to speak when the spreading light also betrayed the *Surprise* to a distant vessel in the east, which instantly burst into a perfect frenzy of gunfire, like a small and solitary battle.

"Jump up the masthead, Braithwaite," he said, "and tell me what you make of her."

The expected answer came floating down. "That French brig, sir. Signalling like fury. And I believe I make out a sail bearing something north of her."

It was just as he had feared: Linois had sent the brig northwards early in the night, and now she was reporting the presence of the *Surprise*, if not of the China Fleet, to her friends over the horizon.

The long-drawn-out ruse had failed. He had meant to draw Linois so far to the south and west during the night that the *Surprise*, doubling back towards the China Fleet in the darkness, would be far out of sight by morning. With the frigate's great speed (and how they had cracked on!) he should have done it: yet he had not. Either one of the French squadron had caught the gleam of her sails as she ran northwards through the pursuing line, or Linois had had an intuition that something was amiss – that he was being attempted to be made a fool of – and had called off the chase, sending the brig back to his old cruising-ground and then following her with the rest of his ships after an hour or so, crowding sail for the track of the China Fleet. Yet his ruse had not failed entirely: it had gained essential time. How much time? Jack set course for the Indiamen and made his way into the crosstrees: the accursed brig lay some 4 leagues off, still carrying on like a Guy Fawkes night, and the farther sail perhaps as much again – he would scarcely have seen her but for the purity of the horizon at this hour, which magnified the nick of her topgallants in the line of brilliant sky. He had no doubt that she was one of the frigates, and that the whole of Linois's squadron, less the corvette, was strung out on the likely passage of the Indiamen. They could outsail the convoy; and with this unvarying monsoon there was no avoiding them. But they could not outsail the convoy by a great deal: and it would take Linois the greater part of the day to concentrate his force and come up with the China Fleet.

The Senior Captains came hurrying aboard the *Surprise*, headed by Mr Muffit, their Commodore. The signal flying from the frigate's maintruck and the Commodore's energetic gathering of the stragglers had given them a general idea of the situation; they were anxious, disturbed, grave; but some, alas, were also garrulous, given to exclamation, to blaming the authorities for not protecting them, and to theories about where Linois had really been all this time. The Company's service was a capable, disciplined body, but its regulations required the Commodore to listen to the views of his Captains in council before any decisive action; and like all councils of war this was wordy, indefinite, inclined to pessimism. Jack had never so regretted the superior rigour of the Royal Navy as he did during the vague discourse of a Mr Craig, who was concerned to show what might have been the case, had they not waited for the Botany Bay ship and the two Portuguese.

"Gentlemen," cried Jack at last, addressing himself to the three or four other determined men at the table, "this is no time for talking. There are only two things for it: we must either run or fight. If you run, Linois will snap up your fleet piecemeal, for I can stop only one of his frigates, while the *Marengo* can sail 5 leagues to your 3 and blow any two of you out of the water. If we fight, if we concentrate our force, we can answer him gun for gun."

"Who is to fight the guns?" asked a voice.

"I will come to that, sir. What is more, Linois is a year out of a dockyard and he is 3,000 miles from the Isle of France: he is short of stores, and single spar or 50 fathom of 2-inch rope is of a hundred times more consequence to him that it is to us – I doubt there is a spare topmast in his whole squadron. In duty he must not risk grave damage: he must not press home his attack against a determined resistance."

"How do you know he has not refitted in Batavia?"

"We will leave that for the moment, if you please," said Jack. "We have no time to lose. Here is my plan. You have three more ships than Linois reckoned for: the three best-armed ships will wear men-of-war pendants and the blue ensign –"

"We are not allowed to wear Royal Navy colours."

"Will you give me leave to proceed, sir? That is entirely my responsibility, and I will take it upon myself to give the necessary permission. The larger Indiamen will form in line-of-battle, taking all available men out of the rest of the convoy to work the guns and sending the smaller ships away to leeward. I shall send an officer aboard each ship supposed to be a man-of-war, and all the quarter-gunners I can spare. With a close, well-formed line, our numbers are such that we can double upon his van or rear and overwhelm him with numbers: with one or two of your fine ships on one side of him and *Surprise* on the other, I will answer for it if we can beat the 74, let alone the frigates."

"Hear him, hear him," cried Mr Muffit, taking Jack by the hand. "That's the spirit, God's my life!"

In the confusion of voices it became clear that although there was eager and indeed enthusiastic support, one captain even beating the table and roaring, "We'll thump 'em again and again," there were others who were not of the same opinion. Who had ever heard of merchant ships with encumbered decks and few hands holding out for five minutes against powerful men-of-war? Most of them had only miserable 18 pounder cannonades – a far, far better plan was to separate: some would surely escape – the *Dorsetshire* was certain she could outrun the French – could the gentleman give any example of a ship with a 270 pound broadside resisting an enemy that could throw 950 pounds? "Whisht, Mr Craig," said Muffit before Jack could reply. "Do you not know Captain Aubrey is the gentleman who commanded the *Sophie* brig when she took the *Cacafuego*, a thirty-two-gun frigate? And I believe, sir, *Sophie* threw no great broadside?"

"Twenty-eight pounds," said Jack, reddening.

"Why," cried Craig. "I spoke only out of my duty to the Company. I honour the gentleman, I am sure, and I am sorry I did not just recollect his name. He will not find me shy, I believe. I spoke only for the Company and my cargo; not for myself."

"I believe, gentlemen," said Muffit, "that the sense of the council is in favour of Captain Aubrey's plan, as I am myself. I hear no dissentient voice. Gentlemen, I desire you will repair aboard your ships, fill powder, clear away your guns, and attend to Captain Aubrey's signals."

*   *   *

Aboard the *Surprise*, Jack called his officers to the cabin and said, "Mr Pullings, you will proceed to the *Lushington* Indiaman with Collins, Haverhill and Pollyblank. Mr Babbington to *Royal George* with the brothers Moss. Mr Braithwaite, to the brig to repeat signals: take the spare set with you. Mr Bowes, can I persuade you to look to the *Earl Camden*'s guns? I know you can point them better than any of us."

The Purser flushed bright with pleasure, and chuckled: if the Captain wished, he would certainly abandon his cheese and candles, though he did not know how he should like it; and he begged for Evans and Strawberry Joe.

"That is settled, then," said Jack. "Now, gentlemen, this is a delicate business: we must not offend the Company's officers, and some of them are very touchy – the least sense of ill-feeling would be disastrous. The men must be made to understand that thoroughly: no pride, no distance, no reference to tea-waggons, or how we do things in the Navy. Our one aim must be to keep their guns firing briskly, to engage Linois closely, and to wound his spars and rigging as much as ever we can. Hulling him or killing his people is beside the point: he would give his bosun for a stuns'l boom, and with the best will in the world we shall never sink a seventy-four. We must fire like Frenchmen for once. Mr Stourton, you and I will work out a list of the gunners we can spare, and while I am sharing them among the Indiamen, you will take the ship to the eastward and watch Linois's motions."

Within an hour the line had formed, fifteen handsome Indiamen under easy sail a cable's length apart, and a fast-sailing brig to repeat signals; boats plied to and from the smaller ships bringing volunteers for the guns; and all that forenoon Jack hurried up and down the line in his barge, dispensing officers, gunners, discreet advice and encouragement, and stores of affability. This affability was rarely forced, for most of the Captains were right seamen, and given their fiery Commodore's strong lead they set to with a determination that made Jack love them. Decks were clearing fast; the three ships chosen for pendants, the *Lushington*, the *Royal George* and the *Earl Camden*, began to look even more like men-of-war, with whitewashers over their sides disguising them fast, and royal yards crossed; and the guns ran in and out without a pause. Yet there were some awkward captains, lukewarm, despondent and re- served, two of them timid old fools; and the passengers were the cruellest trial – Atkins and the other members of Mr Stanhope's suite could be dealt with, but the women and the important civilians called for personal interviews and for explanations; one lady, darting from an unlikely hatch, told him she should countenance no violence whatsoever – Linois should be rea- soned with – his passions would certainly yield to reason – and Jack was kept very busy. It was only from time to time, as he sat in the barge next to Church, his solemn aide-de-camp, that he had leisure to ponder the remark 'How do you know he has not refitted in Batavia?"

He did not know it: yet his whole strategy must be based upon that assumption. He did not *know* it, but still he was willing to risk everything upon his intuition's being sound: for it was a matter of intuition – Linois's cautious handling of his ship, a thousand details that Jack could hardly name, but that con- trasted strongly with the carefree Linois of the Mediterranean with Toulon and its naval stores a few days' sail away. Yet moral certainty could fade: he was not infallible, and Linois was old in war, a resourceful, dangerous opponent.

Dinner aboard the *Lushington* with Captain Muffit was a relief. Not only was Jack desperately sharp-set, having missed his breakfast, but Muffit was a man after his own heart: they saw eye to eye on the formation of the line, the way to conduct the action – aggressive tactics rather than defence – and on the right dinner to restore a worn and badgered spirit.

Church appeared while they were drinking coffee. "*Surprise* signalling, sir, if you please," he said. "*Sémillante, Marengo* and *Belle Poule* bearing east by south about 4 leagues: *Marengo* has backed topsails."

"He is waiting for *Berceau* to come up," said Jack. "We shall not see him for an hour or two. What do you say, sir, to a turn on deck?"

Left alone, the Midshipman silently devoured the remains of the pudding, pocketed two French rolls, and darted after his Captain, who was standing with the Commodore on the poop, watching the last boats pull away from the line, filled with passengers bound for the hypothetical safety of the leeward division.

"I cannot tell you, sir," said Muffit in a low voice, "what a feeling of peace it gives me to see them go: deep, abiding peace. You gentlemen have your admirals and commissioners, no doubt, and indeed the enemy to bring your spirits low; but passengers . . . 'Captain, there are mice in this ship! They have ate my bonnet and two pairs of gloves. I shall complain to the directors: my cousin is a director, sir.' 'Captain, why cannot I get a soft-boiled egg in this ship? I told the young man at India House my child could not possibly be expected to digest a hard yolk.' 'Captain, there are no cupboards, no drawers in my cabin, nowhere to hang anything, no room, no room, no room, d'ye hear me, sir?' There will be all the room you merit where you are going to – ten brimstone shrews packing into one cabin in a country ship, ha ha. How I love to see 'em go; the distance cannot be too great for me."

"Let us increase it, then. Give them leave to part company, throw out the signal to tack in succession again, and there you have two birds in one bush. It is a poor heart that never rejoices."

The flags ran up, the ships to leeward acknowledged and made sail, and the line prepared to go about. First the *Alfred*, then the *Coutts*, then the *Wexford*, and now the *Lushington*: as she approached the troubled wake where the *Wexford* had begun her turn, Mr Muffit took over from his chief mate and put her about himself, smooth, steady, and exact. The *Lushington* swung through 90 degrees and the *Surprise* came into view on her port bow. The sight of her low checkered hull and her towering masts lifted Jack's heart, and his grave face broke into a loving smile; but after this second's indulgence his eyes searched beyond her, and there, clear on the horizon, were the topgallantsails of Linois's squadron.

The *Lushington* steadied on her course. Mr Muffit stepped back from the rail, mopping his face, for the turn had brought the sun full on to the poop, where the awning had long since been replaced by splinter-netting, which gave no protection from the fiery beams: he hurried to the side and stood watching the centre and the rear. The line was re-formed, heading south-east with the larboard tacks aboard, a line of ships a mile and a half long, lying between the enemy and the rest of the convoy, a line of concentrated fire, nowhere strong, but moderately for-midable from its quantity and from the mutual support of the close order. A trim line, too: the *Ganges* and the *Bombay Castle* were sagging away a little to leeward, but their intervals were correct. The East India Captains could handle their ships, of that there was no doubt. They had performed this manoeuvre three times already and never had there been a blunder nor even a hesitation. Slow, of course, compared with the navy; but uncommon sure. They could handle their ships: could they fight them too? That was the question.

"I admire the regularity of your line, sir," said Jack. "The Channel Fleet could not keep station better."

"I am happy to hear you say so," said Muffit. "We may not have your heavy crews, but we do try to do things seaman-like. Though between you and me and the binnacle," he added in a personal aside, "I dare say the presence of your people may have something to do with it. There is not one of us would not sooner lose an eye-tooth than miss stays with a King's officer looking on."

"That reminds me," said Jack, "should you dislike wearing the King's coat for the occasion, you and the gentlemen who are to have pendants? Linois is devilish sly, and if his spyglass picks up the Company's uniform in ships that are supposed to be men-of-war, he will smoke what we are about: it might en-courage him to make a bolder stroke than we should care for."

It was a wounding suggestion; it was not happily expressed; Muffit felt it keenly. He weighed the possible advantage, the extreme gravity of the situation, and after a moment he said he should be honoured – most happy.

"Then let us recall the frigate and I will send across all the coats we possess."

The *Surprise* came running down the wind, rounded-to outside the line and lay there with her foretopsail to the mast, looking as easy and elegant as a thoroughbred.

"Good-bye, Captain Muffit," said Jack, shaking his hand. "I do not suppose we shall see one another again before the old gentleman is with us: but we are of one mind, I am sure. And you must allow me to add, that I am very happy to have such a colleague."

"Sir," said Captain Muffit, with an iron grasp, "you do me altogether too much honour."

The lively pleasure of being aboard his own ship gain – her quick life and response after the heavy deliberation of the Indiaman – her uncluttered decks, a clean sweep fore and aft – the perfect familiarity of everything about her, including the remote sound of Stephen's 'cello somewhere below, improvising on a theme Jack knew well but could not name.

The frigate moved up the head of the line, and on his strangely thin quarterdeck – only the more vapid youngsters left and the Master, apart from Etherege and Stourton – he listened to his First Lieutenant's report of Linois's motions. The report confirmed his own impressions: the Admiral had gathered his force, and his apparent delay was in fact an attempt at gaining the weather-gauge and at making sure of what he was about before committing himself.

"I dare say he will put about as soon as every he fetches our wake," he observed, "and then he will move faster. But even so, I doubt he will be up with us much before sunset." He gave directions for making free with all the officer's coats aboard and walked over to the taffrail, where Mr White was standing alone, disconsolate and wan.

"I believe, sir, this is your first taste of warfare," he said. "I am afraid you must find it pretty wearisome, with no cabin and no proper meals."

"Oh, I do not mind that in the least, sir," cried the chaplain. "But I must confess that in my ignorance I had expected something more, shall I say, exciting? These slow, remote manoeuvres, this prolonged anxious anticipation, formed no part of my image of a battle. Drums and trumpets, banners, stirring exhortations, martial cries, a plunging into the thick of the fray, the shouting of captains – this, rather than interminable waiting in discomfort, in suspended animation, had been my uninformed idea. You will not misunderstand me if I say, I wonder you can stand the boredom."

"It is use, no doubt. War is nine parts boredom, and we grow used to it in the service. But the last hour makes up for all, believe me. I think you may be assured of some excitement tomorrow, or perhaps even this evening. No trumpets, I am afraid, nor exhortations, but I shall do my best in the shouting line, and I dare say you will find the guns dispel the tedium. You will like that, I am sure: it raises a man's spirits amazingly."

"Your remark is no doubt very just; and it reminds me of my duty. Would not a spiritual, as well as a physical preparation be proper?"

"Why," said Jack, considering, "we should all be most grateful, I am sure, for a Te Deum when the business is done. But at this moment, I fear it is not possible to rig church." He had served under blue-light captains and he had gone into bloody action with psalms drifting in the wake, and he disliked it extremely. "But if it *were* possible," he went on, "and if I may say so without levity, I should pray for a swell, a really heavy swell. Mr Church, signal, *tack in succession*. All hands about ship." He mounted the hammock-netting to watch the brig that lay outside the line, where all the long file could see her: a great deal would depend on Braithwaite's promptness in repeating signals. The hoist ran up, the signal-gun fired to windward. "I shall give them a moment to brood over it," he said inwardly, paused until he saw the scurrying stop on the forecastle of the *Alfred*, just astern, and then cried "Ready oh! Helm's a-lee."

This movement brought the Indiamen to the point where the *Surprise* had turned, while the *Surprise*, on the opposite tack, passed each in succession, the whole line describing a sharp follow-my-leader curve; and as they passed he stared at each with the most concentrated attention. The *Alfred*, the *Coutts*, each with one of his quartermasters aboard: in her zeal the *Coutts* ran her bowsprit over the *Alfred*'s taffrail, but they felt apart with no more damage than hard words and a shrill piping in the Lascar tongue. The *Wexford*, a handsome ship in capital order; she could give the rest her maintopsail and still keep her station; a fine eager captain who had fought his way out of a cloud of Borneo pirates last year. Now the *Lushington*, with Pullings standing next to Mr Muffit on the quarter-deck – he

could see his grin from here. And there were several other Royal
Navy coats aboard her. *Ganges, Exeter* and *Abergavenny*: she
still had water-butts on her deck: what was her captain thinking
of? Gloag, a weak man, and old. "God," he thought, "never let
me outlive my wits." Now a gap in the centre for the *Surprise*.
Addington, a flash, nasty ship: *Bombay Castle*, somewhat to
leeward – her bosun and Old Reliable were still at work on the
breechings of her guns. *Camden*, and there was Bowes limping
aft as fast as he could go to move his hat as the *Surprise* went by.
He had never made a man so happy as when he entrusted
Camden's guns to the Purser: yet Bowes was not a bloody-
minded man at all. *Cumberland*, a heavy unweatherly lump,
crowding sail to keep station. *Hope*, with another dismal old
brute in command – lukewarm, punctilious. *Royal George*, and
she was a beauty; you would have sworn she was a postship. His
second-best coat stood there on the quarterdeck, its epaulette
shining in the sun: rather large for her captain, but he would do
it no discredit – the best of them all after Muffit. He and
Babbington were laughing, side by side abaft the davits. *Dorset*
with more European seamen than usual, but only a miserable
tier of popguns. *Ocean*, a doubtful quantity.

"Sir," said Stourton, "Linois is putting about, if you please."
"So he is," said Jack, glancing aft. "He has fetched our wake
at last. It is time to take our station. Mr Church, signal, *reduce
sail*. Mr Harrowby, be so good as to place the ship between
Addington and *Abergavenny*." Up until the present Linois had
been continually manoeuvring to gain the wind, and to gather
his forces, making short tacks, standing now towards the Indiamen, now from them. But he had formed his line at last, and this
movement was one of direct pursuit.

While the *Surprise* lay to he turned his glass to the French
Squadron: not that there was any need for a telescope to see
their positions, for they were all hull-up – it was the detail of
their trim that would tell him what was going on in Linois's
mind. What he saw gave him no comfort. The French ships
were crowding sail as though they had not a care in the world.
In the van the *Sémillante* was already throwing a fine bow-
wave; close behind *Marengo* was setting her royals; and

although the *Belle Poule* lay quarter of a mile astern, she was drawing up. Then there was the *Berceau*: how she managed to spread so much canvas after the drubbing she had received he could not conceive – an astonishing feat: very fine seamen aboard the *Berceau*.

In the present position, with the Indiamen under easy sail on the starboard tack with the wind two points free, and Linois 5 miles away, coming after them from the eastwards on the same tack, Jack could delay the action by hauling his wind – delay it until the morning, unless Linois chose to risk a night-action. There was a good deal to be said for delay – rest, food, greater preparation; and their sailing-order was not what he could have wished. But, on the other hand, a bold front was the very essence of the thing. Linois must be made to believe that the China Fleet had an escort, not a powerful escort perhaps, but strong enough to inflict serious damage, with the help of the armed Indiamen, if he pushed home his attack. As for the sailing-order, there would be too much risk of confusion if he changed it now; they were not used to these manoeuvres; and in any case, once the melee began, once the smoke, din and confusion of close action did away with the rigid discipline of the line and with communication, those captains who really meant to lay their ships alongside an enemy would do so: the others would not.

The tactics that he had agreed upon with Muffit and that had been explained to the Captains were those of close, enveloping action: the line of battle to be maintained until the last moment and then to double upon the French ships, to take them between two or even three broadsides, overwhelming them with numbers, however weak the fire of each Company ship. If a regular doubling was not possible, then each Captain was to use his judgment to bring about the same position – a cluster of ships round every Frenchman, cutting up his sails and rigging at the closest range.

Now, after hours of reflection, he still thought this idea the best: close range was essential to make the indifferent guns bite hard; and if he were Linois, he should very much dislike being surrounded, hampered, and battered by a determined swarm, above all if some men-of-war were mingled with the Indiamen. His greatest dread, after the doubtful fighting qualities of the merchantmen, was that of a distant cannonade, with the heavy, well-pointed French guns hitting his ships from 1,000 yards.

Linois vanished behind the foresail of the *Addington* as the *Surprise* glided into her place in the centre of the line. Jack looked up at the masthead, and felt a sudden overwhelming weariness: his mind was running clear and sharp, and the continual variation of the opposed forces presented itself as a hard, distinct point on a graph; but his arms and legs were drained of strength. "By God," he thought, "I am growing old: yesterday's brush and talking to all these people has knocked me up. But at least Linois is still older. If he comes on, maybe he will make a blunder. God send he makes a blunder. Bonden," he cried, "run up to the masthead and tell me how they bear."

They bore 3 points on the quarter: 2½ points on the quarter: *Belle Poule* had set her forestay-sail and she had closed with the two-decker: they were coming up hand over fist. The hails followed one another at steady intervals, and all the time the sun sank in the west. When at last Bonden reported the *Sémillante* at extreme random-shot of the rear of the line, Jack said to the Signal-Midshipman, "Mr Lee, *edge away 1 point*; and get the next hoists ready: *prepare to wear all together at the gun: course south-east by east: van engage to windward on coming up, centre and rear to leeward*."

This was the aggressive manoeuvre of a commander eager to bring on a decisive action. Wearing would reverse the order of sailing and send the whole line fast and straight for the French squadron close-hauled on the opposite tack – a line that would divide on coming up and threaten to take them between two fires. It would throw away the advantage of the wind, but he dared not tack all together – too dangerous an evolution by far in close order – and even this simultaneous wearing was dangerous enough, although a few minutes of edging away would make it safer. Indeed, Linois might well take it as a mark of confidence.

Now they had edged away from the wind; the line was slanting farther south, with the wind just before the beam. "Carry on, Mr Lee," he said, and turned to watch the repeating-brig. The signals ran up aboard her, brisk and clear. "I must give the Indiamen time to make them out," he said, deliberately pacing to and fro. The slow-match for the signal-gun sent its acrid smoke across the deck, and he found his breath coming short: everything, *everything*, depended on this manoeuvre being carried out correctly. If they turned in a disordered heap, if there was irresolution, Linois would smoke his game and in five minutes he would be among them, firing both sides with his 36 and 24 pounders. Another turn: another. "Fire," he said. "All hands wear ship."

Up and down the line of orders echoed, the bosuns' pipes shrilled out. The ships began their turn, bringing the wind aft, right astern, on the larboard quarter, on to the beam and beyond, the yards coming round, round, and harder round until the whole line, with scarcely an irregularity, was close-hauled on the larboard tack, each having turned in its place, so that now the *Ocean* led and the *Alfred* brought up the rear.

A beautifully-executed evolution, almost faultless. "Mr Lee: *make more sail: hoist colours.*" Blue, because Admiral Hervey in Bombay was a vice-admiral of the blue. The *Surprise*, being under Admiralty orders, wore the white. Handsome colours, and imposing: but the speed of the line did not increase: "Signal: *Ocean make more sail: repeat Ocean make more sail*," cried Jack. "And give him two guns."

Ahead of them now, and broad on the larboard bow, there was the French squadron in a rigid line, colours flying: the Admirals' flag at the mizen. The two lines were drawing together at a combined speed of 14 knots: in less than five minutes they would be within range.

Jack ran forward, and as he reached the forecastle Linois fired a gun. But a blank gun, a signal-gun, and its smoke had hardly cleared before the French ships hauled their wind, heading north-north-west and declining the engagement.

Back on his quarterdeck Jack signalled, *tack in succession*, and the line came about, stretching towards the setting sun. In the depths the 'cello was still singing away, deep and meditative; and all at once the elusive name came to him – it was the Boccherini Suite in D minor. He smiled, a great smile filled with many kinds of happiness. "Well, gentlemen," he said, "that was pretty creditable in the Indiamen, hey, hey?"

"I should scarcely have believed it, sir," said Stourton. "Not a single ship fell foul of another. It was giving them time to edge away that did it, no doubt."

"Linois did not care for it," said Etherege. "But until the very last moment I did not think he would sheer off, night-action or no night-action."

Harrowby said, "The Company Officers are a well-behaved set of men. Many of them are serious."

Jack laughed aloud. Out of piety or superstition he would not even formulate the thought, "He mistook the situation: he has made his blunder", far less put it into words: he touched a belaying-pin and said, "He will spend the night plying to windward, while we lie to. His people will be worn out for the morning action. Ours must get all the rest we can manage: and food. Mr Stourton, since we have lost our Purser, I must ask you to see to the serving-out of the provisions. Let the men make a good hearty supper – there are some hams in my store-room. Where is my steward? Pass the word for –"

"Here I am sir, and have been a-standing by the bitts this half-glass and more," said Killick in his disagreeable injured whine, "a-holding of this sanglewich and this here mug of wine."

The burgundy went down more gratefully than any wine he had ever drunk, strengthening his heart, dispelling weariness.

"So there is to be no battle after all?" said the Chaplain, moving from the shadows and addressing either Etherege or the Master. "They appear to be slanting off at a great pace. Can it be timidity? I have often heard that the French are great cowards."

"No, no, don't you believe it, Mr White," said Jack. "They have tanned my hide many a time, I can tell you. No, no: Linois is only reculing pour mew sauter, as he would say. You shall not be disappointed; I believe we may promise you a brisk cannonade in the morning. So perhaps you might be well advised to turn in directly and get all the sleep you can. I shall do the same, once I have seen the Captains."

All that night they lay to, with stern-lanterns and toplights right along the line, each watch in turn at quarters and fifty night-glasses trained on Admiral Linois's lights as he worked up to windward. In the middle watch Jack woke for a few minutes to find the ship pitching heavily: his prayer had been answered, and a heavy swell was setting in from the south. He need not dread the Frenchmen's distant fire. Accuracy, long range and a calm sea were birds tarred with the same feather.

Dawn broke calm, sweet and clear over the troubled sea, and it showed the French and British lines 3 miles apart. Linois had, of course, spent all the night in beating up, so that now he had the weather-gauge without any sort of a doubt – now he could bring on the action whenever he chose. He had the power, but did not seem inclined to use it. His squadron backed and filled, rolling and pitching on the swell. After some time the *Sémillante* left her station, came down to reconnoitre within gunshot, and returned: still the French hung aloof, lying there on the beam of the English line, with their heads north-west; and the heat of the day increased.

The swell from some distant southern tempest ran across the unvarying north-east monsoon, and every few minutes the sharp choppy seas sent an agreeable spray flying over the *Surprise*'s quarterdeck. "If we engage her from the leeward," observed Jack, with his eyes fixed on the *Marengo*, "she will find it damned uncomfortable to open her lower ports." She carried her lower guns high, like most French line-of-battle ships, but even so, with her side pressed down by this fine breeze and with such a sea running, her lower deck would be flooded – all the more so in that she was somewhat crank, somewhat inclined to lie over, no doubt from want of stores deep in her hold. If Linois could not use his lower tier, his heaviest guns, the match would be more nearly even: was that the reason why he was lying there backing and filling, when he was master of the situation, with a convoy worth six millions under his lee? What was in his mind? Plain hesitation? Had he been painfully impressed by the sight of the British line lying to all night, a long string of lights, inviting action in the morning instead of silently dispersing in the darkness, which they would surely have done if yesterday's bold advance had been a ruse?

"Pipe the hands to breakfast" he said. "And Mr Church, be

so good as to let Killick know that if my coffee is not on deck in fifteen seconds he will be crucified at noon. Doctor, a very good morning to you. Ain't it a pure day? Here is the coffee at last – will you take a cup? Did you sleep? Ha, ha, what a capital thing it is to sleep." He had had five hours in his wool-lined well, and now new vigorous life flowed through him. He knew he was committed to an extremely dangerous undertaking, but he also knew that he should either succeed or that he should fail creditably. It would be a near-run thing in either event, but he had not launched himself, his ship, and fifteen hundred other men into a foolhardy enterprise: the anxiety was gone. One of the reasons for this was the new feeling right along the line-of-battle: the Captains had handled their ships well and they knew it; the success of their manoeuvre and Linois's retreat had done wonders for the fighting spirit of those who had been somewhat backward, and now there was a unanimity, a readiness to fall in with the plan of attack, that delighted him.

However, he knew how early-morning sprightliness could anger his friend, and he contented himself with walking up and down, balancing his coffee-cup against the heavy motion of a ship hove-to, and champing a ship's biscuit dipped in ghee.

Breakfast was over, and still the French squadron made no move. "We must help him to make up his mind," said Jack. The signals ran up: the British line filled on the starboard tack and stood away to the westward under topsails and courses alone. At once the frigate's motion became easier, a smooth, even glide; and at once the French ships in the distance wore round on the opposite tack, slanting down southwards for the Indiamen.

"At last," said Jack. "Now just what will he do?" When he had watched them long enough to be sure that this was not an idle move but the certain beginning from which all things must follow he said, "Stephen, it is time for you to go below. Mr Stourton, beat to quarters."

The drum, more stirring even than a trumpet, volleyed and thundered. But there was nothing to be done: the *Surprise* had long been stripped for battle, her yards puddened and slung with chains, splinter-netting rigged, powder filled and waiting, shot of all kinds at hand, match smoking in little tubs along the deck; the men ran to their stations and stood or knelt there, gazing out over their guns at the enemy. The French were coming down under easy sail, the *Marengo* leading: it was not clear what they meant to do, but the general opinion among the older seamen was that they would presently wear round on to the same tack as the Indiamen, steer a parallel course and engage the centre and van in the usual way, using their greater speed to pass along it; whereas others thought Linois might cross their wake and haul up to engage from leeward so that he could use his lower guns, now shut up tight behind their port-lids, with green water dashing against them. At all events they and all the frigate's company were convinced that the time of slow manoeuvring was over – that in a quarter of an hour the dust would begin to fly: and there was silence throughout the ship, a grave silence, not without anxiety, and an urgent longing for it to start.

Jack was too much taken up with watching his line and with interpreting Linois's movements to feel much of this brooding impatience; but he, too, was eager for the moment of grappling and of certainty, for he knew very well that he was faced with a formidable opponent, capable of daring, unusual tactics. Linois's next move took him by surprise, however: the Admiral, judging that the head of the long British line was sufficiently advanced for his purposes, and knowing that the Indiamen could neither tack nor sail at any great speed, suddenly crowded sail. It was a well-concerted manoeuvre: every French ship and even the brig blossomed out in a great spread of white canvas: royals appeared, studdingsails stretched out like wings, doubling the breadth of the ships and giving them a great and menacing beauty as they ran down upon the merchantmen. For a moment he could understand neither their course nor their evolution, but then it came to him with instant conviction. "By God," he said, "he means to break the line. Mr Lee: *tack in succession: make all practicable sail.*"

As the signal broke out, it became even more certain that this was so. Linois was setting his heavy ship straight at the gap between the *Hope* and the *Cumberland*, two of the weakest ships. He meant to pass through the line, cut off the rear, leave a ship or two to deal with what his fire had left, luff up and range along the lee of the line, firing his full broadside.

Jack snatched Stourton's speaking-trumpet, sprang to the taffrail and hailed his next astern with all his force: "*Addington*, back your topsail. I am tacking out of the line." Turning he cried, "All hands about ship. Hard over. Harrowby, lay me athwart the *Marengo*'s hawse."

Now the long hard training told: the frigate turned in a tight smooth curve with never a check, moving faster and faster as they packed on sail after sail. She tore through the water with her lee-chains deep in white foam, heading close-hauled for the point where her course would cut the *Marengo*'s, somewhere short of the British line if this speed could be maintained. He must take her down and hold the *Marengo* until the van ships could follow him, could reach him and give the *Surprise* their support. With her speed it was possible, so long as he lost no important spars; to be sure, it meant running straight into *Marengo*'s broadside, yet it might be done, particularly in such a sea. But if he did it, if he was not dismasted, how long could he hold her? How long would it take for the van to reach him? He dared not disrupt the line: the merchantmen's safety depended entirely on its strength and unity and the mutual support of its combined fire in close order.

Poised at the break of the quarterdeck he checked the position once more: the *Surprise* had already passed three ships, the *Addington*, *Bombay Castle* and *Camden*, moving up in the opposite direction towards their turning-point; and they were making sail – the gap had closed. On the port bow, a long mile away to the north-east, the *Marengo* with white water breaking against her bows. On the port quarter, still a mile away, the *Alfred* and the *Coutts* had made their turn and they were setting topgallantsails: the *Wexford* was in stays, and it looked as though the eager *Lushington* might fall foul of her. He nodded: it could be done – indeed, there was no choice.

He jumped down the ladder and hurried along the guncrews; and he spoke to them with a particular friendliness, a kind of intimacy: they were old shipmates now; he knew each man, and he liked the greater part of them. They were to be sure not to waste a shot – to fire high for this spell, on the upward roll – ball and then chain as soon as it would fetch – the ship might get a bit of a drubbing as they ran down, but they were not to mind it: the Frenchman could not open his lower ports, and they should serve him out once they got snug athwart his bows – he knew they would fire steady – let them watch Old Reliable: he had never wasted a shot all this commission – and they were to mind their priming. Old Reliable winked his only eye and gave a chuckle.

The first ranging shot from the *Marengo* plunged into the sea 100 yards out on the larboard beam, sending up a tall white plume, torn away by the wind. Another, closer and to starboard. A pause, and now the *Marengo*'s side disappeared behind a white cloud of smoke, spreading from her bows to her quarter: four shots of the thundering broadside struck home, three hitting the frigate's bows and one her cathead.

He looked at his watch, told his clerk to note down the time, and kept it in his hand as he paced up and down with Stourton at his side until the next great rippling crash. Far more accurate: white water leapt all round her, topmast high, so many 24-pound shot struck home that her hull rang again: way was momentarily checked: she staggered; holes appeared in her fore and mainsails, and a clutter of blocks fell on to the splinter-netting over the waist. "Just under two minutes," he observed. "Indifferent brisk." The *Surprise* took no more than one minute twenty seconds between broadsides. "But thank God her lower ports are shut." Before *Marengo* fired the next the frigate would be quarter of a mile nearer.

The *Sémillante*, *Marengo*'s next astern, opened fire with her forward guns. He saw one ball travelling from him, racing astern, as he reached the taffrail in his ritual to and fro, a distinct ball with a kind of slight halo about it.

"Mr Stourton, the bow gun may fire." It would do no harm; it might do good, even at this range; and the din would relieve the silent men. The two minutes were gone: some seconds past: and the *Marengo*'s careful, deliberate broadside came, hitting the *Surprise* like a hammer, barely a shot astray. And immediately after that six guns from the *Sémillante*, all high and wide.

Stourton reported, "Spritsail yard gone in the slings, sir. The carpenter finds 3 foot in the well: he is plugging a couple of holes under the water-line, not very low." As he spoke the bow gun roared out and the encouraging, heady smell of powder-smoke came aft.

"Warm work, Mr Stourton," said Jack, smiling. "But at least *Sémillante* cannot reach us again. The angle is too narrow. When *Marengo* starts firing grape, let the men lie down at their guns."

Fine on the port bow he could see the last of the *Marengo*'s guns running out. They were waiting for the roll. He glanced round his sparse quarterdeck before he turned in his walk. Bonden and Carlow at the wheel, Harrowby behind them, conning the ship; Stourton calling out an order at the hances – sail-trimmers to the foretopsail bowline – over to leeward the Signal-Midshipman, then Callow with his bandaged head to run messages, and young Nevin, the clerk, with his slate in his hand; Etherege watching the Indiamen through his little pocket-glass. All the Marines, apart from the sentry at the hatchway, were scattered among the gun-crews.

The crash of the broadside, and of the bow-gun, and of the twenty shot hitting her, came in one breath – an extreme violence of noise. He saw the wheel disintegrate, Harrowby jerked backwards to the taffrail, cut in two; and forward there was a screaming. Instantly he bent to the speaking-tube that led below, to the men posted at the relieving-tackles that could take over from the wheel. "Below there. Does she steer?"

"Yes, sir."

"Thus, very well thus. Keep her dyce, d'ye hear me?"

Three guns had been dismounted, and splinters, bits of carriage, bits of rail, booms, shattered boats littered the decks as far aft as the mainmast, together with scores of hammocks torn from their netting: the jibboom lurched from side to side, its cap shot through: cannon-balls, scattered from their racks and garlands, rumbled about the heaving deck: but far more dangerous were the loose guns running free – concentrated, lethal weight, gone mad. He plunged into the disorder forward – few officers, little co-ordination – catching up a bloody hammock as he ran. Two tons of metal, once the cherished larboard chaser, poised motionless on the top of the roll, ready to rush back across the deck and smash its way through the starboard side: he clapped the hammock under it and whipped a line round the swell of its muzzle, calling for men to make it fast to a stanchion; and as he called a loose 36-pound shot ran crack against his ankle, bringing him down. Stourton was at the next, a carronade still in its carriage, trying to hold it with a handspike as it threatened to plunge down the fore hatchway and thence through the frigate's bottom: the coamings round the hole yielded like cardboard: then the forward pitch took off the strain – the gun rolled towards the bows, and as it gathered speed they tripped it, throwing it over on to its side. But the same pitch, the same shift of slope, working upon the loose gun amidships, under the gangway, sent it faster and faster through the confused group of men, each with his own notion of how to stop it, so that it ran full tilt against the side abaft the fore-chains, smashed through and plunged into the sea. Oh, for his officers! – high discipline did away with the men's initiative – but those he had left were hard at their duty: Rattray out on the perilous bowsprit already with two of his mates, gammoning the jibboom before it carried away; Etherege with half a dozen Marines tossing the balls over the side or securing them; Callow and his boat's crew heaving the wreckage of the launch free of the guns.

He darted a look at the *Marengo*. All but two of her guns were run out again: "Lie flat," he roared, and for the space of the rising wave there was silence all along the deck, broken only by the wind, the racing water, and an odd ball grumbling down the gangway. The full broadside and the howl of grape tearing over the deck; but too high, a little hurried. Rattray and his mates were still there, working with concentrated fury and bawling for 10 fathom of 2-inch rope and more handspikes. The *Surprise* was still on her headlong course, her way only slightly checked by the loss of her outer jib and the riddling of her sails: and now the rear Indiamen opened fire from half a mile. There were holes in the *Marengo*'s foretopsails. And he doubted she would get in another broadside before the *Surprise* was so close on her bow that the broadside guns would no longer bear – could not be trained far enough forward to reach her. If the *Marengo* yawed off her course to bring the *Surprise* into her fire, then Linois's plan was defeated: at this speed a yaw would carry the two-decker east of the unbroken line.

He limped back to the quarterdeck, where young Nevin was on his hands and knees, being sick. "All's well, Bonden?" he asked, kneeling to the tube. "Below there. Ease her half a point. Another half. Belay." She was steering heavy now.

"Prime, sir," said Bonden. "Just my left arm sprung. Carlow copped it."

"Give me a hand with t'other, then," said Jack, and they slid Harrowby over the taffrail. Away astern, beyond the splash of the body, six of the Indiamen were already round: they were coming down under a fine press of sail, but they were still a long way off. Wide on the port bow the *Marengo* was almost within his reach at last. "Stand to your guns," he cried. "Hard for'ard. Do not waste a shot. Wait for it. Wait for it."

"Five foot water in the well, sir," said Stourton.

Jack nodded. "Half a point," he called down the pipe again, and again the ghostly voice answered "Half a point it is, sir." Heavy she might be, heavy she was; but unless she foundered in the next minute he would hit the *Marengo*, hit her very, very hard. For as the *Surprise* came closer to crossing the *Marengo*'s bows, so her silent broadside would come into play at last, and at close range.

Musketry crackling on the *Marengo*'s forecastle: her Marines packed into her bows and foretop. Another 100 yards, and unless *Marengo* yawed he would rake her: and if she did yaw then there they would lie, broadside to broadside and fight it out.

"Mr Stourton, some hands to clew up and to back the fore-topsail. Callow, Lee, Church, jump along for'ard." Closer, closer: the *Marengo* was still coming along with a splendid bow-wave; the *Surprise* was moving slower. She would cross the *Marengo* at something under 200 yards, and already she was so near the two-decker that the Indiamen had stopped firing from fear of hitting her. Still closer, for the full force of the blow: the crews crouched tense over their pointed guns, shifting them a trifle for the aim with a total concentration, indifferent to the musket-balls.

"Fire," he said, as the upward roll began. The guns went off in a long roar: the smoke cleared, and there was the *Marengo*'s head and forecastle swept clean – ropes dangling, a staysail flying wild.

"Too low," he cried. "Pitch 'em up; pitch 'em up. Callow, Church – pitch 'em up." There was no point in merely killing Frenchmen: it was rigging, spars, masts that counted, not the blood that now ran from the *Marengo*'s bow scuppers, crimson against her streak of white. The grunting, furious work of running in, swabbing, loading, ramming, running out; and number three, the fastest gun, fired first.

"Clew up," he shouted above the thunder. "Back foretop-sail." The *Surprise* slowed, lost her way, and lay shrouded in her own smoke right athwart the *Marengo*'s bows, hammering her as fast as ever the guns could fire. The third broadside merged into the fourth: the firing was continuous now, and Stourton and the Midshipmen ran up and down the line, pointing, heaving, translating their Captain's hoarse barks into directed fire – a tempest of chain. After their drubbing the men were a little out of hand, and now they could serve the French-men out their fire was somewhat wild and often too low: but at this range not a shot flew wide. The powder-boys ran, the cartridges came up in a racing stream, the gun-crews cheered like maniacs, stripped to the waist, pouring with sweat, taking their sweet revenge; thumping it into her, cramming their guns to the muzzle. But it was too good to last. Through the smoke it was clear that Linois meant to run the *Surprise* aboard – run the small frigate bodily down or board her.

"Drop the forecourse. Fill foretopsail," he cried with the full force of his lungs: and down the tube, "2 points off." He must at all costs keep on the *Marengo*'s bows and keep hitting her – she was a slaughter-house forward, but nothing vital had yet carried away. The *Surprise* forged on in a sluggish, heavy turn, and the two-decker's side came into view. They were opening their lower ports, running out the great 36-pounders in spite of the sea. One shift of her helm to bring them to bear and the *Surprise* would have the whole shattering broadside within pistol-shot. Then they could clap the lower ports to, for she would be sunk.

Etherege, with four muskets and his servant to load them, was firing steadily at the *Marengo*'s foretop, picking off any man who showed. Half a mile astern, the British van opened fire on the *Sémillante* and *Belle Poule*, who had been reaching them this last five minutes: smoke everywhere, and the thunder of the broadsides deadened the breeze.

"Port, port, hard a-port," he called down the tube; and straightening, "Maincourse, there." Where was her speed, poor dear *Surprise*? She could just keep ahead of the *Marengo*, but only by falling away from the wind so far that her guns could not bear and her stern was pointing at the *Marengo*'s bows. Fire slackened, died away, and the men stared aft at the *Marengo*: two spokes of her wheel would bring the Frenchman's broadside round – already they could see the double line of muzzles projecting from their ports. Why did she not yaw? Why was she signalling?

A great bellowing of guns to starboard told them why. The *Royal George*, followed by the two ships astern of her, had left the line, the holy line, and they were coming up fast to engage the *Marengo* on the other side while the van was closing in from the west, threatening to envelop him – the one manoeuvre that Linois dreaded.

The *Marengo* hauled her wind, and her swing brought the frigate's guns into play again. They blazed out, and the two-decker instantly replied with a ragged burst from her upper starboard guns so close that her shot went high over the frigate's deck and the burning wads came aboard – so close that they could see the faces glaring from the ports, a biscuit-toss away. For a moment the two ships lay broadside to broadside. Through a gap torn in the *Marengo*'s quarterdeck bulwark Jack saw the Admiral sitting on a chair; there was a grave expression on his face, and he was pointing at something aloft. Jack had often sat at his table and he instantly recognised the characteristic sideways lift of his head. Now the *Marengo*'s turn carried her farther still. Another burst from her poop carronades and she was round, close-hauled, presenting her stern to a raking fire from the frigate's remaining guns – two more were dismounted and one had burst – a fire that smashed in her stern gallery. Another broadside as she moved away, gathering speed, and a prodigious cheer as her cross-jack yard came down, followed by her mizen and topgallantmast. Then she was out of range, and the *Surprise*, though desperately willing, could not come round nor move fast enough through the sea to bring her into reach again.

The whole French line had worn together: they hauled close to the wind, passed between the converging lines of Indiamen, and stood on.

"Mr Lee," said Jack. "*General chase.*"

It would not do. The Indiamen chased, cracking on until their skysails carried away, but still the French squadron had the heels of them; and when Linois tacked to the eastward, Jack recalled them.

The *Lushington* was the first to reach him, and Captain Muffit came aboard. His red face, glorious with triumph, came up the side like a rising sun; but as he stepped on to the bloody quarter-deck his look changed to shocked astonishment. "Oh my God," he cried, looking at the wreckage fore and aft – seven guns dismantled, four ports beat into one, the boats on the booms utterly destroyed, shattered spars everywhere, water pouring from her lee-scuppers as the pumps brought it gushing up from below, tangled rope, splinters knee-deep in the waist, gaping holes in the bulwarks, fore and mainmast cut almost through in several places, 24-pound balls lodged deep. "My God, you have suffered terribly. I give you the joy of victory," he said, taking Jack's hand in both of his, "but you have suffered most terribly. Your losses must be shocking, I am afraid."

Jack was worn now, and very tired: his foot hurt him abominably, swollen inside his boot. "Thank you, Captain," he said. "He handled us roughly, and but for the *George* coming up so nobly, I believe he must have sunk us. But we lost very few men. Mr Harrowby, alas, and two others, with a long score of wounded: but a light bill for such warm work. And we paid him back. Yes, yes: we paid him back, by God."

"Eight foot 3 inches of water in the well, if you please, sir," said the carpenter. "And it gains on us."

"Can I be of any use, sir?" cried Muffit. "Our carpenters, bosuns, hands to pump?"

"I should take it kindly if I might have my officers and men back, and any help you can spare. She will not swim another hour."

"Instantly, sir, instantly," cried Muffit, starting to the side, now very near the water. "Lord, what a battering," he said, pausing for a last look.

"Ay," said Jack. "And where I shall replace all my gear this side of Bombay I do not know – not a spar in the ship. My comfort is that Linois is even worse."

"Oh, as for masts, spars, boats, cordage, stores, the Company will be delighted – oh, they will think the world of you, sir, in Calcutta – nothing too much, I do assure you. Your splendid action has certainly preserved the fleet, as I shall tell 'em. Yardarm to yardarm with a 74! May I give you a tow?"

Jack's foot gave him a monstrous twinge. "No, sir," he said sharply. "I will escort you to Calcutta, if you choose, since I presume you will not remain at sea with Linois abroad; but I will not be towed, not while I have a mast standing."

THE ENEMY WITHIN

Jane Jackson

At the outset of the Napoleonic War the British retained superiority at sea whilst the French had a superior land army. As a consequence there was much threat but little action. Napoleon had called upon Spain to provide him with ships, but Spain was not able to and sent funds instead. It was a strange phony war where military intelligence was crucial. In the meantime Napoleon's ambitions grew. He sought the security of a dynastic succession and, in May 1804, he was proclaimed Emperor of France.

Those were the events prior to the following story. Jane Jackson has been writing for over twenty years and is the author of around twenty books, mostly contemporary romances under the alias Dana James, but also several historical romances. Her latest books are A Place of Birds *(1997) and* The Iron Road *(1999).*

With a strong north-westerly breeze on her starboard quarter and foam peeling back from her raked stem, the schooner *Mouette* sliced through breaking wave-crests, braving the foul December weather on yet another mission of stealth and secrecy. As 1804 drew to a close the endless autumn gales were acquiring a fierce edge rare in the Mediterranean.

Mouette was neither king's ship nor scavenger, but any thinking her easy prey would be quickly undeceived. For her captain had paid for extra barrels of powder from his own pocket, and drilled his gun-crews until the schooner could strike with the speed and cunning of a serpent.

Lieutenant Luke Trethowan emerged from the companion-way and, after an automatic glance at the two huge fore-and-aft sails, crossed to the starboard rail, pleased that Kempe had anticipated his order to take in the topsails. The gusty wind was increasing and *Mouette* sailed faster with the centre of effort closer to her hull. He raised the glass and studied the distant coast, aware of the crew's growing anticipation.

Hand-picked from as rough and wild a bunch as had ever set foot in His Majesty's ships of war, he had moulded them into a proud, close-knit band. The miracle – for such it was – had been brought about by tough discipline; the knowledge that he asked nothing of them he had not done himself; decent food that kept them fit; and constant exercising of the schooner's guns.

Eighteen months of fierce actions against prowling priva-teers, and guardships inevitably their superior in size and firepower, had won him their total trust, and built a pride both in themselves and the schooner. Breton-built, she was herself a prize, and Luke commanded her, not under the English flag, but that of either France or Spain as expediency and their mission dictated. And just as the ship sailed under false colours, so too did her captain and crew.

Instead of the white breeches, silk stockings and double-breasted coat with gold buttons and gold lace to which his Royal Naval rank entitled him, Luke wore a faded, salt-stained jacket devoid of all decoration, dark blue trousers and boots. Kempe, and Garrett the Master, were similarly clad. And the crew sported a collection of garments that would shame the crew of a sallee rover.

"One reef on both gaffs, and take in the flying jib, Mr Kempe," Luke said over his shoulder. "Bear away, Mr Garrett. We will excite less interest if we arrive *after* the sun has gone down." He resumed his study of the Spanish coast. Three points off the starboard bow he could see the tall light marking the end of the Mole. On the far side of the harbour entrance, atop rocky cliffs, the long, low walls and tower of Monjui fort lay gold-washed in the sun's dying rays.

An hour later, a shadow in the dusk, *Mouette* slipped into Barcelona harbour, past the Lazareto and Spanish ships of war: fewer than he had expected. A small brig hailed them and the crew froze. Standing forward of the wheel, Luke cupped hands around his mouth and responded in fluent Catalan, cursing the wind and a lazy good-for-nothing crew. It would be just his luck, he grumbled, if she'd got tired of waiting. As a laughing retort floated across the water the men resumed their tasks.

As *Mouette* turned into the wind, Luke gave a signal and the cutter was swiftly lowered. Containing Kempe, coxswain Joseph Kelly, and four seamen with an oar each, it pulled silently away. Luke watched it disappear. If all had gone to plan, the envoy would have made his escape from Madrid and be waiting for them.

Sheltered by surrounding hills the black water rippled like oiled silk, reflecting the lights ashore and on the anchored ships. Under the pretence of jammed lifts and jeers the schooner was turned about so that her long bowsprit pointed once more towards the harbour entrance. Luke peered across the water to the wharf. How long dare they wait? A cold breath feathered across his cheek and stirred the dark, unkempt hair that curled on his collar. Lifting his head he sniffed. Another storm was coming.

He heard muffled oars, the soft drip of water, then a whispered password as a darker shadow approached. With a gentle bump the cutter came alongside. Glancing down, Luke was startled to see not one passenger but two.

"Fore and main, staysail and jib, Mr Veale," he ordered

quietly. Already the crew had the cutter hoisted inboard. Turning to tell the Master their course, he watched Kempe usher the two passengers to the companionway. The second figure was shrouded in a hooded cloak. He stiffened. *A woman?* Before he could speak they vanished below.

Outside the harbour the rising wind tore the tops off the waves, and flung spume across the canting deck as *Mouette* reared and plunged. It would be a hard beat back to the *Victory*.

Kempe reappeared, carefully expressionless. "Begging your pardon, sir, but – I didn't know we were expecting –"

"Nor did I, Mr Kempe. Where are they?"

"In the saloon. I thought it best until –"

"Quite so. My apologies to Mr Garrett."

"He takes the other sea-berth?"

Luke nodded. Seeing the carpenter's frowning gesticulations Luke realised that sailing into the wind in such heavy seas was subjecting *Mouette*'s hull to a severe pounding. He looked up at the straining canvas. "A second reef in the fore and main, and the staysail, Mr Veale. And if it gets worse, take in the fore gaff."

"Ah, Captain," the envoy struggled to his feet, his face pallid and sweat-sheened in the lamplight. But as he extended a hand, the ship's violent motion threw him back onto the wooden bench behind the long table. Hearing a soft gasp Luke glanced round and met the eyes of the other passenger. The shock was brutal: a kick in the chest that stopped his breath. *Emily?* His face stiffened as he fought for control. Shielded from the envoy's gaze, her eyes signalled both plea and warning.

"Lieutenant," Luke corrected, turning quickly to the envoy. The dryness in his throat roughened his voice. "Lieutenant Luke Trethowan."

"Marcus Reid-Stewart." The attempted smile changed to concern. "Is something wrong, Lieutenant? You look uncommonly pale."

"Bad weather and little sleep," Luke was terse. "Forgive me, but I expected only one passenger."

"Indeed? I cannot think why. My wife could not have remained behind without me."

"Sir, conditions are hardly suitable —"

"They will suffice," the envoy interrupted. "Despite my
wife's close acquaintance with the Queen, she would have been
in far greater danger remaining at the Spanish court than from
any conditions we might encounter aboard your ship."

I wouldn't count on it. But Luke saw no point in warning of the
impending storm, nor of privateers roaming the area hungry for
treasure and important passengers who could be ransomed for
gold.

"If you will show us which cabin we are to occupy, we will
detain you no longer. It is vital I reach Lord Nelson as quickly
as possible. I have information for him of the utmost importance."

Luke nodded briefly, noting the ashen face and glassy eyes.
Marcus Reid-Stewart would be puking his guts up within the
hour. Something about the envoy made him bristle. *The fact
that he was Emily's husband?* "Sir, this is a comparatively small
ship with limited facilities. You will occupy Mr Kempe's cabin:
the door to the right at the bottom of the companionway. My
steward will prepare quarters for your wife." Careful not to look
at Emily, Luke left the saloon.

The walls of his day cabin tapered with the narrowing of the
ship towards the stern. A chart was spread over the truncated
triangular table. On either side of the table, padded wooden
benches with hinged seats provided stowage for charts, books
and spare clothes. His dress uniform and shore rig remained in
his sea chest. Above each bench a sea-berth was concealed
behind sliding doors.

But he saw none of it. Having believed the scars long-healed
he was astounded by his own reaction. *Emily Grenville.* His
mouth twisted in a smile that mingled self-mockery with pain.

There had been other women in the ten years since she had
left Cornwall for London. And in that time he had known
laughter and genuine affection. But he had not loved again. War
held fewer risks.

He wrote up the log. The watch changed. And the schooner
battled on through the storm. Above the howl of the wind and
the crash of waves against the hull, he heard a knock. Expecting

his steward to enter with a plate of cold food – the galley fire
would have been doused for safety – he didn't bother to reply.
The knock was repeated. Impatiently he wrenched the door
open.

"I apologise for disturbing you." Emily was distant, aloof.
Then he noticed her hands were so tightly clasped the knuckles
gleamed white and bloodless. "Do you have a doctor on board?"
The husky rasp stirred vivid memories. He fought them,
equally cool.

"No. Why?"

"My husband . . . is not a good sailor."

"I am told water and lemon juice sometimes help. Ask my
steward to prepare a jug."

"Thank you." She turned to leave. But Luke held the door
shut.

"What are you doing here?"

Her back was toward him. "My husband told you. It was no
longer safe for us in Spain."

He hissed with impatience. "You know what I mean."

"No," she said quietly. "I do not. Now please –"

"Did you find it? Whatever it was you were seeking?" He
could not hide his bitterness.

She turned slowly and raised her eyes to his. "It would be
better for you if you didn't ask these questions. The past cannot
be recalled – or changed," she added softly.

He felt the kick again. "But I am asking. I have a –"

"Do not speak of *rights*. You have none."

"But I . . ." *loved you. Sweet Christ, I still love you.* "I have an
interest. After all, we were close once."

"When I left Falmouth, I wasn't running *to*, I was running
from. How could I know what I was looking for?"

"Why do you not want your husband to know that we are . . .
old friends?"

She shrugged, attempting indifference. "Recalling the past
can serve no purpose."

"Is it so easy to forget, then?"

Her eyes were bleak and her voice so quiet he barely caught
the words. "I cannot afford to remember."

"Why?"

"Because . . ." Shaking her head she looked away.

Luke felt a sinking sensation in his chest. "Emily? What happened?"

She took a deep breath as if to steady herself. "I had defied my family. For various reasons I could not return home. I had no money, and nothing to recommend me except my looks. Having been continually reminded by my governess that overt intelligence and too ready a wit were considered most unbecoming in a *respectable* young lady, I had no choice – if I wanted to eat – but to forfeit respectability."

As he tried, and clearly failed, to contain his horror her brief smile reflected pity. "So I became an artist's model: under an assumed name, naturally."

Distraught, he missed her irony. "You sold your body?"

"No," she corrected. "I sold the right to paint my image. And I learned much about men's desire to own, to win, to be the first, the best. As I became known, I was invited to parties and salons. The kind," her level gaze held his, "attended by government ministers and men of letters seeking amusement and relaxation: gatherings to which wives are not invited."

She was goading him, not defiant, yet deliberately inviting his disgust.

"And is that where you met your husband? How romantic."

Her barely perceptible flinch filled him with a shame that was immediately swamped by fury. Damn her. He had every right.

"No. It was my kinsman, Baron Grenville, who arranged the introduction. And before you ask, yes, he was aware of my . . . circumstances."

There was far more to this that he was being told. "But your husband is not?"

"I think it unlikely."

"And are you happy?"

Agony flared in her eyes, but was so quickly gone he thought he had imagined it. "I have debts to honour and promises to keep. Happiness is not a consideration. However, he is not unkind. Now you must excuse me."

Convinced now she was hiding far more than she had disclosed, Luke did not move. "Why, Emily? I would have –" he was silenced by her fingers on his lips.

Instantly withdrawing her hand she looked away "It is too late. Too much has happened. Besides . . ." Shaking her head she turned to the door.

He stood back. After all, she could not go far.

Restless and wakeful, he had been aware of the storm easing during the early hours. Already the schooner rode more comfortably. Jones brought him hot water, which meant the galley stove had been re-lit.

As he went about the day's business, Luke's thoughts kept straying to Emily and their conversation of the previous evening. *Debts to honour and promises to keep.* To whom? He compared the girl he had known to the woman she had become. Men tested by war and the pressures of command exhibited similar change. Some it broke – others revealed a maturing of character, but such experience exacted a high price. She had not uttered a word of complaint, yet it was clear that in some way she had suffered deeply.

It was no concern of his. She was another man's wife and beyond his reach. And yet . . . Her shock had been as great as his own. And behind it – warmth? Relief? It made no sense.

"Sir?"

His deputy's approach forced Emily Grenville from his mind.

Yet at noon, when dinner was piped, something drove him from his day cabin to the saloon. She was already seated at the table, alone. Pale and strained, with dark shadows beneath her eyes, she spoke little and left early.

She did not appear at supper. But Jones volunteered that he had given the lady sufficient bread, cheese, fruit and wine for two. "So it looks like the gentleman is recovering, sir."

The following morning he was woken from fragmented dreams by a shout.

"Deck! Sail on the larboard bow. French privateer."

The *Marquise*. It had to be. Leaping from his cot into shirt, trousers and boots, he reached the top of the companionway in time to hear the lookout's excited yell. "There's two ships! The other one's English, a merchantman by the looks of her. The Frenchie's –" The rolling boom of cannon fire cut him off.

Crossing the freshly scrubbed deck to the rail, Luke raised his glass, impervious to the damp chill. The crew watched him, their anticipation almost tangible.

"Bring her up, Mr Garrett, but hold her 6 points off the wind. We should appear curious but no threat."

As the schooner altered course, Marcus Reid-Stewart blundered onto the deck puffy-eyed and dishevelled, his greatcoat thrown hastily over his night-attire.

"What's happening? I heard gunfire. Why are you altering course? Your orders were to convey me safely from Barcelona to the flagship."

Luke continued his intent study of the two ships. "That merchantman is no match for the *Marquise*."

"It is not our concern." The envoy was brusque. "You must resume your course at once. I have information of vital importance to Admiral Nelson."

"And that merchantman might be carrying desperately needed supplies for the fleet patrolling off Toulon."

"Even so –"

Ignoring him, Luke lowered the glass. "All hands to stations, Mr Kempe." The nature of their missions meant that *Mouette's* guns had been fired more in practice than in combat. And the envoy was right: the duel in progress a few cable-lengths away was not his concern. But the men needed the catharsis of real action. *And so, God help him, did he.*

As the order was passed, grinning men tumbled over each other in their haste to reach their appointed place, having no need of the starter: that short length of hard rope used by the bosun's mates on men judged slow or lazy.

"French colours, if you please." This ruse coupled with the schooner's recognisably-Breton hull shape, would enable them to close on the privateer without arousing suspicion.

"You can't do that!" The envoy was visibly shocked. "Where is your sense of honour?"

Luke glanced at him, perplexed. "This is war, not a game. That is an English merchant ship under attack. Honour demands we do not abandon her. But as the privateer is bigger than *Mouette*, disguise is our only protection."

"And if it is not enough, what then? You have absolutely no right to take such a risk. You have orders. It is your duty –"

"Enough, sir," Luke snapped. "I need no reminder of my duty. The decisions, and the responsibility, are mine. I suggest you return to your cabin." He turned his back.

As the envoy retreated down the companionway, swiftly followed by Kempe and the two ship's boys who were bound for the locked cupboard containing the powder barrels and prepared cartridges, Luke wondered at Reid-Stewart's reluctance to attack the privateer. But there was no time now to pursue the thought.

As covers were whipped off the shot garlands and the deck was strewn with sand – to afford bare feet more purchase should blood be spilled – he raised his glass once more. Below him, designated firemen filled buckets and placed them beside the guns, and the bosun brought the tubs in which slow matches smouldered.

"Loose your guns," Luke ordered. With two men on side-tackles the four 4–pounders – each a 6–foot-long barrel mounted on a heavy oak carriage – were released. After the wooden plugs were removed from the barrels the guns, two on each side and all having a crew of four, were run out again. The boys ran from gun to gun with the cartridges – tightly-packed cloth bags of powder that the sponger pushed into the barrel and rammed home.

Luke weighed his options. With the privateer and the merchantman both wreathed in smoke, it was difficult to see what damage had been sustained. English naval strategy was to aim for the enemy's hull. Though rarely sinking a ship, this caused numerous injuries among the crew, disabled guns, and started fires that frequently blew up the magazine. But to act thus might betray his identity. Better to continue his masquerade and aim for the masts and rigging.

"Load chain shot!"

The crews worked swiftly, their movements smooth and practised. The balls were loaded, the wad rammed down.

"Run out!"

"Prime!" Each gun-captain pierced the flannel cartridge inside the gun and poured in priming powder.

"Point your guns!" Using handspikes, wedges and ropes the guns were levered into position. With a palm over the priming powder to prevent it blowing away, the starboard gun-captains sighted along the barrel. On the opposite side, the sponger took the slow match from its tub and blew gently so it glowed red.

"Bring her up another point, Mr Garrett."

Deafened by the noise borne towards them on the wind, eyes streaming and throats burning from the acrid smoke, *Mouette*'s crew waited. A momentary shift in the breeze allowed Luke a clear view of both ships. The merchantman's foremast had snapped at the foretop and hung in a tangle of broken spars and ripped canvas. At first glance the privateer appeared relatively unscathed. But screams and curses told a different story. Blinking hard, Luke pressed the glass to his stinging eye once more. He hadn't imagined it. The French ship had a slight but definite list. *Mouette* edged closer.

The privateer's crew sighted her and cheers rang out. Still Luke waited. The cheers died and he heard the soft hiss of Garrett's indrawn breath. Just a few more yards . . .

"Starboard guns fire!"

The slow match was pressed onto the priming powder. There was a hiss, a flash, and as the gun crews covered their ears and jumped aside, the guns roared, spitting crimson flame, thick smoke and fragments of wad as they recoiled hard against the tackles.

Aboard the privateer, bellows of shock and disbelief were lost beneath a series of sharp cracks as spars splintered, tearing sails and snapping ropes as they fell.

"Bear away, Mr Garrett." The schooner swung to starboard and parallel to the privateer. "Larboard guns: wait, wait. Fire!" Before the thunderous blast had faded, they heard a long, rending groan, hoarse cries of fear, then the ear-splitting crash of the privateer's mainmast toppling to the deck.

With a mighty cheer, *Mouette*'s gun-crews leapt forward to swab out and re-load.

"Resume your course, Mr Garrett." Satisfaction surged through Luke. While the privateer wallowed helplessly, the merchantman was taking the opportunity to make good her escape. Her damage was considerable, but already he could see fresh spars being hauled up, rigging replaced and new sails bent on.

"Put up the guns, Mr Kempe."

"Aye, sir."

"There's two captains who'll be wondering what the 'ell 'appened," Garrett grinned from behind the wheel.

"We'd best not linger then," Luke replied. "T'gallant, and jib topsail, Mr Veale." Men swarmed up the windward ratlines, and made fast sheets and halyards.

Bowsed tight against the side, wedges in place behind the trucks, the guns were secured. The slow matches were dowsed, fire-buckets emptied, powder barrels and unused cartridges locked away, and the deck washed clean of sand.

By the time breakfast was piped there was little, apart from a residual buzz of excitement among the crew, to show that *Mouette* had taken part in an action.

"I intend to lodge an official complaint." Marcus Reid-Stewart's face was the colour of suet, save for two red patches high on his cheeks. Seated beside him, eyes lowered, Emily crumbled a piece of bread into crumbs. "Your action was most ill-advised —"

"You forget yourself, sir," Luke cut him short. "*I* command this ship. And the action was successful."

"Even so, Lieutenant, you would do well to remember that your future depends upon my safe arrival aboard the *Victory*. How much time has been lost in this morning's escapade?"

The envoy's arrogance stung, but Luke held onto his temper. "None. If the wind holds we should sight the flagship this afternoon." Emily looked up quickly, but bowed her head again before he could read her expression.

Six hours later Luke's anger still burned. The crew, sensing his mood, made sure he found no cause for complaint.

As *Mouette* closed on the *Victory* it occurred to Luke that the term "wooden wall" might have been coined especially for her.

The huge vessel teemed with men: the marines' scarlet uniforms a bright contrast to the officers' blue coats and the sailors' checked shirts and red neckerchiefs.

Leaving Garrett at the wheel and Lieutenant Kempe in command, Luke followed the envoy and Emily down onto *Mouette*'s cutter for the short trip. The three tiers of windows in *Victory*'s squared-off off stern galleries towered high above them as they approached on the leeward side. Then, with oars shipped and the cutter hooked on, Luke was piped aboard through the ornately carved and canopied entry-port. Returning the First Lieutenant's salute, he turned to introduce the envoy and noticed that Emily's face was paper-white.

"Are you unwell?" he whispered.

Without meeting his eyes, she gave her head a quick shake and moved to take the arm her husband extended. He leaned heavily on her, dwarfed by his heavy coat as, guided by another lieutenant, they climbed the companionway and moved aft to the Admiral's quarters. Glancing at the envoy, Luke detected tightly repressed excitement. The prospect of meeting Admiral Nelson? Or did Marcus Reid-Stewart anticipate a reward – career advancement perhaps? – in return for the information he brought?

In the great cabin the rich panelling, buttoned leather, cream and gold paint-work, and maroon velvet with braided silk tassels all faded to insignificance as a small, one-armed figure rose from behind a polished circular table strewn with papers.

Concern rose in Luke at the Admiral's visible exhaustion. His seasickness was common knowledge and for months the Mediterranean had suffered uncommonly bad weather. Yet despite obvious physical frailty, his personality was so powerful, so magnetic, that for a moment Luke did not even notice the huge Captain Hardy who dared not cross the cabin upright for fear of cracking his skull on the beams.

"Mr Reid-Stewart," Nelson smiled. "I am delighted to see you safe and well."

"Thank you, sir. I am much relieved to be here: particularly since Lieutenant Trethowan prefers glory hunting to obeying orders. May I present my wife?"

Standing rigidly to attention, his jaws clamped tight, Luke watched Nelson gallantly raise Emily's proffered hand to his lips and murmur a few words. Then the bright, penetrating gaze was turned on him. "Glory-hunting, Lieutenant?"

"We came upon the *Marquise*, my lord, attacking one of our merchantmen." As Nelson's fine-boned features sharpened in anticipation, Luke continued. "We only had time for two broadsides, but we crippled her."

"And the merchant ship?"

"Under way with a jury rig before the smoke had cleared, sir."

"Well done indeed, Lieutenant." Nelson beamed with satisfaction. "My mother always hated the French." As he turned to Reid-Stewart who, assisted by Emily, was seated on one of the chairs at the table, his expression hardened fractionally. "Lieutenant Trethowan obeyed the first rule of the sea, saving the lives of his countrymen. That has precedence over any orders, Mr Reid-Stewart. However, as you are not a sailor you could not be expected to know that."

Luke noticed that despite the bitter cold, untouched by the small stove, beads of perspiration gleamed on the envoy's forehead and upper lip.

"Now, sir," Nelson leaned forward, his good eye bright. "What news?"

Marcus Reid-Stewart's tongue darted across his lips. "You are aware, my lord, of the capture eight weeks ago of four Spanish treasure ships by English frigates?"

Anger deepened the lines on Nelson's face. "I am indeed. Had Mr Pitt despatched a larger force, the Spaniards could have surrendered the ships with honour intact. But the loss of so many lives – not to mention a large portion of the treasure – gave Bonaparte just the lever he needed to force Spain to declare war on England. Thus our Prime Minister brought about the very situation he feared. God save us from politicians!"

"Well, sir, during the past five weeks Spanish warships have been sailing up the coast to Toulon to join those of France."

"So, we will face a combined fleet. Maybe now they will find their courage and come out. We have waited long enough. But what I need from you, sir, what I hope with all my heart you can supply, is their destination."

"I can, sir. They are bound for Egypt."

Emily cleared her throat. "My lord, I wonder if –"

"Not now, my dear," Reid-Stewart overrode her.

Clearly deep in thought, Nelson appeared oblivious to the exchange.

Ignoring her husband and startling Luke, Emily repeated, "My lord?"

Nelson looked up, frowning.

"That is incorrect." Emily's voice was firm and clear. "The true destination of the combined fleet is Ireland." As everyone gaped at her she lifted her chin, visibly nervous but determined. "My lord, the English government's continued refusal to grant Catholic emancipation has greatly increased Irish sympathy for the Revolution. Bonaparte is trading on this, and plans to use Ireland as a base from which to launch his invasion of England."

"My Lord," the envoy spluttered, having found his tongue at last, "I beg you to forgive this foolishness. My wife –"

"One moment." Nelson raised his hand, and such was his power that though the envoy's mouth remained open, no sound emerged. But Nelson's gaze was fixed on Emily. "How do you know this?"

"Sir, one of the reasons I was sent to Spain was to discover this very information."

"One of the reasons?"

Luke could not have moved had his life depended on it.

"There were others."

"Sir, I must apologise. This is most embarrassing." The flush suffusing Marcus Reid-Stewart's face drained to leave his skin grey. "My wife was not *sent* to Spain. She simply accompanied me."

Emily's gaze did not leave the admiral. "May I explain, my lord?"

Nelson gestured. "Indeed, I should be most grateful."

"Sir, I really don't think –"

The admiral's raised palm silenced him.

"My lord, Baron Grenville, who was until recently Mr Pitt's foreign minister, is my kinsman. When I found myself in desperate circumstances it was to him that I turned for assistance, which he generously gave. My contact with various senior politicians had afforded me insight into the views of both government and opposition concerning the war with France, and Baron Grenville found this information of great interest and significance."

Watching and listening, Luke felt that Emily, known and loved for so many years, was suddenly a stranger.

"The consensus on both sides of the House was that the Peace of Amiens was little more than a cynical ploy by Bonaparte to buy time to re-group his forces. And Baron Grenville believed it vital to obtain accurate information regarding his plans for Spain."

Debts to honour and promises to keep. Now Luke understood.

"A woman," Emily continued, "would be less likely to arouse suspicion. And as I speak Italian and Spanish, Lord Grenville believed I was in an excellent position to win the Queen's friendship and confidence. However, I would not have been received at the Spanish court unmarried. So, under the patronage of Baron Grenville, I returned to society as a wealthy widow and immediately attracted the attentions of Mr Reid-Stewart. However, though Mr Reid-Stewart's ability and ambition were not in doubt, his superiors were less certain of his loyalty."

"I beg you, sir, stop this now." Marcus Reid-Stewart's face was a mask of anguish. "My wife is not well. She lost a child some years ago. Her grief was such that since then she has been prey to wild fancies. Baron Grenville is indeed a distant relative of hers. But all else is the product of a fevered imagination. She craves attention and will say and do anything to gain it. I do most humbly beg your pardon on her behalf, and ask that you show the forbearance due to one so pitiably afflicted. *I* am the government envoy. I have a letter of credence to prove it. And my information is accurate, as events will soon show."

"I commend your concern. Yet your wife seems uncommon lucid and well informed," Nelson was thoughtful. "It can do no harm to let her speak. Madam?"

All eyes returned to Emily, who might have been carved from marble. But for himself, Luke no longer knew what to think. *A child? When? Who?*

"I have no such letter, my lord."

"There." The envoy made to rise. "With your permission, sir, we will retire —"

"With secrecy so vital," Emily continued, cutting him short, "such documents were considered dangerous. But I can tell you that Baron Grenville discussed his plan with both Earl Spencer and Sir Sidney Smith, and they share his concern regarding Bonaparte's ambitions."

Nelson's mouth tightened at the mention of Sir Sidney Smith, whom he was known to consider insufferably arrogant, and his thoughtful frown deepened. As he turned for a private word with Captain Hardy, the Lieutenant, acting on some prearranged signal, asked the envoy if he would care for a glass of wine. Luke used the moment.

"Is it true? You lost a child?" he asked softly.

She gave the briefest of nods, her face expressionless, her eyes dark pools of pain as she whispered, "My son died three years ago. He was six. My lord," she addressed Nelson as he turned from Hardy. "I will tell you what I discovered. It is for you to judge who is telling the truth."

"You're saying there's more?"

"Indeed, my lord. I learned of a plot that will make Spain not an ally of France, but a subject. Manuel de Godoy, the former Prime Minister who was also the Queen's lover, has uncovered a conspiracy between Bonaparte and Ferdinand, Prince of Asturias and heir to the Spanish throne."

"*What?*"

"That is not all —"

"Sir," the envoy broke in, "I beg you to stop this now. My wife is deranged. The continuing strain of life at court; our hasty flight; then being exposed to action while on our way here —"

"Far from pleading our nation's cause, my lord," Emily's voice held utter contempt. "Mr Reid-Stewart was paid a large sum of money by Prince Ferdinand to give you false information."

The envoy sprang to his feet, his face working, and with a backward sweep of his arm hurled Emily against the Lieutenant. "You fools!" he snarled. "Don't you know you are defeated?" Drawing a pistol from inside his greatcoat he aimed it at Nelson. "Without its famed Commander-in-Chief to give it heart, the English Navy is nothing."

Luke saw the envoy's finger curl around the trigger. As Hardy lunged forward, shielding Nelson with his own body. Emily screamed. And Luke, bending low, rammed his elbow hard into the envoy's belly. Marcus Reid-Stewart's breath exploded from his lungs, his arm flew up, and the pistol fired. Feeling searing heat as the ball grazed his cheek, Luke crashed his fist against the envoy's jaw. Marcus Reid-Stewart sprawled, bloody and unconscious, on the carpet as the door burst open and marines poured in.

"Find him a berth in the fo'c'sle," Hardy growled. "He will fight for England whether he likes it or not."

Taking Emily's hand, Nelson bowed over it. "I commend your bravery, madam. England owes you a great debt of gratitude. Lieutenant Trethowan, I am placing Mrs Reid-Stewart in your care. You will see her safely home, deliver my despatches to the Admiralty, then report back to me."

Luke's split knuckles throbbed, his cheek burned, and his nerves were taut from the aftermath of shock and sudden, violent action. He wrestled with the huge grin, and gave the proudest salute of his life. "Aye, sir."

But back on board the schooner, Emily kept to her cabin, even more elusive than on their passage from Barcelona. With extraordinary self-restraint, aided by a fear of saying the wrong thing, Luke did not approach her for thirty-six hours. Eventually he could stand it no longer. Yet unwilling to intrude on her privacy, he sent Jones with a note asking her to come to his day cabin. Then he waited unable to sit still or concentrate.

When at last it came, the quiet knock made him jump up so fast he jarred his thighs against the table, and cracked his head on the lamp swinging from the deckhead. Feeling a total fool, and more nervous than he had ever been in his life, he cleared his throat. "Come in."

Sitting on the bench seat opposite, her head bent, hands out of sight on her lap, she simply waited.

"The child," Luke swallowed. "Was he mine?"

"Yes."

Anger was crushed beneath an avalanche of questions. Why had she not told him? What had he looked like, this son he'd never known? *How had he died?* He needed answers, but they could wait. He yearned to comfort her, but didn't know how. Hating his helplessness and ineptitude, he reached across the table, his hand open, palm up, offering whatever she would take.

She shook her head, a small, hopeless movement. "No, Luke. Too much has happened. There is too much in my past."

"I am part of that past. Besides," he went on before she could speak, "weighed against your courage, anything else is of little account."

She looked at him for the first time, and he saw how drawn her face was, how red her eyes from weeping. "Don't you understand? We can't go back. Nor can we pretend –"

"I don't want to go back. The past is over. We cannot change it, only learn from it. I never thought to see – then when you came on board –" His voice thickened and he glanced away, fearful of shaming himself. "Emily, I can't lose you again. Please."

After what seemed an eternity her fingers slipped, light and tentative, across his palm. He enfolded them with his own.

THE VICTORY

John Frizell

*Once upon a time Trafalgar Day (21 October) was a cause
for national celebration, but in recent times its significance
seems to be forgotten. The decisive victory of Horatio Nelson
and Cuthbert Collingwood, over a combined French and
Spanish fleet under Pierre de Villeneuve (who subsequently
committed suicide rather than face the wrath of Napoleon),
was the ultimate proof of Britain's supremacy over the seas.
Although Napoleon had already moved away from plans for
an invasion of Britain, because of the grip the British fleet
had in the English Channel, this proved once and for all how
futile such an attempt would be. The victory was, of course,
tinged by the loss of Nelson, shot by a sniper. But the loss to
the French and Spanish was overwhelming, with the deaths
of 14,000 seamen and the loss of eighteen ships. Britain lost
no ships, although 1,500 officers and men were killed.*

*The following story is set in the aftermath of Trafalgar
when there are some scores to settle. John Frizell was born
near Vancouver, Canada, and grew up in a small coastal
town accessible only from the sea. After earning a master's*

degree in biochemistry, he joined the environmental group Greenpeace and soon set sail in a refitted subchaser in pursuit of whaling ships in the Pacific Ocean.

He was crawling carefully through low bush, wearing seaman's trousers, a patched brown shirt and a sword belt with weapons and ammunition. The conspicuous red uniform that marked him as a Lieutenant of Marines was neatly folded a mile back by the side of the game trail they were following. The *Angelica*'s senior midshipman, scandalised by the lieutenant's lack of proper uniform, followed closely behind, sweating profusely in his dark wool. Aromatic bushes enveloped them in the scent of herbs. The area was too coarse for grazing but a chance encounter with a hunter was still a possibility.

Matthew pulled himself into a sitting position in the shadow of a large rock and gestured to the sailor to join him. There was a small rise behind the rock so they risked no silhouette; a sentry sweeping the shore with a telescope would see them, otherwise they were safe. They looked out over a natural harbour of stunning beauty. Miles away, at the end of a long finger of sparkling blue water, a small town clung to a hillside. Much closer, less than a mile from where they sat, was the harbour mouth – a narrow gap formed by rock cliffs on both sides which ran for about a quarter mile inland before dropping to rolling hills. Matthew was sitting on the rolling hills and to his right, across the water, a battery of five heavy guns perched on the cliff top commanding both the sea and the harbour mouth.

Matthew took pen, paper and straightedge from a pouch, sighted angles to the battery, sketched and calculated ratios. The privateer they had chased for a day and a night lay moored to a buoy just inside the harbour entrance, half a mile away, looking trim and pretty against the blue water.

"Why are they anchored so far from the town, sir?" asked the midshipman.

Matthew considered. Spain's government had always been the weak partner in its alliance with France. Spain had long been little more than a puppet of France, and with the loss of its fleet at Trafalgar, six months ago, the Spanish people were beginning to resent their rulers. That resentment might extend to a private ship of war which must work closely with the French.

"Perhaps they feel it is in their best interests, Mr Beer," said Matthew and returned to his study of the scene. There was a boom across the harbour mouth, and the privateer was far enough out that the guns of the battery could sweep all around her. A cutting out expedition, either by day or by night, would be suicide.

"We are in luck, Mr Beer," said Matthew. "I believe that this attack can go ahead."

"What do you mean?" asked the midshipman. "The captain has ordered this attack."

Matthew gave him a cold stare.

"The captain has ordered it, sir."

The captain had only given those orders after Matthew had pointed out a place on the hillside above the harbour which seemed to be masked from the battery; British guns placed there could engage the privateer. But when the orders came, they were most unexpected. Matthew had been given command of a shore party comprised mostly of his marines. A dozen seamen under a midshipman were attached to work the guns.

Matthew guessed that the reason for this extraordinary arrangement was to protect his captain. Captain Harvey's father was a Lord, his uncle the comptroller of the navy. Interest had made him a commander at eighteen and made him captain of a 400-ton ship sloop which was bigger and more heavily armed than some post ships. He could expect to be made post soon, provided he did not disgrace himself. Success here would be to the credit of the *Angelica* and her captain. Failure would be of a land-based expedition under marine command – little to do with the ship.

Matthew could not afford to fail. It had strained his interest and his family's resources to purchase his commission and he was nearing thirty, growing old in his rank. He was the only officer on the ship who did not come from a well-bred family. His only chance of promotion was through victory. If he could destroy the privateer it would be his victory. He spread his drawing out on the ground.

"It was not possible to be sure of the angles from the ship, Mr Beer, and there is only one area on this slope where two guns can go. Were the innermost gun of the battery able to reach that place, we would be slaughtered."

"But one British sailor is a match for any three Spaniards, and so the same must be true for guns, sir. So our two 6-pound shot, times three, gives 36. More than a 32 pounder. Do you see, sir?"

"That's bollocks, Mr Beer. Fine for the men to believe, but don't you go believing it. It is being out of the line of fire that makes us a match for them."

Of course they would be within the ship's arc of fire. But how deadly that would be depended on the guns behind the gunports and how well they were served. Carronades, a common armament for a privateer, would be hopelessly inaccurate at the limit of their half mile range. Matthew folded his drawing, beckoned to the midshipman and started the long crawl back.

The sun had been down for three hours when Matthew set foot on the beach of the landing site. The sand swarmed with men. Guns, kegs of powder, shot, timbers and all the other gear were being quietly and cheerfully landed. The men were a pleasant surprise. The *Angelica*'s first lieutenant, doubtless concerned with weakening the ship if the shore party were lost, had picked the worst men in the crew, but in the day that had passed since then, they had all been replaced by volunteers. Both of the master gunner's mates were there. Landsmen and ordinary seamen had been replaced by able-bodied seamen.

The guns were Captain Harvey's personal property, beautiful slender weapons, made by an armory now defunct. "Mind that you bring those guns back, Simmonds. You'll never see the like of those again," had been the captain's parting words to him.

The first gun was slung in its rope cradle and twenty-four men gripped their handles. The brass gun, lighter than iron, rose smoothly into the air and the men set out with a marine leading the way, his red coat black in the bright moonlight. Four journeys would bring the guns and all the stores to dead ground below the crest of the slope. Once the moon had set, they would carry the guns over the crest and set up their battery on the slope.

The track grew rougher as the men laboured forward, roots and bushes snatching at their feet. Matthew heard the muffled oaths when a man stumbled, and grunts of the others as they took his share of the weight. Twice men brought down their neighbours, and the gun fell, luckily without injury. It took much longer than Matthew had reckoned on to bring the chaser to its marshalling point. The second one took longer and cost him his first casualty – a marine with a crushed foot. The man was a good soldier but there was nothing Matthew could do to help him; tomorrow he would lose his foot and with it his profession. The *Angelica*'s surgeon was a former butcher who had bought a surgeon's commission from the Sick and Injured Board and he knew no medical treatment other than amputation. The moon set before the men, quieter and less cheerful, completed the final carry.

Matthew sheltered behind a bush and used a moment of light from a dark lantern to look at his watch. They were badly behind time. If the battery were not established by dawn, their chance of surprise would be gone and chances of success would be much diminished. He fought down the urge to set the men to work and ordered biscuit, cheese and water issued. He ate his rations standing, walking among the men, asking each little group how they did and sniffing carefully for liquor.

The places he had mapped seemed further apart in the enveloping darkness. He found them and led the working parties by hand, each to its place.

The sailors and some marines built the gun emplacements under Mr Beer. Matthew's party of marines dug a firepit behind the rock that had earlier sheltered him. He opened the dark lantern enough to illuminate the work as two men, a former builder and a farm labourer, began to build a dry stone wall around the pit. Others brought up chunks of wood. He left his sergeant to supervise fitting of the grid and loading it with shot and went to check on the guns.

His night vision was poor, thanks to the lantern light, but he could clearly see that there was only one dark clump of men where there should have been two. Lengths of timber had been neatly bolted together to form a smooth wooden floor, a platform which, unlike the deck of a ship, would neither roll nor pitch. But the two platforms were side by side.

"Mr Beer, one of these platforms is in the wrong place."

Work stopped. The men crowded round.

"Begging your pardon, sir," said one of the gunner's mates, "But it makes 'em deadly. Two shot hitting side by side will punch in his timbers where one would not."

He pointed across the water. Matthew glanced toward the privateer and found to his horror that he could see it, looming grey across the water. It was almost dawn. He looked down at the little bit of gundeck that the sailors had created on a Spanish hillside.

"That is very well by sea. But by land we disperse our guns. We spread them out."

The men muttered.

"But Wilks is right," said Matthew. "Two balls striking together will shatter his timbers. We will honour the traditions of the sea by aiming both guns at the same point and we will follow the traditions of the land by dispersing our guns. Marines, bring your spades. Mr Beer, please be so kind as to have your men pick up the inland platform and follow me."

The Mediterranean sunrise came much faster than in England. It started while the marines were digging in the second platform. He ordered the mix of shush and gunpowder poured into the fire pit and lighted. The sun was above the horizon before the flames licked up, sending a column of greasy black smoke into the air.

The ship awoke. There was a flurry of activity on deck and Matthew did not need a telescope to see men pointing. The odds had turned decisively against him. The guns were not yet in position and surprise was gone. If he withdrew immediately, he could get both of the captain's guns back safely and his marines, sniping from the excellent cover of the hills, would cover the retreat and provide an impressive list of enemy casualties should a sortie be launched. A retreat was the right thing to do, just as he would forfeit his stake rather than bet on a weak hand of cards.

"Your orders, sir," said Beer,

The ship was launching a boat.

Matthew had felt the fighting madness that drives men to

think only of injury to the enemy without regard to themselves. What he felt now, an awareness that another chance might not come again and that odds did not matter, was not quite the same. He waved his men into cover, slipped behind a rock to get his own red uniform out of sight and searched the scene, looking for reasons to support the decision he wanted to make. The battery seemed completely unaware. The ship seemed more concerned than alarmed.

"The seamen are to bring up the guns, Mr Beer, but quietly. No cheering. And throw some branches on them so they are not so obvious."

With only the seamen to carry the guns, each man had to bear twice what he had carried before, but with the enemy in sight and full daylight to show them their footing, the men fairly ran down the slope with the guns. The privateer had her boat in the water and men were climbing into it but they did not speed up as the guns were carried into place.

The shot in the firepit would boil spit but not make it dance, as the artilleryman had said it should. He encouraged the man with the bellows to pump harder. The seaward gun, closest to the harbour mouth, was mounted first. The landward gun, closest to the town, was ready a few minutes later. Their crews clumped tightly around them, rammers and heaving bars ready.

"Open fire on the ship with cold shot, Mr Beer."

Beer was staring at the boat. It was crammed with men, more men than there were in the landing party, and it was pulling clear of the privateer, pulling toward them.

"We came to destroy a privateer, not a ship's launch. Open fire."

The first gun sent a plume of water over the privateer's deck. The second raised no splash at all, earning her crew the bottle of neat rum Matthew had promised for the first hit. The activity on the privateer's deck increased. Gun ports started to open. Matthew thought he heard a trumpet from the battery and the red and yellow flag of Spain ran up its flag staff.

The guns fired again and this time there were no splashes. The gunner's mates knew their work. Beer trained a telescope on the ship then looked at Matthew and shook his head. With his bare eye, Matthew could see long guns, not carronades, poking out of the privateer's ports, and a ship moored in a sheltered harbour is almost as good a platform for gunnery as the land. But Matthew's target was nearly 100 feet long. His guns and crews presented individual targets no more than a yard wide.

Before the guns fired again, Matthew was back at the firepit. The wheeze of the bellows was louder than the crackling of the flames and the grid was beginning to glow. The heat over the grid threatened to set his uniform alight. He picked up a long stick and touched it to the nearest shot. The end of the stick burst into flames. He signalled to his corporal who took the giant tongs the armourer had made and, with the motion he had rehearsed a hundred times with cold shot, picked up the hot iron sphere and deposited it onto an iron stretcher. Two marines set off to the first gun and the second carrying team moved into place. Shot from the ship hummed through the air. A 4-pounder ball smacked into the ground near Matthew then bounced high.

The rhythm of the gun teams changed as they added a wet wad on top of their dry wad then fumbled with bars, unable just to pick up the shot and insert it. The boat was slowing. To the seaward, the cliffs of the harbour mouth offered no landing spot. The slope below the guns ended in sheer drop into the sea. Further down the harbour was a beach, ideal for landing, but to reach the beach meant crossing the stream of shot passing from ship to shore and shore to ship. The boat picked up speed again and made for a partly submerged ledge of rock that offered a passable landing point at the break where the cliffs became hills.

Half a dozen hot shot had gone on board the privateer and Matthew waited for it to burst into flames. Although he had told Captain Harvey that he understood the use of heated shot and had seen it in action, he had not mentioned that his one glimpse of a battery firing red hot balls had been from a mile away or that his knowledge was based on a conversation with an artilleryman over beer. But all seamen feared heated shot – it could not be long now. Already he could see results. Buckets tied to ropes were being thrown over the side and hauled up.

The fore-and aft-most guns had fired twice then stopped. Smoke jetted from a midship gun and Matthew counted slowly to himself. On three there was a ripping sound as a ball tore through the shrubs, followed by a clang as it hit a rock and rolled away. It was bigger than the others, an 8-pounder or a 6. The familiar power smoke smell of battle was mixed with the aromatic tang of sage and rosemary chopped by the bouncing cannon ball.

"Concentrate your fire amidships please, Mr Beer."

"Aye, aye, sir," said Beer and looked beseechingly at him, then at the boat. It had covered half the distance to the landing site. It would be there in three or four minutes.

"Fire on the ship, Mr Beer. But when that boat is within 200 yards you may give it a round of grape from the seaward gun. And if that does not discourage them, canister from both guns when they are 10 yards off the shore."

Beer's face shone with murderous glee. The stretcher men trotted by and Matthew glanced at them just as a cannonball hit the leading man, cutting his arm off and punching through his body, throwing a long spray of blood that covered the earth, pointing like an accusing finger back at the torn body. Flames leapt up where the glowing shot from the stretcher struck the ground. Fear soaked into Matthew, making it hard to think. He had been afraid before, usually while waiting to board an enemy, but always the intensity of the fighting, the extraordinary concentration and awareness necessary to survive in a swirling mass of armed men hacking and shooting at each other, had burned it away. There had been no time for fear. But here on an exposed hillside, swept with cannonballs, it was different.

The seaward gun, laid by Beer and a gunner's mate, fired its grape with deadly accuracy. Water leapt up around the boat and Matthew could see ripples among its crew as the grape went home. Oars dragged in the water. Then the boat crabbed its way around in an awkward circle and went back the way it had come.

The men cheered. Matthew opened his mouth to admonish them and realised it was the crew of the landward gun who were cheering. They were pointing at the battery. A block of stone was falling from the parapet of the most inland battery gun, bouncing down the cliffs. Why had the fools fired on the battery? And how had a 6-pounder done that? He could see tiny figures swarming over the parapet with gleaming tools in

their hands. The Spanish were demolishing part of their parapet so they could bring a gun into play.

"They have breached their own defences," said Beer. "The
gun's crew is visible. May I engage the battery, sir?"

A counter battery-duel between two 6-pounders in the open
and a 32-pounder with partial protection, with the heavy gun
able to draw on four complete gun crews for replacements, did
not appeal to Matthew. And the frantic activity on the privateer
seemed to be paying off; there was no smoke coming from her
and a crew appeared to be returning to the aftermost gun.

"Fire on the ship, Mr Beer."

A second block of stone fell from the battery.

The first of the heavy shot struck an outcrop of bare rock 50
yards from the landward gun with an enormous clang and then
bounced over the hill and disappeared. The men laughed in
derision and fired well-aimed shot into the ship. Matthew saw
flames burst from the deck, but a moment later bucket men
doused them.

If he retreated now, he could go with honour and bring the
captain's guns back safely. No one would blame him for
retreating under such odds. There would be no promotion
but his men would not be exposed to slaughter. The fountain
of blood from poor Williams sprayed into his mind again. Still,
the battery gun was firing at dispersed men. A man hit by a 32-
pound ball was no more dead than one hit by a 4-pounder.

As he struggled with the decision, a second 32-pounder ball
struck wide of the landward gun. His need for victory warred
with his common sense. Fear made it hard to think. The heavy
gun did not make the odds much worse. Unless it hit one of his
guns. But it did not appear very accurate. A third wide shot
confirmed his opinion.

"Sir, we have only a dozen rounds left per gun," said Beer.

"Then make them count, Mr Beer."

A 4-pound shot whipped by with a sound like ripping cloth.
It ricocheted off a boulder, twisted sideways and bounded along
the ground to take the foot off the rammer of the seaward gun.

The stretchermen went by, carrying a pair of balls that glowed
a dull yellow. Matthew stopped them, ordered a round of cold

shot, and stopped the bellows man. The artilleryman had been very clear on this point – if the shot went above red hot it would burn through the wet wad and set the gun off prematurely. "And you'll never steady the gun's crew again," the officer had told him, "Not after their mates have been crushed by the recoil. You may get them to work the gun but they won't stand behind it and aim it, not when they know it can go off by itself."

The launch passed behind the ship. Its crew would no doubt go on board to fight fires. But a moment later it reappeared, followed by two smaller boats. The Spanish were coming on with far more determination then he had expected. He should have sunk the launch instead of merely scaring it off. He called Beer to fire the cold shot at the launch, but as he did, the guns went off, firing at the ship. He had missed his chance; the boats were moving quickly at long range, a hit was uncertain. The shot had cooled to a cherry red. Beer was looking at him. Matthew pointed at the ship and sent the stretchermen on their way.

The three boats had over a hundred men in them and they were circling wide to land on the beach. Say five minutes for them to land and the best part of ten for the men to scramble across the hills and reach the guns. Matthew signalled his sergeant.

"Johnson. Take nine men to within musket shot of where those boats land. Engage them and fall back in skirmish order with strong flanks and a weak centre so they move into a column. Do you see that bare patch with one bush growing in the middle? Make sure it takes them twenty minutes to reach it."

Johnson, who had happily accepted orders to attack at ten-to-one odds, now seemed flustered. Matthew dug out his pocket watch and handed it to his sergeant.

The seaward 6-pounder fired, and he saw the black blur of the ball, like a line being written in charcoal, constantly erased from its trailing end as it curved down toward a perfect hit on the privateer's deck. A fountain of smoke shot from the midships gun as the privateer replied. A thump and the crash of shot hitting timber came together as the ball from the 8-pounder bounced just short of the seaward gun and struck full on its undercarriage, propelling the recoiling gun into the air and reducing the carriage to shattered wreckage. Miraculously the crew were unhurt. The gunner's mate struggled to his feet.

"Brown. Get this gun moving back to the ship."

Matthew inspected the fire pit. All the remaining shot were glowing red on the rack. He pointed at the bellows man, the fire tender and two stretcher men.

"You, you, you and you. Go with Brown, do what he says."

Brown looked at the eight men and the half-ton gun.

"But sir –"

"I know how much it weighs. Take it in short carries and rests. Roll it. I don't care what you do but get it back to the boat."

Matthew loaded a stretcher, took one end and led off to the remaining gun.

The sound of a single volley came from down the slope and Matthew frowned. But half a minute later came the first of the single shots and he relaxed. His marines could fire three aimed shots a minute under perfect conditions, a bit less than two a minute if they had to move between shots. The enemy would receive a musket ball every four or five seconds, enough to slow a headlong rush. Matthew tipped the stretcher against the mouth of the gun and a seaman pushed the glowing ball home with a metal bar.

A 32-pounder ball landed in a patch of gravel just short of the gun and bounced harmlessly overhead. The gravel sprayed like grapeshot into the crew. One man came up clawing at his face, a mask of blood obscuring his wounds. The gunner's mate did not come up at all. The gun sat untended, hissing softly as the red-hot shot burned its way through the wet wad. Beer was on his hands and knees behind the gun. Matthew dragged him clear and fired the gun without attempting to aim it. He helped Beer to his feet and set out for more hot shot and more men.

His right leg stung and the red of his uniform was being stained a darker red. He pulled down his trousers and found a shard of rock embedded in his upper leg, blood dribbling from the wound. He grasped it with both hands and pulled. Fire washed through his leg, then the rock was free in his hands. The dribble of blood became a stream. He folded a handkerchief, tied it around the wound and limped on to the fire pit where he loaded two more shot and, together with the remaining fire tender, carried them to the gun. They left the stretcher propped between two rocks, and returned for the other stretcher and the last of the shot. His right boot squelched with every step he took. He was very tired.

The crackle of musketry was getting closer. The privateer was still not burning.

"Mr Beer. Kindly put these last two shot into the privateer. Then load with grape and double canister, and point the gun at that bush in the middle of that bare patch."

Beer made no objection to a load that was as likely as not to make the gun explode. Matthew sank onto a rock and watched the crew sponge, load and fire, sponge, load and fire. This gun was lost. The ten marines were covering the retreat. Five of his little force were wounded or dead and the wounded could not walk without help. With only a dozen men he could not bring back both guns. He had left it too long. His skirmishers could slow a hundred men but they could not stop them. The retreating force with the wounded and the gun would be caught before they reached the boat.

The activity around the gun died away. He sent Beer and the crew to reinforce the party carrying the other gun, and then dragged Williams' body over to the gun and propped it against the carriage. The body of the master's mate he left where it was, sprawled beside the platform. He took a piece of slow match, blew on it to make sure it was well alight, and lay down beside the gun, his blood soaked-leg outstretched – another body among a slaughtered crew. His fear was gone and it was very comfortable on the ground. Comfort in battle. He could see himself back in the *Angelica*'s wardroom, telling them of this experience, and he felt a giddiness, like a bottle too many at a wardroom dinner. As he drifted into unconsciousness his muscles relaxed. His head rolled sideways until his face touched the tip of the burning slow match.

He jerked awake. There were voices speaking Spanish right in front of him and a forest of legs approaching. The voice of his sergeant yelling orders was coming from behind. He had been overrun.

He heaved himself up onto his knees. A Spanish seaman with a cutlass ran at him. Matthew's sword was in its scabbard; he could not draw it in time to defend himself. He whipped the slow match through the air and ground the glowing end into the powder heaped on the touch hole. A hiss was followed by a shattering explosion as the overcharged gun fired. He staggered to his feet. The man with the cutlass was gone. A solid trail of gore showed where 18 pounds of musket balls and grapeshot had torn the length of the straggling column.

Matthew turned and ran, expecting the impact of a ball or blade. He was half way to the top of the hill when he tripped and the ground shot up to meet him. Before he could regain his feet, strong arms gripped his waist. He groped for his sword to cut them away.

"Sir, don't be daft. It's me sir. I'll hit you, sir, if you try to cut me."

Sergeant Johnson's words filtered through the ringing of Matthew's ears into his dazed brain. He leaned on the man and put one foot in front of the other until they cleared the crest of the hill. He began giving orders for covering the retreat, but lost consciousness and fell to the ground.

The sergeant cut open the leg of his lieutenant's uniform. Blood oozed from the cut as if the cloth were flesh. The ground under the leg was already soaked with blood. A stream of blood leaked through a sodden handkerchief. The sergeant cut it away, wrapped the wound tightly with a length of rag from the supply he always carried in battle, and looked closely at the pallor of the lieutenant's tanned face.

"He might live. Phillips, Jackson, get him back to the ship. Don't let that surgeon near him."

Matthew did not hear his men's steady volleys from cover which kept the shattered enemy force pinned down, unaware that only eight men stood between them and bloody revenge. On board the privateer one of the fires smouldering underneath the deck burst out, billowing up into the rigging and turning the ship into a giant torch. Screams of despair burst from the Spanish seamen huddled on the slope, but Matthew was too far away to hear them, even if he had been conscious. He was still unconscious when he was gently lifted up the *Angelica*'s side and carried down to his cabin.

Sergeant Johnson knocked on the door of Matthew's cabin and entered. He asked after his health and offered rum and lemon juice. He had a bottle of wine in his other hand.

"As long as I don't move the leg, I'm fine," said Matthew. It was almost true. He was floating on a cloud made partly of opium, partly of rum, but mostly of happiness in his victory and dreams of the future.

Corporal Jackson squeezed in after his sergeant, carrying a fried egg balanced on a piece of real bread. Matthew looked at them suspiciously. They had been waiting on him like this since he awoke, two days and a night after the battle. They were good men, but not this good.

"What is wrong?" he asked.

Nothing was wrong they said, but their lies were transparent.

"Jackson. Go and tell Mr Beer that I would be obliged to him if were to visit me when he has a moment."

"It's not his fault sir."

"*What* is not his fault?"

"The captain did it, sir."

"What did the captain do?"

"It's in his dispatch, sir," said Johnson. "Beer was in command at the moment the privateer caught fire and he gave Beer credit for the victory. The seamen all say that Lieutenant Beer is going to be given his own ship in a week or two. Then Beer's family will make sure that the captain gets his promotion to post captain."

Matthew slumped back in his hanging cot and waved his marines away. Then he struggled to a sitting position and called Johnson back.

"Yes sir?"

"You can leave that bottle of wine."

A MURDEROUS CONFLICT

Frederick Marryat

Captain Frederick Marryat (1792–1848) was the first popular writer of naval stories of the Napoleonic period. They were written from direct personal experience. The young Marryat had an unhappy home life and a passion for the sea. He ran away to sea three times before he formally entered the service in 1806 as a volunteer on the thirty-eight-gun frigate Impérieuse. *He saw service in the North Sea, the Mediterranean and the West Indies, and also served in the war against the United States in 1812. He was granted a commission as lieutenant in 1813 and promoted to commander in 1815, at the remarkably young age of 23. However, he did not receive a command until 1820 with the sloop* Beaver. *Marryat was an extremely brave officer, frequently mentioned in despatches, and a recipient of the Gold Medal from the Humane Society for rescuing the lives of others while placing his own life in peril.*

Always impulsive, and never one to see eye-to-eye with authority, Marryat eventually resigned his commission in 1828 after an argument with the Admiralty. After an abortive attempt to stand for Parliament, he settled down to write novels. Having frittered away his father's fortune, and with a large family, Marryat was forced to write quickly for money (which he spent just as quickly). He averaged a book or two a year for the next twenty years. Today he is probably best known for his children's book The Children of the New Forest *(1847), but in his day his most popular books were his sea stories. These began with* Frank Mildmay *(1829) and* The King's Own *(1830) and reached their peak with* Peter Simple *(1834),* Mr Midshipman Easy *(1836) and* Masterman Ready *(1842). Marryat was one of the first to shift these stories to suit younger readers, and he frequently referred to his leading character as "our hero". Nevertheless the stories are full of the grim realism of naval life, and Marryat pulled no punches.*

The following story is from Mr Midshipman Easy *and almost certainly relates to a real incident which took place between the* Impérieuse *and a privateer off Corsica in 1808.*

Despatches from the commander-in-chief required Captain Wilson to make all possible haste in fitting, and then to proceed and cruise off Corsica, to fall in with a Russian frigate which was on that coast; if not there, to obtain intelligence, and to follow her wherever she might be.

All was now bustle and activity on board of the *Aurora*. Captain Wilson, with Jack Easy and Gascoigne, quitted the governor's house and repaired on board, where they remained day and night. On the third day the *Aurora* was complete and ready for sea, and about noon sailed out of Valette Harbour.

In a week the *Aurora* had gained the coast of Corsica, and there was no need of sending look-out men to the mast-head, for one of the officers or midshipmen was there from daylight to dark. She ran up the coast to the northward without seeing the object of her pursuit, or obtaining any intelligence.

Calms and light airs detained them for a few days, when a northerly breeze enabled them to run down the eastern side of the island. It was on the eighteenth day after they had quitted Malta, that a large vessel was seen ahead about 18 miles off. The men were then at breakfast.

"A frigate, Captain Wilson, I'm sure of it," said Mr Hawkins, the chaplain, whose anxiety induced him to go to the mast-head.

"How is she steering?"

"The same way as we are."

The *Aurora* was under all possible sail, and when the hands were piped to dinner, it was thought that they had neared the chase about 2 miles.

"This will be a long chase; a stern chase always is," observed Martin to Gascoigne.

"Yes, I'm afraid so – but I'm more afraid of her escaping."

"That's not unlikely either," replied the mate.

"You are one of Job's comforters, Martin," replied Gascoigne.

"Then I'm not so often disappointed," replied the mate. "There are two points to be ascertained: the first is, whether we shall come up with the vessel or lose her; the next is, if we do come up with her, whether she is the vessel we are looking for."

"You seem very indifferent about it."

"Indeed, I am not: I am the oldest passed midshipman in the ship, and the taking of the frigate will, if I live, give me my promotion, and if I'm killed, I shan't want it. But I've been so often disappointed, that I now make sure of nothing until I have it."

"Well, for your sake, Martin, I will still hope that the vessel is the one we seek, that we shall not be killed, and that you will gain your promotion."

"I thank you, Easy – I wish I was one that dared hope as you do."

Poor Martin! He had long felt how bitter it was to meet disappointment upon disappointment. How true it is, that hope deferred maketh the heart sick! And his anticipations of early days, the buoyant calculations of youth, had been one by one crushed, and now, having served his time nearly three times over, the reaction had become too painful, and, as he truly said, he dared not hope: still his temper was not soured, but chastened.

"She has hauled her wind, sir," hailed the second lieutenant from the topmast cross-trees.

"What think you of that, Martin?" observed Jack.

"Either that she is an English frigate, or that she is a vessel commanded by a very brave fellow, and well-manned."

It was sunset before the *Aurora* had arrived within 2 miles of the vessel; the private signal had been thrown out, but had not been answered, either because it was too dark to make out the colours of the flags, or that these were unknown to an enemy. The stranger had hoisted the English colours, but that was no satisfactory proof of her being a friend; and just before dark she had put her head towards the *Aurora*, who had now come stem down to her. The ship's company of the *Aurora* were all at their quarters, as a few minutes would now decide whether they had to deal with a friend or foe.

There is no situation perhaps more difficult, and demanding so much caution, as the occasional meeting with a doubtful ship. On the one hand, it being necessary to be fully prepared, and not allow the enemy the advantage which may be derived from your inaction; and on the other, the necessity of prudence, that you may not assault your friends and countrymen. Captain Wilson had hoisted the private night-signal, but here again it was difficult, from his sails intervening, for the other ship to make it out. Before the two frigates were within three cables' length of each other, Captain Wilson determined that there should be no mistake from any want of precautions on his part, hauled up his courses and brailed up his driver that the night-signal might be clearly seen.

Lights were seen abaft on the quarter-deck of the other vessel, as if they were about to answer, but she continued to keep the *Aurora* to leeward at about half a cable's length, and as the foremost guns of each vessel were abreast of each other, hailed in English:

"Ship ahoy! what ship's that?"

"His Majesty's Ship *Aurora*," replied Captain Wilson, who stood on the hammocks. "What ship's that?"

By this time the other frigate had passed half her length clear of the beam of the *Aurora*, and at the same time that a pretended reply of "His Majesty's Ship . . ." was heard, a broadside from her guns, which had been trained aft on purpose, was poured into the *Aurora*, and at so short a distance, doing considerable execution. The crew of the *Aurora*, hearing the hailing in English, and the vessel passing them apparently without firing, had imagined that she had been one of their own cruisers. The captains of the guns had dropped their lanyards in disappointment, and the silence which had been maintained as the two vessels met was just breaking up in various ways of lamentation at their bad luck, when the broadside was poured in, thundering in their ears, and the ripping and tearing of the beams and planks, astonished their senses. Many were carried down below, but it was difficult to say whether indignation at the enemy's ruse, or satisfaction at discovering that they were not called to quarters in vain, most predominated. At all events, it was answered by three voluntary cheers, which drowned the cries of those who were being assisted to the cockpit.

"Man the larboard guns and about ship!" cried Captain Wilson, leaping off the hammocks. "Look out, my lads, and rake her in stays! We'll pay him off for that foul play before we've done with him. Look out, my lads, and take good aim as she pays round."

The *Aurora* was put about, and her broadside poured into the stern of the Russian frigate – for such she was. It was almost dark, but the enemy, who appeared as anxious as the *Aurora* to come to action, hauled up her courses to await her coming up. In five minutes the two vessels were alongside, exchanging murderous broadsides at little more than pistol-shot – running slowly in for the land, then not more than 5 miles distant. The skin-clad mountaineers of Corsica were aroused by the furious cannonading, watching the incessant flashes of the guns, and listening to their reverberating roar.

After half-an-hour's fierce combat, during which the fire of both vessels was kept up with undiminished vigour, Captain Wilson went down on the main-deck, and himself separately pointed each gun after it was loaded; those amidships being direct for the main-channels of the enemy's ship, while those abaft the beam were gradually trained more and more forward, and those before the beam more and more aft, so as to throw all their shot nearly into one focus, giving directions that they were all to be fired at once, at the word of command. The enemy, not aware of the cause of the delay, imagined that the fire of the *Aurora* had slackened, and loudly cheered. At the word given, the broadside was poured in, and, dark as it was, the effects from it were evident. Two of the midship ports of the antagonist were blown into one, and her mainmast was seen to totter, and then to fall over the side. The *Aurora* then set her courses, which had been hauled up, and shooting ahead, took up a raking position, while the Russian was still hampered with her wreck, and poured in grape and cannister from her upper deck carronades to impede their labours on deck, while she continued her destructive fire upon the hull of the enemy from the main-deck battery.

The moon now burst out from a low bank of clouds, and enabled them to accomplish their work with more precision. In a quarter of an hour the Russian was totally dismasted, and Captain Wilson ordered half of his remaining ship's company to repair the damages, which had been most severe, whilst the larboard men at quarters continued the fire from the main-deck. The enemy continued to return the fire from four guns, two on each of her decks, which she could still make bear upon the *Aurora*, but after some time even these ceased, either from the men having deserted them, or from their being dismounted. Observing that the fire from her antagonist had ceased, the *Aurora* also discontinued, and the jolly-boat astern being still uninjured, the second lieutenant was deputed to pull alongside of the frigate to ascertain if she had struck.

The beams of the bright moon silvered the rippling water as the boat shoved off; and Captain Wilson and his officers, who were still unhurt, leant over the shattered sides of the *Aurora*, waiting for a reply: suddenly the silence of the night was broken upon a loud splash from the bows of the Russian frigate, then about three cables' length distant.

"What could that be?" cried Captain Wilson. "Her anchor's down. Mr Jones a lead over the side, and see what water we have."

Mr Jones had long been carried down below, severed in two with a round shot – but a man leaped into the chains, and lowering down the lead sounded in 7 fathoms.

"Then I suspect he will give us more trouble yet," observed Captain Wilson; and so indeed it proved, for the Russian captain, in reply to the second lieutenant, had told him in

English, "that he would answer that question with his broadside," and before the boat was dropped astern, he had warped round with the springs on his cable, and had recommenced his fire upon the *Aurora*.

Captain Wilson made sail upon his ship, and sailed round and round the anchored vessel, so as to give her two broadsides to her one, and from the slowness with which she worked at her springs upon her cables, it was evident that she must be now very weak-handed. Still the pertinacity and decided courage of the Russian captain convinced Captain Wilson, that, in all probability, he would sink at his anchor before he would haul down his colours; and not only would he lose more of the *Aurora*'s men, but also the Russian vessel, unless he took a more decided step. Captain Wilson, therefore, resolved to try her by the board. Having poured in a raking fire, he stood off for a few moments, during which he called the officers and men on deck, and stated his intention. He then went about, and himself conning the *Aurora*, ran her on board the Russian, pouring in his reserved broadside as the vessels came into collision, and heading his men as they leaped on the enemy's decks.

Although, as Captain Wilson had imagined, the Russian frigate had not many men to oppose to the *Aurora*'s, the deck was obstinately defended, the voice and the arm of the Russian captain were to be heard and seen everywhere, and his men, encouraged by him, were cut down by numbers where they stood.

Easy, who had the good fortune to be still unhurt, was for a little while close to Captain Wilson when he boarded, and was about to oppose his unequal force against that of the Russian captain, when he was pulled back by the collar by Mr Hawkins, the chaplain, who rushed in advance with a sabre in his hand. The opponents were well matched, and it may be said that, with little interruption, a hand-to-hand conflict ensued, for the moon lighted up the scene of carnage, and they were well able to distinguish each other's faces. At last, the chaplain's sword broke: he rushed in, drove the hilt into his antagonist's face, closed with him, and they both fell down the hatchway together. After this, the deck was gained, or rather cleared, by the crew of the *Aurora*, for few could be said to have resisted, and in a minute or two the frigate was in their possession. The chaplain and the Russian captain were hoisted up, still clinging to each other, both senseless from the fall, but neither of them dead, although bleeding from several wounds.

As soon as the main deck had been cleared, Captain Wilson ordered the hatches to be put on, and left a party on board while he hastened to attend to the condition of his own ship and ship's company.

It was daylight before anything like order had been restored to the decks of the *Aurora*; the water was still smooth, and instead of letting go her own anchor, she had hung on with a hawser to the prize, but her sails had been furled, her decks cleared, guns secured, and the buckets were dashing away the blood from her planks, and the carriages of the guns, when the sun rose and shone upon them. The numerous wounded had, by this time, been put into their hammocks, although there were still one or two cases of amputation to be performed.

The carpenter had repaired all shot-holes under or too near the water-line, and then had proceeded to sound the well of the prize; but although her upper works had been dreadfully shattered, there was no reason to suppose that she had received any serious injury below, and therefore the hatches still remained on, although a few hands were put to the pumps to try if she had made any water. It was not until the *Aurora* presented a more cheerful appearance that Captain Wilson went over to the other ship, whose deck, now that the light of heaven enabled them to witness all the horrors even to minuteness, presented a shocking spectacle of blood and carnage. Body after body was thrown over; the wounded were supplied with water and such assistance as could be rendered until the surgeons could attend them; the hatches were then taken off, and the remainder of her crew ordered on deck; about two hundred obeyed the summons, but the lower deck was as crowded with killed and wounded as was the upper. For the present the prisoners were handed over down into the fore-hold of the *Aurora*, which had been prepared for their reception, and the work of separation of the dead from the living then underwent. After this, such repairs as were immediately necessary were made, and a portion of the *Aurora*'s crew, under the orders of the second lieutenant, were sent on board to take charge of her. It was not till the evening of the day after this night conflict that the *Aurora* was in a situation to make sail. All hands were then sent on board of the *Trident*, for such was the name of the Russian frigate, to fit her out as soon as possible. Before morning – for there was no relaxation from their fatigue, nor was there any wish for it – all was completed, and the two frigates, although in a shattered condition, were prepared to meet any common conflict with the elements. The *Aurora* made sail with the *Trident* in tow; the hammocks were allowed to be taken down, and the watch below permitted to repose.

In this murderous conflict the *Trident* had more than two hundred men killed and wounded. The *Aurora*'s loss had not been so great, but still it was severe, having lost sixty-five men and officers. Among the fallen there were Mr Jones, the master, the third lieutenant Mr Arkwright, and two midshipmen killed. Mr Pottyfar, the first lieutenant, severely wounded at the commencement of the action. Martin the master's mate, and Gascoigne, the first mortally, and the second badly, wounded. Our hero had also received a slight cutlass wound, which obliged him to wear his arm, for a short time, in a sling.

Among the ship's company who were wounded was Mesty; he had been hurt with a splinter before the *Trident* was taken by the board, but had remained on deck, and had followed our hero, watching over him and protecting him as a father. He had done even more, for he had with Jack thrown himself before Captain Wilson, at a time that he had received such a blow with the flat of a sword as to stun him, and bring him down on his knee. And Jack had taken good care that Captain Wilson should not be ignorant, as he really would have been, of this timely service on the part of Mesty, who certainly, although with a great deal of "*sang froid*" in his composition when in repose, was a fiend incarnate when his blood was up.

"But you must have been with Mesty," observed Captain Wilson, "when he did me the service."

"I was with him, sir," replied Jack, with great modesty, "but was of very little service."

"How is your friend Gascoigne this evening?"

"Oh, not very bad, sir – he wants a glass of grog."

"And Mr Martin?"

Jack shook his head.

"Why the surgeon thinks he will do well."

"Yes, sir, and so I told Martin; but he said that it was very well to give him hope – but that he thought otherwise."

"You must manage him, Mr Easy; tell him that he is sure of his promotion."

"I have, sir, but he won't believe it. He never will believe it till he has his commission signed. I really think that an acting order would do more than the doctor can."

"Well, Mr Easy, he shall have one to-morrow morning. Have you seen Mr Pottyfar? He, I am afraid, is very bad."

"Very bad, sir; and they say is worse every day, and yet his wound is healthy, and ought to be doing well."

Such was the conversation between Jack and his captain, as they sat at breakfast on the third morning after the action.

The next day Easy took down an acting order for Martin, and put it into his hands. The mate read it over as he lay bandaged in his hammock.

"It's only an acting order, Jack," said he; "it may not be confirmed."

Jack swore, by all the articles of war, that it would be, but Martin replied that he was sure it never would.

"No, no," said the mate, "I knew very well that I never should be made. If it is not confirmed, I may live; but if it is, I am sure to die."

Every one that went to Martin's hammock wished him joy of his promotion; but six days after the action, poor Martin's remains were consigned to the deep.

The next person who followed him was Mr Pottyfar, the first lieutenant, who had contrived, wounded as he was, to reach a packet of the universal medicine, and had taken so many bottles before he was found out, that he was one morning found dead in his bed, with more than two dozen empty phials under his pillow, and by the side of his mattress. He was not buried with his hands in his pockets, but when sewed up in his hammock, they were, at all events, laid in the right position.

HORNBLOWER'S
CHARITABLE OFFERING

C. S. Forester

The name of Hornblower is synonymous with Napoleonic sea stories, so much so that C. Northcote Parkinson was able to write a fictionalized biography, The Life and Times of Horatio Hornblower *(1970), which is in itself an excellent study of the period. The Hornblower series covers the whole of the Napoleonic period from 1794 to 1823. The character of Hornblower is a mixture of several characters, including Horatio Nelson and, apparently, Admiral James Alexander Gordon, though first and foremost it was an exploration of the individual that Forester himself would like to have been. In addition to the novels about Horatio Hornblower, Forester wrote several short stories, few of which have been reprinted. The following story is particularly interesting because it relates to the same episode as the Cutcliffe Hyne story which follows on.*

Although Napoleon regarded Spain as an ally during his wars in Europe, it was an enforced partnership. Napoleon treated Spain as a puppet kingdom. In 1808 he ejected the Spanish royal family and set up his elder brother, Joseph, as king of Spain. Joseph was never accepted by the Spanish and there were rebellions throughout the country. In July 1808 a French corps under General Pierre Dupont was besieged by the Spanish at Baylen and was forced to surrender to General Francisco Castaños. 17,500 French soldiers were captured. The Spanish did not treat them lightly. French prisoners-of-war were held on the tiny island of Cabrera, south of Majorca, where they were pretty much forgotten and left to look after themselves. That's the background to the next two stories.

HMS *SUTHERLAND* of two decks and seventy-four guns, Captain Horatio Hornblower, was on her way north from Gibraltar to her rendezvous in the Western Mediterranean. To port lay the coast of Spain; to starboard, and barely in sight, just peeping over the horizon, lay the hilltops of one of the Balearic Islands, Ibiza. Spain was now an ally of England, and it was no business of the *Sutherland*'s to intercept Spanish trade or fight Spanish ships of war. Only the French were now enemies, and the French conquest of Spain had not progressed as far south yet as Valencia. It was to take a hand in the struggle in Catalonia that the *Sutherland* – at least so Hornblower suspected – was being sent north. Meanwhile he had little enough to worry him; a full crew, a wellfound ship, and nothing special to do until he reached his rendezvous. It was a period of transition, from one duty to another, and Hornblower revelled in the feeling of suspended animation and freedom. The *Sutherland* was laying over her ponderous bulk as she stood to the north close-hauled to a fine easterly wind, and Hornblower paced his deck breathing deep of the crisp air and the healing sunshine.

It was the look-out at the foretop masthead who broke into the happy neutrality of his mood.

"Deck, there! If you please, sir, there's something adrift right ahead; might just be wreckage, sir – can't rightly tell yet."

"Right ahead?"

"Aye aye, sir. We're coming right up to it. Might be a raft, sir – think I can see a man – two men, perhaps, sir."

There was an obvious explanation of the presence of a raft with men on it at sea in wartime – they might be the survivors of a battle to the death, here where the struggle for the mastery of the sea was being fought out. The *Sutherland* could run down to investigate without fear; there was a curious shifting sensation in Hornblower's skull when he thought of the numerous inventors who were putting forward suggestions by which small boats could explode by charges of gunpowder against the side of a ship of the line. If ever they should succeed in their wild schemes the day of the battleship's magnificent security would be over and instead the utmost caution would be necessary in approaching strange objects. But that was all nonsense, of course, and Hornblower shrugged it away from him carelessly; the ridiculous train of thought had occupied his mind during all the minutes necessary to raise the strange object to within sight of the deck.

"It's a raft, sure enough, sir," said Lieutenant Bush, glass to eye, and gazing across the sunlit water. "There's one man waving, and I think there's another one there, too."

"Heave to when you get to wind'ard of her," ordered Hornblower.

Bush took the *Sutherland* up close to the strange object, and hove to neatly.

"Queer sort of raft," he said, peering over the dancing water as the *Sutherland*'s leeway carried her down to it.

It was nothing more than a couple of logs bound crudely together; the waves broke over it so that the two men on it were to some extent always submerged. One man was kneeling, holding a crude paddle in his hand, while the other lay with occasionally even his head buried under the water which washed over his body.

"Heave 'em a line," said Hornblower.

But even the man who was kneeling was too weak for the deftly-cast rope to be of use to him. He fumbled with it and lost his grip, his head falling forward with exhaustion. The quarter-boat had finally to be hoisted out and the two men brought on board in a bos'un's chair swung from the main-yard arm. They lay there brown and naked, like the Indians of San Salvador, and most desperately emaciated; every bone was standing out clear and well defined, as though straining against the leathery skin stretched over it. Their long lank hair and beards dripped water on the deck. One lay motionless, the other held out a feeble hand to them as they stared down at them; with a croaking voice he pointed down his throat.

"Thirsty, poor devil," said Bush; a gesture from Hornblower had already sent one of the hands running for water.

The castaways drank eagerly, and to Hornblower and Bush it was as if a miracle were being performed before their eyes, almost like the raising of the dead, to see the astonishing effect of the water upon them. They revived magically; the one who had lain upon the deck, and whose head had had to be supported to allow him to drink, sat up. A death's head smile split his lean face.

"I expect they're hungry as well," said Bush. "They look as if they might be."

It only called for a nod from Hornblower for somebody to go and seek for food for them.

"Who are you?" asked Hornblower.

"François," said the stronger one. He had blue eyes which looked oddly out of place in his brown face.

"Frenchies, by God!" said Bush.

"Where do you come from?" asked Hornblower, repeating himself in limping French when he saw he was not understood.

The blue-eyed one extended an arm like a stick towards the Balearics to windward.

"Cabrera," he said. "We were prisoners."

Hornblower and Bush exchanged glances and Bush whistled – Bush could at least understand the gesture and the first word of the reply. Cabrera was a previously uninhabited islet which the Spaniards were using as a camp for their French prisoners of war.

The dark-eyed castaway was speaking rapidly in a hoarse voice.

"You won't send us back there, monsieur?" he said. "Make us your prisoners instead. We cannot –"

He became unintelligible with weakness and excitement. Bush, observant as usual, was yet puzzled by what he could see.

"I can understand their being thirsty," he said, "but they couldn't have got as thin as that just coming from Cabrera. They could have paddled that raft of theirs here in a couple of days, even without a wind."

"When did you leave Cabrera?" asked Hornblower.

"Yesterday."

Hornblower translated to Bush.

"That sunburn of theirs is months old," said Bush. "The fellows can't have worn a pair of breeches in weeks. There must be funny doings in Cabrera."

"Tell me," said Hornblower to the castaways, "how did you become – like this?"

It was a long story, the longer as it was interrupted while the castaways ate and drank, and while Hornblower translated the more sensational parts to Bush.

There were twenty-thousand of the poor devils – mainly the army which had surrendered at Baylen, but prisoners taken in a hundred other skirmishes as well – who had annoyed their Spanish captors inexpressibly while they were kept on the mainland by their continual attempts to escape. Finally the Spaniards had taken the whole twenty-thousand and dumped them down on the island of Cabrera, a mere rock of only a few square miles. That had been two years ago; there was no need for any Spanish garrison on the island itself – British sea power made it impossible for any French ship to attempt a rescue, and there was nothing with which to make boats except for rare driftwood. For two years these twenty-thousand miserable wretches had lived on the rock, scraping holes for shelter from the summer sun and winter storms.

"There are only two wells, monsieur," said the blue-eyed Frenchman, "and sometimes they run dry. But often it rains."

Hornblower's mathematical mind dealt with the time-problem of supplying twenty-thousand men with water from two wells. Each man would be lucky if he got one drink a day, even if the wells never ran dry.

Of course there was no fuel on the island – not one of the

twenty-thousand had seen a spark of fire for two years, and no clothing had survived two years of exposure and wear.

The Spaniards landed food for them at intervals, which was eaten raw.

"It is never enough, monsieur," explained the Frenchman – Hornblower was acquainted with Spanish methods, and could understand – "and sometimes it does not come at all. Because of the wind, monsieur. When the wind is in the east, monsieur, we starve."

Bush was looking at the chart and the sailing directions for the Western Mediterranean.

"That's right, sir," he announced. "There's only one landing beach, and that's on the east. It's impracticable to land in easterly winds. It mentions the two wells and says there's no wood."

"They are supposed to bring food twice a week, monsieur," said the Frenchman. "But sometimes it has been three weeks before they have been able to put it ashore."

"Three weeks!"

"Yes, monsieur."

"But – but –"

"Those of us who are wise have little stores hidden away in the rocks for those times, monsieur. We have to defend them, of course. And as for the others – There is usually plenty of one kind of food for them to eat, monsieur. There are not twenty-thousand of us by now."

Hornblower looked out through the cabin window at the dull smudge on the horizon where, in this enlightened nineteenth century, actual cannibalism was still taking place.

"God bless us all!" said Bush, solemnly.

"There had been no food for a week when we escaped yesterday, monsieur. But easterly winds always bring drift-wood, as well as famine. We found two tree-trunks, Marcel and I. There were many who wanted to take the chance, monsieur. But we are strong, stronger than most on the island."

The Frenchman looked almost with complacency down at his skinny arms.

"Yes indeed we are," said Marcel. "Even if your ship had not seen us, we might have reached Spain alive. I suppose our Emperor has now conquered all the mainland?"

"Not yet," replied Hornblower briefly. He was not prepared at short notice to try to explain the vast chaos which was acquiring the name of the Peninsular War.

"The Spaniards still hold Valencia," he said. "If you had managed to get there they would only have sent you back to Cabrera."

The Frenchmen looked at each other; they would have grown voluble again, but Hornblower checked them testily.

"Go and try to sleep," he said, and he stamped out of the cabin.

Up on deck the air seemed purer, after the foul pictures which the Frenchmen's stories had called up in his mind. Hornblower loathed human suffering; he walked his deck tormented by the thought of the starving Frenchmen on Cabrera. This brisk Levanter, blowing from the east, would go on blowing for another week at least, if he could read weather signs – and he thought he could. It was none of his business to worry about French prisoners of war in Spanish hands. Cabrera lay out of his course. British government stores should be conserved strictly for the use of his own ship. He would have the devil's own time explaining to his admiral if he did anything to relieve the misery on Cabrera. No sensible man would attempt it; every sensible man would shrug his shoulders and do his best to forget about this whole beastly business of Frenchmen devouring their own dead among the rocks of Cabrera. Yet by laying the *Sutherland* as close to the wind as she would lie he could just fetch the island now. Any further delay would mean a long beat to windward. Hornblower crossed the deck and gave his orders, and without another word, solely by the look in his eye, he dared his lieutenants to question him as to his intentions. Then he went back to his walk, pacing up and down, up and down, trying to think out a method of how to land stores on a surf-beaten beach.

That queer mathematical ability of his was working to its utmost. Into his mind there came a whole series of ballistic formulae. Scientific gunnery was in its infancy, in its utter babyhood; it was only in the last few years that the arsenal authorities at Woolwich had begun to experiment practically in the endeavour to obtain data as to the behaviour of the weapons they turned out in such numbers. And most of their attention had been devoted to the big ships' guns and not to the little 6-pounder boat gun whose employment was contemplated by Hornblower. And besides that, he was intending to use the 6-pounder in a way that had never been contemplated by the Woolwich authorities or by anyone else at all, as far as he knew. So far, nobody had thought of employing a gun to bridge a gap with a line as he was thinking of doing. If his plan did not succeed, he would have to think of another one – but he thought it was worth trying.

He broke off his train of thought to issue a whole series of orders to his puzzled subordinates. The blacksmith was given orders to forge an iron rod with a loop at the end and to wrap it with oakum and twine to fit the bore of the long boat's 6-pounder. The bos'un had to get out 100 fathoms of the finest hemp line that the ship possessed and work it into utter flexibility by straining every inch round a belaying-pin and then coil it away with perfect symmetry into one of the oaken fire-buckets. The cooper and his mates were set to work breaking out beef casks, half emptying them, and then heading them up securely. A puzzled bos'un's mate was set to work with half a dozen hands linking these twenty half-empty casks into an immense chain, like beads on a string where every bead was represented by a cask containing 2-hundredweight of meat connected with its fellows by 60 yards of cable. The deck of the *Sutherland* presented a pretty tangle to any possible observer by the time all these operations were well started. And through the gathering evening the *Sutherland* held her course steadily, closehauled for Cabrera.

At dawn she was there, and the earliest hint of daylight found her nosing her way cautiously towards the beach, from which even here, with the wind in the wrong direction, could be heard the thunderous beat of the surf.

"That's the dagos' victualling-ship, I'll lay a guinea," said Bush with his glass to his eye.

It was a small brig, hull down and hove to, over on the horizon.

"Yes," said Hornblower – the speech deserved no more ample rejoinder. He was much too occupied looking through his own glass at the craggy beach of rock on which the Spaniards had seen fit to place twenty-thousand men. It was just a grey fragment, one single ridge projecting like a tooth from the blue Mediterranean, its steep slopes unrelieved by any trace of green. Around its foot the rollers broke into white fountains of spray – Hornblower could see the waves reaching 20 or 30 feet up the cliffs as they beat upon them – save in the centre where a long flurry of foam revealed the landing beach and all its dangers. It was a wicked enough place.

"Can't blame the dagos for not landing stores here in an easterly wind," said Bush, and this time he received no answer at all.

"Hoist out the long-boat," Hornblower rasped; when approaching a difficult task he would take out no insurance by minor politeness for his subordinates' sympathy in the event of failure.

The bos'un's mates twittered on their pipes while Harrison, the bos'un, repeated the order in his resounding bellow. The tackles were manned and the long-boat was swung up from her chocks and hoisted overside. The long-boat's crew stood fending her off as the *Sutherland* surged in the choppy sea.

"I'm going in her, Mr Bush," said Hornblower briefly.

He took hold of one of the falls and lowered himself down; his unathletic figure dangled in ungainly fashion while the long-boat's crew fell over each other in their haste to protect his fall. It was a source of continual inward disturbance to Hornblower that the poorest topman in his whole ship was better on a rope than he was himself. He managed just well enough, and with only a small loss of dignity, with a 3-foot drop as a result of his not quite correctly estimating the relative movements of the ship and the boat. Somebody picked up his hat and gave it to him and he clapped it on his head again.

"Give way," he snapped, and the long-boat crept under oars over the surging sea towards the distant beach.

Now, with his glass, Hornblower could see little figures pouring down to the water's edge on Cabrera. They were all as naked as the two men he picked up yesterday; Hornblower wondered what it was like to climb about with a bare skin over the jagged rocks of Cabrera; he wondered what it was like to try and live naked through a winter storm with only a hollow in a rock for shelter. He felt sick with the thought of all the horror and misery which that jagged lump of rock must have witnessed for the past two years. He was glad he was going to make this small attempt at relief. He put away his glass and walked forward between the rowers to where the 6-pounder was mounted in the bows.

At his command, one of the crew broke open a paper cartridge, poured the powder into the muzzle of the gun and rammed the wad home upon the charge. Another hand knotted the line to the queer missile which the blacksmith had prepared. Hornblower dropped the thing into the muzzle of the gun and rammed it down. He twirled the elevating screw; the wedges slid from under the breech of the gun, and the muzzle cocked itself up as the gun rested at its fullest elevation. He gauged the strength of the wind and glanced round him trying to predict the motion of the boat in the choppy sea. Then he pulled the lanyard, and the gun roared out.

At his elbow the line suddenly came to life, whirring viciously as it shot from the tub; the smoke vanished just in time to give him a glimpse of the line hanging in an arc in the air before the projectile fell into the surf and the line after it. A little groan went up from the crew of the long-boat – they had been taking the usual childlike interest in the novelty of all this, to be expected of sailors welcoming any break in the monotony of a long voyage.

"Get that line in again," said Hornblower sitting down on a thwart. "Make those coils absolutely smooth."

That was one comforting piece of knowledge which the study of scientific gunnery had given him; because one first shot had failed was no proof at all that the twentieth would not succeed. And this time line and projectile would be wet and heavier; the gun would be hot and would react differently; the likelihood that the boat would be at the same angle to the horizon on the waves was very remote; and in any case the trial shot had indicated that they must move a little farther up the coast to make the proper allowance for the wind. He ordered a double wad to be put on top of the new charge so as to keep the wet projectile from damping the powder while the long-boat crept a few yards north along the edge of the surf.

When the gun was fired again, it looked for a second as if the shot would be successful, but it dropped into the surf 10 yards from the waiting crowd – and for all practical purposes 10 yards were as effective as 100. The third and fourth and fifth shots failed by even wider margins. It began to look to Hornblower as if the initial velocity were insufficient – perhaps the pull of the line as it ran out was stronger than he had allowed for. At the risk of straining the gun, he could increase the powder charge; there was an additional risk in that because the line might break and the projectile fly free, in which case it would go clean through somebody in the crowd on the beach. But when the sixth and seventh shots also failed, Hornblower decided to take the risk. He put in a charge and a half of powder and rammed it well down. Then he ordered the whole crew aft as far as possible into the stern sheets of the boat – if the gun should burst, he wanted only a minimum of casualties, and it seemed perfectly logical to him that he should take the risk of pulling the lanyard himself instead of ordering someone else to do so.

He took a last glance down at the line and then jerked the lanyard. The gun went off with a crash which jerked the whole long-boat sternwards, and the gun itself leapt in its carriage with a clatter. But the stout metal held firm, and the projectile, trailing its curved arc of line, cleared the water's edge and dropped into the waiting crowd.

Communication was established, but it was a frail enough bond, because those madmen on shore had no sooner grabbed the line than they began to haul it in. Hornblower cursed himself for not having seen this development; he snatched up his speaking trumpet and groped wildly in his mind for a French phrase which might be the equivalent of "Avast heaving!" or "Belay!"

"*Doucement! Doucement!*" he roared.

He waved his arms frantically and danced about in the bows of the boat. Perhaps the wind carried his words down to the beach, or perhaps his gestures were understood. Someone was taking charge of proceedings; there was a swirl in the crowd and the line ceased to run out. Hornblower swung the long-boat cautiously round and pulled slowly towards the *Sutherland*, paying out the line behind him until he could signal for his gig and row back to his ship to supervise the rest of the operation.

The immense string of half-empty casks was dropped into the sea, and the launch took it in tow and began to drag it slowly up to the long-boat. Half empty, the casks rode high in the water. That would get them through the worst of the surf, and if the Frenchmen pulled in fast enough, most of the casks could be expected to reach land still containing most of their contents – and if the worst came to the worst, the contents would be thrown up on to the beach soon enough. Meat which had already been six months in a cask would not be much spoiled by an additional immersion in sea water.

Hornblower dashed back into his gig to supervise the final operation. The heavier line was bent on to the light one which had been thrown on shore, and Hornblower stood up again with his speaking trumpet.

"*Tirez! Tirez!*" he yelled, and waved the instrument at the crowd.

They understood him and began to pull in. The heavy rope crept in after the line, and then the long string of casks followed. Hornblower watched their course anxiously enough, as the big ungainly objects, black in the white foam under the dazzling sun, crept towards the shore. But even without watching them he could have guessed at their safe arrival, for as each one reached the beach, there was a wild swirl in the crowd as the starving men smashed the casks to pieces with rocks and fought over the contents.

Hornblower did not wait to see the end. He wanted no further reminder of the beastliness and horror of it all, and he had himself rowed back to his ship and the boats hoisted in. He would not look back again at the island as the *Sutherland* braced her yards round and went on to her delayed rendezvous. The Spanish victualling-brig was coming down towards them under full sail. She passed the *Sutherland* close astern, and an irate officer hailed through a speaking trumpet:

"What you mean, sir?" he shouted. "What you mean inter-fering? Cabrera our country – you not must go there!"

"God damn you!" said Bush beside Hornblower as the words reached him. "Shall I give him a shot, sir?"

After what they had seen, the crew of the *Sutherland* would have thoroughly approved of such an action, but Hornblower felt he had done enough towards provoking an international incident between England and her ally as it was. He put his hand to his ear and made a gesture to indicate that he could not hear. The Spaniard repeated himself, bawling and raving and dancing on his deck until Hornblower almost came to hope that he would burst a blood-vessel. It was only a schoolboy trick, but it raised a laugh among the officers and men of the *Sutherland*, and that was what Hornblower was after. In these dreary times of war and at moments of tension between allies, a laugh was worth a great deal.

And then he turned back towards routine. But a new wave of depressed realization flooded over him. The relief of Cabrera had cost his ship hundreds of fathoms of line and hundreds of fathoms of cable, a score of beef casks and a whole day's time. What oppressed Hornblower was the prospect or having to account for all this. There would be at least a dozen letters and reports to write upon the subject, and that would be only the beginning, because My Lords of the Admiralty, when the letters reached them, would certainly demand further explanations, and explanations beyond those, and further explanations still – Hornblower could see those letters stretching to the crack of doom.

Then he caught sight of his two French prisoners down on the main-deck. They were clothed and shaved and looked new men, but Hornblower found no pleasure in the sight of them. To him they represented another whole series of letters and reports which he would have to write, and he groaned at the prospect. For a moment he almost wished that the *Sutherland* had never sighted them, that they had drifted on to meet their death in the desolate Mediterranean. He realized at once that this was not true, and groaned at his hard-heartedness while he paced the deck and breathed free air. But all the same, this work of charity was going to cost him a devil of a lot of trouble.

THE ESCAPE AGENTS

C. J. Cutcliffe Hyne

This story also uses as its basic premise the imprisonment of Dupont's soldiers by the Spanish on the island of Cabrera following the siege of Baylen. It comes from the book The Escape Agents *(1911) by Charles John Cutcliffe Hyne (1865–1944). At the start of the book, Napoleon has employed two totally disparate individuals to engineer the escape of the French captives – an American, Major Joseph Colt, and a French* vivandière, *Clarice de la Plage. The following picks up from the start of their enterprise.*

Hyne was a prolific author best known in his day for a long-running series of stories about a wily old sea-dog, Captain Kettle, that began in The Adventures of Captain Kettle *(1898). He also wrote an intriguing lost-race novel set on Atlantis,* The Lost Continent *(1900).*

1. The First Fifty-Four.

"It looks to me," said Sergeant Colorado appreciatively, "as if they would end up by contriving a shipwreck out of it." He made a telescope of his hands, and peered hard through the spindrift. "And even if she breaks up and sinks in deep water – which is probable, with our beastly luck – the bodies should have clothes on them when they begin to come ashore. Name of Mahomet! But I have almost forgotten the feel of breeches! And as for a shirt, well, one wore shirts, I believe, once when one was a French soldier, but here on this disgusting Cabrera – I ask you even to figure to yourself the luxury of wearing a shirt!"

"It looks to me," said the small man, with the bandy legs, "as if they were trying to pile her up purposely. And, as I was a sailor during the ten years before I joined the army of the accursed Dupont, perhaps my opinion is better than that of laymen."

"My dear Monsieur Jean Baptiste Rousseau," the lanky sergeant bawled back at him through the gale, "conjure me that ship ashore on this infernal isle, and I'll quarrel with you on no matter of professional knowledge whatever. I want breeches. I starve for breeches. And I'd dearly love a shirt. But let them escape their shipwreck – as every selfish brute of a sailor does when we start praying for him to be thrown here on Cabrera – and I'll send my seconds to you, and see the colour of your insides before a dozen hours are over."

The dull thump of a heavy gun came to them down the wind.

"There's the Britisher loosing off a fore-deck carronade again. Might as well try to shoot a horn off the moon as hit a ship in that sea with a little sawn-off, wide-mouthed dog of a 4-pounder carronade like the bulldog's got. Face of a pig! What a shot! He's nicked the fellow's fore-topsailyard."

The sound of the gun carried sullenly over the isle, and of the 5,500 French prisoners of war who were marooned there, just seven had sufficient energy and curiosity to join Sergeant Colorado and the bandy-legged Rousseau, and watch listlessly with them the manoeuvres of the two brigs.

With one brig, the clumsy, leewardly Britisher, they were

bitterly well-acquainted, and that she still sailed the Mediterranean was a standing proof of the inefficacy of their daily prayers and vituperation. She had been set to patrol the seas round their prison by the brutal island sea-power in the north, and time after time had she caught boat-loads of men escaping, flogged them soundly for contravention of rule, and sent them contemptuously back upon the island again. She was captained by one Meadey, a small, dandified, proud, old, and disappointed man, who preserved an iron discipline amongst his own crew, handled his clumsy vessel with almost supernatural skill, and observed a ferocious contempt for all men and things which did not happen to be of British birth and origin. As Captain Meadey, with his ruffled shirt and his gold-buckled shoes, sailed across the vision of each of the 5,500 prisoners at least once per diem, it may be plainly understood that his claim to be the best-cursed man in the Mediterranean rested on no slender foundation.

The other brig, the nimble-heeled polacre, had been sighted by the prisoners the day before, and had obviously tried to communicate with the island. Twice she had run in, and twice Meadey's ponderous *Frolic* had worried her off. She was a heavily-sparred little thing, with an astonishing turn of speed in a light breeze, and she played with His Britannic Majesty's twenty-gun war brig in a way that rasped on Captain Meadey's nerves.

At the third attempt the pole-masted brig ran in close enough to the rocks for a man in her main rigging to attempt to bawl a message through a speaking-trumpet. He was a tall, sallow-faced man, with a black whisker. They had noted him before as smoking incessantly at a long clay pipe. And his French was fluent, inaccurate, and delivered with a fine nasal accent. The prisoners, who were clustered like limpets on the rocks, could pick up one sentence in ten.

"*Take you right back . . . French soldiers have no use for this brand of treatment . . . Emperor Bonaparte had me come . . . us two, Escape Agents . . . You swim off . . . Pick you up . . . My Land! yes!*" . . .

And then the bellow of the voice was blown beyond earshot, though the pipe wagged at them, emphasising further sentences. All the afternoon it had been breezing up, and a heavy sea was beginning to run that knocked the speed out of the polacre. On the other hand it was just the *Frolic*'s weather, and under Meadey's magnificent handling she soon made things very warm indeed for the other brig. Even now the intruder might have run to sea, and, once driven off debatable waters, would probably have been spared further interference. But it seemed she was captained by someone as dogged as Meadey himself; and though it was plain she was very short-handed, she stuck to her plan of making short boards due north and south just a mile to eastward of the rocks.

"Face of a pig!" screamed the sailor Rousseau. "What did I tell you? Look, they are deliberating starting sheets and heading for in-shore. They are deliberately intending to pile her up. There is that long fellow with the black whiskers at the wheel himself, and looking for a soft spot to beach her on."

"We want no more lodgers on this island," grumbled another of the prisoners. "The Spaniards will not increase the ration, and we're three parts starved as it is."

"Toad-brain!" said Sergeant Colorado, "and who was it that ever dreamed of getting those gentlemen ashore alive except your particularly ugly self? We invite them to join us as corpses. Afterwards we take their breeches and wear them. Time was when I should not have cared to wear a dead man's breeks. But here on this beastly Cabrera I am not so nice."

"She will strike on the outer reef if she sticks to her present course," said Rousseau, "and not so much as a spar will come to shore here. With this wind the current will set due south. Those that want pickings must swim for them." He began to clamber down the cliffs. "I'd risk drowning for a cask of good salt-horse. Face of a pig! But think of having one good square meal again!"

Nearer and nearer the polacre rushed into the rocks, rearing madly over the creaming seas. For a time she was plain to all their eyes, and then something of the suddenest she was blotted from sight. A white squall, that typical pest of the Mediterranean, swept down on her through the gale, and before that merciless impact of rain and spindrift and shouting wind, the prisoners on the edge of the island had to turn away their faces.

There they lay whilst the rain flogged them, and the wind blew their shaggy hair into fluttering flags, and yelped at them with an impish frenzy; and when at length the white squall blew through, the polacre brig was not, and out at sea, on Meadey's hateful *Frolic*, a couple of top-men were lashing a besom to her main royal truck. Captain John William Meadey, R.N., was pointing out in his agreeable fashion that he had swept the seas.

At the sight of that nautical insult the Frenchmen on the rocks danced and screamed in an ecstasy of rage; but the hunger-pinch in their bellies, and the bareness of their limbs, soon drove them back to business. They spread amongst the rocks, holding there against the surf, and peered with smarting eyes for any possible thing that would alleviate their condition.

It was Sergeant Colorado himself that found the black-whiskered man who had bawled at them through the speaking trumpet.

They had all seen the fellow swimming strongly shorewards through the surf, and there had been many fears that he would be thoughtless enough to reach the rocks alive. But some piece of floating wreckage stunned him, and he disappeared; and it was fully an hour later that the blue-faced Sergeant found him cast up limp and sprawling under a rick of seaweed.

"Wearer of breeches," said Sergeant Colorado, "I bid you welcome, and promise you decent burial in return for your clothes. Name of Mahomet! To think how I shall revel in wearing that shirt of yours."

He began with vigorous hands to pull away the seaweed, and presently got the body cleared.

"And now," said the Sergeant, "I'll trouble you first of all for your coat, as I feel sure you have no further use for it."

The grizzled old soldier proceeded with a deft thoroughness which proved that he was by no means unused to such post-mortem spoliation, and until he arrived at loosening the supports of the coveted breeches, there was no interruption. But as he was stooping down to disentangle the last reluctant button, a bunch of fingers reached up from below him, and the sergeant sprang back with a yell, and began fumbling tenderly with both hands at his right eye.

The man with the black whiskers drew himself shakily up, and spat sea water.

"You blue-faced cannibal," he gasped presently, when Sergeant Colorado showed further signs of returning to his task, "if you touch my suspenders again, I'll have your eye clean out next time, and bite it in two."

"Name of Mahomet! But here again is my usual luck! Here is monsieur sitting up and recovering his undesirable life. I imagined monsieur had no further use for clothes, and here on this beastly Cabrera we have been forced of late to go for the most part naked."

" 'Monsieur' be hanged! I am Major Joseph Colt. Don't you know enough to salute your officer?"

Sergeant Colorado smacked his bare heels together and saluted. "I have spread your coat out to dry, Major. I thought it might be a little damp for you."

"Thanks," said Colt drily, "I like a thoughtful man." He turned to the coat and, after a fumble, produced the bowl and stem of a pipe in sections, which he blew clear of water and screwed together. His tobacco was in a water-tight box along with flint, steel and tinder, and presently he was drawing smoke from the long tube with an air of great contentment.

"Well, Sergeant," he said at last, "it's a rough way of landing at a place, but I've got here in spite of all their teeth, and that's the main thing. One item for congratulation, though, I'm glad I didn't bring Miss Clarice along."

"What, the late *vivandière* of the 82nd of the Line!" The old sinner grinned. "Well, we have women on the island certainly, but I shouldn't recommend it as quite the place for an officer to bring his ladylove to."

"My Land! but you'll get it in the neck before I'm done with you if you sing any more of that tune. Miss Clarice is no more my ladylove than she is yours. As a point of fact, I believe she's engaged to a Monsieur Legros, or Le Sage, 'way over in Paris. But, anyway, she's down in this section, same as I am, by Emperor Bonaparte's orders, to see you prisoners out of this Cabrera, and back to your work in the army again. In fact, the

Emperor has created a new billet especially for Miss Clarice and me – he's named us his Escape Agents."

"Live the Emperor!" Sergeant Colorado hit his chest. "I was with him in Italy and Egypt. I helped him sweep out Austria and the German States. The Emperor can do no wrong, and if he has appointed you, Major, to get the 5,500 of us out of this hole, it is because you are the best man in the world for the job. But," the Sergeant rubbed his great hammer-headed nose, "to brigade you with Mademoiselle Clarice is curious, even for the Emperor."

"She is far more fitted for the job than I. But I want you to know right here that we work entirely independent of one another. And to take the snigger further off your ugly chops, I am going to tell you once and for always that I'm engaged to be married to a Miss Patience Collier, of 207, Pilgrim Avenue, Boston, Massachusetts, in my own country, and anyone I have to remind of that too often will need a doctor badly, and probably an undertaker. You understand that?"

Sergeant Colorado saluted stiffly. "I can take an order, Major, and carry it out exactly. And if my talk has more of freedom in it than you find to your taste, you must remember I'm an old soldier and have been admitted to intimacy with men who are now marshals of the Empire. Moreover, we prisoners here have lived as savages so long that we have almost forgot what French discipline is like."

Major Colt pulled deeply at his pipe. "So you have known other men who have climbed to be marshals, eh?"

"Berthier, Marmont, Massena – there's three for you, Major, anyway. Who knows but what there's a *bâton* carved with the name of Marshal Colt stored up somewhere?"

"I'm mighty tickled to think there is."

"Well, you bring the 5,500 of us here back to the Emperor again, and he'll draw the *bâton* out of store quick enough. But perhaps that's what you're after."

"Well," drawled Colt, "I'm not here for the climate, I guess, and it would be too flattering to say I'd come for the society – Land of Columbia! Here's Meadey sent for me already!"

Sergeant Colorado turned sharply round, and saw advancing

fourteen sturdy sailormen, cutlass at hip, club-butted pistol in belt, unmistakable Britons. They all rolled to exactly the same angle in their walk, and had their pigtails served to a precise pattern. Beside them marched a contemptuous officer in a uniform that was spruce, stiff, and finely faded. And behind, and on either flank, hovered a rabble of ragged, naked prisoners spitting hate.

The Britishers marched on to near where Sergeant Colorado stood, halted to a cold and formal word of command, and scanned the coast line. Then the officer, in vilely accented grammatical French (after the pattern set by his Grace the Iron Duke), made pronouncement as follows:

"*Order begins.*

"*Any salvage from polacre brig to be given up to authorities duly appointed to receive same at once. And prisoner concealing same to be flogged.*

"*Any body or bodies coming ashore from wreck to be pointed out to authorities before touched. Any prisoner stealing from or searching same to be flogged.*

"*Any survivor or survivors coming ashore alive from wreck to be reported at once to authorities. Any prisoner concealing or failing to report same to be flogged.*

"*Order ends.*"

The chilly Englishman folded the paper and put it back into his pocket, and "here then," thought Sergeant Colorado, terminates the usefulness of this Yankee Major.

He turned his head to see how the escape-agent, who a minute before had talked so feelingly of *bâtons*, would take the check, but to his amazement the man was gone. There was the imprint on the rick of seaweed to point out where he had sat; a splash of wet on the shingle showed where he had emptied the sea water from his shoes; and in the air was the scent of his tobacco.

The Sergeant lifted up his great bottle nose and sniffed appreciatively. Yes, although there was still a stiff breeze, the odour from that quaint long pipe lingered delicately. But of the man, look though one might over every rock within sight, there was not the dimmest trace.

"Name of Mahomet! –"

"If you have a report to make," rasped the Lieutenant Cabott, "make it, and don't stand there spluttering and swearing at nothing. Just like a Frenchman, wasting his wind swearing at nothing."

"My officer, the man was here – a man thrown up from that wreck – and saw you come up, and therefore unless you admit your eyes are worse than a French officer's, you must have seen him. Now he is gone. It was no business of mine to guard him; but as he was under your eyes all the time you must have seen him go."

"You blue-nosed son of Belial!" snapped Cabott, "you'll be getting your back scratched if you don't take a pull on your jaw tackle" – and then to his men: "Spread out there, my lads, and hunt this fellow up."

Merrily frolicked the sailors amongst the rocks, and half-a-dozen times they thought they had their man, but it always turned out to be one of the *bona fide* French prisoners; and in the end they were called in by their chilly officer, who led them back again to the *Frolic*'s cutter.

In the meanwhile, Major Joseph Colt was making himself at home elsewhere, and attending to his creature comforts with the ease of an old campaigner.

At the first sight of the English, he had clapped down to the ground behind the rick of seaweed. He was a man bred up to such quick alarms as these, and every rock and every fold of the ground had already mapped themselves in his eye by instinct. Moreover, his Indian training had taught him how to keep his body always in cover, whilst at the same time moving with the extreme of rapidity.

For a dozen yards he progressed snake-fashion below a ridge not more than a foot in height. Then behind a deeper fold of the ground he straddled along at a fine pace, crouching on all fours, and presently he was running on his two feet at a good round speed. Each footstep was studied. He did not think it likely that there was a tracker amongst those English sailors; but he never took superfluous chances; and so he left no foot-marks. But he was by no means flurried. He unscrewed and stowed away the parts of his long pipe as he ran.

By the time Cabott began his proclamation, Major Colt was in the sea, first wading and then swimming; and by the time that chilly islander had reached his last paragraph, the American had pulled out into the mouth of a cave which he had noted some hours before when coasting by in the polacre.

He had with him a small lobster and a handful of shellfish, which he had gathered *en roule*, and felt ready to stay hidden for a week if necessary.

The cave, as it turned out on inspection, ran upwards and inland, and at its upper end was (as caves go) tolerably dry. A great straggle of dry wood, the jetsam of the Mediterranean, filled the cave's middle part.

"Here," thought Colt, "are the materials for a boat, anyway"; and with characteristic promptitude he pulled out spars which would make keel-piece, stem and stern-post and ribs, and saw to it that enough timber remained over to dub into the requisite planking. But a sheath knife was the only cutting tool he then possessed; and, even for an American with a frontier training, that is short allowance with which to attack so large a piece of carpentry. An axe, or preferably of course an adze, was an early requisite, and so for the time he halted, screwed together, filled, and lit his pipe, and in contemplative clouds of tobacco smoke tried to evolve some scheme by which this weapon might be materialised.

From this mechanical reverie he was aroused, somewhat of the most abruptly, by a giggle – a giggle, too, of unmistakably female timbre.

Major Colt's pipe was quenched with a plug of sand, and Major Colt's person was clapped into a shadowed fret of the rock with the quickness of a thought; and then he had the mortification to hear a comment which made him rapidly emerge again with angular dignity.

Said the voice: "Why, it's that Yankee officer that was with Dupont. The one old poker-back Meadey's sent ice-cream Cabott for. And now he's shut his eyes and thinks he can't be seen. My!" And then as he came out into sight: "Good-day, Major."

"Good-day." Colt looked up and saw the faces of two comely

damsels laughing down at him from the head of a hill of sand which he had thought before ran up in one unbroken sweep to the cavern's roof. "I didn't know there was a back door to my cave."

"Well, we call it our cave," said the darker lady, shaking her curls. "Permit me to present you to my friend Mademoiselle Kabak. I am Mademoiselle La Rueuse."

"I make my salutation. You followed the army, I believe?"

"When there was an army, my brave one. But we are Frenchwomen of the Empire, and adapt ourselves finely to circumstances. Behold us now as cave-dwellers."

"I am sure you act the part charmingly."

"Ah, monsieur! What discernment. Once I was on the stage in Paris, and I left it because they said I could neither act nor kick. You say I can act, Monsieur the Major; presently you shall see my high kick, and I will convince you there also."

"Yes," said Colt drily, "we'll get on to that later. But just now I want your kind assistance in another direction. I want a boat. To build a boat I must have an axe. Can you find one, or beg or steal an axe?"

"Is this boat for yourself?" inquired the dark-haired Mademoiselle La Rueuse, pushing away the sand, and coming into fuller view.

"Sure!"

"Because you talked to that blue-nosed old sergeant of a partnership. You said the Emperor had appointed you as one of his Escape-Agents, and that stuck-up chit, Sophie de la Plage, was the other."

"Miss de la Plage is the other Escape-Agent, and I want to tell you right here that she is neither stuck-up nor a chit – whatever that may be. She is a very high-toned young lady, and, as far as an engaged man may, I admire her exceedingly."

"Ah, you're engaged to Sophie, are you?"

"I am not," snapped Colt. "I am engaged to a lady in Boston, America, who finds employment there as a schoolmarm, and is a very different sort of young person."

"And Boston must be so very far away for an ardent soldier's sweetheart. Well, we all must find our consolations."

"Madam," said Colt savagely, "I could swear right here, but I wouldn't like you to hear me. If I thought you actress enough to play another part, I'd ask you to talk about something else."

The other woman, a stout, placid blonde, here joined in. "Oh, stow it, you two, or, as sure as my name's Kabak, I'll begin using language myself next, and you know what that means. Now, Major, you want to pay your footing, don't you? Yes? Well, hand up that lobster."

"Catch!"

"Good. You are hereby enrolled as a Free Miserable of Cabrera, with authority to go starving as long as you can stand it, and full leave to forage at all times and get nothing for your pains. I don't suppose they'll give you a ration, and if they do the rations are not worth the having."

"But if you please, mademoiselle –"

"Don't call me mademoiselle. I am just Kabak."

"Right. What I want, Kabak, is that axe."

"There is one axe on the island – figure it: one axe to build the huts and cut the firewood for 5,500 men – and if you want it you must hire it. The tariff is six sous the day."

"That goes. I'll take it for a week, and as I guess there's a commission payable on this deal, if I give you a five-franc bill that will be okay."

Now from the first, Major Colt had little hope of building his boat without disturbance. The women in the further cave – there turned out to be four of them all told – were merely camp-followers, and were constantly squabbling. It seemed quite too much to hope for that his presence there and his occupation should remain for long unreported. So he was constantly plotting and scheming to find some other means to deport the first batch of prisoners, but always without effect. Invariably, when he had a new plan formed, some item of it in re-testing proved faulty, and there he was left to begin again afresh. Still he was getting together admirable material to send to that fair historian, Miss Collier, of Boston, for her "Conduct of the Continental Wars."

At the same time he was not idle. He worked ten diligent hours a day at his boat. He was one of those men who always thought best and most clearly when strenuously employed. Between whiles, when he was not sleeping, he foraged. There was no ration served out to him by the Spanish authorities, who, indeed, were unaware of his existence there, and for foraging purposes the island and the smaller islets round it were very barren. The 5,500 prisoners were all in a state of semi-starvation, and half of them were on the constant prowl for food.

But all the world over there is the one man who can grow fat where the thousand will starve, and Major Joseph Colt was one of these exceptions, though in actual girth fatness was not his to acquire. He was always lean and lanky in figure, and his blue-black cheekbones and jaw were always strongly outlined. But he needed food in plenty to keep his machinery going at its accustomed high pressure, and he saw to it that he had it. He charmed out rabbits that no one else could lure from their burrows, he caught fish which had refused every other hook, he found edible roots and salads at whose existence none of the prisoners had so much as guessed.

And still work on the boat progressed, till at length she stood upon her rollers, completed. La Rueuse, Kabak, and the other two women had developed an unexpected fidelity. In return for the surplus meats of his forays, they vied with one another in doing him small kindnesses. And in return for a certain angular deference he paid them – a deference of which they saw little enough elsewhere – they all of them gave "this dear Joe" an affection which was quite open and unrestrained; and, what was far more to his taste, added every possible assistance to his scheme which lay in their power.

Upon matters advanced then to this stage, descended one day Mademoiselle Clarice de la Plage in fine millinery, and under official escort. She had arrived in Majorca, it appeared, a week ago, and on landing at Palma had brought with her baggage labelled "Countess Czerny, Vienna." She spoke Spanish and English with fluent inaccuracy, and because there was no one in the city to examine her, they took it on trust that her native tongue was some Hungarian dialect with an unspellable name. Austria was the chronic enemy of Bonaparte, and any enemy of France was a friend of the Spaniards. Even Captain J. W.

Meadey, who came ashore at Palma one day to make things unpleasant for his beef contractor, was acidly civil to her.

The Countess, it appeared, wished to revel in the sight of enemies in misfortune, and, this being quite comprehensible to the Spanish mind, she was taken over to Cabrera by the next supply boat, assigned quarters, and given the run of the island. It was all ridiculously easy, as she assured Colt with sly malice, when he told his own hard struggle to get a footing.

But, in point of fact, she had moved always in a halo of danger, and knew it. As Mademoiselle Clarice, *vivandière* of the late 82nd Regiment of the Line, she had been for various reasons one of the best known figures in Dupont's army, and many of the tattered, shaggy prisoners stared at her in open recognition. So far she had met their looks with clever winks – with whole volleys of winks – and none of them named her as countrywoman. But she knew she was every moment in danger of being denounced as what she was, and once caught, she was quite certain the Spaniards would put her down as a spy. They had a perfect mania for discovering spies. And their treatment of them – a very final treatment – was too horrible to think about.

The British, she heard, only shot or hanged spies, and, although so far the bag had been all of the other sex, she wondered whether Captain Meadey would hang a female spy if he caught one.

It was Sergeant Colorado who first put her in the way of finding Colt. That grizzled old warrior had one day met her on one of her promenades, had heard her addressed as Countess, and had promptly doubled up in a fit of silent laughter. Later she got him alone, and gave him her views of his indiscretion. "And to think that you, you of all fellows, should behave so to me. Why from my canteen alone came half the liquor which coloured that great bottle nose of thine. And there's a score of drinks owing for yet."

"Which shall be paid for honourably, mademoiselle, when my purse refills. Name of Mahomet! yes. But in the meanwhile one can serve. Will you accept service, mademoiselle? I know your business here, Major Colt told it to me."

"Ah," she said quickly, "now, there is how you can wipe off your score. Take me to Major Colt."

This, as it turned out, was no easy task. The Sergeant had not seen or heard of Colt since the day of his landing, and, indeed, being well occupied with his own hunger and miseries, had let him drop from memory without ten more thoughts. But to serve Mademoiselle Clarice – and possibly to acquire further benefits – he was ready to exert himself, and did so to such good purpose that at the end of a week he had the American's earth located.

With the four nymphs of the outer cave Clarice had a preliminary skirmish that left many ruffled tempers. They did not approve of her, and said so. She very openly did not approve of them. La Rueuse recommended her to leave the Escape-Agency business to people who understood it, and to go back to the army as a *vivandière*, or to the stage as an actress. Clarice regretted she could not suggest that La Rueuse should again become an actress, seeing that she had never been one at all. They all called each other "dear" very effusively, and any spiteful cut they omitted was one they did not think of.

As a consequence, when at last she did come face to face with Colt, she was flushed of cheek, and her temper beneath was ruffled; and when in his second sentence the tall American extolled the services of La Rueuse and her friends, Mademoiselle Clarice let him grasp the situation in rapid phrase.

"I can't understand any man letting such hussies wait upon him. Least of all, a man who so continually prated about his girl in Boston – Conyer, I think you said the name was."

"Collier, Miss. I have noted before that you have a difficulty in remembering names. There was your own *fiancé*, for instance – Monsieur Legrand – Lesage – Lequelque chose –"

The lady wagged a slim brown finger at him. "Monsieur evades the point! Monsieur is aware of his guilt."

"I'm nothing of the kind. I'm down here on business, and I had to make use of such employees as came to hand. If you haven't forgot Emperor Bonaparte's commission, you're down on business, too, and I guess we'd better get back to that right now, and leave frills alone."

"If a further recitation of Monsieur the Major's tastes can be avoided, let us get to the 'business,' as you name it, at once."

"Sure! Well, miss, that's the boat I built, with – er – some help. With crowding she could carry fifteen men. Yes, I had reckoned on sending a first consignment of fifteen men back to Emperor Bonaparte's service. But there will be fourteen now, and the odd seat will be for you. Indeed, I just freeze to think of the risks you have run already."

"Pooh! I am not like your Boston schoolmarm. I have no nerves to stay atwittering."

"No. But it is the Boston schoolmarm that I shall marry."

"Meaning that you wouldn't marry me if I were the last woman on earth? Dear Mary! Do you think I'd have you, even if I were not engaged already to Monsieur Le Brun? What a prospect for any woman who becomes your wife, to be dragged back to your savage America, there to be scalped by the Red Indians! No, Monsieur the Major, be faithful to your Miss Patience Collier, or you will die a bachelor. There is no woman in Europe who would go to the backwoods, as I daresay you have found even with La Rueuse and Kabak, and those creatures."

"Then," snapped Colt, "as I have no intention of breaking my word to Miss Collier, we will take it I am well suited, and drop the subject if you please. There will be no moon tomorrow night, and, if the sea is sufficiently smooth, the boat will take you off then. I will arrange to-night for the fourteen men who shall accompany you. There is a bandy-legged little sailor-man, Jean Baptiste Rousseau, who shall be in command."

"And this boatful is the limit of your ambitions for the time?"

"For the time, yes. My brig was wrecked."

"But my ship was not. How do you suppose I got to Majorca? Flew there? No, Monsieur, I came in an abominable little craft, named a felucca, manned by sailors who adore me. I earned money for her hire by singing and dancing, and acting in Marseilles. Oh, I know, Monsieur, that the Emperor and others have said I am no actress, but still I can earn money on the stage, and good money, too. And my felucca waits now every night behind Formentera yonder."

"Good. I guess you've seen me, and gone ten better. How many men will she hold?"

"Say three loads of your boat."

Colt pulled at his square black whisker. "Well," he said with a sigh. "I guess the Emperor will have to enter up the first forty men delivered on this contract to your account, Miss Clarice."

"Not at all, Monsieur. Without your boat, and without your ferriage across to Formentera, none could get away. So I am afraid the men will have to go down to the joint account of the pair of us, and I can only hope that Miss Collier will not disapprove of the partnership. Perhaps it would be one of the things best left out from the notes you send her for that history she is writing."

"Miss Collier," retorted Colt, "when I parted from her in Boston, gave me instructions to 'get on,' and secure a high position in the French Army. Well, I guess I'm doing it. She didn't mention any limitations about the methods. I have to use what help I can."

"There's one lot of help you'll not use again," snapped Clarice, "and that's those four creatures in the other cave there. They go off by the first boat, or nobody goes off at all. Mind that."

"But, my good girl, the Emperor wants men – soldiers – not women camp-followers."

"I know as well as you do what the Emperor wants, and I know better still what he will get, and that's La Rueuse, and Kabak, and the two others in the first batch. Come, Monsieur, have you no gallantry? Surely it should be the poor weak women to be rescued first!"

Major Colt rubbed hard at his chin. "The Emperor's orders were for men," he persisted. "He said nothing about women."

"Bah, you incorrigible! You philanderer! You want to keep the creatures here to enjoy their pawings, and listen to their silly flatteries."

"They shall go by the first boat, Miss, and be hanged to them. There shall be five of you in that boat, and I hope your tongues will keep you warm."

"Ah, but," said Clarice, sweetly, "I do not go in the boat. I stay here. I have my reputation to make as well as you have yourself. And it is only on Cabrera that I can make it."

The night following came away moonless and black, and, as the sea was smooth, Major Colt crammed no less than eighteen of the prisoners into his boat. A layer of them had to lie on the floorboards, it is true, but they had served too long an apprenticeship to discomfort on Cabrera to mind such small inconvenience as that.

They reached the felucca and were discharged on her, and then Colt ordered the sailor Rousseau to help him row back to the boat.

"Face of a pig!" screamed the bandy-legged Jean Baptiste, "and here was I picturing myself with a full belly at last. And now you ask me to go back to that beastly island again and starve? Never will I budge from here." After which he seated himself sturdily on his thwart, and they rowed off.

On the next night and the next, cargoes of gaunt, shaggy prisoners were taken off to the felucca, which then hove her anchors from the Balearics, and in due time discharged her freight at Toulon. The hungry J.B. Rousseau was with them, very much to his satisfaction, and Colt rowed back the heavy boat alone.

That night, so it happened, Captain Meadey had in mind to give certain of his crew a little boat-exercise, and whilst he sailed the *Frolic* round Cabrera one way, Lieutenant Cabott was set to circumnavigate the island on the opposite course.

It was Cabott who picked up the phosphorescence of Colt's oar-blades against the blackness, and very promptly turned his ten-man-power boat towards the glow, and ran him aboard. Colt had the sense not to resist, but gave instead such explanation as his wit suggested.

One hour later, an elderly, dandified Captain Meadey received this same contemptuous lieutenant on his quarter-deck in the light of a battle lantern, and heard the curt report that he had captured an Englishman who was a born liar.

"Send him aft," said Meadey, and Colt came to him under escort. "My officer tells me you call yourself an Englishman."

"That is so," said Colt. The men around sniggered openly at the accent.

"You're a liar. Also an American. But I am short of hands, and will overlook both offences. You may consider yourself pressed."

"My Land! But I don't."

"If you do your duty," said the chilly Englishman, "you will get what you're entitled to. If you don't you will be flogged. Get forward."

Now Major Joseph Colt was cool and calculating, and the least impulsive man on earth, but Captain Meadey was too much for him. Here was the type of man who had made the American colonists revolt, and Colt was his father's son. His sheath knife was still inside his shirt, and he was within an ace of drawing it and making a rush on the Captain and holding him, knife at throat, a hostage for his own freedom, when of a sudden he halted, and drew back with a cough and a gasp. Clarice de la Plage stepped out of the blackness into the circle of the battle lantern's light.

"An addition to your crew, Captain Meadey? Oh, I am so glad you are going to be kind to 'im."

And then Colt saw the pity glow in her eyes, and her lips – her clever, stage-trained lips – deliberately frame the words, "Poor Joe!"

Major Colt marvelled at her impudence in addressing him by his Christian name.

But on consideration he rather liked it.

As he went forward between the rows of guns, he wondered rather curiously why he should like it. He wondered also how she had come on board the *Frolic*. But as she was there, he felt half reconciled to being there himself for the time being. He somehow seemed to himself responsible just now for the safety of this girl, Clarice de la Plage.

But at the same time he wondered rather uneasily if Miss Collier, of Boston, Massachusetts, would altogether approve of his interest.

2. The Yellow Galley-Full.

Major Joseph Colt stood 6-feet-2 on his bare heels, and as the 'tween decks of H.B.M. twenty-gun brig *Frolic* offered only some 5-feet-7 of head room, he did most of his travelling below bent into the form of an ess.

Like all tall men, Colt was used to keeping his head out of collision, and so avoided actual bumps and abrasions. But his height extracted constant sarcasms from both his stumpy fellow seamen and the stocky petty officers, and like all United States citizens of that period he was perilously sensitive to any criticism which came from British lips.

The clumsy little war-brig hung on to the coasts of Cabrera through gale and calm, guarding the 5,450 half starved and wholly savage French prisoners, ready to spit red battle at a hundred seconds' notice, and carrying on always her own domestic affairs under the iron discipline of Captain John Benjamin Meadey.

Every morning, whether the brig beat wetly through a gale, or grilled under an outrageous sun, gratings were rigged in the gangway, and the cat-o'-nine-tails scored the backs of sundry members of the crew. It was Captain J. B. Meadey's theory that plenty of flogging made his men both tough and smart; and whatever may be said for the specific, there is no doubt that, as nautical fighting material, the *Frolic*'s crew were hard to beat. They accounted themselves the equal of four times their number of Frenchmen, and six times their number of Spaniards, and on at least nine separate occasions had proved this balance to be satisfactorily correct. The trifle that half their sea fights were won by superior seamanship and gunnery was left out of the record. It was an unscientific age, and any advantage that was gained otherwise than by personal bravery was rather looked upon as hitting below the belt.

In the *Frolic*'s forecastle there was Joseph Colt, ordinary seaman and pressed man, and aft (where she had usurped Meadey's own sleeping cabin as boudoir and sanctum) was domiciled a bright little woman with a remarkably neat ankle, who styled herself Countess Czerny, but who was more widely (and more accurately) known in French Army circles as Mademoiselle Clarice de la Plage.

The *Frolic*'s officers understood that Captain Meadey himself had rescued the lady from the insults of Spaniards one evening in Cabrera, and the detail that Meadey had dined rather opulently before his trip ashore, and had swallowed far more muddy port than was good for him, weighed with them as nothing in the transaction. All English gentlemen did drink as much port as they could get hold of in the year 1810, or they were not gentlemen; and anything bad about a Spaniard was easily understandable. That at least was the way the *Frolic* looked at the matter. The average Briton of the period had a far greater contempt for his ally the Spaniard as a man, than for his hereditary enemy the Frenchman.

To see Captain Meadey, who had a most insular and ferocious contempt for all unmentionable foreigners, doing the amiable to Clarice was a sight for the gods. By right of proprietorship over all the oceans, the British sea officers of those days had an intimate acquaintance with charts, harbours, sea-borne commerce, and coastal ports; they were mightily self-complacent in view of the fact that they held the seas in the teeth of Bonaparte; and they had a good deal of contempt for those who arranged land affairs and allowed the French to beat them. Accordingly, to avoid being mixed up in any way with these incompetents, they took a frigid pride in knowing nothing about the land and the ways thereof, and on the *Frolic*, which was as eminently British a brig as ever designer bungled, there was not a man who could have drawn any fuller map than a mere coastline of Europe.

Austria they knew as a name, but beyond that it was to them merely a blank piece of territory of vague size, peopled apparently by a soldiery uniformed in white coats, who got more lickings from Bonaparte than did most of their neighbours.

Came then among this ship's company Mademoiselle Clarice de la Plage, a lady of nimble wit and a highly fascinating manner. She said she was Countess Czerny, and, because no one could disprove the statement, they took it for fact. She knew the Czerny country – as a point of fact she had bivouacked amongst the ruins of the old chateau when she was a *vivandière* with the conquering French Army – and she told them all about the place and its histories and its beauties, and they listened, politely uninterested. It was the morning after her arrival on board, and Captain John Benjamin Meadey, who had a bad headache, broke in upon the subject by asking where he could put her ashore.

But Clarice by this time was getting a more full measure of her entertainer. She was desolated to think what inconvenience her intrusion amongst so many gallant officers could have caused. But she had a mission. On her estate of Czerny she had fighting cocks; she had come to Spain for more birds to improve the strain.

Englishwomen at that time did not often take interest in sport, and certainly they never fought cocks. Englishmen did, and cock-fighting happened to be a passion with J. B. Meadey. Of course, to an Austrian woman anything was possible; and, at any rate, this taste seemed a creditable one. His interest in her grew. He had fighting cocks in his hen coops – it was from them, by the way, that the lady had got her pointer – and he insisted on displaying to her their qualities.

Now Mademoiselle Clarice knew poultry only from the mess-table point of view. But she was an actress, and as she was acting then, as she told herself, to an audience which could throw her a noosed rope in adverse criticism, she did her best.

"Devilish smart young woman that," condescended Captain Meadey an hour afterwards to his second in command, Lieutenant Cabott. "Smart for a foreigner, that is. Knows a thing or two about game fowl, I can tell you. Pity she isn't an Englishwoman. What the blazes she wants to go back to that dashed place of hers in Austria for, damned me if I can see."

"The lady wants to have another look at Boney, perhaps, sir. She knows she won't see much of him aboard here? Boney's not likely to call on us, eh, sir?"

They both laughed at this bright joke, and then said Cabott: "Bo's'n's mate reported that new hand we pressed last night, sir, is showing ugly."

"Then the bo's'n's mate will probably provide him with physic at the gangway to-morrow."

"Oh, I have him in irons already, sir. The fellow complained to me that he was a free-born American citizen, and when I promised that we'd make an honest man of him instead before the end of the commission, he was insolent to me. I promised him the cat, of course. I should say, sir, three dozen will meet the case."

"Six dozen," said Captain Meadey pompously. "I always support my officers, Mr Cabott, in matters of discipline. By the way, I wish you'd call away a cutter, and go over yourself to that yellow-painted gunboat, and find out what's wrong between her skipper and the Countess here. I didn't quite understand the matter last night. Fact is, I was thinking over something else at the time, and just took the young lady away principally because she wanted to come."

"Quite so, sir."

"I know I gave the fellow some good straight English, and he seemed annoyed. I remember he said that he would come and take the Countess back by force. Of course, you will tell him that if he tries that on, I shall fire into him at once. You can tell him I am Captain John Benjamin Meadey, and don't stand dictating to from any Jack Spaniard living."

"Certainly, sir."

"That's all, Mr Cabott. You may call away your boat. And, oh! by the way, if you can manage to get me a bag of small red maize from anywhere, I'd be obliged to you. The butcher tells me we're out of corn, and he's been obliged to feed my game birds this last week on ship's biscuit, and they've distinctly lost brightness. The Countess noticed it at once, and she says there's nothing like small red maize, steeped in a little beer, for bringing them round."

"Very good, sir," said Lieutenant Cabott, and took himself off upon his errands.

Captain Meadey rejoined his guest on the quarter-deck. "I've sent off," said he, "an officer and boat's crew to teach manners to that Jack Spaniard you were foul of last night. By the way, I didn't quite catch what the bother was about. If the fools can't speak English how can they expect one to understand them?"

"A law ought to be passed," said the lady pleasantly, "that all peoples that are not English should be taught English without further delay."

"Now, that's a very sound idea," said Meadey, "and," he added thoughtfully, "it would really be worth their while. It would save them a tremendous lot of trouble in making themselves understood. I always think a man must be abominably handicapped in having to *sacré-parlez-vous* all day long when he wants to say anything. Now, there's your own example. You were brought up, I suppose, to speak Carpathian, or some language like that, all c's and z's and j's, that you have to translate with your hands and feet as you go along. But your people had you taught English, and you can see for yourself how much more useful and easy it is."

"English is a most noble and melodious tongue as one hears it spoken here on the *Frolic*, Captain Meadey."

"Of course it is, of course. No one could help seeing that. Why, if you stayed with us a bit longer, and practised, I don't believe anyone would guess you were a foreigner."

"Ah, Captain, you are holding out too dazzling hopes. But when I have done my errand I must get back to my own poor country again."

Captain Meadey stared down upon his guest. She was a devilish smart little woman he told himself, and what few foreign notions she had left could be soon knocked out of her. He was a bachelor, and getting on. He felt that he might do worse. He rubbed his hands, and looked at her with a very appreciative eye.

"If I could only find a boat," said the lady, "however small, and a couple of sailors to man her, I could slip across to my friends in Italy."

"You don't seem to get on very well with Spaniards," observed Meadey thoughtfully, "and that's a fact."

"I suppose you couldn't wink at letting me have a crew of those poor French prisoners?"

"Impossible, madam; impossible. Indeed, I'm surprised at your asking it. As an Austrian you ought to hate a Frenchman worse than I do, and I hate 'em as badly as I hate the devil."

"My dear Captain Meadey, was I proposing to do the

wretches any special benefit? Once ashore on Austrian territory they would be prisoners just as much as they are here. But, yes, Captain, I can assure you that in one point the poor Austrian can beat the proud Briton."

"I don't take you. How do you mean, madam?"

"Why, in hatred of the French, Austria is far ahead of you. No, I think you might trust any Austrian not to be over kind to French prisoners."

But Captain Meadey shook his head obstinately, and Clarice dared not press the question further just then. Still, Meadey was perceptibly thawing, pompous island bear though he was, and there, under the warm Mediterranean sunshine, she set herself to further fascinate him, whilst on the snow-white deck planks their shadows danced round them to the swing of the brig.

In the meanwhile, away below in the cable tier, with his heels handcuffed to an iron "horse," sat Joseph Colt awaiting stripes. For the pain of the flogging he was not much concerned. He had stood up once, tied to a Huron torture stake, and had watched unmoved a fellow white man killed with very horrid circumstance, and had only escaped his turn through a fortunate capture of whiskey by the Indians. He was a man absolutely stoical in this respect; but when it came to insult and indignity at the cousinly hands of the British, he was a mere bundle of hysterical nerves.

It made him rage to think that after the contemptuous Lieutenant Cabott, other members of the *Frolic*'s ship's company had set themselves out to draw him, and he had been fool enough to let them do it to the top of their bent.

So as he sat there, with his heels in the bilboes, he bit his thumbs in an ecstasy of rage, and, could he have had the ordering of it, he would have ruthlessly sent every Englishman on the *Frolic* to death to the accompaniment of torture.

By degrees, as the first flux of his rage wore through, shreds of his old scheming coolness returned to him, and he began to make explorations with a view to finding some plan for escape, or, at least, revenge. His prison was in black darkness. He commenced to fumble over it with his fingers in every direction to the limit of his reach.

He was built in on all sides with great knees and massive planking of heart of oak. His head as he sat was a good fathom below the brig's water-line. Down in that darkness there he saw red when he thought of the torture-stake ahead of him – for that was how he classed Captain Meadey's grating and cat-o'-nine-tails – and if with his teeth and talons he could have torn a hole through the ship's side and scuttled her he would have drowned himself without a pang. But, as it was, he could only rub his chin in impotence.

Then a sound came to him; it was a snore, an unmistakable snore. For an hour previous the marine sentry outside the door had been thoughtfully hiccoughing the vapour of new rum, and here the man had fallen off to sleep. The discovery thrilled him.

He unlatched the clumsy door, and softly fastened it back upon its hook. Then he leaned forward upon his knees, stretching out as far through the doorway as his shackled ankles would permit. Not a fibre of his clothing rustled; not the slightest clank came from his irons; the Indian training held good.

Major Colt was a very tall man, and his arms were abnormally long even for his height. The drowsy sentry was almost beyond his reach. Only with his finger tips could he touch the man's bayonet, and the weapon was tight in its scabbard. But even those finger tips could grip with the strength of a hand vice. He strained and strained, and stretched out a further quarter of an inch. He got another finger-nail on to the scabbard, pressing downwards, and by hair's-breadth pulls drew the weapon out.

Presently, and with the same quickness and the same caution against noise, he was squatted back in his prison with a British bayonet in his hand.

He slipped the weapon inside one of his leg-irons and strained at it. The fetter opened with ridiculous ease under the leverage. Another wrench at the other ankle, and he was free. Free and armed. Outside the door the sentry snored and exhaled a stale vapour of rum. Colt emptied the priming from his musket, took the lantern which stood at his feet, and stole on down the dark alleyway. He had it in mind then to reach the magazine, stab the sentry, lay a minute's train of powder, fire this, fight his way on deck and overboard, and leave the brig to blow up behind him as a salve for his ruffled honour.

As a point of fact, he would have failed in this attempt. The magazine was aft, and heavily locked, and its keys were in Captain Meadey's cabin. But, as it was, his attention was turned to another scheme for revenge. He passed a gloomy cabin with the unlatched door swinging idly as the *Frolic* shouldered over the swells. The dim lantern light showed him a sea-chest, with lid thrown back, and inside the orderly array of a ship carpenter's tools. There was a 2-inch auger, bright, new, and sharp. A gush of joy well-nigh choked him as he stooped and took it in his hand. Also there were some small shot-plugs newly made.

It was back in his prison that he started to scuttle the brig, boring vertically downwards through her floor, and plugging each hole as he made it. The auger bit finely, and his jarred nerves were soothed as the piles of wet oak chips grew.

But after boring the fifth hole, of a sudden Colt stopped, and plucked vexedly at his square black whisker. "My land!" he said, "just consider me for a fool! Here's my girl has me come to Europe to get on and secure a position, and here am I wasting time just to scratch even with John Bull Meadey and Ice-Cream Cabott. Moreover, unless I light out of here quick, it strikes me I shall drown, and that stops promotion anyway." He dropped the auger and pulled out the plugs. Water whistled into the *Frolic* in five steady fountains.

Outside the door the sentry snored, and exhaled more rum. The gloomy, unventilated labyrinths of the brig beyond the carpenter's cabin were still strange to him, and though he moved in the shadows with all the stealth and quietness of his Indian training, he bumped into hammocks and aroused men here and there. One and all they spotted him in some undefinable way, and lent venom to their comment with some gibe at his nationality. Colt came very near to slipping the marine's bayonet into some of them.

That he must have escaped from his irons, one and all of these aroused sleepers on the lower decks knew full well, but they made no effort at interference. "Run, Yankee, run!" they scoffed. "John Benjamin will score up your rebel hide finely to-morrow."

But Colt had no mind to go out on to the upper deck, and there be forced to surrender at discretion. He found the one gun-port that was triced up to give air to the lower deck. Blackness and the sea were outside, and he leaped into these with a beaver's splashless dive, and was swallowed out of sight.

Only the lower deck knew, and though they were just as willing as their betters to chaff the Yankee, still, of course, they were loyal to the lower deck. So no alarm was given from below that Ordinary Seaman Colt was attempting to desert, and the upper deck knew nothing of it till the master-at-arms made his report next morning. Then, of course it did not take long to discover the sudden leak which had kept the *Frolic*'s crew so hard at work all night.

In the meanwhile Colt swam away from the brig under water till he nearly burst, dived again as soon as he had breathed, and so on, till he had run her out of sight in the darkness. On one side the low hills of Cabrera loomed black through the purple blackness of the night, and for that destination he swam, and presently was encouraged by hearing behind him the dim bellow of distant orders, and then the unmistakable *cluck-clank* of hard-driven pumps.

"I guess," he mused as he swam, "I guess I'm causing that push of Britishers considerable pain at the pump breaks, any-way. If I could only have scuttled that cursed *Frolic* completely, my land! but I should have been a big man. Still, when I send the facts home to Boston, and Patience Collier works them up into her "Conduct of the French War," I reckon they'll add to the sale of that volume. Gee! It's just the thing to sell a book on our side."

The water was warm, the sea smooth, and Colt was a strong man and a powerful swimmer. The black outline of Cabrera came nearer to him and more near, and he had decided in his own mind exactly where he would land, where he could conceal himself, and how he would set about getting away with the next batch of those prisoners which the great Emperor wanted so badly for his army. But there was no escape-agency business for him that night, and it was out of a quite unexpected quarter that the interruption came.

To his ear there drifted the faint thud of rowlocks, irregularly pressed. At first he thought it was a small boat which was coming towards him; but as it drew more near he diagnosed it for one of the Spanish war-galleys which helped the *Frolic* to guard the island; and presently when it loomed into sight, he could see the great oars hitting the water one after another, like a peal of bells.

"Well," thought Colt, "there is plenty of room in the Mediterranean for both of us," and kept on his course. But the galley, it soon appeared, had a helmsman as bad as her rowers, and she steered the vilest course imaginable, yawing to this side and that, till there was no deciding what her intended course might be. And then, as she drew still more near, Colt found her suddenly on the top of him, dived to clear her, and thereupon very nearly lost his life. Some spiteful (or, it is more probable, unskilful) slave dug his oar down to beyond the prescribed depth, hit the American on the head, and stunned him deep down there below the surface.

As it happened, the wash of the oars brought him up again, where he was seen – and ignored. The Spanish watch officer was too idle or too callous to bring-to for a mere anonymous swimmer.

But another galley was close upon her heels – they were hunting in couples it appeared – and someone hailed. She yawed, either through bad steering or design, and a couple of slaves fished up the flotsam with a boat-hook. Spanish galley slaves always appreciated getting an extra hand on board who might possibly be set to an oar.

The night passed on, and the galley thumped and lurched on her way round the island, guarding always against escape of the French prisoners. On her foredeck lay her new acquisition, left there to die or survive, as he thought fit. The slaves were callous, the officers and crew careless, as to the result. If he survived they could inquire as to who he was, and, anyway, that was for *mañana*. The Spaniards were an incurious race, and very much impressed with the futility of doing anything to-day that there was the least chance of putting off till to-morrow.

In due time Joseph came by his wits again, and there was the sun up, and genially employed in drying for him his sodden clothing. The musky smell of the slaves made him cough and spit, and presently he was aware that his head ached as though someone had been endeavouring to chop it in two. That and a further odour of garlic gave him the clue to recent proceedings, and he sat up and propped his back against the galley's bulwark.

His survival was languidly reported to an officer on the quarter-deck, and he was ordered aft, and went there in somewhat tottery fashion. As an officer in General Dupont's army he had fought against Spaniards in Spain, and had caused casualties to many of them. But he saw no necessity to mention this. He stated the solid fact that he was a citizen of the United States, and the officer bowed and gave him a civil smile.

"But how did the *señor* come to be in the water?"

An answer to this might be awkward. Colt squeezed his muddled wits for a diplomatic reply.

"There was no vessel near the *señor*," the officer went on languidly, "except that detestable *Frolic*."

"Oh, detestable, is she?" thought Colt. "Well, I'll risk telling I was pressed on her against my will, and was escaping." He did so, and was promptly shaken by the hand and invited below to breakfast.

"Bully for me," thought Colt, but did not say so aloud. Instead, he went below, availed himself of what primitive toilet appliances the galley offered, and presently was seated in a tiny cabin, eating an olla which was largely made up of heat, garlic, and high-flavoured Mallorquin olive oil.

Don Randolphe, the galley's captain, was a long and melancholy Spaniard, with a square-cut whisker, almost of the pattern of Major Colt's own. The situation explained itself quickly.

"The diplomatists of my country," said Don Randolphe, "have made an alliance with these detestable British; and perhaps at the time it was necessary to use any stone which one could throw at the French. But their presence is hateful, and their manners are a constant insult."

Major Colt hit the table. "My land! Cap, but you should hear an American talk about them!"

"Figure to yourself an instance. Three evenings ago I was ashore to see these French cattle, and to rub my hands and think that we could hold so many of the Corsican's men to such an abominable imprisonment. There was a lady there, an Austrian, the Countess Czerny. At least she called herself an Austrian, but I have my doubts."

"Ah!"

"Of course, you have met her, Don José. Now, what do you think? Is she Austrian?"

"How should I know? Me meet her? Where can I have seen her?"

"Why, on the detestable *Frolic*."

"Oh, to be sure; on the *Frolic!* Why, you see, Cap, I was forward, and she was aft, and we didn't have much truck. So if the lady says she's Austrian, I guess you'd better take her as such. But might I ask what you were doing with this Countess?"

Don Randolphe preened himself in his melancholy way. "Why, *señor*, one does not so often see a woman on this service that one can afford to neglect opportunities."

"I see. Thought you saw your way to do a bit of lady-sparking; and then up came John Bull Meadey and wanted to punch your head?"

The Spanish captain's face-muscles tightened. "Ah, you also are Anglo-Saxon. You speak lightly. You cannot understand how a Latin feels when his honour is touched. You would never grasp my feelings towards Captain Meadey."

"Sir, you're making a very considerable error. I tell you, you can't guess anything bad I wouldn't like to do to J.B. Meadey. He treated me worse'n if I was a yellow dog, and, so far's it doesn't clash with other business in hand, I've got to get square with him."

"Then rest content, Don José. Presently your vengeance shall be carried out completely and horribly – by other hands."

The American did not show enthusiasm. "I guess you mean it very kindly, Cap, but if it's all the same to you, I rather fancy I'm competent to settle up my own accounts, and if they have to be somewhat long outstanding, I don't forget to clap on reasonable interest. I picture myself one day with a hand on the back of John Bull Meadey's collar, and then if I don't get my shoe-toe six times hard into his posteriors, I'm content to have that negligence mentioned in a history of the war now being written by Miss Patience Collier, of Boston."

The captain of the galley looked mystified. "You speak of things, Don José, which are beyond me."

"Sir, I am a free American, and hate all Britishers in a way that would surprise you."

"Then, why do you not rejoice when I tell you that shortly he will be punished? Listen, Don José! I shall set two sets of dogs mutually to worry and tear one another. On that island are French curs innumerable." He waved a hand to where Cabrera baked under the midday sunshine. "To-night the *Frolic* anchors inshore off the castle. News will be taken to *Señor* Meadey of a landing of Frenchmen come to rescue prisoners. Meadey and half his crew will go ashore to capture these. While they are gone, a great mass of the French prisoners will find boats on the beach, will put off under the darkness, and will take the *Frolic*. Many of the dogs on both sides will be killed. Then will return Meadey and his men. They will go aboard unsuspecting, will be surprised, and killed. And so is wiped out the detestable Captain Meadey."

"This is playing my game," thought Colt. "A nice brig-load of the prisoners should escape. But they shan't do it, all the same. It's not a fair trick. Besides, I don't approve of Jack Spaniards putting their knives into white men, even though they are a pack of stuck-up Britishers."

"Afterwards, of course, Don José, we shall deal with the *Frolic*. There will be four galleys of us lying off her bow and her quarter, and when we perceive she is out of the hands of our dear ally, the detestable Britisher, we shall open fire on her – the four against the one – and sink her. So will end the *Frolic*. And so will be cured your wounded honour, Don José, and mine. May I offer you cigarettes?"

"Thanks, no." Colt pulled from his pocket three tubes and a bowl, and screwed them together. "I'll put your tobacco, if you'll give me a load, in this. There's nothing like a cool, long pipe for a pleasant smoke, especially if you want to put in a big think as well."

"Well, *señor*, with permission, I will leave you to it. It is my hour for siesta. May I offer you a cabin?"

"Why, if it is the same to you, I'd rather sit right here on deck. I guess I'm a man that wants to get too much out of life to have any immediate use for sleeping when the sun's turned on."

Now, as Colt knew full well, the great Emperor looked more to results than means, and if he could contrive to bring three or four hundred men back to the eagles, with a British twenty gun brig thrown in as a *bonne bouche*, that act would go a long way to sending him up in the scale of promotion and bringing him nearer to that marshal's *bâton* which he so ardently coveted, and which he had marked for his own.

As to his own personal scruples, they must be neglected for the time being, and of all British subjects, surely Captain Meadey deserved least consideration from him.

Supposing (he told himself) he were boarding the *Frolic* with a crew of Americans, he would tomahawk Meadey with his own hands as soon as look at him; so why be scrupulous of doing the same thing by deputy without risk?

Miss Collier had bidden him come to Europe to "get on", and to take the *Frolic* into Toulon full of Frenchmen would be doing this. He set his jaw, and proceeded to think out a process of persuading the captain of the galley to set him ashore.

As it turned out, his diplomacy to this end went very much astray. He first of all ruffled Don Randolphe's temper, and next aroused his suspicions, and in the end, when, after nightfall, the galley had swept up to moorings in the little harbour of Cabrera, near the ruined castle, he got ashore by the simplest of all means.

The captain and those of the officers he had spoken to were below; he was pacing the deck in sulky solitude under the stars; and a boat came alongside with a message from the shore commandant.

Major Colt walked to the gangway, stepped calmly down into the boat, and there was no one near who dreamed of questioning him.

He got ashore with an equal lack of formality, and a minute later had strolled away into the friendly darkness. He could have laughed aloud at the easiness of it all.

Time pressed. If Don Randolphe was to be believed, the plot for the capture of the *Frolic* was already afoot, and Colt had no mind that any boarding-party should go off to the *Frolic* without his company. In the first place, he had his personal account with Meadey to square, though it irked him horribly to let. Frenchmen be mixed up in this adjustment; and, in the second place, once the brig was captured, it must be his part to see that Clarice got clear.

Don Randolphe, it must be remembered, had only divulged half his plot to the French prisoners. They knew he wished them to take the British brig: they did not know he intended to silence them with his own guns immediately afterwards. Colt felt he must be there in person to attend to Don Randolphe.

Again and again Colt came across batches of prisoners, or went into their rude huts and tried to get in touch with those who were in the secret. Some regarded him with open suspicion; others took him for what he said he was; and others remembered him as a major in General Dupont's army. But none had heard of any scheme to take the *Frolic*. Or, what was far more to the point, no one owned up to having heard of such a scheme.

The warm night passed on, and Colt grew more insistent in his inquiries. There was a curious wakefulness over the isle that made him sure that something was afoot. When 5,450 men all whisper together, a noise goes up like the subdued hum of machinery. But one and all they most exasperatingly kept him out of their councils.

Then Major Colt got a shock. A voice from the blackness of a hut's doorway said: "Joe! You! – and they told me he was dead! Dear Mary!"

"Clarice!" cried Colt. "I beg your pardon, Miss Clarice, I should have said. My land! how did you get here?"

"Come in here out of the moonlight, monsieur. I squeeze your hand, Monsieur Joe. Word was brought to Captain Meadey that there had been a landing of French escape-agents, and he has come ashore with fifty of his crew to capture them."

"But why are you here?"

"Oh, that was simple, once I heard he was going ashore. The brightness of his fighting-cock's plumage was dulled; he told me so, the dear, heavy creature, and I agreed with him. There was no cure for it like the leaves of a certain herb, boiled in a little port, and served with red pepper. What was the name of the herb? Well, I could only think of the Hungarian name, and nearly blew out a tooth in saying it. It grew largely on my estate of – I nearly forgot that name too, but got it in time – estate of Czerny, and also, Monsieur Joe, on Cabrera. No, I could not describe the herb, but I would in part discharge myself of the enormous obligation under which the great, the magnificent, Meadey, had placed me. I would go ashore and find it myself."

"Well?"

"I must own he did not see it at first, but I wheedled him into it. Oh, I can do anything with the dear Meadey – 'Jack' he desires that I should call him. Figure it to yourself, Monsieur Joe, he wants to marry me."

"Here, miss," said Colt sharply, "I can't spend all the night chattering like this. You and I are here on Cabrera as Emperor Bonaparte's escape agents, and if we don't want to be superseded, we must get to business right now. Whose hut is this you are in? Who is that sniggering there in the darkness?"

"Sergeant Colorado, my major."

"Come now, are you as behindhand as all these other fools? Do you know anything about this attack on the brig?"

"The men are to muster for it an hour after midnight, Monsieur the Major, and because we have no watches, and the parish clock does not chime to-night, the intelligent Spaniard has given to one of us a pistol with which to sound *réveille*. At the noise of the first pistol shot, those of us who feel inclined, get to the harbour. At the sound of the second shot, some swim, and the rest take what boats are there on offer. We reach the brig. We take her. There it is – all."

"How are you armed?"

Sergeant Colorado thrust out a large lean hand into the

moonlight, and showed a heavy knob of jagged rock – "It will serve, Monsieur the Major, till I can borrow a more polite weapon."

Colt tugged vexedly at his square black whisker. At last: "Here," he said, "sergeant, you go and play outside. I've something to say to mademoiselle."

Sergeant Colorado saluted, grinned and went.

"I suppose," said Colt, "you hardly want me to set these wolves to cut John Bull Meadey's throat now, miss?"

"But tell me," said Clarice sweetly; "do you want to do it yourself, Monsieur Joe?"

"Well, I do. I want to handle Meadey myself. I want badly to handle him. But I don't want any Frenchman or Spaniard to do it for me, and that's a fact."

"But still, you are in the Emperor's service, and the Emperor's enemies should be your enemies."

"They are miss, they are. Only, when I entered that service I made one proviso: I wasn't to be called upon to fight against Britain. My land! hark to that."

Crack!

The sharp whip of a pistol-shot divided the night outside.

"It seems to me," said the *vivandière*, "that there's little time left now for monsieur to argue out these niceties further. This poor Captain Meadey, that had been so gallant to me, I have a tenderness for him. But with a Frenchwoman the Emperor must come first."

"Right," said Colt, with sudden inspiration. "Emperor Bonapartè shall come first. You stay here. You'll be safer on the island."

"No, Monsieur Joe," said the little woman. "I am accustomed to the fighting line, and I shall come with you."

Outside, in the warm darkness, there came the noise of bare feet padding quickly over the bare earth, and Colt and Clarice de la Plage (after another moment's talk) ran from one to the other, quietly passing the word. The English brig, they said, was too ugly for them. These perfidious British were so full of their own undesirable fog, that they had forgotten how to sleep. Besides, even if they took her, there was a calm, and they could not sail her away. Now, the galleys had oars, and the yellow-painted galley in particular was swift and easily handled.

Against the Spaniards these prisoners were always especially bitter. It was the Spaniards who had originally broken the terms of the capitulation, and, instead of sending them back to France, had marooned them on this desolate Cabrera; it was the Spaniards who had starved them there; it was the Spaniards who had heaped upon them a thousand indignities. The British they merely disliked with a national enmity. For the Spaniards each separate prisoner had a venomous personal hatred.

By the time they had reached the harbour, word had been passed, and each man of the storming party knew of the change of plan. They were desperate fellows all, unarmed except for sticks and stones, volunteers for this most forlorn of all forlorn hopes. None of the women prisoners were there. The only member of the gentler sex with the storming party was an ex-*vivandière*, who wore a face of easy assurance, and carried a tongue of the most cheerful, but who was inwardly half-frozen with terror at what was to happen.

As it chanced, the languid watch-officer of the yellow-painted Spanish galley, with infinite carelessness, had paid out his head warp from the buoy, and let his vessel's stern come within a fathom of the stone quay. A plank bridged the two – it saved the trouble of getting a boat into the water – and that it placed every throat on board in jeopardy did not trouble the languid officer. It did not occur to him that the 5,450 French prisoners that he insulted on every possible occasion should ever resent their treatment.

Then *crack*, another pistol-shot snapped out, and from behind every rock, every wall, every building, from out of every patch of shadow there issued men, dumb, half-naked, shaggy men, who ran swiftly on naked feet, making for the galley's stern.

A great bottle-nosed sergeant and a tall black-whiskered man raced for first place. Bottle-nose was on the plank first, but black-whisker jumped and landed on the galley's rail ahead of him. Of their following, only a few could use the plank, many jumped and missed, and of those on the brink of the quay, scores were thrust over into the water by those pressing on behind. The watch on the galley's deck fought savagely, the galley's crew poured up from below and fought savagely also. At them the stormers raged with teeth and talon, with jagged rock and with weapons snatched from the fallen. It was just a shambles of a fight.

In the water some drowned, some doggedly held on till they scrambled on board, some struggled back to the shore. On the galley men hacked, and stabbed, and strangled, and there was only one who gave a thought or a care to any wounded, and that was a woman.

Then it began to be plain that the French were getting the upper hand. The tall, sallow, black-whiskered man, who seemed to be everywhere, and to see everything and to fight harder than anybody else, jumped on a gun and bawled above the din: "Over the side with them now – slaves and all!"

The order was carried out with a furious rush.

"Now then, we must light out of this right now. All you gentlemen to the oars, and row like galley-slaves, or slaves you'll be for the rest of your lives, with Meadey's cat-o'-nine-tails to help you on. Now, cast off those warps."

Away they went with a roar and a rattle of sound. The other galleys were awake and buzzing, and one had cast loose and was under oars. Upon her Colt bore down, threatening to ram. Where upon she dodged, and fouled one of her friends. Shot came after them fast and thick. But the hot, still night was too dark for accurate aim, and away they tore out on to the open sea without further scathe.

And then came the time to sort out the dead for over-side, and to give more care for the wounded than Clarice could contrive with her crude, first-aid appliances during the thick of the fight.

When dawn burned up egg-yellow over distant Minorca, the galley had rounded the westernmost cliffs of Majorca, and was heading north for France over a desert sea. The shaggy, half-naked prisoners bent lustily to the oars.

Mademoiselle Clarice came aft on to the quarter-deck, and brought up her hand in military salute to Major Joseph Colt, who was still at the galley's tiller.

"Of sound men, and those wounded which are likely to recover, there are one hundred and eighteen, Monsieur the Major. A tidy mouthful, even for the Emperor."

"Tidy enough. Are you sound, Clarice? What's that blood on your sleeve, girl? My land! I felt as if I was stabbed myself when I saw you down, with that great gawky Randolphe standing over you with his knife, and I couldn't get near."

"Ah, but he was the jealous one, monsieur. However the good Sergeant Bottle-nose plucked him from me and threw him over the side. This blood – that's the sergeant's. Just a scratch on the wrist. I mended it for him, and kissed his purple cheek for a reward."

"You are mighty free with your kisses, miss."

"To those I don't care about, yes. Will you have one, Joe?"

"I guess not."

Mademoiselle Clarice de la Plage stood in the sunlight, and addressed the East: "Now what is it, I ask you, that this dear Joe desires? Meadey, Don Randolphe, Sergeant Colorado, all of whom I care nothing about, I kiss those, and he resents it. I would kiss this dear Joe also, to show I care nothing about him too, but he will not let me. There is a Miss Patience Conyers that he prates about –"

"Collier."

"Miss Patience Collier, a schoolmarms and writer of history in distant, very distant Boston. Now, if he really loved this Miss Collier, to whom he is affianced, he would take a kiss from me, as that would show he knew I cared nothing for him, and did not mind. But, no, he will not, this dear Joe. I wonder what does he really wish for?"

"Miss," said Colt savagely, "if it were a thing any American could do to a woman, there are times when I should like to take you up and shake you. You are that exasperating. I keep on telling you I am properly engaged, and have to stick to it."

"La – la!" said Clarice. "But I wager that I do not appear in the 'History of the Wars,' which the correct Miss Collier is writing for the enlightenment of Boston. La-la! dear Joseph."

3. The Pirate

The captain of the pirate was a Portuguese, and carried the name of Hernando de Soto in deference to the feelings of his friends when his time should come for the gallows. The mate was a Frenchman, wore his own name, Georges Chobar, and gloried in piling infamies upon it. The second mate was a Moor of Algiers, decked out in the style and clothing of a Spaniard. Call him Pedro, and he would beam upon you. Slip out Ali, and if the night was sufficiently dark, it was odds on your feeling the chill of his knife.

Half of the crew of this pirate felucca were as great a mix of nationalities as the afterguard; the other half were African Moors or African negroes.

A pirate she was, open and confessed, flying any flag that came first to the halliards, a pariah in every sea; and one would have thought that to put a woman on such a craft was to enlarge the limits of calamity. Yet there was a woman on this dark schooner, a Mademoiselle Clarice de la Plage, and she was there moreover, by her own free will and choice. Into such desperate situations could the glamour of Bonaparte lure even a woman who had once known and appreciated all the delicacies and dainties of Paris.

Out of all that wild ship's company there was only one man she could trust, and he was an American – one Joseph Colt. But then he also was in the service of the great Emperor, and, as it happened, they were partners in the same enterprise. Major Joseph Colt was the pirate's purser, and for the one and only time in his ambitious life he was not anxious to climb to a higher grade in the service. There was only one other English speaker on board, a half-witted creature called Trotter, but he never seemed clear whether his nationality was British or American, and he was a man who had brought unreliability up to the level of a fine art.

The tale of their arrival on this picaroon was sufficiently adventurous. They had stolen a Spanish galley, and in her had carried stolen French prisoners from Cabrera, and brought them back to Toulon, there to rejoin the Imperial eagles. They had set off back to the Balearic Islands for another load, but the very first night they dropped the French land the galley and her feeble crew had been snapped up by a pirate out of Algiers. Into her hold they were clapped, with the promise of slavery later on in Algiers city; and because the Dey of Algiers cared not one jot for Bonaparte or anybody else, they were morally sure that this promise would be faithfully carried out.

The pirate, however, had been successful; she had made many captures, and had sent away many men as prize crews; and because slaves were a commodity marketable in Algiers, she had a fine assortment of sailormen sandwiched in between the pilfered bales in her hold.

Amongst these an insurrectionary movement was already on foot when the galley's contingent arrived, and that night it gushed over into activity. They gained the deck. The Moorish captain rushed up, and was promptly killed. A couple of his men followed him over the side, and the two parties were within an ace of commencing a mutual massacre. But the Moorish first lieutenant, Ali (who called himself Pedro), jumped into the forerigging, and howled out for a parley and a truce.

The Moors, it seemed, were sick of their present employ. They were pirates, with all the risks and without any of the more pleasing emoluments of piracy. If caught they were hanged; if they turned their cruises to a profit, that profit went to His Highness the Dey. They had for long enough wanted to go a-pirating on their own account, and only the captain (just recently deceased) had stood in the way. Now that he was removed, the advantages of a free commission seemed still more pleasing. They even went further, they suggested a joint-stock concern for all hands.

The Europeans from the hold were struck by the fairness of the proposition. They had got what they were fighting for – liberty; and now they began to look a little to the future. Even if they did capture the felucca, how were they to decide where to take her? They were of too many nationalities for all to agree. The world was full of war. The French, British, Spanish, Russians, Austrians were all fighting this week or next in the year 1810, and taking from each other eagles, territory, ships, anything they could capture. Why not set up a new nation of their own – the Felucca Nation, for example – and make war themselves? It would be no more risky than fighting for other people, and they could see to it that the plums and prizes did not go astray.

The beauty of the scheme struck the majority as marvellous – and the small minority held their tongues. Major Colt was amongst that minority, and so also was Mademoiselle Clarice, and they would very much like to have offered an alternative plan. But some wit knocked out the gangway, and rigged a plank outboard by which objectors might leave the ship if they found existing arrangements damaging to their tastes; and this chilled the critics. So all hands fell to electing officers.

On the strength of her previous practice as *vivandière*, Mademoiselle Clarice was named purser's assistant (with special reference to the grog department), and nurse to any wounded that the carpenter might find necessary to whittle down. There was no one on board, it appeared, who was qualified to act as surgeon, but the carpenter was a handy man, and said that after a few trials he had no doubt he could amputate as well as anybody.

In view of mademoiselle's election, Colt saw to it that he was appointed purser. He had no following to support him, and he proposed and seconded himself in the teeth of another candidate who was strongly supported.

"I hate to think I'm pushing in where I'm not exactly wanted," the tall American explained civilly, "but if there's any gentleman here with an eye on that pursership, he's just got to fight me right now; and when I've shown up the colour of his inside I'm ready for the next, and so on for as many times as there are applicants. But it's just the one office I've got use for on this ship, and it won't do for anybody to forget it."

Upon this the other candidate discovered that a knowledge of reading and writing was one of a purser's necessary equipments; acknowledged himself illiterate; and gracefully stepped out of the contest. So Joseph Colt went below and took possession of his official quarters. Mr Trotter alone deigned to applaud the election – after it had been made.

To these quarters presently he inducted Mademoiselle Clarice. "There, miss," he said, "that room's yours, and the bolt you see at the back of the door I fixed up out of a crowbar. I guess you'll be a sight safer there than anywhere else on this packet."

"Oh, Joe, you are good to me."

"I'm just doing what any American would, Miss Clarice."

"More, far more."

"Not at all. You must see for yourself that I am remembering all the time that I am behaving as an engaged man should. I have always Miss Collier of Boston at the back of my mind."

"And for that matter I, too, am, of course, faithful to the dear memory of Monsieur le Brunn, to whom I also am affianced."

"But I thought the gentleman's name was le Sage. Well, never mind, miss. Anyway, each knows the other's engaged, and that's the main thing. Now I'm an American, and you're a lady, and you're just now in a blistering fix, and I want to say right here that I'm going to see you safe out of it. And that's the job I'm going to attend to next."

"But surely, Monsieur Joe, the Emperor has named you his chief Escape Agent, and your duty is first and foremost towards him?"

Major Colt pulled at his square black whisker. "I guess Emperor Bonaparte must wait a bit."

"And there's your own promotion to be thought about. You will never reach that marshal's *bâton*, my major, if you lose thought of it for even one little moment."

"That *bâton*," said Colt stubbornly, "is in store just now, and there, if you please, we'll leave it for the present. Miss, I want to warn you particularly about that man Ali, who calls himself Pedro. He's no Spaniard any more than I am a Mohawk. He's a Moor right through to the finger-nails, and though I'm sure you've too much sense to have any use for bigamists of his description, I've seen you smile at him in a way that's given the creature obvious pleasure."

"Why, dear Joe, I must smile at someone, and he's the least detestable of the bunch. Now there's that hateful captain, for instance; you cannot say that I smiled more than twice at Captain Hernando de Soto, as he calls himself."

Major Colt rubbed vexedly at his blue-black chin. "I don't see why you need smile at any of them. You know what they are. Mr Satan out for a week-end from down below would be reliable and a gentleman compared with any one of the gang. And yet you can laugh with them, and throw pleasant, easy words. My Land! For ten sous I believe you'd kiss that Ali."

"Dear Mary! and why not? Is it your prim Miss Collier of Boston who has taught you that all kisses leave a taste?"

"Miss Collier," began Colt, "holds that a kiss is only permissible between engaged people"; but when, in answer to Clarice's shrill laughter, he would have added his own adherence to these views, the conversation was ended and changed to something of the suddenest. From overhead came the crash and concussion of guns, and almost simultaneously there was added to this the din of shot striking their own vessel.

"That calls me to deck," said Colt. "I'd hate to be killed on a ship like this, but I guess if some of us don't fight there's the alternative of being hanged as pirates. You'll excuse me, miss, for what I'm going to do, but fighting here's no part of your job at any rate, so I'll just keep you out of mischief's way." With which he slipped out of the cabin, and hasped the door on the outside, in spite of Clarice's shrill and scathing disapproval.

On deck the scene was none of the most encouraging. A night, black and starless, hung over the sea. The watch of the picaroon had, it appeared, seen the other vessel a bare two cables' length away, and had forthwith fired into her without measuring her size. But the stranger travelled with guns loaded, and must have had linstocks smouldering in tubs alongside of them. She returned the shot almost before the flashes had left the enemy's guns.

The pirates from below poured out on deck, and for a moment showed a very lively panic. The other vessel – a heavily sparred brig they made her out to be – had gone about, and was brazenly coming after them. They were men of a dozen nations and tongues, and Captain Hernando de Soto's vitriolic Portuguese, though well intentioned, reached the inner feelings of but few of them. The renegade, Pedro Ali, a man full of hot courage, was for accepting battle. "The brig trimmed deep,"

said Ali, "and promised rich pickings." But, "Let us get away,"
pleaded others; and presently pistols began to crack between
these two parties, and there was every man fighting a neighbour
for his own hand.

Now inside Major Joseph Colt there were lungs of brass, and,
indeed, the envious freely said that he had fairly shouted his
way up out of the ranks of the French army, and then on up
through the commissioned grades. He had been cradled on a
frontier where the Indian warwhoop was common music, and in
the warmth of action no one could deny that he had the knack of
putting a certain terrifying ferocity into his yell.

He yelled here; moreover, he backed his words with a hail of
blows from an ash belaying pin on all who attempted to fight
with him or with anyone else, till presently he was left gnashing
and shouting in the middle of an empty circle.

"Shoot that American," said somebody.

"Just you dare!" snarled Colt. "I'll kill the man that shoots
me."

No one laughed, and, what is more to the point, no one pulled
a trigger.

"Now," said Colt, "who wants hanging? Speak up quick,
please. There's the hangman so close astern that you can hear
the creaking of his gear if you listen, and I tell you my neck
tickles already."

Once more uprose a yammer of voices, and once more Colt
yelled them into silence. "Looks as if he could make a right
smart speech," said Trotter. "Let's hear what he's to say."

"You lunk-headed scum, that's a British brig-o-war you've
run foul of. That's the *Frolic* that patrols round Cabrera in the
Balearic Islands to keep the French prisoners from escaping."

"What! You know her?" gasped Captain de Soto.

"My Land!" shouted the exasperated American, "how
could I tell you her name if I didn't? John Bull Meadey's
her captain, and he'll hang every son-of-a-dog here if he takes
the felucca, and try us afterwards. Want to ask any more fool
questions?"

Apparently they did not. The great majority of them might
not understand the tall westerner's words, but his gestures bit

home, and the glare of his fierce dark face from beside a battle-lantern brought back discipline. Captain and mates screamed their orders, and the crew jumped to duty without help from the flying belaying pins. The felucca bore away till she had both of the brig's masts in one in the dimness behind her, and then with her own great lateens goosewinged, and half of her crew aft on the poop to bring her by the stern, she fled like some great scared seafowl down wind into the night.

Long after they had congratulated themselves on having shaken off Captain J.B. Meadey's pursuit, that worthy man rounded the *Frolic* to, and with a promise to each of his gun captains who made a miss of three dozen at the gangway next morning, let loose the whole of his starboard broadside into the darkness. Two trundling round-shot from the carronades smashed into the crowd on the pirate's poop, and killed five men there by way of leavetaking.

The escape, and the demise of their friends, had small enough effect on the spirits of the survivors when the Mediterranean sun rose next morning into a pleasant turquoise sky to warm their bodies; and as in the course of the day they overtook and captured a small wine ship out of Valencia, by nightfall they were roaring songs in twenty different tongues, and firing off the felucca's guns at intervals by way of accompaniment. The unspeakable Trotter had daubed his face black with a paste of gunpowder and water, and lurched about howling that he was the devil.

It was whilst this concert was at its height that Major Colt again went down to see Clarice.

For a minute, when he had thrown open the door, the thin little woman glowered at him in tight-lipped fury.

Then: "You savage," she hissed, "you American savage to dare to chain me up here whilst brave men are on deck standing shot."

But Colt was not to be intimidated even by her. "Brave men do you call them? Say mad dogs, and you'll be nearer the mark."

"Oh, poof! You do not understand a little soldierly enthusiasm. To me it would have been nothing. Monsieur the Major, whilst I was *viviandière* with the French armies, I have seen the sack of Saragossa, yes, and the sack of four other cities, and know what even French soldiers can do. These boys here would not terrify me half so much as did the lonely blackness of this cabin. Major Colt, you forget, the light went out."

"The darkness doesn't appear to have hurt you, miss and I tell you again it has been no place for you on deck. I don't guess, I know. Once whilst I was trading cutlery to a Mohawk tribe way out West by the Great Lakes, they lifted the scalp of a business rival who represented a firewater firm, and drank his samples. Well, miss, if I compared those Indians to wild beasts, it would be insulting the beasts. But I say to you straight, I'd rather be there than here as an insurance proposition."

"Poof! I tell you. The *cher* Pedro Ali would be my escort. I am sure he would be most gallant."

"That blighted renegade," said Colt grimly, "has been making such remarks about you already that I have had to attend to him."

"What did he say?"

"He said you must be lonely down below alone, and proposed to come and comfort you. The rest of the beastly crew cheered him on."

"The brutes!" said Mademoiselle Clarice with a shiver.

"Precisely. But they kept the ring fairly enough whilst he and I had it out."

"So you dissuaded him, my Joe?"

"I set him off to swim home if he can find the way."

"You killed him?"

"To be exact, I flung him overboard."

The little woman's eyes brightened. She put out a slim brown hand and reached up and patted the tall American on the shoulder. "Once when I was on the stage I acted in a play of the classic time. There was a knight in it, and the knight fought for his ladylove and rescued her. Did you ever fight for Miss Collier of Boston, dear Joe?"

"Miss Collier," snapped Major Colt, "occupies far too lady-like a position ever to want fighting about. If you'd taught school yourself, Miss Clarice, you'd have felt the dignity of it."

"And Miss Collier also writes history?" suggested Clarice sweetly.

"She does. She is writing a book on the 'Conduct of the European Wars,' and from time to time I send her a batch of material."

"I can picture her, this Boston miss, so prim and accurate, that never kisses any except her dear *fiancé*, who is away from her so savage America, and, therefore, cannot be kissed at all. Dear Mary! what an image of a perfect woman! Now I am different; I could not stand up, stiff and demure and sharp-voiced, to teach school, nor could I sit, in dull patience and write out history that was sent to me. No, myself I am small, and I am thin, but I am very full of hot blood. Once I was an actress, till the greatest man on earth bid me cease acting. So now I take my pleasure as you take yours, my Joe, in making history for others to write about."

Major Colt pulled vexedly at his square black whisker. "I am afraid, miss, that you and I are of too different temperaments to have much in common. I am afraid you will never appreciate Miss Collier as I do." He took out the joints of his long pipe and screwed them together, and fitted on the bowl. "But we're getting away from the matter in hand. With permission I'm going away to find a bunk now to have a smoke and a sleep, and see if that won't show me a way out of the bad mess we're in. I just want to ask one favour, miss."

"Well?"

"Keep yourself snug behind a barred door till I come again."

"If it will make you rest more soundly, *mon brave*, I promise. And here is something to direct your night thoughts. You told me once that Mademoiselle Collier (after teaching you Euclid) had sent you to Europe to 'get on.' "

Major Colt sheathed his knife, and repocketed the plug from which he had been shredding tobacco. "Yes," he admitted, "that is so."

"Then be ambitious here. You are not safe as purser. Meadey would hang a pirate's purser without a qualm if he caught him, and he could do no more to a pirate captain. Be ambitious, dear Joe. Send de Soto after Ali, and be captain yourself, and then you can best give directions about how to save our necks."

"I don't know," said Colt, fumbling for his flint and steel. "I want to be quit of this ship, not captain of her. Besides, I hated Ali, and de Soto isn't such a bad sort of cut-throat. I noticed he was civil to yourself."

The *vivandière* shrugged. "Oh, if Monsieur the Major must deal tenderly with all my admirers, it will be hard to give so much as a rough word to any of this crew. Captain de Soto certainly did kiss me with much tenderness when we parted."

Major Joseph Colt blew on his smouldering tinder with such violence that it flamed extravagantly. "I've no right to interfere with your tastes in kissing, I know, miss, but I'll see to it that de Soto at any rate ceases from troubling in that direction. I bid you good-night," he snapped, and gave an angular bow, and stalked away, puffing volumes.

Overhead the drunken crew danced madly and filled the warm night with their shoutings. And punctuating the whole were occasional pistol shots, and now and then a scream.

The 'tween decks of the lurching felucca were full of noise and smells, and they had small allowance of head-room. Colt had to bend almost double as he walked, and Clarice leaned out of her cabin doorway and watched his tall stooping figure with a tender eye. "If it were not for thoughts of that ridiculous stiff schoolmistress in Boston (wherever that may be), I'd like to tell my hero that I shall die of sheer terror if I have to stay in this awful ship much longer. But whilst he continues to speak of her, never shall he learn it. Dear Mary! What a thickness is this bar he has fitted to my door. How he cares for me! Well, never girl needed care more."

Once more through the gloom of that night the drunken crew sighted a sail, fired into her, and again caught a tartar. Major Joseph Colt awoke to the bellow of guns. He was refreshed with a four hours' sleep, and after satisfying himself that Clarice was safe, he went cautiously out on deck.

The stranger was a big barque of nationality undistinguishable; but she was heavily armed and heavily manned; moreover, her guns were admirably served. The pirates fought with a savage ferocity, and some considerable skill with weapons. But discipline was not theirs. Twice they stopped their fire to clear the decks, and many wounded went over into that black night sea with the dead, so that full space might be left to fight the guns. But the barque held steadily to her distance and poured in a merciless fire; and then of a sudden the wind dropped.

There was nothing for it now but to fight the felucca till she sank, and this her crew with shouts prepared to do. It was probable the barque would take no notice of an offer to surrender; and even if they were granted quarter for the moment, it would be merely to spare them for an inevitable hanging in the near future. Sailormen of honest extraction had a short way with pirates in the crude year 1810.

As purser, Major Joseph Colt had no fighting station; but it was not in the nature of the man, when battle was lit, to keep aloof from the entertainment. The blood in his veins ran scalding hot, and it was the itch for a fight that had driven him to Europe, quite as much as the "get on" advice of Miss Patience Collier. So after his first eruption on deck, he employed himself for a while in carrying wounded men down the hatchways. But presently, when a powder-monkey dropped, he found himself handing ammunition; and next he thrust himself in to lay and aim one of the broadside guns, vice a Moorish gun captain, who was hopelessly incompetent.

Splinters flew, and round shot hummed around him, but Colt's iron coolness was unsuffled, and his gun was the best fought in the ship.

Then came the dropping of the wind, and the pirate's desperate resolve to die fighting; and it was there that Major Colt's genius for success was forced to show itself. He left his gun, jumped up on the break of the poop, and by sheer weight of lung, even in the midst of that furiously-contested action, got himself attention.

"Who wants to die?" he shouted above the din of firing. He had a heavy flint lock pistol in either hand, held muzzle up, ready to drop into instant use, and there was a look in his grim, dark eyes that got the attention of the men who were even then prepared to glare unawed into the face of death.

"You may be ready to quit the earth, you scum, and I daresay it is the best thing that could happen to most of you. But I'm not. I've got a lot of work mapped out for me on ahead, and I can't afford to die and leave it. My Land! no. So I'll just have to save your blackguard necks along with my own, whether I like it or not. Now attend to me, you gun-captains. You all see that big white splinter mark on the barque's water-line there, just abaft of midships? I want all of you to lay your guns on to that, and lay them true. You're to fire when I give the word, and not before or after. Any gun captain who misses his aim I'll pistol with my own hand, and promote the number two of that gun to be captain. So turn-to again, you no-nation swine, and fight for your dirty necks."

The guns were loaded, run out, laid; Colt bawled an order to fire, and the felucca reeled to the shock of the discharge. The barque also reeled, and white splinters sprang in bristles from an ugly wound in her side.

The pirates sponged their guns, reloaded, clapped on to the breech-tackles, and ran them out. But the barque's crew fired no more, applying themselves instead with a sudden industry to pumps and bucket-chains, and Major Colt saw that it was wisdom to accept the involuntary armistice.

"Hold your fire," he ordered, and when one gun barked in spite of his prohibition, he dropped a pistol on to the man who pulled the lanyard, and shot him through the head. "That's my cure for a hound who didn't know that discipline had arrived on board here. There are more pills from the same box if any others of you want doctoring. I guess we'll quit this neighbourhood before that big fellow has cured his stomach ache, and can attend to us again."

De Soto came across the poop. "I thank you for your help," he said. "That lesson was needed."

"Say 'sir' when you address me."

De Soto's hand slid to his belt, and he promptly found himself looking down the barrel of Major Colt's pistol.

"I shall be very pleased to serve under you, sir."

"I thought you would be. Now see to it that you don't play any monkey tricks, or you'll get it quick and sudden where the chicken got the axe." Major Colt raised his voice again. "Men and officers! There's been a new election of captain on this packet, and the officer who's promoted gets the job because he's the best man on board. Anybody dispute that?"

No one did. Indeed, the American's demeanour so jumped with their fancy, that they gave him what they intended for a cheer, each pirate of them shouting in his native mother tongue.

"Mark, I don't want to be captain of your old iniquity shop. But you made me so frightened I just had to elect myself. I've worn this scalp so long that I've grown to like it, and I tell you I've never before felt it so loose as it's been since I've travelled in your undesirable society. I just hate this pirating idea; but if it's got to be, I'm going to have it run on sound, safe, commercial lines. Fall to at those sweeps, you. Mr de Soto, stave every liquor cask there is on board, and then see the decks swabbed up and holy-stoned. For the future I wish this ship kept as clean as one of those blistered British men-o-war, and for that I hold you responsible."

Now a gap occurs here in the records that have been placed at my disposal; but to a certain extent this can be bridged from hints let drop here and there in the context. It is pretty plain that for the moment neither of the Escape Agents saw a way to get back to the work which Bonaparte had given them on Cabrera; and so the best was made of the alternative. The felucca was sailed towards the Eastern Mediterranean, because, as Major Colt stated, all Greeks and Turks were pirates themselves anyway, and so it was no robbery to play the pirate amongst them. And amongst the islands of Greece she plied with industry her nefarious trade. At the end of that time she sailed back west for the Balearics, carefully dodging the English cruisers, which were just then strung out across the Mediterranean for the especial benefit of the French.

It is rather laughable to think of the means taken to induce this crew of hopeless rapscallions to lend their services to the cause of the Emperor Bonaparte, for which no single man of them cared one jot; and the key to the whole mystery may be given in the one word discipline. Scattered over the face of the seas in the year 1810 were many thousands of men who earned a precarious livelihood by following the industry of pirating, and without exception these had all tried honest seafaring first, and thrown it over because the smallness of the profits and the heaviness of the discipline irked them. They thirsted for gold easily won, for women slaves, for wild drinking bouts; and all their brains and thews were tuned to reach these ideals. Beyond these they asked for nothing. A short life, and a wet and merry one, was their motto. Discipline they scoffed at, and openly told their captains that Jack was as good as his master. As for holystoning decks, or keeping their vessels dandified, they would as soon have thought of carrying a chaplain.

Enter then upon such a society, Joseph Colt, United States subject, with ideas of his own upon tidiness and discipline, and a strong enough personality to see to it that his theories were carried into practice. "You're a sickening lot of swine to start upon," he informed his crew with grim emphasis; "but my Land! I'll make you into the most efficient pirates in the Eastern Mediterranean before I'm through with you. You shall never throw it in my teeth that you were hanged as nobodies."

Accordingly he practised them with cutlass and small arms, drilled them at the great guns, exercised them at sail drill, landing drill, boarding, skirmishing, scouting, in fact made them perfect in all the manoeuvres which could possibly occur to the mind of a major of French infantry, with an Indian training, suddenly promoted to a sea captaincy. Between whiles he made them holystone, paint, scrub, and polish; and he beat loiterers over the head with a brass pistol butt. He seldom went below, still more seldom slept. He sat for the most part on the after skylight, smoking at a long, many-jointed pipe, and looking grim, and black, and savage. The crew feared him more than anything in earth or sea, and hated him and their sad hard lot with a hate that was almost pathetic.

"How long?" was the question Clarice put to him every day, and his reply was always: "As short a time as I can make it."

Once when they had taken a prize, and she was more than usually anxious to be gone from the horrors of her present situation, "My Land! miss," he snapped out, "do you think I forget what I came to Europe for? I'm tickled to think there's a marshal's *baton* somewhere in store for me, and if I don't soon get to work trying for it again, I guess Emperor Bonaparte will forget I'm in the contest."

In the meanwhile they appear to have been taking ships, easing them of money, food, valuables, and ammunition, treating their crews and passengers with a fine courtesy, and then letting them go little harmed. Colt would permit no liquor to be looted, neither would he allow his crew to go ashore at any port to spend their money in a regulation piratical debauch. And the pirates, worn thin with hard work, clicked their dry tongues, patted the useless gold in their pockets, and swore that if this were piracy, then a moral life was the life for them.

To his crew, then, in this chastened mood, Major Joseph Colt at last made a proposal.

They all had money saved now. How would it suit them to settle down ashore, each man as a respectable householder?

Some of them looked glum; the rest grinned; they thought they were to be treated to a specimen of Major Colt's grisly humour.

"Beg pardon, Captain," said Trotter, "is this the South Seas you've got in view?"

"France."

Mr Trotter passed two fingers tenderly round his neck, to hint that the very idea made him feel the twitch of the rope.

"I can dump you down in France, and guarantee that the old record against each of you shall be wiped clean. On terms. I know quite well you'll be up to your old iniquities again twenty hours after you've landed, but that's no concern of mine. As I say, I can set you ashore free men, on terms. Question is, do you want to hear how?"

There was no doubt that they did. In spite of the new discipline, they fairly yelled for information; and when they were told that a free pardon could be earned by anything so ridiculously easy as lifting a cargo of Cabrera prisoners from under the noses of Captain Meadey and H.B.M.S. *Frolic*, their enthusiasm knew no bounds. Heavens! how sick they were of being hard-driven, thirsty outlaws.

Major Colt was quick to catch their mood before the rebound.

They were lying at somebody else's anchor and cable in a bay at the back of Zante, waiting for the passing trader. They did not trouble to weigh. They manned halliards, and the great lateens were mastheaded. The stolen cable was slipped and went to join its anchor on the sea floor; and as the huge triangular sails filled and drew, that rascally crew danced and sang from sheer light-hearted joy. Honesty fairly oozed from them. Just outside they came upon a current boat, romping home light, her cargo sold, and its price in good red gold (so they told themselves) in her cabin locker. They ran down close and wished the scared Greeks good voyage and profitable commerce. For themselves, they said they had gone out of business.

Now in their present reckless mood, the pirates (so sick were they of sober piracy) would have attacked Captain Meadey's *Frolic* herself had they been so ordered. And, indeed, Colt had no little trouble to hold them in hand till a moonless night would give him the weather he needed. But till that date occurred he was resolute in keeping Cabrera out of sight, even from his mast-trucks ; and so to fill in time ran to Alcudia Bay in Majorca for wood and water.

It was here, during one of his brief snatches of sleep, that Clarice deserted, leaving in her place a letter. His brown cheek grew sallow as he read it :

Dear Joe,

The trouble is, how are we to let those so ragged prisoners on Cabrera know that they must stand in readiness the instant we come for them? You could do it, or I could. But you cannot leave your detestable ship, or, to be exact, I dare not be left on her without you. Oh, *mon cher*, I am an amazing coward. So I will make my way to the island. Remember I can swim there if the need arrives; and when the dark nights come, and you see three camp fires in a triangle, with the point towards the beach, that is where the passengers will be awaiting. So come there also for

Your comrade,
Clarice.

Postscriptum. Could your Miss P.C., of 2907, Pilgrim Avenue, Boston, swim back to an island where those detestable Spaniards had threatened to kill her already?

Now the crew of the felucca – had little love for Major Joseph Colt, as has already been plainly stated; indeed, he imagined them to be mere callous brutes, who could carry no affection for anyone except themselves; and so it came to him as somewhat of a shock to learn that they had in a way set up the *vivandière* as their goddess. It seemed she had told Trotter, who was in the boat's crew that had set her ashore, something of the nature of her errand, and Trotter spread the news. The crew were on fire. Sooner than Meadey or the Spaniards, yes, or the beastly French prisoners should so much as hurt the little finger of Mademoiselle Clarice, they were ready to cut the throats of every living soul in the Mediterranean.

In fact their mood jumped with his most intimate desires; but still there was need for patience till the time came. However willing the felucca's desperate crew might be, Colt knew quite well they were no match for the hateful *Frolic*.

But time and the moon move on at their own pace. The date arrived as set forth in the calendar. The felucca moved out of harbour. Night came away moonless, starless, and blessedly thick with a drizzle of rain. Major Colt ran his vessel down the Majorcan coast, and into the strait between it and Cabrera. Three tiny crumbs of light threw him the longed-for signal.

He ran in towards the Cabreran rocks, and cast off two fisher boats he had in tow. They rowed off softly into the wet darkness and faded out of sight. He dared show no light, not even the glow of a pipe, to guide them back, and he stared after them into the gloom, and was torn with the most heavy anxiety; but in an hour's time they returned to him, full of shaggy, half-naked men, who had once been conquering French soldiers.

There was no Clarice with them.

Again they went off, and again returned. It was not till the third lot of boat loads came off that she rejoined.

The felucca had been lying with stripped masts in the trough, so as not to court inspection; but now word was passed, and the great lateens soared aloft with eager speed. The boats were cast adrift. The felucca sprang out on her race for France and the Eagles.

The *vivandière* came up to Major Colt on the poop.

"Come aboard, Captain," said she, saluting.

"I saw you. I couldn't come down to the gangway to meet you. I am a little upset." He gripped her hand and looked down at her with something in his black eye that made her thrill.

But she took his mood lightly as usual. "Dear Mary! Major Colt, but I thought you were going to kiss me!"

He sighed heavily. "I fear it would not be right to go so far as that. You see, my comrade, I am an engaged man."

Trotter came up to them grinning, and saluting: "This crew wishes to say, miss, how very happy they are to see you safe and sound amongst them once more. Captain, you'll make a good story out of this for that young lady in Boston. I'll send the crew's account of it myself if you like." He saluted again and went forward.

"You've no idea, miss," said Colt gloomily, "how little things do get distorted as they drift across the Western Ocean, even when you feel sure they're just a private matter of your own. We are taking back to the Emperor one hundred and three of his soldiers, and of our forty-seven scoundrels on the felucca, when they have had their spree, I daresay as many as forty will be glad enough to enlist. It would look very pleasant printed in a history book, with one's name tacked on; but I guess, miss, we'll have to suppress it."

THE COMMANDER'S WIFE

Harriet Hudson

*Up until now I have said little about Napoleon's private life.
His love affair with Josephine de Beauharnais is well known,
though she was six years older than Bonaparte and already
thirty-two by the time they married in 1796. Their marriage
was childless and Napoleon's desire for an heir led, reluctantly, to a divorce in 1809. Four months later Napoleon
married Marie Louise, the daughter of Francis, emperor of
Austria, and the grand-niece of Marie Antoinette. His son
and heir, also called Napoleon, was born in March 1811.*

*Harriet Hudson is the pen name of Amy Myers. Under her
own name she is best known for her books about Victorian/
Edwardian master-chef and sleuth August Didier, which
began with* Murder in Pug's Parlour *(1987). As Harriet
Hudson she is best known for a number of novels set in the late
nineteenth and early twentieth centuries, such as* The Woo-
ing of Katie May *and* The Sun in Glory. *Under the alias
Alice Carr she has written a series of novels, starting with*
The Last Summer *(1996), which explores the change in
society during the First World War.*

"So, Madame Baste, I trust this will suit your convenience?"

Philip Carteret's voice was cold as befitted the captain of one of His Majesty's thirty-eight-gun frigates in speaking to an enemy hostage. Such a prisoner could not normally expect such regard from the captain himself, but this was the wife of the commander of the French fleet, Rear-Admiral Baste, and there were no quarters aboard the *Naiad* for women, nor aboard any of His Majesty's Ships of the line in this year of 1811. The days when sailors brought their wives or other women to enliven their days in harbour were past, and navy rules strictly forbade their presence under sail.

The woman cast a quick glance at the Spartan day-cabin, showing little appreciation of his having vacated his own quarters on the upper deck for her benefit and safety. His possessions were few-deliberately so-but he resented this speedy dismissal of their worth. A perfunctory *"Merci, Capitaine Carteret"* was all the thanks he received for his consideration.

She spoke with a thick accent, obviously some province of France far from Paris. Her eyes were cast down, and the hood of her cloak hid most of her face from view. She was far from tall, and though he guessed she was only in her early or middle twenties, the enveloping black cloth suggested a dumpy figure beneath. Yet he watched as she turned away from him to gaze through the stern windows at the receding English coastline. For some reason he was unwilling to leave. He felt impelled to impress upon her the lengths to which he was going for her comfort. Even now, he could change his mind, and she would remain a prisoner in Deal Castle. It had been he who had received her on the *Naiad* with the grand words: "Madame, we shall return you to your husband's arms at Boulogne. His Majesty's Navy does not wage war with women as weapons."

She understood English, he had been informed, and so she could not claim non-comprehension. It irritated him that she did not acknowledge her good fortune at her release.

In these days one must take care. The Eagle Emperor Napoleon was flexing his wings again, and might yet fly against England. The invasion scare of seven years earlier had once more reared its head, at least for those with eyes to see. Kentish mothers had never ceased to scare their misbehaving children with "Boney will get you", and now, unknown to them, they might have good reason again. The French fleet had been gradually building up strength, the Boulogne harbour fortifications were formidable, and there were indications that Napoleon was still intent on fulfilling his long-held dream: conquest of England. The alternative was Russia, and while the Emperor deliberated whether to turn west or east, England must hold her breath – and her navy ready.

Sixteen days earlier, on 3 September, there had been ominous signs at Boulogne where the main body of the French flotilla was moored along the coast of the bay. Two ten-gun brig-sloops had awaited their chance of intercepting any French vessels foolish enough to leave the safety of numbers. They were not disappointed, and although outmatched in gunpowder and numbers when they attacked the rear of the flotilla, acquitted themselves most gallantly. Two days later, deserters from the French admiral's ship had brought them in addition to useful information a rare prize as a hostage to prove their good will.

Madame Baste had been held in Deal Castle and was willing enough to co-operate, until the powers-that-be found her information to be of little use, and belatedly decided in favour of chivalry. Philip Carteret was requested – not ordered – to take her back to the shores of her native land and bide his opportunity to fly the white flag of truce to return her safely.

Very well, he had determined that Admiral Baste's wife must be treated as he would have wished his own had she been so captured. Jennifer, his beloved Jenny, had died in childbed two years earlier and the pain still stabbed.

Still he stood there hesitating, he knew not why. At last the woman rose to remove her cloak, and he saw with surprise that, despite a dowdy, brown morning gown, she was attractive, with fair hair that fell in unruly curls in the current fashion, and blue eyes. Moreover, he had been wrong. Her figure was perfect. But she had no beauty. Beauty requires animation and she had none. Where Jenny's eyes had danced and sparkled, this woman's were melancholy and her face a blank slate.

"You stare, *monsieur le capitaine*." There was hauteur in her voice.

"My apologies, madame." He bowed. "I trust you will dine with me here this evening?"

She did not answer and he was affronted at her fear. Did the woman think he *wanted* to dine with her?

"Madame, let me make myself clear. I fear you *must* dine with me or you do not dine at all – unless your taste is for the hands' mess or the officers' wardroom. Neither is seemly company for an admiral's wife." He wondered whether she was harbouring fears on any other score, but was diffident about putting this into words. At length he said: "As to these quarters thereafter, they are yours alone. The sleeping cabin lacks a goose-feather bed, but I trust you will find the swinging cot comfortable. Moreover," he added coldly, "there will be two sentries, not the usual one, on guard outside. You will rest undisturbed."

She coloured. "I thank you, Captain."

Philip would far rather have dined in the wardroom, and he returned to his quarters at eight bells at the end of the second dog-watch in evil mood. By this time the *Naiad* was at anchor off the Boulogne road – and tomorrow his primary mission must begin. The secondary mission, to return intelligence of the French intention, might be aided by the former, but he was well aware that even a flag of truce might not be sufficient to ensure his ship's safety.

Madame, he saw, had changed her gown, and seeing his glance she explained in halting English that it was provided by the wife of the Warden of the Cinque Ports. So that was why it hung so loosely over that intriguingly fine figure. If the lemon silk tunic dress had clung closer, she could grace any court, a fitting spouse for an admiral. She was more than attractive, Philip now realised, as he admired the regular features, the peachlike skin, and the swell of her breast under the low-necklined bodice. Her apathy remained, however. Or perhaps it was remoteness, as though so eager to return to her husband, she had no spark of gratitude for her deliverance. How different to his Jenny, with her lively face and interest in all and everything.

"Where does madame live in France?" His question was merely to break the silence that fell as they tackled the hot-top dried-pea soup in the dining cabin. He raised his eyebrows when she did not reply. "Come, madame," he said scathingly, "this is not information that Fouché would disapprove of your giving me."

"You know Fouché?" The woman was frowning.

"Napoleon's spymaster is known to us by repute. He is a brilliant man at his job, even if one despises the job."

She ignored this. "I live in Boulogne," she answered shortly.

"Then you can see little of your husband." He was surprised. He would have expected their home to be at Cherbourg.

"I have a child," she said after a moment. "My son needs my company." Another surprise. Why had she not made much of this son at Deal to plead for her release?

"Your Emperor also now has a son, madame. Napoleon is a new man, so they say, with his baby son and new wife."

She stared at him coldly. "He is the Emperor. He must have an heir."

An heir? This was going too far. "Napoleon and his empire with him will take a tumble if he invades England."

She shrugged, returning to her soup. "Everyone believes he will turn to Russia, not England. It is logical, so my husband says, for Poland looks to Napoleon for its salvation."

"Poland? There is no Poland. It belongs to Russia and to France. Poland is divided into pieces and consumed at Napoleon's pleasure." He tossed back the last of his sack, his tongue not so guarded now as it had been.

"There is still a free Poland."

"Free?" He laughed. "You are blind in France, madame. The King of Saxony rules the so-called independent Grand Duchy of Warsaw, and he is Napoleon's pawn."

"No!"

"Yes. Moreover if Napoleon intends to march on Russia, why does he increase the number of ships of the line in Boulogne harbour? What does Admiral Baste say about that, when he talks with his wife?"

"Captain," she interrupted, a flush sparking up on her cheek, "am I to be interrogated yet again? Do you suppose that because I am wife to the fleet commander that makes me privy to the highest secrets of state? Must I answer? Is this ship another prison?"

It was the first sign of animation he had seen in her, and he sat still, astounded. He had been wrong. This woman was more than attractive, she had come alive. Her face was transformed, as she gazed at him with indignant eyes, as blue as the cornflowers in the English meadows, and fringed with dark, curling eyelashes, eyes that mesmerised as they sparkled. He had to struggle not to beg her pardon, to remember he was Captain Philip Carteret of His Majesty's frigate *Naiad* and in charge merely of a hostage to be returned to the enemy.

"If I so choose, madame, yes." His voice was controlled again now, despite the turmoil within him.

The blue eyes had ice in them now. "I do not dine with inquisitors." She pushed her plate away, rising to her feet.

"A pity. This beef is excellent." He continued eating calmly, to let her wrestle with the fact that there was nowhere for her to go, save the sleeping cabin or the galley. If she retreated to either she would appear ridiculous, and that, he banked on, she would never choose. He could feel the tension between them, as taut as an anchor rope in a storm. He would remain to finish his meal. What would she do?

She laughed, again taking him by surprise. "Very well, Captain. I should not like to play you at chess. It seems I must return to my 'rosbif' of old England."

"Your health, madame." Philip raised his glass: the ship was rolling at anchor now, and the claret slid from side to side in a battle of its own with the goblet. He looked straight at her and wondered that he could ever have thought that face plain. Gazing at him in amusement was the most beautiful woman he had ever seen, and that beauty was warm and alive, not cold and calculating, like Emma Hamilton's. Her face, her eyes, bore such a sweet and innocent expression that he must have surely been blind to think her dowdy when first he saw her. And gentle, too. The thought came to him that this woman responded to love, that she bestowed and she received, and in her path of life she chose when and with whom she walked in her loveliness. But that implied . . . hastily, he pulled himself back from such mad imaginings, and raised his glass again.

"To your husband, madame," he said slowly. "The admiral is a most fortunate man. No wonder you were aboard his prame when the deserters took you. He would not choose to have you far from him." And would pay much to get you back, was his unbidden thought.

The smile disappeared and her eyes dropped once more.

"Thank you, Captain," she managed to say, but he saw with alarm that there were tears on her face.

"You will be with him tomorrow," he vowed. She said nothing in reply and he realised in one great surge of inexplicable pleasure that he had mistaken the situation. "Are you not happy with him?" he asked fiercely. It was important for him to know. "Is that why you are apart so much?"

She raised a look of such agony that the question was answered for him. "He no longer loves me, captain. He loves another, though he still cares for me as a friend."

"Then why return?" Was this Philip Carteret, a captain known for his steady reliability, so out of control, so suddenly concerned? "You would not be ill-treated in England."

"My son is in France," she replied. "That is why I must return. And moreover, my husband still needs me."

"But does not deserve you." On an impulse he lifted his goblet once more. "Then let us drink the end of war between us two –" he paused deliberately, then added – "nations."

He thought she would refuse, but she lifted hers too. "To my country," she said gently.

She had rejected him.

"You are hard, madame," he replied sadly. "Do you not believe there should be peace between nations as there is love between two people?"

"Sometimes one must choose."

"And you choose – France."

The wine seemed to be mocking him. This woman was mocking him. Ships were a kingdom unto themselves. Back lay England, forward France, but here they remained between the two. He had thought he was in command, but he was wrong.

She ruled this kingdom, not he. He searched for some way to penetrate her armour, and returned to the route that had worked earlier.

"Methinks you do not approve of your new Empress. Perhaps you believe Revolutionary France should not be ruled by a niece of Marie-Antoinette? Yet Marie-Louise has given Napoleon a child. She has achieved more than Josephine could. It is as well for England that he did not marry the Grand Duchess Anne, the Tsar's sister. Such an alliance would have banished the last hopes of freedom for many lands, Poland in particular. The Habsburg Marie-Louise was a wiser choice. Napoleon has everything now, save love, so they say. He should not have cast off his first Empress or his mistress so lightly. Your husband should have a care if he thinks to follow his example."

She was silent.

"Come," he continued, "do not be offended. I make idle chatter only, and only repeat what is said by all the world."

What was happening to him? Why should he care if he'd offended her? Surely he was too mature to be besotted by a pretty face? He raised his glass again so abruptly the wine slopped, angry with himself and with her for making him so.

"I must make the loyal toast, madame, I bid you drink. Madame, the King." Philip remained seated in the time-honoured naval tradition, but she had risen, obviously angry.

"The King," she repeated.

"Thank you, madame," he said quietly.

"One moment, Captain, before I resume my seat. I too have a loyal toast and for this you *will* stand." Surprised, he obeyed.

"The Emperor Napoleon." She lifted her goblet.

Philip glared at her angrily, muscles twitching in his cheeks with fury. He held his glass high. "The Emperor Napoleon *the Second*. May he never follow in his father's butchering footsteps."

He spluttered as the contents of the glass were dashed in his face. "By God, madame . . ."

He broke off, appalled. His adversary was no longer in command, no longer defiant. She was weeping, her head in her hands. In her eagerness to vanquish her he had gone too far.

He took one of her hands to his lips, and when there no reaction took her into his arms. "Forgive me, pray forgive me," he murmured against the golden hair.

She gently removed herself from his embrace. "I should ask your forgiveness, Captain," she said sadly. "You have given me hospitality, which I have repaid by challenging your authority. My husband would be the first to condemn such behaviour."

"Even through your tears, your beauty shines out."

She dismissed this impatiently. "The looks God gave me. I claim no credit."

"No. He gave you eyes as blue as the sea on a fine summer's day, hair spun from gold, and skin as soft as rose petals, but they do not add up to beauty. Your beauty comes from your gentle nature, from your compassion, your loyalty – and your courage."

Why had he added that last word? Why had the wife of Admiral Baste been so easily captured? Why had she been aboard his prame? Why did she know the name of Fouché? Why so strong in situations that would give most women the vapours? Slowly his brain began to disentangle the answer.

A pause. "You are kind, sir. I do not deserve that."

Even as he longed to take her in his arms again, to woo her to himself, the puzzle became complete, and the knowledge horrified him.

"Madame," he asked abruptly, "what did you think of our England while you were in Deal? Did you admire our new fortifications and our Martello Towers in defence of our coastline, and observe the numbers of our troops in their red jackets?"

She gasped, but met his eye bravely, as she replied in a low voice, "I did. I also heard tell of the great new canal zigzagging back over the marshes for defence; I heard also –" she glanced at him – "that so little is invasion now feared by the people, that the canal is open to the public, not just the military."

"Those who govern Britain know that Napoleon is unpredictable, and that every move he makes – even, perhaps, the conquest of Russia – is with the ultimate aim of invading our islands. The people at large may believe he has forgotten his dream, but that will change when I return, if I have further news of the Emperor's fleet a-building. The dragon stirs in his lair, but St George will outwit him yet."

What now? Here in this self-contained world, he stood with an avowed spy. Philip fought the conflicts within him. His duty was to return her to Britain. If he did so, however, he must surrender her and he shuddered to think of her fate. If he did not, he too would be a traitor. He could not do it.

"This was some plan of your husband's, was it not?" he asked eagerly, seizing her hands in his. "He sent you with so-called deserters, knowing we would not hold a woman hostage in England, but that before you returned you would have gathered much information on our defences."

"It was my suggestion, not his," she retorted quickly, pulling away from him. "And Fouché agreed at once. So, Captain, I am a spy. Will you hang me from the yardarm? It is your right."

"You know that I will not."

"You should."

"When you return to France," he said desperately, "you must tell your husband and Fouché how strong the English defences are, and what vast numbers of troops are held ready to fight invasion. Then Napoleon will abandon his plans for England for good and turn towards Russia."

"No. I will say that England believes the threat is past."

"If it were my wife, in your situation, I would want her to say anything, true or false, that might save her life."

"You are married?"

"A widower now, and were our countries not at war –"

"My son, Captain," she reminded him gently.

"After the war?"

She sighed. "Perhaps. Who knows? Don't look so sad, my Philip."

She pronounced his name in the French manner, and he thought he would die for love of her.

"Were this two nights hence, a Saturday, there would be another toast in the wardroom, madame. 'Sweethearts and wives.' Will you drink it with me now?"

"Ah yes, I will drink to that," she replied sadly.

"Then let me address you as a lover would."

She hesitated. "Very well. My name is Marie."

"Sweethearts, Marie." He raised his glass to her.

"And wives, my Philip."

Their goblets clinked, but Philip's hand shook. "How can I bear it?" he whispered. "A lifetime apart."

"But still a night together," she said softly.

At noon on the following day, 20 September, the *Naiad* was still at anchor off the Boulogne road; officers and hands observed with astonishment the activity in Boulogne harbour. There was a general bustle about the scene not fully explained by the proximity of a British frigate, and Philip watched for some time to choose his moment carefully before he flew the flag of truce for parley. Then she would leave him. He knew that, and was resigned to it. But he had a responsibility to his ship and to his crew not to provide obvious prey for the Frenchmen.

A strong south-south-westerly was brewing up, and he must make a move soon. At his side on the quarter-deck, shrouded once more in her black cloak, stood Madame Baste. The more he thought of her thus, the less he would remember his Marie of those precious few hours. Never had his sleeping cabin with all its discomforts offered such perfume, such tenderness, such dreams.

"Signal midshipman!" he barked, "make –" He broke off, unable to believe what the view through the telescope was telling him. This was no moment for relinquishing prisoners. At the maintopgallant masthead of the central prame waved –

"The imperial flame," Philip said softly to himself, then shouted aloud in triumph: "By God, we have a prize today. Old Boney himself is aboard." Who could have expected this? This was intelligence to bear home in triumph – and soberness. For if Napoleon was here to inspect his fleet, it could mean only one thing. The invasion would soon be a reality.

"The Emperor?" Marie cried out in agitation. "I must return. My husband needs me."

He did not hear her; he was too busy watching the upheaval in the harbour, ready to cast anchor at the slightest sign that the activity was threatening the *Naiad*. There was no gunfire; instead the imperial flame was lowered, as Napoleon left to inspect other vessels, and the flag of Rear-Admiral Baste was hoisted.

"Your husband's flag flies once more at the mizzen, madame," he exclaimed, "but I see he is replaced by another as commander of the fleet today."

"May I go to him now?"

"No, madame, you may not."

She raised startled eyes to his and he turned away to avoid the accusation he saw in them.

"Napoleon is here for some purpose, perhaps to launch the invasion. A mere inspection at such a time? Never."

Even now, there were indications that the prames under Rear-Admiral Baste were about to head towards the *Naiad*. To weigh with this wind and flood-tide would distance the frigate still further from the prames, and let Napoleon assume the British Navy was turning tail. No, he would remain at anchor here, with springs on his cable, and let the commander come to him. Even the Emperor himself, if he wished. *Why* was he here? To launch an invasion? There was no sign of troop preparations. To inspect the fleet? Possible, by mere coincidence. Or had he heard from Fouché of Marie's mission? Had he learned from his spies in England of her return and come to hear at first hand what information she brought? Or was this visit to find out for himself whether His Majesty's Navy still believed in attack, not defence. If so, the *Naiad* – and its captain – would be ready to prove it.

He turned to Marie again. "Madame," he said evenly. "I regret you must wait a while longer. Pray retire to your quarters. There is something here I do not understand, and I may yet have need of a hostage."

She did not move, nor even seem to hear him, her eyes were fixed on the now billowing sails of the French prames steering north towards the *Naiad*. "I will stay here," she answered him at last.

"You must take shelter. Your husband is under way with six other armed prames. He flies no flag of truce."

"If I am seen, there will be no risk to your frigate."

Philip hardened himself, as she pitted her will against his.

Napoleon's presence had changed everything. "You can see the Emperor's barge rowing him from ship to ship. Until I know what his intentions are, you, madame, must retire. That is my *order*." Then gently he added, "Marie, there may be issues at stake that make the fate of you, of me, and even of the *Naiad* and her crew, immaterial compared with that of my country."

She bowed her head, and to his relief she withdrew without further question. Philip forced himself to put her and the pain that still stabbed at his heart aside so that he could concentrate on the enemy. The prames were drawing closer. No matter; their twelve guns posed little threat to a thirty-eight-gun frigate, and it was the admiral's next move that would indicate Napoleon's plans. He crisply snapped out his commands, from the quarterdeck. The decks were cleared for action, the guns run out.

"Mr Peyton, larboard side to fire at my command."

The prames, in line, were almost within gunshot range now, and the first round of fire from the admiral's ship cracked the air.

"Fire!"

As the *Naiad* replied to the French challenge, the foremost prame tacked, and as each prame in turn took its place to fire, each time the *Naiad* responded, although the distance between them was too great for serious engagement. It therefore followed that the admiral's plan was merely to force the *Naiad* away. No prying telescopes should be trained upon Boulogne. It also followed, Philip reasoned, that Admiral Baste could not know of his wife's presence aboard. Or was it that he waited for the *Naiad* to fly the flag of truce first, and this show of force was to hurry her into doing so?

"Brigs, sir,". yelled the look-out. So, the Admiral was to be reinforced. In all, ten four-gun brigs arrived, and a bomb-sloop.

"Weigh, Mr Peyton!"

If he could get to windward of the enemy, he could chase the admiral back to his lair, and by heaven, the *Naiad* would not deliver its precious hostage until he knew what game the Emperor played. At 7.30 that night Philip dropped anchor in the same position, well satisfied. He had shown the admiral the

Naiad was built for fighting, and that it would take more than Napoleon's presence to frighten her away.

"The eyes of the fleet" was how Admiral Nelson had described the role of a frigate, and he would not have been disappointed in the *Naiad*.

"Casualties, Mr Peyton?"

"None, sir."

"Damage, then?"

"Only a little to the canvas, sir."

Philip relaxed. The spars were intact. Tomorrow he was convinced the admiral would come again, and this time show his hand more clearly. And tomorrow Marie would be returned to her husband.

But what of tonight? She was silent at dinner that evening, and weary from the tensions of the day, so was he. The nearness of their parting pressed in more closely in the confines of the day cabin, as he found himself torn between his duty and his desire.

He knew which he must choose. There could be no sweet love for the *Naiad*'s captain this evening, for tomorrow must end what had begun today. He was almost sure now that Admiral Baste did *not* wish to drive the *Naiad* away, but was intent on drawing her closer to within range of the shore batteries; he aimed perhaps to both regain Marie and take a fine prize as well. Did that explain why they did not yet ask for parley?

Philip decided he would appear to play their game. However, when the Rear-Admiral's ships left the security of their shore batteries tomorrow – as he would ensure they would – they would find more guns blazing than those of the *Naiad*. He would signal the rest of the British inshore squadron to be ready for him to join them on the far side of the bay. When Marie was back in her husband's unloving arms, it would be at a place and time of *his* choosing, not Rear-Admiral Baste's. If he played his own game aright, the *Naiad* had a unique opportunity to show Napoleon what fighting strength still lay in England. The *Naiad* would go in full sail to attack; and the prize would be hers, not the enemy's. None other than Rear-Admiral Baste's prame itself. The admiral would be reunited with his wife – but aboard the *Naiad*. Both would return to England. What would happen then, he dared not let himself consider.

"Madame, I must bid you goodnight."

"Philip?" There was a question in her eyes, as he rose so abruptly to take his leave, and his resolve all but crumbled.

"Tomorrow, Marie," he said unsteadily. "I will return you to your husband's arms as you wish."

"And tonight, Philip, the captain must sleep alone," she returned sadly. "I understand."

He must go quickly, before his resolve weakened. He kissed her lips and then her eyes, bidding her gently goodnight. "The admiral's wife must sleep here alone, but Marie will rest tonight and forever within my heart."

Little sleep came to him, however, as unanswered questions raced round and round his mind, and one question above all. When dawn came, however, the crispness of the September air, and the smell of the salt in his nostrils, exhilarated him as he weighed and set sail to join the rest of the squadron as soon as he saw movement from the admiral's prames. Formed in line, heads to the west-north-west, colours hoisted, were the ten-gun brigs *Rinaldo* and *Redpole*, the eighteen-gun sloop *Castilian* and an eight-gun cutter, *Viper*. Heading for them in two lines were the French prames, brigs and bomb-sloop, and leading the weather line was the prame flying the admiral's flag.

The admiral would expect a repetition of yesterday, but today the *Naiad* with colours hoisted, would enter the lions' den to tweak the Emperor's nose.

"Helm, larboard hard over!"

The admiral's prame had fired its first broadside.

"Mr Peyton, all guns to bear," Philip roared.

The French were crowding sail, as they suddenly realised they had ventured outside the protection of their shore batteries. *Redpole* and *Rinaldo* were making for the sternmost prame on the lee line, but the *Naiad* had more important prey. Closer, closer – Philip cursed. This admiral had the luck of the devil. Prames were flat-bottomed, drawing little water, and now shoal water would prevent his frigate from reaching his quarry.

"Helm a-larboard. Steady, as she goes."

"Aye-aye, sir."

So be it, the admiral would escape, but Napoleon, who must surely be watching the engagement from the shore batteries, would still have his nose tweaked. He would risk taking the *Naiad* right between the two lines of prames to bear up to the sternmost prame, already crippled with gunfire. He would board and carry her. Shortly afterwards, he was watching the ensuing struggle dispassionately from the quarter-deck. This was war, all his faculties were needed for judgement, not for pity for the many dead, and the brave but futile resistance of the French officers and men. That would come later.

At last the *Naiad* had her prize. She stood away with the *Ville de Lyon* in tow. The admiral may have escaped him, but Philip's mission to shake Napoleon had been fulfilled.

First to count the cost, and then he would rejoice in victory and congratulate himself on putting up a display of English grit before Napoleon that must surely give him second thoughts about any invasion of England's shores.

The loss was greater than yesterday, with sixteen casualties. Two seamen had been killed by shot as had a lieutenant of marines, twelve seamen were wounded and young Midshipman Dover was dead. Only yesterday, Philip grieved, he had been receiving Philip's orders, eager, lively, capable. A likeable lad, too. War was harsh. It gave and it took away; on its chessboard he and Marie were merely pawns. There was one more casualty upon the *Naiad* moreover. Its captain had been wounded – although his wound was not physical.

Still splashed with blood from his visit to the surgeon's bay, he went to fetch Marie from his cabin. "Marie," he said quietly, "it is time to leave."

Enveloped in her black cloak, she followed him onto the quarterdeck.

He handed her his telescope: "There, Marie, is your husband's prame. We will send you by a ship's boat under a flag of truce, back to your husband's arms, as I promised." He hesitated, unwilling even now to seek confirmation of his suspicions. "One thing, Marie, I must know before you go. Your presence aboard must be known, and the Emperor himself thinks your information of such value he has come in person. That information has now been superseded. Napoleon has seen with his own eyes that England does not lack the will to fight."

He paused, then asked the damning question. "Marie, who *is* your husband? For sure, he is not the French fleet admiral, as you claimed, or he would by now have flown a flag of truce for parley. Tell me, you need not fear I shall change my mind now."

She had flushed. "I have dealt as fairly with you as I could, Philip. My home is in Boulogne, but not this seaport. Boulogne is also a village near Paris. And Rear-Admiral Baste is not my husband, nor am I French. You assumed both wrongly. But I *am* the commander's wife, in the eyes of God at least. He is the commander of the Boulogne flotilla, as he is of all the ships of France and most of Europe."

"Marie?" he whispered in disbelief, for even his wildest imaginings had not taken him as far.

"Dearest Philip, that is why I cannot stay. I love Napoleon still, although he has no further use for me, his once adored mistress, for he has a legal wife who has borne him a son. To him I am now only a friend, but I am proud to be so, and while my advice and love can serve him, they shall do so, whether I live in Paris or return to my native Poland. How could I not love Napoleon? I bore his first son. Alexander is over a year old now."

"Poland?"

"That is why I wished the Emperor to invade England, and gladly carried out the mission I proposed to Fouché. I saw this as the only way left to save my country from falling entirely under Russian domination. If," she spoke unwillingly, "Napoleon marches against the Tsar, I fear even his might will be defeated, and Russia will take the pitiful remains of Poland into its greedy arms for ever."

"So you, my love –" he cried in anguish.

She drew the hood of her cloak over the golden hair as she prepared to leave. "Yes, Philip. I was the Emperor's sweetheart. My name is Marie Walewska."

DAVY JONES AND
THE YANKEE PRIVATEER

Michael Scott

The war in the West Indies is easily overlooked because of the general interest and fascination with the war in Europe, but considerable action was seen throughout the period of the Napoleonic Wars in the Caribbean where French, Spanish and English fought to gain or retain possessions. Several islands changed hands. Trinidad, for instance, had been Spanish since Columbus claimed it in 1498, and it remained so until the British captured it in 1797. Its capital is still called Port of Spain. Martinique, Guadaloupe and other islands switched hands between the French and British and French again. The whole Caribbean was a volatile area because of the richness in trade.

Michael Scott (1789–1835) was a Glaswegian merchant who went to seek his fortune in Jamaica, living there for most of the years between 1806 and 1822. He was witness to many incidents and captured these in Tom Cringle's Log, *which was serialized in* Blackwood's

*Magazine between 1829 and 1833 and proved immensely
popular. The following self-contained episode is from the
very start of the book, and brings home starkly the reality
of life in the Caribbean.*

1

The evening was closing in dark and rainy, with every appearance of a gale from the westward, and the weather had become
so thick and boisterous that the lieutenant of the watch had
ordered the look-out at the mast-head down on deck. The man
on his way down had gone into the maintop to bring away some
things he had placed there in going aloft, and was in the act of
leaving it, when he sung out:

"A sail on the weather-bow."

"What does she look like?"

"Can't rightly say, sir; she is in the middle of the thick
weather to windward."

"Stay where you are a little; Jenkins, jump forward, and see
what you can make of her from the foreyard."

Whilst the topman was obeying his instructions, the look-out
again hailed: "She is a ship, sir, close hauled on the same tack;
the weather clears, and I can see her now."

The wind ever since noon had been blowing in heavy squalls
with appalling lulls between them. One of these gusts had been
so violent as to bury in the sea the lee-guns in the waist,
although the brig had nothing set but her close-reefed maintopsail, and reefed foresail. It was now spending its fury, and
she was beginning to roll heavily, when, with a suddenness
almost incredible to one unacquainted with these latitudes, the
veil of mist that had hung to windward the whole day was rent
and drawn aside, and the red and level rays of the setting sun
flashed at once, through a long arch of glowing clouds, on the
black hull and tall spars of His Britannic Majesty's sloop, *Torch*.
And, true enough, we were not the only spectators of this

gloomy splendour; for, right in the wake of the moon-like sun, now half sunk in the sea, at the distance of a mile or more, lay a long warlike-looking craft, apparently a frigate or heavy corvette, rolling heavily and silently in the trough of the sea, with her masts, yards, and the scanty sail she had set, in strong relief against the glorious horizon.

Jenkins now hailed from the foreyard: "The strange sail is bearing up, sir."

As he spoke, a flash was seen, followed, after what seemed a long interval, by the deadened report of the gun, as if it had been an echo, and the sharp, half-ringing half-hissing sound of the shot. It fell short, but close to us, and was evidently thrown from a heavy cannon, from the length of the range.

Mr Splinter, the first lieutenant, jumped from the gun he stood on: "Quartermaster, keep her away a bit," and dived into the cabin to make his report.

Captain Deadeye was a staid, stiff-rumped, wall-eyed, old first-lieutenantish-looking veteran, with his coat of a regular Rodney cut, broad skirts, long waist, and stand-up collar, over which dangled either a queue, or a marlinspike with a tuft of oakum at the end of it – it would have puzzled old Nick to say which. His lower spars were cased in tight unmentionables of what had once been white kerseymere, and long boots, the coal-scuttle tops of which served as scuppers to carry off the drainings from his coat-flaps in bad weather; he was, in fact, the "last of the sea-monsters," but, like all his tribe, as brave as steel, and, when put to it, as alert as a cat.

He no sooner heard Splinter's report, than he sprang up the ladder, brushing the tumbler of swizzle he had just brewed clean out of the fiddle into the lap of Mr Saveall, the purser, who had dined with him, and nearly extinguishing the said purser, by his arm striking the bowl of the pipe he was smoking, thereby forcing the shank half-way down his throat.

"My glass, Wilson," to his steward.

"She is close to, sir; you can see her plainly without it," said Mr Treenail, the second lieutenant, from the weather nettings, where he was reconnoitring.

After a long look through his starboard blinker (his other

skylight had been shut up ever since Aboukir), Deadeye gave orders to "clear away the weather-bow gun"; and as it was now getting too dark for flags to be seen distinctly, he desired that three lanterns might be got ready for hoisting vertically in the main-rigging.

"All ready forward there?"

"All ready, sir."

"Then hoist away the lights, and throw a shot across her forefoot – Fire!" Bang went our carronade, but our friend to windward paid no regard to the private signal; he had shaken a reef out of his topsails, and was coming down fast upon us.

It was clear that old Blowhard had at first taken him for one of our own cruisers, and meant to *signalise* him, "all regular and ship-shape," to use his own expression. Most of us, however, thought it would have been wiser to have made sail, and widened our distance a little, in place of bothering with old-fashioned manœuvres, which might end in our catching a tartar; but the skipper had been all his life in line-of-battle ships, or heavy frigates; and it was a tough job, under any circumstances, to persuade him of the propriety of 'up-stick-and-away,' as we soon felt to our cost.

The enemy, for such he evidently was, now all at once yawed, and indulged us with a sight of his teeth; and there he was, fifteen ports of a side on his maindeck, with the due quantum of carronades on his quarterdeck and forecastle; whilst his short lower masts, white canvas, and the tremendous hoist in his topsails, showed him to be a heavy American frigate; and it was equally certain that he had cleverly hooked us under his lee, within comfortable range of his long twenty-fours. To convince the most unbelieving, three jets of flame, amidst wreaths of white smoke, now glanced from his maindeck; but in this instance, the sound of the cannon was followed by a sharp crackle and a shower of splinters from the foreyard.

It was clear we had got an ugly customer – poor Jenkins now called to Treenail, who was standing forward near the gun which had been fired: "Och, sir, and it's badly wounded we are here."

The officer was a Patlander, as well as the seaman. "Which of you, my boy?" – the glowing seriousness of the affair in no way checking his propensity to fun – "Which of you – you, or the yard?"

"Both of us, your honour; but the yard badliest."

"The devil! Come down, then, or get into the top, and I will have you looked after presently."

The poor fellow crawled off the yard into the foretop, as he was ordered, where he was found after the brush, badly wounded by a splinter in the breast.

Jonathan, no doubt, 'calculated,' as well he might, that this taste of his quality would be quite sufficient for a little eighteen-gun sloop close under his lee; but the fight was not to be so easily taken out of Deadeye, although even to his optic it was now high time to be off.

"All hands make sail, Mr Splinter; that chap is too heavy for us. Mr Kelson," to the carpenter, "jump up and see what the foreyard will carry. Keep her away, my man," to the seaman at the helm. "Crack on, Mr Splinter, set the fore-topsail, shake all the reefs out, and loose topgallant-sails; stand by to sheet home; and see all clear to rig the booms out, if the breeze lulls."

In less than a minute we were bowling along before it; but the wind was breezing up again, and no one could say how long the wounded foreyard would carry the weight and drag off the sails. To mend the matter, Jonathan was coming up hand over hand with the freshening breeze, under a press of canvas; it was clear that escape was next to impossible.

"Clear away the larboard guns!" I absolutely jumped off the deck with astonishment – who could have spoken it? It appeared such downright madness to show fight under the very muzzles of the guns of an enemy, half of whose broadside was sufficient to sink us. It was the captain, however, and there was nothing for it but to obey.

In an instant was heard, through the whistling of the breeze, the creaking and screaming of the carronade slides, the rattling of the carriage of the long twelve-pounder amidships, the thumping and punching of handspikes, and the dancing and jumping of Jack himself, as the guns were being shotted and run out. In a few seconds all was still again, but the rushing sound of the vessel going through the water, and of the rising gale amongst the rigging.

The men stood clustered at their quarters, their cutlasses buckled round their waists, all without jackets and waistcoats, and many with nothing but their trousers on.

"Now, men, mind your aim; our only chance is to wing him. I will yaw the ship, and as your guns come to bear, slap it right into his bows. Starboard your helm, my man, and bring her to the wind." As she came round, blaze went our carronades and long-gun in succession, with good will and good aim, and down came his fore-topsail on the cap, with all the superincumbent spars and gear; the head of the topmast had been shot away. The men instinctively cheered. "That will do; now knock off, my boys, and let us run for it. Keep her away again; make all sail."

Jonathan was for an instant paralyzed by our impudence; but just as we were getting before the wind, he yawed, and let drive his whole broadside; and fearfully did it transmogrify us. Half an hour before we were as gay a little sloop as ever floated, with a crew of 120 as fine fellows as ever manned a British man-of-war. The iron-shower sped – ten of the 120 never saw the sun rise again; seventeen more were wounded, three mortally; we had eight shots between wind and water, our maintop-mast shot away as clean as a carrot, and our hull and rigging otherwise regularly cut to pieces. Another broadside succeeded; but by this time we had bore up – thanks to the loss of our after-sail, we could do nothing else; and what was better luck still, whilst the loss of our maintop-mast paid the brig off on the one hand, the loss of head-sail in the frigate brought her as quickly to the wind on the other: thus, most of her shot fell astern of us; and, before she could bear up again in chase, the squall struck her, and carried her maintop-mast overboard.

This gave us a start, crippled and bedevilled though we were; and as the night fell, we contrived to lose sight of our large friend. With breathless anxiety did we carry on through that night, expecting every lurch to send our remaining topmast by the board; but the weather moderated, and next morning the sun shone on our bloodstained decks, at anchor off the entrance to St George's harbour.

2

I was the mate of the morning watch, and, as day dawned, I had amused myself with other younkers over the side, examining the shot holes and other injuries sustained from the fire of the frigate, and contrasting the clean, sharp, well-defined apertures, made by the 24-pound shot from the long guns, with the bruised and splintered ones from the 32-pound carronades; but the men had begun to wash down the decks, and the first gush of clotted blood and water from the scuppers fairly turned me sick. I turned away, when Mr Kennedy, our gunner, a good steady old Scotchman, with whom I was a bit of a favourite, came up to me: "Mr Cringle, the captain has sent for you; poor Mr Johnstone is fast going, he wants to see you."

I knew my young messmate had been wounded, for I had seen him carried below after the frigate's second broadside; but the excitement of a boy, who had seldom smelt powder fired in anger before, had kept me on deck the whole night, and it never once occurred to me to ask for him, until the old gunner spoke.

I hastened down to our small confined berth, where I saw a sight that quickly brought me to myself. Poor Johnstone was indeed going; a grape-shot had struck him, and torn his belly open. There he lay in his bloody hammock on the deck, pale and motionless as if he had already departed, except a slight twitching at the corners of his mouth, and a convulsive contraction and distension of his nostrils. His brown ringlets still clustered over his marble forehead, but they were drenched in the cold sweat of death. The surgeon could do nothing for him, and had left him; but our old captain – bless him for it – I little expected from his usual crusty bearing, to find him so employed – had knelt by his side, and, whilst he read from the Prayer Book one of those beautiful petitions in our Church service to Almighty God, for mercy to the passing soul of one so young, and so early cut off, the tears trickled down the old man's cheeks, and filled the furrows worn in them by the washing up of many a salt spray. On the other side of his narrow bed, fomenting the rigid muscles of his neck and chest, sat Mistress Connolly, one of three women on board – a rough-enough creature, heaven knows! in common weather; but her stifled sobs showed that the mournful sight had stirred up all the woman within her. She had opened the bosom of the poor boy's shirt, and untying the riband that fastened a small gold crucifix round his neck, she placed it in his cold hand. The young midshipman was of a respectable family in Limerick, her native place, and a Catholic – another strand of the cord that bound her to him. When the captain finished reading, he bent over the departing youth, and kissed his cheek. "Your young messmate just now desired to see you, Mr Cringle, but it is too late, he is insensible and dying." Whilst he spoke, a strong shiver passed through the boy's frame, his face became slightly convulsed, and all was over!

The captain rose, and Connolly, with a delicacy of feeling which many might not have looked for in her situation, spread one of our clean mess table-cloths over the body. "And is it really gone you are, my poor dear boy!" forgetting all difference of rank in the fulness of her heart. "Who will tell this to your mother, and nobody here to wake you but ould Kate Connolly, and no time will they be giving me, nor whisky. Ochon! ochon!"

But enough and to spare of this piping work. The boatswain's whistle now called me to the gangway, to superintend the handing up, from a shore boat alongside, a supply of the grand staples of the island – ducks and onions. The three 'Mudians in her were characteristic samples of the inhabitants. Their faces and skins, where exposed, were not tanned, but absolutely burnt into a fiery-red colour by the sun. They guessed and drawled like any buck-skin from Virginia, superadding to their accomplishments their insular peculiarity of always shutting one eye when they spoke to you. They are all Yankees at bottom; and if they could get their 365 'islands' – so they call the large stones on which they live – under weigh, they would not be long in towing them into the Chesapeake.

The word had been passed to get six of the larboard-guns and all the shot over to the other side, to give the brig a list of a streak or two a-starboard, so that the stage on which the carpenter and his crew were at work over the side, stopping the shot holes about the water-line, might swing clear of the wash of the sea. I had jumped from the nettings, where I was perched, to assist in unbolting one of the carronade slides, when I slipped and capsized against a peg sticking out of one of the scuppers. I took it for something else, and damned the ring-bolt incontinently. Caboose, the cook, was passing with his mate, a Jamaica negro of the name of John Crow, at the time. "Don't damn the remains of your fellow-mortals, Master Cringle; that is my leg." The cook of a man-of-war is no small beer; he is his Majesty's warrant-officer, a much bigger wig than a poor little mid, with whom it is condescension on his part to jest.

It seems to be a sort of rule, that no old sailor who has not lost a limb, or an eye at least, shall be eligible to the office, but as the kind of maiming is so far circumscribed that all cooks must have two arms, a laughable proportion of them have but one leg. Besides the honour, the perquisites are good; accordingly, all old quartermasters, captains of tops, etc., look forward to the cookdom, as the cardinals look to the popedom; and really there is some analogy between them, for neither are preferred from any especial fitness for the office. A cardinal is made pope because he is old, infirm, and imbecile; our friend Caboose was made cook because he had been Lord Nelson's coxswain, was a drunken rascal, and had a wooden leg; for, as to his gastronomical qualifications, he knew no more of the science than just sufficient to watch the copper where the salt junk and potatoes were boiling. Having been a little in the wind overnight, he had quartered himself, in the superabundance of his heroism, at a gun where he had no business to be, and in running it out, he had jammed his toe in a scupper hole, so fast that there was no extricating him; and not-withstanding his piteous entreaty, "to be eased out handsomely, as the leg was made out of a plank of the Victory, and the ring at the end out of one of her bolts," the captain of the gun finding, after a stout pull, that the man was like to come "home in his hand *without* the leg," was forced "to break him short off," as he phrased it, to get him out of the way, and let the carriage traverse. In the morning when he sobered, he had quite forgotten where the leg was, and how he broke it; he therefore got Kelson to splice the stump with the butt-end of the mop; but in the hurry it had been left 3 inches too long, so he had to jerk himself up to the top of his peg at every step. The doctor, glad to breathe the fresh air after the horrible work he had gone through, was leaning over the side speaking to Kelson. When I fell, he turned round and drew Cookee's fire on himself. "Doctor, you have not prescribed for me yet."

"No, Caboose, I have not; what is wrong?"

"Wrong, sir? Why, I have lost my leg, and the captain's clerk says I am not in the return! Look here, sir, had Doctor Kelson not coopered me, where should I have been? Why, doctor, had I been looked after, amputation might have been unnecessary; a *fish* might have done, whereas I have had to be *spliced*."

He was here cut short by the voice of his mate, who had gone forward to slay a pig for the gunroom mess. "Oh, Lad, oh! Massa Caboose! dem dam Yankee! De Purser killed, massa! Dem shoot him troo de head! Oh, Lad!"

Captain Deadeye had come on deck. "You John Crow, what *is* wrong with you?"

"Why, de Purser killed, captain, dat all."

"Purser killed? – Doctor, is Saveall hurt?"

Treenail could stand it no longer. "No, sir, no; it is one of the gunroom pigs that we shipped at Halifax three cruises ago; I am sure I don't know how he survived one, but the seamen took a fancy to him, and nicknamed him the Purser. You know, sir, they make pets of anything, and everything at a pinch!"

Here John Crow drew the carcass from the hog-pen, and sure enough a shot had cut the poor Purser's head nearly off. Blackee looked at him with a most whimsical expression; they say no one can fathom a negro's affection for a pig. "Poor Purser! De people call him Purser, sir, because him knowing chap; him cabbage all de grub, slush, and stuff in him own corner, and give only de small bit, and de bad piece, to de oder pig; so, Captain –"

Splinter saw the poor fellow was like to get into a scrape. "That will do, John Crow; forward with you now, and lend a hand to cat the anchor. All hands up anchor!" The boatswain's hoarse voice repeated the command, and he in turn was re-echoed by his mates, the capstan was manned, and the crew stamped round to a point of war most villanously performed by a bad drummer and a worse fifer, in as high glee as if those who were killed had been snug and well in their hammocks on the berth-deck, in place of at the bottom of the sea, with each a shot at his feet. We weighed, and began to work up, tack and tack, towards the island of Ireland, where the arsenal is, amongst a perfect labyrinth of shoals, through which the 'Mudian pilot *cunned* the ship with great skill, taking his stand, to our no small wonderment, not at the gangway or poop, as usual, but on the bowsprit end, so that he might see the rocks under foot and shun them accordingly, for they are so steep and numerous (they look like large fish in the clear water), and the channel is so intricate, that you have to go quite close to them. At noon we arrived at the anchorage, and hauled our moorings on board.

3

We had refitted, and been four days at sea, on our voyage to Jamaica, when the gun-room officers gave our mess a blow-out.

The increased motion and rushing of the vessel through the water, the groaning of the masts, the howling of the rising gale, and the frequent trampling of the watch on deck, were prophetic of wet jackets to some of us; still, midshipman-like, we were as happy as a good dinner and some wine could make us, until the old gunner shoved his weather-beaten phiz and bald pate in at the door. "Beg pardon, Mr Splinter, but if you will spare Mr Cringle on the fore-castle for an hour until the moon rises."

("Spare," quotha, "is His Majesty's officer a joint stool?")

"Why, Mr Kennedy, why? Here, man, take a glass of grog."

"I thank you, sir. It is coming on a roughish night, sir; the running ships should be crossing us hereabouts; indeed, more than once I thought there was a strange sail close aboard of us, the scud is flying so low, and in such white flakes; and none of us have an eye like Mr Cringle, unless it be John Crow, and he is all but frozen."

"Well, Tom, I suppose you *will* go" – *Anglice*, from a first lieutenant to a mid – "Brush instanter."

Having changed my uniform, for shag-trowsers, pea-jacket, and south-west cap, I went forward, and took my station, in no pleasant humour, on the stowed jib, with my arm round the stay. I had been half an hour there, the weather was getting worse, the rain was beating in my face, and the spray from the stem was flashing over me, as it roared through the waste of sparkling and hissing waters. I turned my back to the weather for a moment, to press my hand on my strained eyes. When I opened them again, I saw the gunner's gaunt, high-featured visage thrust anxiously forward; his profile looked as if rubbed over with phosphorus, and his whole person as if we had been playing at snap-dragon. "What has come over you, Mr Kennedy? Who is burning the blue light now?"

"A wiser man than I must tell you that; look forward, Mr Cringle – look there; what do your books say to that?"

I looked forth, and saw, at the extreme end of the jib-boom, what I had read of certainly, but never expected to see: a pale, greenish, glow-worm coloured flame, of the size and shape of the frosted glass-shade over the swinging lamp in the gun-room. It drew out and flattened as the vessel pitched and rose again, and as she sheered about, it wavered round the point that seemed to attract it, like a soapsud bubble blown from a tobacco pipe before it is shaken into the air; at the core it was comparatively bright, but gradually faded into a halo. It shed a baleful and ominous light on the surrounding objects; the group of sailors on the forecastle looked like spectres, and they shrunk together, and whispered when it began to roll slowly along the spar towards where the boatswain was sitting at my feet. At this instant something slid down the stay, and a cold, clammy hand passed round my neck. I was within an ace of losing my hold, and tumbling overboard. "Heaven have mercy on me, what's that?"

"It's that skylarking son of a gun, Jem Sparkle's monkey, sir. You, Jem, you'll never rest till that brute is made shark bait of."

But Jackoo vanished up the stay again, chuckling and grinning in the ghostly radiance, as if he had been the "Spirit of the Lamp." The light was still there, but a cloud of mist, like a burst of vapour from a steam boiler, came down upon the gale, and flew past, when it disappeared. I followed the white mass as it sailed down the wind; it did not, as it appeared to me, vanish in the darkness, but seemed to remain in sight to leeward, as if checked by a sudden flaw; yet none of our sails were taken aback. A thought flashed on me. I peered still more intensely into the night. I was now certain. "A sail, broad on the lee bow."

The ship was in a buzz in a moment. The captain answered from the quarterdeck: "Thank you, Mr Cringle. How shall we steer?"

"Keep her away a couple of points, sir – steady."

"Steady," sung the man at the helm; and the slow, melancholy cadence, although a familiar sound to me, now moaned through the rushing of the wind, and smote upon my heart as if it had been the wailing of a spirit.

I turned to the boatswain, who was standing beside me. "Is that you, or *Davy* steering, Mr Nipper? If you had not been here bodily at my elbow, I could have sworn that was your *voice*."

When the gunner made the same remark, it startled the poor fellow; he tried to take it as a joke, but could not. "There may be a laced hammock with a shot in it, for some of us ere morning."

At this moment, to my dismay, the object we were chasing shortened, gradually fell abeam of us, and finally disappeared. "The Flying Dutchman."

"I can't see her at all now."

"She will be a fore-and-aft-rigged vessel that has tacked, sir." And sure enough, after a few seconds, I saw the white object lengthen, and draw out again abaft our beam.

"The chase has tacked, sir, put the helm down, or she will go to windward of us."

We tacked also, and time it was we did so, for the rising moon now showed us a large schooner under a crowd of sail. We edged down on her, when, finding her manœuvre detected, she brailed up her flat sails, and bore up before the wind. This was our best point of sailing, and we cracked on, the captain rubbing his hands: "It's my turn to be the *big un* this time." Although blowing a strong north-wester, it was now clear moonlight, and we hammered away from our bow guns; but whenever a shot told against the rigging, the injury was repaired as if by magic. It was evident we had repeatedly hulled her, from the glimmering white streaks along her counter and across her stern, occasioned by the splintering of the timber, but it seemed to produce no effect.

At length we drew well up on her quarter. She continued all black hull and white sail, not a soul to be seen on deck, except a dark object, which we took for the man at the helm. "What schooner's that?" No answer. "Heave-to, or I'll sink you." Still all silent. "Sergeant Armstrong, do you think you could pick off that chap at the wheel?" The marine jumped on the forecastle, and levelled his piece, when a musket-shot from the schooner crashed through his skull, and he fell dead. The old skipper's blood was up. "Forecastle, there! Mr Nipper, clap a canister of grape over the round shot into the boat-gun, and give it to him."

"Ay, ay, sir!" gleefully rejoined the boatswain, forgetting the augury and everything else in the excitement of the moment. In a twinkling, the square foresail, topsail, topgallant, royal, and studdingsail haulyards were let go by the run on board of the schooner, as if they had been shot away, and he put his helm hard aport, as if to round to.

"Rake him, sir, or give him the stem. He has *not* surrendered. I know their game. Give him your broadside, sir, or he is off to windward of you like a shot. No, no! we have him now; heave to, Mr Splinter, heave-to!" We did so, and that so suddenly that the studdingsail booms snapped like pipe-shanks, short off by the irons. Notwithstanding, we had shot 200 yards to leeward before we could lay our maintopsail to the mast. I ran to windward. The schooner's yards and rigging were now black with men, clustered like bees swarming, her square-sails were being close furled, her fore-and-aft sails set, and away she was, close-hauled and dead to windward of us.

"So much for undervaluing our American friends," grumbled Mr Splinter.

We made all sail in chase, blazing away to little purpose; we had no chance on a bowline, and when our *amigo* had satisfied himself of his superiority by one or two short tacks, he deliberately hauled down his flying jib and gaff-topsail, took a reef in his mainsail, triced up the bunt of his foresail, and fired his long thirty-two at us. The shot came in at the third aftermost port on the starboard side, and dismounted the carronade, smashing the slide, and wounding three men. The second shot missed, and as it was madness to remain to be peppered, probably winged, whilst every one of ours fell short, we reluctantly kept away on our course, having the gratification of hearing a clear well-blown bugle on board the schooner play up "Yankee Doodle."

As the brig fell off, our long gun was run out to have a parting crack at her, when the third and last shot from the schooner struck the sill of the mid-ship port, and made the white splinters fly from the solid oak like bright silver sparks in the moonlight. A sharp piercing cry rose into the air – my soul identified that death-shriek with the voice that I had heard, and I saw the man who was standing with the lanyard of the lock in his hand drop heavily across the breech, and discharge the gun in his fall. Thereupon a blood-red glare shot up into the cold blue sky, as if a volcano had burst forth from beneath the mighty deep, followed by a roar, and a shattering crash, and a mingling of unearthly cries and groans, and a concussion of the air, and of the water, as if our whole broadside had been fired at once. Then a solitary splash here, and a dip there, and short sharp yells, and low, choking bubbling moans, as the hissing fragments of the noble vessel we had seen fell into the sea, and the last of her gallant crew vanished for ever beneath that pale broad moon. *We were alone*, and once more all was dark, and wild, and stormy. Fearfully had that ball sped, fired by a dead man's hand. But what is it that clings, black and doubled, across that fatal cannon, dripping and heavy, and choking the scuppers with clotted gore, and swaying to and fro with the motion of the vessel, like a bloody fleece?

"Who is it that was hit at the gun there?"

"Mr Nipper, the boatswain, sir. The last shot has cut him in two."

THE NANTUCKET
SLEIGH-RIDE

Peter Garratt

Throughout the Napoleonic War and the War of 1812, the Americans pursued their whaling endeavours throughout the Atlantic. The whaling ships and their crew tried to avoid their involvement in the war but sometimes that proved impossible. In the following story Peter Garratt (b. 1949) brings together events in 1813 with a fascinating preview of events in another great book of the sea, Herman Melville's Moby Dick.

The bookseller looked offended by my simple statement of fact. He enquired with a sneer: "So when did you see this remarkable freak of nature?"

I told him it had been many years before, when I had just been given my first command, and was at once ordered to Halifax in Nova Scotia, to protect a convoy from American privateers, and later join our own blockade.

We stayed in Halifax till it was almost spring. H.M.S. *Montgomery* needed repairs, and no one would be looking for whale-fish on the Grand Banks at that season. It was a hard winter, the same one we later learned put paid to Boney's trip to Moscow. I gave my ship's master, Mr Ahab, leave for Christmas to visit relatives who lived down the coast. When he had not returned a month into the New Year, I concluded he must have jumped ship to more distant kin. That was not a total surprise. He had not protested at being impressed, indeed had taken the King's Bounty to aid his promotion. But that had been before his fellow Johnathans (as we called Americans in those days) joined in the war, effectively siding with the Frenchies against their former countrymen. Mr Ahab said only that he knew more of Boney's ways than President Madison or Congress did. He was a man who preferred his own counsel. I decided it would do the crew's morale no favours to imprison so important an officer, and gave him the leave.

It was a hard, cold place, though they say Canada can be even worse further from the sea. For provisions we shipped mostly salt cod, and it wasn't easy to get the fresh produce men need to keep them from the scurvy. I had to drive a hard bargain to get a tiny consignment of limes, and the only fruits available in quantity were cranberries. Men were another problem. I admired the hardiness of the locals, and dearly wished to recruit some, but few took the bounty, and nearly all the English or Scottish born for some reason held exemptions from the press. Most already belonged to the militia, or had joined in fear of an invasion from the south. They were men who would defend their homes fiercely, but did not understand the greater aims of strategy. In the end I recruited a man born in the colony, named Fryzer, to be my new master: he was a skilled navigator and knew much of the whale-fishery, though he told me he had never worked in it. He advised me also about the locals: I did not wish to go to war short handed, given the inevitability of putting some of my crew into prizes. I was reduced to signing on half-breeds, runaway slaves, and even a couple of redskins who knew some English and had been to sea. I drew the line at Canadian Frenchies, except for one Lavelle I signed as assistant

cook. Fryzer assured me the French in the colony were loyal to
His Majesty, and had little time for Boney and less for the
Johnathans to the south, but none came forward, and I thought
it imprudent to press them.

Nevertheless, by the beginning of Lent I had assembled an
almost adequate crew. The repair work had been done, and as
Shrove Tuesday was a fine day for the season and latitude, I
mustered the men on deck. I allowed Mr Paul, ship's chaplain,
only a brief sermon before serving them all pancakes with a little
lime and rather more cranberry, and warmed them with mulled
wine instead of the usual grog.

The wind was light and off the sea. I savoured great lungfulls
as it diluted and swept away the equally agreeable smell of wine
mulling and pancakes frying. We were well into the great
harbour, but it was a clear day, and I could see right out to
the ocean. At first I took no notice of a single-masted fishing
smack making toward us, thinking it a local vessel which had
taken advantage of the better weather, but when it made right
for us, it crossed my mind to wonder if the Johnathans could
have hit on the idea of using a fireship. The United States did
not have a full navy at the time: there were privateers enough,
but they were short of warships to match a forty-two-gun
frigate like *Montgomery*. Surprise and fire might be their best
weapons.

I observed carefully as the smack came closer. There were no
obvious war-like preparations, but she flew no flag. I gave
orders for the challenge signal to be flown, and for the marines
to ready their weapons. I could see men rushing about on the
deck and an ancient Jack ensign being hoisted. It lacked the
third cross, so clearly dated from before the Act of Union with
Ireland. Indeed, it was so faded and moth-eaten that I guessed
it had been hidden in some unsavoury hole since before the
great rebellion in America.

The smack came alongside, and I decided to allow the crew
on board. Their leader was a tall, rangy young man with dark
hair and intense eyes. He wore our uniform, not surprisingly, as
he was still officially my ship's master, Mr Ahab. He saluted
correctly, and said: "I have been detained on family business,

Captain Thomas, and am greatly relieved to find you still in port."

I studied him carefully. I knew he must have been south, and the obvious thought came to me that he had returned as a spy, or, more likely, as he would be unable to communicate with the Johnathans from aboard ship, as a saboteur. This latter speculation was reinforced when he indicated that six or more others from the smack, who were joining him on *Montgomery*'s deck, were, as he put it: "Good men of Nantucket, the finest seamen in the world when it comes to finding whales, which I dare say is the best and only way you'll find whale-catchers willing to serve under you as seamen. Though not," and here he cast an anxious glance at the redcoats who were still at attention with fixed bayonets, "as marines or cutlass cut-throat men. For we hold with the Society of Friends, and though we fear not the fiercest monster of the deep, and hunt him down with lance and harpoon, the Book forbids us take up arms against men!"

I had known Mr Ahab was a Quaker, but that had not stopped him taking the King's bounty and serving against the French. But then he had been far from his own people, and now he was in their midst. The sun was below the mains'l arm, and it was getting cold. I invited, or rather instructed, Mr Ahab to come to my cabin, along with Mr Brown, First Officer, and Matthews, Lieutenant of Marines, excellent fellows of sound judgement. I also invited Mr Paul to join us. He made a study of religious customs on the wild fringes of civilization.

I studied Ahab closely. He did not seem anxious, as one would assume any but the most hardened spy to be during such an investigation. Instead, he seemed suffused with anger against his own people, apart from such few as had come with him. He sat on the edge of his seat, and without waiting for me to begin interrogating, launched into a diatribe concerning his recent adventures. "Captain Thomas, I am aware you have been inconvenienced by these delays I have been unable to avoid, but not a half, no, not a quarter, as much as I have been inconvenienced!" I began to ask a question, but he ranted on: "You will be aware, sir, that I accepted your bounty because, from the very earliest part of my life, I have been cheated and misused by those who should have been my protectors and my friends!"

I replied, or rather inserted a comment, that I had not been aware of that, for he had previously spoken little of himself. I knew he had left Nantucket in a whaler as a young man, but had done his schooling and had not been a cabin boy. At some point he had signed on a Dundee ship as harpooner, but when I met him he was spending his share of the proceeds on a course of study at St Andrews. When offered the bounty but threatened with impressment unless he could prove his exemption, he enquired at once as to whether by volunteering he could learn the art of navigation, and thus came willingly, unlike most of the Johnathans we took on before they entered the war. He went on:

"Sir, it would be easy for a man in my position to plead that I am from a family Loyalist by conviction, but that would be a false witness to bear. My cousin Saul, who lives here in Nova Scotia, once owned a store in Boston, but being a Friend, he was forced out for loyalty, not to the King, but to God.

"Similarly, my father was traduced. He was a whaler-captain, sir, and he owned a half-share in his own ship. He too was a man who rendered unto God, not Caesar. But he had a misfortune sent to try him, that he was forced by unfavourable winds into the harbour at Boston, when on his way home to Nantucket. Now, it so happened that feeling ran very high against Caesar the King Georgius in Boston in those days, because of atrocities taught of in our schoolrooms but not in yours. Now, it came to the militia captains of Boston, that they had an American ship in their harbour that did not belong to any of their neighbours. And also that it was a better ship, being built to round the Horn into the great Southern Ocean, and not merely to paddle like a duck in the Atlantic. So, in the name of liberty, they attempted to impress my father, or at least his ship. For when he was ordered to cut gunports in her sides, he replied that of course he believed in the great cause of no taxation without representation, but added that the Hebrews had not been represented at the court of Caesar, but our Lord cut no gunports against that injustice!

"But the city fathers of Boston are Puritans, sir, men who

read the book with their lips, but do not know it in their hearts, and they seized the ship, and with it the cargo, and those of the crew, who, for want of their share of the proceeds, would sign up for anything!"

I had known none of this sad tale. I said indignantly: "So, your family lost its ship!"

"Not quite, for the war was almost over. I myself was born on the day it ended. I have never been a subject of your king, though I take his silver. The cousins who owned the other shares petitioned the courts of Massachusetts for the return of the ship. This was granted, though with the proviso that my father's share was given to his brother, a Cain, sir, to his Abel, a sailor who could run before the wind, but not tack into it.

"Though my father was allowed to keep his house, he never got another command, or even a mate's berth. After some hard years, he signed before the mast on an ill-run ship which never returned. Had my mother not inherited a small share of a different ship, we would have hungered badly.

"My uncle was not totally devoid of any sense of justice, and having no heir of his own body, made known his intention to bequeath his share of the ship back to me. For that reason, I requested my cousin Saul to send him word, that on no account should the ship be risked at sea during this war."

"You sent him word of our planned blockade?" Matthews asked sharply.

"Not of your exact plans. The whole world knows there is a general blockade during war with England. Besides, in the end I sent him no word at all, for Saul informed me my uncle had recently died.

"This made me apprehensive, for I learned that the other share holders, mostly cousins on the other side to Saul, were disputing the Will, which was spoken but unwritten. Therefore, when the weather eased a little after Christmas, I dared risk the passage south to Nantucket, for I knew that if I delayed, then custom would ossify the ownership in undeserving hands."

"So," I asked sharply. "You have been to the territory of the King's enemies! Were you arrested for wearing his uniform, or did you disguise it?"

"Neither. In Nantucket, they study profit, not war. I calculated that if I warned them against risking their ships at sea
during this conflict, they would not enqire deeply as to the
source of that useful intelligence."

Mr Paul nodded sympathetically, but the others were looking
perturbed (unless one counted the portraits of His Majesty and
the Prince Regent). For though it would suit the King's business well enough if the Nantucketers sulked unprofitably in
port for the duration, for the officers and crew, and indeed
myself, the chance to take prizes was the main compensation for
the dangers of the war. I said: "Just how much intelligence did
you give them?"

"None at all they put to use. I meant mainly to reclaim my
own ship, and spoke privately to my cousins to keep her in port
till the issue of the disputed ownership was settled. To my
amazement, they denied that any dispute was in progress,
maintaining the ship was entirely theirs, and they would do
with her as they chose. When I protested in most vigorous
terms against this crime and folly, they took the whole matter to
the town meeting, where some who were not Friends named
me, *me*, as a traitor for protesting at this theft, and threatened to
put me in the jailhouse if I went to court to secure my
property!"

"What!" I exclaimed, and all the others indicated equal
shock, that the former colonies had fallen into such an anarchic
state that so important a matter as property could be settled by a
town meeting. "So, for that reason, you returned at once to His
Majesty's service?"

"Like Jeremiah, I delivered my warning, and was ignored.
For though they supply no ships to the American fleet, they
consider it the equal to yours, and greed has so blinded them
that under its protection they mean to continue their business
entirely as usual!"

I though it politic not to ask what he would have done, had
the meeting ruled in his favour. Such a speculation would have
achieved nothing. Mr Ahab had seen for himself that revolution
against established law does not lead to justice. I therefore
reinstated him as ship's master. Mr Fryzer's warrant had not

arrived from the Navy Board, hardly surprising in view of the weather. During his time on board, Fryzer had shown an unexpected knowledge of ordnance, and the previous incumbent never having fully recovered from a bout of the Yellow Jack, I made Fryzer acting gunner in his place.

Later that day, I was summoned aboard the flagship to receive sailing orders from Vice-Admiral Pringle. His huge cabin was decorated with portraits of Nelson and the entire board of Admiralty as well as royalty. He warmed me with a glass of mulled wine as I briefly described Mr Ahab's adventures. I had decided to give him a chance to overrule me on the latter's Warrant if he wished, but he shook his head:

"New England was a hotbed of sedition in the revolutionary war, but this time those former colonies have taken a more sensible approach. They voted against the war, and have protested against being dragged into it. For a while we held off extending the blockade to their ports, hoping they could persuade Mr Madison to see sense. That is why we left their whalers in peace last year. But the war goes on, Canada is still in danger, and the blockade must be extended. Though, if you stop a captain who can produce receipts to show he had recently sold us certain essential supplies, use your discretion."

He explained that a close blockade would be attempted on the American coast, but there were too many small ports for all to be watched. "Merchantmen can vary their routes when past the close blockade, but whalers of course have to follow the habits of whales!"

I said I had recruited two experts on the New England whale fishery, and he looked pleased. We went over the chart in detail. We both knew that the Greenland type of whale, which our own fishermen call "the right whale to hunt", had once visited the Grand Banks and other Banks closer to New England in great numbers every spring and summer, but was now getting scarce there. Despite the wine, I think it sobered both of us to think that unwise hunting had so reduced this mother-of-plenty, that the Nantucketers now preferred to hunt the far more dangerous Sperm Whale, even though they sometimes had to sail right down to the Southern Ocean in search of it. My own ship, I pointed out, was only provisioned for the Banks.

He shrugged: "This little war won't last that long. Mop up any Johnathan whalers who venture onto the Banks. They'll soon hear, if they haven't already, that their new ally General Bonaparte met his match in Russia."

"What, from the Russian army?"

"No, from the cold and the snow."

I was reminded of that as we put out to sea the next morning on a brisk westerly. The sea was not heavy, but it was a wind which had blown through the frozen heart of Canada, where Lent is too early for the snow and ice to melt. It being Ash Wednesday, Mr Paul tried to encourage the men to chant seasonal hymns, but they preferred an old whaling song:

> The cold coast of Greenland is bare and unfair?
> No seedtime nor harvest is ever known there.
> The sweet bird he sings out in mountain and vale,
> But there's no bird in Greenland to sing to the whale.

The sky was clear, but I could see heavy clouds on the northern horizon. I mustered the men and gave them a little speech, assuring them that we were not going to Greenland, but they did not seem reassured, so I set a course south of west. Fryzer had told me that whales migrated like birds: they wintered in waters of their own choice in the tropics, but in spring were drawn north to banks where fish were plentiful. He said it was still early in the year for them to have reached the Grand Banks, so I resolved to try my luck on Stellwagon's Bank, which is further south and nearer to New England.

The wind shifting, I was able to head due south the next morning. We were out of sight of land, but birds were passing above us, leading the way north. Around ten I was looking for a sail I had glimpsed on the horizon ahead when I lowered my telescope and observed that although there was quite a swell, a patch of water about the size of a large ship had gone unseasonably flat less than a quarter of a mile ahead. As I wondered what this could mean, an enormous grey-black head burst out of the water. Nothing I had ever seen compared to it: within seconds the great back of the monster was in sight, and with an audible hiss like the valve of a steam engine, a spout of vapour shot into the air. Someone shouted "there she blows" and the whole crew raced onto the deck, the officers hurrying to join me on the quarterdeck.

Of course, I had seen whales many times before, but never as big as this nor as close to the ship. Usually, those which approach are no more than large dolphins. As I watched, the first whale lowered its head back into the sea and its back revolved forward, revealing the dorsal fin: at the same time another monster broke the surface and spouted, if possible even bigger than the first.

I turned angrily to Fryzer and said: "You assured me there would be no whales this far north at this season, yet here we are well off the bank, and there are two bearing straight down on me! Are they dangerous?"

As I spoke the first whale seemed to notice us. It came up again vertically, and at some speed, so the whole of its head and part of its body were out of the water. I could see its eyes, on the sides of its head, trying to focus on us. They were almost on a level with the quarterdeck, while the tip of the snout looked as if it would reach to the fores'l arm. I noticed that although the back and the left side of the mouth and throat were grey, almost black, the whole right side of the lower jaw was an unnervingly pure white. Then it plunged forward again with a tremendous crashing and boiling of the sea, so I fancied I got some of the salt spray even where I stood.

Meanwhile, Fryzer was shaking his head. "They're not dangerous. At least, not to you. Those whales are finbacks. They're bigger than a 'right' whale, at least in length, and also faster, so when the time comes, they can swim ahead of the others and sometimes reach northern waters earlier."

Mr Ahab added: "If you could contrive to put a harpoon i' one, then there'd be a danger! As you see, they've no fear ships, so you could maybe make fast. But if you tried to hol or haul him in, why he'd drag you to the ends of the earth. could load your boat with enough line to hold that lo then he'd drag out the rest of the line and leave you alone on the sea wondering how to get back to your ship, if you could still see her!"

Fryzer added: "Of course, every whaler you meet will tell you of a man he met once in a tavern in another town, who told how once they killed a finback whale. And they all say the same, these friends of friends of drinking companions: at the moment the brute spouted red, and they were sure they had it, it plunged into the depths and never rose again, almost taking boat and crew with it, so these strangers' claims could never be put to proof!"

The whales rose again, this time only showing their backs and spouting. Fryzer explained that the spout was an exhalation of breath, the whale not being a true fish, but breathing air like a mammal. Mr Ahab looked at him in shock. "How can you deny that a whale is a fish? Does it not say in the Good Book that the prophet Jonah was swallowed by a great fish? Looking on these, do you prefer to think he was swallowed by a haddock or a mackerel?"

They rose now beside the ship, so close that a Frenchman could have hit one with a musket, had he been mad enough to provoke it: these vast animals were almost as long as the ship. I commented that this seemed the ultimate of God's creations: so vast and terrible that even the boldest and most skilful dare not tackle it. Robinson, the surgeon, mentioned reading of an even huger beast, lurking of course in the fabled Southern Seas, which was similar to the finback except for being blue in colour. An argument developed, Fryzer maintaining that a whale could no more be blue than a cat or dog, when Mr Ahab exclaimed: "There is another vast beast, the most fabulous in the world, so rare that some say there is one only. And this singular monstrosity is similar in form to the Sperm Whale, but bigger than most in size and pure white in colour."

Fryzer scoffed: "White whales are quite common off Canada. They are known as belugas and no more than large porpoises!"

By this time the two finbacks were well behind us, and now they disappeared below for the last time. Mr Ahab pointed at em angrily and shouted: "These whales are not pursuable because they live faithful to the Lord's Commandment, two by two. But your Sperm Whale is a tyrant fish, each bull seeking a whole hareem of females, and for that sinful life the Lord gives them to us, if we are bold enough. But some there are who outgrow their sin, and swim alone as tyrants of the whole ocean, and these, sir, these tyrants are to your finback as King Georgius is to the Mayor of Boston! And the White Whale is the vastest of them all, a veritable Bonaparte of whales!"

He turned and stormed below. Fryzer remarked that most sailors had a wife in every port, but whalers were monogamous as they put into port very seldom. It crossed my mind that it might have been something, or someone, some Jezebel, other than a ship which had not been waiting for Ahab when he went home.

With fair weather we continued south, then inclined a little east, until by my reckoning we were close to Stellwagon's Bank. Dolphins began to play around us, and we saw a few finbacks in the distance, but none approached us. The only American ships we saw were tiny fishing smacks, too small to be worth taking, so I contented myself with ordering them back to port on pain of being certainly taken or sunk the next time. On the third day on the Bank, already quite far south, I was sweeping the empty horizon while remarking to Mr Brown that Admiral Pringle's tactics seemed to be working, when I saw a sight which would have made any sailor's blood run cold: a cloud of smoke on the horizon. I shouted orders to cram on all sail, and make towards it with all possible speed. Mr Ahab had been off duty, but after a while he joined me on the quarter-deck, to assess the change in our course. I explained that I could see smoke, and that the masts of a ship were now visible. "I don't think it's an engagement. I think we would hear the ordnance even at this range. Some poor devil's got his ship on fire, with no one to help him but us!"

"Let me see." He borrowed my telescope, studied the just-visible smoking ship for a little, then said: "I don't think it's an accidental fire."

"What do you mean? What else could it be?"

He gave me an odd look. "Have you never heard of a furnace being used on a ship?"

"No. Unless you count tugs." I paused. In coffee houses near the Admiralty, one encountered men with sketch-pads, who sought one's interest in plans for steam engines so light and powerful they could be used in sea-going ships. Such plans always required a great deal of money to get them from drawing board to shipyard. Our Lancashire neighbours rented land to the cotton trade, and the engines I had seen in these mills would require a barge the size of Noah's Ark to keep them afloat with no room for ordnance. Nonetheless, Mr Ahab was looking very confident in a mysterious way, so I snapped: "Are you saying your Johnathan friends – or whatever you now call them – have invented a steam and furnace engine that can put to sea?"

"No. Look closely! It may be to your advantage!" I almost snatched the telescope. The whole of the mystery ship was now visible above the horizon. All sails were furled, and the whole stream of smoke rose from just forward of the mainmast. I could see an American flag but no distress signal: though as far as I could judge she was very low in the water.

As we got closer, Mr Ahab said he believed she was our exact quarry, a whaling ship, and probably from New England. The crew would have recently taken a whale-fish, and still being some way from land, would have hove to in order to cut it up and render down the oil for blubber there at sea.

So it proved. As we got closer, I saw what had to be a dead whale afloat, tethered to the ship's side: men stood on it hacking at its outer layer of blubber with great machetes called flensing knives. They were hacking in such a way that the blubber could be pulled from the dead monster in a continuous strip, as if they had captured an orange made for Titans and were peeling it. On the deck, more flensers were cutting up the blubber and putting it into a furnace, which stood most dangerously on the deck between the masts. This, I learned, was called a try-works.

The most surprising thing was this: though the ship's look-outs had sung-out our approach, our ensign was clearly visible and our guns run out, no one took much notice. They were working and sweating away over their foully smoking furnace as

if they were already in hell, and nothing, not even the approach
of an enemy forty-two, could interfere with their labours. I had
the order to heave to flown, and was about to have a shot put
across their bows when I realised they were simply ignoring us,
not trying to escape. I would just have to board and see what
happened. I even considered using the dead whale as a fender:
but as we got closer I noticed the fins of sharks in the bloodstained water around it, and gave the order to put hard to
starboard, to cross the whaler's stern and then board her own
starboard side.

As we came alongside, they at last noticed what was happening, and desisted from their labours. We were now downwind of
them, and smoke hideous as that which comes from burnt flesh
(as I later learned this did) blew into our faces. I thought it a
satanic weapon of the enemy, that they assumed none less
accustomed to it than they could bear it at all, but our marines
were of sterner stuff than I, and soon the ship was secure.

I found the captain who identified himself as one Bildad, his
ship the *Enterprise of Nantucket*. He was a tall, rangy fellow who
at once started to abuse me: "What's the meaning of this, sir?
My men are all Independent-born, after the Declaration, and
you have no claim to press them for your God-forsaken war
with the French. And as you can hardly say we are bound for a
Frenchie port, you can get your men off my ship this instant,
and read the lads' papers later if you insist!"

I wanted nothing more than to get my men off that ship, for
she was dangerously low in the water at the best of times. But we
had work to do, and a war to fight. I said: "Sir, you act as if
ignorant that your President Madison has joined the war, and
sided with the French! All your ports are under blockade, and
this ship is forfeit as a prize of war!"

A shudder ran across the deck. The tall Bildad seemed to
shrink, like a dragon which had discovered itself to be a tortoise,
and skulked back into its shell. He said plaintively: "Sir, we are
not men of war. We have been working these last two years in
waters in the furthest ocean known only to us, scarcely spoken
of even in Nantucket, where there is no king nor president save
the great Sperm Whale, whom your Limey whalers do not dare

depose. We reaped a bountiful harvest, and have returned at our own pace, and saw no sails, doubtless because of this blockade you speak of. So we are no part of this war, and deserve to keep our ship."

I felt a little sympathy, but had my own crew to consider. I think even they might have hesitated, had it not been for the hateful furnace, now roaring away almost out of control. Flames were shooting out of its brick base and endangering the rigging; smoke affronted our throats as if the worst street of industrial Blackburn had been infernally transported out into the pure air of the sea, where poisoning is usually the one danger one does not face. I shouted, or rather gasped: "Shut down that furnace! Is this ship not loaded down enough, that you need light another altar to Mammon? This is a prize, and she will be properly conducted. Dowse that furnace, I say!"

Now the whalers stirred a little, as if it had only now dawned on them that their two years of obsessive labour, out of touch with the civilized world, had been in vain. One man who had been cutting the blubber, an Indian of some kind, darker than a Redskin and more tattooed, gave an evil cry, raised his flensing-knife and rushed at me, swinging it like a sabre, though it was bigger and heavier than any sword. I ducked back smartly, and the blow just missed my head, though it carried away my hat. A couple of shots rang out, but none hit my assailant. Most of my marines had to keep their guns and bayonets on the rest of the crew: meanwhile the Indian had slipped on the greasy deck, but he recovered his balance at once and flew at me again. He was strong as a horse, but luckily no swordsman: I had my cutlass out, and managed to parry him, knocking the great flensing knife out of his hand, and just as well, for my own blade snapped with the impact. Now Matthews and some of his men had their pistols on him, and seeing that none of the others had actually joined his revolt, he too surrendered.

Throughout my time at sea, I have fought to conceal a touch of the asthma, a disease for which I find sea-air the best remedy. I am lucky that though there are many steam-mills in Lancashire, my father has resisted allowing any on his estate. (Though he did allow a canal to be driven through it. Navigation is always beneficial.) So it seemed just that these whalers had suffered a fate they would have escaped had the bump of greed been less obvious on their skulls. Having sailed half-way round the world already overloaded with whale-oil, and miraculously been delivered almost home, they had to take yet another of the beasts that laid the golden oil, not reckoning that the smoke of that last rendering would bring a final end to their adventure. I ordered they be taken below decks on the *Montgomery*, though I made it clear that if any would take the King's Bounty, he would get his share of this prize, as well as any others we might take. Next, I made the prize safe as best I could. I had the dead whale cut loose and all its remains thrown over the side. The ship was still overloaded, and as I had no idea when or if she would be used for whaling again, I had the try-works detached from the deck, which was done with some difficulty, and thrown overboard as well. Thus lightened, I concluded the ship could be got safely to Halifax. In charge of her I put Mr Barnes, my senior midshipman: he was a man quite capable of passing the examination for lieutenant, but for some reason never wrote off to take it: I felt the experience would do him good.

Soon after I was approached by the oldest of my Redskins. he was a sensible type named White Blanket who had adjusted well to civilized ways without totally abandoning his own. He said: "Captain, that man who attacked you wishes to send his apologies. He would like to take your King's Bounty."

"What, do you know him? Is he one of your tribe?"

"No, he was signed from an island in the South Sea, where he says his father is a King, though kings there have many wives and more children. His name is Quohog. He says he formerly admired the Nantucket men, for their daring in taking whales, but cannot understand why they let the ship go without fighting. I explained to him that King Jorjie is a far greater king than King President Madison, and he wishes to serve him. He says he is an expert seaman as well as a harpooner."

I had Quohog brought to my cabin, and explained to him

carefully that I was not looking to recruit a harpooner. He shrugged:

"You want to find Nantucket men, stop them getting home?" I nodded, and he said: "American hunt 'parm whale, and I find him for you." He went to the cabin window, and pointed at something just below the surface, near our wake. "See him 'quid there? My eye good for 'quid. Usually 'quid swim very deep, down in bowels of sea. Hard work for whale. But when he swim near surface, Holly Day for whale, and for whaler. I find him for you. If you see him 'quid, soon you see him 'parm whale!"

He swore the oath correctly, but insisted on adding an addendum under his breath to whatever dark South Sea deity he followed. I had doubts about signing a man into the crew who was an unknown, and obviously a Paynim, but I had little choice, for I needed every hand I could get. Our next two prizes, another inbound whaler and a merchantman illegally carrying slaves, were not so easily taken as the first, but take them we did. A few of the slaves had been born to captivity, knew English, and eagerly took the bounty, on being told they were now free men and could therefore be pressed, but I was still very short of experienced men. Indeed, I considered after a few more days on the Bank without sighting a sail that it might be prudent to put back to Halifax myself, but by then there was a serious blow from the north, which soon turned into a near storm, and I had no choice but to run before it.

We were carried through heavy seas for two days. Even Williams, the ship's cat, stayed below. I have seen worse storms, but it had a bad effect on the less experienced men. Many were observed throwing up over the side, and a few didn't reach it. Some tried to blame Lavelle's cooking, but the true cause was obvious. For myself, I judged the ship to not be in serious danger, and quite enjoyed the storm, though I was unable to take bearings.

On the third morning, I made a guess at our position as off Virginia or North Carolina. The wind dropped a little, though the sky was overcast and there were frequent squalls of rain. I was trying to decide if it was yet worth the effort of trying to tack back the way we had come, when we observed a ship beating into the wind and making very slow progress. The captain identified his vessel as Portuguese, carrying coffee from Brazil to Halifax. I suspected he might try to run the blockade into Boston or New York, but, Portugal being an ally, felt it best not to enquire too closely. My forbearance was rewarded when I was given intelligence that Johnathan ships were hunting the Sperm Whale only a short distance to the south. I was told that on this occasion an American government ship escorted them, but much smaller than ours, a corvette by the description.

I asked Mr Ahab bluntly if he intended to fight, and for whom.

"No one. But I have taken your silver, and will help you find the sperm whales, and those who challenge them."

I knew he meant to find the White Whale, or some other vast Leviathan, but by this time I too was fascinated and I let him set the course he chose. Whether he had some secret I lacked, or succeeded by pure luck alone, I cannot say. It must have been around noon that the wind, still high, took us into a dense squall. We emerged into a clear patch of turbulent green sea, with another squall about a mile ahead. Near the edge of that curtain of rain, our lookout hollered he could just see whale-boats. Before I could examine them closely, he was shouting, "There she blows", and one whale's back, then a half a dozen more broke the surface. Mr Ahab almost jumped up and down with excitement. I studied them closely: they were grey, and had no fins on their backs: the spouts were different also, Mr Ahab explaining that these were definitely Sperm Whale spouts. After a minute they disappeared, and when they returned, one of them raised its whole head vertically out of the water. I had learned that this was called spy-hopping. As far as I could judge, this creature, though vast by any human standard, was no more than two-thirds the size of the finback which had similarly spied on us. It was entirely grey, and its jaw was a totally different shape.

By this time, Fryzer had joined us. He said these whales were fleeing the boats which were just getting clear of the far curtain of rain. He also observed that when Sperm Whales are chased they always seemed to swim into the wind, so the pursuer had to work his oars all the way and could get no advantage from his sail. Mr Ahab commented:

"Aye. Your Sperm Whale is a cunning and worthy adversary, while the 'right' whale is a dullard any fool with a harpoon could bring in."

We were now very close to the fleeing whales. Fryzer commented: "They'll dive soon. Another thing, you can't always tell where they'll come up from the direction they set out in. Let's see how the lads in the boats are doing." He borrowed the telescope. "Hey, it looks as if they've caught them a Beluga. Unless that is the fabulous White Whale!"

A small white animal was struggling in the water in front of one of the boats. I could see a harpoon in its side, and the line running back to the boat. I say small, but the creature was small only in comparison to the others. It was at least as big as the boat it was fast to. Mr Ahab said:

"I think you'll see soon, that's a calf white sperm, spawn of the Great White!" As if on a cue, it spy-hopped, and I saw it looked indeed like a white miniature of the sperm-whales, all of which had now disappeared. The young one had been trying to escape, but in doing so had actually been towing the boat. It now swam back towards its tormentors, evidently meaning to try and swamp the boat, as I had heard whales sometimes did. The men paddled, and the steersmen deftly managed to get the boat out of the creature's way, which was just as well, because it was at least the size of a large elephant. It tried twice more to charge the boat, and each time it narrowly missed, though the boat rocked wildly. I said:

"They don't seem to be trying to finish it off."

Mr Ahab replied: "No. That'll be the youngest. They'll be hoping its mother, and perhaps some of the others, will come back to help, thus saving them the effort of more rowing against this gale."

Then it again tried to escape, pulling the boat behind it by the harpoon stuck in its flesh. Mr Ahab said: "That's what we call the Nantucket Sleigh-ride. With a big whale in a temper, it's the most difficult thing in the world, steering a boat that's being pulled by a steed that's furious with his driver – knowing when to make fast the line, when to haul in, when to pay some out, and when, alas, to cut the line and sacrifice the quarry. I sometimes think the whole of a man's life is like that sleighride, knowing when to endure and when to act, when to make war, and what season to make peace, whom to attack with an iron, and whom to greet with the Book, whether to serve a king or a republic, to render to God or to Caesar."

At that moment, Mr Paul rushed up to me. "There's a commotion down below. Some of the men are panicking. You'd better come."

He led the way down into the depths of the ship, below the gun-decks and the waterline, where in charge of the prisoners I had put my Redskins and half-breeds. I found them good fellows, surprisingly easy to teach seamanship and civilized ways, but the Johnathans for some reason never became aware of that fact, and lived in great terror of them. This time, however, they seemed to be letting me down. Below decks the ship was full of strange noises, not just the creakings of her timbers in the near-storm, but some of the musical squeakings and groanings one often hears at sea, that some say are the voices of whales. These sounds had an eerie quality I had not heard before, and to add to it all, the voices of my Indians could be heard shouting and chanting.

I should say that White Blanket, though educated on a Mission, knew many old Indian ways, and was regarded as something of a medicine man by his own people and, indeed, many of the hands. Even Robinson found his herbs useful. His most treasured possession was a glass, not any old trader's tumbler, but a very fine Italian glass, which tongue-waggers said he had traded for enough land to make a farm. Now he sat huddled against the ship's side, glass pressed against it and ear to the glass, shuddering, weeping, and speaking fast and loud in his own language: most of the natives and some other hands were crowded round him, trying to make a chant out of his words: from behind the bulkheads where the prisoners were confined during an action, a great gabble arose, apparently to the effect they were afraid of a massacre, if the ship went into battle and looked likely to lose.

I shouted above this din for everyone to be quiet, without much luck. Quohog, who had become White Blanket's special friend, shouted: "Him say glass show him voice of the sea. Him say Jonny Whaler do bad thing to whales, Whale Spirit call to him."

"Nonsense!" I shouted, but White Blanket lowered his glass and replied:

"Listen! Just listen!"

I took the glass gingerly and put it to the oaken side of the frigate. At once I could hear less of the ship's own sounds and more of those from outside. They did have a quality I had not heard before: though they were like the sound of no bird or land animal, I felt I could hear pain, pain and terror. Whether they were really the voices of the harpooned baby whale and its mother I cannot say: but I knew I didn't want any of my men listening to them for longer. I ordered them all to get up on deck and put themselves under Mr Matthew's command on pain of flogging: then stormed up there myself, almost dragging White Blanket.

On the quarterdeck, I found we were very close to the whaleboats. Mr Ahab had been right: several of the big whales had turned back and were blowing at the surface not far from the boats, and the three boats which were not fast to the little one were heading toward them, harpooners ready in their bows. They were some way to port, but the boat fast to the small, white whale was directly ahead. I guessed that most of the crew would feel as I did, that this whaling was an unsporting business, and it would be good for morale to teach them a lesson, so I told the steersman to make straight for the fast boat. The men on it were so caught up in what they were doing they made no effort at evading action till it was too late: the whale-calf dived, and as they paid out the line, they were caught up in our bow-wave and scraped along the ship's side. They shouted and cursed, most un-Quakerish terms, and as they went past our stern, the harpooner, a big swarthy character in a red kerchief, snarled and hurled a harpoon directly at me. At first

I though he could not throw it upward with much force or accuracy; but finding it flying straight at my face, ducked, not like Hector avoiding the spear of Achilles, but like a fool who wound up sprawled on his own deck. The harpoon flew over me, fell to the deck, and then rattled backward, pulled by the line toward the boat. It had wicked barbs, and as I staggered to my feet on the swaying deck, one of these caught fast on the guardrail. I saw the harpooner curse his stupidity and reach for a knife to cut the line, but too late: the boat was already half-flooded, and as it dragged behind *Montgomery*, it was totally swamped, turning over and pitching its crew into the waves.

I had assumed the other boats would come to the rescue, but none did. They were very near to the most forward of the great whales, which I assumed to be the mother. Several harpoons flew, and one of them struck home, in the animal's side, I suppose where the shoulder would be. The mother whale shuddered, dived, then reappeared swimming very rapidly on a course which would cross our wake, where the little white whale had also reappeared. The harpooner hurled a second weapon, which narrowly missed the mother's tail, then did an extraordinary thing. He ducked down into the boat and seemed to be crawling along the bottom, between the oarsmen's legs, and the steersman appeared to be doing the same thing. I exclaimed: "What! Are those fellows totally mad?" Mr Ahab replied:

"No. It is a great tradition of the whale-fishery that the steersman, who is a ship's mate, goes to the front to despatch the beast with a lance, after the harpooner has made fast: the *coup de grace* is delivered by a gentleman."

"Gentleman! Sir, you speak often of these brutes as if they had the cunning minds of men, but I ask you, is it the act of a true gentleman to seek to master a cunning brute by exploiting the one act the creature does which is not at all brutish?"

He said that such tactics were used by the whale-fishers of all nations, to which I could only reply that I now doubted that whales were fish. "They are warm, sir, and seem to have a disposition more like horse or dogs. And a gentleman, sir, would treat them as he treats his horse or his hound!"

He made no reply, nor had the chance to, for at that moment two things happened. The lookout called that he could see the whaling ship, our main target. Behind, something far more remarkable happened. It was as if a sailor had made a model boat, about the size that would fit into a quart bottle, but instead had floated it on a rather rough, grey-green pool. And then a swimmer had crept underneath, and suddenly struck upward with his fist, catching the boat amidships and sending it flying into the air. But what smashed the boat fast to the mother whale was no fist but the head of a great Sperm Whale, moving so fast out of the depths that it leaped the whole of its vast length out of the sea. Vast, I say, because it was at least as big as the finback I had seen, and the whole of its body as white as the finner's jaw; whiter than a dove or an arctic bear. No man has ever seen a sight more remarkable, not only for the size and colour of the beast, but for its actions. Having disposed of one boat, it seemed to twist in the air with the grace of a gymnast, until it saw the next pursuing boat, and toppled itself over in that direction. It fell back into the sea like a Titan from Olympus, making a tidal wave which swept over the boat, and could almost have swamped a man-of-war: I felt it above the remains of the storm-swell at the distance I was.

Mr Ahab had fallen completely silent. He stared spellbound at the place where the White Whale had crashed into the water. Eventually the mighty beast appeared again, close to the last boat. It did not breach again, but beat the water with its tail, and this alone was enough to half-flood the boat.

Meanwhile, we were getting closer to the whaling ship. With four boats out, I knew there would only be a handful of men aboard, and so it proved. She was beating painfully against the wind with a minimum of sail. That left her skipper with a hard choice. He could put about, cram on as much extra sail as his few hands could manage, and try to lose us in the doubtful light, in which case he would have to leave most of his shipmates to the mercy of the seas and the White Whale, or he could surrender. That is what he did.

The Captain's name was Peleg, and he turned out to be a more agreeable fellow than Bildad, perhaps because the ship, the

Pequod, was fresh out of Nantucket without a barrel of oil in her. It was a great relief to be able to replenish my supplies, especially limes and lime juice. Captain Peleg had mixed feelings about what had happened: he knew the White Whale was in the area, and had warned his mates about tangling with it if they could find easier prey. They had lowered the boats without telling him that the whales sung for included a white calf, doubtless, as he put it, more drawn to glory than profit. I told him quite bluntly that if a creature was rare and remarkable, it was sad to lower boats for it for either reason. We beat back in company to the scene of the disaster, where we found all but two of the boatwrecked whalers clinging to wreckage. It did not seem the enraged whales had attacked any of them in the water.

I now had the supplies to patrol for a little longer if I wished, though now very short of men. I decided to take a chance, my lieutenants having gone off on previous prizes, and gave Mr Ahab the opportunity to get the *Pequod* to Halifax. I had felt obliged to apologise to him for doubting his story of the White Whale, and he had accepted that like a gentleman. The only other possibility would have been Fryzer, and I needed him for his skill at gunnery. Nevertheless, I put a squad of marines aboard as well.

No sooner had I despatched Mr Ahab with his new command, than the lookout shouted a sail heading toward us from the south-west. She was an armed three-master, about the size of a corvette, flying an American flag and sailing as close to the wind as possible, thus making just north of east. Her captain had the impudence to signal me to heave to. I gave the order for the guns, which had just been put away, to be run out, and continued tacking slowly northward till he was just in range, at which point I put about and ran before the wind across his bow, giving him a broadside from my twenty-fours. The shot roared and the familiar stink of gunsmoke afflicted me, until the wind swept it away. I saw I had caught him a couple of times at least, but the reply from his bow-chaser fell well short. The American ship was no more than a twenty, and I thought that having satisfied his honour, her captain would now break off: instead he swung round and started to follow me downwind.

This gave me a problem. I could see men swarming on his deck, and clearly his best plan was to board. Short-handed as I was, it was a very good plan, if he could get close enough. For my part, I didn't have the men to fight for another prize and take one home, so I ordered Fryzer to concentrate his men on the twenty-fours. I swung far enough into the wind to give the American one broadside, then around to give him the other. Obviously, he was able to creep up on me, and he did so, till I noticed he was definitely down by the bow. He had taken several hits on the waterline there, and must have sprung quite a leak. He was well within range for his main armament, twelves I assumed, when he swung round and gave me his first broadside. Instead of trading blows to the hull like a drunken prizefighter, he fired at maximum elevation into my rigging. At this he did very well: my mizzen-top was loosened on his first salvo, and the foretopgallant came right down on the second.

I could see his pumpers were losing their battle against the leaks. *Montgomery* was starting to slow, but he would have to make his move to board soon. When my maintop came down, with a shriek from the lookout in the crow's nest I could hear above the guns, I ordered Fryzer to concentrate on the starboard broadside, with all guns firing into the American's rigging. He swung towards me again, on course to board, so close the wind carried the sulphur stench of his gunsmoke to me. We fired repeatedly but only holed his sails. Small-arms crackled from his tops, we were out of musket range but the Americans had their accursed rifle guns. I was about to order grape loaded, when one of our twenty-fours smashed down the whole of his foremast. Next the mainmast went just below the mainsail arm. With two masts hanging over his starboard side like unwanted rudders, the whole ship was pulled round to starboard, listing badly in that direction, and I guessed the water must be almost at the starboard gunports, if not already flooding in there. I imagined his men must be struggling to push the guns up the sloping deck, secure them, and close the ports at the same time, and concluded he had no option but to strike his colours. But that was not his plan: he carried on firing and I had to return, till the water lapped his quarter-deck: then the ship, which by now I could see was the U.S.S. *Egret*, eventually sank without ever surrendering.

Happily, the skipper, Captain Schwalbe, was one of the men we managed to rescue from the heaving green sea. This left me with far more prisoners than crew, half of them fighting men from the *Egret*, a loose mizzen-top and no main or fore tops at all. Luckily, the hull was intact, though the figurehead, a piece by the Irish woodcarver Sexton, which represented Deidre of the Sorrows, had been slightly nicked.

The *Pequod* was still in the area, having waited out the outcome of the action. She carried no guns, and had taken no part in it. Though some of my marines were aboard, it occurred to me that Mr Ahab was a skilled enough seaman to have driven me towards the *Egret*'s boarding parties while appearing to try to help. He had stuck to his word to help but not fight. I therefore signalled him to return.

The wind was dropping, but the sea was still high and grey-green. I could just see patches of clear sky near the horizon, with blue sea beneath them. We had hove to, and were still sur-rounded by wreckage from the *Egret*, spars, chests, barrels, bits of cabin furniture. I was looking closely for any survivors we had missed, when I saw, about a mile to the north, the family of Sperm Whales we had encountered earlier. First the small white one appeared, then the larger grey sperms, and finally the vast, white giant himself. I noticed that the white calf and the grey next to it still had the harpoons in them, and the others formed a ring round them. Through my telescope, I saw the backfins of sharks following the trail of blood, though these did not venture an attack while I was watching.

The main group of whales continued southward, swimming far more slowly than before, apart from the big white one. I saw him surface briefly behind the group, possibly trying to dis-perse the sharks: then he appeared much closer than the others to *Montgomery*. He lifted his head out of the water, spy-hop-ping. He stared at us very intently for what seemed like a long time. I stared back, and for a moment seemed to look right into the eyes of Leviathan. I wondered if such a cunning, ancient creature could have curiosity, and try to assess the dangerousness of ships according to how they looked and acted. After he submerged, I noticed the main group continued along the surface, but altered course slightly, to pass us a good mile to the east, as if they knew the range of our guns. Soon after, they disappeared on one of their longer dives, the giant at a distance from the others, as if he was the protector of the family group, but no longer a full part of it.

By this time the *Pequod* was quite close. I ordered Ahab to come alongside, and called him to my cabin, where I told him he had conducted himself like a British officer, and that I was reclaiming my marines and entrusting him with getting the bulk of my prisoners back to Halifax. I kept only the officers and a few wounded Robinson said could not be moved. Mr Ahab thanked me very politely. He kept the close counsel which was typical of him when not discussing whales or his personal grievances. I hoped this indicated he had matured enough to put his unhappy past behind him, but could not read him in this mood, so as a precaution I remembered that the harpooners from the whalers were counted as petty officers, and I kept them back too. The *Pequod* left under full sail, with a cargo of prisoners, crewed by half-breeds and pressed men: *Montgomery* followed, crewed entirely by men I could rely on. Frankly, I thought it wiser to risk an empty prize than a frigate.

The storm died, and the wind shifted to the southwest. I let it carry me well out to sea before swinging back to Halifax. Twice we spotted topgallants on the horizon which could have been American warships: we didn't try to find out and they didn't see us. After all, there was less of us to see.

We reached Halifax after all of our prizes. All, that is, save the *Pequod*. We commenced the work of repair, and, the war still dragging on, of re-supplying and raising more men. Three rich prizes having come in, this was not so difficult as before.

Admiral Pringle was not so impressed. "You entrusted a prize to a Johnathan, and a damned rum fellow by the sound of it! What do you think he's done? Changed sides, I suppose!"

"I don't think so." I hesitated. "I didn't leave him any

harpooners, but that's a job he could do himself. He knew I
thought of whaling as a sordid trade unbecoming an officer, but
that was something I never convinced him of. To him, it was far
more important to prove himself as a whaler than an officer. I
think he's gone after the White Whale."

"Rum fellow. It's not as if it's the kind of beastie you could
stuff and hang over your mantelpiece! Who'd know he'd caught
it?"

"He'd know." I am not a speculative man, but I added: "It's
an American thing. Discontent with what you have. Always
believing the dream that there's something bigger and better,
over the western horizon."

"Well, you'd better catch him! This war doesn't look like
ending, and the damn Johnathans are giving us a harder time
than twice the number of French could manage. They've almost
won control of the Lakes, and I'm not having them getting their
morale up at sea. Load provisions to get you to the South Seas if
you like, take as many prizes as you like, but get that one back!"

On that second voyage, we sailed much further than on the first,
but took fewer prizes. It was not difficult to raise men. They
had heard the prizes were rich, and that I had taken several.
Quohog was one who sailed with me. He had taken against all
Nantucketers, and promised to find them for me. He was
obsessed with their food: squid. "If you see him 'quid, soon
you see him 'parm whale." But the sea is vast, and life short. A
year passed, and we caught only rumours. They said the White
Whale had been seen in warm waters and cold, in the north and
the south, off the Island of Mocha and in the Straights of Moby.
I was told that all hunted him and that all fled him: that the
Pequod was close behind his flukes, and that Ahab would sail the
world endlessly and never find him.

Hunting one such rumour, I put back into the South Atlantic.
I stopped a British whaler for news, and he told me the war with
America had ended. High time, for our supplies were low and
stank of mould and the crew were muttering for their share of
the few prizes we had taken. A cold wind was blowing out of the
dark south. I crammed on sail and started to run before it.

It was near evening on the second day of peace that the
lookout sang for Sperm Whales, some distance to the north-
west. They were heading rapidly upwind, and my pulse still
quickened at the thought they might be under chase. I did not
alter course, and they passed us well to the west. Someone
called that there was a white whale among them: as usual, it was
on the outskirts of the group, and came a little closer than the
rest. It spy-hopped once, and I was sure from the size it was the
immense one I had seen before, huge and white as an iceberg in
that southern sea. After that, I noticed the whales circling
slightly into our wake, as if they felt we were friends and
wanted to put us between them and the hunters.

By this time a sail had been sighted due north. He was right
on the horizon when the whales were already behind us, beating
slowly into the wind, and I guess losing ground on his prey. I
cannot say what ship that was. Before I could make a definite
identification, he turned into the wind and ran before us. It was
near sundown, and later I lost him in the dark. I cannot say if
that ship was the *Pequod*, and Ahab, facing a choice of Nemesis,
chose discretion; or else some less obsessed whaler, simply
giving up an impossible chase.

I could have kept looking for Ahab as a deserter worthy of
punishment, but by that time I had come to see his obsession as
a curse, and wished him no worse harm.

On the way back to Halifax, I put into Nantucket. There was
no news of Ahab there. And so it continues, though I heard he
did eventually return home, for a while. I kept on hearing
rumours of the White Whale in every port, that it was huger
than an iceberg and twice as dangerous. I met an American
called Reynolds who claimed that Ahab had chased the White
Whale of Mocha till it smashed his boat and snapped off his leg.
Much later, after I retired from the sea, I heard more distant
rumours that, even then, Ahab had continued, that his whole
ship's company had perished in his last battle with the whale,
save for a man called Ishmael Melville, who had written a book
about it.

And that was the story I told to the book dealer in Cambridge,
a former university man, asking if he could get this book about

the White Whale. He scoffed at me, saying he could, and it might be an excellently written tale, but that it was a romance, not a serious work, for the White Whale did not exist.

"Is that so?" I enquired. "And what gave rise to such a sceptical notion?"

"Why, the book isn't really about a whale at all. It's a symbol. It's like the Holy Grail, an unreal thing men seek, only, being Americans, in this romance they have to kill their whale, rather than commune with their Grail."

I declined to buy a book of his poems he tried to sell me.

DAWN'S EARLY LIGHT

Kenneth B. Atkinson

The continued British blockade of the French ports throughout the first decade of the nineteenth century had led to increased tension with the United States whose trade Britain was disrupting. In 1812 matters came to a head and war was declared between the two countries on 18 June. Britain was able to switch many of its forces to combat America because Napoleon had transferred his energies to his disastrous attempt to conquer Russia. The war with America, usually known as the War of 1812, though most action occurred in 1813, was an opportunity for the British to gain revenge for their ignominious defeat forty years earlier. Britain developed grandiose invasion plans, and British forces got as far as capturing and burning the White House in 1814. The following story explores just one incident during the Anglo-American War.

The US Frigate *Invincible* – forty-four guns – rolled in the trough of a running sea. Captain Blades, standing in the shrouds, moved his telescope a point studying an approaching sail, his high-boned face in silhouette against a pitiless blue sky. Aft, his men sweated with a damaged rudder.

It was late afternoon, 10 August, 1813.

Without question the stranger was British, and a man-o'-war. The red-figured ensign snaking from the main truck was the Royal Cross of St George.

Grimly lowering his glass, Blades descended from the rat-lines. In a dozen long strides he was at the taffrail where his sailing master, Hogan, bellowed orders at the seamen in the boats below. Beside him in silent contrast stood Mr Adams, first lieutenant, fresh-faced and twenty-two.

"She's British," said the captain tersely, pointing with his chin toward the cloud of sail.

Eyes met significantly.

Blades glanced toward the boats below. "When will you be done?" He betrayed no illusions. The rudder had been wrenched loose in a squall the night before.

"Another three hours, sir." Under bushy brows Hogan's pale eyes flashed venom. "Let's be fightin' thim black haythens."

Blades shook his head. "We can't even haul anchor. Anyhow, yonder's no frigate. She's a ship of the line, likely seventy guns."

The Irishman glowered, all his people's hate for the British in his wind-bitten face. "An' behould, a true-born Hogan o' Dundalk atwiddlin' his thumbs."

Blades turned, went below, trying to rid his mind of stinking English prisons . . . losing the *Invincible*. Something choked him. He loved this trim cruiser. He could make her give him anything. By the feel of her deck he knew her moods.

In his cabin he turned over a letter in his sinewy duelist's hands. The water flashed blue through the stern windows and he paused. The envelope, containing his orders, was unaddressed. But on the back, pressed in red wax, was the Navy Department's eagle. It was not to be opened till off Halifax, yet a day's sail north. Again he cursed Commodore Jacoby's cautious secrecy.

"We can't take chances," the latter had told him heavily, finger tips together. "No one must know."

He'd talked on . . . sedition in Massachusetts . . . enemy agents, while Blades brooded on the devious minds of politicians turned commodores.

Now, however, floundering before a powerful enemy, the captain felt no scruple in opening his orders – burning them before he was captured.

He winced. From the first the *Invincible* had been a part of him. With his own money he had bought better food for the gun-decks, special sights for the long 24-pounders. To him the war was personal. He was furious when people didn't care whether Americans were pressed in sight of their own shores.

Late sunlight glowed on the seal. He wasn't of a high-flown imagination; yet the possibilities of his orders for an instant brought a fleeting vision, foreign chancelleries, parliaments. . . .

Awed by a daring inspiration he glanced out toward the British man-o'-war. She was nearly within gunshot.

Abruptly he picked up a quill, dipped it and addressed the blank letter.

To His Britannic Majesty's Foreign Secretary.

A touch of humor in his deep-set eyes, he drew the shadings and flourishes affected by diplomatic secretaries. With close scrutiny a sailor's hand, but good enough. He sanded the ink, put the letter in his pocket.

Stooping through the door, he bumped into Michael, the lame, dwarfed cabin boy whom he'd plucked a month before from the Boston constables. The lad's pinched face was pale. "Sir, they're saying that's a British man-o'-war –" His voice faltered, off key.

Blades gripped his shoulder, felt the quivering muscles and recalled his own midshipman days, running orders on bloody decks. He'd grown fond of this youngster who'd hidden on his frigate, chased for a tavern pickpocket. None such aboard, he'd sworn; later offered him the sea – or jail.

"Do you think . . . ?" Michael went on. He had the wizened look of a gnome. "Do you think we'll be taken?"

Blades lowered his voice confidentially. "Not if there's another way."

On deck, he was in time to see the Englishman come about and belch a fluff of white, erased quickly by the wind. A boom; a cannon ball screaming overhead. To larboard spumed water.

"What orders, sir?" asked Adams, running up.

"Dip the colors."

The lieutenant licked his lips. "You mean haul 'em down?"

"Oh no. Half-way down and back again." He looked up at the star-circled ensign, symbol of all he cared about. "And hurry on that rudder."

Furtively his men watched him. Why weren't the drums beating them to quarters? Blades spread his rusty-booted legs, staring calmly over their heads. His blue coat was faded. A battered cocked hat tilted over his intense eyes.

Covertly he knew they called him "Black Dick," not for his strictness, but for a day off Guadeloupe. Face sooted with gun smoke, cutlass slashing, he had led them boarding. He watched the flag dipped.

No response. Blades smiled a little, picturing the quandary aboard the enemy. Presently her beakhead swung. A hail came shouted down wind. "What frigate is that?"

The captain knew how to make his voice like battle bugles, or wheedling with flattery. Now he made it insolent, bawling through a speaking trumpet. "United States Frigate *Invincible*, Captain Blades."

The reply was instant and ominous. "His Majesty's Ship *Sphinx*, Captain Brydges. Do you surrender?"

Tersely, Blades continued with his phantasy. "Diplomatic dispatches for His Majesty's Foreign Secretary."

Again the British seemed mystified. Finally came another short hail. "We're sending a boat."

The captain watched calmly as a long-boat put out, oarblades glinting in the waning sunlight. It swarmed with armed men and his eyebrows bent in surprise at sight of a captain's epaulets in the sternsheets.

Why he came in person was shortly explained by his curiosity and concern. Sword clanking, a saturnine lieutenant at his heels, Captain Brydges clambered to the deck flushed and perspiring. His right sleeve hung empty. Followed twenty redcoated marines to line up along the rail with bayoneted muskets.

In a hundred ports, Blades had seen this florid, gross-mouthed breed. More privilege than intelligence; an appetite for drink and flogging sailors. He saluted, wooden faced. "I regret you felt the need to board us." Blades' tone was silky, slightly injured. "My mission is diplomatic."

Ignoring the salute, the Englishman, arrogant and super-cilious, surveyed the officers, the seamen at attention. His little eyes, peering from twin areas of pouchy flesh, returned to Blades whom he looked up and down with curling lip. But the anxiety which had brought him was apparent.

"There were rumors at Plymouth that you Yankees would be suing for peace. You had letters for all His Majesty's men-of-war, of course. Show me them."

"I have the letter to your foreign minister," said Blades, fists tight knots behind his back. Naturally, this obnoxious captain would expect the United States to apologize for every ship at sea.

"No papers stating your mission?" There was a muddy cruelty in the Briton's eyes, something in his voice like a cat-o'-nine-tails.

"Why should I?" asked Blades, remembering, as if yesterday, a British flogging through the fleet he'd witnessed at Gibraltar – and that same muddy look of cruelty. "I have the dispatch itself."

"Highly irregular," pronounced Brydges through puffy lips, love of forms and formalities in every thread of gold braid. "Let me see it."

Haughty as a Mohawk chieftain, Blades looked the Briton over from his black half-boots and white pantaloons to the royal anchor on his hat. Studiedly deliberate, he took out the envelope.

Brydges snatched it, peered at the inscription, the official seal. "I shall have to open this."

"You shall not."

Blades' tone was flat and deadly, and the Briton's eyes flamed as if an upstart powder monkey had affronted him. They met an agate gaze, fought for supremacy and jerked away. Angrily he tapped the letter on his rolled lapel, brows stormy. He looked toward his own ship, and back.

Perhaps it was Blades' stern self-assurance, perhaps the suspected contents of the letter, diplomatic uncertainties. Brydges waxed more conciliating.

"Possibly you're not lying." He frowned importantly. "But it's all too irregular. My duty to my king and country," he went on smugly, "demands that you accompany me to Halifax, where Admiral Sawyer can decide."

Blades breathed easier. For the moment ship and orders were safe. Now to rid himself of Brydges.

"That will delay you and parley between our governments. We could never keep up with you," he improvised smoothly. "Our rudder's shattered and we're fouled with barnacles."

"I shall have to brook the delay. Do you know anything of this letter? These parlies?" Brydges' china-blue eyes studied Blades shrewdly.

"Nothing."

"Well, you wouldn't tell." The Englishman shrugged his gold epaulets. "Consider your frigate under, ah, detention, and set sail as soon as possible."

Blades burned with humiliation. "I appear to have no choice." He held out his hand for the letter.

Unpleasantly sure of himself Brydges stepped back and put it in his inside pocket. "This," he announced, "I shall keep as hostage of your good behavior."

Raging behind a face stiff as porcelain Richard Blades calculated swiftly. Brydges turned away, paunch bulging into silhouette, and all at once Blades smiled.

"Captain," his flashing teeth courted favor, "don't think us poor losers. We must come if you insist. Meantime, let's forget our differences. I can't sail till I rig a new rudder. You and the lieutenant have dinner with me."

He signaled to a seaman for chairs. "While we're waiting – a bottle of brandy. Some very special *Étoile*."

Alert with suspicion, Brydges mumbled regrets, backing off awkwardly.

"Is the captain afraid?" insinuated Blades.

Trapped, Brydges hesitated. Actually, he'd run little risk, his heavy batteries covering the *Invincible*. Too, enemy commanders usually exchanged courtesies. In the end, perhaps the *Étoile* decided him.

"We shall be pleased," he condescended.

Excusing himself, Blades went below and called Michael. "Were you a good pickpocket?"

At the twinkle in the captain's eye Michael squared his narrow shoulders. "Pretty good, sir."

Blades instructed swiftly – smoke the lantern glasses in the forward cabin. Presently, he was back on deck with a bottle and a case of silver cups.

Half an hour later, mellowed by the spirits, Captain Brydges and his second, Mr Sellers, followed Blades to dinner, where Adams and the sailing master joined them.

The British captain's pudgy hand seemed lost without a brandy glass. They were no more than seated when he lumbered to his feet, liquor slopping on his fingers. "The King!" he gestured belligerently.

Blades stepped hard on Hogan's toe as he heard the latter's sharp breath. "Your *health*, sir," he said courteously, stared the Briton down, and drank.

Dinner progressed. Brydges grew boastful – his mighty ship, his service at Trafalgar. "Nelson gave his life," he pronounced pompously and held up his glass, drank some silent toast. He pointed to his empty sleeve. "I gave this."

" 'Twas gin'rous of ye," said Hogan, brittlely sarcastic. Brydges glared and Blades switched the topic, a little tipsily, "I hear Bonaparte –" he hiccoughed – "He's won again at Lützen."

"That butcher!" sneered Brydges. But under the yellow lantern, swinging slowly, he peered at Blades as if speculating on his knowledge of the Emperor. Mr Sellers, a languid-voiced

fellow with narrow chin and white protruding teeth, mumbled
of Austria's joining the allies.

"Slow but sure is the just revenge of Britain," he repeated,
apparently by formula. Sleepily he blinked.

"Too shlow for Naplo –" Blades struggled with his tongue,
"– for Napoleon."

Hogan twirled his glass by the stem. "Your fine Wellington'll
be runnin' for his life by snowfall."

Brydges, red-faced and coat undone, revealing a corner of the
letter, cursed in angry profusion. Running? He had some of the
Duke's veterans aboard – to lead the invasion of New York. And
he had muskets, munitions.

To Blades the boast seemed too hilarious to be borne. He
threw back his head and his laughter filled the cabin. "Those
redcoats'll be dead within a month."

Brydges choked over his brandy. "Your filthy Yankee militia!
They'll be crushed like reeds – that is if we're still at war," he
added, as if suddenly thinking. But Blades refused to let the
subject drop. Michael limped in with the pudding and he grew
even more boisterous.

"One filthy Yankee," he announced thickly, "can kill a hun-
der-erd filthy Englishmen." His fist banged the table, upsetting
his brandy with a crash.

Cursing, Brydges pushed back from the glinting pool, while
Blades tried to follow Michael's swiftness in the dim light. He
merely saw a flash, a slight twitch of Brydges' coat.

Mumbling about the rudder, Blades rose, leaving Hogan and
Mr Adams to entertain the guests. In his after cabin Michael,
eyes shining, waited with the letter. The captain broke the seal.

He was ordered, Jacoby had written, to cruise off Nova Scotia
– at all cost capture or delay any British ship he thought carried
soldiery or munitions. In a week Captain Tate with the
Independence and two sloops-of-war would follow to take command.

Idiot! To imagine he could know by simply looking which
British vessels bore troops. As for delaying ships-of-the-line . . .

He shrugged, staring unseeingly at Michael. No escaping
Brydges now; he must stop those soldiers and munitions. Few,

but tough as iron, the regulars would be the backbone of a larger Canadian militia. New heart for the enemy, guns to help Ojibway savages burn and scalp along the border, storm down through New York.

Again his eyes returned to the letter, caught a gleam. Swiftly he sought paper, and his pen began to scratch.

Finishing, he put the sheet in the envelope and considered. How to seal the eagle?

A button glinted on his sleeve and he turned it in his fingers. Then he moved with decision. He patched the broken seal and pressed the button deep in the hot smear. A sorry looking bird, but an eagle.

"Michael" – the boy was watching curiously – "can you put this back where you got it?"

"I think so, sir."

"Good. There'll be an opportunity."

Returning, he saw that Brydges had had little chance to think about the letter. Sailing Master Hogan was taunting the guests wickedly with Irish abuse. ". . . and 'tis the lucky haythens ye are," he was jibing as the captain sat down.

Haughtily, the Briton cursed him for a black papist.

Through a long evening glasses lifted, tinkled and were endlessly replenished, though Brydges showed only a spreading net of tiny red lines across his eyeballs.

Blades marveled at his liquid capacity, but when they rose to leave it was no surprise that the Briton stumbled, falling heavily – over his host's foot. Helped up by Mr Adams and the cabin boy he damned the *Invincible*'s rough decks.

The captain saluted blandly as the English officers departed.

The night sky glittered and Captain Blades awaited moonset, an hour after they were under way, before showing that the letter was insufficient security.

Sending all who could be spared below, he ordered Hogan to draw away gradually from the *Sphinx*. He explained the content of his orders, his plan to lure Brydges south toward Tate's squadron. "We mustn't gain on him. I said our bottom's fouled and he'll hope to overtake us."

At times the sailing master overstepped his rank. "How do ye know he'll follow us an' not be headin' straight for the St Lawrence?"

Blades considered him, listening to the *cheep* and whine of the rigging. Properly skilled at navigation, just the right roughness and physique, but with all the ill-judged impertinence of his race. He smiled. "There's bait in that letter Michael slipped back in his pocket when I tripped him after dinner."

"But –" Hogan curbed his curiosity. Saluting, he turned on his heel to direct the helmsman.

Shortly, Blades saw the lights of the *Sphinx* drift slowly off to starboard as they veered from the course. A challenge came bellowed across the water. Where was he going?

Blades lifted his speaking trumpet. "Trouble with the rudder again," he called placatingly.

A pause, an evident consultation. Then: "Get back on the course or we'll put a prize crew aboard."

The captain's lips tightened as he studied the widening gap of dark water. A good broadside could still leave him brokenwinged and sinking. From the *Sphinx* he heard the high call of pipes and his spine crawled cold.

Silently the two vessels rushed on, the *Sphinx* veering south to draw closer, battle lanterns sparking into life. Too slowly the interval increased. As Blades stared against the dark a red flash split the night, followed by a heavy boom and scream of roundshot overhead. Men swore softly.

His voice rang. "Royals! Lights out!"

The darkness was convulsed with dim shapes, thudding feet, and shrilling boat-swain's whistles. Seamen swarmed aloft and loosed the royal sails. Blocks creaked and the great sheets snapped taut.

Overside the water swashed by; silence from the *Sphinx*. Unconsciously Blades braced himself, the frigate creaking slowly to her roll. Then like magic came flame and a stunning crash – shot tearing through the rigging. Broken spars hurtled to the deck. A shriek from the helmsman ended in a gasp and men running.

Beneath the binnacle blood welled darkly. But there was no

time. Blades grabbed the spinning helm and bawled his command.

"Wear full away!"

Safe now to bare the stern. Brydges would need time to reload, couldn't show his starboard guns without losing distance. Blades had his wounded carried to the cockpit – five hit by flying splinters – and took stock. Foretruck gone. Foreroyal and topgallants hanging useless. He had them cut loose. Watching from the taffrail he saw that they were out of range.

About now Brydges would be opening a sealed letter. And the snare within, Richard Blades told himself, was baited well.

Yet he stood long, staring out beyond the phosphorescent wake; later slept brokenly, dreaming of Brydges turning back to send his redcoats wielding bloody scalping knives. But at dawn the *Sphinx* still plowed after them, sails pink in the sun.

A day and a half the chase continued, the *Invincible* now running in contempt or faltering artfully to make Brydges blaze away with his bow chaser, the balls splashing astern.

The second morning sails swam over the horizon. Tate's squadron? A brief scrutiny through his glass and Blades was reassured. Brydges showed no sign of giving up.

The captain faced the wind. From the west.

Two hours later, up to the squadron, Blades, with Adams and the sailing master, watched signal flags break out aloft the *Independence*. Tate, senior officer, was giving his commands.

"Anyhow," observed Blades, "we'll have the weather gauge." Adams looked slightly pale.

The little pennants, daubs of bright color, fluttered upward. *The Invincible to take her place behind the Independence.*

Blades wore around and took his place in the line. Behind came the sloops *Firefly* and *Yellowjacket*. The *Sphinx* was trying to beat to windward, gain the weather gauge herself. "But we can sail closer hauled," Blades' thoughts ran comfortingly. "We'll keep that advantage – offset a little Brydges' 36-pounders." Then Tate signaled again.

At my lead wear to starboard across enemy's course.

"He's wantin' to give Brydges a chance," observed Hogan acidly. "Divil a fine business *this!*"

Blades frowned. "Obey orders! Mr Adams acknowledge that signal."

Inwardly he boiled. Giving up the weather gauge! Tate, he remembered, was a political appointee, his experience in fighting trivial and flimsy. True, Brydges must advance into raking fire, guns idle. But theirs was inferior artillery. Tate would gain a few raking broadsides at the cost of doubling the *Sphinx*'s power to maneuver.

He cursed with a gloomy precision. To windward the ships could lick past the Briton like a scorpion, every barb dealing poison, and curling back repeat the deadly work. If only Bainbridge or Decatur, those artists with the long guns, commanded the *Independence*!

He shrugged, turned to the first lieutenant. "Mr Adams, beat to quarters."

To rattling drums partitions were removed, furniture buried in the hold, hammocks netted atop bulwarks – to stop musket balls. Sand was sprinkled on the decks, gunports lifted, guns unleashed and tompions taken from the muzzles. Aloft they shortened sail, clewed up courses and hung the yards with chains.

To catch splinters they spread a net from mainmast to mizzen. It made a slanting sunlit pattern on the quarter-deck where Blades waited alert and poised to open fire.

Bearing down, the *Sphinx* came frowning, long shadows under bellied-out sails, still beating to windward.

She was but half a mile off, and Tate hadn't yet turned across her course. Blades felt a rush of hope as the flagship ran up new signal flags. But his lips compressed tight as he spelled out the command. *Fire at sails and riggings*. The *Independence* was finally turning, sails squaring.

"Depress your metal," Blades yelled at Adams, choking with exasperation. Tate was leaving the *Sphinx*'s fighting men untouched; trying to cripple the ship herself.

The *Invincible* followed on around and gun crews leaned on their pinch bars, pulled out the quoins to lower the breeches.

Tate's 24-pounders roared and holes dotted the *Sphinx*'s sails, spars disengaged themselves, falling lazily. Adams was at the Captain's elbow. "Shall I fire?" Blades nodded.

Giving up the weather gauge had taken Brydges full of surprise. Before he could come about, bring his batteries to bear, in her turn the *Invincible* was on him.

"Blo-o-o-w your matches," the cry sounded down the decks. "Take off your aprons."

"Fire!"

The frigate jerked with a shattering roar. Through the smoke Blades saw a British yardarm fall, its sail crumpling like paper. "Reload!" his voice was hoarse. "Scrap-iron and chain shot."

Ahead Tate turned south, showing starboard guns and leading the squadron into U-shape. Kicking white spray, the *Sphinx* rushed toward the bend scornful of the sloops. The *Invincible* was quiet, save for screeching blocks, guns rumbling back into battery.

Blades turned to Adams. Unconsciously his hand, on his sword hilt, was jerking out the weapon, slamming it back in its scabbard. "Fire again when she overtakes us."

Her figurehead showed – an armored Mars. Brydges, he knew, would not aim at sails. His shoulders ached with waiting. Fragments of the past came together in his mind; climbing the shrouds on his first man-of-war – the *Philadelphia*, it had later burned at Tripoli – a day of battle on the *Constitution*.

Firing handsomely, the two sloops crossed the Briton's bows and turned, clearing Brydges' guns. But the latter was intent on the frigates which had lost ground maneuvering.

Blades, to ease his nerves, pulled the plugs of wool from his ears, inspected them and put them back. Then the *Sphinx*'s towering sails were opposite, the captain felt a sting of air against his cheek. Flame and smoke leaped toward them with a roar, instantly blotted out, answered, by his own batteries.

The *Invincible* shuddered. Screams rose from hatchways. Searching human targets, the *Sphinx* had fired on the downward roll, her heavy balls smashing into gun ports or through the hull along the water line. Again he cursed Tate. Shooting at sails! At windmills!

Squinting into acrid smoke he called harshly, "Mr Adams! The carpenter! Have him plug those holes."

Adams, boyish face startled, sped away, leaping over corpses.

Forty minutes and a standoff.

Hounds of Triton! How long could they continue? Blades stepped up on a shattered carronade, eyes raking about. Crippled, *Independence* wobbled with a shot through her rudder-post. Burning sullenly, *Firefly* and *Yellowjacket* pillared up black smoke. The *Invincible* was a bloody abattoir – half her batteries out – only hope now her sails, still standing, drawing wind.

But if evil chance had maimed Tate, he'd been incredibly successful in crippling his enemy aloft instead of striking at his men. *Sphinx* had lost her foremast, sky gaped through riddled sails, masts tottered unsupported. Only blazing guns showed the life still in her. Blades stepped down unable to suppress a surge of admiration.

Playing for position now, he needed all the genius of his sailing master.

If the *Sphinx* limped toward the floundering *Independence*, Blades was on her bows to pour in a few round shot, slipping off before the Englishman could come about and fire.

Yet Brydges held the odds.

Sucking on a lemon to assuage his throat, Blades paced the quarter-deck, feverish with holding off the inevitable. Parry as he would Brydges' lunges, the latter grilled him constantly at long range, mercilessly accurate.

Adams came up with a worried face, pantaloons splashed red. "We're making water, sir, despite the pumps. Do you think –?" His voice ended dead and Blades saw his eyes widen.

"Look!" He pointed with a shaking hand. "He's signaling *withdraw*."

The captain turned his haggard face toward the *Independence*. If Tate was giving up . . . He cursed silently, squinting against the smoke. Through the rifts he saw the signal flags. His heart raged.

Withdraw? When he wasn't through with Brydges?

Wheeling, he clamped Adams' arms as if to beat him against

the mast. "You lie! You didn't see any such signal. Do you understand?"

The terrified boy nodded and abruptly Blades was calm, patted Adams on the shoulder. A cold purpose had invaded him. Tate, the fool, had let the British gunners go, ordered him to fire at sails. Very well. His jaw hardened. They'd shoot every stick from that haughty deck.

"Hogan! Quick, man!"

The sailing master hurried forward.

"Close in at once."

Hogan's eyes gleamed.

The air rang with commands, feet pounded the decks.

Under full canvas they headed for the *Sphinx*, slowly wallowing toward the *Independence* with another load of flame and iron. Through the yellow haze she loomed grotesque and stark, foremast gone and shreds of sail flapping.

There would be a short interval of waiting. For a moment in the swirling smoke Blades saw again the yelling Moslems at Tripoli. That was long ago. Woodenly he took another lemon from the box by the mizzenmast, and cut off the end with his dirk.

At their posts, matches flaring, the gunners stood waiting. They had their orders. Gun muzzles looked upward, gorged with star-shell and chain shot. Richard Blades spat out a seed, glanced toward the *Sphinx*. Beneath his feet groaned the pumps.

One could perhaps count to three . . .

From the Briton burst orange flame. The air vibrated, rose to a screaming crescendo and exploded as his own guns roared back. There was a quick wild instant of round shot flinging heads and arms, smoke and shrieks of pain.

But above the *Sphinx* there was another noise, a great cracking, and Americans forgot shattered bodies to cheer as Brydges' mainmast toppled like a falling pine, dragging sails into the sea. Frenzied little dots of figures cut with axes at the wreckage. Then the scene was yellowed out in smoke.

"Starboard the helm!" bawled Blades, eye measuring the Briton's bows for a raking broadside. Remnants of gun crews heaved with sponge and rammer. The helmsman swung the wheel – and the wind shifted again, quartering off the beakhead. Brydges, who had dropped astern, began to come ahead, wreckage now cleared, drawing parallel with the *Invincible*.

Through the smoke, sun filtered on the shredded remnants of the *Sphinx*'s sails. Blades heard a high-pitched command, followed by a blaze of guns, a crash. His mind told him that the ships had fired together, and he felt stinging driven particles like sharp glass against his cheeks – a numb blow in the shoulder.

He was spinning, falling to the deck.

The sanded planks he felt first, then the shocking pain above his armpit. He found he could still curse. The face of a sailor swam overhead. Hands lifted him. Hands pulled a wooden splinter from his shoulder.

Shrilling throats below deck, the lazy roll of the *Invincible*, told him what Brydges' broadside had done.

Lieutenant Adams came running.

"We're sinking!" He gulped. "You're hurt, sir! We can't hold out ten minutes."

"I know, I know, we're sinking. Keep quiet!" Blades wasn't looking at him. Horribly his shoulder ached. But the wind – it was even stronger now – seemed a cooling drug against his face. He was gazing at the *Sphinx*. "Look!"

The enemy's remaining mast, rigging shot away, was tilting, strained by the remnants of sail bellied out by the wind. Tiny figures, like maggots crawling on a skeleton, struggled to furl the tattered canvas. The wind blew harder.

The mast toppled – fell – and the little figures disengaging from the yards waved puny arms falling.

Blades whipped his men to final effort, cast overboard all dismounted cannon. Those they could fire were shifted to larboard. Overbalanced thus the frigate listed sharply, but the gaping holes were lifted above water; pumpmen checked the flood.

This done, Blades came about to occupy position aft the *Sphinx*'s stern. Methodically he pumped shot through her poop windows. Ten minutes and she struck her flag.

*   *   *

Later, the next week, Captain Blades leaned against the rail listening amiably to his sailing master.

Luck, Hogan labeled their recent success. Brydges should have sunk them all.

The captain, his arm in a sling, stared across blue water toward the *Sphinx*, rolling in tow of the *Independence*. He privately agreed.

"Ye were lucky, too," Hogan warmed to his subject, "to have Brydges follow us away from the St Lawrence."

"There was bait," Blades reminded.

"Bait!" Hogan spat to leeward.

"The letter," Blades went on, "introduced me as an emissary to Napoleon, who frightens Englishmen more than you do, my friend. There was reference to American co-operation with France. It was me he wanted when he read that."

"Faith! But it was addressed to the King's minister," objected Hogan.

"So I pointed out in the letter," answered Blades dryly. "I said it was to quell suspicion should we fall into British hands."

THE LAST BATTLE

Walter Wood

*Napoleon's downfall started because of the failure of his
Russian campaign. The Napoleonic War ended with the
Battle of Waterloo in 1815. Napoleon was exiled to St
Helena where he died six years later. Alas, as we have seen
throughout history, when one conflict ends, another is
seldom far away. Yet, the decade following Waterloo
was a surprisingly peaceful one, with few major battles.*

*The last two stories in this book select two specific
examples of subsequent battles to demonstrate the changes
that were ahead. "The Last Battle" concerns the Battle of
Navarino in 1827, which was the last battle between
sailing ships. Since 1821, Greece had been struggling for
independence from the Turkish Empire. She was assisted
by her allies, and the decisive battle came at Navarino
where the combined English, French and Russian fleet
faced the Turko-Egyptian fleet. The following story
was pieced together by Walter Wood (1866–1961) from
his discussion with one of the last survivors of the battle,
Admiral Sir Erasmus Ommanney (1814–1904), nearly*

eighty years after the events. Ommanney is cast as the first person narrator.

"I was a midshipman in the *Albion*," said the Admiral, "one of the British ships of the line at Navarino. The *Albion* was commanded by my uncle, Captain Ommanney, and I was acting as his aide-de-camp. She and the *Genoa* each carried seventy four guns, the *Asia* having eighty four. These were our three line-of-battleships. Then there were the *Dartmouth*, of forty two; the *Talbot*, twenty-eight; the *Rose*, eighteen; and the *Mosquito*, *Brisk* and *Philomel*, of ten guns each, and a tender or cutter called the *Hind*. In all we had a dozen British ships. There were seven French ships, including three of the line, and eight Russian – four line-of-battleships and four frigates. In all the allies had twenty-four ships.

"The enemy, who was known as the Ottoman Force, had a combined fleet of Turkish and Egyptian ships, amongst them being three line-of-battleships, seventeen frigates, thirty corvettes, and twenty-eight brigs, six fire brigs, five schooners, and forty-one transports – a total of 130. They were anchored in the port of Navarino, which was like a bottle, the neck being the entrance.

On the right of the entrance were the castle and batteries, and on the left more batteries and the Isle of Navarino. Besides these land guns, there were the guns of the Turkish and Egyptian ships, which were moored in the form of a crescent. It was a very strong and fine position for the enemy, being the work of a renegade Frenchman, who had been in the French navy. His idea was to leave room enough for the allies to enter the harbour, then to form his complete circle, and having surrounded his enemy to destroy him. There was a perfect semicircle of guns afloat, helped by the batteries ashore, and it was into the arms of this crescent, so to speak, that we sailed on 20 October, 1827.

"The allies entered the harbour in two columns, the British and French forming the weather or starboard line, and the Russians the lee line. The *Asia* led the way, followed by the

Genoa and the *Albion*. The British entered first, the French next, and then the Russians.

"The ships were all in line-of-battle, and presented a most beautiful sight. They were, of course, all under sail, because those were the days before steam was in use in the Navy. Many of the officers present, too, were men who had fought with Nelson. Sir Edward Codrington, our admiral, for instance, commanded the *Orion* at Trafalgar, and was one of the captains under Lord Howe on the "Glorious First of June," 1794.

"It must be borne in mind that the Turkish and Egyptian ships fought at their moorings, with bare masts and yards, and it was simply a case of going in under their very guns, and smashing away broadside to broadside, seeing who could smash the hardest, and which side could first blow the other out of the water. In that respect Navarino was a unique engagement, because by far the most of the old battles with sail were fought when the ships were under way and could be handled. It was because of this confined area of operations, this fighting in fixed positions, and the impossibility of escape for any ship, that Navarino was such a sanguinary struggle.

"In the letter which I sent home two days after the fight, I gave some brief details of what we in the *Albion* did, and they are confirmed by my log. The actual fierce fighting lasted four hours. We had scarcely anchored when it began."

Codrington's orders, it should be said, were that no shot was to be fired unless the enemy fired first; and obeying this instruction the *Asia*, *Genoa*, and *Albion*, with loaded guns and men at their quarters, silently passed up the harbour to the moorings which had been most carefully chosen for them, as well as for the rest of the ships of the allies. These stately ships, indeed, were sailing into what was literally a vast gun-trap, for on the right and left were batteries ashore, and sweeping out ahead was the crescent formed by the warships of the enemy. Both in his batteries and on board his ships the enemy was seen to be on the alert and prepared for battle. The fight actually began with firing on a boat which the *Dartmouth* had sent to one of the fire vessels, and so smart was the discharge of musketry that the lieutenant and several of the boat's crew were killed or wounded. That was the signal for action, and instantly a furious struggle was in progress.

"The battle opened with this firing at the *Dartmouth*," continued the Admiral, "and immediately the signal was made to engage the enemy. The *Albion* was attacked by two sail of the line and a frigate; but in about a couple of minutes we had forced the frigate to surrender, and she was on fire. It was a sudden change from perfect quietness to deafening uproar, for there had seemed every likelihood of the enemy striking without coming to blows.

"As soon as we got into the harbour we anchored, and had just manned the rigging to furl sails when we were fired upon. "Down, men, to your guns!" came the order, and the men tumbled below from aloft as we drifted towards the frigate, which was a double-banked Turkish ship.

"We got so closely locked together with the Turk as to make it possible to board her. The first lieutenant and the first division of boarders scrambled on to her, and soon mastered her. But they were forced to hurry back to the *Albion*, as the frigate was found to be on fire.

"In spite, however, of their natural hurry to get clear of a ship that might blow up at any moment, three of the *Albion*'s men ran up the fore-rigging, made a dash at the top, where some Turks were stationed, and seizing two of them hurled them headlong overboard.

"There were many other daring acts and displays of courage. An Irishman seized a musket, and with a roar of 'Make way there!' he swept a road through the Turks by swinging his weapon from side to side with crushing force. One of my fellow-midshipmen, named Hicks, was amongst the boarders, many of whom had forgotten to take their pistols. Hicks shouted to the first lieutenant, 'Give them cold shot, sir!' and the boarders did, for they picked up the cold shot which was lying about ready for the guns, and hurled it down upon the Turks.

"Another midshipman, named Langtrey, slashed at a slackened cable of the frigate with an axe that Boteler handed to him from the wardroom windows, at the same time encouraging him to persevere. And Langtrey did persevere, too, although he was working in one of the cutters, which was swamped and flush with the water.

"Langtrey stuck gamely to his work until the cable nearly parted and he was almost exhausted. The danger and pluck of the achievement will be best understood when it is stated that the frigate was burning fiercely and was expected to blow up every second. As a matter of fact she exploded with a terrible crash and blaze when the *Albion* was only about 100 yards away.

"Curiously enough, the gunners of the *Albion* felt no immediate ill-effects from the explosion; but below the case was very different. There the concussion of the disaster was so great that the gunner, who was in the magazine, thought it was his own ship which was destroyed, and he and his men rushed out, but had the presence of mind to lock the door.

"As it was, the *Albion* had a wonderful escape, for adjoining the magazine was a room in which three lamps were burning, so that the men who were filling powder could see what they were doing. The explosion shook two of the panes of glass out of their sashes, but, most luckily, the panes were not on the magazine side, or the powder dust would have been ignited and the *Albion* would have been blown to fragments.

"It is astonishing, indeed, how many and narrow were the *Albion*'s escapes. On two occasions she was on fire, and each time the firemen were called to extinguish the flames. One of the most zealous of the firemen was the chaplain, who, although he was himself wounded, rushed up from the gloomy cockpit when he heard the alarm, and, in addition to bearing a hand with the flames, shared in the boarding, and varied his attentions to the dying and wounded by fighting.

"The danger did not come solely from the enemy, either, for Boteler made an awful discovery while moving about at his quarters and ordering the men to fire at certain ships. The *Albion* by that time was thick with a choking yellow smoke, which was highly inflammable. On approaching his cabin he found that one of the men, a silly, stupid fellow, had taken down a valuable fowling-piece from a hook in the beam overhead. The fellow was squatting down, and actually snapping the flint-lock of the weapon over some loose powder which was scattered on

the deck! Boteler naturally kicked him away, and the captain of
the gun near, seeing what had happened, gave him a stunning
box on the ear as he got on his legs, while the second captain
followed the blow up with another that nearly floored the man
again.

"The cannonade was soon heavy and furious, and those being
the days of very smoky powder, the air became so thick that we
seldom saw beyond the length of the ship – about 200 feet –
while often enough it was impossible to distinguish friend from
foe.

"For a full hour and a half the *Albion* was very hotly engaged;
then the French flagship, *La Syrène*, of sixty guns, came up and
took the fire off us.

"By this time we were in the very thick of the battle, and there
were many grand but awful spectacles. I was, of course, a very
little fellow at the time, but I saw the fight from start to finish
and witnessed pretty nearly everything that went on in and
about the *Albion*.

"Soon after the blowing up of the frigate we had boarded and
cut adrift, Boteler ran on deck for a moment to try to get a
general view of the fight. He shook hands with the captain, who
was frowning, and shaking his head, and touching his nose,
where one or two drops of blood were falling.

"Then, there was Commander Campbell; he fought with a
bloodstained stained handkerchief bound round his head, but
not much hurt; and last, as also least, my own small self, my
hands on my knees, looking with straining eyes through the
spare quarter-deck port.

"I must pause for a minute to tell of an incident that
happened on board, showing how the old school of British tars
behaved, and how sportsmanlike they were, even in the heat of
battle.

"At Boteler's quarters there was a squabble amongst the
powder-boys, who were waiting for powder to take to the guns.
Boteler demanded to know what the row was about, and the
answer was that a big lad, named Knight, was getting all the
powder.

"Knight was certainly greedy, for he had three cartridges in his box, and so Boteler pulled his ear and told him to be off. Then Boteler had to go away, but on coming back two minutes later he found Knight and another boy fighting, and most of the men of the crews of two guns standing round and encouraging them! They were even more interested in the fight between the powderboys than with the Turks for the time being. Boteler turned to the captain of one of the guns, and angrily asked him what he could be about to abandon his weapon at a time like that?

"The man replied: 'Beg your pardon, sir; but we couldn't help it!' and with that they went back to their guns willingly enough.

"When the French flagship came up and took the fire off us, matters became easier so far as the *Albion* was concerned, but the worst of the battle was by no means over. We were yet to witness its most terrible features. The ships were suffering greatly, and the surgeons were busy in the cockpits with the wounded, while the dead on board the ships of the line were numerous.

"The *Genoa* in this respect was the heaviest loser. Amongst her twenty-six killed was her brave captain, Bathurst, who was Commodore of the Fleet. He was wounded early in the action by a splinter, which struck off his hat. Then a shot carried away the tails of his coat, and a third came which mortally wounded him. It passed not only through his body, but also through the bulwarks near him.

"The Commodore lived until next morning, having received the personal thanks of the Admiral for his gallant conduct. Bathurst was a noble and unselfish fellow, and his last words were inquiries about his own wounded officers. His body was brought to England and buried at Plymouth with full honours two days after Christmas."

The *Asia*, too, was having a life-and-death encounter with the Infidels, who neither gave nor took quarter, and who perished rather than surrender. The sullen Turk refused to yield on any terms, and when the worst came to the worst he either blew up his ship and died with her, or escaped to the shore. Codrington had placed the *Asia* alongside the ship of the

Capitana Bey, the Turkish Commander-in-Chief, and the *Asia* was even nearer to the flagship of the Egyptian Commander-in-Chief.

The *Asia* set herself deliberately to destroy her great and imposing enemies, and pounding steadily at them with all the zeal and skill of the gunners, she smashed the Turk on her right and the Egyptian on her left. Codrington's gunners worked, as he himself said, and he knew well what gunnery was, with a "precision which looked like mere exercise," and so devastating was the fire upon the Turkish flagship in particular, that she looked as if her sides had been tasted by the adze.

The Turkish Admiral fought with all the fatalistic valour of the Infidel, and fought until his ship was a veritable shambles, for when at last she was driven away from the *Asia*'s side, no fewer than 650 of her crew of 850 had been killed. It was impossible to see whether she surrendered, for her masts had been shot away, and Codrington could not even send a boat, because these little craft were so badly damaged by shot and bullet that not one of them would float.

So this furious, bloody, and destructive fight in a confined area, between ships which were anchored in one spot, and forts bellowing thunder, continued for four hours. The water was discoloured with blood, the air was dense with battle-smoke, and the crashing of the guns was ceaseless. There were the piercing cries of the combatants and the reverberation of the artillery in the neighbouring hills. The water, too, was strewn with wreckage and the slain, while to every spar and shattered boats men were clinging, making a last despairing fight for life.

Most terrible of all the struggles to witness were those of Greek slaves, who, still shackled, had somehow managed to escape from the ships in which they were cruelly held prisoners. No mercy had been shown to these hapless wretches by their conquerors and captors, and while ashore the Greeks were homeless and starving – some were actually feeding on boiled grass – matters afloat were infinitely worse, for the slaves could not even attempt to escape from certain and appalling death. Of those who were blown skywards or into the water, many were helplessly manacled to floating wreckage.

"We saved no fewer than fifty of these poor slaves, and took them on board the *Albion*," said Admiral Ommanney. "We saved others, too – amongst them, I remember, was the secretary, or some such official of the Turkish admiral, whose arm was badly injured. The arm was amputated, and my uncle took the Turk to Malta in his cabin.

"As I have said, the *Albion* was very hotly engaged for an hour and a half, but the heavy firing went on until about five o'clock in the afternoon. The battle, however, did not really finish until midnight. The crews were utterly exhausted by their labours during the fight and the work of preparation which preceded it, and it was only with the greatest difficulty that they were kept from sleeping at their guns. They remained at their quarters, ready instantly to renew the battle, although, as a matter of fact, the firing had been so severe and continuous that the fleet had run short of powder and shot.

"When the lull in the firing came, we were faced with another danger – one which was always present in the old days of wooden fighting ships, and that was the danger of fire. In this case it arose chiefly from the floating ships, which were blazing, helpless hulks, drifting where the tide carried them, and ready to set in flames anything with which they came in contact. The danger, of course, was intensified by the narrow area of battle, and was infinitely greater in the confined harbour in which we fought than would have been the case in open water. For a long time after our victory was assured these wandering masses of fire were a source of intense anxiety to us; but, as it happened, we kept free of any very serious calamity.

"The battle was full of strange and striking incidents, and many of these I witnessed personally in or from the *Albion*. We, like the other ships, had on board Greek pilots, who were stationed on the poop, and one of the most interesting features of the battle was to watch them potting at the Turks. Whenever they saw a chance of hitting a Turk they let fly at him.

"I saw a very strange thing in the *Albion* during the fight. We had a captain of marines, called Stevens, who had always a conviction that he would be killed in action. So strong was this premonition that he shook hands with Boteler on the poop, and said farewell to him, at the same time begging him to see that his few personal belongings should be sent to Canterbury, where both were then living.

"Strangely enough, poor Stevens' fear was realised, for he was cut in two by a shot which also carried away one of his hands. The hand was picked up by a young marine, who put it in his forage cap and then replaced the cap on his head, so that he could keep his relic safe until the action ended. When the fight ceased the marine went to Lieutenant Anderson, produced the hand, and holding it up by the finger, asked what he should do with it. The answer was, of course, stern and prompt – the ghastly relic had to go overboard, where the body of the officer had gone as soon as he was killed.

"The finest and most terrible sight I ever witnessed was the blowing up of the Turkish ships during and after the battle. Ship after ship was destroyed, mostly by the Turks themselves, so that they should not fall into our hands, and having blown them up the Turks tried to escape either by swimming or rowing ashore. Some of them succeeded, and could be seen crawling up the rocky cliffs of old Navarino. It was not the custom of the Turks to strike their colours in action, but when the worst came to the worst they deserted their ships and swam ashore, when, of course, they got the chance.

"The Turks carried no surgeons in their ships, and the wounded were simply left to die. Many helpless men were abandoned in the ships which were foundering and exploding. The Greeks were used as galley slaves, not kept as prisoners of war, and many of them were deliberately deserted, in company with the dead and dying, before the whole were blown up together. Of these poor slaves many, happily, were saved by other ships as well as the *Albion*, and as soon as they were got on board their fetters were knocked off and they were free.

"In the morning after the battle I went on board one of the Turkish ships with Boteler. It was a most shocking sight. There were dead bodies all about, and the stench was so overpowering that I could hardly stay below. Boy-like, I looked about me to see if there were anything worth taking, but there was not, for the Turks had broken everything, as if with the deliberate intention of preventing us from getting their belongings. The ship, a corvette, was quite deserted, only one man having any life in him, and he was half dead.

"Bad as this spectacle was, Boteler told me it was nothing to be compared with the Turkish admiral's ship, which he afterwards boarded. This ship was foul of another, and each had only one mast standing, besides being a pitiful wreck. These two ships between them had more than 1000 men killed and wounded. Boteler and his people got some trophies from them, including a gorgeous hanging compass of crimson and gold and many colours from the admiral's cabin. The Turks bowed and *salaamed* to this compass as Lieutenant Anderson carried it across the deck to the barge which was alongside."

Amongst the brilliant acts of that memorable day there was none more daring and courageous than the conduct of the cutter *Hind*, of 160 tons, which was tender to the *Asia*.

She was commanded by Lieutenant John Robb, who had a crew of thirty, and mounted eight light carronades. She became entangled with a large Turkish frigate, and the Turks repeatedly tried to board her. She defended herself in the most valiant fashion, and even the surgeon, who was getting ready for an amputation, dashed up from below on hearing the call: "All hands repel boarders!"

The Turks at last, in savage desperation, manned a large boat, and it seemed as if the doom of the *Hind* were assured; but two carronades, loaded to the muzzle with grape and canister, utterly destroyed both boat and Turks. The *Hind* lost half her crew in killed and wounded, and so great was the glory with which she covered herself that she won the proud name of "His Majesty's line-of-battle cutter."

Codrington, the admiral, seemed to bear a charmed life. His escapes from death were marvellous. So that he might command a good view of the battle, he stood on the poop of the *Asia*, the most exposed part of the ship. He was talking with the master, when a shot came and killed the latter at his side. A shot killed an officer of marines who was on the quarter-deck, just below the poop. The admiral left the poop only once, to go forward to talk to the boatswain, and, while talking to him, the boatswain also was killed at his side. A bullet went through his hat, in which it made two holes, and another bullet went through his loose coat-sleeve. Another bullet smashed his gold watch. When on the poop he stooped his head under a rolled awning, and, while bent like that, a shot passed through the awning's folds. At another time, he had just turned from a spot on the poop when the place where he had been standing was covered with wreckage from aloft, which would have crushed and buried him. And yet, throughout the battle, when men were being slain and wounded everywhere around him, Codrington escaped uninjured!

One of the most famous and amazing stories of this great and lurid battle was that the bitterness which still prevailed between the French and the Russians, owing to the prolonged Napoleonic wars, led to deliberate mutual attacks, although nominally the two nations were friendly allies. It must not be forgotten that only fifteen years had elapsed since Napoleon had tried to sack Moscow and destroy the power of Russia, and that Navarino was fought only a dozen years after Waterloo and twenty-two after Trafalgar.

In the whole of naval history there is no more striking instance of strange bedfellows than this of Navarino, for here, joined together against a common enemy, were British, French and Russians. Only a few years later there was to be another change of allies – in the Crimea, when British and French were banded together to fight the Russians, and, stranger still, the Turks, who had been the enemy of the combined three, had thrown in their lot with the Saxons and the Latins against the Slav.

The story then was told, and widely credited, that instead of uniting their efforts for the downfall of the common foe, the French and Russians actually turned their guns upon each other during the fight and did a great deal of mutual mischief. I questioned Admiral Ommanney particularly on this point, and he replied: "I think the proper explanation of the story will be found in the fact that the battle-smoke was so dense, enveloping everything like a thick white fog, that it was impossible to distinguish friend from foe, and at times some of the ships of the allies fired into each other because they could not help it."

As a matter of fact, the *Albion* herself fired into the French ship *Breslau*, and the French returned the compliment with energy. When the fight was over some of the *Albion*'s shot was found sticking in the *Breslau*'s foremast, and Boteler was told by one of the French officers that they thought some of the shot came from the *Albion*. Certainly the *Breslau*'s attention gained for her the friendly name of the *Albion*'s "chum."

The victorious fleets left Navarino on 25 October and reached Malta on 3 November. The getting to sea was a period of intense anxiety, for the ships were crippled and were actually becalmed between the threatening batteries, which were still manned by the merciless Turks. But the seamen were standing grimly at their guns, and the Infidels did not fire at the bluff broad-sides which had already wrought such havoc.

The conquering ships, with the help of all the boats which could be spared, slowly and majestically got clear of the harbour and sailed into a night of heavy rains and squalls, with a contrary wind, accompanied by thunder and lightning – an elemental paean on the downfall of the Infidel and the triumph of the Christian in the Bay of Navarino.

THE STOLEN COMMAND

Walter Jon Williams

Time marches on. This final story is set during the American Civil War when the ironclad steam ships were appearing. In 1862 the North launched a riverine offensive to seize control of the Mississippi and cut the Confederacy in two.

Walter Jon Williams (b. 1953) wrote a series of books, starting with The Privateer *(1981), set during the American Revolution and the War of 1812 following the exploits of the Markham family. Since then he has concentrated successfully on science fiction, and this story marks a welcome return to his nautical work.*

1

Jase Miller first saw the iron monster in its improvised drydock off the Yazoo. The huge creature had her nose into the land and showed her armored backside to the river. Her twin stacks and rust-red casemate loomed above the flat Old River country like a visitation from another world. Laboring blacks swarmed over the thing like ants. Even over the sound of the *General Bee*'s engine, Jase could hear the ring of hammers on railroad iron.

"There she lies," he thought, "and I am going to have her or get hung."

"Not as big as I thought," said Ensign Harry Klee, who had seen *Louisiana* before she burned.

"Big enough," said Jase, and wondered again how he would steal her. By indirections find directions out, he thought.

He signaled the engine room for ahead slow, then tapped the bell twice to send a leadsman to the bow for soundings. *General Bee* dropped off its bow wave, slowed in the murky water. Shoreward, a cottonmouth moccasin bared its fangs from the safety of an oak limb.

Strange country, Jase thought. He was a salt-water sailor, and unused to the ways of rivers. The meandering Yazoo country was simultaneously open and constricted – absolutely flat, though with all its sight lines hemmed in by dense hardwood forests. Cypress, willows, cottonwoods, all thirsty trees that clung to the banks of the river. Everything that stood was strung with vines. There were alligators here, and snakes; herons and cormorants flocked in thousands.

And it was hot. Hot as a boiler room. Jase yearned for a sea breeze.

"By the mark three!" sang the leadsman. "Half less three! By the mark twain!"

Jase maneuvered the tug toward the bank, signaled astern slow, and brought the *Bee* gently to ground on Yazoo mud. The levee began to fill with curious bystanders.

Ensign Klee's huge body almost blocked the pilothouse window. "Any of them look like much a senator to you, Jase?" he said.

Jase peered around Klee. "May be the fellow in the top hat."

Harry Klee squinted and spat. "He looks more like an undertaker."

"Guess I'll go ashore and find out."

Jase rolled down his shirt sleeves and put on his grey uniform jacket – visiting a former senator required a degree of formality – then he adjusted his straw boater and made his way past the 30-pound Parrott rifle on the foredeck. Once there, he discovered that the mechanism for lowering the gangway had jammed.

"Sorry, sir," said Castor, one of the twins, in his Cockney accent. "I'll 'ave it fixed in a tick."

Jase looked at the group of people standing on the levee and felt his temper rise. He decided he was not about to stand and be gawked at while he waited for the gangway to be repaired, so he dropped off the bow and waded to the land, wet above the knee. The Yazoo mud took one of his boots, which did not improve his temper. He splashed ashore and mounted the 4-foot-high levee in one stride.

"Senator Pendergas?" he asked the fellow in the top hat.

The man shook his head. "That's the general there," he said, "coming this way."

The senator – now a general – was a broad, round-headed man in shirt sleeves, striped uniform pants held across his big belly by red suspenders. His shirt front was stained with tobacco. When Jase saluted him, Pendergas held out one big hand and waited for Jase to shake it. Jase did as the man seemed to want.

"Lieutenant Jase Miller, C.S.N., commanding the *General Bee*," Jase said.

"Glad to meet you," Pendergas said, for all the world as if Jase was a constituent.

"Let me have men about me that are fat," Jase thought, "Sleek-headed men and such as sleep o' nights." And felt inwardly pleased.

"You got any engineers?" The senator asked. "I'm having problems with my engines."

"I've got navy engineers," Jase said. Because Pendergas was army, and so was his boat apparently. And on account of the first point, Jase aimed to change the second.

Pendergas looked at him with little eyes half-hidden by lids of fat. "We can work something out, I reckon."

"I am ordered to co-operate with you, sir."

Pendergas spat tobacco onto the grass. "Well, that's good.

Because you and me, that's all the South has to defend Vicksburg."

Which was, Jase reflected, sadly true. A few months ago Flag Officer Davis had taken Memphis with his Yankee river squadron. Farragut had captured New Orleans with his salt-water flotilla, then steamed up the Mississippi, right past Vicksburg's batteries, to join Davis north of the city. With the two Yankee fleets united, it was clear that Vicksburg was next on their agenda, and the South didn't have much to stop them.

Pendergas looked down at Jase's stocking foot. "Ain't the Navy issuing full sets of boots these days?"

"The Navy issued the full set," Jase said, "but nobody told me the Yazoo River was planning on collecting a toll."

Pendergas curled a lip at this sorry example of wit. "Let's hope the Yankees don't get the other," he said. "And your boat with it."

There was a rushing sound as the *Bee* blew steam. Pendergas' little eyes almost disappeared into his fleshy face as he looked at the *General Bee*.

"What kind of boat has the navy given me, Jase?"

Chill mirth crept round Jase's brain. So Pendergas thought the navy had given him a boat, did he? They would see whose boat would be given to whom.

"Armed tugboat, sir, escaped from New Orleans before it fell," he said. "We carry a 30-pound Parrott bow chaser, a 20-pound Parrott aft, and a 24-pound smoothbore on each broadside."

Pendergas' lip curled again. "And no more armor than a country whorehouse," he said.

"Oh, a little more than that," Jase said. He had built waist-high log structures around the cannon to protect the gunners, and stacked bales of cotton around the pilot house, the boiler, and wherever else he thought it might do any good, but there wasn't much else that could be done. The *Bee* had been built as a tugboat, taken into the navy because the navy had no other vessels, and then named after a man who had been dead since First Manassas. None of these omens seemed particularly auspicious.

"Well," Pendergas said, "come and look at *Arcola*, and I'll show you the boat the army's going to use to clean Farragut off the river." He turned toward the rust-red monster he was building in his cotton field, and raised his voice. "Argus! Argus McBride!"

Limping on his one stocking foot, Jase followed the senator toward the drydock. McBride turned out to be an old man, with a shock of white hair and a handshake dry as sand.

"Formerly of the New Orleans, Galveston, and Great Northern Railroad," Pendergas said proudly. "He's rebuilding *Arcola* for me."

Argus looked at Jase skeptically. "You wouldn't know anything about triple-expansion marine engines, would you?"

"I'm your man," said Jase.

The senator clapped Jase on the shoulder. "Good boy! I knew we could use you!"

"If you like, I will send for my chief," Jase said, "and we'll look at the engines together."

While they waited for Chief Tyrus to come from *General Bee*, Pendergas and Argus proudly showed them over the armored ram they were building on the Yazoo.

Arcola had started life as the *Mingo*, one of the Ellet rams that had sunk the entire Confederate River Defense Fleet in about ten minutes during the Battle of Memphis a few months ago. A few days after the battle, *Mingo* had blown its boiler while on patrol, drifted down the Mississippi, and come aground on a sand bar, where it was captured by a corporal's guard that rowed over from shore. "*My* corporal's guard!" Pendergas bellowed in amusement, and jabbed Jase in the ribs with an elbow.

President Jefferson Davis, who had served Mississippi in the Senate alongside Pendergas, had obliged his colleague at the war's start with a brigadier's commission. But – possibly because Senate experience had given the President a good notion of Pendergas' capabilities – Pendergas had never actually been given the opportunity to command a combat unit. Until his corporal's guard rowed out to the sandbar to demand *Mingo*'s surrender, Pendergas' sole war experience had been to raise regiments and supplies in safe rear areas, which he shipped off north to the fighting army.

Pendergas knew an opportunity when he saw it. He hauled *Mingo* off the sand and hid her up the Yazoo, on one of his plantations. His slaves dug day and night to build a drydock here in his cotton field while he assembled the men and equipment necessary to turn his captured Yankee boat into a monster that would devour the republic that gave it birth.

Argus showed Jase the foot-thick wooden bulkheads that ran the length of the boat, to strengthen it for ramming, and the bows packed with timber to increase the power of the blow. The two triple-expansion engines, driving screw propellers, were braced for the shock of ramming and were able to drive the *Mingo* at 15 knots.

The Yankee *Mingo*, built purely as a ram, carried no armor or guns, but Argus had changed that. He had covered the ram with a 2-foot-thick casemate of oak, angled like a pitched roof, so that shot would bounce off, and then plated the oak with two layers of railroad iron, the rails ingeniously rolled and slotted, riveted and spiked and racked together to present a smooth rust-red surface impenetrable to enemy shot. A pilothouse had been built atop the casemate forward, steel bars stacked like the logs of a frontier cabin and welded into a roughly pyramidal shape, with an open top.

Bellona's bridegroom lapp'd in proof, Jase thought.

While building his ram the senator had also been scavenging guns. A massive 10-inch Dahlgren smoothbore was to be mounted forward, pivoting on tracks so that it could fire from forward, port, or starboard gunports. A 7-inch Brooke rifle was to be similarly mounted in the stern. Each broadside consisted of three bottle-shaped 32-pound smoothbore cannon, making six altogether. Rather than being placed opposite each other on each broadside, the guns were staggered down the length of the narrow ram, to allow each big gun room for recoil.

Jase wondered if either Argus or Pendergas realized how much the iron and guns would degrade the ram's performance. They wouldn't be getting 15 knots out of this boat ever again. They'd be lucky to see half that.

And they didn't seem to know anything about ballast, either. All that iron topside was going to make the ram roll like a drunken whore unless they stowed more weight below the waterline.

Still, it would be a good boat, more than a match for anything the Yankees had in the water. Jase's mouth watered at the thought of commanding her.

"We can't seem to get the carriages right," Argus said. "That's why the guns ain't in her. None of us have ever made gun carriages before."

"My men can help you with that," Jase said.

"I'm gonna knock Farragut's flagship to splinters," Pendergas said, "see if I don't."

Jase kept silent on this point. He had plans of his own.

2

Jase and his officers, Harry Klee and Chief Tyrus, were invited to the big house for supper. Jase always enjoyed the sight of Klee's huge body stuffed into a dress uniform, the cannonball-shaped head glowering from beneath a cocked hat while his thick neck bulged out from around the collar and neckcloth.

The Senator's plantation house was a quarter-mile inland through cotton fields. Long Shanks – which Jase imagined was Longchamps creatively spelled by its owner – was a big place of raw red brick and cypress wood. It was too new to have acquired the white plaster and stately pillared portico that would eventually turn it into a miniature Greek temple somehow misplaced in the bogs of Mississippi. Folks hereabouts even hired artists from Europe to paint false grain on their cypress wood to make it look like a less common brand of timber.

Jase thought it was pretty odd what rich people spent their money on, but he watched the rich carefully when he could. He aimed to be rich himself, and he wanted to learn their ways.

Mrs Pendergas was as stout as her husband and chewed at least as much tobacco, spitting with casual accuracy into a silver ladies' spittoon designed so as not to get tobacco juice on her skirts. Jase bowed over her hand when he was introduced – on one fat finger there was a diamond the size of a robin's egg – and when he straightened he saw a fat crab louse sitting on Mrs

Pendergas' head. The louse eyed him with the same suspicion that the senator's lady was displaying at just that moment.

Jase promised himself he would find reason not to accept any offer to lodge at Long Shanks. At least he knew his own boat was clean of vermin.

Interesting, Jase thought, these Mississippi gentry. Out east, in the Carolina tidewater where Jase had been raised, the planters made a display of their manners and elegance and breeding, but Mississippi had been raw frontier just a generation ago, nothing but swamp and cypress, and the folks who lived here were still people of the frontier. Very little on the Yazoo had been papered over – neither the plantation houses nor the people had gained a veneer of elegance, and life was still lived in the raw. Ambition was for masters, submission for slaves, and sheer violence was the means to wealth.

They had come out West to get rich, these people. Jase figured it was something he and the planters had in common.

Accompanying them was one of Pendergas' aides, a young soft-spoken artillery lieutenant that the Senator introduced, with a twinkle in his eye, as "Euphemism." There was obviously a story behind this, one that Euphemism thought a good deal less funny that Pendergas, but the young lieutenant was so quiet and retiring that Jase thought it better not to ask.

The Pendergas' kept a good cook, though. Navy vittles had sharpened Jase's appetite for the real thing, and he tucked into the pickled oysters, goose, beefsteak, and fresh greens with a will, and washed it down with the senator's French champagne. The dinner conversation focused on the war, and on the senator's opinions of the various commanders, none of which were favorable.

The meal ended. "Where are you getting crew?" Jase asked, as he accepted one of the senator's cigars and strolled to the drawing room.

"Called for volunteers among artillery batteries," Pendergas said. "Got sixty gunners that way. Got the beginnings of an engine room crew from the railroads and some unemployed steamboat men." He lit a lucifer match and paused with his cigar half-raised to his lips. "We'll fill up the crew with field hands. Servants."

The senator puffed his cigar alight while Jase exchanged glances with Harry Klee. "You're using slaves to fill up your crew?" Harry asked.

"Servants," Pendergas nodded, using the euphemism common among planters. "The niggers can haul ropes and shovel coal as well as anyone." He saw the dubious look on Harry's face and tried to reassure him. "It'll be white men who steer the boat and point the guns, don't worry."

And old trick, Jase knew, to make money. Some planters had tried it in the Old Navy – they put their slaves on board as crew, and while the slaves worked, the owners pocketed the slaves' pay for themselves. The practice wasn't common, because most navy captains refused outright to enroll slaves, but some captains with Southern sympathies had permitted the practice.

But even the most fire-eating Southern captain, no matter how colossal his greed, had ever for an instant considered putting sixty or eighty slaves on his warship. The idea was sheer lunacy.

Harry Klee's thick neck swelled inside his collar. "But, General Pendergas," he said, "slaves – servants – they won't fight for you. Not like free men."

The senator gave Klee a complacent look. "They'll do what I tell 'em. They always do." His diamond stickpin glittered in the lantern light. "They'll all tell you, Boss Pendergas is a fair man. The whip and the branding iron only for those who deserve it, apple jack on Sundays, and I keep my drivers away from their women. Everybody works hard at Long Shanks, but nobody works harder than me." He nodded. "So they'll fight for me, I reckon. They know what's good for me is good for them."

"But sir –" Harry was about to continue his protest, but Jase caught his eye and gave a slight shake of the head.

The last thing he wanted was to keep Pendergas clear of disaster.

Jase looked at the senator. "Well, how you make up your crew is your business," he said. "But what your gun crews'll need is training, and my boys from the *Bee*'ll be happy to provide it."

"Thankee," Pendergas said.

"In fact, once your men get to know the ropes a little, we might have some competition between your men and mine."

A red reflection glowed briefly in the senator's eyes as he drew at his cigar. "Perhaps a little wager on the outcome?" he suggested.

Jase smiled. "I think the navy would be happy to bet on a sure thing," he said.

"A sure thing?" Pendergas seemed amused. "You figure your little boat's able to give my boys a challenge?

"I'm counting on it," Jase said, and took a long pull on his cigar.

3

"I want you to mix with *Arcola's* crew," Jase told Harry and Tyrus as they strolled back to the levee. "Get to know them. Get to be their friends. I'll make sure you have access to the *Bee's* spirit locker – they're going to be thirsty men after working on that monster all day." He smiled. "Have less than thou showest, speak less than thou knowest, lend less than thou owest."

"Ain't got money to lend nowheres, anyhow," Klee said. "Those white crew, they ain't gonna be happy to work with blacks."

"And it's *dangerous*," Tyrus said. "Asking a slave to fight for his master is like asking a steer to fight for the honor of the slaughterhouse. The quicker the *Arcola* surrenders, the sooner the blacks get their freedom."

"I want you to point this out to the senator's crew," Jase said. "And every time you catch any of the officers or crew making a mistake, I want you to point that out, too. I want you to let them know that they ain't getting proper instruction from proper sailors." He smiled. "Once Pendergas' crew realizes that the senator plans on taking 'em straight out on their lonesomes to fight Farragut's whole fleet, with niggers making up half the crew and no real officers among 'em, I figure they'll be looking for a way out." He looked out at the *General Bee*, lying like a shadow against the levee. "And a way out," he said, "is just what we'll give 'em."

4

Jase had grown up on the Charleston waterfront, the scrawny red-haired runt in a litter of roughneck brothers. As a boy he wandered over the wharfs, imagining Spanish galleons choked with gold as his eyes roamed over the ships. Charleston's elegant gentry didn't give a damn whether he was educated or not, but his parents did – his God-fearing mother made sure he had his letters, and his father, a saloon keeper, pounded pieces of the Bible and Shakespeare into him with a stick. But the sea was what drew him, and when he was twelve he took his first voyage, as a captain's servant, past brick Fort Sumter to Havana.

He alternated working on ships with working in his father's saloon until his maternal uncle was finally rewarded for a lifetime of toadying the Democrats with a postmaster's job in Alexandria, Virginia. This was close enough to Washington for him to get within smelling distance of some real patronage: soon all Jase's relations were working for the post office. And Jase himself, somewhat to his surprise, found himself with an appointment to the Naval Academy.

Annapolis was easier than he'd expected. He already knew practical seamanship and navigation: spherical trigonometry was as natural to him as breathing. The discipline and hazing were mild, and far less arbitrary, than what he got at home from his parents and brothers.

Relations between the South Carolina wharf rat and other young naval gentlemen were more problematical. They had money, connections, and social elegance: Jase had a world of experience that, at Annapolis, didn't count for a damn. He hated the Southerners because they were rich, lazy, and stupid. He hated the Yankees because they were rich, ambitious, and Yankees. He kept his chin tucked and his fists clenched. He got a reputation as a vicious fighter, a wolverine with whom, in the end, it was easiest not to tangle.

When he finally got his commission he was glad to be at sea again. All he needed was a good war and he'd make himself rich off prize money. In the absence of prize money, he'd settle for a ship of his own. Instead there were long cruises to show the flag in the Mediterranean and mind-numbing months off Guinea on anti-slavery patrol.

Jase hoarded his meager lieutenant's pay and dreamed of war and command. Not for the sake of glory – though he had no objection to a scrap with the Limey or the Frog – but because it would be an opportunity to get rich. Just let me loose on an enemy, he thought, and I'll strangle him with one hand and empty his pockets with the other.

When the Union crumbled, Jase took his time deciding which way to jump. He had no reason to love the Confederacy. The people running the rebellion were his worst nightmare, but on the other hand he hated the Yankees six ways from Sunday. He didn't want to fight his own family: he knew his brothers would join the C.S.A. When he finally joined the navy, he was put to work building a ropewalk in Mobile.

He should have joined a blockade runner, he thought. Where the money was.

But friends in the navy came through for him. One certain officer was asked to undertake a delicate mission on the Mississippi, and the officer – who Jase knew to be honest, honorable, and a bad liar – instead recommended a certain Lieutenant Miller, who had none of these disadvantages.

Jase took the railroad north to Richmond and a meeting with Secretary of the Navy Mallory. He told the Secretary that he had some conditions. He wanted to hand-pick his own crew from anyone in the South, in or out of the service. He wanted his back covered in Richmond, particularly with the Secretary of War.

Mallory saw the sense of these requests, and acceded entirely. The loss of both Mississippi flotillas had led to an unusual degree of clarity in the thinking of the Navy Department.

Harry Klee was at loose ends after the *Louisiana* had been scuttled, and Jase took him on as executive officer. The Jackson twins were found on a Charleston blockade runner. Chief Tyrus was brought out of the shipyards in Charleston, where he'd been converting vessels of blockade runners, and the Gunner, Faren Smith, the finest cannoneer and rifleman Jase had ever known, was found amid the wreckage of the River Defense

Fleet. Other people were found here and there. Though not a few of them were inexperienced at theft, none of them had stolen an entire warship before.

5

Under Jase's direction, the senator's workmen put together massive gun truck carriages of cypress wood strapped with iron. Carpenters assembled a simulated gun deck on the levee, protected with revetments and cotton bales, where the guns could be pointed out over the Yazoo and crews could be trained while workmen still labored on the ironclad. The battery could also be used to protect *Arcola* in case the Yankees decided to venture up the Yazoo. Crewmen from the *General Bee* came ashore to instruct the ironclad's crew in gunnery.

Since there were no real seamen in *Arcola*'s crew, nobody wondered why the little *Bee*, a tiny vessel in a service strapped for volunteers, was 50 per cent over complement. Jase had, like Fortinbras, shark'd up a list of lawless resolutes, and the list was a long one.

The ironclad's crews proved no better than expected. The militia artillerymen that Pendergas had scavenged from his training units knew how their jobs well enough, given that they'd trained on little 6-pound brass howitzers instead of hulking iron naval-guns, but the militiamen hated the blacks like poison. They demonstrated on every possible occasion that they'd rather curse and kick their black fellow crewmen than fight the Yankees. The slaves knew better than to disclose the hatred they doubtless felt for the whites, but they showed no enthusiasm for their task, and little bits of sabotage kept occurring. Friction primers would go missing, the special ammunition for the Brooke rifle would be placed by the wrong gun, handspikes and priming irons would not be ready to hand when they were needed. On one occasion, the guns' wooden tompions were seen floating down the Yazoo. These incidents drove the white gunners into near-frenzy.

Senator Pendergas pronounced himself pleased with his gunners' progress. Jase smiled and bided his time.

Jase formed some of the *Bee*'s men into a baseball team, and navy played army almost every afternoon, following drill. With Faren Smith's pitching, Castor Jackson stealing bases, and Castor's twin Put-Up-Your-Dukes and Harry Klee regularly belting the ball into the bayou, the navy won on a regular basis. Army discontent increased. Jase let it simmer.

Pendergas seemed unaware of the tensions within his command. He busied himself with the grand plans for the conclusion of the war once the President gave him the troops, and with plotting the destruction of Farragut's fleet, which he figured would be the work of an afternoon. On occasion, though, he relaxed to the extent of attending a baseball game.

"Your center fielder," he nodded on one such occasion, "I've been thinking he looks familiar."

Jase took a draw on one of the senator's cigars. "His name is Pedaiah Jackson," he said.

Pendergas gave him a squint-eyed look. "The prizefighter? The one they call Put-Up-Your-Dukes – Dukes for short?"

"That's the one."

"I saw him beat Tommy Corcoran down in Orleans in '58. He was a champ, wasn't he?"

"Heavyweight champion of Great Britain and Ireland," Jase said, "till the law found out about the wives he had stashed all over the kingdom, and he had to take a long sea voyage." On the *U.S.S. Constellation*, as it happened, where Jase was serving as third lieutenant.

Pendergas spat tobacco into the grass and ground it in with his shoe. "Interesting crew you've got, Miller."

Jase nodded at the field. "That's Jackson's twin brother Castor at shortstop. My quartermaster."

The senator scratched his beard thoughtfully. "There's a prizefighter up in Yazoo City called Tom Amboise. People call him 'King.' A blacksmith. Killed a man in the ring up in Memphis with his bare fists."

"I heard of him," Jase said.

"You reckon Dukes would fight him? Barehanded, of course? I'd put up a good cash prize. We could stage the fight up in

Yazoo City, and I could commission a special train from Jackson for all the sportin' gents."

Jase concealed his inward smile. "Talk to Jackson about it. But I don't want him fighting as long as we're working on the *Arcola*. Launch the ram and get the men trained, and then I figure I can release Dukes from duty for a few days."

The senator spat. "Gives me more time for putting up placards and spreading the word." And placing bets, Jase figured.

"Well, then," Jase said. "If Jackson is willing."

Pendergas peered at him. "Is Jackson in training?"

"I've never seen him come close to losing."

Pendergas smiled as he placed mental bets against the local man-killer. Things were coming together pretty well.

6

Placards for the prize fight started going up on the same day that *Arcola* was launched. The earthen embankment that separated the makeshift drydock from the Yazoo was torn away, and foaming river water spilled into the gap. As slaves worked madly with shovels and barrows, the water climbed the ram's wooden hull to the belt of iron at the waterline. The cradle on which *Arcola* rested gave a series of groans. People cheered. Guns fired a salute. Flags waved. A militia band – boys and elderly men – played "Bonnie Blue Flag." Pendergas, grandly dressed in a soft pearl-grey uniform, waved his forage cap at the crowd.

A gun fired. The army battle flag, the red square with the blue saltire and white stars, rose on the ram's flagstaff.

Jase, aboard *General Bee*, did not like that flag there, and reckoned he would have to change it. He ordered ahead slow. The tugboat's bronze screw propeller thrashed brown water. Warps tautened, creaked.

The ram groaned but refused to move from its cradle. The railroad iron was weighing it down. Jase increased *Bee*'s power until there was nothing but white froth under its stern counter. *Arcola* did not move.

Harry Klee beat upon the frame of the pilothouse door with

one huge fist. "Those army dung-throwers! They've stranded *Arcola* in her own dry dock!"

Jase jangled bells to signal engine stop. "We'll get her afloat."

"Hope she's not stuck till the river rises!"

Mule teams were mobilized, harnessed to warps, and lined up on the levees. The ironclad was lightened by the weight of its anchor and chain, its cookstove, a pair of anvils, carpenter's stores, and the contents of the paint locker. Again Jase signaled *Bee*'s engine room ahead slow. Mule drivers cracked whips. Again the flags waved. Again the people cheered. Again Pendergas waved his cap. Again the strains of "Bonnie Blue Flag" were heard.

Again the ironclad failed to move. Pendergas threw his forage cap onto the levee and kicked it into the Yazoo. Jase lit a cigar while Harry Klee cursed and fumed.

"Calm down, Harry," he said. "This is just dandy." Then he went ashore to tell Pendergas he had a plan.

The crowds had gone home by the time *Arcola* was floated. The ironclad's boilers were filled with water. Jase warped a coal barge into the drydock until its bows touched *Arcola*'s flat stern. Just enough coal was shifted into the ram's bunkers to get up steam, then the barge was warped away again. It was the middle of the night before the steam pressure was sufficient to crank the engines, but that wasn't enough for Jase. He had Chief Tyrus tie down the safety valves and ordered more coal thrown into the fireboxes.

The mules were harnessed once more. Harry Klee took position in *Bee*'s wheelhouse. Jase stood in the armored pilot's station atop the front of the ironclad's casemate, Castor Jackson and three others stood at the wheel just below him, and Chief Tyrus attended the engines. The other crew were hustled ashore, and were probably glad to be there. Jase wished he could blow a steam whistle to let everyone know when to start, but *Arcola* lacked that piece of equipment. Maybe a whistle was beneath the dignity of an armored terror such as the ram.

Arcola's pilot house lacked a roof, so Jase just chinned himself up, got one foot onto the casemate, and stood. The day's heat still rose from the railroad iron. He had Castor hand him up a battle lantern, and he waved it at Klee. *Bee*, which had a whistle, promptly gave out with a series of blasts, and over the silent river Jase heard the sound of *General Bee*'s engines begin to thump. Whips cracked. Wood groaned as it took the strain.

Jase looked down into the ram and called to Castor. "Signal astern slow." Castor expertly played the ropes that rang bells in the engine room, and was answered by huge, solid, tooth-rattling crashes as *Arcola*'s engines engaged, then a surge as the twin 8-foot-diameter propellers began to bite water. White water streamed alongside *Arcola*'s flank. Jase felt the ram shudder, heard submerged wood groan.

"Half astern," he ordered. Bells jangled in the engine room. Tongues of flame licked from the twin stacks. The hawsers that connected *General Bee* to *Arcola* were so taut that water shot from the coils as they took the strain. The ram's air intakes, huge metal bells shaped like ear trumpets, began to howl with the force of the gale sucked into the boilers. Wood moaned like a giant in torment. The water in the drydock surged back from the propellers, turned to froth. A shudder ran the length of the ram, and Jase felt the trembling in his bones. Jase saw Pendergas on the edge of the drydock, pacing up and down, shouting at him. He had a feeling that the senator wanted Jase to shut everything down and wait for the Yazoo to rise.

Jase looked left and right, watching the water surge along the ironclad. Gauged his moment.

"Astern full." Spray from the propellers flew 20 feet high, a wave inundating Pendergas in his new uniform. Pendergas kept shouting. A series of bangs like cannon shots sounded through the air. *Arcola* jerked on the ways and Jase almost tumbled down the inclined iron casemate. There was a surge, the bow rose as if to a wave, and *Arcola* leaped like a racehorse from the drydock, scattering behind it the hardwood wedges that had held it in its cradle.

"Engines stop! Helm hard a-port! Hard down!"

Jase had calculated that *Arcola*'s propellers would pull so much water into the drydock that its water level would rise several feet above the level of the Yazoo. The rising water, more than the power of the propellers, floated the ram free.

Castor and his mates flung themselves on the wheel's spokes, trying to get the big rudder over before *Arcola* speared itself, stern-first, onto the opposite bank of the Yazoo. Harry Klee had to maneuver nimbly in midstream to avoid being rammed as *Arcola* shot past *General Bee*; he had his own rudder hard over and was steaming upstream at full ahead. *Arcola* had only begun its turn before the hawsers connecting it to *General Bee* cracked taut, and the ram snapped stern-to-current with a jerk that almost sent Jase tumbling. *Arcola* rolled madly for a moment – Jase remembered that she was unballasted, topheavy, and watched in horror as creamy water licked the gunports – but the boat righted itself, and Jase breathed easy.

Steam flew high and white as Chief Tyrus valved the boilers. The rushing steam made so much noise that for a few moments Jase didn't hear the screams and shrieks rising from the Yazoo. He looked in puzzlement at the water, then saw heads breaking surface in foam.

Mules. No provision had been made for untying the mule trains that had helped to run *Arcola* out of its dock. The ram, which probably weighed 1,000 tons with the armor on her, had dragged the animals out into the river, helpless as birds in a net. To judge from the cursing that was emanating from the vicinity of the struggling animals, some of the mule handlers had been dragged into the water as well.

Jase gazed in horror at the thrashing men and animals, tangled together in their harness. It was the sailor's worst nightmare: in the water, drowning because you were tangled in your own equipment. *Arcola* was killing them. He shouted to Castor, ran down the casemate to the foredeck, and tried hauling on the lines with his bare hands, but it was useless. Even with Castor's help, he wasn't strong enough. The river had the men and animals, and there was nothing to be done.

Two men drowned, and twenty-four mules, before *Arcola* was laid alongside the levee. Because the men were free whites, Pendergas would pay compensation for the mules only.

Jase thought of the old pagan days, when the launch of a ship would mean the sacrifice of men and animals, and he wondered if the dark old gods of the Yazoo had just conferred a blessing on the ironclad and its mission.

7

The day after *Arcola*'s launch, army and navy met for their gunnery competition. *Arcola* fired first, the smoothbores pounding away at targets set on rafts in the Yazoo while the Brooke rifle fired at targets on the far bank. Both Jase and Pendergas pretended not to notice when one of the loaders dropped a 32-pound solid onto the bare foot of one of the blacks, or when a fistfight developed among the crew of the 10-inch Dahlgren.

Army demolished the targets in four and a half minutes. The *Bee*'s well-trained crews beat the army men by more than half. Jase's shellbacks were all picked men, but Pendergas couldn't know that.

Pendergas gave Jase a thoughtful look as he paid over 200 silver dollars. "That was . . . impressive, lieutenant."

"My gunners have had more practice. Yours will improve."

The senator said nothing, only spat a meditative quid of tobacco onto the grass.

"You'll win your money back in the prize fight, and then some," Jase consoled him.

Pendergas then had his bugler call his men to receive their pay. The pay was in Confederate scrip, stuff so badly printed that the ink stuck to the fingers and the bills turned to compost in the soldiers' pockets. Sutlers and merchants would only take scrip at a discount. Jase wondered if the wages that Pendergas was collecting on behalf of his slaves were paid in scrip, or in specie. Jase reckoned the latter.

This was better and better. Jase called for *General Bee*'s pay chest, which Secretary Benjamin had provided, and handed out his own crew's wages – all in silver.

"Be sure to tell your friends in the army," he admonished his men, "that the navy pays in silver, because we all get prize money for our captures. Too bad they're not in the navy, eh?"

Wine maketh merry, he thought, but money answereth all things.

He observed thoughtful expressions on the faces of a great many army men that day.

8

Arcola was ballasted with leftover railroad iron and 50 tons of pig iron brought in barges from Yazoo City. Her guns were hoisted into her, and she began her trials, steaming up and down the Yazoo while her crew accustomed themselves to sweating inside a baking iron box while working alongside enormous, fast, and highly dangerous machinery. Jase was pleased by the speed he could get out of the ram despite all the armor topside. Ten knots, he judged, if he had the current with him.

After the trials came the fight between Dukes and the local champion Amboise. Since prizefights were illegal, the fight couldn't take place in Yazoo City, but in a pasture outside of town along the railroad track. Shortly after noon a train whistle blew, and the first of the chartered specials chugged into sight, packed with the sporting crowd brought in from Jackson. Jase looked at the rich planters with their diamond stickpins and silver-headed canes, and he reckoned that he'd never seen so many men out of uniform since the war began. And, since there were silks and jewels everywhere on display, it was difficult to tell the fancy ladies from the respectable women by the scale of their finery alone except that the ladies refused so much as to look at the strutting town girls.

The planters' women, Jase figured, were practiced at not seeing what their menfolk got up to, their amorous night raids in the slave quarters especially.

Harry Klee appeared with a silver bowl of his special milk punch. Jase poured into it the contents of a bottle labeled Tincture of Opium and offered it to the Senator and his lady.

Jase instructed Dukes to drag out the fight as long as possible. It was the eighty-fourth round before the exhausted blacksmith dropped his guard enough to let Dukes drive a punch straight into his throat. Amboise gagged and bent over, clutching his windpipe. Dukes volleyed a half-dozen unanswered punches to his head, then hammered him in the temple with one solid fist. There was a crack like a wooden mallet banging home a fid. Amboise dropped like a sack of beets. He convulsed, ugly little twitches running over his body. His supporters stormed the ring and carried him away before the referee finished counting him out.

Whether the cause was the punch to the throat, the fist to the temple, or the quality of the medical care – the ring doctor had passed out from drink about the fortieth round – the word soon passed through the crowd that Amboise was dead. Which didn't stop the band from playing "Dixie," or Jase and the Senator from collecting their winnings.

The Senator's pupils were wide as platters when he returned to the grandstand with his winnings to find his wife was sound asleep, slumped in her finery. From her throat issued delicate, ladylike snores.

"Maybe you should get a hotel room tonight," Jase suggested. "We can return to Long Shanks in the morning."

The Senator considered. The opiate hadn't affected him at all, other than to increase his air of jollification. "Bound to be some parties in Yazoo City tonight." He jingled the gold and silver in his pocket. "And it's not me who will be paying."

"I'm going to get Dukes out of sight," Jase said, "before somebody thinks to arrest him for killing that boy."

"They won't serve a warrant on a navy ship," Pendergas said. Jase nodded. "Then I know where to hide him."

He needn't have drugged the punch after all, he thought. The possibility of a murder warrant was enough excuse to get everyone aboard the *Bee* and head down the Yazoo.

Amboise had become another sacrifice to Jase's success.

9

It was two in the morning when *General Bee* pulled up to Long Shanks Landing. Jase was surprised to see the levee alight with torches and lanterns, and the ironclad abuzz with activity.

"We got a wire, sir. Yankees coming up the river," said the

man Pendergas had left in charge, the artillery officer known as Euphemism. "Two Eads ironclads, *Clasher* and *General Stone*, and a double-ended gunboat."

Sudden fire blazed through Jase's veins. "Have you got steam up?" he demanded.

"Steam's down, sir."

"*Well get it up, you fool!*" If the Yankee squadron caught *Arcola* tied to the bank and unable to move, Jase and his crew might as well all be in Paris for all the good they'd do.

The army lieutenant's eyes widened, and he turned to give the order, then hesitated. "Where's General Pendergas, sir?" he asked.

"In Yazoo City! Now get that steam up!" He turned to Harry Klee. "You'll take command of the *Bee*. Get that torpedo ready."

Klee grinned. "Lovely, Captain. Couldn't have worked out better."

Most of *General Bee*'s crew poured off the tugboat to help ready *Arcola* for combat. Jase had a pair of coal barges warped alongside *Arcola* on the river side so that the Yank boats couldn't ram her while she was helpless against the bank. Harry Klee took the *Bee* down river on a reconnaissance.

Jase brought order to the *Arcola*, had the gunners standing by their pieces, the guns loaded and run out the ports while the stokers worked like fury to raise steam. When one of Pendergas' officers volunteered to ride to the telegraph office and send the Senator a wire, Jase cursed him, called him a coward, and ordered him back to his post.

The last thing he wanted was for Pendergas to show up on a chartered boat just in time to make himself a hero.

At five in the morning Chief Tyrus reported that *Arcola* had a full head of steam. The National squadron hadn't turned up. *Bee* returned at dawn without having scented any Yanks. Jase sent the crew to breakfast by watches and had a chat with Harry Klee.

"How's Put-Up-Your-Dukes?" he asked.

"Not talking much," Klee said, "But I reckon he's all right." He spat. "You think those Yankee boats even exist?"

Jase stroked his unshaven jaw as he gave the matter his consideration. "That wire was pretty specific, down to the names of the Eads boats," he said. "We've got to assume that the Yanks have a squadron up the Yazoo somewhere. What with all the boasting our papers have been doing about this ram, it may be that Farragut or Flag Officer Davis decided to see what all the boasting is all about."

"Lucky they didn't send the whole fleet." Klee cocked an eye at the starboard watch, eating breakfast in the Senator's cotton field while the port watch stood by the guns. "You planning on reading 'em your commission?" he asked.

Jase slapped an insect. "They'll like the news a sight better if we sink some Yankee ironclads first," he said.

"You reckon they'll follow you?"

"I don't plan on giving 'em any choice, Harry."

After breakfast he had both crews mustered on the levee. Jase and Harry Klee climbed the sloping red side of the ram, turned to face the men he wanted to lead down the Yazoo. The whites stood in ranks, most of them in uniform. The slaves slumped behind, silent and resentful.

"I'm not a politician," he told them. "I'm a navy man, and I don't give speeches."

"Rude am I in my speech," he thought to himself with amusement, "And little bless'd with the soft phrase of peace." Father, your Shakespeare is more useful than you knew.

"There are two Yankee ironclads on the Yazoo!" Jase said. "They've heard we're up here, and they're looking for us. If they find us now, with *Arcola* tied to the bank, we'll be trapped like rats in a hole." He gestured down the river, a clenched fist. "If we go to find *them*, the fight will be even!" He raised his voice. "That's all the South has ever asked. A fair chance! An even fight! Am I right, boys?"

There was a cheer. Jase observed Tyrus and Faren Smith among the *Bee*'s men, keeping the cheer going longer than might otherwise have been the case.

Jase grinned and threw out his chest. Give 'em a little Harry Fifth, he thought. "I don't want anyone on board *Arcola* who isn't ready to get himself a bellyful of Yankees!" he said. "I don't want anyone with me just because he's *ordered* to be there. And that includes *servants*!"

"You in the back!" he said, craning over the ranked white faces on the levee. "The Confederacy thanks you for your contribution, but you will not be required for the coming battle. You are dismissed!"

The blacks moved away, casting glances of hate or contempt over their shoulders, while the white crewmen cheered. They didn't need any prompting this time. Some of them even threw dirt clods after the retreating slaves.

Jase felt a moment of quiet triumph. If he had to build morale by uniting white against black, or black against white, or for that matter by getting them all to whip a cringing cur dog, then that's what he'd do.

"And as for the rest of you – " He took off his straw hat and waved it at the hatchway. "Any man of you who wants a scrap with the Yank, take your stations!"

The crewmen cheered again as they poured onto the ironclad. Harry Klee had the watch and quarter bills ready – the *new* watch and quarter bills, the ones that distributed two-thirds of *General Bee*'s complement over the ram, and put them in charge of all *Arcola*'s departments.

"Raise the flag, sir?" Harry Klee asked.

"Ay," Jase said. "And let's make it the naval ensign, shall we?"

Klee got an ensign from the *Bee*, the rectangular flag with its white and red stripes, the blue canton with the circle of stars, and sent it up *Arcola*'s flagstaff. Jase saluted the ensign as it rose, and felt a thrill rocket up his spine. His flag. His boat. His command.

It would take more than Pendergas to take it away from him. And more than a Yankee flotilla, too.

He was about to enter the boat when he saw Lieutenant Euphemism hovering uncertainly by the hatch. He approached, happy to see the lieutenant salute him.

"Yes, Lieutenant?" Jase said. "Do you have a question?"

"To tell you the truth, Lieutenant – Captain – Lieutenant – I have been superseded in command of the starboard battery by one of your men."

"You are not superseded," Jase said. "You hold the same post you always did. But I did put someone more experienced over you."

"I'm not certain you have the authority to do such a thing." Euphemism's eyes rose to the flagstaff. "I do not believe I would feel comfortable serving aboard a navy boat. Perhaps I will ride to the station and wire General Pendergas."

"You'll miss the fight."

"I'm not sure it's my fight, sir, properly speaking."

Jase gave the young man a thoughtful nod. "As you choose. I want only volunteers for this mission."

The lieutenant touched his cap brim. "Much obliged, sir."

"But you should know, Lieutenant, that if you wire the Senator, there may be unfortunate consequences?"

The lieutenant smiled. "For you, sir?"

Jase laughed, to the lieutenant's surprise. "Lord, no," he said. "What I meant is that if you miss this fight, you should ask for a transfer out of this department. Because you'll never be able to walk aboard *Arcola* again and hold your head up."

The lieutenant stared, then swallowed, hard. Jase stepped back from the hatchway, gestured for the man to enter. "Come along, sir," he said. "You can wire the Senator from Vicksburg as well as anywhere."

Euphemism pondered for a moment, then smiled, touched his cap again, and entered the ram.

Let the Senator stay away for the next fifteen minutes, Jase thought, and the ram is mine.

10

Black smoke poured from *Arcola*'s twin stacks as the ram thrust down the Yazoo. The foredeck before the casemate was almost awash with brown water. Jase sat on the edge of the roofless pilot house, his seaman's soul thrilling to the glory of it all.

"Who is she that looketh forth as the morning sun," he thought, "fair as the moon, clear as the sun, and terrible as an army with banners?"

Arcola. His *Arcola*.

Oh, *Arcola* was a sweet boat! Fast despite her size and weight, trim, born for the water. Engines tuned to a fare-thee-well, and if she was a little hesitant to answer the big rudder, well, that was just because all the iron gave her momentum. It was a flaw for which a commander sensitive to her ways could compensate, and Jase had learned her well in her trials.

Sitting next to Jase was the Gunner, Faren Smith, who held an English-made Armstrong target rifle casually across his knees – even as Nimrod the mighty hunter before the Lord, Jase thought.

Jase glanced over his shoulder and saw *General Bee* following two cable-lengths behind. *Bee* towed a pair of coal barges which would be cut adrift on the appearance of any Nationals. Above *Bee*'s foredeck towered a pair of wooden sheers that supported a 40-foot boom with a homemade tin canister on the end, Harry Klee's spar torpedo. Behind the foredeck gun stood Dukes. It would be the big prizefighter's job to place the canister under an enemy hull, then touch off the 50 pounds of black powder in the tin bucket.

The thing that most worried Jase was that he and Klee would be unable to communicate with one another once the fight started. Each would have to remember his part in the plan. But there were several plans depending on different contingencies, and it was more than possible to confuse one with the other, and of course, there came a time in any fight when the plan went straight to hell . . .

"Smoke downriver, boss," Faren Smith said. Jase turned abruptly, scanned the river ahead, saw nothing.

"To the right, above the trees."

Jase corrected his gaze, saw the black smudge billowing above a tangle of cypress. Coal smoke, all right. A lot of smoke, which meant more than one boat.

Jase felt his heart shift to a higher rate of speed, like an engine with the throttles opened. He turned again, waved at the tugboat following behind, pointed to the smoke rising over the cypress. He saw Harry Klee wave back from the pilothouse, then saw a plume of steam rise as Klee blew the whistle twice, the sound unheard over the throb of *Arcola*'s engines.

Jase dropped through the pilot house to the main deck, where Castor stood by the wheel. The inside of the ironclad was hot as a blacksmith's forge, and the clank and hiss of the engines hammered on the ears. "Captain on deck!" someone yelled. The crew shuffled into a state of attention. They'd been at quarters since leaving Long Shanks, the boat cleared for action, guns loaded but not run out the ports.

"Yankees around the bend!" Jase shouted. "Run out the broadside guns!"

Guarding against abrasions with their leather waist protectors, the crewmen threw their weight onto the gun tackles, their bodies leaning almost to the deck as they hauled the heavy iron 32-pounders to the ports. Jase walked swiftly aft, to the hatchway, then dived down the companion to the engine room.

Gleaming piston rods slammed back and forth in the red light of the furnace. The monster cranks of the shafts flung themselves up, then down into their wells, a terrible lunging movement that could crush a man as easily as a boot could squash a beetle. Stokers stood stripped to the waist and leaned on their shovels, sweat making pale tracks in their coats of coal dust.

"Yankees!" Jase shouted to Chief Tyrus. "Stand by to ram!"

Tyrus nodded. Jase ran back up the companion, traveled the length of the gun deck. Forward of the wheel he saw daylight gleaming on the big Dahlgren pivot gun. The iron shutters that closed its three hatches were open on account of the heat. He paused next to Castor, ordered, "Close those shutters forrard." he said. No sense in letting a lucky Yankee shot fly in and drive the length of the boat.

Then he jumped up into the pilothouse again. Faren Smith still sat on the edge of the hatch, legs dangling, rifle across his knees. "I want you to aim the first shot from the Dahlgren," Jase told him. "After that, you can come up here and use that Whitworth."

"Ay, sir." Smith swung down, made his way to the gun deck.

Jase looked over his shoulder, saw the *Bee* following, its men at quarters, the spar torpedo poised high in the air.

He hoped the torpedo wasn't a dud. They were tricky things. He looked forward, gauged the approaching boats by their smoke. "Steer a point to port," he told Castor. Take the turn wide, he thought. Let's not risk running aground on that point, not now.

The point neared. Jase felt sweat trickling down the back of his neck.

"Full speed!" he shouted down to Castor. "Hard a-star-board!"

Castor already had his hand on the bell line to the engine room. He signaled madly, then threw himself onto the wheel along with his three quartermaster's mates. There was a moment's hesitation as the rudder bit, and then the ram heeled into the turn, white water creaming along its side.

The point fell astern, with its tangle of cypress and flock of roosting cormorants, and a new vista opened up. Jase felt a rocket of pure terror fly up his spine as, a bare three-quarters of a mile away, he saw the Federal squadron.

He had known the Eads ironclads were big, but these were the size of *islands*, islands forged of iron and studded over with batteries of artillery. The Northern engineer James Eads had started with the flat-bottomed hulls of big Mississippi steamers, then plated them over with a slab-sided iron casemate sloped at 45 degrees. A conical pilot house perched atop the casemate forward, and behind the twin stacks reared a tall pair of humps, the armored housing for the twin paddle wheels.

But what made the Eads boats dangerous was their firepower. Where the *Arcola* had a single gun firing forward, *Clasher* and *General Stone* had four. Where *Arcola* had three guns on the broadside, the Yankee boats had five. And where *Arcola* had a single gun firing astern, the Eads ironclads carried two.

Arcola's advantages were its speed, its ram, and the greater thickness of Argus McBride's ingenious armor. As Jase stared through the steel pilot house bars at the Yankee flotilla, they seemed scant advantage enough.

If it goes badly, he consoled himself, he could run away. With its twin screws, *Arcola* was faster than these big paddle boats.

And at least the Yankees were moving up the Yazoo one at a time, not as Jase had feared in line abreast, presenting Jase with an iron wall. The boat in the lead, judging by the gilt-trimmed letters that scrolled out on a graceful wrought-iron arch between the stacks, was the *Clasher*. The *Stone* followed. If the double-ended gunboat was present, it was behind the *Stone*, and Jase could not see her.

"Wheel amidship," he called down. "Stand by the bow gun."

Arcola lurched and shuddered as Chief Tyrus fed more steam to the engines. Jase could see Castor fighting the wheel as the power came unevenly to the screws.

"Port your helm. Meet her. Hold her so."

Jase aimed *Arcola* right for *Clasher*'s bows, as if intending a head-on collision. The impact would probably be suicidal for both boats, but if he could panic *Clasher*'s helmsman into turning, then he would be able to ram the Yank broadside and sink her.

Jase ducked beneath the hatch coaming, shouted along the gun deck.

"Stand by your guns!" he shouted. "You're going to have all the time you need to aim, so make each shot count."

There was a sudden bang, and Jase straightened just as a solid iron shot shrieked right overhead, a sound that made him duck again. *Clasher* had fired one of its bow guns. Jase's heart hammered. This was all happening very fast.

Another gun went off, and for a moment Jase was staring right at an advancing iron ball that seemed aimed right between his eyes. Terror sang along Jase's nerves. But the shot dropped at the last instant, and then Jase felt the impact, heard iron clang and timbers groan. Sparks flew, and then Jase saw the 42 pound solid shot shooting straight up into the sky as it bounded off *Arcola*'s slanting casemate.

Another bang, then a series of splashes to port as a clean miss skipped along the surface of the Yazoo. And then another impact, another screech of iron, as *Arcola*'s armor absorbed the last of round of *Clasher*'s forward battery.

"Run out the forward gun! Fire at will!"

The forward iron shutter was thrown open with a clang, then trunnions rumbled on the deck as the 10-inch Dahlgren was hauled out the port. Jase stared at the oncoming bow wave as *Clasher*'s massive prow shouldered aside the brown river water.

The Yankee was not turning. That damned Eads boat had to be at least 50 feet wide.

Lord, Jase thought, they were coming together fast. Let him not mistime this. Shoot, shoot, shoot *now*, he mentally urged Faren Smith.

Too late. He ducked below the coaming to shout at Castor. "Port your helm! Signal the engine room for half ahead! Ready the port broadside!"

Just then the bow gun went off, its roar hammering Jase's ears in the confined space of the casemate. There was an almost immediate clang as *Clasher*'s armor received the 10-inch ball. Jase straightened and looked forward just as the rudder began to bite, the planking tilting under his feet, the boat slowing as the big rudder acted as a brake. As the gunsmoke cleared he saw a dimple on *Clasher*'s casemate iron where the Dahlgren had struck. There was no other effect.

That huge prow seemed only *yards* away. Jase's mouth went dry. If he had mistimed, it would be the *Clasher* that rammed *Arcola*, not the other way around.

"Helm to starboard!" Jase shouted. Castor flung the wheel the other way, throwing his weight on the spokes. The blunt Yankee prow creamed closer. *Arcola* shuddered as the rudder bit and slewed to the left.

"Brace for collision!" Jase yelled. He'd mistimed, damn it.

There was an impact, then a sound of rending timbers as *Arcola*'s port bow struck the port bow of *Clasher*. Jase clung to the bars of the pilot house as the collision tried to take him off his feet. Timbers shrieked as *Arcola* scraped along *Clasher*'s port side, the huge Eads boat shouldering the ram aside as if it were a piece of driftwood. A laugh forced its way past Jase's throat. He hadn't managed to kill his boat on the Yankee's prow after all.

"Port battery!" he shrieked with relief. "Fire as you bear!"

And then Faren Smith hopped up beside him, the Armstrong rifle in his hands. "Shoot the helmsman, sir?" he offered.

"If you like," Jase said, but his words were drowned by the storming of the broadside guns, *Clasher* and *Arcola* firing at such close range that the muzzles almost touched. Flame and smoke shot up between the iron casemates, and the clang of iron sounded like anvils ringing beneath the hammers of giants Splinters flew through the air as *Arcola*'s longboat was demolished. Crewmen of both vessels cheered. Smith aimed and fired his rifle in the din, and Jase didn't even hear him.

"Missed, sir," he reported, and began to reload.

Jase peered through gunsmoke. "Starboard a point. Meet her. Run the Dahlgren out the port side."

That would put *Arcola* on a slightly diverging course. He wanted to get as close to the starboard bank as possible so that he would have room to turn the ram around.

The second Eads boat, *General Stone*, was hidden behind *Clasher* and had very possibly not even known what was going on until the first shot was fired. *Stone* followed *Clasher* at two cables' distance. A canvas awning was spread over the flat roof of *Stone*'s casemate, and bulwarks of sandbags and timber had been constructed beneath the awning. Jase saw people running along the top of the casemate, arms glittering, and realized that *Stone* carried a company of infantry on its roof, probably with the intention of using them to burn a few plantations or gins while they passed through the interior of Mississippi.

Two cables behind the *Stone* came the double-ender gunboat. Pointed at each end, with rudders fore and aft and a pair of paddle wheels right amidship, the gunboat could go as fast astern as forward. Though it was ideal for reconnaissance missions up creeks and bayous, in a battle between ironclads it was outclassed.

He heard the clang of iron shutters and the rumble of trunnions as the reloaded port battery began to roll out the ports.

"At the second boat," he called, "fire as you bear."

The Dahlgren's mighty boom concussed the water with its fury. Its iron shutter slammed shut as the huge smoothbore recoiled into the casemate. From *Stone* came a clang, and Jase saw infantryman dive for cover as the 10 inch ball struck the Yankee's slanted armor and bounded over their heads in a trail of sparks.

"Look at the *Bee*, sir!" Faren Smith called in delight. "Look at her take on that big Yankee!"

Jase turned to see the *General Bee*, flame shooting from her stacks, firing its guns as she ran along the side of the *Clasher*. The Eads ironclad hadn't reloaded its broadside yet and weren't able to reply. Jase saw the spar torpedo dip, saw Dukes and another crewman wrestling with the ungainly butt-end of the spar. And then the torpedo splashed white as it hit the Yazoo, and the force of the water immediately wrenched it from the prizefighter's hands as it slewed under the *Clasher*'s hull.

"My God," Jase said, knowing what was about to happen. He saw the boxer's arm jerk the lanyard, and then the river rose beneath the Yankee boat as the 50 pounds of gunpowder went off beneath its flat bottom.

Water splashed *out* the gunports, he saw, blasted up right through *Clasher*'s bottom. The sound echoed off the trees. The explosion heeled *Bee* far over to starboard, and for a moment Jase's heart stopped as the tugboat was poised on the edge of a capsize. But then *Bee* righted itself, and the *Clasher*'s gunports filled with struggling figures as nearly 200 crewmen tried to abandon ship at the same instant. Boilers began to thunder as river water found the fires. Steam gushed from every port. The two tall stacks toppled into the river.

There was nothing to keep the *Clasher* afloat. It was made of iron, and it sank fast. In a few brief seconds, all that was left on the surface was foam and struggling figures.

Then *Arcola* and *General Stone* began to exchange broadsides, and the river filled with the sound of iron hammering iron. The infantry on *Stone*'s casemate lowered their muskets and began to fire by platoon volleys, and Jase winced as musket balls whined off the pilot house. Faren Smith waited for the shooting to die down, then popped above the pilot house, leveled his rifle, and fired.

"Got an officer, sir," he said conversationally. "Only infantry, though."

The double-ender's bow gun fired, and the shot screamed overhead. There was a crash as it landed in trees. Jase glanced at the river bank to starboard, the cypress standing in the brown water. Gauged his motion. Felt sweat trickle down his nose. He tried to remember that the boat hesitated when the helm was put down hard, that she didn't answer the wheel directly.

"Hard a-port!" he called. "Engines ahead full. Run the Dahlgren out forrard. Starboard battery, stand by to fire at the gunboat."

Arcola heeled as the rudder bit water. *General Bee* maneuvered sharply to avoid collision as the ram crossed its bows. The starboard battery lashed out at the double-ender, but Jase's eyes were on the *Stone*.

"Rudder amidships. Steady as she goes."

Jase jerked around at the sound of a bang aft, afraid he'd been hit, but then he saw the plume of gunsmoke and realized that the Brooke rifle, trained aft, had fired as it bore on the double-ender. *Bee*, having crossed *Arcola*'s wake, was aimed for the double-ender as well. Its bow gun barked out, and Jase saw splinters fly from the Yankee boat.

Jase returned his attention to the *Stone*. The Yankee's stern guns rolled out the ports as the Confederate ram fell into her wake, and both fired at almost the same instant. One hissing shot punched a hole in *Arcola*'s starboard funnel. The other missed. *Arcola*'s 10-inch Dahlgren fired in reply, and as the shot struck home Jase was pleased to hear the crack of broken iron plate.

The Yankee's rear armor wasn't as thick as that in front. If he could keep on the *Stone*'s vulnerable tail, the huge Dahlgren was going to break down the enemy's defenses.

Cannon boomed as *General Bee* engaged the double-ender. Jase ignored it: Harry Klee was on his own.

Arcola's big bronze screws bit the water. Her speed grew. *General Stone* loomed closer, a gun-studded wall of iron.

"Brace for ramming!" Jase called.

Arcola smashed into *Stone*'s stern with a sound like thunder, the ram's iron-plated beak punching through timber. Jase didn't think he could sink *General Stone* this way, but hoped he could disable the Yankee's rudder. If *Stone* lost its rudder, it might slew broadside-to-current and Jase could ram it broadside.

Iron shutters parted with a clang, and *Stone*'s aft battery began to run out. "Engines half ahead," Jase called. The boats drew apart as *Stone*'s guns fired. Jase felt *Arcola* shudder, heard oaken timbers crack. *Arcola*'s bow gun blasted out again. Again there was that satisfying smash as the 10-inch solid struck home.

Faren Smith's Whitworth cracked. "Another officer," he reported, but then musket balls began to whine around the pilot house as the infantry atop the enemy leveled their weapons and began to fire. Jase hunched low, peering through the lowest slit at the looming enemy. He was acutely aware that he and Smith were the only targets a whole company of infantry could find to shoot at.

"Engines ahead full!"

Jase rammed again, jolting the *Stone* with another smashing blow from behind. A swarm of musket balls pelted the pilot house. Jase wondered if he should order the Dahlgren loaded with grapeshot and blow those footsoldiers off their perch, but decided his best chance for ending the fight was to keep hammering at *Stone*'s vulnerable stern.

This went on for at least fifteen minutes. *General Stone* plodded upriver, with *Arcola* pursuing, ramming her stern whenever the opportunity presented itself. *Stone* was going to have to do *something*: she was running in the wrong direction, deeper into enemy-held Mississippi, and the Confederate ram lay between the Yank and its base. But if *Stone* tried to turn around, *Arcola* would ram her broadside and put her on the bottom of the Yazoo.

"Sir! Sir!" Jase looked in surprise to see a powder-streaked army lieutenant, the man called Euphemism. "That last shot knocked away the flagstaff!" Euphemism shouted. "Our flag's lying on the casemate where I can't reach it through the gunport!"

Jase winced as a musket ball whined through one of the pilot house slits, ricocheted off iron, then buried itself in the oaken coaming. "Very good, Lieutenant," he said, unable to think of a remark more suitable to the occasion.

"Sir!" Euphemism sounded desperate. "It's not good at all! We're not flying a flag! The Yankees could think we're trying to surrender!"

Jase looked at Smith. Smith shrugged. "Let 'em," Jase said. "No!" Euphemism shouted. "We've got to keep the flag flying!"

Jase watched in surprise as Euphemism chinned himself up to the open hatch atop, then sprang onto the casemate and ran aft. He picked up the remains of the flagstaff and stood straddling the casemate's spine, waving the flag like fury and shouting defiance at the Yanks.

"And the navy flag, too," Jase said.

"Well," Faren Smith said, as surprised as Jase, "at least it gives the infantry someone else to shoot at."

And indeed the infantry seemed happy to devote their attention to Euphemism. He stood amid the bullets' hail as he shouted and waved his flag and his fist. The Yanks' efforts, however, did not seem blessed by any great accuracy. Though they shot off his cap, and at one point knocked him down, he just got back to his feet and yelled at them to try harder.

Finally the Dahlgren smoothbore did its work: the big gun boomed, and the thunderous concussion was followed by a crack, then a rapid series of clangs. The 10-inch solid shot had penetrated *Stone*'s rear armor, traveled the length of the boat, then began bounding inside like a mad thing, upending guns, taking off arms and heads like the devil's own executioner. Once the boat's iron armor had been penetrated, the same armor that protected the ship from attack would not let the shot *out*: it bounced around inside, like a seed shaken in a gourd, until it got tired.

"Three cheers!" Jase shouted. "We've raked her!"

The third cheer rang out just as *Stone* began a lumbering turn. The raking shot had convinced the skipper he had to try something before the Dahlgren gutted his boat.

"Starboard your helm!" Jase called. "Ring for full ahead."

Arcola's ram caught the *Stone* dead amidship. There was the crash of timbers, the scream of tortured oak. "Engines half astern," Jase called. He suspected he hadn't gained quite enough momentum to do mortal damage. He backed *Arcola* for a cable's length while the *Stone*'s paddle wheels thrashed white water in an effort to get the big boat around, and then Jase ordered full ahead and speared *General Stone* on the iron-sheathed ram.

There was a colossal wrench, a rending of timbers, a crash of machinery. Jase felt *Arcola* pitch forward, heard the gurgle of water as it crept up the casement. "Astern full!" he shouted. *General Stone* was filling with water and would drag *Arcola* to the bottom unless Jase could get the ram out of the enemy boat.

The ram's engines shuddered to a stop, then reversed with a hiss of steam. Jase felt his boat tilt downward. He could hear the gurgle and suck of water. He had to get the boat reversed before her screws pitched up out of the water. *Stone*'s broadside guns roared, hammering Rebel iron. The big bronze screws turned the water white under *Arcola*'s stern. Then, with a moan of broken timber, the ram pulled free. Water gushed into the enemy boat, and her crew began to pour out her hatches.

"Port your helm! All stop!"

Silence fell on the torpid river, and then Jase heard the distant sound of two shots. *General Bee*'s action with the double-ender was proceeding, out of sight, downstream.

And then *Arcola*'s crew began to cheer. Jase leaned wearily against the side of the pilot house and grinned at Faren Smith.

"Well," he thought, "the boat is mine now, whatever anyone else might think."

11

Accompanied by *General Bee*, *Arcola* pulled up to the levee below the fortress city of Vicksburg, protected by the 100 heavy guns on the city's red clay bluffs. *Arcola* sported a new flagstaff, jury-rigged by Euphemism, on which flaunted the bullet-torn navy flag. *Bee* had reclaimed its coal barges, on which slouched about a hundred soggy Yankees picked up off the river. The rest of the Federals had got ashore and were wandering in the swamps of the Yazoo, where they would eventually be rounded up, no doubt, by the militia.

Harry Klee had won his running fight with the Yankee double-ender by putting an explosive shell into one of its paddleboxes. With one paddle wrecked, the gunboat had veered straight into the bank, where her crew had set her afire. The double-ender blew up when the fires reached its magazine, and its crew had joined the scattered refugees on the shore.

Bee was somewhat the worse for wear. Its stack was riddled and leaking, and its superstructure had been hit by enemy shot that had punched clean through the wood-sided tug, though without harming either its crew or its machinery. The Yanks' accuracy had put Klee in a temper, which he relieved by cursing at the prisoners as they were marched to the city under guard.

Jase sent Dukes to the telegraph office to send a wire to Richmond announcing the victory, then mustered the two crews on the levee, lit a cigar, and called for *Arcola*'s pay chest. But first, he took from his chest two letters he had been saving, each from Secretary of the Navy Stephen Mallory.

The first letter commissioned *Arcola* as a vessel in the Confederate Navy. The second placed Jase in command of her, and assigned him and *Arcola* to special duty on the Mississippi, as described in sealed orders to be opened later at the captain's discretion. Jase read the letters aloud to the assembled crewmen, then smiled and drew on his cigar as Faren Smith and Castor led the cheers.

"There," he thought, "let Pendergas try to get me out of the boat now."

He saw the Army crewmen exchanging uncertain glances, and saw the uncertainty increase as he ordered the muster rolls produced and the pay chest opened.

"In the navy," he said, "we are entitled to head money for the crew of the Yankee boats we sank this morning. I have every expectation that Congress may award prize money as well. I intend to pay all navy men their share, in advance, in silver. Unfortunately I can't do this for you army boys – " He smiled. "Unless, of course, you choose to enlist in the navy and remain with *Arcola*. Ensign Klee," pointing with his cigar at Klee, "will be happy to put you on our muster rolls. Now – " He cleared his throat and tried to look serious. "Some of you may wonder whether you can serve simultaneously in the army and navy. My own guess is that people like us need not worry about it, that these are matters for people in Richmond to fuss over.

What I *do* know is that if you put your name on the dotted line yonder, you can receive your head money in silver. Anyone for the navy – " He took off his straw boater and flourished it in Klee's direction. "Form up before Mr Klee!"

A cheer rose as the army men broke ranks. Jase watched them and savored his cigar. He became aware that Euphemism was limping toward him.

"You're not wounded, I hope?" Jase said.

"A few scratches," Euphemism said, and patted at some tears in his uniform jacket. "The Yankees shot off the heel off my boot."

"That's a brave thing you did, sir," Jase said. "I won't venture to speak to its wisdom."

"Wise or not, it was necessary," Euphemism said briefly, and Jase wondered if it was necessary to the cause, to the laws of war, or to Euphemism, a proof of his own courage under fire. The Army man held out his hand. "I wonder if I might see your orders, sir?"

Jase handed over the two letters from Secretary Mallory. Euphemism read them with a polite frown. "These appear to be perfectly genuine," he said. "But I observe that these are dated nearly a month ago."

"That is correct."

Euphemism looked up at Jase from beneath the brim of his cap. He stroked his mustache thoughtfully. "This usurpation of yours appears to have been planned in high places, sir."

Jase found himself in an expansive mood. "Let us say, Lieutenant, that you, I, and Richmond alike meditated on the capacities of General Pendergas, and came to identical conclusions."

Euphemism frowned.

"We can enlist you as an ensign," Jason said. "That is the naval equivalent of your present army rank – with your commission dating from this morning, before the fight on the Yazoo. Your position on *Arcola* will remain unchanged."

"I'm flattered, Captain." Euphemism tilted his head, affected to consider the offer. "I'm afraid not, sir," he said. "I fear I can serve a single master only."

"As you wish," Jase said. "But I hope you will remain on *Arcola*." The crew, Jase suspected, would admire Euphemism for his bravery, if nothing else.

"I will remain unless orders take me elsewhere."

"I'm happy to hear it." Jase offered Euphemism his hand, and Euphemism took it. "By the way," he asked, "why do people call you Euphemism?"

The army man stiffened. "My real name is Ronald Fux, sir. F-U-X, like the composer."

Jase tried very hard not to smile. He failed. "Very well, Lieutenant," he said. "Welcome aboard."

"Your servant, sir." Touching his cap brim. "What happens next?"

Jase glanced uneasily up the river. "The crew will be permitted to celebrate tonight. But in the morning, I want everyone at stations. Once Farragut finds out I've sunk his boats, he's going to come looking for us. He's not one to let this sort of insult stand."

"Perhaps he will not find out."

Jase laughed. "He'll find out from our newspapers! I'm sure enterprising Vicksburg newsboys sell the local rags to the Yankees every day."

Euphemism's mustache gave a twitch. "I hadn't considered that."

"I think we'll be in a scrap before the week is out. Probably in two or three days."

There was a blare of brass on the bluff above their heads, and then the thump of a drum. "Bonnie Blue Flag?" Jase wondered aloud, "or Dixie?"

Euphemism tilted his head, listened for a moment. "Hail to the Chief," he said.

"I think you may be right."

The band came marching down the bluff to the river, followed by most of the town's civilian population. News had reached the population of *Arcola*'s victory on the Yazoo.

Which meant, Jase thought as he doffed his boater to wave it at the crowd, that Farragut would find out tomorrow.

12

Tomorrow brought Pendergas, the Senator and his wife bellowing into town on a special early morning train. Jase traveled up the bluff to meet them at the headquarters of General Van Dorn, who commanded the department. Van Dorn was thin, shorter even than Jase, and pugnacious; he was an able general who had never won a battle, and Jase reckoned that Van Dorn wasn't about to win this one, either. Pendergas demanded his ironclad. Jase refused to give it to him, and showed his authorization from Secretary Mallory. Tobacco juice sprayed from Pendergas' lips as he shouted that *Arcola* did not belong to the Secretary of the Navy. Jase replied that, on the contrary, it did. Pendergas demanded that Van Dorn put Jase under arrest. Jase suggested that if he were to be placed under arrest, it should be the Department of the Navy, not the War Department, that should do it; and further offered the opinion that in light of the losing battles of Belmont, Forts Henry and Donaldson, New Orleans, Island Number Ten, Shiloh, Memphis, and Corinth – he tactfully avoided mention Van Dorn's own defeat at Pea Ridge – he, Lientenar Jase Miller, was the only successful Confederate commander west of Virginia, and that to place him under arrest would irretrievably damage the morale of the civilian population.

"Besides," Jase said, "my crew is personally loyal to me, and will fight for no one else."

"*You bribed them!*" Mrs Pendergas roared.

"I paid them their wages," Jase said, "which is more than the Senator ever did."

"*Snake in the grass!*" she screamed, and went for his eyes. For a few exciting moments Jase dodged about General Van Dorn's office, feeling like the *Bee* beset by an Eads ironclad, until Van Dorn and the Senator between them got ahold of Madame Pendergas and wrestled her into a chair.

Van Dorn looked as if a 20-pound Parrott rifle had just gone off next to his ear. "Gentlemen," he said, "this is out of my sphere. All I can do is wire Richmond."

"Your servant, sir," Jase said, saluted smartly, and made his way out.

13

Pendergas came to *Arcola's* berth the next day to make a speech from the levee, and win back the hearts of his crew. The army men ignored him, and the navy men jeered. Van Dorn sat in his headquarters and did nothing. And that night, Farragut came down the Mississippi with his whole fleet, all the huge black sea-going frigates with their towering masts, their wooden hulls, and their long, flashing broadsides.

Farragut wanted no part of *Arcola*, that was clear. He kept to the right bank, away from the ram and Vicksburg's river batteries. His ships were silhouetted by bonfires the rebels had prepared on the far bank, and *Arcola* and Vicksburg's hundred guns fired away for over an hour while the Federals fired back. Only an occasional shot rang on *Arcola's* armor: it was likely that in the dark, with all targets obscured by gunsmoke, the Federals had no idea clear where *Arcola* was berthed, and apparently they weren't about to venture close enough to find out.

Dawn light revealed no wreckage, no toppled masts or gutted hulls, and this suggested that the Federals had paraded past Vicksburg without loss to themselves. The Confederates had suffered nothing except for six men wounded by a gun that burst in one of the river batteries.

Farragut was taking his wooden ships back to salt water. The band marched forth for another impromptu parade, and the people of the town swarmed into the batteries and down to the waterfront to rain on their heroes both garlands and whiskey.

Vicksburg was saved, and it was Jase that had saved it. In the midst of the celebrations came a telegram from Richmond announcing Jase's promotion to commander for his action on the Yazoo. The ram was his – his alone – his till death, either his own or that of the boat.

No one could take *Arcola* from him now.

A CHECKLIST
OF SEA STORIES OF
THE PERIOD 1790–1820

This bibliography is a selective listing of the key works of fiction set during the above period. Where possible the book titles are listed in chronological sequence of the historical events, which may not always correspond with the original order of publication. Dates of first publication only are given, though alternate titles are shown. Many of these titles are no longer in print.

Bulmer, Kenneth (writing as Adam Hardy). Series featuring George Abercrombie Fox: *The Press Gang* (1972); *Prize Money* (1973); *Siege* (1973; US *Savage Siege*); *Treasure* (1973; US *Treasure Map*); *Powder Monkey* (1973; US *Sailor's Blood*); *Blood for Breakfast* (1973; US *Sea of Gold*); *Court Martial* (1974); *Battle Smoke* (1974); *Cut and Thrust* (1975); *Boarders Away!* (1975); *Fireship* (1975); *Blood Beach* (1975); *Sea Flame* (1976); *Close Quarters* (1977).

Challoner, Robert. Series featuring Commander Lord Charles Oakshott: *Run out the Guns* (1984); *Give Fire!* (1986); *Into Battle* (1987).

Chamier, Captain Frederick. *Ben Brace: The Last of Nelson's Agamemnons* (1836); *Tom Bowling: A Tale of the Sea* (1839).

Connery, Tom. Series featuring George Markham, Royal Marines: *A Shred of Honour* (1996); *Honour Redeemed* (1997); *Honour Be Damned* (1998).

Conrad, Joseph. *The Rover* (1924).

Cooper, James Fenimore. *Wing-and-Wing* (1842).

Donachie, David. Series featuring Harry Ludlow: *The Devil's Own Luck* (1991); *The Dying Trade* (1993); *A Hanging Matter* (1994); *An Element of Chance* (1994); *The Scent of Betrayal* (1996); *A Game of Bones* (1997).

Forester, C. S. Series featuring Horatio Hornblower: *Mr Midshipman Hornblower* (1950); *Lieutenant Hornblower* (1954); *Hornblower and the Hotspur* (1962); *Hornblower and the Crisis* (1967); *Hornblower and the Antropos* (1953); *The Happy Return* (1937; US *Beat to Quarters*); *Ship of the Line* (1938); *Flying Colours* (1939); *Commodore Hornblower* (1945); *Lord Hornblower* (1948); *Admiral Hornblower in the West Indies* (1958). Short stories will be found in *The Hornblower Companion* (1964) and *Hornblower – One More Time* (limited edition, 1976).

Gerson, Noel Bertram. *The Nelson Touch* (1960).

Glascock, William Nugent. *A Naval Sketch-Book* (1826); *Sailors and Saints* (1829); *Tales of a Tar* (1836); *Land Sharks and Sea Gulls* (1838).

Hall, James Norman. *Doctor Dogbody's Leg* (1937).

Hardy, Adam. *See* Bulmer, Kenneth.

Henty, G. A. *By Conduct and Courage* (1904).

Hyne, C. J. Cutcliffe. *The Escape Agents* (1911).

Kent, Alexander. Series featuring Richard Bolitho: *Richard Bolitho – Midshipman* (1975); *Midshipman Bolitho and the Avenger* (1978); *Stand into Danger* (1980); *In Gallant Company* (1977); *Sloop of War* (1972); *To Glory We Steer* (1968); *Command a King's Ship* (1973); *Passage to Mutiny* (1976); *With All Dispatch* (1988); *Form Line of Battle!* (1969); *Enemy in Sight!* (1970); *The Flag Captain* (1971); *Signal, Close Action!* (1974); *The Inshore Squadron* (1977); *A Tradition of Victory* (1981); *Success to the Brave* (1983); *Colours Aloft!* (1986); *Honour This Day* (1987); *The Only Victor* (1990); *Beyond the Reef* (1992); *The Darkening Sea* (1993); *For My Country's Freedom* (1995); *Cross of St George* (1996); *Sword of Honour* (1998).

Kingston, W. H. G. *Will Weatherhelm: or, The Yarn of an Old Sailor* (1859); *Adrift in a Boat* (1869).

Kippax, Frank. *See* Needle, Jan.

Lambdin, Dewey. Series featuring Alan Lewrie: *The King's Coat* (1989); *The French Admiral* (1989); *The King's Commission* (1991); *The King's Privateer* (1992); *The Gun Ketch* (1993); *H.M.S. Cockerel* (1995); *A King's Commander* (1997); *Jester's Fortune* (1999).

Marryat, Captain Frederick. *The Naval Officer: or, Scenes and Adventures in the Life of Frank Mildmay* (1829); *The King's Own* (1830); *Newton Foster: or, The Merchant Service* (1832); *Peter Simple* (1834); *Mr Midshipman Easy* (1834); *The Three Cutters* (1836); *Masterman Ready* (1841); *The Phantom Ship* (1839).

Maynard, Kenneth. Series featuring Matthew Lamb: *Lieutenant Lamb* (1984); *First Lieutenant* (1985); *Lamb in Command* (1986); *Lamb's Mixed Fortunes* (1987).

Meacham, Ellis K. Series featuring Percival Merewether of the East India Company: *The East Indiaman* (1968); *On the Company's Service* (1971); *For King and Company* (1976).

Needle, Jan. Series featuring William Bentley: *A Fine Boy for Killing* (1979; revised 1996); *The Wicked Trade* (1998).

O'Brian, Patrick. Series featuring Jack Aubrey and Stephen Maturin: *Master and Commander* (1969); *Post Captain* (1972); *H.M.S. Surprise* (1973); *Mauritius Command* (1977); *Desolation Island* (1978); *The Fortune of War* (1979); *The Surgeon's Mate* (1980); *The Ionian Mission* (1981); *Treason's Harbour* (1983); *The Far Side of the World* (1984); *The Reverse of the Medal* (1986); *The Letter of Marque* (1988); *The Thirteen Gun Salute* (1989); *The Nutmeg of Consolation* (1991); *Clarissa Oakes* (1992; US *The Truelove*); *The Wine-Dark Sea* (1993); *The Commodore* (1994); *The Yellow Admiral* (1996); *The Hundred Days* (1998). Background to these books will also be found in *A Sea of Words* (1995) and *Harbors and High Seas* (1996), both by Dean King and John B. Hattendorf.

Parkinson, C. Northcote. *The Life and Times of Horatio Hornblower* (1970). Series featuring Richard Delancey: *The Guernseyman* (1982); *Devil to Pay* (1973); *The Fireship* (1975); *Touch and Go* (1977); *So Near, So Far* (1981; US *Near and Far*); *Dead Reckoning* (1978).

Pope, Dudley. Series featuring Nicholas Ramage: *Ramage* (1965); *Ramage and the Drumbeat* (1968); *Ramage and the Freebooters* (1969); *Governor Ramage* (1973); *Ramage's Prize* (1974); *Ramage and the Guillotine* (1975); *Ramage's Diamond* (1976); *Ramage's Mutiny* (1977); *Ramage and the Rebels* (1978); *The Ramage Touch* (1979); *Ramage's Signal* (1980); *Ramage and the Renegades* (1981); *Ramage's Devil* (1982); *Ramage's Trial*

(1984); *Ramage's Challenge* (1985); *Ramage at Trafalgar* (1986); *Ramage and the Saracens* (1988); *Ramage and the Dido* (1989).

Scott, Michael. *Tom Cringle's Log* (1836).

Styles, Showell. *Path to Glory* (1952); *Mr Nelson's Ladies* (1953); *The Admiral's Fancy* (1956); *The Frigate Captain* (1956); *The Sea Officer* (1961); *Sea Road to Camperdown* (1968); *Vincey Joe at Quiberon* (1971); *The Malta Frigate* (1983); *Stella and the Fireships* (1985); *The Lee Shore* (1986); *The Quarterdeck Ladder* (1989); *Nelson's Midshipman* (1991); *The Independent Cruise* (1992).
Series featuring Septimus Quinn: *Midshipman Quinn* (1957); *Quinn of the Fury* (1961); *Midshipman Quinn and Denise the Spy* (1961); *Quinn at Trafalgar* (1965).
Series featuring Michael Fitton: *A Sword for Mr Fitton* (1975); *Mr Fitton's Commission* (1977); *The Baltic Convoy* (1978); *The Gun Brig Captain* (1987); *H.M.S. Cracker* (1988); *A Ship for Mr Fitton* (1991); *Mr Fitton's Prize* (1993); *Mr Fitton and the Black Legion* (1994); *Mr Fitton in Command* (1995); *The Twelve-Gun Cutter* (1996); *Lieutenant Fitton* (1997); *Mr Fitton at the Helm* (1998); *The Martinique Mission* (1999).

Trelawny, Edward John. *Adventures of a Younger Man* (1831).

Weiser, Bruce. Series featuring Nicholas Chenevix: *The French Impostor* (1980); *Dispatch from Cadiz* (1981).

White, Simon. Series featuring Captain Jethro "Cocky" Penhaligon: *The English Captain* (1977); *Clear for Action* (1978); *His Majesty's Frigate* (1979).

Wibberly, Leonard. Series featuring the Treegate family: *Leopard's Prey* (1971); *Red Pawns* (1973); *The Last Battle* (1976).

Wilkins, Vaughan. *Napoleon's Submarine* (1944).

Williams, (Walter) Jon. Series featuring the Markham family, known as Privateers and Gentlemen: *The Privateer* (1981); *The Yankee* (1981); *The Raider* (1981); *The Macedonian* (1984); *Cat Island* (1984).

Woodman, Richard. Series featuring Nathaniel Drinkwater: *An Eye of the Fleet* (1981); *A King's Cutter* (1982); *A Brig of War* (1983); *The Bomb Vessel* (1984); *The Corvette* (1985); *1805* (1985; US *Decision at Trafalgar*); *Baltic Mission* (1986); *In Distant Waters* (1988); *A Private Revenge* (1989); *Under False Colours* (1991); *The Flying Squadron* (1992); *Beneath the Aurora* (1995); *The Shadow of the Eagle* (1997); *Ebb Tide* (1998).